ROMANZO CRIMINALE

ROMANZO CRIMINALE

GIANCARLO DE CATALDO

Translated from the Italian
BY ANTONY SHUGAAR

CORVUS

First published in Italy in 2002 by Giulio Einaudi editore S.p.A.

Published in trade paperback in Great Britain in 2015 by Corvus,
an imprint of Atlantic Books Ltd.

10 9 8 7 6 5 4 3 2 1

A CIP catalogue record for this book is available from the British Library.

Trade paperback ISBN: 978 0 85789 372 7
E-book ISBN: 978 0 85789 373 4

Printed in Great Britain.

Corvus
An imprint of Atlantic Books Ltd
Ormond House
26–27 Boswell Street
London
WC1N 3JZ

www.corvus-books.co.uk

For Tiziana

Special thanks go to Bruno Pari, '*er più de li macellari*', for his lessons in '*romanità*', and to P. G. Di Cara for the quote from Bernardo Provenzano and his review of the dialogue in Sicilian dialect.

The restriction of bloodshed to a minimum, its rationalization, is a business principle.

Bertolt Brecht, *Notes to the Threepenny Opera*

I urge you always to be calm and righteous, fair and consistent, may you successfully benefit from your experience of the experiences you suffer, do not discredit all that they tell you, always seek the truth before speaking, and remember that it is never enough to have one piece of evidence in order to undertake a decision. In order to be certain in a decision, you must have three pieces of evidence, and fairness and consistency. May the Lord bless you and protect you.

Bernardo Provenzano, July 1994

Table of Contents

Prologue
Rome, Now

HE CROUCHED BETWEEN two parked cars, curled into a ball. He covered his face as best he could and waited for the next blow. There were four of them.

The little man was particularly vicious; a knife scar ran the length of his cheek. Between assaults, he traded witty observations with a girlfriend on his mobile phone: a running commentary on the beating. Fortunately, they were punching blindly. This was their idea of fun. They're young enough to be my own kids, he thought. Except for the African, of course. A gang of wild, reckless lowlifes. Only a few years ago, he thought, if they'd so much as heard his name, they would have just shot themselves in the head to avoid tasting his vengeance. A few years ago. Before everything changed. It had been a brief, fatal moment of carelessness. The hobnailed boot caught him right in the temple. He slithered down into blackness.

'Time to go,' ordered the little man. 'I'd say this one's not getting back on his feet!'

But he did. It was already dark by the time he picked himself up. His ribcage was in flames, his thoughts were muddled. A short way up the street there was a water fountain. He washed off the dried blood and drank down a long gulp of water that tasted of iron. Now he was on his feet. He was walking. On the street, cars went by, stereos blasting, while knots of young men toyed with their mobile phones and laughed scornfully at his lurching gait. The windows were lit by the bluish glow of thousands of television sets. A little further on: a brightly lit shop window. He eyed his reflection in the glass: a man hobbling in pain, coat torn and matted with blood, thinning greasy hair, rotten teeth. An

1

old man. Look what he'd become. A siren sailed past. Instinctively he flattened against the wall. But they weren't looking for him. No one was looking for him now.

'I was with Libano!' he murmured, almost incredulous, as if he had suddenly come into possession of someone else's memories. They'd taken his money, but the lowlifes had overlooked his passport and ticket. As well as his Rolex, sewn into an inside pocket. They were having too much fun to search him thoroughly. A smile flickered across his face. They'd be breaking their teeth on some tough bread crust, no question.

Passengers wouldn't be called for boarding for another three hours. There was enough time. The gypsy camp was about half a mile away.

The African was the first to see him coming. He stepped over to the little man, who was making out with his girlfriend, and told him that grandpa was back.

'Didn't we kill him?'

'How would I know? But here he is!'

He strolled easily across the piazza, looking around him with a foolish smile, as if begging pardon for the intrusion. The other lowlifes glanced idly at him as he went by, and then returned to their own business.

The little man told the girl to go for a walk, and then stood waiting, arms folded across his chest. The African and the two others – a very tall hooligan with a pockmarked face and a fat thug with tattoos – flanked him on either side.

'Good evening,' he said. 'You've got something that belongs to me. I want it back!'

The little man turned to the others. 'He hasn't had his fill!'

They laughed.

He shook his head and pulled out the piece. 'Everyone flat on the pavement!' he said in a grim voice.

The African reared back. The little guy spat on the ground, unimpressed.

'Sure, let's play ring-around-the-rosy! Who are you trying to scare, with that pop-gun!'

He looked down apologetically at the little .22 calibre semi-automatic that the gypsy had given him in exchange for the Rolex.

'You're right, it's small…but if you know how to use it…'

He fired without aiming, and without taking his eyes off the little man. The African dropped with a howl, clutching at his knee. Suddenly, there was a deep silence.

'Clear out, everyone!' he ordered without turning around. 'All but these four!'

The little man waved his hands in the air, as if to placate him.

'All right, all right, we'll work this out…But you just keep cool, right?'

'All of you, down on the ground, I said,' he repeated quietly.

The little guy and the others knelt down. The African was rolling and keening in agony.

'I gave the money to my girl,' the little man snivelled. 'Let me call her on my mobile phone, and she'll bring it back, all right?'

'Shut up. Let me think…'

How long could it be until boarding time was called? An hour? A little longer? The girl could be back here in a couple of minutes. He'd have his money back. Venezuela awaited him. It might take some time and effort to fit in, but…it shouldn't be that difficult, down there…right. The smart thing would be to relent, at this point. But when had he ever done the smart thing? When had any of them ever been smart? And then, the little man's fear…the smell of the street…Hadn't all of them always lived just for moments like this?

He leaned down over the little man and whispered his name into his ear. The little man started trembling.

'You ever heard of me?' he asked softly.

The little man nodded.

He smiled. Then he delicately lodged the barrel of the gun against the little man's forehead and shot him between the eyes. Indifferent to the sobbing, the sound of running footsteps, the approaching sirens, he turned his back and aimed his gun at the bastard moon. With all the breath he could muster, he shouted:

'I was with Libano!'

PART ONE

Genesis
1977–78

I

DANDI WAS BORN where Rome still belongs to Romans: in the apartment blocks of Tor di Nona.

When he was twelve, they'd deported him to Infernetto. Written on the eviction order, signed by the mayor, were the words: 'Reconstruction of decrepit buildings in the historic section of central Rome.' That reconstruction had been dragging on for a lifetime now, but Dandi never tired of saying that, one day, sooner or later, he'd move back to the centre of Rome. As a boss. And everyone would bow to him as he went by.

But for now he was living with his wife in a two-room flat with a view of the huge gasometers, the Gazometro.

Libano walked there from Testaccio. It wasn't far, but August perspiration was pasting his black shirt to his virile, hairy chest. As he walked, he felt a growing fury at the little delinquent.

Dandi opened the door with a bewildered expression on his face. He was dressed in a red polka-dot dressing gown. He'd once chanced to read a few pages from a book about Beau Brummel. Ever since, he'd been a sharp dresser. And that's why he was known as Dandi.

'I need the motorcycle.'

'Quiet. Gina's sleeping. What's up?'

'They stole my Mini.'

'So?'

'The duffel bag was inside.'

'Let's go.'

The hot scirocco wind was actually agreeable, as they rode out on the

Kawasaki. They hurtled down the road, until they reached the Magliana water-pumping station. There they parked the bike in front of a badly rusted iron security shutter and set off on foot into the big meadow. The hut stood between an abandoned wreck of a building and a warehouse full of junk. The door was bolted shut; it was dark inside.

'He's not back yet,' decided Libano.

'Who is it?'

'Some idiot. The nephew of Franco, the barkeep.'

Dandi nodded. They sat down on an old hollow tree stump. Dandi pulled out a joint. Libano sucked down a couple of puffs and passed it back to him. This was no time to get wasted. For a while, they sat in silence. Dandi closed his eyes and savoured the relaxed pleasure of the hash.

'We're wasting time,' said Libano.

'Sooner or later the motherfucker has to come back home.'

'That's not what I'm talking about. I mean, in general: we're wasting time.'

Dandi opened his eyes. His partner was restless.

Libano was short, dark and bluff, and his nickname – Lebanon – was a tribute to his Levantine appearance. He was born in San Cosimato, in the heart of Trastevere, but his people were from Calabria. They'd known each other all their lives. They'd run a gang of kids when they were small, and now they were an enforcement squad.

'I'm thinking about the baron, Dandi.'

'We've talked about this a hundred times, Libano. The time isn't right. There's too few of us. And it belongs to Terribile. There's no way he'd okay it.'

'That's exactly it, Dandi. I'm sick of asking permission. Let's just do it.'

'You may be right. But we're still outnumbered.'

'For now… That's true for now,' Libano ended the discussion thoughtfully.

A fat yellow moon had taken possession of the horizon.

Libano was right. They needed to think about setting up operations on their own. But a squad made up of four youngsters didn't have much of a future. Organization. How many times had they talked about it? But how to get started? And who with?

A dog started barking.

'You hear that?'

Footsteps on the asphalt. Whoever this was, he wasn't trying to hide. They both crept over to a pile of truck tyres. The young punk, skinny and misshapen, lurched along as he walked. When he was within range, they nodded in agreement and moved fast.

Libano grabbed him from behind, pinning him so he was helpless. Dandi kicked him hard in the stomach. The punk whimpered and slumped to the ground. Libano plunged the punk's face into the dry earth, pulled out his revolver, and planted the muzzle at the base of his neck.

'You know who I am, you idiot?'

The punk nodded furiously. Libano pulled his gun away.

'Get up.'

The punk got to his knees.

'He stinks like a goat,' said Dandi in disgust.

'That's the smack. He's wasted. Get up, I said.'

The young punk struggled to get to his feet, flailing. Libano smiled.

'I promised your uncle I would take it easy on you, but don't test my patience. Answer yes or no, don't say anything else.'

The punk stared at him, dazed and confused. His face was covered with red sores. Dandi kicked him once in the jaw.

'Yes or no?'

'Yes.'

'Good,' Libano continued. 'You stole the Mini in Testaccio, right?'

'Yes.'

'Did you look in the boot?'

'No.'

'Are you sure?'

'Yes.'

'Lucky for you. Where's the car now?'

'I don't have it anymore...'

Dandi limited himself to a sharp smack to the nape of the neck. The punk started whimpering. Libano sighed.

'Did you sell it?'

'Yes.'

'To who?'

The punk fell to his knees again. He couldn't say. Those people were dangerous. They'd kill him.

'Bad situation, eh, kid?' said Libano. 'If you talk, *they'll* shoot you. And if you *don't* talk, *we'll* shoot you...'

'Libano, once I saw a Western—' began Dandi.

'What's that got to do with this?'

'You'll see, you'll see. There was a horse that had been injured, poor thing, it was on its last legs...and the owner didn't know what to do...Poor animal, he looks up at his master with these big pitiful eyes...Why do I have to go on suffering, it was saying...'

'Aaahh! Now I get you! So finally he puts the horse out of its misery, right? Bam!'

'Exactly!' said Dandi.

'But...but, Dandi, look, there's something I don't understand.'

'Then ask me, Libano!'

'The horse in the film, you said it was injured...And this kid, from what I can see, he's perfectly healthy...'

Dandi shot the punk in the knee. The punk grabbed his leg and started screaming.

'Take another look, Libano!'

'You're right, Dandi. He's hurt badly! He's in terrible pain! What do you say, should we help him out? Put him out of his misery?'

The punk talked.

II

NOW FREDDO – ITALIAN for 'cold', a reference to his icy composure – had the Mini. Libano knew nothing about him, but Dandi had crossed paths with him once or twice. He was a serious operator, not much of a talker, and he had a certain amount of experience with post offices. He'd been arrested once for extorting money from a chef, but he'd been acquitted after the victim retracted his testimony. A trustworthy individual, in other words.

Still, they had their guns at the ready when they kicked in the door of the abandoned warehouse behind the restaurant Il Fungo.

Libano found the light switch. Aside from a strong smell of petrol, there was only the bodywork of a stripped Fiat 850 and, behind a plate-glass window that had seen better days, what looked like a small accountant's office.

They stared at one another in dismay. It had seemed at the time that the punk was telling the truth, but you can never be sure about that kind of thing. Libano was starting to regret the partial mercy he had shown, when they heard a noise behind them.

They turned around slowly. There were four of them. They must have waited for them in the street, concealed somewhere, perhaps inside a car. Libano scanned them rapidly: two short men, dressed in gym shorts and T-shirts, both with the same brutish face, like a pair of badly formed twins; then a bearded man built like a wrestler, with one eye looking towards India, the other looking at America; and in the middle, the youngest of the group – dark, curly hair, skinny as a rail. Freddo. Practically a child. A penetrating glare. Focused, determined.

Meanwhile, Dandi studied the arsenal: three semi-automatics – and Freddo was holding a long-barrelled revolver. A Colt, .38 calibre. A handsome beast: reliable, traditional.

'How's it going, Freddo?' asked Libano.

'We were expecting you.'

A tight situation. Clearly not a good one. The other guys were feeling relaxed and in control. If not, they'd have opened fire immediately. Freddo seemed perfectly capable of controlling his men. Libano decided it was no accident that he'd picked up that moniker, and flashed him a vaguely friendly smile. Freddo barely moved his head, and the cross-eyed guy strolled away unhurriedly towards the office, careful not to wander into the line of fire. A minute later, a boxer's equipment bag was tossed to the floor at Libano's feet. The duffel bag in question.

'Open it up and take a look. It's all there. Four Berettas, two Tanfoglios, the clips and the ammunition,' said Freddo.

'I trust you, Freddo. I've heard a lot about you.'

'You must be Libano. It's too late for the Mini, though. Sorry about that.'

He said it with an odd sneer. That must be what passes for a smile with him.

11

'No big thing. It was insured.'

What tension was still in the air subsided in a collective burst of laughter. Everyone lowered their weapons. Dandi suggested going for a drink at the Re di Picche, a bar named after the King of Spades. Libano asked to use the phone, if there was one. The cross-eyed wrestler escorted him into the office. From there, he called Franco the bartender and told him where he could go get his nephew.

'He's still all in one piece, relax. He might walk with a limp now, but he got off easy.'

Freddo introduced the Buffoni brothers and Fierolocchio, the cross-eyed guy. The gambling den, the Re di Picche, was winding down for the night, aside from the bartender in a bow tie and a couple of wrecked-looking whores with bags under their eyes. They ordered a bottle of champagne and a deck of cards, and killed a few more hours playing a listless game of *zecchinetta*. There was something in the air, something that was bound to come out sooner or later. They just didn't know where to begin. Dandi and the Buffoni boys were ready to call it quits by the time the sun came up. Fierolocchio had fallen asleep, his head on the card table. Freddo offered to give Libano a ride to Trastevere. They climbed into his VW Golf hatchback, and Libano tested the ice.

'This Re di Picche strikes me as a real shithole.'

'You can say that again.'

'Who owns the place?'

'Officially it belongs to some woman named Rosa, a geriatric whore. But the real owner is Terribile...'

'Terribile this, Terribile that...I'm getting sick of tripping over this fucking Terribile every time I turn around. Senile old fuck without an ounce of brains in his head. If he had people like us working for him, we could turn a dive like this into a goldmine...'

Freddo said nothing, apparently concentrating on his driving. But there was a gleam in his eye. Libano decided to double down.

'Just think, Freddo: a few poker tables, a dealer, a nice fat ante, high table stakes, but strictly for a select clientele. A cosy little spot. Some girls – the right kind of girls, not those worn-out hookers. A barman who knows how to pour...What could you pull in with a place like that, eh? Think about it. How much a month? How much a week?'

'A lot of cash. But you'd need at least that much just to get started.'

'Anything's possible. All you need is to find the right people.'

Freddo slammed on the brakes at the corner of Viale Trastevere and Via di San Francesco a Ripa and glared at him in his angry, inscrutable way.

'What do you have in mind?'

'A kidnapping.'

'Who?'

'Baron Rosellini. The one who runs horses.'

'Why him?'

'He's methodical. Sticks to a routine, follows a schedule. Piece of cake.'

'Kidnappings are never a piece of cake. How many men do you think?'

'Twenty or so...Maybe we could pull it off with fifteen.'

'I've got the guys you saw. How many of you are there?'

'Aside from me and Dandi, Satana and Scrocchiazeppi.'

'Four and four makes eight. Less than half.'

'You don't think we can come up with the rest?'

'Give me two weeks.'

Libano slumped back against the car seat, refreshed. Now, finally, this was starting to look like living.

III

KIDNAPPING THE BARON had been child's play. Just as he'd expected. Libano reserved the right to wait until the kidnapping had taken place to announce the identity of the phone contact. There had been some grumbling, but Freddo had made his authority felt. The alliance was starting to hum. They were going to go far – very, very far. Together. As for the phone contact, Libano had an idea all of his own. Something that had a lot to do with loyalty, fear and domination over weaker vessels. As soon as he got home, he called Franco the barkeep and told him to send the punk around.

He showed up not half an hour later, his eyes still puffy with sleep. He was limping on his wounded leg, but at least he'd taken a shower, and

13

he didn't stink the way he did before. Libano invited him to take a seat in one of the armchairs draped in black fabric. The punk hesitated, his curiosity piqued by the bust on the side table, a purchase from the Porta Portese market.

'Who's that?'

'Mussolini.'

'Who's he?'

'A great man. Sit down.'

The punk did as he was told. A savage fear glittered in his eyes.

'How's your leg?'

'So-so. I'm doing physiotherapy...'

'Still shooting up?'

'I'm clean, I swear.'

'My arse. You want some work?'

'What kind of work?'

'You want it? Yes or no.'

The boy trembled from head to foot. Libano struggled to suppress a smile.

'What's your name?'

'Lorenzo.'

'You look like a mouse, all hunched over and tight. A sorcio, a little scrabbly mouse, definitely... Well: yes or no?'

'Yes.'

'Correct answer. You just joined up, Sorcio. Now off you go to Florence, and until I say you can, no more needles. As for the job, I need you to make a few phone calls.'

Freddo got home at dawn, too. Gigio was waiting for him outside the front door, shivering with cold.

'What are you doing out here?'

'I'm not setting foot in that place again.'

'Did Papa beat you up again?'

Gigio shook his head no.

'So, what happened?'

'I've had it! School's a disaster, and I never have enough money. Why don't you let me come work for you? I'm begging you...'

Gigio was six years younger than him. Polio had done a number on his leg, and his brain had never been anything to write home about either. Freddo felt a strange fondness for that unlucky younger brother of his. A different life, why not? There's no law that says you can't change your fate, is there? In one of his rare moments of fantasy, he'd dreamed of Gigio becoming a doctor. He reached into his pocket and handed the boy a hundred-thousand lire note.

'Now go home, change clothes, and go to school. Or I swear I'll break your nose and your jaw. Understood?'

Gigio hunched his shoulders and tucked his head in. He'd do as he was told, like always. And he'd stay out of all this mess, like always.

Once he was alone, Freddo flopped down onto the bed, without even taking off his boots.

IV

JUDICIAL REPORT ON THE KIDNAPPING FOR PURPOSES OF EXTORTION OF BARON VALDEMARO ROSELLINI
by Commissario Nicola Scialoja

From the investigations conducted concerning the crime in question the following facts have emerged:

BARON ROSELLINI, at the time of the kidnapping, was driving his own vehicle, a camel-brown Mercedes turbo diesel. The kidnapping took place near La Storta, on the Via del Casale di San Nicola. The victim's car was forced to brake to a halt at a sharp angle in the middle of the road by two other vehicles. According to the eyewitness account of Oscar Marussi, who was at the wheel of his own car, a FIAT 131, and was right behind the victim, the other cars were a CITROEN DS 21 and a light blue ALFETTA 1750. Marussi also reported that the two vehicles sped up next to the baron's Mercedes, forcing it to a stop, whereupon four men got out of the ALFETTA, seized the baron, and dragged him over to the CITROEN, shoving him into the vehicle. The CITROEN took off immediately, heading towards Rome, while the remaining four criminals, after threatening

Marussi, drove off as well, three of them aboard the ALFETTA, the fourth taking possession of the baron's Mercedes. That car was found the following day on the Via Cristoforo Colombo, at number 459.

Telephone contacts with the victim's family were made from areas outside the district (geographic regions other than Lazio) in order to thwart the tracing equipment installed by the SIP phone company.

All the same, from the tape recordings made by the personnel operating on the incoming equipment in the home of the victim, it emerged that the phone contact, always the same person, can be identified as a male, presumably no older than twenty-five to twenty-eight, and without any distinctive regional accent, or at least tending to simulate a variety of regional accents.

The family received five (5) written communications demanding a payment of ransom. They were composed in a technique involving a collage of various letters cut out of the most widely circulated Roman daily newspapers (*Il Messaggero* and *Paese Sera* and, on one occasion, *Il Secolo d'Italia*, an extreme right-wing publication).

The phone calls demanded an initial ransom of ten billion lire, then dropped to seven, and finally settled on three billion lire. According to statements by the family of Baron Rosellini, it would appear that this last sum was the amount actually paid.

The first message was left on 29 December 1977 near Piazza Cavour, and contained three Polaroid photographs depicting the victim of the kidnapping holding a copy of *Il Messaggero*.

On 2 January 1978, at 1600 hours, an appointment was made at the Bar Cubana, where the victim's son, ALESSANDRO, waited in vain for a phone call that appears to have been made only after he left the premises. That same day, another appointment, at the Bar Georgia, was likewise unsuccessful.

On 11 February a message was reported to have been left by the kidnappers in a trash receptacle on the Lungotevere di Pietra Papa, but without results.

On 15 February, ALESSANDRO ROSELLINI was summoned to the Termini train station, to retrieve a message left in an automatic photo booth. The message, composed with the usual technique of

16

letters cut from newspapers, ordered him to travel to Torvajanica. Upon arriving in this location, the young man found a second message, which set another meeting at the diner at the Pontecorvo service station on the Autostrada del Sole. No one came to that meeting, either.

The telephone contact criticized Rosellini, saying that he had been followed by three police teams.

On 23 February, another appointment was made at the restaurant Il Fungo at EUR, but again, no one showed up.

The same thing happened on 27 February in Piancastagnaio, near Siena.

On 2 March, on the Via Cassia, near the exit for Monterosi di Viterbo, the ransom was finally paid. The witness – who in that setting, by express order of the judicial authority with appropriate jurisdiction, was not being followed – reported that, on the orders of three individuals with their faces concealed who were seated in a parked FIAT van with a Viterbo (VT) registration plate, he had thrown out the bag containing the money.

The cash from the ransom was traced to various locations around Italy, but no successful investigative leads were developed as a result.

There is no need to point out that the failure of the hostage to return home, even after the full payment of the ransom, clearly indicates that this crime culminated in the most tragic of outcomes.

V

THE PROBLEM ORIGINATED with the Catanians from Casal del Marmo. What happened was the baron caught a glimpse of the face of one of his captors. He therefore had to be eliminated. Even if they'd had the chance – and they didn't, they'd only been informed after it was all said and done – neither Libano nor Freddo would have lifted a finger to save the baron. For that matter, it was a lot less risky without live witnesses. But after giving Feccia – whose name roughly meant Filth – his share of the take, they decided to put an end to their dealings with those dilettantes. Bufalo, a young man from Acilia who was built like a refrigerator and had procured the chloroform and the Alfetta 1750, suggested wiping out the whole gang. But their giddy euphoria at successfully receiving the ransom won out: after paying those idiots from Casal del Marmo their share of the ransom, they still had two and a half billion to divvy up – according to the shares assigned during the planning phase. Two and a half billion to split ten ways.

Libano had summoned them all to the apartment at San Cosimato. Everyone was there. Along with Dandi, there was Botola, a short, thickset guy from the Piramide district, skilled with a pistol; Satana, something of a nut, but a good guy in a fight, with a light dusting of red hair on his head and dressed in a black jumpsuit that Diabolik would have been proud to wear; Scrocchiazeppi...In other words, the gang was all there, with the exception of Sorcio. Libano was suspending judgment on him for the moment: he'd clearly been high when he made a couple of the phone calls, and had come dangerously close to screwing up the whole operation. All things considered, though, he hadn't done too badly. In any case, he'd pay for his screw-ups by forfeiting his share of the loot.

Right, the money. He had never seen that much money in one place, not even in a film. Still, the thing that he found most compelling was watching the reactions of the others. The Buffoni twins, for instance: Aldo – or Carlo, it was so hard to tell them apart – were trying to make themselves a hat with the notes. And Carlo – or Aldo – explained:

'Fuck that arsehole of a father of mine, who wanted to send us to work for a boss.'

Bufalo had bought a vial of cocaine on credit, and he was sitting there in a stunned daze looking at the plunder, his nose all floury, every once in a while slipping into a sort of death-grin sigh (heh! hee! heh heh!). Dandi was leafing through a Ferragamo catalogue and a brochure from an art exhibition. Fierolocchio had pulled out of his pocket a crumpled piece of scrap paper covered with phone numbers.

'The finest pussy in Rome!'

Beers and joints were being passed from hand to hand, and understandably everyone was thinking about the fastest, stupidest way to run through their share of the take from the kidnapping. Almost everyone. Freddo was standing off to one side. He was looking out the window: a grey dawn rising over the marketplace, a dense, chilly drizzle that penetrated into your bones.

'Time to divvy the take?' Libano suggested.

Bufalo had emerged from his drug-induced coma. 'All right then: five hundred million lire went to the shitheads. So amen, we're done with them. We have two and a half billion left over. That's four hundred million apiece for Libano and Freddo. That's a fair share; after all, they came up with the idea, right? That leaves one billion seven hundred. There's eight of us, meaning two hundred million apiece. And the hundred million left over we can go shoot at the various floating card games. What do you say to that, huh?'

What need was there even to answer? They all threw themselves onto the plunder, even Scrocchiazeppi, skinny as he was – if you so much as bumped him with your shoulder there'd be nothing left of him. Only Libano and Freddo held back from the scrum: one of them with a hand resting on Il Duce's oversized bald head and the other leaning against the window, a cigarette butt clamped between his teeth.

Libano decided to play his ace card.

'Hold on, comrades!'

'Now what the hell does he want?' They all turned to stare at him, the way you would a lunatic wandering down the street. Bufalo even had his hand on the holster under his armpit. Suspicious, all of them smelling a trap. Libano sat there in his armchair, arms spread wide in a reassuring gesture. Freddo observed the situation with his usual intense focus.

'Here's what I'm thinking: now here we have two and a half billion lire. Which is quite a different matter from me having four hundred million, and you having two hundred, plus the hundred for the gambling dens...'

'What the fuck are you talking about?' Fierolocchio objected.

'Shut up,' Freddo broke in. 'Go on, Libano.'

'You, Dandi, I'll start with you because we've been friends all our lives...Now, the first thing you're going to do is update your wardrobe, because you're Dandi, and if not, what kind of a Dandi would you be, right?'

'To tell the truth, the Kawasaki's looking a little beat up too...'

Scattered laughter. Bufalo's hand fell away from the holster. Libano had a chance to catch his breath.

'And you, Scrocchiazeppi…I dropped by Bandiera & Bedetti this morning: I've got my eye on a couple of Rolexes that'd make your eyes pop out of your head…Fierolocchio, for you…pussy, cocaine and champagne?'

'Sure, it's the finest life has to offer, right?'

More laughter. Libano was starting to get worked up. Even Bufalo was beginning to show a glimmer of interest.

'What I'm trying to say is: we all have things we want, certain ambitions…'

'We deserve what's fair; we want what we've got coming to us!' Satana raised his voice.

Heads nodded.

Libano stated his agreement. 'What we've got coming to us is just one thing: the best there is.'

'Then what are we waiting for? Let's divvy the take!'

Satana would be the hardest one to win over, Libano could tell. For now, he spoke to him alone, staring into his small, delirious eyes.

'So we split the take today. And tomorrow or the next day, before you know it, we're back where we started. Cars get old, coke gets snorted, pussy dries out from a shortage of liquidity – and when I say liquidity, Fierolo, I mean cash. But what if we didn't divvy up the two billion five? What if we kept it all united? What if we all stayed united? Do you have any idea what we could achieve? Instead of owning just a little, we could own more – a lot more. And the more we have, the more we can get…You remember the priest, Satana? To those who have much, much will be given…That's what we ought to do: take less today so we can have everything tomorrow.'

'Wait a second, let me get this straight…' ventured Bufalo, definitely intrigued.

Libano smiled at him, but his eyes sought out Freddo. But who could say where Freddo was, lost in thought, standing there stiff, motionless, his eyes a pair of narrow slits.

'Bufalo, here's how I see it: let's stay a team. We'll take what little money we need for petty expenses…let's say fifty million lire apiece…'

'Same for you?' Bufalo's jaw dropped.

'Same for me. Even split all around!'

'All around, same for everyone?' Satana asked, a mocking note in his voice, with a baffled glance in Freddo's direction. Freddo was the other lion in the pride. It was up to him to issue a verdict. But Freddo didn't move a muscle, his eyes roaming restlessly from the bust to the ugly framed mirror with the figurine of the Madonna under a glass bell, to the armchairs draped in black, to the stereo fenced in Via Sannio.

'Fifty million lire times ten – that is, if we're all in on this – means two billion lire left over,' Scrocchiazeppi pointed out.

'Two billion lire is a nice, solid foundation,' Libano persisted. 'We're going to need guns and a safe place to keep them. Let's say that we could invest a billion and a half, maybe a billion eight, for our little shared enterprise...'

'So just what is this enterprise?'

'You still don't get it, Satana? I want the same thing the rest of you want!'

'What's that?'

'Rome.'

'Ba-boom! Mussolini has spoken! How the fuck do you think you're going to take over Rome?'

'By asking politely, and if that doesn't work, we'll just have to turn nasty, you stupid shit. We'll use drugs. We'll use gambling...'

Then all hell broke loose. Everyone wanted to have their say: words, threats, outlandish gestures. Libano got slowly to his feet and went over to stand next to Freddo. They exchanged an intense glance. A silence ran between them that isolated them from the rest of those present. Freddo extracted a revolver from his pocket and slammed it down hard on the side table.

'Shut up for a second.'

He hadn't even needed to raise his voice.

'Libano has a point. If we split the money up, then it's no good to anyone. If we split up, we're no good to each other. Victory comes from unity. You've convinced me, Libano. An even split for everyone, and the rest goes into a general fund. Maybe we put something aside for urgent cases – say one of us winds up in jail, or has family problems...'

'That's only reasonable,' said Libano. 'When times are lean, we can finance our operation with this...let's call it a strategic reserve. A couple

21

of hundred thousand lire a month will come out of it anyway.'

'I'm with you,' said Dandi. The Kawasaki could wait; the historic heart of Rome, on the other hand...

'Comrade, this is a great idea,' snarled Bufalo, and went over and planted a resounding smack on Libano's back. 'Money, after all, is only good for one thing, and that's to avoid problems. How can you compare it to the street?'

Fierolocchio said yes: he could still afford a couple of weeks of wall-to-wall sex, even if all he had was fifty million lire.

Scrocchiazeppi said yes: he'd find some other way of getting hold of the Rolex. The usual way.

Botola said yes: he lived alone with his mama and he'd promised her a washing machine, a dishwasher and a brand-new colour TV.

Aldo and Carlo said yes: Freddo's word was law, as far as they were concerned.

When his turn came, Satana stopped to count the two hundred million lire, with a provocative manner.

'I'm getting the impression you're not on-board,' Libano challenged him.

'I'm getting the impression you've had a massive stroke.'

'Hey, Satana,' Dandi waded in, 'it's not our fault if the last strokes you remember involved the parish priest!'

Cruel laughter. And a vicious glare from Satana.

'First: we're talking about gambling. And everyone knows that Terribile controls the gambling around here...'

'We'll talk to him,' Fierolocchio suggested, in a conciliatory tone of voice.

'So what if he tells us to go fuck ourselves?'

'We'll shoot him.' Bufalo liquidated the problem seraphically.

'We'll shoot Terribile? Exactly who here is going to shoot Terribile? You?'

'Sure, I'll shoot him. And if you don't like it, I'll shoot you too, you piece of shit!'

Bufalo was scowling. And Satana already had his hand in his pocket. Libano tried to calm the waters. The only thing missing now was a knife fight out in the street with the money out for all to see. 'Hold on, hold on.

So Satana's not in on it? Fine, we'll do it without him. Satana, you take your share and go where you like. We can still be friends.'

But Satana wouldn't drop the subject.

'Second,' he resumed, ignoring the suggestion, 'we're talking about drugs. That's the Neapolitans' territory; they control that market. Now what are you going to do, Bufalo – shoot the Neapolitans, too?'

'You're wrong there, Satana,' Dandi broke in. 'Puma's been importing shit from China for years and no one ever said a word to him...'

'What are you wasting your time on this animal for?' Bufalo muttered.

Satana didn't hear him, or pretended he hadn't heard him. Now he had it in for Dandi.

'Puma kicks back a share to the Calabrians. Or didn't you know that?'

'We're not going to kick back a penny to anyone,' Libano said very clearly. 'If anything, we can make deals between equals...'

'Aw, you want to take over Rome, Libano, but no one's ever going to take over this city. Anyway, what do you know about it? You're half African...'

All eyes darted from Satana to Libano. Libano sighed. Would he and Freddo ever manage to get these boys' feral nature under control? These people could flare up over nothing, and what you needed to get ahead in this world was a cold, clear mind. Satana was mocking him provocatively. If Libano failed to pay him back for his insult, he'd lose the respect of the others. He flashed a faint smile, shook his head, and let fly with a straight-armed slap that left a bright red mark on Satana's cheek.

'I'll kill you, you bastard!'

There was bound to be a reaction, but Satana had been lightning fast, catching him off guard. Knocked off balance by a hip thrust worthy of the viper that he was, Libano found himself with a pistol jammed against his throat. Luckily, Freddo was on guard: a sharp knee to the kidneys and Satana sprawled out like an empty sack. Bufalo had grabbed the handgun, which slid out of Satana's grasp as he fell.

'Now let's have a little fun with him!'

But Freddo grabbed the gun out of his hands and helped Satana back to his feet.

'Now take your money and get lost, and just thank your lucky stars that we're in such a good mood...'

Satana nodded, glowering. Before folding his tent and stealing away, he took a look around the entire panorama of the newly founded organization.

'These two arseholes have set you up. You'll figure it out, sooner or later!'

The minute he walked out the door, Bufalo took off after him. Libano stood in his way.

'Where do you think you're going?'

'To deck that miserable turncoat, no?'

'You're not going to deck anybody at all, Bufalo.' Freddo's tone of voice made it clear that the point wasn't open for discussion.

'We're an association now, comrade,' Dandi explained. 'We make all our decisions together and nobody's an independent operator anymore.'

Bufalo nodded in agreement.

Alliances
February 1978

I

SATANA WASN'T WRONG. If you wanted to be a player in the narcotics market, you'd have to strike a deal of some kind with the Neapolitans. And that meant working with Mario the Sardinian. Bufalo arranged for the meet. When he felt like thinking, Bufalo was actually pretty sharp on things like that. The guarantor was Trentadenari, a guy from Forcella who was originally with the Giuliano gang. Then there'd been a quarrel with the Licciardiellos, allies of the Giulianos, and two 'Ndrangheta Santisti – made men – went down in a pool of blood. Trentadenari went to Cutolo for protection, and he was welcomed with open arms into the NCO – the Nuova Camorra Organizzata, or New Organized Camorra. Finally, in the aftermath of a peace talk between *cumparielli*, or Mafiosi, over pasta and fish – *trenette con moscardini and pesce cappone all'acqua pazza* – the mob tribunal had acquitted him, and now Trentadenari was considered by both factions to be a reliable intermediary. Not bad for a guy who had defected not once but twice, winning a reputation as well as the moniker of a Judas – in fact, Trentadenari meant 'thirty pieces of silver'.

Trentadenari had attended the Genovesi high school, and he came from a respectable family. He boasted a formidable network of contacts and fine manners. He was a big hulk of a beast, stood six foot two, and was arabesqued from head to foot with tattoos that – he claimed – went perfectly with the flashy Marinella neckties that he loved to wear even at home, in the nude. With the money he made dealing cocaine, he'd had his oversized apartment decorated in the latest Paolo Portoghesi style. The place was in the EUR district, near the homes of certain Roman nobility.

'The princess is a real lady,' he liked to say, as he showed his guests the veranda overlooking a courtyard filled with towering magnolias and classical Italian garden hedges. 'Too bad she's a Communist. I have to say I can't figure out these rich folk that trend Red!'

Libano had to agree. He was a long-time Fascist; the way he saw it, right wing meant order and organization. Which is what he was trying to do with the gang – impose order and organization on a band of undisciplined hotheads. Power must reward those who see clearly and have the strength to impose their vision.

While Bufalo and Trentadenari exchanged hugs and a series of jovial insults, Freddo and Libano inspected the place. It all seemed safe and secure enough. Dandi, on the other hand, was knocked out by the sheer magnificence of Casa Trentadenari. Designer furniture, little round glass tables, a stereo system with ultramodern speakers, a cinema-quality screen, an immense living room with sprawling sofas…Now that's what you call style! That's definitely what you call living…Trentadenari locked arms with him, all friendly.

'So you like it, eh? If I tell you how much the architect bled me for all this…But you see the professional touch, right? Let me put on a little music.'

Gloomy droning church music poured out of the enormous speakers. Bufalo put his hands over his ears. Libano asked, wryly, whether the architect had picked the records too. Trentadenari explained with a laugh that it was 'mood music' that he used to seduce lady psychologists, lady journalists, and even a lady lawyer or two.

'Even lady lawyers?'

'They're the biggest sluts of them all!'

Mario the Sardinian kept them waiting until sunset, when they were all starting to get sick of the music and Trentadenari's over-abundant hail-fellow-well-met routine. He'd brought Ricotta with him. Libano was astonished to see an old fellow gangster he'd long since given up for buried, if not underground, after years of jail time.

'I had a good lawyer. He pleaded me down to concurrent sentences and now here I stand!'

Mario the Sardinian, known as Sardo, had escaped from the criminal insane asylum of Aversa two months earlier, while out on probationary leave. Accused of attempted murder, extortion and armed robbery, a psychiatric evaluation had allowed him to pull off a finding of mental infirmity. And he'd earned it, no question about that: at his first session, he'd pissed on the psychiatrist's papers; at the second session, the doctor had shown up with four guards and Mario had remained closed in a wall of silence; during their third meeting, he broke down sobbing like a little boy, demanding a pacifier and a baby bottle. The tests and evaluations dragged out for over a year, amid general dismay. In the end, Mario had won the trust of the prison chaplain and, in a bid to overcome the psychiatrist's flagging objections, he'd staged a fake suicide attempt, in which he supposedly tried to suffocate himself with an overdose of consecrated communion wafers. When all was said and done, he'd been declared clinically insane, something of a menace to society, but only just, keep that in mind, eh! His escape – theoretically a mistake, since it was only three months until his next psychiatric exam – had been in compliance with a specific order issued by Cutolo. Sardo and Professor Cervellone had met, in fact, at the Aversa asylum, and Sardo had kept after him with such persistence that in the end Cutolo decided to go ahead and baptize and bless him, appointing him the underboss of Rome. In a sense, Libano and his men had played a role in Cutolo's decision to send his new lieutenant to the territory of Rome: 'prison radio', as the prison grapevine was known, was reporting that the Rosellini kidnapping was the handiwork of Cutolo's Neapolitans, and the Camorra boss had ordered an investigation into those claims.

'And instead it turns out it was you guys!'

'And instead it turns out it was us.'

'It went pretty well, considering it was your first job,' Sardo conceded.

He was almost completely bald, short, squat, his forehead grooved with an ancient knife scar. When he said jump, Ricotta leapt straight into the air, and even Trentadenari treated him with considerable deference. Libano disliked him immediately. Impossible to say what the inscrutable Freddo thought of him.

'We've got some money to invest and we'd like to put it into a shipment of shit,' Dandi explained.

'How much money?' Sardo asked flatly.

'One, one and a half...'

'We can make that happen. Trentadenari has established a good network with the South Americans. I'll procure the coke for you and I'll authorize you to put it on the market, as long as you stay out of Terribile's territory. I get seventy-five per cent of your profit and ten per cent of the overall capital investment.'

That's worse than the deal you'd get borrowing money from Cravattaro in Campo de' Fiori, Dandi decided instinctively. Libano stroked his chin. Freddo sat there, his eyes half-lidded. Bufalo seemed to be making an effort to follow the conversation, leaning forward to grasp the transitions that escaped him. Trentadenari, feigning indifference, was rolling a spliff. Ricotta knotted and unknotted a garish tie, decorated with a yellow sun and a black moon.

'Maybe Dandi failed to make himself clear,' Libano said, unruffled. 'We're not asking for anyone's authorization, and we couldn't give less of a shit about Terribile. We're offering you a business deal. A fifty-fifty cut, from start to finish. You sell us the shit at the price that we set and we split the profit. For all of Rome...'

The Sardinian got a nasty look on his face.

'Do you understand who you're talking to, Libano?'

'If we didn't, we wouldn't be here,' said Freddo drily.

The Sardinian stared at him with a look of astonishment. There was something imposing about Freddo, Libano decided.

'Let's say that we did this deal. If you want to cover all of Rome, you need a hell of a lot of people. How many men do you have?'

'Fifteen or so,' Dandi ventured.

'That won't be enough.'

'We can find more men, no problem,' Dandi insisted.

'They still won't be enough.'

'You could get in on it yourself,' Freddo suggested. 'With some of your own men, I mean...'

'A joint operation, in other words.'

'I think I said that, no?'

Sardo turned to Libano.

'How do you plan to proceed?'

'By organizing the network into zones. Each zone includes two or three quarters. Each quarter has six or seven ants and a horse overseeing them.

28

The ants report to the horses and the horses report to us. Considering it all, we'd have, maybe, eight zones...'

'What about the competition?'

'We can work out an understanding with Puma. We've known each other all our lives. Everyone else is just small fry...'

'And Terribile?'

'If he's open to it, fine. Otherwise...' Libano let his voice trail off at the end of the phrase, but it was hard to miss his meaning.

Sardo scratched his scar. 'You're asking a lot. Nothing like this has ever been done before in Rome...'

'So much the better. That means we'll be the first. You and us. Together.'

Freddo again. Decisive; cold, hard steel. A boss.

'Together? Maybe. But just one boss. Me,' said Sardo.

'I'm hungry,' Dandi ventured.

A long silence followed. Bufalo and Trentadenari exchanged a glance and headed for the door. Ricotta followed them.

Out in the street, signs of winter: girls in maxi skirts and a dark, ominous sky, with rumblings of thunder. Bufalo and Trentadenari dragged Ricotta into a nearby *rosticceria*, where they ordered roast chicken, potatoes and pizza for everyone.

'You think this'll work out?' Trentadenari asked.

Bufalo spread his arms in an agnostic shrug. And added that Sardo was a real arsehole.

'No, don't say that, Mario's just that way. You'll see, in the end it'll work out...'

'A greedy arsehole,' Bufalo confirmed.

On the way back, Ricotta informed them that the Court of Cassation had ordered the burning of Pasolini's last film. They couldn't have cared less about the fact, but they let him talk because he was a friend. When Ricotta was a kid, he'd put in a few cameo appearances, in Rome's Faggotville, Borgata Finocchio. The word was that Pasolini in person had taught him to read and write. He'd never become an intellectual, but as soon as he got out of prison, he'd gone on a pilgrimage to the Idroscalo, where that nutcase Pino la Rana had murdered the queer poet.

They got back just in time for the round of hugs goodbye. Dandi informed them of the terms they'd struck: 50 per cent for everyone, and an extra five in cash to Sardo for 'staking his name and guaranteeing the good outcome of the deal'. They'd handle the cash receipts fifty-fifty, Trentadenari and Dandi, which is to say, one from each gang. As for who would be boss, they'd come to a compromise: they'd all ask Puma to take on the role of guarantor, a non-partisan arbiter. Obviously, Sardo was convinced he was the top dog, no matter what anyone said. The first shipment of coke would come in fifteen days from then, via Buenos Aires. So it was a done deal.

As he watched the way Libano, Freddo and Dandi exchanged glances behind Sardo's back, it became clear to Bufalo that it wouldn't last long.

'Take it from me,' he whispered to Ricotta, 'forget about that guy. You're one of us.'

II

PUMA HAD COME into the world forty-two years ago, and half of that time on earth he'd spent variously in the Albergo Roma and the Regina.* For the past few years he'd been living with a Colombian girl twenty years younger than him, a mestiza with an Indio nose, the niece of a gangland soldier in the ranks of the Calì cartel. The couple lived with their newborn son, Rodomiro, in a small villa on the Via Cassia.

Four of them went to the meeting: Dandi and Freddo representing one side, Trentadenari and Ricotta on the other. Puma was waiting for them in the yard, with his baby in his arms and a large German shepherd that sniffed at them uneasily, wagging his long thick tail. The Colombian girl served alcohol and fruit tart. Trentadenari, in his usual colourful language, set forth the terms of the proposed deal. Puma let him talk without blinking an eye. And in the end, with all eyes trained on him, he said no.

'Hey, Puma, what are you talking about? We're practically handing you the gold medal!' Ricotta blurted out.

The dog snarled. The baby started whining. The Colombian girl

* Underworld slang for the prisons of Rebibbia and Regina Coeli.

30

appeared inside the house, looking out a window. Puma handed the baby to her and lit the stub of a Tuscan cigar.

'I'm retiring, Ricotta. Tell Libano and Sardo, tell everyone you know, especially the cops...'

Everyone laughed. Puma took two deep drags on his cigar.

'I'm tired. I already have everything I need: this house, a little money in the bank...Maria Dolores...the baby boy...did you see how handsome he is? No, I'm tired. I've had enough of this life...'

'You're talking bullshit, Puma. In just four days, I know you're taking delivery of a kilo from the Chinaman via Palermo. Everyone in Rome knows about it.'

Puma turned slowly to look at Freddo.

'If you let me keep that kilo, you'd be doing me a favour. I'd be in your debt. If you want to take it, go right ahead. This is my last shipment. It's up to you. I'm going to kick the dust off my shoes. That's right, I'm getting out of Rome entirely...'

His unruffled calm had made quite an impression on Freddo. Puma never talked just to hear the sound of his voice. If he said he was getting out, it meant he really was getting out. Was it a matter of age? Was he really as worn out as he was trying to make them believe? Freddo couldn't seem to make all the parts add up.

'Plus, you guys know, I've been in the underworld for twenty-five years now. I've seen it all and I've done it all. What do guys say these days? I've got a very presentable résumé. But there's two things I just can't stomach: kidnapping and murder. I've never nabbed anybody, and I've never killed anybody either...'

'We were as sorry about what happened to the baron as anybody,' Dandi ventured, 'but what were we supposed to do about it?'

'That's not what I'm talking about, boys. The past isn't what worries me...'

'Then what's worrying you?' Freddo asked.

'The future. What's about to happen to every one of us...That's why I'm stepping aside, Freddo...'

'Why, what's about to happen, in your opinion?'

Ricotta was all puffed up: chest thrust forward and the usual ridiculous tie fluttering in the breeze. Trentadenari, who had indulged in a nice little cashmere jumper from Cenci for the occasion, gazed at him with a look of commiseration.

'What's going to happen is you're all going to tear each other limb from limb like a group of pigs. You're going to finish each other off like so many dogs. I guarantee it. And I don't want to be there when it happens.'

'Come on, boys,' Trentadenari exploded. 'Now the old man's casting the evil eye!'

They beat a tactical retreat back to Rome in irritated silence. Freddo couldn't get over it. It wasn't so much the refusal; what worried him was the fact that Puma had seemed to be trying to show them all a different path, a different way of life. How absurd was that? They might as well just go back and finish voc-tech school and take a job under some boss. Wind up like his father: nine-to-five, weekly pay cheque, flaccid balls like a couple of flat tyres. Puma was just a creaky old geezer going senile.

Trentadenari insisted on taking him to dinner with the lady lawyer he'd picked up a couple of weeks ago and had been dating ever since. But Freddo wanted to spend the rest of the evening by himself. Get wrecked on a bottle of wine, sitting in front of the mirror that, with the bed and the café table, constituted the only furniture in the studio apartment on Via Alessandro Severo. But first he had an age-old promise to keep. He asked Trentadenari to drop him off at Mangione's, where he ordered a motor scooter for Gigio.

III

PATRIZIA COULDN'T HAVE been any older than twenty-two, maybe twenty-three. She had dark hair, smooth, soft skin, small firm breasts, perfectly waxed armpits, long legs, and an arse that would tear your heart out of your chest. When she opened the door, in a black negligee and a micro bra that slipped down to reveal the already engorged areola of one tit, Dandi decided he'd done well to trust the recommendation of Fierolocchio, the gang's top expert on whores. Compared with Gina, who was growing visibly fatter day by day, and was already starting to overdo it with the beer and the pills, this young girl was a goddess. And

32

the place might be small, but it was cosy and inviting. On the bed, neatly made with fresh clean sheets, a few plush animals were arranged.

'I charge a hundred if you want it normal, and a hundred and fifty for extras,' Patrizia announced. Her voice was low, hoarse and indifferent.

Dandi flashed his wallet, stuffed with cash. A greedy gleam lit up her eyes. Dandi counted out three fifty-thousand lire notes and tucked them into her micro bra. Patrizia started to strip.

'You want a little floor show?'

Dandi didn't even bother to reply. Either he fucked her in the next ten seconds or he was going to explode. He lunged at her and seized her by the hips with his big rough hands. He spun her around, pulled out his dick, and shoved it in from behind. He came after four thrusts, grunting like a pig. While she went off to get cleaned up, he stretched out among the stuffed animals and lit a cigarette. The intensity of the orgasm had left him sore all over, with a diffuse stabbing pain and a vague sense of dissatisfaction.

'Are you still here?'

Her coldness, the undertone of disgust in the way she looked at him...Patrizia got him steamed up. Till he couldn't stand it.

'You have a boss?' he asked.

'What are you talking about?'

'A boss...a pimp...someone to take care of you...'

'That's none of your business, is it?'

'Do you or don't you?'

'There was a guy who tried, and he's still sobbing bitterly, rueing the day.'

'Are you with somebody?'

'Would you happen to be from the police?'

Dandi burst out laughing. She stood there, aloof and distant, toying with the hem of her panties. Her black lace panties. Dandi already felt the urge to go a second round.

'Come over here,' he said, all polite.

She didn't move an inch.

'You paid, you played, now what do you want?'

With a sigh he grabbed his wallet and tossed it in her direction. She caught it on the fly.

'What are you worth, in your opinion?'

'Are you sure you can afford me?'

'Take as much as you need.'

'I need it all.'

'Then take it all!'

For the first time, she seemed genuinely hesitant.

'I want to be with you,' he said softly.

'I told you: I don't want a pimp.'

'Who's talking about being your pimp? I said I want to be with you: be with you be with you. Get it? We'd go out together, get dinner in a restaurant at night, I'd come see you whenever I felt like it and you'd always be there waiting for me. I'd introduce you to my friends…boyfriend/girlfriend, that sort of thing…'

Patrizia laughed. The sight of her tits bouncing up and down made him feel a little crazy.

'You've got a nerve! Do this, do that, as if your money was better than anybody else's. Who the hell do you think you are? I don't even know your name.'

'I'm Dandi. And I'm a classy guy…'

'Oh really? Classy how?'

'A beautiful apartment, designed by an architect. A painting by Schifano on the wall – the painter who buys his shit from Sardo; we call him "Ski Jump" for all the snow he goes through – an antique secretary desk, oriental carpets, good music, fine champagne…Classy, right? Have you ever seen a fashion show? That's what I have in mind for you, darling…'

She bent over double laughing.

'Classy! He fucks like a wild animal! Wham, bam, ooh, how exciting. There. All done. And now he says he's classy!'

'Then why don't you teach me how?'

She shot him a long, appraising look. Was he worth the effort? Why not? He wasn't anything special to look at, he had a bit of a stink on him, and he was completely clueless in bed. Still, he had more than enough energy. And he sure wasn't shy. Above all: what did she have to lose by trying?'

'Go take a shower, *caro*,' she commanded him, sweetly.

Dandi shot out of the room in a state of high excitement. Once she heard the water running in the shower, Patrizia emptied his wallet and tucked the cash away in the drawer of her bedside table.

When he got back, he found her sprawled out on the bed, legs spread-eagled.

IV

LIBANO COULDN'T BELIEVE his eyes. He flashed a worried look at Bufalo, who was dancing around him like a clumsy bear on his hind legs, and wondered for the dozenth time if he wasn't the butt of some kind of prank.

'Come on, Libano! This is serious, deadly serious, the most serious thing in the world!'

'Serious, but unbelievable!'

'Exactly. Who'd ever think to look here?'

Right. Who'd ever think to look in the ministry? But that's exactly where they were standing. Out in front of the ministry at the EUR, just a short walk from the police station, a quarter mile from the metro station. In the background was the Fungo, the iconic, towering mush-room-shaped water tank; in their ears the roar of traffic on the Via Cristoforo Colombo. They were at the ministry.

Bufalo whistled and a tall grey-haired man dressed in jacket and tie emerged from the shadows of the portico. His name was Ziccone, amiably nicknamed 'the Tic'. Government usher by profession. He was a sweet-smelling, slightly oily individual, with the hoarse voice of a habitual snorter of large quantities of cocaine. There seemed to be a strong bond of conviviality between him and Bufalo. Ziccone ran a steady stream of bets out at the racetrack and, when necessary, he could arrange for small-scale lines of credit. He was available to make short-term investments and to do special favours. Like finding facilities to set up a secret armoury. Right in the basement of the government ministry.

Ziccone led them through a cramped door, covered with graffiti carved by teenage wankers, and into the cellar. Down here, he said, was where the deputy custodian lived. A diminutive grey-haired man, who seemed slow on the uptake – they'd be passing him a monthly payment of six hundred thousand lire to keep an eye on the merchandise. The pint-sized custodian – Brugli, he introduced himself as in a whiny wheeze – handed Libano two bristling key chains, showed them how to work the locks and the most convenient route through the corridors. There was no danger of unwanted surprises: that wing of the government building had been empty for years. Still, Libano pointed out, they had a custodian on salary.

'Because there used to be a passageway that led to the minister's private secretarial pool,' Ziccone explained. 'They walled it up, but nobody's figured that out yet, so Brugli still has a job.'

They drove back to town, calling down benedictions on the blessed bureaucracy that would let them take care of their own fucking business right under the benevolent eyes of the state. Ziccone was paid off with two grams of coke that he snorted up right then and there, so hungrily that Bufalo himself urged him to take it easy. Then Libano dropped the two of them off in a gambling den on the Via Aurelia and went in search of Freddo. But nobody had seen him at Franco's bar – the only one in the bar was Sorcio, scratching the zits on his neck with a blank expression – and Freddo's home phone rang and rang, but nobody picked up. Libano was getting a little tense. Between one call and the next, he managed to find out from Fierolocchio where he could find Dandi, and went straight there.

He had to wait forty-five minutes outside the small street door on the Via Cavour, and it was a good thing his car was clean and he'd left the house without his rod. Dandi showed up reeling like a sailor, and was amazed to find Libano waiting for him. Libano cut the conversation short, asking him about the meeting with Puma. When he heard that it hadn't gone well, he snorted in annoyance. Oh well, take the bad with the good. They'd find another solution. In turn, he told Dandi about the store room in the ministry. They had a good long belly laugh, then Dandi suddenly turned deadly serious and told him that he was in love.

'With that whore?' Libano asked, stunned. 'You don't even know who she is...'

'So? You know what they say: love at first sight...'

'I don't like it. Keep your mouth shut around her!'

'Two months, no more, and I'm moving in with her.'

'What about Gina?'

'Aw, Libano, cut it out! I don't feel like thinking about that right now. What do you know about it? Come to think of it: why don't you have a girlfriend? You wouldn't happen to be a faggot, by any chance? Look, I don't have any hang-ups about that...Should I call you Fifi?'

No, he was no faggot. He liked women, and then some. But how could he explain it to Dandi? It's a matter of military security, he wanted to say to him. We're at war. And when you're at war, you can't afford distractions. Not that a quick fuck now and then wouldn't come in handy, but...emotional involvement, that was out of the question. He had to keep himself clean and...what was the word? That's right – celibate, in a certain sense. Like a priest. There'd be plenty of time later. First, though, they needed to win this war. Take control of the city.

Dandi understood that this wasn't the time for it and went back to his motorcycle. He wanted to tell everyone about Patrizia. He decided to start with Trentadenari. He could even squeeze a little advice out of him. The Neapolitan had more than enough class for the two of them.

But that night Trentadenari had too much gorgeous company to listen to what Dandi had to say. He came to the door dressed in a bathrobe, his nose smeared white with coke and his eyes crazed with excitement, preceded by the undertow of music from inside the apartment.

'Come in, come in, my friend, we were just saying that we needed a fourth guest to round out the table!'

Dandi took a quick look. Two female shapes were squirming on the big white couch. A head of curly blonde hair emerged from the welter of limbs. Dandi locked eyes with the lady lawyer, Mariano. The other woman was a stranger, and something about her cried out junkie. The lady lawyer nodded hello, and then dived back between her partner's legs.

'Well, you want to join in, Dandi? Trust me, it's worth it...'

He declined the offer without a second thought. He couldn't think about anyone but Patrizia.

COMMISSARIO NICOLA SCIALOJA was a restless young man. Twice he'd requested a transfer to the anti-terrorism division and twice he'd been turned down. Politically not quite kosher. A few months ago he'd had a romantic liaison with a young woman from the Autonomia movement, the daughter of a big fish in the Bank of Italy. She lived in a big mansard apartment with a view of Villa Pamphili. She was raising funds for political prisoners. One night she'd asked him why he hadn't stayed at home in the small town he'd grown up in, instead of coming to seek his fortune in the big city of Rome. The affair ended then and there.

His colleagues considered him either a mama's boy or a weirdo, or perhaps both at the same time. In theory, he was an investigator, but in practice he was ineffective. The night they'd kidnapped Baron Rosellini, he was standing in for a more experienced colleague busy searching for – it went without saying – a Red Brigades lair. He'd found himself working side by side with the assistant district attorney, Borgia. They'd got along instinctively. They were both tall and lanky, both totally lacking political protection or mentors, both working on the outskirts of the spotlit stage. Borgia managed to get him assigned to the judicial police squad. The final report on the baron's kidnapping had met with approval. Borgia had complimented him, in the presence of the chief of the mobile squad. They wound up having a beer together on their lunch break. The café on the Via Golametto, across from the main entrance of the Hall of Justice, was teeming with gesticulating lawyers, weary-looking magistrates and cops with arrogant voices. The air was redolent with the smells of stale smoke, coffee grounds, and a hot griddle of sizzling hamburger patties and sliced cheese. Borgia was tired. His wife was expecting a baby. His home life was rife with tension.

'I'm almost thirty,' he said, 'and my life's about to change.'

Scialoja told him about Sandra, the girl from Autonomia Operaia. He hadn't yet completely recovered. Borgia consoled him with a hint of envy: lucky you, you're still a free man. A senior officer from the vice squad walked in. They exchanged a nod of salutation. The senior officer whispered something in the cashier's ear. Scialoja saw her blush. The senior officer gave him a wink.

All charges dropped, case closed. Because the suspects were so many John Does.

Borgia was telling him that even though it was a good report, they hadn't been able to pin down any solid elements. The baron was a goner. Neither hide nor hair of the kidnappers.

'The DA says that my team is a little…how to put this…overstaffed,' Borgia murmured.

So Borgia was about to send him back to where he'd come from. Pushing papers. Looking for another opportunity. There had been no results. Success had escaped his grasp. There had been no arrests. Without arrests, you won't get anywhere. That's rule number one. Scialoja decided to skip the intermediate steps.

'I need a little more time,' he said abruptly.

'If it was up to me…We really worked very well together. But the thing is that equal opportunity isn't really the fashion in the prosecutor's office…The thing is, I'm just a recent arrival. Things would be different if we were trying to catch someone in the Red Brigades. But I'm afraid that, right now, the way things stand, the poor baron…'

Borgia was uncomfortable. He examined his watch. Time to get back to his desk. The cop insisted it was his treat. The ADA accepted the gesture. Left sitting alone at the table, Scialoja ordered another beer. The senior officer from the vice squad, two tables over, was leafing through the *Corriere dello Sport*. Every so often he'd lower the pages of his newspaper and try to catch the cashier's eye, but she avoided his glance. She couldn't have been any older than twenty-two, maybe twenty-three. She was petite, fair-skinned, flat-chested, with a disgruntled expression and no apparent allure. Scialoja paid the bill. The senior officer from the vice squad caught up with him at the front gate of the Hall of Justice.

'I heard they're shipping you back to deskwork.'

'That's the way it looks.'

'You could come work for us…'

'Thanks, but no thanks. I don't think I'm cut out to be a whoremonger.'

'Always the perfect gentleman, eh, Dotto'? Well, too bad for you. You don't know what you're missing…'

'Like, for instance?'

'I saw the way you were staring at the little blonde working at the counter...'

'What little blonde?'

'The cashier.'

'You were the one who was staring at her, not me.'

'Excellent. You're observant. She gets fifty thousand lire a trick. If you want, I'll give you the address.'

'What are you talking about?'

'She looks like a perfectly ordinary young girl, doesn't she? Nothing special about her, right? Well, she's a part-time whore. She gets off work at six in the evening and then she goes to turn tricks in a little apartment right behind the Vatican. Rome is full of girls like her. They put aside a little money and then marry the first sucker to take them for a soap-and-water saint. Part-time whores are a gold mine of interesting information. If you'll allow me the play on words, they live in constant terror of having the trick turned on them. Men just love to confide in their whores. A good cop could roll around in this mud for a whole career. And make plenty of arrests. Give it some thought, my boy!'

Scialoja said that he'd certainly consider it. He watched him stroll away with the swaggering gait of a guy in his forties with testosterone to spare. With a quiver of horror, he considered the greasy hair, the rotting teeth, the oily skin. To be a cop. To wallow in corruption. To wind up like that. One day. One day in the very near future.

He went back into the café. Straight to the cash register. He bought a pack of cigarettes, a box of liquorice, two bars of milk chocolate. Just so he could look her in the eye. To search for the telltale signs that he'd failed to see. But there were no signs.

For the rest of the afternoon he rattled around in his small two-room apartment, WWII-era, out in the university district, with a tiny, increasingly empty refrigerator, a tidal wave of dusty old books, and an old black-and-white television with bad reception that only got RAI, public broadcasting. He pondered the boundaries between good and evil, questioned his own place in the world. He yearned for glory, he yearned for the girls he lacked the courage to approach, he yearned for a change of some kind. They shouldn't have tossed him off the case. He wasn't going to let them send him back to be a paper-pusher in an office.

He plunged into the Rosellini file. Anonymous tips that came up empty. Informants who were peddling smoke. Inconclusive interviews with persons of interest. False alarms. Delirious pathological liars. Dead ends, all of them. He wondered whether any leads could come out of the money laundering. A small portion of the ransom had consisted of marked notes. Less than 5 per cent. Slipped into the bag of cash without the knowledge of the family members. Some of those banknotes had subsequently surfaced. Someone had drawn up a list. Three notes in Sardinia. The carabinieri had put the screws on the Sardinians. Nothing. A dozen or so notes in Calabria. The treasury police had twisted the ear of a few 'Ndrangheta small fry. Plenty more of nothing. A number of banknotes had been found in Rome. Seven fifty-thousand lire notes and four hundred-thousand lire notes, making eleven banknotes in Rome out of the total twenty-four that had surfaced. Scialoja picked up paper and pen and sketched a diagram. Banknotes in Monteverde: two. Banknotes in the Esquiline neighbourhood: nine. Nine banknotes in the same neighbourhood. A smoke shop. A clothing store. A perfume shop. Another smoke shop. A lingerie shop. Another perfume shop. A beauty salon. A shoe store. Another lingerie shop. All between Via Urbana, Via Paolina, Via di Santa Maria Maggiore and Via Cavour. An area just a few hundred metres square. The shopkeepers had all been interviewed and reports filed: I don't remember, I don't know, perhaps they were chance clients, walk-ins. Always customers in the same part of town. But what if it was a single customer? Smoke shop. Lingerie shop. Beauty salon. Perfume shop. It was a woman. A woman.

Scialoja rummaged through his tiny refrigerator. He slammed the door, upset. He went downstairs to eat dinner in a student cafeteria. The students were calling out, talking loudly or necking. He'd only stopped being a student himself a few years ago. He still lived like a student. All he was lacking was a student girlfriend. He thought back to the cashier in the café on the Via Golametto. Sex scenes drilled into his mind. Him and the girl from the café. The girl from the bar and his senior colleague from the vice squad. Her and Borgia. Solitude was starting to get to his brain. He finished the overcooked chicken and the *cicorietta all'agro* and went back to his file.

A woman. A woman from the Esquiline neighbourhood. How many

possibilities? Ten thousand. Twenty thousand? He was dreaming at this point. There was nothing here that justified an additional report. He was wasting time. He'd wind up on the vice squad. Or in an administrative office somewhere. Stamping passports.

He went to sleep. He dreamed of the girl from the café. He woke up in the middle of a wet dream. He checked the dates. The notes hadn't all been spent on the same day. Nine visits to various shops over a twenty-day period. Lingerie shops. A woman. A woman who smokes. A whore. A gang kidnaps the baron. The family pays the ransom but the victim never returns home. The kidnappers split up the loot. One kidnapper pays a woman with cash from the ransom. The woman spends one banknote, then another. The kidnapper comes back to see her again. He pays her again. More banknotes. She works the Esquiline district. The kidnapper is a faithful customer. Scialoja felt he was getting closer to a solution. Sleep had fled. His visions were of a different nature now. An arrest. A chain of arrests. Young officer solves the Rosellini case. Now all he had to do was talk Borgia into it. He needed men. Resources. Most of all, he needed time.

The next morning Borgia didn't even give him a chance to open his mouth. His assignment to the judicial police squad had been revoked. He was once again subject to scheduling by the head of the mobile squad. Effective immediately. Scialoja had twenty or so days of unused paid holiday. He decided to invest the time in a bet on his future. He celebrated with a Campari at the bar in the Via Golametto. Instead of the young female cashier there was a bearded student who read Wittgenstein on his break.

Business, Politics
March–April 1978

I

THE PLAN WAS that Trentadenari would go pick up the courier at Fiumicino airport. Alone. Libano had insisted on having one of them go with him. Sardo pitched a fit: one man attracts less notice than two; this was a bad beginning if it meant they didn't feel they could trust him. Freddo cut the objections short: either we do it the way we say, or the deal is off. Sardo gave in. Bufalo was the second man. He liked the Neapolitan: he kept up a rapid-fire running patter of bullshit and there was no danger of getting bored. If there was one thing Bufalo feared more than anything else on earth it was boredom. Boredom sucks you down like a black hole, and to avoid it you'd do things that right then and there you didn't think twice about, but later you had real trouble on your hands.

When not one but two mestizos – a man and a woman – emerged from passport and customs control, struggling with a large heavy suit-case apiece, it dawned on Bufalo why Libano had insisted on the point, and his admiration grew. Libano was a guy who could think clearly. Libano was a guy who could read the cards. They'd discussed one ship-ment, but Sardo was expecting two. You get it? That bastard. They hadn't even become partners yet and he was already trying to scrape a little off the top for himself!

Trentadenari immediately grasped the implications, too. Bufalo saw him turn pale and slapped him on the back.

'I didn't know a thing about this, I swear it!'

'I believe you, I believe you. But your boss better watch his step!'

They headed back to Rome in two separate cabs. Another security measure devised by Libano. Bufalo drew the taxi with the woman courier, an Indio with a pockmarked face who smelled of sweat and cheap perfume. She looked out the window and grinned idiotically. Bufalo decided he wouldn't fuck her if she was the last woman on the planet. Trentadenari had climbed into the other taxi with the tall guy who looked like a homelier version of Tomás Milián as the petty thief Monnezza. The man was scared and in pain: he kept looking over his shoulder and every so often he clenched his jaw in a grimace of discomfort. He probably swallowed something like forty ovules, Trentadenari mused, and he's shit out of luck if one of them breaks open inside him.

But nothing went wrong, and an hour later they were all in Libano's apartment. Libano was sprawled in an armchair, poring through a horse racing sheet. Sardo, Freddo, Ricotta and Dandi were playing poker, cursing their miserable hands. Of all people, who'd have ever expected it, Sorcio was there, translucent as a cavefish, looking as if he were about to melt, shaking with an unhealthy tremor.

Bufalo and Trentadenari acknowledged each other with a nod and handed over the suitcases to Sardo. Sardo put on a show that was worth paying for a ticket: nobody had told him it was a double shipment, the Chileans must have been trying to pull a fast one, in business you're only as good as your word, ain't that a shame, and so on. Freddo stopped him short.

'Forget about it. Double the shipment, double the business. Same rules apply.'

Bufalo laughed. Sardo shot him a malevolent glare. Ricotta picked his nose, and Dandi watched him with disgust. Libano emerged from his torpor and pushed forward the suitcases containing the money. The Indio courier asked if she could go to the bathroom: she had all the ovules in her body, and the time had come to extrude them.

Sorcio walked over to Libano and stared at him with pleading eyes. Libano pulled a tobacco pouch out of his pocket, opened one of the suitcases containing the shit, rummaged through clothing, bags, toiletry kits, lifted the false bottom, and hefted the various bulging bags of snow. He pulled out one, tore it open with his teeth, careful not to spill so much as a floury smear of drugs, poured ten grams or so into the pouch, and tossed it to Sorcio.

'Thanks, Libano! You're great!'

'That comes out of your end,' Sardo pointed out brusquely.

'Somebody give him a C note, he's starting to get worked up,' Dandi commented acidly.

Sorcio had padded off into the kitchen to cook up a needle for himself the way God commands. Sardo clicked open the suitcases with the money and called Ricotta: give me a little help counting up the cash, four eyes are better than two. Freddo and Libano started weighing the shit.

The Monnezza-looking Chilean had been standing, rigid, the whole time, one hand resting on Il Duce's big old head. He looked pale and dangerously sick. Trentadenari took pity and handed him a tall glassful of whiskey.

'*Guaglio*', it's all going to be all right. All okay, *capito*?'

The Indio woman appeared at the bathroom door. Now someone had to fish the ovules out of the toilet and clean them off. A shitty job, to say the least. Not men's work. Work for rats. For mice.

'Sorcio!' Libano shouted.

The kid came in from the kitchen, feet dragging, his eyes quiescent with the joy of his happy spike. Libano pointed to the toilet. Sorcio trudged off, head down.

And finally everyone understood why he had been summoned: once again, Libano had thought of everything, literally every last thing.

II

Patrizia had a girlfriend. Daniela didn't dye her hair or shave her armpits, but she'd already made a couple of pornos. The three-way left Dandi deeply unsatisfied; it was a different thing with Patrizia alone. The line of coke he'd snorted hadn't revved him up the way it should have. In fact, after a mere half gram, he felt a wave of sadness wash over him that was more powerful than anything he could remember even as a boy, on Sunday afternoons, when he and Libano went out to steal tyres and motor scooters and would stop, staring out over the sea at Ostia without any idea of what would happen, the next day or even the next minute…

They wound up sending her girlfriend away and lazing around the apartment watching television. Patrizia wanted to go out: a little dinner, then dancing or a film. But Dandi got it stuck in his head that they needed to make proper love, and so they wound up doing nothing. They fell asleep watching an old comedy routine by Alighiero Noschese.

At midnight Patrizia woke up ravenously hungry. Dandi walked in on her wolfing down chocolate ice cream, and the sight of her, naked, legs tucked beneath her as she sat eating in the black leather armchair, finally rekindled some healthy physical desire. He had to have his Patrizia! She let him have his way without responding all that much. Anyway, Dandi was a fast learner and he was already starting to shed some of his cruder ways. As for pleasure, Patrizia had long ago figured out that pleasure's out there for the taking, everywhere, except between your legs.

The phone call from Libano caught Dandi by surprise, awakening him in the midst of a Western-film nightmare where he was the marshal with a silver star and Patrizia was a squaw who was letting the head of the black-hatted bad guys fuck her in the arse.

'They kidnapped Moro.'

'Who?'

'Moro, the guy from the Christian Democratic Party.'

'You want to talk about that later?'

Dandi slammed down the receiver and rolled over. Patrizia was still asleep, or at least pretending to be. He slid a hand between her legs, just to see what would happen. She pulled free of him with a snarling grunt. The phone rang again.

'Listen to me, you idiot: the Red Brigades have kidnapped Aldo Moro, the leader of the Christian Democrats, and killed his five police body-guards in the process…'

'Hey, Libano, that's their fucking problem, isn't it?'

'No. It's our fucking problem, too. I want to see you in an hour at the monument.'

Patrizia made things perfectly clear: a shower first thing or no sex for Dandi. Dandi obeyed reluctantly. Still, he managed to get everything done just in time, and at 10.30 he was there, ready and waiting as per appointment.

Libano, however, was running late. Dandi waved hello to Cravattaro, who was on his way to collect the vigorish payments from the market stalls, and then lit a cigarette as he stood waiting at the foot of the statue of that monk the priests burned at the stake so many years ago. Campo de' Fiori stank of rot and smog. Newsboys were strolling up and down calling out the headlines of the special editions of *Paese Sera* and *Il Messaggero*. Everyone was whispering about this Moro guy. As far as Dandi was concerned, the terrorists were an annoyance: road blocks, constant document checks, all-points suspect bulletins. Little room to operate, and getting more dangerous by the moment. Still, they were folks who knew what they were doing. Guys with balls. Too bad they were wasting all their time on politics!

Giordano Bruno, covered with shit-spewing pigeons, couldn't care less. He looked down on them from his vantage point, Bruno did. Dandi thought how horrible it must be to be burned alive. A few years ago he remembered reading in the paper about a student who burned himself alive in protest. Arsehole. When his time came, he hoped it would take the form of a cold, unannounced bullet. Amen.

Libano pulled up on his motorbike and waved for him to climb on behind him. They roared off down the narrow lanes, crossing Via del Pellegrino, emerged into the Largo della Moretta, and pulled onto the Lungotevere, running along the Tiber. Libano was grim, focused.

Mario the Sardinian, AKA Sardo, was waiting for them under the Magliana bridge. He was wearing a heavy white jacket, a pair of mirrored sunglasses, and a tricolour necktie, and he carried a crocodile skin attaché case.

'What's all this? Your imitation of a businessman?'

Sardo ignored Dandi's dumb joke and brought them up to speed on the situation.

'Cutolo reached out to me. We have to do something for Moro.'

'Do what?' Libano asked.

'He wasn't specific. I think we're supposed to find where they're holding him, break in, liberate him, something like that...'

'We're supposed to do what?' Dandi asked in amazement.

'Either us or the police. As long as we can come up with the information.'

'Hey, Sardo, did we get enlisted without being told about it? Since when did we become the white hats?'

'Maybe we did, Dandi, maybe we did. Think of it this way: those arsehole cops don't have the slightest idea of which way to turn. So they're asking Cutolo for help. Cutolo knows that in Rome he can count on me. And I'm counting on you!'

'And what's in it for us?' Dandi insisted.

Libano intervened.

'This is supposed to be some kind of barter, right, Sardo? I give you this today and tomorrow you give me that...'

Sardo nodded.

'We can do this,' Libano concluded, 'but where do we start?'

'I'll let you know,' Sardo said.

III

PUMA WAS HAVING problems with his kilo of coke. He'd handed over half the kilo wholesale to a group of Calabrians on their way to Buccinasco, on the outskirts of Milan: shit that would be used to seal an understanding between Turatello and the Catanians under Epaminonda il Tebano, up north. But Puma didn't even want to hear about that kind of thing. He'd decided to get out of the business, full stop. So, rather than eat his losses, he'd decided to liquidate that half kilo of coke, selling it to Freddo at cost. Freddo put in every penny that remained to him from his end of the kidnapping ransom. So when it came time to divvy up shares, alongside the 1.3 kilos of brown sugar brought by the Chilean couriers, there was also a half kilo of Colombian pink that Puma had already cut with amphetamines and lidocaine.

They had all gathered in Sorcio's shack. The Buffoni brothers were in charge of cutting the dope: 33 per cent, because flooding the market with excessively pure shit meant massacring the clientele, shooting themselves in the foot. And 3.9 kilos of heroin retail was interesting business.

Bufalo, Trentadenari and Ricotta had done a good job with their recruitment drive. Sardo's men were there and so were all the kids they'd managed to round up. Libano had drawn up a chart with the division into zones. As each batch of baggies with the stepped-on shit was ready, they'd deliver them to a horse and carefully note down weight and placement. A record needed to be kept of everything. It all had to be minutely described and regulated.

'It looks like an assembly line to me!' Dandi observed. 'Who'd have thought I was going to wind up working in a factory after all!'

'Working for the award-winning purveyors of product, Smack, Coke and Sons!' laughed Bufalo.

'This is just to get started,' Libano reassured them. 'Before long the business will practically run itself...'

Delivery notes
17 March 1978

ZONE // QUANTITY // DISTRICT BOSS // HORSES

Magliana, Monteverde, Portuense // 700 g // Trentadenari, Bufalo // Orzobimbo, Pescofresco

Trullo // 700 g // Buffoni brothers // Minchione, Palla di Neve

Garbatella, Tormarancia // 700 g // Scrocchiazeppi, Fierolocchio // Giamesbond, 'O Marocco

Trastevere, Torpignattara, Centocelle // 1500 g // Dandi, Libano, Botola, Freddo, Sorcio, Petulante

Ostia-Acilia // 150 g // Sardo // Brigantino

Viale Marconi // 150 g // Ricotta // Sadico

There was to be no market in Testaccio, as they'd decided to accept Botola's request. It was all his mama's fault: she couldn't stand to see the piazza of her proletarian childhood invaded by a horde of scab-ridden junkies. As for the half kilo of cocaine, Trentadenari's proposal had been approved. They'd exchange the cocaine ounce for ounce for Thai heroin, already 25 per cent cut. The deal was with a couple of his old comrades from Naples. The five hundred grams of Thai smack would then be subdivided between the groups of Ostia-Acilia and Viale Marconi (two hundred grams for each group), and the remaining hundred grams would be split between Garbatella and Trullo.

The last one to leave was Sadico, a gimp from Via Oderisi da Gubbio, who'd earned his moniker – the Sadist – through a bad habit of beating the prostitutes on whom he spent all his money.

Three of them remained in the shack: Sorcio – who'd managed to cadge an extra shot for himself – Freddo and Libano. Libano lit two Marlboros and handed one to Freddo. There was a smile on his face. The smile of a true friend.

'You know, Freddo, that half kilo of coke...'

'Yeah?'

'It was your idea, you put up the money. If you'd gone ahead and sold it and kept the proceeds, nobody could have said a thing against you.'

'It was the right thing to split it up, equal shares...'

'How many of the others do you think would have done the same thing?'

'What do I know? You, Bufalo, maybe Fierolocchio...'

'Dandi.'

'Dandi, sure, of course...'

'But the others wouldn't have, eh?'

'No, not the others.'

'Well, we need to get to the point where the others do the same thing without thinking twice. All the others – even Ricotta, even Sardo...'

'Why's that?'

'Because the day we can get everyone to think the same way – when that day comes, no one will be able to stop us...'

'What if someone's not down with it?'

'Then it'll be time to get rid of them!'

But Freddo wasn't opening up. He was still so reserved, shut up tight, impenetrable. Libano slapped him on the back.

'We'll pull this off, partner.'

'Sure.'

'And we'll open that club.'

'Maybe.'

'At seventy or eighty thousand lire a gram, we'll be making a lot of money. We'll put part of it in the general fund, part of it we'll reinvest, part we distribute to the boys and part we'll use to open that club.'

'Could be.'

'Wow, hold it down with all the enthusiasm!'

'I heard we're supposed to be doing something about Moro.'

Libano crushed out his cigarette and lit another. 'That's a good thing.'

'Politics is never a good thing, Libano. I smell a trap.'

'What are you talking about! Let's say we really do find that poor bastard: we'll be doing a favour for the government, and the government will turn a blind eye... That's what we're talking about now, Freddo: it's a high-stakes game!'

Freddo shrugged. That was the way Freddo was. He was always expecting a nasty surprise, any minute, from any direction. It was just when things seemed to be falling into place that the devil would stick his tail in.

IV

SCIALOJA HAD BEEN forced to bring his colleague from the vice squad in on it. What he needed from him was a list of whores working the Esquiline hill. No part-time whores or common streetwalkers: he only wanted call girls above a certain level. He'd been forced to lay out his theory.

'Say I'm a gangland criminal and I've just laid hands on a major payoff. I'm horny as hell. I want nothing but the best.'

The colleague had his doubts. In the end, he gave Scialoja a list of five names and a photograph to go with each name. In exchange, Scialoja had to promise he'd share the arrests with his colleague. That is, if there were any arrests. If the whore contributed in any way to those arrests. If there even was a whore at all. Scialoja showed the pictures to the shop-keepers. One of the two guys who ran the smoke shop recognized all five of the hookers. Big smokers: multiple packs a day. The man's palms were glistening with sweat. No doubt about it: he'd found his way into bed with at least one of them, maybe more. The woman who ran the perfume shop down the street recognized none of them. The sales girl at the lingerie shop recognized girl three. Scialoja checked the accompanying file: Vallesi, Cinzia, twenty-four. Stage name: Patrizia. Expelled from the city limits of Vicenza and Catania. No convictions.

Scialoja went back to the perfume shop and demanded that the woman rummage a little more insistently through her memory. 'Maybe' this face looks familiar, but 'I couldn't be 100 per cent certain'. 'It could be' that the young lady purchased an item or two from the shop. 'Perhaps' she paid in cash. It was a slender lead, but it was the only lead he had.

Early the following morning, Scialoja went to see Borgia. He told him everything, or nearly everything. He suggested applying a little pressure to the girl. Have her tailed. She'd lead them to the kidnapper. But they'd need staff and resources.

Borgia was in a foul mood. He had the slightly bruised features of someone who'd been up until all hours dealing with the exaggerated fears of a pregnant wife. Staff? Resources? With every man in uniform the length of Italy trying to track down poor Aldo Moro? Sheer madness!

They parted ways with a tense farewell.

Scialoja had an address. He spent two days of his precious holiday time staking out the beat-up old street door in the Via di Santa Maria Maggiore. She showed up around eleven in the morning and didn't leave again until seven at night. To look at her, so to speak, in civilian clothes, she had a certain something, a touch of class. Impossible to tell her apart from any young secretary or university student determined to earn her degree. There was no concierge in this apartment building. Men came in, men went out. It was pointless work, a complete waste of time. Scialoja was looking for a professional criminal. But it was impossible to distinguish a hardworking head of household coming home from the office from a john looking to purchase sex.

On the third night, Scialoja decided to take his chance when she went out. Like all whores who aspire to a certain tone, she kept home and workplace separate. Home was in the Borgata Giardinetti, where the city goes to die in the embrace of the Via Casilina and the on-ramp to the Rome beltway, the Grande Raccordo Anulare. She went upstairs to get changed, came back down wearing an evening gown, and climbed into her wheezy old Fiat 500. She carefully tucked the long skirt with its dizzying slit up the side beneath her, gave her make-up a quick check in the rear-view mirror, and was gone. Scialoja gave her a fifteen-minute head start to limit the risk of unexpected returns home. Then he made his move.

The street was deserted. The street door was wide open. On the downstairs panel of buzzers, her real name appeared. It was a third-floor apartment. The door had an ordinary Yale lock, without any dead bolts or reinforcement back-up rings, and it gave right in to his pass key. He didn't know what he was looking for. He didn't even know whether Patrizia was the right woman. But he had to get inside. He was about to commit a certain number of crimes. He was irreparably undermining the investigation. Just one quick look around. A matter of five minutes, no more. He carefully shut the door behind him. Turned on the light. A neat, well kept little apartment. The smell of floor wax in the air. Wallpaper with a puppy-dog pattern. A sofa, a television set. In the other room, a full-size bed, a small dressing table in very poor taste, an armoire full of clothing and an incredible collection of women's shoes. Lots of handbags. Three drawers crammed with lingerie: all of it quite refined, nothing flashy. Ah, of course, she doesn't entertain customers here. Here she's just the amiable Signorina Cinzia, the well-mannered third-floor neighbour...

A faint, early-morning scent wafted off of the clothing. Feminine, no doubt about it, but it didn't suggest sex; rather, it hinted at a long, lazy awakening, the leisurely morning of a little girl still warm from the bed. Cinzia: the good little girl, still part *bambina*. In the fourth drawer, photographs and school notebooks. Cinzia at age seven. In the background, the beach at Capocotta. Litter and sweaty bodybuilders in high-waisted swimsuits. A man with a thick moustache held her hand. She was glaring into the lens with a furrowed brow. Cinzia at her first communion. The man with a moustache had a few grey hairs, and in this picture she was taller. The man was wearing the uniform of a non-commissioned officer in the Italian navy. Her gaze: lost in the middle distance, over there somewhere. No mother bubbling over with joy and excitement. Cinzia was motherless. Cinzia didn't grow up on the street. Cinzia already more than adolescent. In the glare of a flashbulb, in a discotheque. Arms wrapped around a dance floor Casanova, his shirt unbuttoned to the navel. Looked like a young man from a good family. Cinzia in a miniskirt. Her gaze: focused, with a hint of greedy rapacity.

Scialoja put everything away and did a perfunctory search of the rest of the apartment. No sign of any male presence. Patrizia had no pimp or protector. In the washing machine he found a key. There was a little lockbox high up in the overhead toilet cistern. How naïve: he had to smile. He was starting to get a better idea of her. In the lockbox: some loose change, a few rings, gold earrings, a bankbook in which, in a neat, somewhat hesitant hand, she had kept records of periodic deposits. The treasury of Patrizia, the good and thrifty little girl. Three folded sheets of paper. A photo of Raquel Welch in a swimsuit, taken from a pulp scandal sheet, with a caption that read: *The secret love affair of the most beautiful woman on earth*. A brochure featuring the latest jewellery from Bulgari. And a pamphlet touting: *The trip of your dreams to the tropical islands*. Cinzia's dreams. Well, there you go: a quick tour of the world of a girl who trades pussy for cash.

Scialoja knew that the smart thing was to beat it out of there fast. He decided to stay anyway. It had excited him to violate the privacy and intimacy of a stranger. He turned off all the lights, checked to make sure that his duty revolver was in order, and got comfortable on the sofa. Anyone with money could have Patrizia, but he was going to take Cinzia. It might be a long wait.

V

THEY'D CAUGHT SORCIO while he was delivering a packet of baggies to two ants from Cinecittà. The ants had taken off running like the wind, leaving the shit behind them on the ground. There were six of them: the four Gemito brothers, Checco Bonaventura from Spinaceto, and Saverio Solfatara, a Sicilian who'd done seven years seclusion in an asylum for the criminally insane. They'd dragged Sorcio into a big open field and forced him to swallow a gram of dope. Then they'd broken one of his arms and left him there, sprawled in a puddle of his own vomit. It was a miracle that the kid had survived, and now he was under police guard and hospital arrest at the Ospedale San Camillo. Franco the barkeep was the one who'd told them what had happened. Libano and Freddo had decided that none of them should go to visit him in the hospital: too risky. Before Libano let Franco go, he'd handed him ten million lire for the kid's medical care and other expenses.

So Terribile had struck a blow. He'd taken it out on the most helpless of them all, that miserable loser Sorcio. This was a full-fledged declaration of war. This was something they couldn't ignore. Bufalo, who was present with Dandi, Trentadenari and Ricotta at this plenary session of the executive council, suggested getting their weapons at the ministry and going to unleash a nice warm bloodbath.

'I know where to find that piece of shit!' he shouted. 'What are we waiting for? He's not expecting us! We'll catch him off guard and leave him dead. Let's go right this second!'

'Oh, I know where to find that miserable turncoat myself,' Libano replied calmly. 'He's holed up in a bunker in Garbatella. Bulletproof glass and bodyguards all over the place. And if there's a time when he expects us to come for him, that would be now...'

'So we're supposed to just let this stand? We take our medicine and say amen?'

'Not on your life. We're going to wait until the time is right, that's all.'

'Wait until the time is right! And when is the time going to be right?'

Libano looked over to Freddo for support. Freddo gestured for him to go on.

'We're not strong enough right now. The boys are still afraid of Terribile.'

'Let's kill him and call it even!'

'We can't go there right now. He's on the alert, don't you get that, Bufalo? Let's even say that we managed to break our way in. How many of us would die in the process? One of us? Two? We can't afford to lose a single guy!'

Bufalo turned to look at Freddo. Freddo slowly nodded his head.

'Right now a shoot-out would be suicidal.'

'So what are we supposed to do?' Bufalo asked.

'The first thing we need to take care of is moving this shipment of product. The whole shipment. Without any further losses. And if we want to do that, there's only one way. We're going to have to cut a deal with Terribile.'

Pandemonium broke out in the room. Bufalo started pounding the big bust of Mussolini's head. Dandi did his best to placate Trentadenari, who was shouting threats in dialect. Ricotta was frantically searching for the scrap of paper with the secure phone number for Sardo, who had gone to consult with Cutolo on the matter of Aldo Moro. Freddo waited for the hubbub to die down. Then he asked Libano to go ahead and explain his proposal.

'We offer him a ten per cent cut in exchange for freedom to deal on the street without problems...'

'But you said you'd never pay for protection!' Bufalo objected furiously, his eyes bloodshot.

'Cut it out,' Freddo murmured.

'We're just pretending, lulling him along, acting as if we acknowledge his authority,' Libano went on. 'We'll tell him he's still the boss, still the top banana. We'll let him believe he's won just as long as it takes us – two, maybe three months – then, once we've moved the entire shipment, once every last baggie's sold, we'll order another. and then we'll offer him twenty per cent. At that point he's feeling safe, perfectly safe. He's sleeping on velvet...And that's exactly when we'll take him out. We're in no hurry. We'll do it at a time of our choosing. With a method of our choosing. At a place of our choosing!'

They called on Puma to help organize the meeting. A man of his word, Puma: he'd sold the villa in record time and now he was enjoying his infant son and mestizo girlfriend in the cool green hills of Acquapendente. It hadn't been easy to talk him into it, but in the end Dandi pulled it off by kidding around and caressing the baby. Terribile set the rules of the meet: no weapons, only two men from their side, while he had the right to bring all the men he wanted. The setting: the ancient Roman ruins of Ostia, at the beach. Puma was the guarantor for both sides.

While they were driving out for the meeting, Freddo could sense the tension emanating from Libano's skin.

'It's because we're staking it all, going all in,' his partner explained. 'All we need is a little more time, but if Terribile won't give us that time, we won't be able to control the boys anymore. We're going all in on this one.'

That was only a part of the truth. Now that he'd got to know him better, Freddo understood that there was something else going on beneath the surface. Something different, something more personal. He felt a twinge of curiosity, but this was no time to ask questions. Terribile and the four Gemito brothers were waiting for them, hands on their hips. Puma, who was with them, broke away from the group and walked towards them. With the pretext of the usual greetings, he made it clear to them that Terribile was absolutely furious.

'Ah, Libano. How's the kid doing? What is it you call him? Sorcio?'

'He's doing all right, Terribile. He said to give you his regards...'

'Ah, well, that's nice. It means I've saved myself the cost of sending a wreath!'

Libano unfurled his most reassuring smile and put his best foot forward: they'd come in peace, they wanted to come to an understanding and avoid a gang war that would only cause trouble and misery for everyone.

'There's no one who can cause me trouble, you little piece of shit. You're the one who has good reason to be afraid of his own shadow from now on!'

Puma did his best to restore peace. If this was how it was starting out, it promised to end badly. After all, the boys had come to beg Terribile's pardon for having invaded his territory, and it was incumbent upon him to recognize their good will and act a little more reasonable. Terribile seemed to think it over for a little while, and then he turned to Freddo.

'So what the fuck do you have to say about it, eh?'

Freddo pretended he hadn't heard and lit a cigarette. But Terribile kept pushing: and it was who-the-fuck-do-you-think-you-are here and what-the-fuck-are-you-looking-for there, and even a shove for poor Puma who was trying to pour oil on the waters. This was the first time that Freddo had ever seen Terribile. Everybody knew that he'd started out as a car thief, and had then moved up to loan sharking and running whores, and from there to gambling. Terribile was the king of dog- and horse-racing. With the money he'd made on picchetto games (as they called piquet in Rome) he'd opened a couple of butcher shops and a building supplies retailer in Primavalle. He had fifteen hired thugs, and he fenced the swag that bank vault burglars brought him. The Gemito boys were his praetorian guard: they were privileged to work their own extortion and loan-sharking rackets. Freddo summed him up: the brain of a chicken and the fat of a Japanese beef cow. If he'd brought his revolver with him, he would have shot him down then and there. But

Libano stopped him with a glance. When a friend calls for help, you owe him a response.

'We've come to ask forgiveness, Terribile. We made a mistake and now we want to make up for it.'

'Oh, finally someone's starting to talk sense!'

Arrogant, and stupid. While the Gemito boys visibly relaxed, and Puma drew a sigh of relief, Libano formulated his proposal. Terrible let him finish, and then hocked out his counteroffer: 25 per cent immediately, and thirty on the next delivery. No direct involvement in the narcotics trafficking and Centocelle was off-limits. Libano did another ten minutes or so of song and dance about the group of youngsters just making their first faltering steps in the big time, depending for advice and guidance on a venerable and respected leader. They settled on 20 per cent for now and twenty-five on the second shipment. They had to give in on Centocelle. Oh well, they'd take it back on the next round. Terribile and his men headed out without so much as a wave goodbye to Puma.

Once they were alone again, Freddo noticed the half moon that was illuminating the clear, cold early March night and the way Libano was shaking. He was staring out at the amphitheatre's horizon with balled fists, his jaws clenched. He insisted on heading back to Rome solo. Puma offered to give Freddo a ride back. It was on the way back that he learned from Puma the reason for the ancient hatred that Libano felt for Terribile.

'It's an old story, from when they were kids, but what can you do about it? Libano still harbours that grudge...'

Libano was sixteen at the time and he liked a girl from Vicolo del Bologna, in Trastevere – a cute little brunette, the daughter of a policeman, a guard in the *pubblica sicurezza*. They were just starting to kiss and she'd already let him feel her tits the night that Libano decided to impress her by showing up with a big expensive car. The only problem was that he stole the wrong Lancia, and one of Terribile's men had even seen him hot-wiring the vehicle. They grabbed them as they were leaving the pizzeria and dragged them into the presence of the big boss himself. In the back of a gambling den at the Magliana Idrovore, Terribile pissed on him while two of his men forced the little brunette to suck them off. They let them go, and it was just dumb luck that they didn't go ahead and rape her. Libano never saw her again.

'If you ask me, sooner or later Terribile is going to have to pay for all the moves he's pulled, because he's pulled one too many,' Puma concluded. 'But that's why I'm walking away from the game. What can I tell you, Freddo, bloodshed just turns my stomach!'

Freddo decided that the honour of the first shot would be Libano's by rights. But the second shot, he was determined to fire it right into the slimy bastard himself.

VI

THEY SAT WAITING for Dandi, staked out in the countryside surrounding the Gazometro – the big gas holding tank. Scialoja was there too. He wanted to come face to face with the man Patrizia had betrayed. Two hours earlier ADA Borgia had signed the arrest warrants. The kidnapping of Baron Rosellini was the work of a gang consisting of two-bit Roman gangsters. Their names: Dandi, Libano, Freddo, Bufalo, Satana, Botola, and others yet to be identified. The eyewitness Marussi had identified Dandi from a photograph. It was all there in Scialoja's supplementary report. The input came from 'confidential sources'. The photographic identification was a formidable confirmation of the theory. They were going to catch the lot of them. And all at once. Scialoja knew that it would be no easy thing to pull this off in court. Judges dislike tipsters. The eyewitness to the kidnapping might suddenly have a change of heart. They'd need some luck. Some valuable new information might emerge from the searches. One of them might decide to talk. In any case, the battle was just beginning. He needed them to feel his breath on their necks. He needed them to understand they'd been identified. He needed them to tremble in fear. He needed them to make a misstep.

They sat waiting and smoking. Scialoja was thinking about Patrizia. He was thinking about the investigation. Once they'd received the initial tip-off, the rest followed automatically. It took brainwork. It took heart. Patrizia had talked. If only they'd offered Scialoja some minimum level of assistance, some hint of co-operation, he would've immediately assigned six men to tail Dandi day and night, and in less than a week he would've known everything about him that there was to know. But he was working solo. He'd had to come up with a different strategy. Heart and head. He had gone to pay a call on the mobile squad. He'd asked a series of naïve questions. He'd taken old colleagues out to dinner, men who'd never bothered to glance in his direction. He'd flattered them, kissed arse, prodded and poked at them, encouraged their arrogant pride – I want nothing better than to learn at your feet; I'm just a beginner; I'm in need of your help. The senior officers had warmed up, set their wariness aside. Scialoja gathered useful information. In Rome, there'd never been one gang stronger than any of the others. The gangs are born and die in the course of a morning. Here, agreements dissolve at the first gust of a western breeze. Everyone hates everyone else and if they can find a way to arse-fuck each other in turn, they do it gleefully. Which is why anyone who wants to come to Rome does so and commands as he sees fit: Sardinians, Marseillais, Calabrians, Pugliese, even inter-lopers from the adjoining rural Ciociaria, like Lallo lo Zoppo's men, a guy who liked to feed his victims to the hogs. They come and they go, and none of them live long enough to tell their grandchildren the story. Right now the strongman was a certain Terribile. A specialist in extor-tion and gambling. Scialoja had cautiously introduced the topic that mattered most to him: if Terribile was the boss, did it seem likely that as spectacular an undertaking as the kidnapping of Baron Rosellini could have escaped his supervision? He'd heard a hearty burst of laughter in reply. Terribile controls his territory; he's very careful to respect borders. Terribile knows that you have to fit in if you want to survive in Rome. Terribile's not the kind to pull off a kidnapping.

'What about Dandi?' he'd said off-handedly, as if he'd just let it slip.

'Him? He's an airbag, small fry, a complete zero.'

He'd resumed regular police duty eight days before his holiday time was up. His captain had spread his arms wide in mock helplessness: now what am I going to do with my young professor? He'd asked to be assigned to the gambling beat. That was Terribile's territory, right? If he and Dandi were partners in the kidnapping, he'd find out about it. He'd done his homework. Unearthed old criminal complaints, perused forgotten reports. Terribile owned property, controlled men, had connections. He'd identified one foot soldier with more tips on him than a billiard parlour. This Pino Gemito seemed to be a bodyguard of some kind, a side of beef, all muscles and no brains, paid to take his boss's place in jail. Scialoja shouted in his ear that he and his friends were suspects in the baron's kidnapping and murder. He trotted out Dandi's name. He insinuated that a spate of evidence had begun to flow in. It would only be a matter of time before he had them all where he could screw them royally. The muscle-bound Maccabee sat open-mouthed, purple-faced, looking as if he were having a heart attack. It was obvious he didn't know a thing, but there was only one thing Scialoja wanted: to get word to the man's boss. His senior colleagues told him that there was no such thing as solidarity in the *mala* – the Roman underworld. Maybe fear could get someone to squeal. For years, Gemito had been one of the senior officers' favourite informants. That senior officer burst into Scialoja's office and pinned him to the wall.

'If you want to last in here you have to learn the rules, you little piece of shit. What's with this whole kidnapping thing? Do you think that if Terribile had anything to do with it I wouldn't have known about it before anyone else? I'm starting to think that you're not going to last long around here...'

The officer went to pay a call on Terribile in person to reassure him. That whole story was nothing more than a comic sideshow, a piece of opera buffa. The overambitious debut of a half-pint careerist who wasn't destined to last. He had no evidence against Terribile and his men. Terribile thanked him and promised a suitable payback when the time was ripe. But in the meantime, the 'overambitious debut of the half-pint careerist' had planted the seed of an idea. Libano and his rag-arse henchmen were getting to be a little too full of themselves. The opportunity made his mouth water. Why let this chance slip away? The policeman was already on Dandi's trail. Why not gift-wrap the whole gang and hand them over?

When he saw him loom out of the shadowy doorway and head in his direction, Scialoja scrabbled frantically for his department-issued Beretta. But Pino Gemito, hands raised in a sign of surrender, came in peace. He came bearing names, dates, corroborating details, priceless information. There was just one condition: anonymity. Scialoja took the bargain. Pino Gemito had already spread out his merchandise for him to consider. The man had run a considerable risk. He'd taken it right out to the brink. And he'd won. For the moment. Scialoja smoked and bided his time, waiting for his fat pigeon. He still couldn't quite figure out why Patrizia had decided to talk.

Patrizia couldn't seem to wrap her head around it either. It had gone the way it had gone, and that was that. She remembered every detail of that night. She'd come home a little before dawn. When she saw him, she'd let out a scream. Her first thought was: a maniac. But he'd just waved his badge in the air with an ironic look on his face.

'Ciao, Cinzia. I've been waiting for you.'

She'd lunged instinctively for the door.

'Don't try it. I'm bigger than you and I know what I want.'

Something in his tone of voice persuaded her to resign herself to the situation. She'd kicked off her shoes and let her handbag fall to the floor.

'I have to go piss.'

She had been intentionally vulgar and unpleasant. She wanted him to feel the full blast of her scorn. But when she walked past him, she'd caught a distinct whiff of his excitement. He'd grabbed her by the arm.

'Leave the door open.'

'What, you like it filthy?'

'No, I just don't like surprises.'

'I give you my word.'

'Your word as Cinzia or your word as Patrizia?'

She'd locked herself in, and he'd done nothing to stop her. Maybe he was just a horny cop after all. Maybe she'd get off easy, turning a fast trick, and be done with him.

She came back to him dressed in a two-bit kimono with a nasty grin on her face. Ready to take care of business all by herself, as usual. She'd lit an incense stick.

'It cuts the stink of cop.'

He'd peeled off a couple of C notes.

'I don't work here.'

'Ah, of course, I was forgetting... This is the lair of little girl Cinzia...'

Still, he went on waving the banknotes around. In the end she took them, mechanically. And she let her kimono slip open. He sat considering her small breasts, let his inscrutable gaze run over her nude body, sliding to a halt when it reached the chestnut pubic hair of her crotch.

'You like looking?'

She'd moved closer. As long as he got it over with. She was tired. The Arabs at the Hilton had worn her out. She loosened the knot of his tie. He had a decent smell: tobacco and bitter cologne. The smell of a man having his first kinky experience. He'd shoved her away with a sort of leer.

'So you like to do it fully dressed, darling?'

He'd brushed his fingers over her long neck, caressed one of her breasts.

'The ice is starting to melt at last, eh?'

He'd pushed her away again. She had returned to the charge. He'd pushed her away with even greater determination. She'd lost her temper. What kind of game was this guy playing? He'd lit a cigarette. He smiled. He exuded confidence. A young cop. Tall, skinny, handsome, horny. And yet he'd pulled back just at the tastiest moment. Patrizia donned her kimono.

'All right, what's up?'

'Come here. We've got some talking to do.'

'I don't have a thing to say to a cop. Not me.'

'You want a cigarette?'

'Fuck yourself!'

'I could have had you subpoenaed. I could have had you arrested...'

'What for? I'm not doing anything wrong. I'm at home, minding my own business!'

'Oh, we can always come up with a reason. If we make up our minds to. Anyway, here I am...'

'So what about it?'

'You're curious, eh?'

'I'm tired. I'm sleepy. I've had an exhausting evening.'

'Ah, of course, your work...your clients...all those men, coming and going...'

'What are you, anyway? Some kind of sadist? One of those maniacs who get their excitement from tormenting helpless young girls? Well, if that's what you're looking for, you came to the wrong place. There are certain areas I have no interest in exploring. But I can direct you to a couple of friends of mine...'

'Cut it out, Cinzia. I'm just a guy who's trying to do you a favour.'

'Don't call me Cinzia! You paid, didn't you? So call me Patrizia.'

'A big favour…Patrizia.'

'A favour? You're trying to do me a favour? Oh, I get it! Another would-be protector! No, handsome, that's not going to work out. I don't want a boss, and I don't want a pimp. I'm here today and who knows where I'll be tomorrow. If you think that all you have to do is raise your voice and I'll be quaking with fear…'

'You have a customer who's been paying you with dirty money. Cash that comes from a ransom payment, a kidnapping. He gave you at least four marked banknotes. The victim was murdered. This is a case that carries a mandatory life sentence.'

She put her head in her hands. She'd understood immediately. There was only one guy who could have pulled off a stunt like that. That animal who'd been buzzing around her. The swaggering boaster. The idiotic bumpkin. What was his name again? Dandi. The cop had heaved a sigh, all sympathetic now.

'I see you're starting to figure it out. Come on over here.'

She'd gone over and sat down next to him. He'd pulled her closer. The nice cop. The cop with a warm, persuasive voice.

'I'm sure you know who I'm talking about. All I want is that one name. I'll make sure your name is kept out of everything. I swear it. Just give me that name…'

'I don't have any idea who you mean. They come, they pay, I can't possibly know what…'

'I know, you're clear of all this. Just give me the name and I'll leave you alone.'

Patrizia had felt very confused at this point. It seemed like a reasonable offer. But if you ever spill the beans to a cop, you might as well resign yourself to spilling the beans for the rest of your life. You automatically get taken under his wing. And she didn't want protectors of any kind. There was no room in her life for a protector. She'd sworn it on the scar running across Russo's face. Russo had raped her. And Russo had paid. Russo hadn't exactly gone around talking about what had happened to him.

'So?'

'So give me a cigarette.'

She'd leaned forward for him to give her a light. One small breast had slid out of her kimono. She'd caught him glancing at it out of the corner of his eye. She'd sensed his body go rigid. She'd stared at him, blowing tiny smoke rings into the air. He'd returned the look. Their heads brushed against each other, dangerously close. Patrizia had crossed her legs, revealing a glow of tanned thigh. The policeman had gulped. Patrizia had understood that this fleeting glimpse excited him, while seeing her nude, earlier, had left him indifferent. Now he was looking at her the way you look at a whore. She'd understood that the cop was a man like all the others. A man who desired her. If she gave in, if she'd given him the name, then she'd have had a master. The kimono had slid away. She'd run a hand between her legs, impregnating it with her smell, and then she'd caressed his face. She'd started working on one of his ears with her tongue. The policeman had clutched her to him, incapable of controlling himself. She'd started fooling around with his belt.

'The name!' he'd groaned.

'I don't know,' she'd laughed, her mouth plunged into his ear, 'and even if I did I'd never tell you!'

He'd grabbed her and given her a powerful shaking.

'Don't make me lose my temper!'

She'd wriggled out of his grip. She'd dug two fingernails into his neck and scratched hard. Two reddish striations appeared on his skin. Then she'd rolled away to the far end of the sofa. Ready to face down his insults. Ready to defend herself against the predictable violence. The cop had run his hands over his wounds, as if incredulous. He'd stared at her, suddenly aflame with desire. Patrizia had felt her own yen grow. She'd slid over next to him. She started licking the blood that oozed from the cuts. He'd shut his eyes. She'd undressed him. With her claws dug into his back. When she sat down on top of him, he was ready and able. I've won, said her eyes, afterwards. You paid, you came, I didn't talk. He'd seized her arms, shoved her against the wall, forced her to look him in the eye.

'You're a little turtledove.'

'Oh really?'

'Turtledoves start out on the lowest branch and then work their way up to the top of the tree by killing their mates. One at a time. First they approach them, then they do a short dance of submission, and then, once they've earned their mate's trust – zac! – a sharp peck of the beak at the base of the neck. Ah, those sweet, lovely, adorable turtledoves!'

That was the moment when she decided to just go ahead and spill it.

'That money? The guy who gave it to me is someone they call Dandi.'

Scialoja lit yet another of a long chain of cigarettes. The colleague standing lookout on the Via Portuense radioed the arrival of a high-performance vehicle.

'This is it,' murmured the team leader.

They ran a final weapons check. They slid a shot into the chamber. A car was turning into the narrow line, headlights dark. The car came to a halt. A powerful, thickset man stepped out. Dandi. The team leader gave the go sign. Scialoja was the first to reach the objective. Dandi put up no resistance. He was unarmed. While he fastened up the cuffs, Scialoja thought back to his last conversation with Borgia.

'That prostitute…what was her name?'

'Vallesi, Cinzia – stage name Patrizia.'

'That's right. Patrizia. Why isn't there any mention of her in here?'

'It would have been pointless. She'd have just denied everything and wasted our time.'

'Scialoja…'

'What is it, *dottore*?'

'By any chance…you wouldn't have taken advantage of the opportunity…you and that woman…'

'Are you kidding me, *dottore*?'

'Forgive me, I just felt I had to ask.'

He'd lied. He'd been convincing. Strange: he hadn't felt a thing. Strange: it was easy, he'd felt at peace.

VII

THIS WHOLE THING with Moro was turning into a nightmare: exactly what Dandi had said would happen. Roadblocks on every street, suffocating police monitoring, thousands of uniforms circulating freely. The risk of running into a squad of cops loaded for bear was tremendously real, and everyone had to stay out of sight. Freddo had become even more taciturn, if such a thing was possible; when he did open his mouth, it was only to curse the politics that kept them from focusing on more serious matters. Almost everyone agreed with him.

Libano, on the other hand, was in a good mood. The shit was practically selling itself, and moving briskly. In the hot zones, the eggheads in charge of national security had cleverly deployed ordinary conscripted soldiers. They might very well be good at identifying terrorists – how, though? From the way they wore their hair? By smell? – but they were definitely capable of letting a three-ounce baggie sail right under their noses without blinking. The cops had furious bloodshot eyes, almost as if they'd just snorted a line of shit the way Christ almighty commands, but they were baying after the scent of Red Brigades meat with such intensity they were paying little or no attention to anything else. No cop had taken the trouble to devote serious investigative resources to the disappearance of a delivery van loaded with first-class fur coats. This was Bufalo's doing. Sick and tired of sitting on his hands, he'd pulled off the job on a tip from a cop drowning in debt to dog-racing bookies. Once the job went off without a hitch, the cop's debts had been forgiven, and Bufalo had obediently deposited the swag in the general fund. For once, Libano made an exception and let the boys dig in freely. Every member of the gang was allowed to grab one or two items for wives, mothers, sisters, lovers and assorted sluttish chattel. It was only right to put out the word that hard work had its rewards.

And all this thanks to Moro. If for no other reason, the guy deserved a little work to try to get him sprung. Sardo was sure they'd pull it off. Whatever the payoff in the end, Libano certainly didn't mind the opportunity to stick it up a few Commie arses.

Finally, one April morning, Libano told Freddo that they needed to go to a certain place in the Maremma.

'Sardo's found Moro.'

'And he's being held in Tuscany?'

'No. That's where Cutolo is. We're going to have a talk with him.'

Freddo said that he didn't want any part of it. His opinions on this matter were well known, and he didn't intend to let himself get sucked in. Libano asked him to come along: a personal favour to a friend and colleague. Impossible to deny that request. Freddo punished him by maintaining a stubborn silence the whole way up.

The place was a large farmhouse in the far countryside, preparing for spring's reawakening. A couple of tough-looking young men, toting Czech sub-machine guns, were guarding the long driveway. Libano identified himself. The men asked for instructions via walkie-talkie, then waved them through.

Flies, mosquitoes, and an enclosure with a small flock of fat sheep, surrounded by a litter of baby lambs. In the parking area in front of the building stood five or six vehicles. Two individuals who stank of state law enforcement got out of an armoured BMW with tinted glass and a temporary number plate. Sardo was standing in the doorway, waving frantically for them to hurry.

'I'm not going in,' Freddo said decisively. Libano, in exasperation, walked off without a word.

Freddo lit a cigarette and stood contemplating the lambs. They'd take to their heels, suddenly, the whole flock moving as one, for no good reason, in a crazed headlong stampede. Just as suddenly they'd stop stock-still, and then turn and run for shelter under the teats of Mama Sheep. The crunch of footsteps forced him to turn around. The two guards were looking at him, blank-eyed. The smell of government agents became stronger, overwhelming. They asked for a smoke. He handed them the pack. They thanked him with a nod of the head, then the taller of the two clambered over the wooden fence and jumped into the enclosure. The lambs resumed their crazed headlong gallop. One of the slower animals banged right into the man's legs. He seized it with a lightning lunge, snapped its neck with no apparent effort, and threw the lamb over his shoulder. As he strode back past Freddo, he gave a brief wave of the hand.

Freddo felt a shudder pass through him. For an instant, he'd seen Gigio's face on the head of that lamb. Then Libano and Sardo returned, grim-faced, and they all climbed back into the car.

Just how things had gone inside was something Freddo learned during the drive back to Rome. Cutolo had introduced his right-hand man, Pino il Bello – an elegant clotheshorse who would have made Dandi turn green with envy – and two other men in jacket and tie whose identities it was better not to know – Zeta and Pigreco, and no more need be said. But they all treated each other with immense respect. Sardo couldn't wait to spill his news: he'd received a hot tip on where Moro was being held prisoner. Source: a former member of the radical leftist Autonomia Operaia, who had eventually defected to the extreme right wing. A young hothead, but judged reliable. According to the source, Moro was in an apartment not far from the San Camillo hospital. More detailed information could be had, as long as you were willing to spend some money. But the conversation had focused on anything and everything but Aldo Moro. The topics included: Don Rafele's escape from the insane asylum, which he referred to as 'my noisy departure' (the main gate had been blown down with three kilos of TNT); how the organization's business was proceeding in Naples; the kidnapping of De Martino's son ('*na cosa 'e mariuole* – scoundrels were behind it – Professor Cervellone said in colourful dialect); an upcoming trip to America; even the dinner of roast lamb with aromatic herbs that ought to be eaten to honour the holy holiday of Easter, just around the corner. But every time Sardo tried to put a word in, the conversation promptly turned to a new subject. So unmistakable was the tactic that eventually Libano ventured to toss out an acid rejoinder.

'Don Rafe, you summoned us and we are here. But would it be possible to know why you summoned us?'

And Don Rafele had peered at him from behind his lenses, with that half-smile of his that meant everything and nothing, and issued this decree:

'*Guaglio*', do you want to get it into your head that they want that poor Christian dead, not alive?'

And that's the way it went. But Libano refused to resign himself: now that they had the information, they might as well get some cash for it. Maybe sell it to the Christian Democrats; there must be someone in that political party who wanted to try to save Moro's bacon. They only needed to identify the right person and the thing could still be pulled off.

'It seems to me you haven't figured this out,' Sardo said. 'Nobody questions an order from Cutolo.'

'I don't take orders from anyone,' Libano retorted, challenging him.

Sardo left the challenge where it lay, and added that the time had come for him to settle his own accounts with the law.

'A couple of days to settle up my last few things, then I'm turning myself in to the insane asylum of Sant'Efremo. I don't like whatever's in the air. Sooner or later the Red Brigades are going to kill Moro, and then it's going to be anybody's bet.'

They accompanied him to Trentadenari's place. While Libano did his best to persuade him to make one last effort, Freddo couldn't get that lamb's head with Gigio's face out of his mind.

When they said goodnight, in the early hours of the morning, Freddo still hadn't told Libano yes or no.

The mobile squad picked them up at dawn.

Inside and Out

April–July 1978

I

THE FIRST ONE to enter the room was Libano. Right behind him came Freddo. And a few minutes later, one after the other: Scrocchiazeppi, the Buffoni brothers, Fierolocchio, Dandi, Botola, and last of all Satana – who went over and sat in an out-of-the-way corner, head bowed, glowering and gloomy, making it clear to everyone in that room that he wanted nothing to do with certain individuals.

The only one not present for roll call was Bufalo.

As each new arrival entered the room, greetings were exchanged, hands shaken, backs slapped heartily. That they'd all been circulating in criminal circles for years was common knowledge throughout Rome. To pretend they'd never met now would be worse than waving a red cape in front of the bull's nose, and there was surely no point in provoking a reaction from the Man before getting some idea of the lay of the land. What did they know? Anything in particular? Or was this just a fishing expedition – the police trawling for vulnerable fish? How much information did they have? Had some turncoat decided to squeal?

And so, as they sat waiting for the district attorney of the Italian Republic, there was a busy to-and-fro of cigarettes changing hands, a continual by-play of hand gestures and glances, but aside from that, absolute silence. The fact that they were all here together meant something was up. No doubt there was someone watching from behind the one-way mirror, ready to pounce on a frightened expression, an unguarded phrase. A waste of effort; these days not even rank beginners, not even kids still green behind the ears, fell for the old aquarium trick.

71

Leaving aside the distinct possibility that one of the group in this room could very well be the informer.

For two days now they'd been left to steam in the slow cooker of solitary confinement. The law gave the cops every right to do so, and they took advantage of the fact. Two days packed with worries and paranoid fugues for Libano. Impossible to wring any information out of the inmate-orderly, a Marchigiano serving a mandatory life sentence – first he'd cut his wife's throat, then he'd chopped her up into little bits and tossed her down a well. And Libano hadn't bothered to try to work any of the guards. It was possible to glean a little information from the arrest warrant. They'd cited him for the kidnapping of the baron for purposes of extortion, but there was no reference to any homicide. They hadn't dared to push it that far. *Ergo*, as old uncle priest of the church of Francesco d'Assisi had said when he realized that someone had broken into the alms box. *Ergo* they hadn't found the body. *Ergo* they knew something but not everything. *Ergo* the whole thing reeked of an informant. This wouldn't be the first time. It certainly wouldn't be the last. Out of fear or greed, there was always bound to be someone ready to betray, at least in Rome. Sicily was another matter. Down there, no one was willing to turn traitor. Down there, respect was commonplace. Well, time would tell: they'd find a way of changing things in Rome too. Just a matter of being patient. As he sat there smoking his cigarette, nerves on edge, Libano did his best to study the others.

Most of them put on a show of irritation, indifference, arrogance and self-confidence. His eyes happened to lock with Freddo's. They nodded, as if each of them could easily read the other's mind. Freddo too assumed there'd been a turncoat. No one in that group except the two of them was capable of looking past the present; no one seemed able to plan for the future. Without their leadership, the rest of them would scatter in a flash. It would all be over before it even had a chance to get properly started. But here was Dandi, keeping to himself, still dressed in the tracksuit and designer robe he'd been wearing when they came to arrest him. He was as baffled and dismayed as anyone else. Libano decided that Dandi was starting to mature. Maybe that was partly to the credit of that girl Patrizia: a good egg. A whore, but definitely a good egg. Dandi, with her at his side, was turning into more of a man with every day that passed. It

72

wouldn't be a bad thing to put a real woman, a woman with balls, beside each and every kid in the gang. But maybe that was hoping for too much, decided Libano. Anyway, the first order of business was to figure out how to get out of this mess.

In the meantime, the lawyers started to dribble in, one or two at a time. Still no sign of Bufalo. He was the only one missing. An ugly thought started to worm its way into Freddo's head.

The lawyers that they'd appointed at their intake hearing at Regina Coeli prison were all from the usual list of names: Terenzi, Piancastelli, Biancolillo, Domineddò, with their entourage of paralegals and office scuts. Journeymen all, working in the legal penumbra, perfectly respectable practitioners who'd never risen above the level of defending loan sharks and armed robbers, small-time predators on the outskirts of the big, dark forest. Libano was just wondering whether it might not be time to hire someone with more of a name, a bigger reputation, when the lawyer Vasta walked into the room, escorted by a warrant officer, or *maresciallo*, with three stripes on his sleeve. Accompanying the lawyer was a young woman in a business suit, with a head of curly blonde hair. Dandi recognized the girl and shot her a larcenous grin: her surname was Mariano, and she was Trentadenari's girlfriend. She blushed and a glitter of panic appeared in her big blue eyes. Dandi reassured her with an imperceptible tilt of the head. Then he turned to Libano and raised two fingers in a sign of victory.

The less illustrious counsellors, in the meantime, were clustering around Vasta. It was decided that each of them would be assigned two defence attorneys: the one they'd already appointed and Vasta, who'd therefore be able to keep an eye on all the cases simultaneously.

Assistant District Attorney Borgia stepped into the room and informed the lawyers for the defence that they had the right to meet with their clients before their depositions. There was a new face at his side – a young cop, who had a little-boy look about him. Libano felt like laughing out loud. It was with these freshly scrubbed idiots straight out of university that they hoped to ensure the triumph of law and civil order? No doubt about it: they were grasping at straws, is what they were doing!

'We can proceed, Dottore Borgia. My clients intend to invoke their legal right not to answer.'

Vasta had spoken for everyone. The other attorneys nodded. Borgia let slip a nasty snicker. But there was nothing he could do about it. The deposition was therefore a dead letter, little more than a formality. One by one, the defendants were informed of the charges pending against them, they issued their statements of intent to remain silent, and they were escorted back to their cells in solitary confinement. Then, one at a time, they were marched back from solitary confinement to the interview room, where Vasta and Mariano awaited them.

Before morning turned to afternoon, everyone in the group knew what had happened: Bufalo was at the bar downstairs from his apartment playing a hand of zecchinetta when two police cars loaded for bear roared up and screeched to a halt. If the cops sent to get him hadn't been so intent on playing cowboys and Indians, they'd have had no difficulty bringing Bufalo in. But alerted by the noise, he'd slipped out the back way and made good his escape. From the bar he'd headed for Trentadenari's house; Trentadenari had called Mariano; Mariano had called Vasta. Now Bufalo was out of harm's way, and as for the fees, that was taken care of: Trentadenari had already paid a hefty retainer. Libano's system was beginning to hum along nicely. Vasta's report was very encouraging.

'None of the search warrants resulted in any significant finds. The trial looks like it'll be based purely on circumstantial evidence. I don't believe that the prosecuting attorney has any credible witnesses. At the very most, a few confidential sources. But that's not the kind of testimony he can introduce in court. You'll be subjected to confrontations, line-ups, and they'll take your fingerprints. They'll ask each one of you to repeat a phrase into a tape recorder. They're going to use that to try to track down the kidnappers' telephone contact. So if any of you has anything to worry about, it'd probably be a good idea to come up with a bad head cold or something of the sort. Aside from that, we'll appeal to the investigating judge and if that goes badly, there's always the supreme court. Unless something unexpected happens, you'll all be out in two to three months, with a formal apology.'

THEY WERE LET out of solitary confinement after a week. The exercise yard was filled with a bright sunshine that did their bones and their souls a world of good after all that time in the dank, dark cell. Libano and Freddo gave a wide berth to the hoodlums engaged in the usual football game and sat down to study the arrest warrant, their backs resting against the outer wall in the shade of the central guard tower.

'Most of the information is missing here,' said Libano.

'They know the basics, but they don't have the details,' Freddo agreed.

'They don't know anything about Feccia and the other guys from Casal del Marmo.'

'That's why they're only charging us with kidnapping, not murder. Maybe they think the baron's still alive...'

'No. They've figured out he's dead and buried by now. But they lack evidence.'

'They don't have a thing.'

'Not a shred of evidence. Not even a word about the dope...'

'Nope, they've got nothing.'

'Not a single word about Sardo and Trentadenari...'

'Nothing at all.'

So it had been an informant. That much was certain by now. But not someone from inside their group. Even Satana, who was in a cell like everybody else, could safely be considered as out from under suspicion. An outsider, then; someone who was certainly well informed, but that was no problem. In their circle, everyone knew who had taken the baron. Someone on the outskirts of the group, then, or someone who had it in for them, anyway.

'Sorcio?' Freddo ventured.

'I doubt it. Vasta said that they're looking for the telephone contact. If they already had him, they wouldn't be busting our balls with a bunch of voice samples.'

'That could be nothing but a smoke screen...'

'I'd rule that out. Have you taken a look at Borgia? He's...what's the word? An idealist. You can spot the breed from a mile away. No. Here we're taken a pounding from someone who's sworn to fix us good...'

'Vasta says the cop who was with Borgia, the new guy, wrote all the reports.'

'Yeah, I heard that. He doesn't look like much to me, but I could be mistaken…'

'He was the one who got the information.'

'The informant is someone he's handling…'

'The informant is someone from our network.'

'There's a name that comes to mind,' Freddo said with a leer, after a short pause.

'So tell me, comrade: are you thinking what I'm thinking?'

'Well, that depends. What exactly are you thinking?'

'I'm thinking of a guy, and I'm thinking how it chaps this guy's arse that certain fine young citizens are making a career for themselves in this world…'

'A guy whose career is already behind him…'

'Exactly. So instead of retiring the way he ought to, this guy goes in and has a nice little talk with the cops…'

'Why, that's just terrible!'

'You said it, comrade. Just the thought of it is terrible…' He empha-sized the word, dragging it out in his Roman accent: '*Terribile*'.

Who else could have ratted them out if it hadn't been Terribile? If there still could have been any doubt about Terribile's fate, those ever-so-timely arrests were sure to erase them once and for all. The countdown had begun for Terribile; the clock was ticking.

Dandi, who had stopped to pass the time of day with Don Pepe Albanese and two soldiers from his *'ndrina*, did his best to catch their attention with broad gestures. Freddo and Libano sauntered in a leisurely fashion over to the trio. The two soldiers moved out of the way with alacrity, leaving their boss room to hold court. The men exchanged greetings, nodding their heads over and over. Just like the Japanese in the films, Libano thought ironically. Then Don Pepe gestured to the soldier who stood to his right, and the man hastened to pop a cigar-ette between the boss's teeth. The other soldier, just as eagerly, struck a lighter into flame.

'I hear you're making all the right moves.'

They accepted the compliment without twitching a muscle.

'Why don't you come pay a call on me one of these days? I like smart young men. I need people like you for Rome.'

'We don't pay a cut like Puma does, Don Pepe,' Freddo pointed out.

The two gangland soldiers – short, stocky, black as beetles – started to get agitated. Albanese calmed them with an easy-going grimace. He was an old man with long white hair, well manicured fingernails, and a face as smooth as a baby's bottom, scented with scotch pine aftershave.

'I hear that Sardo turned himself in,' the Calabrian resumed, changing the subject.

Libano nodded.

'Why would someone be in such a hurry to get out of general circulation?'

'What can I tell you,' Dandi butted in, 'when a guy isn't used to fresh air, at a certain point he just misses his old familiar haunts...'

Don Pepe smiled. The soldiers smiled.

'You did the right thing by keeping away from this Moro thing,' Albanese said, turning suddenly very serious. 'They asked us to do the same favour, and then they told us they were no longer interested, same as with you. And I have another thing to say to you,' he added, staring intently at Freddo. 'Don't think I didn't understand what you meant, just then. Don't think for a second that you invented life itself, this morning, just because you might have made a little money kidnapping Baron Who-the-Fuck and you think you're the Second Coming of Christ. Maybe before long I'll get out of here, and you'll get out of here too, and then we'll see how things go outside...'

Libano shook his head no. 'I've got something to say to you too, my Calabrian friend: if I were you, I wouldn't sleep all that easy tonight...'

The two soldiers were ready to lunge. But as the conversation heated up, Botola, the Buffoni boys, Scrocchiazeppi and a few other new faces had gathered around Dandi. Don Pepe evaluated the situation with a vague smile on his face.

'No need to get all fired up, Libano. I came in peace. There'll be time to talk things over again, no?'

'Maybe so, maybe so...' Libano conceded, and then he let drop a phrase out of the corner of his mouth, 'And maybe tomorrow you'd be well advised to have yourself shipped north to San Vittore and around here we can breathe some clean air for a change...'

Don Pepe turned around, spat on the ground, snapped his fingers. His soldiers took their positions on either side of him.

Freddo watched the ritual entry of the boss into the prison: the football game had broken off, and the hoodlums, lined up in orderly rows, bowed as the trio went by.

'It's a face-off,' Botola observed. 'I get the feeling we might have just fucked up.'

'No, what in the world are you saying!' Dandi retorted in grim jest. 'We've just rejected an attractive job offer and kicked an all-powerful clan boss in the arse! I think we're going to be resting uneasy tonight, not him!'

'Don't talk nonsense,' Libano cut him off brusquely. 'There was no face-off. They're leaving. He understood that we're the strongest ones here. If we want to, we'll slice and dice his balls tonight.'

'You really want a war with the Calabrians?' asked Dandi in amazement.

'There's no need for that. They're leaving. And anyway, even if we did, don't you know that many enemies bring much honour?'

'And who exactly first preached that sermon?'

'Mussolini!' Libano replied, his chest swelling with pride. He brooked no criticism when it came to his political passions.

'Hey, Libano, you're truly fixated!' laughed Dandi.

III

THE DAYS WENT by. The pre-trial investigation panel had made mincemeat of Vasta's appeal, but the lawyer still insisted he was bound to emerge victorious after he had his day before Italy's supreme court, the Court of Cassation. Vasta wasn't accustomed to losing. The eyewitness to the kidnapping had made a hash of his testimony at the line-up: first he'd identified Dandi, then a cop, then another inmate who had nothing to do with any of it – an unfortunate Yugoslavian who'd been arrested at the border behind the wheel of a semitrailer loaded with heroin.

The days went by. The Calabrians had taken a powder, as predicted, the day after the meeting. Prison radio confirmed Don Pepe's epic rage, but also Libano's considerable foresight: the gang's prestige was growing by leaps and bounds. Tonino Sciacquatore and a couple of the boys from Via della Marranella had made it clear they were 'at their disposal'. Pino Passalacqua had also approached them. Pino was a Sicilian who controlled a couple of gambling dens in Primavalle, a determined guy who didn't talk much, more or less like Freddo. So did Ranocchia, a faggot who had made his bones by procuring female companions for the Bergamelli gang from Marseilles; he was now considered the top dog in the realm of first-class bordellos. Men were lining up to talk to Libano and Freddo. Among those offering their fealty were renegades from the ghetto outskirts of Rome, the *borgata*, their arms as riddled with holes as a piece of Swiss cheese, and tubercular safecrackers. The renegades were drawn by the mirage of easy access to drugs; the safecrackers were eager for a fresh start, a second chance. Libano sat patiently listening to the ridiculous boasts they spread out before him. To each of them he offered a word of encouragement and hope, and issued orders to provide concrete assistance for the grieving widow and the bereft orphan, because hope without bread gives little fruit. Day by day the base expanded, all of them united by a dream of finally counting for something, all of them sick and tired of the aging bosses and the outsiders and foreigners who were calling the shots right in their own city, bossing them around in their own home. All of them feverish with the fantasy of finally taking control of the eternal streetwalker of Rome, with her sidekicks the she-wolf and the suckling twins. Even the guards could see their influence and power grow steadily: courtesies and kindnesses proliferated, mistreatment and abuse diminished. A few of Terribile's underlings grumbled, but the same rule that had broken the power of the Calabrians applied to those bumpkins as well. Would there be a reckoning? Outside, afterwards, when the first one able to make his move would scoop up the ante and all the chips.

Dandi watched and learned. Libano was a born leader. He knew how to keep the bloodthirsty members of his gang at bay and he knew how to stiffen morale when it was flagging.

Libano had decided, for instance, to avoid any contact with Sardo and Trentadenari. He'd even issued an ironbound rule about visiting day: the only ones allowed in were family members, and he expected them to keep their mouths shut too. So Botola could see his mama, who would always and only consider him to be a victim of some monstrous machination on the part of the magistrature. Freddo spent long hours listening to Gigio blow off steam, responding to his heartfelt protests with the anodyne, sensible advice any concerned elder brother would give. The only ones who had regulation wives were the Buffoni brothers: those wives were sisters themselves of course, but the only thing they were interested in was getting a cheque at the end of each month and complaining about the bills and the kid. Libano, on the other hand, truly seemed to be alone in the world: no one ever asked to see him, and he never asked about anyone else.

They used Mariano as a conduit for their communications with the outside world. There was nothing about a female attorney lingering over a conversation with one of her clients to attract special attention. For that matter, guards weren't even allowed to search lawyers. So, when they had a message they needed to get out, they'd write it up and she'd forward it to Trentadenari. It was a system that worked beautifully. There was no shortage of cash and care packages; bountiful assistance went to the families on the outside. All credit was due to the organization that Libano had dreamed up.

The only one who had kicked up a bit of a ruckus was Dandi, whose face darkened when he was told to forget about reaching out to Patrizia. As far as he was concerned, the only thing that mattered on earth was Patrizia, but Libano had yanked the bureaucratic form, the Modello 80 in which Dandi was declaring their co-habitation, right out from under his nose.

'You don't trust her! You were against me from the day I first met her!'

'We established one basic rule and it applies to all of us: no outsiders.'

And so, Dandi was forced to go through the weekly ration of torture with his Gina. Still, Gina was pretty, or she had been once. A fine big girl with plenty of curves and a delightful, innocent smile, but with something not quite right in her head. Not that she ever did anything outright strange: it was just that she increasingly verged on the catatonic. All it took was a beer or a screen in front of her. Or a holy card or saint's image because, among her other fixations, she'd also been swept away by her love for Padre Pio. She would put on weight and then just as suddenly shed it. It was her husband's fault: he'd long ago stopped treating her like a woman. For that matter, if she'd been of sound mind, she never would have fallen for the bullshit of a guy like Dandi in the first place. A guy who was deeply perverted, too: only someone like him would ever have come up with the idea of using poor Gina as an intermediary to get his love letters to Patrizia! But she let him do whatever he wanted, she said yes to anything he asked, even the unpleasant responsibility of acting as go-between with that bored slut who liked to make Gina wait for an hour at a time outside the front door in the street, and then gave her a scant thirty-second audience before dismissing her scornfully.

'She said that she misses you terribly and thinks about you all the time,' she even told Dandi.

There was only one point on which Gina was absolutely unyielding. So he wanted her to act as a go-between? In exchange: the salvation of his immortal soul! And so Dandi was forced to swear that he'd never miss a single mass, that he'd even gulp down the consecrated host after full and proper confession. A promise that was kept thanks to Libano, who had guessed at the upside of this arrangement.

'You go see the chaplain, Don Dante. No, better yet, stick to him like glue and tell him that you've had a mystical crisis.'

'Me? What's up – have you lost your mind, Libano?'

'You, definitely you. That way you'll finally stop talking about this Patrizia all the time and maybe, if we need some news, a little favour or two… The Catholic parish is a nurturing mother, after all, and Don Dante is a fine man and a friend of our friends…'

Moral of the story: Dandi, his soul in full redemption, served mass and spent many a long hour in the library studying up on the fundamental doctrines of Holy Mother Church. Some notes went out to a secret destination – he's a cousin, Padre, so unfortunate, poor fellow, but so respectable; a well-meaning young man, this Neapolitan, he even finished high school. And the serious news reports from the outside world poured in before anyone else had them. Information is the soul of commerce. Take it from Libano.

IV

MAY HAD HAMMERED down on Rome with all the fury of its incandescent spring. But this May was a strange one. A sad one. In a city suspended in a soundproof horror dome, as if it were snowing polystyrene foam. In a city that had been clapped under one of these glass vitrines where old people kept sacred images of the Virgin Mary. Or of a Christ with a bleeding heart and the face of Aldo Moro.

Scialoja dreamed about Aldo Moro at night. Millions of Italians dreamed about Aldo Moro at night. His colleagues dreamed about Aldo Moro at night. They dreamed of dying just like the five martyrs shot down in Via Fani. His colleagues hated the war-mongering Communists, because the Red Brigades terrorists did their killing in the name of Communism. His colleagues hated the Socialists who wanted to negotiate, who were calling for a 'unilateral humanitarian gesture', because you couldn't make deals with hyenas. His colleagues hated the Christian Democrats, with their millennial experience when it comes to martyrdom: the way they prayed with trembling lips and heavy-lidded eyes and then washed their hands of it all like in the old days of Pontius Pilate. His colleagues showed respect only for the elderly Pope who had prayed on his knees to 'the men of the Red Brigades'. In the meantime, they were cleaning and oiling their guns. If I have to be sent into the other world, I just want to take a lot of them with me, these Red bastards.

There was war in the air. There was defeat in the air. The judges didn't know which way to turn. The intellectuals had no idea what to do or say. The 'movement', from the free radio, was establishing a dialectical interaction with the 'misguided comrades'. It was unbelievable that the police couldn't track down the people's prison. In the meantime, the prisoner was writing letters to recipients who hastened to reject them. And the Red Brigades couriers moved freely through the city, from phone boxes to rubbish bins. False reports of sightings came pelting in. They'd searched for Moro in houses on the outskirts of town and at the bottom of an icy lake. The Red Brigades terrorists were in charge of the game, and they were all targets – furious, depressed, helpless. All hanging on the gerund in a communiqué from Moro's captors: we conclude the trial, carrying out the sentence. Which means they hadn't carried it out yet. While there was life there was hope. The investigation into the baron's kidnapping had long ago been forgotten. Everyone was after the elusive guerrillas. Even Borgia, assigned to keep an eye on a number of marginal sectors of the vast opposition movement 'to the left of the extra-parliamentary left wing'. Even Scialoja, who by this point was embedded on an on-going basis with his prosecuting magistrate. After all, since word was that he had a left-wing past, why not make the most of it? Scialoja had let his beard grow. His long-awaited arrival on the anti-terrorism squad had proved to be a profound disappointment. The days passed, between an investigative meeting and the analysis of the ridiculously long-winded documents of the collectives that were sprouting up like mushrooms around the university campus. And at night, dressed as a no-longer-young man, assemblies, where he was expected to fraternize with a horde of youngsters in the throes of the armed struggle, artists of the convoluted rhetorical style that split hairs in two and then in four with their I adhere/I don't adhere. Wannabes, romantics, occasionally unwitting comedians, with that mania for acronyms and accusations that smacked of the Third International. *Avanguardia Operaia* (Workers' Vanguard) accuses the *Movimento Studentesco* (Student Movement) of being the 'new police'. *Lotta Continua* (Constant Struggle) accuses AO of being the 'new new police'. AutOp accuses LC of being the 'new new new police'. All of this under the eyes of the only real police, strategically disseminated in the cardinal points of the parlour, the lecture hall, the cellar café of the moment.

Scialoja, who had even read Che Guevara, was able to understand some of their points of view. But he could not overlook the blood that had been spilled in Via Fani. When you shed blood, you go over to the wrong side. Scialoja imagined the Red Brigades terrorists as short, stout, square, cold, meticulous, banal in their everyday lives, methodical accountants of terror. If there was anything to be caught by fishing, the sea of beards, angry rhetoric and collective rituals was certainly the wrong water to fish in. These people could murder you with quotations from Marx, Deleuze and Guattari. Those others had at the very most a high school equivalency degree or a certificate from a voc-tech school and calluses on their hands, but they could break down a sub-machine gun in forty-five seconds flat. These people were a river of words. Those others were a drizzling rain of lead.

One evening, just like so many others, summoned to attend an extended assembly of the Circle of Countercultural Factory Workers in Via Luigi Luiggi in Garbatella, Scialoja heard someone ask for a light. He rummaged around in his pockets and, without thinking twice about it, handed over his Zippo.

'Thanks, comrade!'

He sensed a mocking, ironic undertone. He looked hard at the other guy, who flashed him a wink. It was Tagliaferri, also known as 'Spillo', because he was tall and skinny as a needle. Operations squad of the carabinieri. A colleague, if the term applied between two corps as different as the police and the paramilitary carabinieri.

'Don't mention it, comrade.'

'You're here too tonight, comrade?'

'That's what was decided, comrade.'

Tagliaferri was a salacious cop from Livorno. He boasted three notches on his standard issue Beretta: three firefights, two of them with Catanese gangsters who'd resettled in Versilia and one with the *Prima Linea* (Front Line) hardliners of Verbania. Never injured, not even a nick.

They moved over to the shadows of a pergola covered with wisteria adjoining a nearby villa. The entrance to the circle was guarded by a couple of lunks who didn't look particularly bright. The comrades trickled in a few at a time. Nobody seemed to pay them any attention. Tagliaferri explained that the group was well known and had been for some time. There were no fugitives; no one was wanted on outstanding warrants. They paid no special attention to security. Still, arrests were expected. The *caramba* – slang for a carabiniere – was more than willing to share what he knew. Scialoja did nothing to encourage him. He sat smoking his cigarette, idly watching the militants stream past, breathing in the faintly alcoholic aroma of the wisteria.

At the art film house in Via Benaco they were showing *Touch of Evil*. He'd have happily watched it again for the eleventh, no, the twelfth time. Every time he saw it the story threw him into a state of crisis. Charlton Heston was a democratic policeman devoted to the protection of civil rights, the kind Scialoja wanted to be. Orson Welles was a bandit in uniform – filthy, greedy and corrupt. A Fascist, just like most of his colleagues. But Heston was also a fool capable of being led by the nose when a bomb-maker spouted tears. While Welles was an investigative genius who could catch the scent of the guilty party when the corpse was still warm. How could you help but admire him?

Scialoja was about to cut a deal with Tagliaferri and take off when he saw her. Tight jeans, white T-shirt, black jacket. She'd walked by less than a yard away from him. She hadn't noticed him. Just another of the many comrades ready to hurl words of flame against the big bosses and the bourgeoisie. If only he'd been so blessed indifferent! Instead he'd jumped at the sight of her. And Tagliaferri had noticed.

'You know her?'

'Never seen her before!'

'That's what I thought. A fine piece of arse, no?'

'Sure.'

'Belli, Sandra. Comrade Belli. A tough one. Once the top brass give us the go-ahead, she'll be the first one we throw in a cell. I'd like to be one to serve that arrest warrant. I'd like to catch her trying to resist arrest. You know the situation: the suspect tries to get funny and you have to get physical with them!'

Scialoja lit another cigarette.

'Arrests,' the *caramba* went on. 'Two, maybe three. For sure, Belli. The little group of the factory workers' circle in and of itself wasn't enough to scare a kitten. Idiots that they were, though, they were trying to establish contact with a clandestine operative of the Roman column of the Red Brigades – Comrade Nardo. A real hard arse. Two documented murders.'

Belli could lead them to this guy, thought Scialoja. There was an operation under way. The time frame was short.

'Maybe tomorrow, maybe next week, who could say...'

'Maybe never,' Scialoja tossed out.

'I'd exclude that possibility. Sooner or later, we're going to take her down.'

The two lunkheads at the front gate of the factory workers' circle let loose a high-pitched whistle. Tagliaferri responded with another equally high-pitched whistle.

'It's all good. We're on our way.'

The lunkheads went in. Tagliaferri slapped Scialoja on the back.

'These guys are such idiots that they've inducted me into the security branch of the organization. I don't know if you got this detail: they sent me over here to check up on you! Shall we go?'

Tagliaferri strode off, certain that Scialoja would follow him. But Scialoja couldn't go in there. Sandra would recognize him at a glance. There was a good chance she'd blow the carabiniere's cover. Scialoja ran after him and fed him one of the most classic excuses. Tagliaferri made a show of empathy.

'A girl? Sure, sure, it's not like there's much to get a hard-on over around here... *Vaya con diòs, compañero!* Just remember: you owe me a favour!'

Scialoja moved his old aubergine Mini Minor into the shadows of the wisteria trees and waited patiently. Three hours and fifty cigarettes later, she emerged, took a look around, and headed off with a determined stride, looking around every five or six steps.

In a little counter-insurgency handbook that circulated around the office, Scialoja had read that, back in the years of the partisan resistance movement, whenever a meeting ended, the most important member of the group was always the first to slip away. Scialoja gave her a fifty-yard head start, then he pulled out. Small knots of people were starting to emerge. Scialoja let the car purr along at walking speed, headlights darkened. Sandra stopped when she came even with a beat-up over-sized Vespa. She rummaged around in her pockets for her keys. Scialoja switched on the headlights. He swung the car perpendicular across the road, blocking one lane of traffic. He got out and walked towards her.

'Ciao, Sandra.'

'Nico? Is that really you? What on earth are you wearing?'

He searched her before she had a chance to recover from her astonishment.

She wasn't armed. He seized her, indifferent to her vociferous objections. He shoved her into the car. Her comrades, back there, hadn't noticed a thing. Congratulations on the tradecraft!

The hole in the wall in the Via del Mattonato was a sort of temple to alternative culture. Four or five small café tables, dim lights, herbal infusions, tea and macrobiotic biscuits. The sickly sweet smell of pot caught in the throat. In the background, music by Claudio Rocchi and Ravi Shankar. The walls were lined with faded batik hangings depicting elephant-headed deities.

'Ganesh, the god who grants impossible wishes,' Sandra said with a wry grin.

'Just like our own St Rita of Cascia.'

'Why, I didn't know you'd turned all sanctimonious.'

'And you all spiritualist.'

'I detest spiritualists. If you ask them, nothing much has happened.'

'I'm with you there. Still, this is a nice, quiet place. A good place to talk.'

'Talk? I thought this was a kidnapping!'

'Sorry, I just had to make sure you weren't armed.'

Sandra shrugged. A petite hippie with a slightly frightened demeanour took their orders. They asked for a bottle of wine. The young girl explained that they had no alcohol licence. They decided to go for a herbal infusion instead.

Sandra lit a cigarette. 'Do you still live in that filthy little two-room apartment in the Via Pavia?'

'And are you still spitting on the family's fine Bukhara rugs?'

'You look well, Nicola. I'd never even guess you were a cop.'

'What, are you propositioning me?' Scialoja asked.

The young hippie waitress brought a wicker tray to their table and set down two steaming mugs.

'Here's to you.' Scialoja raised his mug.

Sandra laughed. He took one of her hands and held it in his. She pulled it away. He looked her right in the eye.

'How deep are you in it with these people?'

'What do you care?'

'I want to understand. You're a member of the bourgeoisie yourself. Why do you hate your own people so bitterly?'

'Because I know them. I know what they're capable of. We have to stop them, before it's too late…'

'And how are you going to stop them? With guns and bullets?'

'Why not? But only when the time is right.'

'Will the time ever be right?'

'Sooner or later. Not now, anyway…'

The herbal infusion had a slightly bitter flavour, or maybe it was just that all the cigarettes he'd smoked had ruined the taste. Scialoja took her hand again. This time, she didn't yank it away.

'Have you ever fired in anger?'

'No.'

'I believe you. But now you have to run, Sandra.'

'You believe me? Oh, I'm touched! Do you really think that I give a damn about what you think?'

'You need to get away, Sandra. Immediately.'

He told her everything. She listened to him without a word. When he was done, she ran a hand through her hair and smiled at him. Then, without warning, she hauled off and slapped him. A few people turned their heads. A spiritualist joined his hands in prayer and intoned 'Om!' The hippie waitress with the frightened expression started trembling. Sandra stood up and strode briskly towards the door.

Scialoja watched her leave, hypnotized by her swinging hips. Was there something about her that reminded him of that other girl – some similarity with Patrizia? Or was that just a fantasy of his? A wave of hot desire swept over him. Follow her. Confront her. Tell her the whole damned story again, from start to finish. Force her to listen. Abduct her, if he had to. Instead he remained motionless. He'd waited for her. He'd talked to her. Now she knew. It was up to her. It was her life. Scialoja lit one last cigarette and asked for another herbal infusion.

On the afternoon of the following day, they found Aldo Moro, dead, in Via Caetani. There were those who speculated that they must have intentionally left him midway between Via delle Botteghe Oscure and Piazza del Gesù – the headquarters respectively of the Italian Communist Party and the Christian Democrats. That way, everyone would understand that this marked the end of the historic compromise between Catholics and Communists. Scialoja flashed his badge, making his way through a crowd seething with dismay, anger and grief. In the trunk of the red Renault lay a huddled body. This was a case of patricide, Scialoja mused. They shot their elderly father, they looked him in the eye as he was dying. The murder of a father. And a father's blood always drips onto the children.

That skinny, bony face, like a bird's; that unshaven grey beard. It all reminded him of his own father's body as it lay in the open casket. The old man had died calling in vain for his distant son. The sick old man he hadn't had a chance to kiss one last time.

V

WHEN WORD GOT out that Moro's corpse had been found, Scrocchiazeppi started laughing and clapped his hands. A grim-faced Libano punched him square in the face.

'What's the matter with you?'

'Not me, you: what the fuck are you laughing about?'

'Well, I don't really know, but one of their guys is dead, no? The enemy, the way you like to say—'

'What enemy are you talking about? If they hadn't picked us all up, we could have saved him, and we would have come off as heroes!'

'What, now you want to be a hero?'

'Well, think of this: they don't search heroes' houses at dawn, searching for drugs...Heroes are above suspicion. But why I am telling you about this, since you don't understand a thing!'

Two months later, the Italian supreme court, the Court of Cassation, nullified the warrants for 'absolute lack of evidence'.

Waiting for them outside the prison gate was Bufalo, his face lit up like the sun itself.

There'd been no way to hold Dandi back. The minute he got out, he rushed over to Trentadenari's to withdraw twenty million lire from the general fund: an advance against profits, we'll settle up later, glad to give you an IOU, what, you don't trust an old comrade, and so on and so forth. Every penny spent on the unforgettable homecoming, his return to Patrizia, something he'd been dreaming of for all those long, interminable months in stir. It was also Trentadenari who offered him invaluable advice on the indispensable accessories that he'd need to procure if he wanted to make a good impression on a classy woman like his Patrizia.

After a steam bath and a trim to get rid of the dry split-ends from prison, Dandi tried to replenish his wardrobe in an expensive down-town store, but the clerk had made him feel like a piece of shit – in fact, he'd actively considered coming back with a pistol and turning the whole place upside down. But Patrizia was more urgent, so he'd turned to the more reassuring and familiar Clarke store newly opened in Viale Marconi. Jacket, trousers, six pairs of socks and silk boxer shorts, three ties the way he liked them – not too flashy – and a coat. While trying on the clothes, he found himself just one dressing room away from a prosecuting attorney that he'd seen plenty of times at the Hotel Regina for his depositions. Funny situation: the prosecuting magistrate and the gangster trying on clothes just six feet apart. No question, the other guy had recognized him too. But these details are overlooked among men of the world. He bought shoes too, four pairs – two pairs of loafers, two pairs of lace-ups – from Boccanera in Testaccio. And for the grand finale, a magnum of champagne and, with the five million lire cash advance, a brand-new Kawa 1300, with temporary tags still on it. Official and completely legal.

Patrizia opened the door, dressed in evening wear. She looked him up and down, coolly surveying the clashing palette of garish colours, sniffed at his aftershave, wrinkled her nose in distaste, and then froze his smile in place with a nasty, acidic sneer.

'Oh, it's you. You could have at least phoned ahead. It's a miracle I was even in. All right, let's go.'

She plucked the magnum of champagne out of his hands, leaving him standing at the door like an idiot, then reappeared after putting the bottle in the fridge, slipped her arm through his, and imperiously dragged him away into the night.

Patrizia was even more beautiful and desirable than he'd remem-bered. Beyond his wildest fantasies. But also cold, distant, unattainable. Winding up in bed together was out of the question. Nothing but a minimal concession: he was allowed to grope her small pointy breasts, and then there was the sweet-smelling clasp of her bare arms around him, afterwards, on the motorcycle roaring towards Climax Seven.

It was a restaurant and piano bar around the corner from Via Veneto with its shoeshine men and whores. Some of the whores he knew by sight, others Patrizia pointed out to him, detailing the specialties of each.

Sitting at a table next to the piano player were two or three football players from the S. S. Lazio team. Also: journalists, industry tycoons, pimps, Arabs, a princess of royal blood holding a tiny lapdog in her arms, a second-rank politician, the chief of staff of a government ministry, a fading actress trying to come to terms with the aftermath of an unsuccessful facelift.

The piano player struck up Patty Pravo's '*La bambola*'. Dandi was drinking. Patrizia talked busily about this and that: excited, unbelievably sexy, unattainable. When the tight sheer T-shirt described in Claudio Baglioni's '*Questo piccolo grande amore*' reached his ears, he was suddenly on the verge of tears: what the hell were the two of them even doing in this shitty bar? What did his little big love – his piccolo grande amore – have to do with these losers?

Then the lights dimmed, a spotlight illuminated a curtain at the far end of the room, and Franco Califano appeared. Dandi felt an electric shock run through him. Franco Califano – the Caliph – was a living legend. He gripped Patrizia's hand tight and murmured tender words of gratitude. The Caliph kicked it over with '*Una ragione di più*'. Suddenly Dandi could no longer hold back his tears: tears of champagne and liberation. When the song was over, he jumped to his feet, clapping like a madman. Everyone turned to stare at him. When he shouted: 'You're the best, Caliph!' the Caliph flashed him a smile. He fell back into his chair, his heart plummeting like a lead weight. Patrizia had left the table. He scanned the room, full of people glaring furiously at him. Ah, there she was: chatting with an elegantly attired couple. The man looked like an intellectual, with tiny round glasses and she... She was Daniela, Patrizia's girlfriend. A sense of foreboding shot through him. The Caliph was singing '*Dammeli per più tardi quegli attimi d'amore*'. Patrizia strolled back to the small round table, swinging her hips.

'I have to go.'

'What?'

'It's work,' she murmured, pointing at the intellectual who was holding Daniela's hand.

'You're not going anywhere.'

He'd raised his voice, perhaps without realizing it. He caught a peeved glare from the Caliph. Alcohol was pulsing through his veins.

'You're not going anywhere,' he repeated in a quieter voice.

Patrizia reacted to that announcement with a disdainful shrug and strode off towards the waiting couple. All three of them vanished behind the red curtain. Dandi had to exert considerable effort to get to his feet. His legs were unsteady. He knocked over a couple of café tables. Indignant looks followed in the wake of his tottering progress towards the door. Shit, he hadn't realized how drunk he was! The Caliph really seemed to have it in for him: *Perché domani o chissà quando le cose potrebbero cambiare e i baci che tu non mi darai…*Because tomorrow, or who knows when, things could change and you'll keep your kisses from me…

Outside, the night air hit his face like a stinging slap. The three of them were climbing into a Porsche Carrera. It took a tremendous force of will, but he managed to grab Patrizia before she made it into the car. The intellectual shot him an anguished look.

'Let me be! I'm working!'

'You're done working. You're my woman now!'

A sudden rush of bouncers. The slamming of car doors. The Porsche screeched away, engine roaring. The bouncers formed a circle around him. One of them had a familiar face. He knew him – he'd served time with Dandi's brother.

'Everything's under control, guys!' the familiar bouncer called out, to keep his colleagues at bay, and then, under his breath, he pleaded: 'Do me a favour, Dandi, don't cause trouble on my watch. I'd lose my job…'

It was Patrizia who dragged him away. Her high heels clicked furiously on the *sampietrini*, Rome's distinctive cobblestones.

'You and me are through, you bastard!'

'No woman of mine has to work. No woman of mine works as a whore!' His words were slurred and there was a reek of vomit on his taste buds.

'You don't even have a woman anymore, you animal!'

He raised one hand to hit her. But he saw something in her eyes that made him decide that physical violence wouldn't be the best choice. He'd definitely lose her for good that way. Patrizia wasn't someone he could tame. The thought of Libano offered a faint light of consolation. Libano would be able to give him the right kind of advice.

'Patrizia, I...'

He might as well have been talking to the wind. Patrizia was disappearing into the club. Dandi braced himself against the wall and puked his heart out.

VI

MEANWHILE, ALL THE others were celebrating at Trentadenari's place.

They'd sold off every last gram of the shipment. After accounting for legal expenses, there was still a net profit that would make your head spin. This time, Libano was lavish with the boys: two hundred million lire apiece. Another six hundred million lire in the general fund, which was operating better than anyone could have hoped. Next: reinvestment. A quarter of the cash went to a loan-sharking operation that was entrusted to Ziccone, the guy who had found them the arms stash in the ministry basement. The rest went for a new shipment of smack – Thai shit this time – already delivered and safely deposited at the same ministry.

Trentadenari had made a rice timbale, *sartù di riso*, and sent for a couple of crates of water buffalo mozzarella produced by a friend down in Casal di Principe: the best mozzarella on earth. They ate, they drank, they passed joints around. Only Libano and Freddo stayed clear-headed, as usual.

There was a new face in attendance. Vanessa. A nurse in her early thirties that Sorcio, still in pretty poor shape after the beating he took, had somehow – no one knew how – managed to recruit during his time in the hospital. She made quite an impression on Trentadenari: blonde and feminine, under her shy, awkward smile you could sense a tiger in bed. Sorcio certainly didn't seem like her type. But she'd had a good effect on him. The youngster seemed to have cleaned up considerably. He was still shooting up, no doubt about it, but he had reduced his doses, and now he could afford a new syringe for every shot. Vanessa didn't look like a junkie at all. Moreover, she was clearly intelligent. She'd knocked with her feet – had to, really, because her hands were so full – and had brought a case of morphine and a few ampules of methadone, just in case. And she was coddling her baby Sorcio like a loving mother.

Then and there, Libano appointed Sorcio to be in charge of the trade in methadone and other legal pharmaceuticals. They could peddle the stuff at a steep mark-up to the recovering junkies on the maintenance programme. It would be a small, independent source of income for the kid and for Vanessa – 15 or 20 per cent of the gross. The rest, of course, would go to the general fund.

Once the distribution of cash was complete, Libano sent everyone home. He, Trentadenari, Bufalo and Freddo stayed behind.

Trentadenari said that, for the moment, Terribile had been as good as his word. No ant or horse had had any more trouble. Now it was time to pay what was owed. Libano changed the subject and asked Bufalo to repeat in front of the others what he had told him that afternoon. Bufalo cleared his throat and spoke up in his big voice.

'A guy from Aversa is going around saying that Sardo is pissed off at us.'

'Really?'

Freddo cocked an eyebrow. Bufalo laughed, and addressed Trentadenari.

'Your boss says that since he went back behind bars, he hasn't been getting much money. He says that his share has gone up to sixty per cent. Starting with this new load. Or no more business.'

Trentadenari was roundly astonished. But all the payments had been made on time and properly received! And to think they'd even bought a brand-new car for Sardo's sister! And to think they'd given three hundred million lire to the courier, and he'd definitely transported it to Switzerland! And to think that not even the Neapolitans had had a single objection to the split!

'I get the idea that sooner or later we're going to have to have a little talk with Sardo,' Freddo observed.

'When he gets out,' Bufalo prophesied, stroking the handle of his revolver.

'One thing at a time,' Libano said, placating them. 'Let's just say that Sardo is pissed off because the judge has issued an order that, instead of the remaining three months, he's going to have to serve the two years of his term in the insane asylum all over again. What's the legal expression? *Ex novo!*'

'Well?' Bufalo asked, slightly disappointed. Sometimes Libano, with his fixation for keeping the peace at all costs, could be exasperating.

'Well, we'll have Trentadenari write him a nice letter and explain to him that everything is running along fine here, but that we still need a little more time to get things under control. Could he try to be patient, and everything's going to work out for the best. A friendly letter, eh?'

Trentadenari was in agreement. Now that the matter of the letter was settled, the next item on the agenda was the shipment of heroin. It was something terrifying to behold, said Trentadenari: thirteen kilos of brown sugar, to be stepped on, minimum, to 35 per cent strength. If they got to work right away, no more than three, four days tops, the smack could already be out on the street.

'Instead, what we're going to do is keep it in storage for a month, month and a half,' Libano said flatly.

The others stared at him in bafflement.

'You know the junkies are already going cold turkey out there!'

'They're drooling for dope on the streets...'

'Libano, this time you've lost me...'

Libano let them vent. Then he lit a cigarette and explained his idea. Unruffled and calm, as always.

'It's the law of supply and demand, comrades. We'll starve them for thirty, maybe forty days. In the meantime, we're going to step on it – not thirty-five per cent, but fifty or sixty per cent. And by the time they're all – and I mean all – panting for it, tongues hanging out, we'll dump the whole load out on the street. At twice the regular price...'

'Fuck!' Bufalo whispered.

Freddo was thinking it over.

'Not a bad idea. But what happens if someone steals our market out from under us?'

'But who?' Libano shot back. 'The Neapolitans are with us. Puma's out of the business. Who are we supposed to be afraid of, Freddo?'

Trentadenari came around at the sound of his voice. Freddo was still putting up some resistance.

'I don't know, Libano. A month and a half seems too long to me...'

'Well,' Libano conceded, 'we can keep them calm with the hashish...'

'Hash is strictly for two-bit thugs,' Bufalo protested indignantly.

'Sure, but in times of no smack,' Libano corrected him, 'hash turns into solid gold!'

They all laughed. Freddo gave his okay.

'Now, for more serious matters,' Libano announced. 'When do we schedule this meeting with Terribile?'

Settling Scores
August–September 1978

I

AT THE LAST minute, Sardo joined the expedition. Nobody could say why, but the probation judge had authorized a pass. Maybe just to sugar-coat the pill, or else because he'd been swayed by the tears of Barbarella, Sardo's beloved sister. It was Sardo who'd introduced her to Ricciolodoro, her current boyfriend, whose nickname Goldilocks described his curly blond mane of hair. And Ricciolodoro had followed Sardo on his leave from the asylum. He'd even joined him aboard the stolen Fiat 131, hotwired by Sorcio, with Freddo at the wheel. The rest of the crew consisted of the Buffoni brothers, Fierolocchio and Bufalo aboard a midnight-blue Fiat 132 hotwired by Scrocchiazeppi. Ricotta didn't come; he'd stayed behind to split up the hashish. Neither did Dandi and Trentadenari because, if by any chance something went wrong, they'd need to have someone on the outside. Also missing from the expedition: Libano. That had been Freddo's idea.

'Everyone knows that you've got it in for Terribile. You'll be the first person they come looking for. Get yourself an alibi and we'll take care of the rest.'

So Trentadenari went out to dinner in Via Garibaldi with Dandi and Counsellor Mariano, who no longer even cared who else might see her out in public with him, and he was forced to listen all night long to Dandi's tale of woe about Patrizia. Libano, who in the end had taken Freddo's advice, holed up in a gambling den in the Monte Mario district. No question, it chapped his arse to be playing the fugitive while all the others were risking their hides on such an important operation. Still, this time Freddo had taught him an invaluable lesson. Freddo had done his thinking for him. When you're in too deep, what happens is your heart manages to muffle your brain, but you always have to think rationally. At the very least, forty stand-up guys saw him lose a car-load of cash at the baccarat table. Because, no matter what cards the dealer laid out in front of him, his mind was somewhere else – it was travelling with the bullet that was going to put an end to Terribile's life, clinging to a vendetta that he'd been dreaming of since he was a kid, beginning with the moment that changed his life forever.

Terribile, after banking his well-earned commission on the shipment, dropped his guard. He walked out his front door relaxed, without body-guards or so much as a cautious look around, and headed off at an easy, arrogant pace towards his Mercedes. Bufalo and Freddo put their cars into gear at the same moment and headed straight for him from both ends of the narrow lane in the heart of Garbatella. Terribile must have sensed something in the roar of the engines, because he immediately took fright and dashed for shelter behind a delivery van, reaching under his suit for his gun as he went. Freddo was the first to reach him. Just a nudge of the bumper and Terribile flew head over heels. Bufalo and Sardo were out of their cars and on top of him immediately, hammers cocked, bullets already in the chamber, and they poured a hail of bullets into his chest – three, four, five shots. Terribile was twisting like a viper. Bufalo and Sardo climbed back into their cars, shouting to go, hit the accelerator, it's all done. But Freddo shifted into neutral, applied the handbrake, got out as cool and calm as could be, indifferent to the insults of his comrades, and walked over to the body. Terribile was gasping and groaning. Freddo leaned over him, pulled out his revolver, and finished him off with a bullet to the back of his head. Terribile convulsed, then it was all over. The whole operation might have lasted forty, fifty seconds, a minute at the very most.

It was dark outside, a light westerly wind was blowing, not a soul in sight. Before pulling away, Bufalo fired a bullet at the only working street lamp. Maybe he was sorry to leave one last bullet in the chamber, or maybe it was his way of expressing his excitement at having committed his first murder.

Yes, because none of them had ever taken the great leap before. Not even the baron's blood was really on their hands; that had been the doing of the guys from Casal del Marmo. If it had been up to them, once they had the ransom, they wouldn't have harmed a hair on his head.

Bufalo was shouting like a lunatic: 'We're unstoppable! Let's go, Rome! Fuck you, Terribile! Fuck you, Terribile!' until Fierolocchio finally had to yank the gun out of his hand. They had to make a stop at a bar to calm everyone's nerves, then they drove the cars to Sacrofano, where they doused them with petrol. From there they drove back home in clean cars.

Freddo drove carefully, respecting signals and traffic signs. That would have been a laugh, to get pulled over with both hands hot. But no one seemed to notice a thing.

'Holy shit, he shot you!'

It was Ricciolodoro who sounded the alarm. Sardo was losing blood from one of his legs. But the excitement of the moment had anesthetized him to all pain.

'You just shot yourself in the leg,' Freddo commented wryly.

Later, when they were all back together in Sacrofano, they ascertained that one of the shots fired by Bufalo had ricocheted off the cobblestones and hit Sardo's thigh. It was just a flesh wound, nothing serious, but he was losing blood and he needed medical care. Scrocchiazeppi volunteered to take care of it. Through Sorcio, he'd reach out to Vanessa, and if they were lucky she'd be working her shift at the hospital. A registered nurse could take care of it without medical charts, official admissions, prying questions. Ricciolodoro went off with them.

The Buffoni brothers stayed behind to burn the cars. Fierolocchio was in charge of taking the weapons back to the ministry. Bufalo was dying to give the news to Libano.

Freddo went back alone. On the drive home, he pushed himself to take a serious accounting of what he felt. Were there any emotions? In a certain sense, it had been a straightforward case of legitimate defence. Sure, they'd planned out Terribile's elimination, but after the shameful way he'd reported them to the cops, they'd really had no alternative. Legitimate defence, straight up. Pre-emptive, okay, but fully justified. He wasn't sorry for the dead man. He felt no fear of the consequences. In fact, he couldn't feel a damned thing. And that final head shot was a gift to Libano, from one friend to another. It was as if he'd pulled the trigger himself.

A patrol car from the mobile squad was waiting for them out front. Freddo wondered how they could have tracked them down so quickly, unless they'd committed some irreparable error, and for a moment he was even tempted to take to his heels. But he could see they were armed and determined, so he decided to come along quietly. If they'd done a paraffin test right then and there, no question, he'd have got life without parole.

II

THERE WAS NO paraffin test. There wasn't even a deposition. Terribile's murder had nothing to do with it at all. The decision to keep Libano out of it proved to have been a good one. Word went out on prison radio that murder charges were filed against three old-school veterans of the loan-sharking circuit. They were completely innocent, but nobody wanted to hear their version. *Raus*, get marching, it's jail for all three of them.

As for the arrest, it was all because of an old warrant that had long ago been spiked following an appeal. Something that had completely slipped Freddo's mind, like something from another life, a different Freddo. It was an extortion involving Tigame, a guy with a wrecker yard in Vitinia, a slimebag who, instead of taking it and shutting up, decided to rear up on his hind legs and object over a few miserable million lire. They'd done everything they could think of to make him pipe down: threatening phone calls, punctured tyres, cans of petrol and severed sheep heads in front of his premises. It hadn't done any good. In fact, he'd filed a criminal complaint, against Freddo and against Fierolocchio and the Buffonis.

Now they were all behind bars, this time in Rebibbia. All of them were fully aware of how flimsy the charges were; so much so that, personally, Freddo was inclined to just let matters play out. Really, a flashback from another lifetime. Why get worked up? And Vasta, who was there within minutes of the first phone call, still smelling of aftershave, took one look through the documentation and listened to the guys' account of what had happened, and actually broke into a faint smile.

'You know when this complaint dates from? November 1977. Almost a year ago. Borgia wasn't happy with the way the baron's kidnapping case went down, so he's determined to grab you by the short hairs. But he's got nothing on you. There are no eyewitnesses. He has nothing but Tigame's word. And Tigame is an ex-con with a rap sheet that looks worse than all of yours put together. It's going to end up just like the last time, take my word for it. Only this time it's going to be faster. Trust me, you're going to be out in twenty days, tops.'

Libano was with Bufalo when they heard about the arrest. Libano grimaced. This was a dangerous time, riddled with unknown factors. They couldn't afford the slightest misstep. Terribile's death threatened to trigger a spiralling vortex of anarchy. There were plenty of other gangs eager to lunge at the opportunity, eager to occupy the space left open by the old boss. Those other groups were starting to fear them, but there just wasn't enough fear on the streets. They needed to lay their claim in an unmistakable manner, establish their mastery, now and forever, over Rome, the old whore. Disrespect shown to one of them meant open defiance of them all.

'Which is to say: one for all and all for one, Bufalo,' Libano summed up, before setting forth his conclusions.

They couldn't allow just any ordinary Tigame to send someone like Freddo to jail and get away with it. An exemplary punishment would be required. Tigame had to die.

'Okay, okay,' Bufalo interrupted, his eyes glittering with that particular, macabre irony of his. 'When you start talking double Dutch I have a hard time following you, Libano. What are we waiting for? Let's grab a couple of rods and get going, no?'

Libano understood that he was calling his bluff. It was always a bad idea to underestimate Bufalo. He'd grown up on the street, and he hadn't the slightest idea of what strategy meant, but deep down he had an instinct, a sort of second sight. He'd figured out that Libano was really trying to talk himself into it.

They grabbed a couple of revolvers from the ministry and stole a motorcycle that some sucker had left parked on the Lungotevere di Pietra Papa, zipped off towards Vitinia without a word, and stood waiting in front of the bar where Tigame showed up every day, still in his greasy overalls, to down his *Sportino Borghetti*, an espresso cocktail. The minute they saw him, they unloaded three shots apiece and roared away into the gathering dark. With a nice touch of class, Bufalo left the motorcycle just a hundred yards from where they stole it.

'You feel a little calmer now, Libano?' was his salutation as he left.

Libano walked down to the riverbank under the Ponte Marconi. His legs were still trembling, but the adrenaline was slowly subsiding. Maybe there had been some concrete reason to eliminate Tigame. Maybe all the fine words he'd reeled out for Bufalo did have a meaning. Maybe. But the truth was that he owed something to himself. To himself and to Freddo. With that whole thing with Terribile, he'd established a pact of friendship. A sacred pact. Once and for all. Sacrificing Tigame had been his way of honouring that pact.

Still, even that wasn't the whole truth.

All plans and projects aside, well beyond any rational considerations, the cement that held everything together was action.

No strategy alone, however sophisticated, could ever make a boss of him. Nothing outweighed action. You had to get your hands dirty. Just like the others. Tigame or someone else in his place amounted to the same thing. They meant nothing; they were nobodies. What mattered was action. He had to show Bufalo how to become like him. And he had to become like Bufalo. Bufalo was born with the idea of action hardwired inside him. Nobody had ever had to tell him how to do it.

As he stood there breathing in the slimy scent of the river, he felt himself regaining mastery of his world. And a growing sense of indomitable power lofted him to stratospheric heights. He could tell that committing that murder had done him good; he could sense the devastating impact of the rite he'd just celebrated, along with Bufalo, in the name of the entire gang. Because they had finally become a gang. United. Invincible.

It had been four days since Terribile's murder.

'IT'S NOT UP to the magistrature, it's up to police and law enforcement in general to combat terrorism. The magistrates are there to monitor and check scrupulously the legality of all police actions. Guarantee civil rights, above all. Guarantee civil rights!'

'Still, when democracy is being actively threatened, certain excessive guarantors of civil rights become a luxury. We should, in that case, overthrow the rule that one is presumed innocent until proven guilty. Let the accused terrorist prove that he is not one, and not the other way around.'

'Preserve the guarantees provided by the rule of law: that's our core value, first and foremost.'

'Decapitate and uproot the foul weed of murderous thuggery: that's our first priority.'

'We may be at war, but it's not a sufficient reason to throw a long-standing tradition of legality overboard.'

'We are at war, and war itself is enough of a reason. When you're at war, you wage war!'

One after another, members of the audience took the floor, an ever-rising tide of opinions being voiced. Minute by minute, the atmosphere of the assembly was heating up, growing progressively more inflammatory. Judges, politicians, lawyers, students, ordinary citizens – they were there to 'review the situation' concerning terrorism. The occasion for the assembly: the passage of more new special laws intended, according to their sponsors, 'to drain the waters in which the fish of the Red Brigades habitually swim.' The divide separating civil rights fanatics and advocates of the gallows was deep, abiding and irreconcilable.

Borgia, who was listening with growing discomfort, disguised among the students in the furthest rows in the rear, was focusing in particular on the speakers who addressed the issue of Aldo Moro. Here also there were two lines of thought. Firstly: we were unable to save his life because there were people who had an interest in letting him die. Every time we were on the verge of taking some significant step forward, the investigation was hamstrung by mysterious entities that intervened, boycotting, cutting off, root and branch. The other line of thought: the Red Brigades only seem invincible because judges and policemen have their hands tied by laws that are excessively permissive towards the wrongdoers.

Borgia turned over and over in his hands a sheet of paper on which he'd jotted down a phrase written by Leonardo Sciascia:

> Anyone can evade the Italian police in its present state of training, organization and management, but it's not so easy to evade the laws of probability. Yet according to the statements broadcast by the Minister of the Interior concerning the operations the police carried out between Moro's abduction and the discovery of his body, the Red Brigades did indeed evade the laws of probability. Which is *realistic*, but can't be *really true*.*

This piece of wisdom from Sciascia, the Maestro of Racalmuto, was his final consolation. Between civil rights fanatics and advocates of the gallows, he was caught midway across the stream, feet wet, at the centre of an uncomfortable ford. We are at war, true, but in any war the means count at least as much as the ends. We are at war, but it is an occult war, a hidden war that no one ever declared. Most important of all, we are in the midst of a battlefield of that war whose boundaries are ill-defined, to say the least. No question: those who pick up weapons and use them are in the wrong, and the country must be defended, one way or another. But what significance was he or anyone to attribute to the ambiguities, the half-truths, the mysteries that studded the investigation into the massacre of Via Fani? When, in the course of a military operation, in the wake of a door-to-door search throughout the entire city, you run up against a locked door, and you fail to break it down. When you learn afterwards that behind that door, that door and no other that you chose not to force open, the captors of the abducted statesmen might very well have been hiding. When you experience such a monstrous twist, live and direct, so to speak, you begin to wonder whether the lack of preparation, the seat-of-the-pants decision-making, the contradictory orders, the helplessness in the face of a powerful enemy and the simple-mindedness of individual officers really are sufficient explanations for everything that happened. Or whether, instead, the widely denounced fecklessness of the investigative effort might not be yet another cunning prank confected

---

* Rabinovitch, S., 'The Moro Arrair', p. 26, *New York Review of Books*, New York, 2004.

by an extremely cunning mastermind, whether at the bottom of everything there could be one of those fanciful illusionists who move with all the talent of a wizard of the cinema along the ridgeline that transforms ally into adversary, victim into executioner. And even if we were to admit, as Scialoja, the ever pragmatic Scialoja, insisted, that there had indeed been an occult intervention, it had come into existence only in a subsequent phase. That is to say, if someone, for their own political calculations, had chosen to lend a hand to the Red Brigades after Moro's abduction – protecting them, providing them with a smoke screen, hindering attempts to capture them – didn't that mean in any case that the good people had some share in the guilt, in the responsibility, having co-operated to a decisive extent in the bloody culmination of the crime, the murderous finale? Perhaps it was this that Sciascia was talking about when he wrote about a 'literary' aspect underlying the fifty-five days that followed the abduction on 16 March. The *realistic*, the apparent, but not the *real*. In the land of Pirandello and Machiavelli.

These are the things that Assistant District Attorney Borgia thought as he left the noisy assembly that was unlikely to provide him with any aid in resolving the persistent doubts that tormented him.

The majority of those who thought the way he did – and there were quite a few – remained on the front line of the battle, perhaps hoping to prevent even worse developments. Borgia chose to step aside because of his point of view, no doubt a dangerous one for an assistant district attorney of the Italian Republic to harbour. He asked to be reassigned to cases involving common criminals. His request was met with no resistance.

Scialoja decided to join Borgia on his new assignment the morning he received a postcard with a picture of the Eiffel Tower. There was no signature, but the message was clear: Sandra had made it safely to Paris. This outcome was confirmed by Maresciallo Tagliaferri, AKA 'Spillo', over an ice-cold slice of watermelon, at one end of the bridge where the year before the police had shot and killed the university student Giorgiana Masi.

'You remember that unbelievable babe? She managed to get away. Dumb luck, if not something worse. These revolutionaries from good families always seem to find a way to get off scot-free!'

The other militants from her group were rotting away in Rebibbia prison. None of them had claimed the status of political prisoners. From various veiled admissions, it emerged that, yes, they had indeed made an attempt to establish contact with a wanted terrorist on the run, suspected of having taken part in the ambush on Via Fani. But they'd done so strictly for humanitarian reasons. Naïve young things that they were, they had hoped to persuade 'Comrade Nardo' to release Moro. Though not because they had any principled objections to the idea of shedding blood in the name of the cause. But rather on the basis of a more 'acute' and 'strategic' political calculus than that followed by the Red Brigades.

To say goodbye to the domain of the political was a relief for both Borgia and Scialoja. And the news of the run of the mill murders, so to speak, of Terribile and Tigame almost cheered them up. At least now they had something concrete to concentrate on. They knew, or fooled themselves into thinking they knew, where the line between them and evil ran.

So then, two murders in four days. A widely feared and respected mob boss like Terribile, and a nobody from the beach towns like Tigame. Both Borgia and Scialoja could guess at the link between the two killings. As was all too often the case, however, they lacked proof. Still, while there might have been ten thousand reasons to rub out Terribile, the murder of the unfortunate Tigame from Vitinia didn't seem to fit into the larger framework. The direct beneficiaries of the elimination of the prosecution's sole witness were right there before their eyes, and the most unassailable alibi on the planet was at their service. If it weren't so tragic, certain aspects of the thing would be distinctly comical. It was as if someone out there had wanted to do Freddo a favour. No question – there was a link. But that didn't amount to evidence, much less proof. Still, something was changing, and fast, within the ranks of organized crime, the mala. An infusion of new people? That wasn't all. A different plan was more what it seemed like. Almost a military strategy. The prelude to a mutation that might perhaps already be underway. And they, of course, would be the last ones to notice, as always.

Borgia sketched out an organizational chart.

'We've got: Freddo, the Buffoni boys and Fierolocchio behind bars.

And out of those involved, according to your…confidential sources, we have Bufalo, Dandi and Libano out on the street.'

Scialoja nodded. They were two groups. They'd joined forces. Now they were a gang. They were sweeping the city.

They interviewed Freddo and Fierolocchio, they interviewed the Buffoni brothers, they interviewed Bufalo, they interviewed Libano. They questioned them twice, three times, four times. They brought them together and confronted them. Nothing. A big fat zero. They were arrogant and self-assured, and occasionally unexpectedly submissive. But, no matter what, they always lied. On those rare occasions when their interrogators had them on the ropes, they'd exchange a glance with their icy-calm lawyer Vasta and choose to invoke their right not to respond. Scialoja started to develop an idea of their personalities. Fierolocchio and the Buffoni boys shouted, hollered, kicked up a ruckus, spat, and fired off defamatory statements and insults involving sexual appraisals. Hooligans. Hired killers. No moral structure. All the same, they refused to sell out.

Libano had an off-kilter smile that no amount of pressure seemed able to wipe off his face. He was cold and brutal. In prison, he'd told a boss of the 'Ndrangheta, the Calabrian mafia, to go fuck himself. He possessed charisma. A born leader. No one but him could have come up with the idea of the kidnapping. Fierolocchio and the Buffoni boys looked at him the way little children look at the Sacred Heart of Jesus during catechism. He was the one who held the rest of them together; he was the cement. Libano was a dead end, a blind alley in investigative terms. Too tough.

Freddo never said a word more than he had to. He never insulted. He revealed nothing about himself. You could never tell what he was actually thinking. Like certain children who have already suffered too much in life and have never developed the ability to express it – all this suffering. Freddo and Libano treated each other as equals. As if each of the two sought in the other the very qualities that he lacked, keeping him from achieving perfection. Was it perhaps a matter of the quantity or quality of their courage? Was it their contempt of danger? Their ability to plan things out? Their life stories could not have been any different. Libano had been born on the streets; Freddo was born to a respectable

107

middle-class family. At a certain point in their lives, their vicious natures had met and mingled. The result was a terrifying force. Scialoja felt it grow like some monstrous organism. In any case, Freddo remained an enigma. Scialoja instinctively disliked him less than the others.

Bufalo, big and brawny, liked playing the bored lunatic, alternating brooding silences with outbursts of fury. But he was no fool: an unmistakable telltale could be glimpsed in certain sudden intervals of heavy-handed camaraderie with the weaker members of the ring, the Buffoni brothers, and the benevolent consideration in which Libano himself seemed to hold Bufalo. The way you do with a young man who has unquestionable talent but also seems to be constantly on the verge of getting himself into some bottomless abyss with no way out. Bufalo was someone who needed to be kept track of. Dangerous, slippery.

Then there was Dandi. Scialoja interviewed him three times. Dandi was the most arrogant of them all. It was a subtle arrogance: studied and self-aware, but at the same time instinctive. He was always perfectly clean-shaven, with well-cut custom-made suits, always respectful towards the ADA. He could be cutting when it came to it, but if you gave him the opportunity, he had plenty to say and a ready wit. He made enormous efforts to behave like a gentleman. Scialoja wondered whether there was a woman behind these aspirations to middle-class appearances. Perhaps Patrizia herself. Perhaps the relationship between those two was more complicated than the usual bond between a whore and one of her dime-a-dozen johns. Dandi lacked Libano's acute intelligence, Bufalo's unpredictability, even the dark strength that seemed to gust out of Freddo's silent spells. But it was as if Dandi, from fraternizing with the others, had managed to pick up a pinch of all those qualities, as if they'd somehow stuck to his skin. If Libano was a born leader, Dandi was a student who might soon overtake his master. It was people of this calibre that they would be taking on.

Scialoja went back on bended knee to the senior colleague on the mobile squad who had the longstanding confidential relationship with Pino Gemito, Terribile's former bodyguard. But Pino Gemito was gone, and wherever he was, he seemed to be sleeping so deeply that the noise of the shots hadn't awakened him. In other words, the old three monkey routine: see no evil, hear no evil, speak no evil.

'This is the true corroborating evidence,' Scialoja commented. 'It was them!'

Borgia nodded.

'If they kill the commanding boss of someone like Pino Gemito and he takes it without a word...'

'It means that they've already taken control!'

Scialoja drew up a little report filled with allusions and equations with three unknowns, three variables: it can be theorized that... There is solid evidence on which to base the theory of a connection between...

Vasta had a hearty laugh and demanded all his clients be released. Borgia voiced his opposition. But only to make his point: the lawyer was right. This time, they wouldn't even make it up to the Court of Cassation. This time the investigating judge himself was going to let them go. While he was signing the four brief notarized pages that would obtain no other effect than to deprive the alleged perpetrators of a few days of freedom, the assistant district attorney tossed out a thought, wondering aloud.

'And yet, I have to wonder... All that money from the kidnapping – what are they doing with it? Can they possibly spend it all on coke and whores?'

Scialoja got rid of his Fidel Castro disguise and went back to Patrizia. On the phone, grim-voiced, she explained, no recognition of the voice on the end of the line, that she only entertained by appointment. Only very well-to-do clients. And the address would be provided only if the caller provided ample references and documentation. How had he come by this number, which wasn't listed on the official bulletin board for whores, the classified ads in the Rome daily, *Il Messaggero*? Who had told him about Patrizia? Scialoja came up with an identity: a businessman in Rome for the night. It was the desk clerk at his hotel who had suggested a pleasant way to kill some time before leaving town. Patrizia gave him the address.

It was a Saturday night. In a downtown shop Scialoja bought a little plush toy tiger. He remembered certain photographs he'd glimpsed in Cinzia's apartment. Even as he stood in front of her door he wondered why he'd decided to make that gesture, and he still didn't know what the answer might be. Patrizia recognized him immediately. She tried to slam the door in his face. He was too fast for her and managed to jam his foot in the door. Patrizia moved aside. He walked in and dropped the plastic bag with the gift-wrapped plush animal on the sofa. She crossed her arms and looked at him.

'Get out of here. I'm expecting someone.'

'Would it be a businessman in Rome for the night?'

She threw her arms open in exasperation. She was wearing a red corset, black silk stockings, and bracelets around her ankles. Scialoja waved hello with his hand.

'Look, the prices have gone up,' she said, face and voice both flinty.

'This time I'm not paying.'

'This time you're not fucking.'

'You owe me, and you're going to work it off.'

'You're nuts!'

He walked around her. He ventured deeper into the apartment. He moved from the front door to the bedroom. He saw the big, impeccably made bed. The collection of whips and riding crops. The plush toys on the bed. The television turned on, with the sound off, showing scene after scene of urban violence. He breathed in the perfume of Patrizia, so different from the scent he remembered from Cinzia's apartment. He went back into the other room. She'd put on a light polo-neck jumper. She was smoking a cigarette on the sofa, legs crossed, pouting, indifferent to the world around her. He lit a cigarette too. He sat down beside her, shoving aside the package with the little gift-wrapped tiger.

He told her that her friend Dandi was a murderer. She told him that she didn't give a damn whether he was or he wasn't. That wasn't any concern of hers. People are born, people die, some live better lives than others. What does it matter? He threatened her: he'd tell Dandi that she was the one who'd ratted him out. She threw her head back and laughed.

'He won't believe you. And even if he did, I'd make sure to change his mind!'

He told her that sooner or later, Dandi was bound to make a misstep. Sooner or later, every criminal in the business sets his foot wrong. They'd catch him. They'd send him up for life without parole. He'd never get out of prison again.

She told him that she found him unappetizing as a man. As a cop? Downright disgusting.

'You wanted a name? You got a name. And what did you do with it?

110

Nothing. But that's not my problem. I work here, do you understand that? And you're wasting my valuable time. *Capito?* So, either out with the money...'

'Or else I'm not fucking, I get it,' he concluded, irony in his voice.

He stood up. He went and peered out the window. A hot, luminous summer evening. Tourists. Happy little families, absorbed in their own affairs, indifferent to the rest of the world. Scialoja felt suddenly grim, hollowed out.

'Maybe some day they'll manage to kill him,' he said softly.

'Who? Dandi? Like I care! Will you get it through your head that I don't give a damn about Dandi, you, and all the other men who pass through, who come and go...? Will you get it through your head that I don't give a damn about anything at all?'

She was beautiful, in the lengthening shadows. She was beautiful as she flew into a rage, pounding her small clenched fists on the arm of the sofa. She was beautiful as he looked at her: the way you look at a woman, not a whore, as he felt a fury steadily mount within him, unable to pin down a reason for it, something he couldn't connect to any loss, even vaguely, any sentiment, any grief. Scialoja picked up the package with the plush tiger and extended it to her.

'This is for you,' he said softly, before turning to go.

Patrizia tore open the gift-wrapping. The stuffed tiger had blue eyes and long whiskers and a sweet, philosophical smile. It was gorgeous. Patrizia clutched it to her breast and started cooing to it and petting it as if it were a baby. She took it into her bedroom and set it on the bed with her other plush toys. She could tell they were all happy together. They were keeping each other company. Patrizia felt a wave of dull anger surge through her. She seized the tiger and ripped off one of its eyes. She grabbed a knife and plunged it into the cloth belly. Calm returned instantly. She extracted the knife blade. She tucked shut the tear in the cloth, did her best to put it right. She put the eye back where it belonged. She lay the tiger on her pillow. That was better, that was all much better.

The smell of the cop still hovered in the bedroom air. Tobacco and sickly sweet. Patrizia glanced at the clock on the wall. Just half an hour until the three football players were due to show up. Daniela was most likely ready and waiting. Patrizia went into the bathroom. She let the water run in the shower. She soaped up between her legs and picked up her razor. Certain clients liked it like that.

IV

OUT ON THE street, in the meantime, word spread about the gang's new vendetta. And if Sardo and Ricciolodoro were taking it easy in the insane asylum, where they had hastened to return, clean and blameless – This scratch on my leg? I fell off my motorcycle, Judge, Your Honour – there was a line of petitioners and office-seekers waiting to see Libano. The rapid punishment inflicted on Tigame had made it clear to the world at large just who they were dealing with.

The Cravattaro of Campo de' Fiori informed Dandi that there were people who wanted to meet with him. So one morning he and Libano made the acquaintance of Nembo Kid.

Nembo Kid was an overgrown boy from Pigneto. Word had it that in the old days he'd hung out with Lallo lo Zoppo's gang, but the subject of that gossip dismissed it as nonsense.

'Me with those Zulus? Don't make me laugh!'

If nothing else, he'd certainly run with the gang from Marseilles under Berenguer and Bergamelli, spent some time in France where he pulled off a few quick heists, and a year or so in Milan, at the court of King Turatello.

'Then all hell broke loose and life got tough. Did you know that Epaminonda il Tebano gave a lion to a politician as a gift?'

According to Cravattaro, Nembo Kid was a guy 'with the right contacts'. Dandi instinctively liked him. He boasted that he knew how to behave in high society. He dressed in a black leather motorcycle racing suit, rode a streamlined bike and was polite to women.

Not long afterwards, in the discreet backroom of a fish restaurant in the Nomentano district, Nembo Kid introduced his 'contacts': the Maestro and Uncle Carlo.

The Maestro had come up in the world through loan sharking, then he'd moved on to real estate investment in Southern Italy and in Sardinia. Uncle Carlo, a distinguished old gent who never said much and respectfully greeted one and all, was introduced as 'a friend from Sicily'.

Dandi and Libano exchanged an eloquent glance. Mafia. And yet, everyone knew they wouldn't hear of the idea of taking orders from anyone else.

The Maestro suggested they all have *linguine ai totani e moscardini*, accompanied by a potent ice-cold Regaleali, and for their main course the obsequious restaurateur displayed a four-pound sea bream with a large harpoon gash in its side. They were alone in the dining room. Two waiters stood guard to ensure that no one disturbed them.

'This is a reliable place,' the Maestro explained. 'The seafood comes through cousins of Uncle Carlo from Mazara.'

But Dandi and Libano, landlubbers both, went for the *bucatini all'am-atriciana* and the grilled lamb, *abbacchio a scottadito*. The Maestro, with a smirk, ordered a bottle of Barolo.

Uncle Carlo said that he'd heard about them from Don Pepe Albanese, and for the first time since they'd met, he smiled.

'To cut a long story short, we might need some good workers for Rome, and it seems to me that we can count on you.'

A proposal like the one Uncle Carlo had just placed before them – so civil, so courteous – left a very different taste in their mouths from the brutal propositions offered by the Calabrian. The Maestro explained that it wasn't customary for a serious group, like the one Uncle Carlo represented, to invade someone else's territory in a high-handed manner. That meant an explicit recognition that this eternal city – where sooner or later everyone gathered whenever a big deal was on the table…those ancient imperial stones…even that dish of *bucatini* that Libano was letting grow cold in the face of the unmistakable evidence that his dream was actually taking shape before him – everything, in other words, was 'their territory'…

'A pipeline with Turkey has been established for some time now,' the Maestro was explaining. 'The route runs through the Balkans. The Hungarians, as you know, pay lip service to the idea that they're Communists, but in reality they couldn't care less, so their banks and transit through their territory are completely secure.'

'For a while,' Uncle Carlo made clear, 'we worked with a family that's close to Don Pepe Albanese –' another smile – 'but lately these old friends of ours have proven to be, somehow…'

'…not quite keeping up with progress,' Nembo Kid broke in.

'Let's put it like that,' Uncle Carlo conceded.

The Mafia had chosen them. But not as thugs and underlings, the way the Calabrians would have demanded. What was being offered here was a partnership among equals, a joint venture, as Uncle Carlo put it. The man was proud of his experience in the field of high finance and, now and then, indulged in some serious reading.

'The shipments ought to be on the order of ten to fifteen kilos of raw material every twenty or twenty-five days,' the Maestro laid out the numbers.

Dandi and Libano turned pale. Nembo Kid smiled.

Uncle Carlo furrowed an eyebrow. 'Are you sure you can take on this kind of work?'

'We'll do our best,' Libano replied seriously. Uncle Carlo seemed to appreciate the modesty.

'The Maestro and Nembo Kid will be your points of contact. Turn to them for any problems you might have. The shipments are to be paid in full, in cash, upon receipt, at current market price. The cutting, the distribution and all profits are for you to keep. For us, it's a deflationary transaction, and in the meantime it gives us a base of operation here in Rome. If the necessity arises, we'll ask you for logistical support and, if needed, the loan of a man or two. Any observations?'

Needless to say, there were no observations. More than a partnership, this was manna from heaven. Dandi and Libano made their farewells, their eyes gleaming. Nembo Kid left with them. Uncle Carlo watched them disappear into the night, gesticulating in their excitement.

'What do you say, Uncle Carlo?' asked the Maestro.

'They strike me as good fellows. Maybe a bit…trashy. They ought to dress a little better, get cleaned up. A little class wouldn't hurt, in other words.'

'They're kids; they'll grow up.'

'It would be a good idea to have Nembo Kid join the group.'

'We've already agreed on that.'

'Then it's done,' Uncle Carlo concluded. And since he really was satisfied, he took care not to smile.

*

Two days later, Don Pepe Albanese, fresh out of Palmi prison because the time limits on preventive incarceration had expired for him, was killed. A sniper popped his brains out of his head with a single bullet from three hundred yards.

'You could see that coming,' Nembo Kid commented while stopping by to sample the coke that the Neapolitans were supplying. When Dandi asked him how he could say such a thing, Nembo explained that Uncle Carlo had smiled when he mentioned the Calabrian's name. Twice.

'The man never smiles, Dandi. Only when he's about to kill someone or when he just has.'

V

AFTER THE AGREEMENT with the Sicilians, the pipelines for transporting smack proliferated, and the manoeuvre designed to raise prices and intensify demand that Libano had dreamt up was sufficient, in and of itself, to increase revenue five-fold. The Neapolitans sent their congratulations, and shipments of cocaine started to come in on a regular basis. For the retail sale of the cocaine, Trentadenari was authorized to explore the availability of personalities from the world of show business. Working alongside him was Nembo Kid, who'd worked his way into the operation with little more than a wink and a nod.

There were even a few crumbs for the Gemito brothers, prostrated with grief at the premature death of Terribile. Having mended their proud ways, the Gemito boys had humbly asked if they could continue running the gambling dens and a couple of piquet tables. Their plea had been graciously accorded. Provided they kicked back 50 per cent of the profits, of course, and took orders from the new organization from now on. It had been Libano's decision, and met with harsh criticism from Bufalo.

'Don't trust them. They're snakes in the grass.'

'They're just little lost orphans. And they already have a network of customers. They could prove useful.'

Libano had found a solution for Dandi and Patrizia's problems as well. Since heartbreak and desire was eating Dandi alive, Libano confronted him with a harsh choice: either he dropped her once and for all, or else he had to make up his mind to keep her just the way she was, because no matter what he might try to do about it, there was no changing her.

'Let me tell you, the usual systems aren't going to work with that one. You know why your girlfriend Patrizia is so determined to be a whore? Because she's not willing to let anyone else order her around!'

'Well, then, what do I have to do?'

'Buy her a bordello all of her own.'

'What? Be a pimp? Me?'

'You have nothing to do with it. She'll run the whole thing herself. That way, she'll have an independent income and the two of you can finally stop busting my balls!'

No sooner said than done. Libano oversaw the details of the bordello in person. With the intermediation of Ranocchia, the great expert in the field of sex for cash, an old three-storey apartment building in Piazza dei Mercanti, in Trastevere, was identified and purchased, pending formal registry. Libano explained to Patrizia that this was an interest-free loan: she need only pay back the initial capital. Once that was done, congratulations, blessings and all best wishes. Now she'd become Dandi's woman. For good. Until death do you part, as Uncle Priest would have put it. And amen. An architect friend of Trentadenari's would take care of the renovation and interior decoration. Patrizia would have a free hand to recruit the girls, set the rates, the working hours, the featured services. Donatella, Nembo Kid's woman – a big brunette with green eyes and a history as a chorus dancer at the Teatro Ambra Jovinelli – had offered to give her a hand running the place, along with Daniela.

Just as their lawyer Vasta had foretold, Freddo and co were released in early October. Freddo left prison unobtrusively, without even waiting for his comrades, who had undoubtedly prepared a fitting welcome home. He spent his first night as a free man with Gigio. Their mother – they only spoke by phone – had informed him that his kid brother was flunking out of school. The boy had lost weight and he was shivering with cold. Freddo suspected he was on drugs. Gigio protested that he never had anything to do with the shit.

'You'd better not. If I find out you're defying my rules, I'll destroy you.'

The next night, Freddo met Libano in front of Franco's bar. Everyone was inside: Bufalo, Trentadenari and the rest. Free champagne for one and all, and anyone that doesn't drink is going to have some explaining to do!

Libano and Freddo embraced.

'Thank you.'

'No, I thank you,' Freddo replied after a brief pause. Then Libano dragged him into his brand-new, bright red Alfetta Spider, and from there he never took his foot off the accelerator until they pulled up outside a huge two-storey villa at the gated community of Olgiata.

'This is the place.'

Freddo looked out at the scraggly lawn, the empty eyeholes of the windows, the solid but grim appearance of the building, the For Sale sign dangling from the rusty wire on the front gate.

'This is what place?'

'The club. Fourteen thousand square feet, two stories; in the cellar, a billiards room and, if you want, an indoor swimming pool. The owner can't refuse. Five hundred million lire and it's all ours. If you're in, we can sign the papers tomorrow.'

They got out of the car. Freddo lit two cigarettes and handed one to Libano. It seemed as if he was having a hard time staying in one place.

'Why me?'

'Listen, Freddo, that whole thing with Terribile, I...'

'You've already thanked me,' Freddo said, cutting him off and turning to walk back to the Alfetta.

Libano followed along behind him, shaking his head. 'So you're not convinced, eh?'

Freddo stopped short. 'No, I'm not convinced.'

'Why not?'

'It's too soon.'

'Too soon for what? What else are we waiting for? Business is going great guns...Rome's stretched out at our feet...We buy this shack and we turn it into the most elegant nightclub in the city: a nice bar on the ground floor, classy floor shows, distinguished clientele. And upstairs, in the private rooms, roulette tables, green felt card tables...'

'They'll never give us the licences. They know who we are.'

'We can use other people's names. It's easy to get a front.'

'I'm just not convinced.'

'Why not?'

'I don't know. Somehow it just doesn't add up.'

There were times when Freddo could be exasperating. Libano wondered if he was afraid of something. Then he thought of the scene with Terribile: from what Bufalo had told him, Freddo had balls and heart, in abundance. This wasn't about fear. Then what could it be?

'This is our dream, Freddo. The great leap forward. All things considered, it didn't even cost us that much to get here. It was enough to have some ideas in our heads, and a little determination. This world is dripping, this city is dripping... They were all just waiting for someone with determination, someone like us, someone with as much heart and brains as us...'

'But why me? Ask Dandi.'

'He's still not ready for this!'

'Ask Bufalo, ask Scrocchiazeppi, ask Trentadenari, ask Sardo...'

'They aren't ready. They're not right. Heart and head, Freddo... There's no one but you and me...'

'I'm just not convinced, Libano. I'm sorry.'

The following morning, Freddo put down a down payment for a detached house in Casalpalocco. There was plenty of room for his parents and for Gigio, and even, if he decided to use it, a bedroom for him. Among the neighbours were a doctor and a lawyer. His father wouldn't hear of taking anything from him, so he was forced to make arrangements with his mother alone. Always by phone. As for Libano's offer, he'd let it drop once and for all with one last 'I'm not convinced'. But he couldn't explain the reason why. He could just tell it wouldn't be a good thing, that was all. For that matter, he'd given up explanations of any kind for some time now.

VI

PATRIZIA WAS FOND of Ranocchia. He was her friend, her confidante. He always had a smile on his face, Ranocchia did. He knew how to jolly her out of it when she was in one of her moods. He knew how to calm her down when she was in a towering rage. But the thing she liked best was when he told her his dreams.

'I'm blonde, I'm five foot eleven, and I've got a pair of spectacular tits on me. I'm at the top of a staircase with a purple railing and I'm holding a bouquet of white irises. Looking up at me is a spectacular flock of magnificent young men, all in tuxedos. The orchestra strikes up 'I Wanna Be Loved By You', and in my slender-fingered, pale white hands there appears, as if by some enchantment, a tiny banjo. The spotlight focuses on me. I start coming down the stairs, one step at a time. The young men are going wild…I can hear them, I can feel their animal heat…I'm their favourite prey. I'm Norma Jean Baker…'

'Who?'

'Marilyn Monroe, silly girl!'

There, it really didn't take much. And her grim thoughts were dispelled, like dry leaves in the wind. Patrizia laughed and laughed. Ranocchia was knee-high to a grasshopper and had greenish skin. In fact, his nickname meant 'frog' as well as 'ugly runt'.

'I'm in the Sonora desert, down in the southernmost part of Arizona. I'm Minnehaha, the queen of all squaws. The scalp-hunters have captured me. I'm tied to a tree, lit up by the light of the full moon. The hunters are going to kill me. But first they're going to take turns raping me. I know that out there somewhere, concealed behind a boulder or a cactus, Golden Serpent, my brave warrior, lies in ambush with his bow and arrows, ready to rescue me. I know it, and I'm all wet down there with anticipation. I just hope and pray that he'll arrive late enough to let me have my full ration of fun with those heathen brutes!'

'Where in the world do you get all these dreams, Ranocchia?'

'From films, dear heart. From the great, wonderful films of the golden age of cinema. What about you? What do you dream about?'

'I never have dreams.'

'Oh, you poor little thing! That's just awful! No one can live without dreams, absolutely no one! Even…even the devil himself! That's right, even the devil has dreams every now and then. And a sweet little angel like you would just…'

'I never have dreams.'

'It's because there's something stuck in that pretty little head of yours that's keeping you from doing it, darling. It's like a boulder. A boulder that's weighing down on you, oppressing you. If only you could make an effort to get that boulder out from inside of you, that damned boulder…'

'That's the last thing on earth I'd want!'

'*Mamma mia*, Patrizia! What a mess you are! You don't know how to dream, and you don't know how to cry! And yet, God, how much nicer you'd look with a few tears running down that wily, razor-sharp little face of yours…'

That's when the two of them were done playing. Patrizia would come up with some excuse or other, put an end to the conversation, and she'd be out of there. It unfailingly happened every time she felt that Ranocchia was getting close to something dangerous. Being forced to take a look inside of herself: that was the one thing that truly scared her.

Ranocchia had a knife scar that ran diagonally across his right cheek.

'One of my fiery lovers,' he loved to say, allusive, winking his luminous eyes, which were surrounded by a fine network of wrinkles that defied any and all beauty creams. And he added, humming the tune of that old song by Tony Renis, '*Quando dico che ti amo*':

'*È la pura, sacrosanta verità!*'

'It's the pure, sacrosanct truth!'

Ranocchia liked to play rough. Born rich, he'd been to school and had always been an odd duck. If Patrizia asked, he'd have cut off his right hand, or possibly both. He'd been the one who talked her into the idea that no self-respecting bordello could do without a nice hot young boy or two on offer.

'For our more refined clientele, the ones who might have slightly particular preferences…'

At first, Patrizia had told him she didn't want to hear about it: not a word about faggots, and especially not about underage boys. Sooner or later, however hard they might try to keep things discreet, the bordello was bound to get a reputation for itself. When that happened, trouble would ensue. Patrizia knew that you could fix anything with the vice squad, unless what was broken was an underage boy. There was a taboo on underage boys. Just let a little boy come through your front door once and you were in the crosshairs for the rest of your life. With a cunningly orchestrated array of tears, wisecracks and bouquets of orchids, Ranocchia managed to strike an agreement: he'd personally run a third-floor bedroom. But in contrast with the arrangement with the girls – some of whom were full-time, long-term residents – the boys, or young men, really, as all were rigorously twenty-one or older, were to be recruited for each client as needed, and they were forbidden to spend the night within the bordello walls.

When he heard that faggots would be on offer, Dandi wasted no time making fun of Ricotta.

'Hey, Rico, you used to hang out with Pasolini: would you happen to have a couple of nice fresh arse cheeks you could spare?'

Ricotta, choking back a bitter taste in his mouth, cursed the day that he let slip that he himself, one time, just once, with the great poet…

If Ranocchia had only liked women, he'd have married Patrizia. She was just his type. Maybe he really was a little bit in love with her. That's why when Agents Zeta and Pigreco showed up, he begged them to forget about the place and leave. But this was just work for Zeta and Pigreco. They had their orders. Orders from the Old Man, in person.

'She'll tell you to go straight to hell,' Ranocchia entreated them.

'So we'll shut the place down,' Zeta replied.

'It's not what you think.'

'Who said anything about thinking? Have I missed something, or isn't it all about ficky-fick?'

'Why on earth do you have to be so damned vulgar!'

'And why do you have to be such a damned faggot?'

'Well, anyway, you'd better find someone else. I'm not doing you this favour. Not even if you kill me.'

'Well, we probably wouldn't kill you, but we could always arrange to send you to prison for a nice long fifteen-year term…'

This was their job. This was extortion. The Old Man liked to say that queers made excellent pasturage: graze there and you were sure to have your fill. Queers were fragile weather vanes; they span with the winds

121

of passion. All queers, sooner or later, wound up making a mistake – to some greater or lesser degree, an irreparable one. And then they wound up on the Old Man's pay book. Thus it always was, and thus it always would be. For all time. So however much he might shrill and keen and curse, Ranocchia still introduced the men to Patrizia as two of his very best clients.

She had them pegged at a single glance: cops, maybe worse. But they were cut from a different cloth than that other odd character who used to pester her before she became Dandi's girlfriend. Scialoja. He smacked of…What was it he smacked of? Ah, tobacco and sickly sweet, that's right. These two stank of leather and metal. Nasty people. Patrizia dismissed poor Ranocchia with a fiery glare.

'You came on the wrong day. This is the girls' day off. But if you give me half an hour, I can call Milly the redhead and Ketty the blonde…'

'What's your hurry!' replied the taller of the two – grey eyes, crew-cut hair, nicely cut suit, astringent cologne.

'Right, why all the rush?' echoed the other one – shorter, stouter, heavier, a creature redolent of hair net, brilliantine and comb-over.

The fox and the cat, Patrizia thought, thinking of the two dubious characters from Pinocchio. They just wanted to take a look around the place. She started the tour on the ground floor. Zeta and Pigreco exclaimed with admiration at the respectability of the furnishings.

'A comfortable little drawing room where you can entertain your clients in perfect seclusion and privacy. Wouldn't a bar be nice in here?'

'There's plenty to drink in all the bedrooms,' she replied in a frosty voice.

'Plenty to drink, and a little cocaine, too, eh?'

'No drugs allowed in here.'

'Oh, that's a pity.'

'Yeah, that's a real pity!'

The bedrooms of love were located on the second and third floors.

'The full-time girls are on the second floor. The other girls are on the third floor.'

'And what's behind that door there?'

'That's in case you like boys.'

'Heavens above! Have you taken us for faggots?'

'No, really, don't tell me you took us for faggots?'

Zeta and Pigreco inspected two bedrooms chosen at random. Nothing had been left to chance. Nothing: from the huge circular bed, to the refrigerator and bar, the erotic prints on the walls, the Super 8 projectors with an ample assortment of porno films, and the cabinets filled with sex accessories of every kind. Each room had its own cosy bathroom. It was anyone's guess how much the renovations had cost. The Old Man, as always, had been right: this was a promising operation.

'Really quite admirable!'

'Yes, really quite so!'

'Still, just a little cold and impersonal, don't you think?'

'Yes, it's a little like a hotel. Maybe some people wouldn't like it!'

'Maybe they wouldn't.'

'And then,' said Patrizia, doing her best to steer them back to the front room, 'we have the dark room in the cellar...'

'Oooh! That sounds sinful!'

'Very sinful!'

Zeta and Pigreco demanded to see it. The dark room smelled of disinfectant. In the middle of the room was a marble table. Hanging on the wall were whips, latex body suits, masks and chains. There were two metal rings set into the wall. Zeta opened a cabinet door and peered inside. It contained an assortment of enema bulbs.

'You understand what these are used for, don't you?' Patrizia asked.

'How disgusting!'

'Yes, truly disgusting!'

'Men are disgusting,' said Patrizia.

'Coming from you...' Zeta sniped.

Pigreco laughed.

They went upstairs. Patrizia renewed her attempts at talking to them about the girls. Zeta got comfortable on a small red loveseat. Pigreco remained standing and lit a cigarette. Patrizia rudely extended an ashtray in his direction.

'Well, it's really a lovely little business you have here. What a pity it would be if something awful were to happen to it...'

'Yes, wouldn't that be terrible. All that money, all that nice furniture...'

'Is this some kind of shake-down for protection?'

'Let's just say it's a proposal you might want to take under consideration...That is, if you were interested...'

'What would you need?'

'A bedroom,' murmured Zeta.

'Or even better, two,' Pigreco ventured.

'I said one!' Zeta glared back.

'It may happen from time to time that clients of some regard frequent the bordello. Very special clients. Important men who, between one commitment and the next in their tumultuous lives, feel the need for a refreshing pause. A brief, innocent breath of oxygen in their sea of daily adversities. It may happen that these men feel the need to vent about some bitterness they feel. Or to rejoice in a success that they've long pursued and finally attained. It would be interesting, in those unguarded moments, to be close at hand. To watch. To listen.'

'I understand. You want to blackmail them.'

Zeta burst into laughter. 'Blackmail someone for a few sexual peccadillos? What an absurd idea! It's not like we're in America, darling. This is Italy. Good old Italy. Here in Italy, the more powerful a man is, and the more of a rutting hog he is, why, the more people like him!'

'We're Roman Catholics, after all!'

'Are you suggesting I become a spy?' Patrizia asked.

'Whatever are you thinking? You just rent us a room – a room from which we can watch without being observed, listen without being overheard – and in exchange we guarantee that no one – and I mean no one, ever, for any reason – will bother you in the slightest!'

'To be exact, two rooms,' Pigreco corrected his colleague, ignoring the daggered look Zeta gave him.

'But you can take your time making up your mind,' Zeta reassured her. 'We'll be back.'

'In the meantime, now that we've met and since it looks like a cosy little place...'

'I'll call the two girls.' Patrizia heaved a sigh.

Zeta shook his head no. Pigreco smiled.

'With a lovely lady like you, right here, ready and waiting...'

'Both at the same time, or one after the other?' she asked coldly, slipping off her jumper.

Zeta admired her cool.

'Go take a stroll,' he ordered his colleague.

Once the two secret agents had finished up, Patrizia called Dandi and told him about the call they'd just paid. Dandi asked her if they'd gotten their dicks wet. Patrizia told him to go to hell.

Dandi reached out to Libano. Libano said that those two were trouble and to steer clear. Old acquaintances of Nembo Kid. He'd tell him all he needed to know when the time came. As for the deal they'd offered, he needed some time to think it over. In any case, he'd take care of it.

Patrizia refused to forgive Ranocchia. She felt betrayed. Off with his head! Ranocchia confessed, weeping, that the two bastards had black-mailed him. Because the one time in his life that in his explorations of the sado-maso world he'd decided to see what it felt like to go sado instead of maso...The poor boy...pure rotten luck...an accident...he'd never meant...just never got back up from the floor...

Patrizia was implacable. Ranocchia found himself out on the street, his pockets stuffed with the cash she owed him and a hole in his heart that he just couldn't patch. He hooked up with a young Arab in Piazza Navona and took him to a little pensione he knew over by the central station. The Arab was carrying a ridiculous knife of some sort, more box-cutter than anything else. As the Arab started cutting away at him, Ranocchia closed his eyes and imagined himself as a painting of St Sebastian.

The Idea
January–June 1979

I

THE FATHERLAND WAS mortally threatened by Red hooligans. The scarlet fangs of the Bolsheviks were about to be plunged into the flesh of the Nation. The Christian Democracy was in cahoots with the Cossacks, who wanted nothing better than to water their warhorses at the fountains in St Peter's Square. Evidently, the lesson of Moro was wasted on them.

The streets were under the control of a horde of youngsters running wild, their minds exalted with Marxist deviationism. The university was a hotbed of subversion. The armed forces were on their last legs. The economy was going to hell in a hand basket, to the enormous satisfaction of Jewish bankers. America was too far away to intervene. This wasn't Chile, and there was certainly no Pinochet on the horizon. Italy needed to work from within. The way they did in Greece. When there was rot in the system, then it was time to overthrow it and put a new system in its place. When a limb was gangrenous, it was time to amputate. Pointless – and suicidal – to wait for the infection to propagate. That was why the time was ripe to aggregate all the opposition forces eager to be done with the old system around an overarching project of purification. Put out the clarion call to all those – in the armed forces, law enforcement, the judiciary, the church, the universities, and even in politics – who were unwilling to give up feebly and eat rice while truckling under and kowtowing to Mongols and Muzhiks. Bring all those forces together, but most important of all, don't overlook the people in the street. Idealist militants, Mafiosi, renegade soldiers, as well as thieves and killers: all those, in other words, that the Communist sob-sisters denounced as 'criminals'. All marching side-by-side in the common battle against the corrupt state that flew the banner of the five-pointed red star. Because it was only through universal destruction today that it would become possible to rebuild in the future. Because it was only by annihilating the old order of today that it would become possible to establish the new order of tomorrow.

When he stopped to catch his breath, and it happened only rarely, between one diatribe and another, Professor Cervellone – jocularly so called, with a name that meant Professor Brainiac – wiped a mono-grammed scarf over his spacious forehead and ran a hand between his thighs, adjusting the sizable junk highlighted by his close-fitting trousers. Then he looked them in the eye one by one, almost feverishly.

They returned those glances with distracted gazes and faint, polite smiles; just enough of a reaction to feign a certain degree of interest. This lukewarm encouragement was enough to send the professor – entirely oblivious to the signals that they were discreetly flashing in his direc-tion – off on a new tirade, his impetus renewed. And so his eyes would range randomly over the walls of his study – prints of hunting scenes; a Futurist scrawl; a giant-format photograph of that famous Japanese writer who committed hara-kiri; streamers and pennants from the late Fascist Republic of Salò; another photograph with a signed dedication by Prince Junio Valerio Borghese, 'To the fiery warriors of the Xª MAS – *eia eia eia alalà*' – halting fleetingly, with an air of reproof, on Dandi, who sat utterly absorbed in filing his fingernails.

'As I was saying… What's needed is the establishment of a coalition of deviants. We need to sow panic among the populace. Unleash a campaign of terror that will make Robespierre look like a piker. Ideally no one will feel safe anymore, in the streets, at the stadium, on a train, even in their own home. People will be forced to ask themselves, in horror: what is this place? How did we get here? And the next question they'll ask will be: who can save us? And they'll come running to us, they'll throw them-selves into our arms. And we'll be ready to welcome them! That's exactly what I have in mind when I speak of a "coalition of deviants". I'm thinking of the arms and legs that will make our new order march!'

Which is to say, Freddo translated, that the professor wanted them to plant a few bombs here and there and shoot a few Reds in the head, while in exchange…Right, what they got in exchange was the darkest part of the equation. The professor swore up and down that the new order was going to take power in an astonishingly short span of time. They themselves would be amazed to learn just how many prominent personalities were fully briefed on the plan and supported its aims. If he failed to share those names now, it was merely out of understandable caution, and because he didn't want to be taken for a raving lunatic. But once the new order had been established, all their sins would be amnestied, all their merits recompensed.

'We'll have to organize an army…We'll need an efficient espionage service…The experience of people like you will prove invaluable…And what you will have done on the behalf of the advent of the new order will never be forgotten…'

To Freddo – for whom the mere sound of the word 'politics' was enough to make him feel like unleashing a bloodbath – the prospect of becoming a general, or master spy, was more irresistible than a film starring Alberto Sordi – Albertone! Sure, and after that a cabinet minister! Ladies and gentlemen, it is my distinct honour to introduce to you His Excellency, Freddo, First Count of Spinaceto, honourable Ambassador of Infernetto!

'You are not criminals, you are authentic soldiers of the national revolution! You steal and you kill with a view to a higher end! Your lives represent the most ruthless j'accuse imaginable levelled against the degenerate flabbiness of the Red Communist horde. What choice, in the world we now live in, is available to a brilliant young man, a talent forged in the tradition, other than that of the daily and self-aware practice of evil?'

What did he know about it!

Even Libano, with all his Fascist impulses, was starting to run out of patience. The whole Moro affair had made him wary. When it came to politics, he had to hand it to Freddo: scepticism was the right approach. The offer itself, moreover, was nothing to write home about. The people who could teach them something were the ones like Uncle Carlo. Whether the Communists or the Fascists wound up winning in the end, the important thing was to remain standing, on the crest of the wave. All the rest was a bunch of dumb show, like the false heroics of the Battle of the Volturno.

Dandi, on the other hand, pocketed his nail file and looked out the window at the grim sunset over the countryside of the Ciociaria, and a sky that was threatening rain or possibly even snow. He might have to miss the evening's entertainment at the Climax Seven. Listening to the advice of that loser Mazzocchio had been an idiotic mistake.

Mazzocchio, who had arranged the meeting, watched as the magnificent project in whose success he'd invested his last few crumbs of credibility slipped through his fingers. After a series of exploits, each one a more spectacular failure than the last, he had been re-admitted to the network through Puma's intercession. Acting as intermediary with the professor was supposed to be his passport to a full gala welcome home. But everything was going terribly wrong. Everything was pointing to a future in which he'd have to go on settling for pennies and peanuts.

The professor, in the meantime, was waving a copy of an old book in the air: a slender volume with a swastika on the cover.

'You'll find it all written in here!' he shouted, waving his arms in a frenzy. 'Read up! Examine the documentation! Read *The Protocols of the Elders of Zion*! The Jewish conspiracy! The Zionist plan for world domination! Read! Develop your culture...'

'Hey, professor, I've had just about enough!'

It had been in the air. The professor had pushed things so far that in the end Freddo had told him where to get off. They all put on their jackets, ready to strike camp, when Mazzocchio blocked them with a hopeful sigh.

'But wait! The professor can help us out as an expert witness...'

Libano shrugged and kept walking, paying him no mind. Still, Dandi had kept the book. He'd seen pictures in a magazine of one of the many houses he'd like to live in. It was full of books. That might be a good sign.

II

MARIANO HAD HER abortion in mid-February. Vanessa, who was becoming day by day an increasingly invaluable member of the group, took care of everything. Trentadenari took her out to dinner the following evening. Mariano had already been packed off to Udine to stay

130

with family. They wrote each other a couple of heart-rending letters, but she was never going to come back. So much the better. Aside from the fact that, somewhere in the Campania region, Trentadenari was already legally married, and that his wife was bringing up their two children, there was no evidence that he'd even been responsible for that short-lived pregnancy. With all the dicks she'd spread her legs for – Mariano, you tell me who the father really was. So as long as we're talking about orgies and group sex, lines of coke and partying down, it's all well and good. But true love was quite another matter, and forget about children. As the great Eduardo De Filippo used to say, they take pieces out of your heart: *'so' piezz' 'e core!'*

Vanessa, on the other hand, was quite a different type of person from that complete slut and half a lesbian, the lady lawyer. Vanessa was poised, elegant and petite – quite striking, with a vague resemblance to that baby-faced actress who allowed herself to be buttered up in *Last Tango in Paris*. That is to say, it was sufficient to see her smile and cross her legs to understand that deep down there was a fiery flame. A flame that first of all needed a little taming. Like all real women, and like all love affairs worthy of their salt, there was no point in trying to hurry things along. Mariano, on the other hand…She'd unzipped his fly the very first time they met, in the law offices of Nino Vasta. No question, a complete slut…

'Would you care for a little more champagne?'

'Thank you, yes.'

What a waste, to see a woman like her with a filthy goat like Sorcio, who was always either tripping or high on junk, and if he couldn't get his hands on actual dope, was capable of huffing a paper bag full of disposable lighter fumes. But Trentadenari knew it was only a matter of time…

In the meantime, they were enjoying their night out at the Climax Seven. Not a shabby little club at all. Popular with the people who mattered. Doing a booming trade, at first glance. But Dandi had heard that Nembo Kid was tightening the screws on the owner: gambling debts, loan sharking, an assortment of compromising photographs of the guy with underage girls…Long story short, three or four months tops and the guy would be forced to hand over the club's licence. Dandi, ever since the night he'd looked like a fool with Patrizia, had sworn to himself that sooner or later, that place would be his. He and Nembo Kid had talked it over with Libano, who, for some reason incomprehensible to them, was holding back. Libano was still pestering Freddo about the villa in Olgiata. But Freddo, then as always, was paying no attention to anybody. When Trentadenari heard what was afoot, he'd hurried to get word to Sardo, who was growing increasingly edgy in the nuthouse. Sardo ordered him to keep the situation under observation. And so, that night, pleasure of their company aside, he was there on a mission.

'Ciao, Vanessa!'

Trentadenari looked up and his eyes took in the smiling face of a tall young man with a handsome dark cloth jacket and a very respectable necktie. Vanessa, who had returned the young man's greeting, introduced him.

'Fabio Santini, an old classmate of mine.'

Before he could even have his suspicions aroused, Trentadenari noticed that with Fabio Santini was a stunning girl with exotic looks and a pair of thighs that seemed to go on forever and a breathtaking miniskirt that made the blood churn in his veins. Fine, no jealousy, no worries. He got politely to his feet and asked the new arrivals to join the party.

Fabio was a facile conversationalist, a guy who seemed all right; the girl, who pointed to herself and said 'Desy', didn't speak a word of Italian. She just kept rubbing up against the young man, whispering filthy nothings into his ear in a mixture of Spanish and who-knows-what dialect. Vanessa was comfortable, at ease with her 'old classmate'. Most likely she'd been to bed with him at some point in the past. One thing was clear, to judge from the mulatto: he knew something about women. He could be a young lawyer, or even a wealthy man of leisure. Whatever he did, Trentadenari liked the kid well enough, and in a while the atmosphere was sufficiently warm that he invited them all back to his place to end the evening there, with the thought that a couple of lines of coke might even oil the skids with the nurse.

Back at the apartment, in the time that it took Trentadenari to put on some of that whiny American music that girls dug so much, Fabio and Desy hoovered up three lines of Bolivian pink. Just as rabid as wildcats, their noses still floury with the dope they'd snorted, the couple catapulted themselves onto the white sofa that in times gone by had been

132

the venue for Mariano's athletic exploits. Vanessa didn't turn her nose up at the coke, but she indulged him with no more than a kiss or two and a quick grope of her tits before announcing that she was just too tired from her long day, and she started her next shift at dawn. Trentadenari, a gentleman to the very last, offered to see her home. Vanessa opted for a taxi. The two lovebirds had found their way to the bedroom without assistance. Left to his own devices, Trentadenari found himself incapable of mastering the desire that Vanessa – unquestionably a first-class *femmina*, a true *baba au rhum*, he mused, licking his lips – had kindled and left unquenched. He was about to reach out to Fierolocchio and have him send over one of his little tricks, when his gaze happened to fall on Fabio Santini's jacket, kicked to the floor at the foot of the sofa during the couple's amorous disporting. Trentadenari leaned over for a better look. If it had been a normal handgun, no problem. But the pistol that protruded from the inside jacket pocket was a Beretta 92S with a double-stack magazine – a regulation-issue weapon for law enforcement professionals. Therefore, one of two conclusions followed by necessity: either the old schoolmate was a stand-up guy, the kind of thug that went around at night with a pistol ripped off of some helpless cop, maybe even a genuine terrorist. The other alternative was this: Fabio himself was actually a law enforcement professional.

The first thing Trentadenari did was to pocket the weapon, then he went to close the sliding bedroom door, behind which the two were going at it with gusto, the *negrita deliciosa* shrieking like some amorous bird of prey. Then Trentadenari proceeded to do a more meticulous search. When he found the badge and ID, complete with photograph and corresponding badge number, it finally became clear to him that he'd actually brought a cop home to party.

And that was only part of the trouble. He could shoot him then and there, him and his mulatto girlfriend, but that opened the door to a series of other problems: bloodstains, to say nothing of the bodies, and most important, the possibility that some snoopy neighbour might have noticed them all come upstairs together. He could suggest they all go out for a stroll along the riverbanks, but the risk of a scheme like that, thrown together on the spur of the moment, terrified him. Still, he had to make up his mind. He wasn't worried about the prospect of a couple of murders: it had happened before back in Naples, and he'd come out of it just fine. But this was a different matter. Here, he was inside his own apartment, the place he lived. And he didn't have the first idea of what to do. So when the big strapping boy emerged from the bedroom, naked and dripping with sweat, at the sight of his open and slightly stoned smile, Trentadenari let a wave of pissed-off fury sweep him away. He let fly with a kick to the testicles, and as the guy was toppling over, astonishment washing over his face, he doubled down with a hook to the back of his neck. Then he jumped on him and started choking him.

'Filthy cop! Piece of shit! What did you have in mind, eh? You come to my house, you have a nice fuck, and the whole time you're nothing but a goddamned cop!'

The other guy struggled wildly, grunting incomprehensible phrases. Trentadenari kept both hands clamped around his neck. The cop's face was turning blue. The mulatto girl stuck her head in, saw what was happening, screamed and bolted for the door. But Trentadenari was too fast for her. He grabbed her around the waist and threw her roughly onto the sofa.

'I'll take care of you soon enough, slut!'

But it had given the cop time to recover, or at least to crawl behind an English antique sideboard for which Trentadenari had paid two million lire in a gallery on Via dei Coronari. The cop had left a trail of blood behind him, like a filthy slug. Oh great, now to make things worse, they were going to ruin his interior decoration too!

'Wait, I can explain…'

'What the fuck are you going to explain? You're a dead man, you understand?'

'No, please, wait. I work for Criminalpol, the criminal police. I can help you…'

Trentadenari, who had already pulled back the hammer, lowered the Beretta.

'I like to snort, friend. And I have to support Desy in the proper style. It's not an easy life…When we met at the club, I hadn't had a taste of the shit in two days. I'm flat broke, friend. Why don't we help each other out? You help me and I'll help you…'

He seemed sincere. But then who wouldn't seem sincere if they found themselves naked, unarmed, and looking down the barrel of an eleven-shot semi-automatic pistol?

'And Vanessa? What does Vanessa know about you?'

'Nothing, I swear it! We really did go to school together. She thinks I'm a reporter. Come on, put down your gun and let's talk it over...'

They wound up coming to an agreement. Fabio would procure back-channel information about trials, if there ever were any, and he'd warn of any upcoming arrest warrants. In exchange, Trentadenari would supply him with cocaine. Fabio promised to introduce him to another couple of enterprising cops looking for opportunities. Trentadenari authorized the two of them to get dressed, but he held onto the Beretta as a little piece of insurance.

'You're going to keep it? What am I going to tell my superiors?'

'Invent some story. Now get the fuck out of here!'

When all was said and done, it had turned out to be a nice piece of luck. They were paying off cops in Naples; in Rome they were going to have to start, sooner or later. Now he knew what he could tell the others: I picked up two or three cops and I'm paying them in cocaine. They may prove useful. Too bad if that wasn't the whole truth. He was hardly married to them, his comrades. They were in business together, but what was the phrase? Here today, who knows where tomorrow?

III

EVEN THOUGH THINGS turned out the way they did with Professor Cervellone, word made its way quickly through the city's quarters that as a gang they leaned right. And so, from sunset till dawn, they found themselves besieged by a student body of overgrown kids sporting buzz cuts, designer jumpers, with words of bloody havoc pouring out of rosebud lips that still smacked of milk. The kids would pretend they'd just happened along, crossing paths at Franco's bar, or in the other places they frequented, such as at the EUR or Fiumicino. These kids seized every opportunity to jump into the conversation, displaying as trophies of combat weapons stolen from the political squad or the *caramba*, as they called the carabinieri. They'd launch into bloodthirsty descriptions of real or alleged exploits. Some of them really had undergone their baptism by fire, but most of them were bluffing. Once the intoxication was over, if they made it out alive and scot-free, they were bound to go running back to mummy's welcoming arms.

There were others. Sellerone, to name one (named 'celery' in Roman dialect in honour of the tall, thin vegetable he so closely resembled), who showed up with the brilliant plan of indoctrinating the *coatti*, the hooligans from the city's periphery, on the model they'd already seen from the professor. Libano had accorded him a half-hour's audience one afternoon when he was in an especially good mood. Two hours earlier, he, Dandi and Nembo Kid had finally agreed to rent the long-desired villa in Olgiata. He'd just have to let Freddo be himself, but if he let himself get caught up in his apprehensions and fears, there was a real danger of growing old without ever getting anything started. Sellerone, a sort of pathetic, worm-eaten intellectual who came from the Castelli Romani and ranted on about the masters of tradition, was trying to explain to him that 'all the men that he'd suppressed in his time' had been 'justly sacrificed on the altar of the Idea'. Leaving aside the fact that Libano had serious doubts that that sad sack have ever actually 'suppressed' anyone, this whole thing of the Idea was starting to become a pain in the arse.

'No, but listen, the Idea... What's in it for you, this big Idea?'

'The Idea isn't about what's in it for you, Libano. The Idea is the exact opposite of that money-grabbing profit motive. The Idea abhors self-interest. All profits are usury, and usury is strictly for Jews...'

'Lemme understand: you want to be poor?'

'Poor in money, maybe, but rich in glory. And rich in traditions!'

A small crowd had gathered to listen to them debate. And when Libano came out with his memorable line, he set off a robust belly laugh among those present.

'But that means you're a Communist!'

Sellerone turned red as a beet and looked like he was about to burst. Libano called over Scrocchiazeppi and asked him to give him his watch. Then he pulled a bunch of keys out of his pocket and laid everything on the bar.

'This is a Rolex, Sellero. And these are the keys to my Alfetta. You know how a person gets things like these? With their heart and with their head. Not with the damned Idea! Can I offer you a piece of advice? Actually, more than advice, it's an opportunity for you…Tomorrow morning a friend is coming in from Sicily. He's a good kid. I need you to go pick him up at the station, help him to carry his luggage, drive him around Rome a little bit and show him the wonders of the Eternal City. Poor guy, he doesn't have much time and he has to catch a train back home tomorrow night. And, oh, I was almost forgetting: he's bringing something with him, and he needs to take something else back home. So you get your car and you do this job for me, you take delivery of his thing and in exchange you give him a thing that I'm going to give you, then, when you're done, you take him back to the station, you make sure he boards the train and the train leaves the station, and only once you've heard the train blow its horn – you know what a train horn sounds like? Bufalo, what's the sound of a train horn?'

'Tooot-toooot-tooot…'

'That's right, perfect. Toot-toot toot-toot…Only once you hear that sound do you get back in your car and drive here. You give me the package the Sicilian brought up and in exchange you'll get the Alfetta and a Rolex just like this one. And I promise you, you'll fall asleep tomorrow night happy as a clam and you'll forget all about the Idea…All right, what do you say? You up for my little errand?'

Sellerone's skin tone had shifted from red to leaden grey. Now the laughter all around him had become open snickering. Libano called for silence. The laughter was stifled.

'Well then, Sellero, let's go!'

'You…you don't believe in a thing, Libano!'

'What are you talking about? I was a Fascist before you even came into the world!'

'What kind of fascism are you talking about!' Sellerone blurted out. 'This is…this is…'

'This is…?' Libano provoked him.

Sellerone couldn't find the words. Or perhaps he simply lacked the courage to say what he really thought. That the story of the 'coalition of deviants', for which the professor had 'infiltrated' him into their midst, was nothing more than a gigantic load of bullshit. He turned on his heel and left, Bufalo's mocking words sailing after him.

'And when you see the Idea, give it my regards!'

But there was one guy who was different from the rest, one guy who wasted no words and who in the end really became one of them. He called himself Nero – not like the emperor, but rather the colour black, the colour of extreme right-wing terror – and he was tall and lanky, just like Freddo, and in fact the two men resembled each other a bit in terms of personality as well. They became friends without a lot of beating around the bush. When they were together, they needed nothing but each others' company to feel comfortable. It was as if everything that one of them kept bottled up tight inside somehow resonated with every-thing the other one was concealing. But what was it they were holding so close to the vest, what could be so heavy that they didn't dare pull it out into the open air? An anger, something unsaid, something unutter-able? Well, it was hard to say, in fact. But they understood each other anyway.

One night, when Freddo was sampling a shipment of coke from the Neapolitans, Nero happened to drop by. They snorted up together and, after they were done, Nero admitted that it was the first time he'd ever snorted coke.

He had to do it. He had to try. You have to try everything in life. His one and only master, his true teacher had taught him that: Julius Evola. A genius relegated to a wheelchair by a bomb during the war. He'd died a few years ago, an old, old man. He lived in a cheap apartment and loved to surround himself with young people. In his youth he'd been a painter. He never talked about politics: only about life. Nero had met him and frequented him when he was still a minor. He'd never forget him.

'Everything, everything, you understand? With him you really grasp the meaning of the Idea. The Idea isn't a bunch of words. The Idea is actions, without words. Everything. The river of life. And when it's over, it's over.'

Freddo felt those words flow down into him like a flume of white hot metal. And he decided to share something with Nero that he'd never told a soul, and that he would never tell another person as long as he lived.

'I've only thought about the end once, Nero. I was five years old and I was staying with the nuns. They'd served me a bowl of disgusting soup and I threw it straight out the window. But the mother superior saw

138

what I'd done, and she made us all go out into the courtyard, and she told me to scoop it all up with a spoon and eat it. Right there, in front of everyone else. Down to the last spoonful. That was the only time in my life I've ever wanted to die. And I decided that I was never going to feel that way again...'

'If you want, I'd be glad to kill that nun for you.'

Freddo smiled.

'Cancer beat you to it.'

'It was probably your prayers. Those things really work, Freddo.'

'You think so?'

'It's part of life, isn't it? So I believe in it!'

The best of friends, in other words. And in fact when Nero asked him for a couple of rods for a personal matter he had to take care of, Freddo didn't say a word: he just handed over a duffel bag containing two revolvers, a semi-automatic handgun, and a Czechoslovakian sub-machine gun that they'd taken off a hothead from the Autonomia Operaia, the left-wing radical group.

IV

FINALLY, THE GAMBLING den opened for business. Within a few days, the team of construction workers hired by Ziccone were finishing up the renovation of Freddo's villa at Casalpalocco. Everyone attended the inauguration of the Full 80. Libano, Scrocchiazeppi, Dandi, Nembo Kid, the Buffoni boys, Botola and even Ricotta in jacket and tie – so outlandish and wrecked that he was given specific orders to stay out of sight. Ricotta, who deep down was basically a good kid, took it the right way and went over and joined Bufalo. They were both on outside guard duty, in case there were any unpleasant surprises, joints in their mouths and hands on their guns, the thought of all the gleaming pussy glittering just a stone's throw away, with a sincere request to leave just a little bit for them, too, poor things.

Fierolocchio, perennially on the prowl, offered to lend a hand or, if needed, both hands to the girls hired by the trio – Patrizia, Daniela and Donatella – as they trotted back and forth between the front entrance room and the upstairs rooms. Freddo was off in a corner conversing with Nero. Sorcio was just getting more and more fucked up, and it was Vanessa's responsibility to keep him under control. Trentadenari, who found Vanessa extremely alluring in a diaphanous one-piece outfit and no bra, was manoeuvring with his usual discretion. He was in no hurry. Destiny, after all, had already determined that sooner or later, with a candy striper like her, things were going to go the way they inevitably would. Cravattaro was there with his wife, who was dripping gold. The Maestro popped his head in, said hello all around, conveyed Uncle Carlo's best wishes.

'I hope he didn't smile when he sent them,' Dandi ventured.

'He was completely deadpan,' the Maestro reassured him.

Puma showed up with his girl Dolores, so fat now that she had become virtually unrecognizable, and so did Mazzocchio, oily as ever.

In other words, it was a celebration. Aside from them, the attendees were mostly guests of honour. High-class people. In a certain sense, anyway. Califano and Fred Bongusto hadn't shown up. When Bufalo suggested the name of Lando Fiorini, there had been a universal turning up of noses. They'd been obliged to fall back on a virtual unknown, Mimino Vitiello, who put on airs as if he were the second coming of Fred Buscaglione and who, with his cockeyed English, mangled covers of songs by Frank Sinatra. They put up with him for fifteen minutes, and then they decided to do without music entirely. Vitiello was sent packing with a rubber cheque: he'd know better than to come back demanding cash once it bounced.

Still, what with actors, football players and wealthy businessmen with their wives in tow, the general level of the evening's entertainment remained quite high. There was also a face they'd never seen before, a highly scented fat man with piggy eyes accompanied by two bodyguards. He was tastefully dressed, and he gorged himself with equal gusto. Not only that, there were even two authentic cops, introduced by Fabio Santini, slapping backs heartily with Trentadenari. One was from the local police station, the other was from Via Genova. With guests like that, there really was nothing to worry about.

Libano told Freddo that the fat guy was known as Secco. Ironic, since 'secco' implied lean and slim.

'I'll introduce you later. We need to talk.'

But Freddo was focused on two friends of Nembo Kid. Strange faces. They reminded him of someone. They were chatting with Nembo, Botola and Dandi.

'Have you ever seen those two?' he asked Nero.

'Complete strangers.'

As he gave his answer, Nero had looked away.

Freddo walked over to the little group clustering around Nembo Kid. Dandi introduced the strangers: they'd given him a hand with the building permits and the alcohol licences for the club, he said. Freddo ignored the hand that the taller of the two extended in his direction. He'd recognized him. The first and only time they'd met was at Cutolo's place.

'Did you like the roast lamb?'

The man smiled and spread both arms wide, as if to say: what are you looking for? Nembo Kid and Dandi exchanged a worried glance. Freddo waved so long with two fingers and strolled off to talk with Bufalo and Ricotta.

Nero was smoking a cigarette, nervous and on edge. He didn't like lying to a friend. But he had no alternative. Seeing the agents Pigreco and Zeta in cheerful conversation with Nembo Kid, Dandi and Botola hadn't surprised him all that much. Those people were always looking for something. They'd first approached him one morning three months ago.

'There are things that the state can neither do nor admit that it's ordered someone to do. And that's why we need smart young men like you,' Pigreco had told him.

Nero, pretending he'd understood, had asked him how much. Pigreco had pulled a number out of his hat. Nero had turned to leave. Zeta called him back, offering double the fee.

'Half up front, the rest when the job is complete.'

Nero had accepted the offer and taken the cash. Before they went their separate ways, Zeta told him that 'they were on the same side'.

The two spies thought they'd recruited him. But that was far from the case. The idea that they attributed to him was not the true Idea. For him, it was nothing but an experiment. One of many. Which is why he'd lied to Freddo. He liked to keep the different spheres of his existence separate. Maybe some day he'd tell him everything, or maybe he never would. In partial justification of his behaviour, it should be noted that the contract had been stipulated before he and Freddo ever met. It was an open retainer: he needed to stand by, ready for action.

Libano finally tracked Freddo down, contemplating the moon, high as a kite, and took him upstairs to the top floor, where they'd set up the gambling room. You entered through a little door marked 'Private'. One of the Buffoni brothers was standing guard. Inside, there were four poker tables, a baccarat table and a collapsible roulette wheel, as well as a small, very well furnished bar and, standing in as the maître d', the actor Bontempi. Just a few years earlier, he'd been one of the best known stars of Italian film. Then cocaine, gambling and whiskey had wrung him dry. Now he could be hired for a flat fee to preside over high-stake card games. He was a ghost of his former self: only a hint of the old charm on his drawn, weary face. Secco, sitting at one of the poker tables, observed the scene. Libano introduced him to Freddo and explained his project.

'Here's the thing. Secco is an artist when it comes to moving money. He's already helped out with Patrizia's…club. My idea is to let him handle the general fund. Or, I should say, a portion of the general fund. He guarantees us a return of forty or forty-five per cent on the capital we invest with him in the first six months.'

Freddo looked at his unctuous would-be business partner.

'What does he know how to do that we don't already know how to do? Loan sharking? Debt collection? Real estate? What do we need another partner for?'

It was obvious that something was eating at Freddo that night, Libano decided, because even before he knew what the subject was, he was on the attack. Secco kept his composure and responded with a broad smile.

'You already have so much to do, lots of different business activities…Me, all I think about is one thing – how to move money. It's my specialty. I'm talking about banks, high finance, stock market, real estate speculation…I'm talking about capital. I take ten per cent and I give you earnings of forty-five, even fifty per cent. It's all I think about…'

There was something about the man that Freddo didn't like. He didn't like the cops downstairs either, for that matter. There was nothing he liked about the whole situation. It was all too confusing. Freddo needed some time to think things through.

'It's just like the human body, Freddo,' Secco continued. 'You have legs to walk with, a head to think with, a heart to make decisions...'

'Heart and head!' Freddo laughed bitterly, and then added, looking straight at Libano: 'We have all we need, Libano. What do we need him for?'

Libano started to get worked up. 'But we can't do it all by ourselves! Around here the turnover is multiplying day by day. And we can't spend all our time doing our own accounting. Soon we're going to have to get back out on the street...'

'How can you be sure of that?'

'I can sense it! Have I ever been wrong? I can sense it! Plus, let's be clear about this: you and I, and maybe Dandi and Nembo Kid – we're people who use our brains. But the others? How long do you think we can keep them on the leash? Any minute now Bufalo, or Scrocchiazeppi, or Trentadenari might fuck up somehow, and it'll be up to us to set matters right. It'll take money, men, ideas... We can't do it all on our own, Freddo! Damn it, take it from me!'

Libano wasn't wrong. Libano had never been wrong. Freddo said that he'd approve the plan only if every one of them were allowed to go on investing their share of the profits just as they each saw fit.

'Whoever thought anything different?' Libano smiled. 'Let's say we have two or three billion lire to divvy up: one, just one miserable billion, we set aside for Secco, and he starts it spinning. Before you know it, you have a billion five...'

'Even a billion seven, if you're lucky,' Secco pointed out.

'A billion seven,' Libano went on. 'And then we take that billion and we hand the seven hundred million back to Secco, and he makes that turn into...'

'Another billion, if you calculate the rate on the first investment...'

'Fine, you've talked me into it,' Freddo cut them off brusquely. He was starting to lose his patience. Then he locked arms with Libano and moved off a little way.

'Downstairs, I saw a couple of shitheads...'

'I know, I know who you mean. But there's nothing to worry about. They're friends of Nembo Kid. They can help us out. Protection, you understand? For us, and for Patrizia too... I'll tell you about it later. How long do you think they'll leave us alone – Borgia, the cops, and the whole Greek chorus? We're famous now, my friend. And we need protection: it's our daily bread!'

Freddo was about to reply when a frantic burst of voices rose from downstairs. Secco leapt to his feet, muttering something about his body-guards. Libano and Freddo rushed down the steps.

Sardo was out on leave again. That insane asylum was leakier than a sieve. Now he was screaming bloody vendetta because not only had they organized that whole casino without breathing a word to him about it, but they hadn't even invited him to the opening night.

Trentadenari, who had managed to corner Vanessa while Sorcio was shooting up in the bathroom, dropped a brilliant wisecrack into the silence electric with tension:

'O Zappatore is here!'

And Sardo had no choice but to swallow his dissatisfaction. In the face of laughter, pistols are no defence.

V

AT THE SIGHT of that bloody mask of a face that kept begging him for more – stab me again, more, I want more, my love – the Arab boy took fright. He'd thrown his clothes back on in great haste, he'd grabbed Ranocchia's wallet on the way out, and he left without looking back. The night porter got suspicious when he saw the Arab rush past, eyes rolling wildly, so he went upstairs to look in on his old friend Ranocchia, a faggot, but a kind and invariably generous one. He used his passkey to open the door to Room 216. Seeing what was inside, he immediately threw up, and then called for an ambulance. Still, Ranocchia was the kind who never died, not even if you killed him. No matter how much blood he'd lost, he still had enough left in his veins to go on playing extreme games of this kind for another ten years.

It took double the anaesthesia to knock him out. Before losing consciousness he'd managed to pour out a torrent of abuse cursing his rescuers, because the last thing he wanted was to be saved. He wanted to die, and die happy. And just because he was different, a pervert, that was no reason to deny him the comfort of his long-sought death. Now, in a miniaturized little room at the polyclinic hospital, bandaged like some obscene mummy, arms immobilized by the IV, still dazed by the drip of sedatives, but kept awake by the incandescent pain of his wounds, he did his best to persuade that tall, dark and handsome policeman that the whole mess had been nothing more than an unsuccessful attempted suicide.

'What about the Arab?'

'There never was any Arab.'

'The night porter saw you both.'

'The night porter must be mistaken.'

'You went upstairs together.'

'Nothing but a coincidence.'

'I'll be forced to have you charged as an accessory after the fact.'

'Do as you see fit.'

Scialoja considered him with a compassionate smile. He was one of the most unsightly creatures he'd ever laid eyes on. He had a criminal record as long as your arm, all for sexual offences. His colleagues from the vice squad told him that he was a well-known bordello impresario. A hardened criminal and ex-convict. His birth family – his father was a university professor, his mother was an architect – had disinherited him and refused to see him. All Scialoja could see was an aging and desperate homosexual. The cuts and wounds had little or nothing to do with it.

'Do you want a glass of water?'

'Don't you see I'm on an IV? I'm not allowed to drink.'

The policeman heaved a sigh. Ranocchia regretted having been so discourteous to him. The poor guy was only doing his job. After all, he'd done his best to be kind. After all, he was fine, big hunk of a man.

'Excuse me,' he murmured. 'All these damned cuts...'

'Forget about it. Why don't you tell me a little bit about you, instead? So you wanted to die. Could I ask why?'

'Well, why do you want to live?'

Scialoja folded up his notebook. 'I'll come back tomorrow. I hope you'll be a little more co-operative then.'

'Don't go!' Ranocchia wheezed. 'Don't go...'

That big, warm body, just footsteps away from his own deteriorating

145

hulk, was instilling in him a dangerous desire to live. Scialoja stood there, waiting, by the door.

'You won't believe it, but it all started out with a woman…'

'Are you in love with her?'

'Strange, isn't it? But that's exactly the way it is. Patrizia is a woman unlike any other…If I told you about her, you'd probably think she was nothing but a whore.'

Scialoja didn't bat an eye. Deep within, however, he savoured his victory. At last, that dreary hospital visit was beginning to pay off. Because Ranocchia meant Patrizia: that was the only reason for his interest in this otherwise undistinguished assault. It had been the night porter who put him on the trail, his tongue miraculously loosened by the paired concepts of murder and accessory that the boys from the mobile squad had shouted into his face. Ranocchia? He lives in Piazza dei Mercanti. The boys from the mobile squad had hurried to Piazza dei Mercanti, and there they'd found: 'Signora Vallesi, Cinzia, an acquaintance of the victim, with absolutely no connection to the criminal acts in question.'

The report wound up in the file of John Doe open cases that lay on Borgia's desk. By now the judge had become the short-order cook left to deal with the scraps and leftovers that the connoisseurs of the prosecuting attorney's office turned up their noses at, scorning it like overripe cheese. Borgia had read the report, had a good, long laugh, and forwarded the documents to Scialoja.

In the meantime, Ranocchia spoke of this impossible dream lover he'd never possess, and his language became increasingly high-flown, verging on the poetic. Scialoja sat there listening, fascinated, tense. Ranocchia asked him to plump up his pillows. It was just an excuse to feel that warm body near him. The policeman leaned over him. He smelled of tobacco and resignation. But his senses were alert, wide awake. Ranocchia suspected that he was starting to show a little too much interest in Patrizia. Ranocchia was proud of his natural talent as a chaperone. A mellifluous smile blossomed onto his lacerated face. Scialoja caught the signal. He took refuge in his policeman's aplomb.

'You still haven't told me why you want to die. Why can't you have her?'

'But I don't want to have her! It's impossible to have Patrizia; no one can have Patrizia, not even the ones who think they hold her solid in their grip...'

'Not even you...'

'Let's just say that she's decided to deny me the further enjoyment of her company.'

'She got tired of seeing you?'

'I introduced her to the wrong people. But I had no choice...'

'Why not?'

'On this matter, if you don't mind, I choose to avail myself of my right not to answer the question.'

Scialoja understood that the magic moment was quickly vanishing.

'Thanks very much. You've been very helpful. I'm going to leave now and let you get some rest...'

Ranocchia burst out laughing. A sudden stab of pain choked his breath. He coughed. He waved for Scialoja to draw nearer.

'If there's one thing I hate, it's being left in peace! But you, on the other hand...'

'Me?'

'You,' he murmured. 'You don't give a damn about me. You don't even give a damn about the investigation. What you're interested in is Patrizia. You want to get to know her. Or maybe you already do know her, eh?'

Scialoja recoiled. Ranocchia grabbed his hand.

'Come back and see me. I'll tell you all about her. I'll tell you her weaknesses. But don't kid yourself – you'll wind up like all the others...'

Scialoja slipped out the door, the faggot's venomous laughter following him as he left, and headed straight over to Piazza dei Mercanti. He took in the building and the high-performance luxury vehicles parked outside the main door. He saw the rough-hewn faces of the two bouncer-type individuals guarding the entrance. He took a quick ride over to the city assessor's office and discovered that the building was in the name of Vallesi, Cinzia, stage name Patrizia. It had been purchased in cash for a sum that was surely bogus. The previous owner, a certain Luciani, was listed as residing in Via Aurelio Saffi. But in Via Aurelio Saffi there were no buildings at all. Only an old trailer parked at the foot of crumbling sheer city walls. Luciani was an immensely fat old man covered with tattoos. He stank of cheap wine and threatened to sic a mangy mutt, clearly the result of countless crossbreeding, on Scialoja. The dog smelled of the sewer and looked unlikely to move even if Luciani had beaten it with a stick. Clearly a front. Scialoja returned with a demijohn of sweet sparkling Olevano wine and persuaded the old man to give him the real name behind the property.

'It was Secco. It was that rotten bastard Secco who made the deal. Motherfucker, the river of money that flowed through my fingers! But never a penny that stuck, eh! Because of all the money I owed Secco…He took away my car and my house too, and now here I sit!'

In the mobile squad's archives there was a very thick file on Secco. Secco owned real estate. Secco moved money. But all of it was hearsay: no one had ever managed to pin Secco down and catch him red-handed. Secco was a cunning operator. Secco basically pickpocketed the building from Luciani and when the dust settled, Patrizia found herself with the deed in hand, free and clear, unencumbered. Secco never did a thing out of the goodness of his heart. So were Secco and Patrizia an item? Was she his girlfriend? What about Dandi? What had become of Dandi?

Scialoja resumed his stakeout. He spotted Patrizia on the third day. She left the building in the morning, accompanied by a girlfriend. They were out for a couple of hours, returning home loaded down with packages and shopping bags. From his vantage point, Scialoja was able to distinguish the names of major fashion labels on the bags. Before entering the building, Patrizia took off her sunglasses and appeared to shoot a glance in his direction. Scialoja instinctively tried to take cover and blend into the background. What an idiot he was! She couldn't have spotted him! Still, that glance had gone straight to his heart.

At certain hours of the day, girls went in; at other times, girls came out. Few men, and all of them clearly well-to-do and distinguished: a television host, a famous journalist, a football star. A couple of determined-looking men in their thirties, politicians or perhaps members of the military, showed up together and were ushered in.

On the fourth day, Dandi appeared. He parked a monstrously large motorcycle, took a bag marked Valentino from the luggage compartment, and walked through the front door, greeted respectfully by the guards. That same afternoon, a few more familiar faces showed up:

Bufalo, a lanky beanpole of a young man with a fidgety demeanour, and Fierolocchio, joined at the hip with a tall attractive job with a bored expression on her face. Scialoja put together an informal report for Borgia: Secco bought Patrizia a bordello all of her own. Among the regulars, 'our boys' have been observed. Secco never does anything out of the goodness of his heart. Secco is working hand-in-hand with the boys. The bordello is an investment.

'Do you remember when you asked me what had become of all of that money from the kidnapping? Well, here's the answer: they're buying and they're investing. They're sinking roots into the cityscape, exactly like the Mafia has always done...'

Borgia found the investigative avenue commendable, but he asked a question that begged the issue of common sense.

'And you say they spent all this money just to give a gift to that woman?'

'Vallesi, Cinzia. Patrizia.'

'Because in the end, she's the owner!'

'She's Dandi's woman.'

Borgia ordered a tax audit. Scialoja cajoled a team of men out of him and headed back to Piazza dei Mercanti. Two officers asked the bouncers at the door for their documents and took them in to police headquarters for questioning. Four more officers stood guard outside to discourage any potential new clients. Scialoja walked in unhindered. He'd need a little time. Patrizia, in a skirt suit, hair fresh from a first-class beauty salon, looked like a corporate executive.

'Ciao, turtle dove. You've certainly come a long way. You've almost reached the summit!'

'Ciao, cop. I don't kid myself for a second. Nothing's easier than to fall.'

If she was surprised by the unexpected visit, she gave no sign of it. There was no sign of fear in her, either. Scialoja thought about how he'd enjoy drinking an ice cold Negroni together. On the beach, or in Piazza Navona perhaps. Patrizia asked him whether he'd like to take a look around or get right down to business.

Scialoja lit a cigarette. 'Aren't you in a hurry!'

'There are people who might not be too pleased to find you here.'

'People like Dandi?'

149

She shrugged her shoulders. He told her that there was no danger of anyone disturbing them. An ironic gleam appeared in her eyes.

'Is this an...official visit?'

'It's not customary to offer a drink here in your place?'

'Only room service, *caro*. Shall I get you a girl?'

He shook his head no. And he gazed at her intensely. A faint smile played over her lips and she replied with another negative shake of the head. Scialoja sighed. Patrizia took a seat, crossing her long legs.

A kitten with sharp claws, who knew how to use them...A kitten who left a mark wherever she'd been...

He angrily stubbed out his cigarette. She never lost control. The situation was becoming paradoxical. Every time he found himself in that woman's presence, the paradox washed over him. He thought back to Ranocchia and his venomous warning. Cinzia had grown up. Even her scent had changed. A slight new edge of bitterness, decisiveness. She was more confident. Every minute spent with her was a challenge. Scialoja yearned to bend that indifferent will to his own intent. He wanted to grope around under her clothing. To dig down, all the way. Down to her soul. If there was one.

'Shall we make a bet, Cinzia?'

'Only if I win in the end.'

'Shall we bet that I can close this place down in...let's say...a week?'

She burst out laughing. That low, ambiguous laughter of hers, deep from the throat.

'Do it and I'll marry you!

Scialoja drew up a detailed report for Borgia. The important thing was to hit them where they lived, take away what mattered most to them: money and property. They should start with the bordello. Raid the place, take down the names of everyone present, confiscate everything in sight, indict Patrizia for running a whorehouse. There was an overabundance of proof. They needed to aim even higher. Hurt them badly. As badly as they could.

Borgia gave in to his scruples. 'This comes under the vice squad's jurisdiction.'

'They're filthy and corrupt. Let's beat them to the draw.'

'There's no direct link with Dandi and the others. They're going to accuse me of violating jurisdiction.'

'And you just let them talk. Let's move now, before it's too late.'

But it was the judge's decision. The report was forwarded to the vice squad. Scialoja didn't like one little bit the lopsided smile on the face of the whoremonger-in-chief when, three days after the forwarding of the documentation, he informed Scialoja that investigations were still underway.

Keeping Up With the Times
July–December 1979

I

ANGIOLETTO WAS STRICTLY small fry, and the night of 15 August, two nameless killers rubbed him out. It was a clean, professional job: seven shots from a semi-automatic pistol, possibly a Smith & Wesson .357 magnum and, just to make sure, a death shot in the back of the head, right behind the mass of golden curls that had given Angioletto his celestial nickname. While he was alive, there'd been little if anything about Angioletto that could have been described as angelic. All the same, a very respectable rap sheet of armed robbery and a few import–export round trips to the cocaine regions of South America hardly seemed like sufficient motivation for such a brutal end. Unless it all had to do with his family ties to Puma, because Angioletto had been – and actually would have gone on being for many years, if he hadn't consumed that unfortunate and difficult-to-digest high-lead-content meal – Puma's sister's man.

And so, as Giuliana wept and wailed over the still-warm corpse, surrounded by officers from the forensics division and the ADA on duty, standing around trying to look busy on the riverside gravel of Ponte Bianco, where the murder had taken place, Puma was already at Franco's bar, pouring out his anger and disappointment.

'I told you how this was going to end, Freddo. And I told you the same thing, Libano. Come on… You're starting to flip out, you two! Now, over a miserable half pound of dope, someone had to go and kill this fine young man. What would it have cost you to come talk to me? We'd have sat down around a table and worked it out! I told him too, poor Angioletto: forget about it, these are people who don't fuck around… But now you guys do whatever you think's right. I'm old school, I won't say a word, but as far as I'm concerned, you're all pieces of shit from now on!'

'Puma,' Freddo said in a serious tone of voice, 'I respect you because of your white hair. Even though when the time was right, you pulled back. But that's water under the bridge. If there was a problem of any kind, we'd have come to see you, we'd have talked it over. We didn't have anything to do with Angioletto!'

Not only had they had nothing to do with it, but they'd never even heard of the man. And having paid their condolences to Puma, they tried to rack their brains to make sense of what had happened. Once Puma had calmed down, he told them that Angioletto, who urgently needed to get his hands on a shipment of dope that had slipped through the fingers of certain people from outside of Rome – there was no time to waste, he wanted to act before someone else beat him to it – had taken out a sixty-million-lire loan. He figured he could pay it back once he'd peddled it on the street, but the lenders were pushing for repayment. There had already been raised voices and harsh words. In short, they'd decided to punish him. Puma had the dope, in a safe place. He'd put two and two together, and that's why he was accusing them.

'In Rome, at this point, all dope runs under your control. I never believed this story about outsiders who let nine ounces of narcotics slip through their fingers. You know what Angioletto was like: he knew how to keep his secrets. But I had told him: I'll go put in a word, we'll come to an agreement. He wouldn't listen. Now you might tell me that you had nothing to do with this, and I might even believe you. But tell me this: who was it?'

Good question. That was something that worried Libano. The appearance of a shipment of dope over which they had no control was a disquieting development. Either one thing or another: a rival organization, or some Judas from within the gang who was trying to do a little freelancing on the side, just like in the old days. Leave aside the fact that the murder threatened to bring Judge Borgia sniffing at their heels. Lately, the only ones who'd been doing any shooting in the streets, aside from the terrorists, was them. Everything pointed to one of two conclusions: either one of them had taken out Angioletto, or else there was someone out there imitating them.

Freddo asked to see the dope. Puma took them to see a parking garage owner on the Via Ostiense. The coke was kept in a safe built into a furred-out wall partition, and covered by the fire extinguisher that the garage was required by law to install. The garage owner was Smorto, a half-pint loser who'd spent half his life behind bars and the other half out on the street, a sometime informant and an equally occasional business partner. Freddo admired the contrivance, but he couldn't help wondering whether Puma had told him everything there was to know. Libano thought the same thing. Ever since he'd refused to become a fully fledged gang member, Puma hadn't been levelling with them. But one thing was certain: that coke didn't come from them. It was a nasty, super-stepped-on excuse for coke that instantly irritated the nostril and inflamed the throat. The kind of thing you'd expect to get from sharp-dressing amateurs freelancing out of some Chilean barrio. Angioletto had lost his mind if he'd really thought that he was going to step up to the big time with such a pathetic deal. Clearly someone had conned him good and proper.

'We'll let you know, Puma. But I'll tell you again: we had nothing to do with this.'

As soon as they made it back to Franco's bar, Libano and Freddo got right down to work. They called the zone captains and ordered a general audit of dope in and dope out. They notified their comrades and, the following evening, at Trentadenari's place, they reviewed the situation. One after another, Dandi, Trentadenari, Botola, the Buffonis, Fierolocchio, Scrocchiazeppi and the rest all sang the same lyrics: for every gram of dope put out on the street, there was a clear and accurate accounting of a corresponding cash return. All the ants and all the horses were on schedule with their payments. No suspicious comings and goings had been reported in any of the districts. Libano personally ticked through the accounts. Everything checked out. So, leaving aside the unlikely eventuality that one of their most trusted comrades had sold them out, no one in the gang had anything to do with Angioletto's murder. Then who had done it?

Scrocchiazeppi ventured a theory of his own. 'The cops killed him. The cocaine comes from a legal confiscation and he went into business with some traitor in uniform.'

Libano assigned Trentadenari to unleash Fabio Santini on the case. If there was a corrupt cop behind that killing, who'd be more likely to find out than him?'

Fierolocchio said that, according to a streetwalker girlfriend of his, someone – though no one could say who – had seen the Bordini brothers hanging around in the area in the days before the killing.

Dandi laughed loudly and with gusto. He'd known the Bordini brothers since nursery school. They were both cracked in the head, sure, but small fry; purse-snatchers, basically. It was impossible to think of them pulling off such a well-planned murder, and such a successful one. Freddo objected that it was still worth investigating in that direction. Botola volunteered.

Ricotta suggested reporting what had happened to Sardo, who after all was still his boss. A silence filled with unstated meaning ensued. Sardo, especially after his latest outburst at the Full 80, was definitely on the down slope. He'd even started to pepper them with threatening letters from the insane asylum. Now he wanted this, and next he wanted that, and nothing was ever good enough for him, and to cut a long story short, sooner or later they were going to have to deal with that problem too. Still, Ricotta, who had a heart of gold – what good would it do to drag him into all that bickering? Not yet, anyway. When the time was ripe, he could choose which side he was on.

'All right, write him a letter and see if he knows anything about it,' Libano conceded ambiguously.

They all burst out laughing. Ricotta's lack of facility with the alphabet was legendary.

It was at that point that Nembo Kid looked around and asked why Bufalo hadn't come.

II

That afternoon, Bufalo had met with Trentadenari and had told him that everything was running smoothly in his zone as well. He added that he was sorry to hear what had happened to Angioletto, but after all, he'd asked for it. He seemed normal, maybe a little revved up, the same old

156

Bufalo as always, in other words. The freak-out wouldn't hit him until a couple of hours later. Still, he'd been wandering around the neighbourhoods for a while now, in the grip of a sense of panic that he wouldn't have known how to describe in words. Maybe he should blame it on the summer, the humidity beading the walls, the foul-smelling blend of muggy air and exhaust fumes. Or maybe it was because of that thing that had gone wrong at the bordello: he'd picked one of the girls Patrizia had made available, but she wouldn't hear of it when he decided to stub out his cigarette on her breast. Actually, Bufalo didn't give a damn about scorching the girl. He was just looking for some way to get worked up, and a picture from a porno mag happened to pop into his head: stuff from years ago, when he made do with jerking off, like all the other kids his age. Thinking back, the whole thing could have been settled peaceably, even then, if only the girl hadn't started screaming that he was a dangerous lunatic, a sadist, and so on and so forth. He would have been happy with a quickie, and the whole thing would have blown over like a soap bubble. But the girl just wouldn't stop screaming. Bufalo, to get her to shut up, closed her mouth for her himself with a short, sharp slap. Not hard, practically a love tap; nothing to complain about. But things went downhill fast after that. Patrizia came charging down into the cellar, she'd grabbed him by the scruff of the neck – she had some muscles, the little sex kitten! – and the next thing Bufalo knew he was out in the street. He couldn't take it out on the women, and he'd been forced to repress his urge to burn the place down. Patrizia was untouchable, and Dandi would never forgive him. Everybody needed to keep cool, that's what Libano would have said. Keep cool! Easy to say!

Not even he could say how the hell he wound up in that toilet of a latteria, or milk bar, over behind the old MiraLanza plant. But when Varighina the albino (his name was dialect for 'bleach'), piece of shit pimp that he was, a complete zero, an absolute nothing, threw some old issue involving debt collection in his face, that's when all the tension and anxiety he was keeping tamped down inside suddenly exploded. He grabbed a handy bottle and broke it over his head. Varighina, his face a mask of blood, took two steps back. Bufalo, head down, butted him right in the belly. Varighina went down. Bufalo was on top of him, both hands around his throat. He'd have throttled him right then and there, in front of at least fifteen witnesses if they hadn't managed to pull him off.

'You're going to pay for this, you son of a bitch!'

Bufalo was already over it, his head of steam subsiding as quick as it had surged. That's just the way he was put together. His vision was clearing; the fog of fury that had filled him was gone. He wasn't even shaking anymore.

'Ah, let's just forget it ever happened,' he said, shaking his big woolly head. But Varighina, doing his best to wipe the blood off his face, seemed determined to hold a grudge.

'What are you, dreaming? I'm not scared of you. I'm not scared of anyone, you piece of shit. I'm gonna fix you good!'

'C'mon, just drop it, trust me...'

'Ah, you wish! You've ruined my face. Just look at it! Don't kid yourself, Bufalo. You think that just because you have two or three friends, the rest of Rome shits its pants when you go by? I'll tell you what: you and Freddo and that other individual, Libano, I'll piss in your mouths, all three of you. Get it?'

'You'd better lay off Libano if you know what's good for you...'

'I'll take a shit on your heads, arseholes!'

What should he do now? Drunk as he was, Bufalo was eager to get home to the peace of his bed. The fifteen people in the latteria, by now, were starting to give him some uncomfortable looks. If he gave them time to get organized, there could be a beat-down in store for him. Still, however, the animal had insulted his friends and would have to pay. But there was no hurry, as Libano always liked to say.

'This doesn't end here,' said Bufalo, and headed for the door. No one dared to stop him. Varighina continued to hurl insults at his retreating back.

Libano got word of Bufalo's night of bravado. Bufalo took the tongue-lashing with his tail between his legs. With all the complicated things going on, he thought this was a good time to start annoying girls? And at Patrizia's, of all places? If it hadn't been Bufalo, a long-time comrade, Dandi would have torn him limb from limb with his own hands. What was he thinking when he decided to insult that poor girl? Was that any way for a man to behave? Cigarettes!

158

'You know the way it is, Libano – sometimes it just comes over me and I don't even know...'

And then that other fuck-up in the latteria! Now they were going to have to go teach a two-bit pimp a lesson. Get their hands dirty with a piece of snot like him when they had all of Rome spread out at their feet!

'I'll go take care of Varighina, Libano!'

'Oh no, my friend. We're all going out on this one!'

So they all went out. Or nearly all of them. A nice big crowd, anyway. Except for Dandi, who was probably best kept out of it, on account of the thing at Patrizia's, the ones who went were Libano, Freddo, Scrocchiazeppi, who had brought the balaclavas, the Buffoni brothers, Fierolocchio and, obviously, Bufalo. Everybody had roundly cursed him, and he rode along in silence, looking sheepish and guilty. It was the middle of the night, but all the windows were open in Varighina's shack. It was brutally hot, their shirts were clinging to their chests and wearing jeans was sheer torture. The beachfront shack was immersed in silence.

An hour earlier, Fierolocchio and Freddo had gotten into an ugly wrangle over the question of the guns. Fierolocchio had dug his heels in about the Czech-made sub-machine gun, the one they'd taken off the left-wing radical, the *autonomo*. Freddo explained that he'd loaned it to Nero.

'Who told you to do that? Go get it back, right now.'

Since the weapons were gang property, and the decision to lend out the sub-machine gun had been made on his own personal initiative, Freddo gave Nero a call. Nero told him that right then and there he wouldn't be able to give the gun back.

'I'll tell you why tomorrow.'

So Fierolocchio was forced to settle for a six-shot snub-nose Colt revolver. Freddo selected a Bernardelli long rifle. The others carried an assortment of carabines and revolvers.

Still, the quarrel wasn't forgotten, and they were all on edge when they kicked in the door of the shack. Bufalo elbowed his way to the front and went in firing, recklessly, without even bothering to aim. The whole place was pitch black. The flashes of gunfire illuminated flaring streaks of human bodies desperately diving for cover under the sheets and behind the furniture. They guessed, more than saw, that they were shooting at two women and two men, and Libano shouted out to aim at their legs. The acrid stench of gunpowder mixed with the stale odour of sweat, filling the summer night. The people in the shack were screaming and begging. Freddo knew that if they'd wanted to kill them, it would have taken no more than three or four well-aimed shots. All that wasted fire-power was so much choreography imposed by Libano. This expedition to root out a few pathetic losers turned his stomach. Still, it was something that had to be done, thanks to that goddamn Bufalo.

'Let's go! Out of here!' Libano barked.

They pulled back, leaving behind them a wake of blood, lights flicking on in the neighbouring shacks, and the moans of the wounded. Unless someone fucked up, there wouldn't be any deaths. Libano had been categorical.

'Every insult has a price. Never overdo it. The minute you step over a certain line, you shorten your life expectancy.'

III

NERO AND FREDDO were strolling side by side along the Tiber, on the Lungotevere della Vittoria.

'I can't give you the guns back.'

'That's a problem.'

'I'm sure it is. Nothing I can do about it. I don't have them anymore.'

'You gave them to someone?'

'Yes.'

'To who?'

'Sellerone.'

Freddo lit a cigarette. Nero probably had his own good reasons for what he'd done. But this new development sounded like a betrayal of trust.

'Sellerone is an idiot, Nero.'

'His Idea doesn't match up with mine, though I have to say it's not all bad...'

'I need those guns back.'

'You'll get them back. It's just a matter of time.'

'I can cover you for a while, but the others are pissed off.'

'Not feeling trustful?'

'I don't trust Sellerone.'

'But you trust me?'

'Yes, blindly.'

Nero nodded. Things were proceeding nicely. This problem too would work itself out. Still, a mistake had been made. Somehow, Freddo and the others would need to be compensated. Nero decided to tell him about the robbery at the savings and loan, the Cassa di Credito.

'That was you?'

'Me and a couple of other guys.'

'Political shit?'

'In part.'

'Nice job,' Freddo complimented him.

'Organization, preparation, meticulous planning…But the notes were marked.'

'You'll need to get them cleaned.'

'I was thinking about contacting some people I know in Milan.'

'Why go so far away? We can talk to Secco…'

'Yes, we can do that.'

'You're going to have to tell the others about it.'

'Everyone has a part to play. I'm strictly responsible for my own.'

'What about the Idea?'

'Everyone has their own Idea, Freddo.'

This was the way things should be between men, thought Freddo as he passed him the cigarette. Not much talking and a deep understanding. Nero took a half-hearted drag and stopped to observe two very blonde girls hurrying towards the Ostello del Flaminio. Half-nude tourists. Big tits and long wading-bird legs.

'You like women, Nero?'

'Do you?'

'Same as anyone.'

'You go to Patrizia much?'

'Never. I said women, not whores.'

'Whores, women…What's the difference? The act itself never varies!'

'Is that really what you think?'

'Not always. But women can be a problem. You can't let them get the upper hand.'

'You just need to find the right one.'

'You think she exists?'

'I haven't found her yet, if she does.'

'I'm not even going to bother looking. Women come and go, Freddo. Like everything in life.'

'Except friendship.'

'Yeah. Except friendship.'

Trentadenari thought that friendship was a fine thing, too. Best of all, it was crucial to have the right friends in the right place, and at the right time. That Fabio Santini, for instance – at first he'd dismissed him as a two-bit punk, but now he was proving to be an invaluable addition! After a rapid investigation, Santini had assured him that no men in uniform had had anything to do with what had happened to Angioletto.

But then, one night when they were at the Climax Seven, the cop dropped his bomb.

'Fifty kilos of super-pure Peshawar white. Confiscated from an Indian courier in transit through Fiumicino. It wasn't even meant for the Italian market. The loser was travelling to London but the dogs caught the scent on him. Now the shit's in the evidence room. I have a friend who works there, a civil servant. Getting in would be child's play. We'll keep our friend happy with chump change. For myself, I want two kilos of coke and a little money to take care of my debts.'

Trentadenari informed Libano and the rest. It looked like an appetizing job, a pushover to all intents and purposes, if what the cop had told them was true. Trentadenari and Botola took it upon themselves to check into the feasibility of the thing. Bufalo, eager to redeem himself as quickly as possible, wanted to take part in the job. But that proved to be impossible when the mobile squad swung by his house to pick him up at the end of August.

In the arrest warrant, there was even mention of possible charges of attempted mass murder. And to think that Varighina, his brother-in-law and their respective harlots had gotten away with a few scratches on their legs!

162

Trentadenari, through the usual Santini, managed to get his hands onto a deposition that was still under pre-trial secrecy and deliver it to their lawyer Vasta. It appeared from the document that Varighina had named Bufalo as one of his likely attackers. It was Borgia's investigation.

Carlo Buffoni suggested killing Varighina once and for all. Freddo countered by suggesting they make a sizable offer for a heartfelt retraction of testimony. If they killed him immediately, in reaction, even a judge less perceptive than Borgia would put two and two together. Libano seconded Freddo's proposal. Freddo went to pay a call on Varighina in the hospital. Varighina took the offer and promised that, the minute he was released, he'd go see the investigating magistrate to retract his statement.

In early September, seeing that Nero had vanished from circulation and the weapons still hadn't been returned, Freddo, Fierolocchio and a couple of horses eager to advance their career picked up Sellerone from in front of the Trastevere train station and took him to a safe house that had been procured by Ziccone, in the Via dell'Imbrecciata neighbourhood.

'You've got one week,' Freddo explained. 'Either you give us the guns or we're going to feed you to the hogs.'

IV

IN PIAZZA DEI Mercanti there was not, and there never had been, a bordello of any description. The repeated investigations, entries, searches and stakeouts had produced absolutely no 'criminally actionable evidence'. It was all the product of the wrong-headed campaign of a policeman who was as naïve as he was zealous. Commissario Scialoja had made a colossal blunder.

'It's a disgrace! You were right all along, sir! I should never have trusted those guys in the vice squad. I made a mistake when I ignored your advice...'

Borgia was furiously waving the report with which the vice squad had placed a massive seal on the investigation. Scialoja had never seen him this angry before. Borgia was looking for comfort and reassurance.

Scialoja avoided the ADA's lucid and indignant glare and took refuge in the smoke of yet another cigarette. Borgia went on venting his legitimate outrage. Scialoja struggled to find the right words to let him down easy.

The night before, Zeta and Pigreco had picked him up at the exit of the independent film club where he'd just watched Altman's *McCabe & Mrs Miller*. He hadn't even seen them coming. He was the last one to exit the cinema, evicted by the weary projectionist. With an unlit cigarette dangling out of the corner of his mouth and the blank gaze of Julie Christie high on opium still filling his eyes and his heart, and the deep baritone voice of Leonard Cohen still resonating in his ears, he noticed a fraction of a second too late a couple of guys bursting straight towards him from behind the huge trunk of a linden tree. He'd instinctively reached for his gun, but the two of them were just too fast. The powerful little guy had decked him with a sharp blow of the knee to his kidneys. The cigarette had disintegrated between his clamped teeth, leaving an acrid aftertaste on his palate. The other man, tall and distinguished in a white linen three-piece suit that gleamed in the starry summer night, had slipped his Beretta out of his reach with a grin of contempt. Then they'd locked arms with him, as if he were just another merrymaker who'd had too much to drink, and frogmarched him off to the nearby secluded gardens of Piazzetta dei Quiriti. The fountain splashed away, the air was redolent with jasmine and desuetude. The tall man offered him a cigarette. Scialoja, still dizzy from the blow he'd taken, accepted with a weary gesture. Zeta and Pigreco identified themselves and flashed their IDs.

'Who's to say those are real?'

'They're real, they're real,' Zeta reassured.

'They're real, and you're in trouble,' the other one had chimed in.

They'd all taken seats on the edge of the fountain. The last pair of lovebirds had flown off, leaving their bench empty. A nocturnal bird of some kind had let loose its strident call. Zeta was filing his fingernails. Scialoja had seen this duo someplace before. He just couldn't recollect where or when.

'Accomplice to terrorism.'

'Aiding and abetting.'

'Association with subversives.'

'Armed conspiracy.'

Scialoja felt a piercing stab of pain grip his stomach.

'I have no idea what you two are even talking about.'

'Sandra Belli. Fugitive from the law, safe in France. You helped her escape.'

'You warned her the raid was imminent.'

'You protected a Red Brigades terrorist.'

'You're in deep shit.'

'In shit right up to your neck.'

'Terrorism is no joking matter.'

'You've gone over to the other side.'

'You're a turncoat cop.'

'You're in deep shit.'

They finally fell silent and sat there staring at him. Sarcastic, contemptuous.

'Sandra's not a terrorist.'

Zeta had laughed. Pigreco had laughed.

'Sure. Sandra's not a terrorist. And Patrizia's not a whore!'

Now Scialoja remembered. He'd seen them on his stakeout of Piazza dei Mercanti. They frequented the bordello. They were protecting the bordello.

'What do you want from me?'

'A deal,' Zeta said with a sigh.

'Deep down, we're on the same side,' Pigreco added.

'Deep down, you're not a bad kid.'

'Just a little naïve.'

'Just a little arrogant.'

'Let's just say that you got a swelled head.'

'Let's just say that reasonable people can always come to an understanding.'

'Let's just say that as far as we're concerned, we're closing the book on the whole story of the Red Brigades terrorist.'

'Let's just say you take a little time off and you forget all about Patrizia and her...'

'Retail establishment?'

'Let's call it that: retail establishment.'

Scialoja lit a cigarette.

'Well? What do you say? It strikes me as a very attractive offer, wouldn't you say...colleague?'

Scialoja took a sharp, angry drag of smoke. 'Listen carefully. I'm not excluding the possibility that Sandra might have fucked up. If so, I'm willing to pay the consequences. But all that has nothing to do with the bordello. It's nothing more than a cover operation. A convenient investment for a major criminal organization. The biggest one that's ever operated in Rome. I'm talking about Mafia, colleagues!'

Zeta put away his nail file with a grimace of disgust. Pigreco spread both arms wide.

'You hear that? He doesn't get it!'

'He doesn't get it!'

'We come in peace...'

'And he drags up the Mafia!'

'What an arsehole!'

'What a complete arsehole!'

'Maybe we failed to make ourselves clear...'

'Maybe we've been too indulgent...'

'Maybe...'

Scialoja had a sudden impulse to dig out the black belt he'd left buried somewhere in the back of his wardrobe. Pigreco had made a ferocious face in his direction.

'Listen up and listen good, you little piece of shit: you're fucked. End of story. Fucked. Got it? One more word out of you and tomorrow night you'll be sitting in the brig at Forte Boccea with a warrant for your arrest fifteen miles long!'

'In other words, we've got you by the balls!'

Before turning to go, Zeta gave him back his gun.

Borgia was now pacing back and forth in his office.

'This thing's not going to end here! I'm going to raise hell! We're going to raise hell! I've already requested a meeting with the chief district attorney. I'm not going to be stopped in my tracks. If they think that all it takes is a little eyewash report to...What the devil, why don't you say anything? You understand that they're accusing you of being a moron, an idiot? Say something, Scialoja!'

166

Scialoja lowered his head. 'I have a feeling they might be right,' he murmured, incapable of looking the other man in the eye.

'What? What on earth are you talking about?'

'They're right. I got it wrong. That's all.'

And that was that. Scialoja made an abrupt about-face. He left both righteous wrath and his own bad conscience to fend for themselves.

For a full week he was absent without leave, then his boss sent a police car to pick him up. He presented him with an immediate transfer order. Scialoja left for Modena with a suitcase full of books and a liver soaked in alcohol.

V

THE TWO GIRLS that Patrizia had selected, a brunette and a natural blonde, were giving the latex dildo a workout. Nero, sitting in the lotus position, was distractedly watching their manoeuvrings on the big four-poster bed with the red canopy. His mind worked back, following the thread of his memories. He'd gone back to that last evening with Evola. The Maestro, by now barely flickering with life, was telling them all the story of Krishna's apparition to Arjuna. Avatar: the godhead manifests itself in moments of crisis to restore man to a state of order. Krishna explains to Arjuna that all action is in and of itself useless and super-fluous, but that if there were no such thing as action, then human beings would think that everything was futile, and they would sink into a mortal slough of despondency. The tedium of inaction, which would inevitably drive mankind to extinction. For that reason, action was necessary, but only if one maintained detachment from the outcome of one's actions. Act, but do not rejoice in action: that was the essence of the matter. While everyone listened raptly to the Maestro's harsh voice, Nero had interrupted him, thus violating a sacred rule.

'But doesn't all this possibly mean just one thing: that action is a posi-tive good in and of itself?'

A scandalized buzz of indignation greeted his intervention. The Maestro had invited him to clarify the concept.

'What I mean to say is: perhaps Krishna is sending an occult message.

He, a god, is face to face with Arjuna, a man. Krishna knows that action is the sole value that mankind can understand. And so he offers it to him on a silver platter...'

'To what end?'

'To ensure that Arjuna will complete the mission with which he himself, the god, has entrusted him. To ensure that he makes up his mind, once and for all, to do so without troubling himself with too many questions...'

'In your opinion, then, this was nothing more than a vulgar technique designed to ensure control? A mere question of power, when all is said and done?'

'Precisely, Maestro.'

'Come back when you are capable of understanding,' the Maestro had said with a smile.

But Nero had never returned. He no longer had any need of teachers. Zarathustra had been clear on that point: you do your teachers a disservice by remaining a pupil all your life. Nothing remained to him from that period of his life but the beauty of the gesture.

The girls were starting to pant. The brunette had noticed the laughter that was starting to play over his elusive lips.

'Don't you dare laugh! We're working here.'

'Excuse me. Please, don't stop.'

He concentrated on them. They were doing everything imaginable to get him excited, and it was starting to work. He slowly let himself get drawn in, with steadily growing conviction. The orgasm started to build up: an angry tide surging up from the depths of his guts. Just when he was about to come, he bit his tongue and pushed it back. He couldn't let that energy get away from him. He'd need it soon. Very soon.

'That's enough.'

The girls flopped down exhausted on the silk sheets. The blonde slid her hand between her legs with a grimace. The brunette unfastened the phallus belted to her waist and dropped it on the nightstand. Even though the two girls were compliments of Patrizia, he paid them generously. They kissed him goodbye, then Nero got dressed, picked up the duffel bag with the weapons, and went to get the Honda with the fake number plates that he'd parked along the riverfront.

Nero knew nothing about the man he'd been assigned to eliminate except that he wrote for a scandal sheet and had managed to annoy the wrong person. As far as he was concerned, the man wasn't even a human being; he was nothing more than a target. The target for his action. They called him the Pidocchio – the louse. When he gave him the go-ahead on the job, Zeta had told him how the nickname had originated. The politician who had it in for him had coined it. It had been at one of the many dinners attended by the great and powerful. Zeta had laughed as he remembered the exact wording.

'One of these days, if he doesn't stop stirring up trouble, I'm going to crush that miserable loudmouth like the louse he is.'

Pidocchio kept a lover in the Nomentano quarter. He went to see her two nights week, regular as clockwork. He never left before ten o'clock. It was now just fifteen minutes until the final deadline.

The Sicilian was already on the spot. They exchanged a nod of greeting. He was a minute, dark kid, with large eyes in which bolts of terror would flash unexpectedly. Semi-illiterate. A son of the country-side. Zeta had told him that as a child he'd been raped by sheepherders. His presence sealed an agreement whose details were known to only a few. Nero wasn't one of those in the know, but it didn't take much to figure it out. All you had to do was stick pins in certain strategic points, draw some lines and see where they intersected. That grey area where the state and the anti-state helped each other out was where he was most comfortable operating. The secret was that all this just disgusted him, and that's why each time he emerged cleaner than before. It was action that, paradoxically, kept him chaste.

A light drizzle began to fall. The Sicilian, who had been assigned duties as a lookout and as backup, had been ordered to intervene, if it proved necessary, only as a fall-back option. That meant that if something went wrong, the Sicilian had orders to finish off Pidocchio and eliminate Nero while he was at it. Nero didn't begrudge him his orders past a certain point. It fit in with a military technique that did not strike him as un-familiar. After all, the same thing applied in reverse: if the Sicilian was in trouble, it would be Nero's job to finish him off. The important thing was to make sure there were no witnesses. Before taking up his post, he scrutinized the long tree-lined street, doing his best to peer at the pitched roofs and windows of the solid, elegant apartment buildings. He couldn't make out any undesired third parties. In any case, if worst came to worst, he had brought a small hand grenade along as well.

Nero went to take shelter from the drizzle under the overhang of a roof. He'd brought a book that he was pretending to read. While the Sicilian might attract a certain amount of notice and curiosity, Nero was in every way indistinguishable from the many young habitués of the *Officina*, the nearby independent left-wing cinema that had already been burned down twice.

The rain had progressed from a mist to a driving downpour, and the street was now deserted. Nero turned up his jacket collar, snapped off the safety, and screwed on the handmade silencer – a metal pipe with a wooden disk, filled with wadded cotton. The handgun was a Tanfoglio; not brand new, but a precision weapon. The clip contained five Fiocchi shells and four modified Winchester shells. The ballistics experts would be tearing their hair out afterwards.

At ten o'clock sharp, the front door swung open. The target, backlit by the dim glow of a ceiling lamp high above, had the tawdry appearance of a wage-slave worn down by the daily grind. He looked around, flicked away the cigarette he was holding between two fingers with an irritated gesture, and headed off down the street. Nero emerged from the shadows and took two or three steps until he was right behind him. The target never even knew he was there. The street was still deserted.

Nero pulled out the gun and fired three shots in rapid succession. The sound of a tin can being crushed. The target twisted around on himself, corkscrewing and grabbing at the empty air, and then fell without a sound. Nero bent down over him. He seemed to be a goner, but you could never be sure. He placed the silencer against his forehead and pulled the trigger for the last time. His skull exploded, blasting fragments of bone, blood and grey matter into the air. Nero had turned aside to avoid the spray.

All done, he signalled to his partner, waving the Tanfoglio. The Sicilian raised an arm in a gesture of farewell and took off at a run towards Piazza Verbano. Nero walked without haste towards the cinema. The idea of spending an hour in that Communist lair struck him as a delightful touch of class. The fundamental problem with the Reds was that they thought of themselves as part of the 'masses'. And they believed in mankind. Masses, no doubt, but masses of idiots.

Manning the box office was an airhead girl with curly hair and a pair of small tits that were something to think about it. She gave Nero an unfriendly look. He filled out a membership application with a fake name, paid, took the ticket she tore off and handed him ungraciously. They were showing a Marx Brothers film: Jews, but funny Jews, at least.

As he was entering the cinema, he heard the first sirens. Nero needed to relax. The murder, the action, had worn him out. The energy that he had created with the help of the two whores, the energy that he had stored up within himself, had vanished in the glare of the gunshots. Tomorrow would be an important day. He'd have to collect the rest of his fee. He'd have to resolve the issue with Sellerone.

The next day, Pigreco handed him the attaché case containing the cash in the atrium of the National Library, along with his compliments for the flawless outcome of the mission. Nero accepted the cash and compliments with a faintly contemptuous smile. The Pidocchio story was on the front pages of every newspaper in the country. Blistering accusations were flying in all directions, naming various alleged masterminds. That miserable hack was starting to look more dangerous dead than he had been alive. Zeta, Pigreco and whoever was giving them orders might very well be in control of the government, but they were behaving like dilettantes who'd never fired a gun in their lives.

At sunset he met Freddo out front of the Trastevere station, where they'd kidnapped Sellerone. Nero handed Freddo the duffel bag with two pistols and an army assault rifle.

'They're not exactly the same ones you gave me, but it's good, safe stuff.'

'Fine. I'll head up and send Sellerone back to you.'

'I'm glad the whole matter has been settled.'

'So am I. Sellerone talks too much, but deep down, you were right, he's a good guy...'

They exchanged a farewell handshake. Freddo had climbed into the VW Golf when Nero called out to him.

'The Tanfoglio's hot.'

Freddo looked him up and down. A baffled glance, a flat phrase.

'Pidocchio.'

'Right.'

'Beware of politicians,' Freddo admonished him, and drove away.

VI

DESPITE THE RETRACTION of testimony and the dropped charges, Bufalo was still stuck in Regina Coeli, and Varighina found himself charged with abetting prostitution. Ever since he'd lost his trusted right-hand man, Scialoja, Borgia had been gnashing his teeth. Apparently his ideas were starting to spread and find favour. In fact, the investigating judge, in his court order rejecting the application for release from preventive custody, had described Bufalo as 'a leading figure of a new form of criminal activity that distinguishes itself by its extreme ruthlessness in terms of methods employed and a total disregard for human life'.

'I'll kill him!' he'd threatened, during a meeting with the lawyer. Vasta had cowed him with an arrogant little smile.

'For so little? You'll be home by Christmas. I guarantee it.'

Maybe so. But in the meantime the days followed one after another, endless and dull. For the first time prison had become a burden to Bufalo. He replayed in his mind scenes from the past, especially that damned afternoon of idiocy. It looked like he might very well ruin everything. But no matter how hard he tried to figure out a reason, or a justification, he always unfailingly came back around to the same point: it's the way I am, there's nothing I can do about it. It happened, that's all.

Luckily, from the outside world, along with the care packages and the money orders from the general fund, nothing but good news was filtering in. The raid on the evidence room had gone as smooth as silk. Trentadenari, Freddo and Botola, with Nero standing lookout, had paid a little courtesy call on the evidence storage room in broad daylight, passing easily through the various checkpoints with the identity badges that Santini's friend had procured for them. The fifty kilos of Peshawar white had been stashed in two aluminium suitcases and trundled out right under the noses of the guards. But maybe that was just one more reason why, with the thought of how much fun the others were having out there, time crept slowly in Bufalo's prison cell.

At Christmas, due to the decision of a maresciallo armed with a remarkable sense of humour, they assigned him a new cellmate: Pischello, just turned eighteen, straight out of juvenile detention centre. His nickname – *pischello*, or 'greenhorn kid' – said it all.

Pischello came in on the right foot: he walked in, greeted them all politely, announced his real name, asked Bufalo permission to set up his bed, and asked whether anyone minded if he smoked. He was a short, slender kid, fresh-faced, with the look of a sly dog, a level gaze and a tweed jacket a film star might wear. Bufalo, who caught a whiff of well-to-do snob, asked him what part of town he came from.

'I was born in Piazza Euclide,' Pischello replied.

'I can't fucking stand pretty boys from Parioli. What are you in for? A few joints?'

'Murder.'

This was starting to look a little more interesting. Pischello didn't have to be asked twice to tell his story. He said that he belonged to a national socialist revolutionary organization and that they had approved the elimination of a turncoat, a lawyer who had sold them out to Almirante's Neo-Fascist MSI. He and four comrades had done all the prep work on the ambush, and the target had been hit and killed by sub-machine gunfire. But something had gone wrong in the escape phase. A *caramba* police car had pulled up, there'd been an exchange of gunfire, and three of them had been captured.

'To make things worse, we killed the wrong man. Someone who looked like the lawyer, but wasn't the lawyer.'

'So now what are you going to do? Say a prayer to St Denial?'

'They basically caught me red-handed.'

'Well?'

'I've already claimed status as a political prisoner.'

'Ooh, another idealist! What a pain in the arse all this politics is getting to be!'

Still, the slick little kid seemed to be okay. Whenever investigating judges came to question him, he either responded with contemptuous

173

silence or chased them away with his cutting wisecracks. On visiting days, a well-dressed woman and a scared-looking little girl came to see him: mother and sister, always loaded down with clean linen, fashionable cashmere jumpers and chocolate cakes that Pischello shared generously with the others. He was a guy who knew how to survive in prison. Ridiculously young, but already displaying the confidence of a veteran, he spent two hours lifting weights in the cell each day, and his things were always neat and tidy. Bufalo had never seen him with a hair out of place or a sock that didn't match his outfit.

Little by little, Bufalo too began to confide. He told him about some – just a selection, eh – of his exploits, talked to him about Libano and Freddo, Trentadenari, Sardo and Dandi, about Patrizia and her girls, the coke and the smack, the gambling dens, about the street, really, and its age-old electric allure. Pischello listened raptly, taking in and registering the details, breaking in rarely and always with cogent questions, and eventually Bufalo started to feel for the first time in his life as if he was someone's big brother. Like another Libano or Freddo, in other words. And it was a new sensation, even a thrilling one. Bufalo had been a loner all his life. The fondness that he was starting to feel towards that kid was doing his heart good. It was even forcing him to use his brain. Not that he lacked intelligence, as Libano had already guessed; it was just that most of the time he seemed to forget to use it. And so it was that Bufalo did the right thing, the smart thing: he talked to Vasta about the kid's situation. Vasta, legal eagle that he was, had heard all about him: good family, influential relatives, plenty of money. Certainly it was a shame to throw your life away like that for a cause, an idea that might even be right but which, without a groundswell of support, was bound to remain a utopian dream. Certainly, if only Pischello had the right sort of counsel in his legal proceedings, from the right kind of lawyer, of course...

'Fine, fine, counsellor, I get your drift. But now what am I supposed to tell this guy?'

Vasta offered some preliminary legal advice. That evening Bufalo confronted Pischello.

'Listen up now: if you stick to this story that you're a political prisoner, the only way you're getting out of this place is feet-first, on a slab!'

'So what should I do?'

'Confess.'

Pischello glared at him, hard-faced.

'You think I'm afraid of prison?'

'No, I got you figured. You're not scared. But sooner or later you're going to get sick of being in here. Just think of all the fun you could be having out in the world, with the right friends, if you follow me...'

Pischello thought it over, snorted, shook his head no.

'Why not?' Bufalo persisted.

'If I talk, I'd be betraying my comrades...'

'Aw, you don't have to name names, you dope! You just have to throw them a bone...Yes, Judge, Your Honour, it was me that done it. I admit my guilt. I'm sincerely sorry for what I've done and I want to make up for the consequences of my act. But I won't name names...'

'You think that would hold them?'

'Pische, listen to me! You've been to school, it's obvious. You come from a good family. You have the added advantage that you were still a minor when you did the crime. With a good lawyer, if you go ahead and confess, they afford you the generic mitigating circumstances, you tell Papa to write a little cheque to the victim's family...And in ten years you're out! Believe me, either you do that or you'll get life without parole...'

Pischello spent the next two days knocking himself silly, lifting weights and doing push-ups. Silent as a doornail. It was clear that he was seriously evaluating the proposal. And he never spoke a word. Kept it all bottled up inside. A true tough guy.

Bufalo, who really didn't know the meaning of patience or the fullness of time, woke him up in the middle of the third night, with the excuse that Pischello was snoring.

'Pische, satisfy a curiosity of mine: how is it that you guys are Fascists but you still address each other as comrades, just like the other guys?'

'Comrade's a fine word. *Camerata* – the term we're theoretically supposed to use as Fascists – smacks of army barracks. Mouldy old terminology. Uninteresting.'

'Have you thought about what I told you?'

'Okay, let's say I'm in. I confess but I won't sell anyone out. Let's say it works out and they believe me. But I'm still cut out of the network for good...'

'Out of what network?'

'Out of my network.'

'In what way?'

'Well, they'll always assume I'm a turncoat...'

'Ah.' Bufalo heaved a sigh of relief. 'If that's all you're worried about, I'll take care of it. Just a word or two to Nero and it's all taken care of...'

'Do you know Nero?'

'Nero's with us.'

After a little more back and forth and hemming and hawing, Pischello finally fired his public defender, appointed Vasta and wrote a long letter to the prosecuting magistrate.

In mid-January the Court of Cassation accepted Vasta's appeal and Bufalo was ordered to be released. He left prison with the certainty that he'd done a good deed: Pischello was becoming a man, and he'd helped him to grow up. Something inside him told Bufalo that the two of them would meet again.

Controlling the Street
1980

I

ON THE AFTERNOON of 7 February, Donatella caught Nembo Kid with a Colombian chick. The two of them were in Fierolocchio's pied-a-terre behind St Paul's Basilica. Nembo did his best to patch things up.

'It's not the way you think... She works at the embassy... I'm putting together a deal...'

After inviting her to collect her oversized bra and her turquoise suspenders, Donatella waited patiently for the big brunette to clear out, then she pulled out her penknife and gave her man a souvenir of the day on his shoulder.

That night, when Nembo Kid showed up at the Full 80 with a grim expression on his face and his arm in a sling, he was greeted by a colossal burst of laughter. The detail that they found particularly hilarious was this: the penknife had actually been a gift from Nembo Kid to Donatella just one week before. For purposes of self-defence, adding meaningly: with all the nut jobs out on the streets these days...

They were still celebrating the commemorative stabbing when Ricotta let the four of them in the front door: young, well put-together, nicely dressed, they'd proffered the correct password when questioned and so he'd assumed they were on the up and up. Mistaken for friends by the actor Bontempi, they were invited to join in the toast. With all the money that their plucked chickens were doubtless going to leave on the gambling tables over the course of that night, they could well afford to be generous with the alcohol. But the four men politely declined the offer and then, one at a time, pulled out their badges and identified themselves as the law. Carabinieri. Bufalo, who was packing his revolver that night, managed to sneak his way to the exit. It struck Libano that the *caramba* had noticed Bufalo's manoeuvre, and yet they let him go without objection. That was the second odd detail, if you counted the password as the first. Third odd detail: ignoring the main party room, which was clean and fully licenced, proper and above-board, and moving quickly before any organized countermove could be set afoot, the officers headed straight upstairs, broke into the casino room, demanded and recorded the identification documents of all those present, and then efficiently proceeded to confiscate playing cards, chips, dice, cheques, cash and IOUs. Finally, the fourth and last odd detail, this one truly unsettling: all of them were then released on their own recognizance, with the sole exception of Dandi, Libano, Nembo Kid and Ricotta, all of whom, before the sun rose on Rome that morning, had been issued a set of sheets and blankets and a comfortable little room in the hotel of Ponte Mammolo – AKA Rebibbia prison. Along with that gift pack came a brand-new arraignment for criminal conspiracy to defraud and illegally operating a gambling establishment. Kid stuff, agreed, but still, this in-again out-again revolving door was turning into a royal pain in the arse.

Now, Rebibbia was a different kettle of fish from Regina Coeli. Sure, there was more room and less stench of human flesh, true enough, but regulations were much more stringent, and a full week had gone by before they were all out of solitary confinement and managed to meet up again. When they finally had a chance to talk during free time in the exercise yard, all four of them were furious, disappointed – and suspicious.

In the last few days, in separate meetings with each of them, Vasta had put on the usual show of chipper optimism.

'The indictment is technically defective as far as games of chance are concerned. The prosecuting magistrate is Sciancarelli, a cretin. You have nothing to worry about. Worst case, once we've got you out of here and back on the street, we can admit that you'd gone to the Full 80 to do a little gambling, and you'll get off with a fine. Unfortunately, they've put police seals on the club, and you're just going to have to resign yourself to the loss. As for the fraud charges, they'd need the gamblers themselves to testify that you were cheating. That strikes me as a remote likelihood at best, and in any case, for now there's nothing of the sort in the documents. Cheer up! At the very latest you're out of here by early April!'

So that was that: the gambling den was gone. A total and considerable loss but, well, nothing you could do about it. As soon as they got out, they'd set up a new one. Bigger and more profitable. There was no shortage of money. But the first thing to do was track down the miserable jackal who was trying to screw them and make whoever it was pay.

Where was the attack coming from this time?

It turned out that Donatella had actually done Nembo Kid a favour: he was admitted to the prison infirmary. There, through the good offices of an orderly, duly bribed with a generous helping of coke, he was smuggled a little powder to snort and a message from Trentadenari: Fabio Santini swore up and down that the mobile squad had been kept completely in the dark. They'd been cut out of the operation and, what made matters even worse, certain carabinieri friends of his had made it clear that the Full 80 bust had been conducted 'on the highest level of secrecy' and 'in accordance with orders from the upper echelons'. Just how high those echelons might be, there was no way of knowing.

Libano, who deep down had been favourably impressed by the lightning-fast, surgical precision of that raid, wondered why the carabinieri had chosen to make those specific arrests. Why the four of them? Why not just haul in everybody? Were they aiming at the bosses, or the people they assumed were the bosses? Then why ignore Freddo? Why haul in Ricotta, who was a good fellow, but in terms of authority, well... Or were they trying to drive a wedge between them? Trying to plant the idea that there was a traitor in their midst? They knew the password, which they changed twice a week. True, there were plenty of gamblers who knew the latest password. Which meant it could have been anyone...

For once, this time, it looked like they didn't have Borgia on their case. And even that could be a signal that there was a problem lurking: just one more hint that there were more enemies out there, manoeuvring in the shadows. Libano had no doubt that he'd be able to beat the rap this time. As always, his main concern was whether the gang would be able to remain intact. True, Freddo and Trentadenari were still out on the street: that meant that, with Dandi and him in stir, the number of clear minds able to move unimpeded had been cut in half. Maybe they could take a risk and give Nero a bigger share of responsibility. But how far could they trust him? That guy came and went, disappeared, clearly had a mind of his own, enough said. And no one seemed able to talk to him but Freddo.

Without a doubt, being back in jail was definitely not a good thing. In the future, they'd need to stay on their toes. Diversify their alliances. As high as they'd managed to climb by now, paying off some crooked cop no longer offered adequate insurance. Maybe, after all, that was exactly the message someone was trying to send…

One evening in early March, they were summoned to the warden's office. But the guard assigned to escort them, instead of heading for the office building, accompanied them to a separate wing undergoing renovation. This wing was slated to house the terrorists, fake and real, that were raining down by the truckload in that period. Paying absolutely no attention to the questions they pelted him with, the guard deposited them in a small interview room illuminated by a flickering, constipated neon light.

'I don't like it,' Ricotta said.

'Stay cool,' Libano philosophized, who had brooded long enough to glimpse a thing or two through the murk.

And in fact, when he saw them emerge from the armour-plated door that the guard had left ajar, he had practically been expecting to be reunited with his old acquaintances Zeta and Pigreco.

'So it was the two of you who pulled this gag!'

Dandi and Nembo Kid were about to lunge at them. Zeta raised his hands in a sign of truce. Pigreco dropped a bindle of cocaine on the table.

Nembo Kid approached the coke cautiously, dipped the tip of his pinkie into it, and tasted it.

'Seems good.'

'Go slow,' Pigreco warned. 'It's eighty-five per cent.'

'You don't have to polish it all off tonight,' Zeta pointed out. 'We're not staying, but it can…'

Dandi got the first snort, followed by Ricotta and Nembo Kid. Zeta and Pigreco pulled up a couple of chairs and got comfortable.

'You're not dipping in, Libano?' Zeta asked.

'Business before pleasure. You're here on business, aren't you?'

'Sure, and maybe you were even expecting our little visit. You're a smart boy, Libano. Which is why we're here...'

Libano strode briskly over to the table, picked up the bindle of coke, folded it up and slipped it into his pocket. Ricotta watched him, open-mouthed. Libano lit a cigarette. Zeta started his spiel.

He was very sorry about what had happened to the gambling den, but it wouldn't take them long to recover from the loss. He'd like them to think of this episode as a small sample of their power. In any case, if this conversation produced the desired results, whatever problems were in the air would vanish like a soap bubble popping. And all of them would profit enormously. Already once before they'd been obliged to step in to rescue the bordello from the meddling of that demented cop, Scialoja, who thought he could step on people's feet without paying the piper. And it had gone smooth as silk, hadn't it? All right then. He wanted them to consider their terms. Zeta spoke at considerable length. All around them, night fell, punctuated by the cadenced footsteps of the guards patrolling. Zeta spoke, and while Dandi, Nembo Kid and Ricotta nodded, increasingly convinced, verging on gleeful excitement, Libano sat back, leaning against the wall. Impassive. Impenetrable. In the end, when Pigreco, who'd never opened his mouth the whole time, asked whether he should assume they had an agreement, Libano made his move. Before the others gave way to their surging enthusiasm, Libano shot Zeta a vicious glare.

'Why didn't you bring in Freddo, too?'

Zeta smiled. 'Maybe it wasn't necessary...'

'You don't get it, do you?'

Zeta and Pigreco exchanged a worried glance.

'Now listen here, Libano...'

'No, you listen to me: we might need you guys, but not as much as you need us. You might own the office buildings, but we own the street. And that's what you want: the street. Because without the street, your office buildings aren't worth a wet rag! Well, there's nobody who knows how to control the street like Freddo. No one. Freddo is the street. So...no Freddo, no deal!'

'Fucking hell, you're right! It's everyone or no one!' shouted Ricotta, slamming a fist down on the table.

Libano looked around, trying to build consensus among his other comrades. But Dandi was muttering something incomprehensible. And Nembo Kid was staring at the floor, hands crammed into his pockets. Libano could smell opportunism in the air. What would become of them all, if anything ever happened to him?

'Without Freddo,' he repeated, driving home his point, 'there's not going to be any deal!'

'We'll have to talk this over with the Old Man.'

'Who's the Old Man?'

'The Old Man is the Old Man.'

'Well, then, you go tell this Old Man as follows, word for word: if there's no Freddo, there's no deal!'

Zeta sighed. Still, in this case, his orders had been reasonably elastic. He needed to go back to the Old Man with results, and this constituted a result. What's more, wisdom dictated that in any negotiation you had to give up something.

'As you like,' he conceded. 'But I'm holding you responsible.'

Libano nodded. He pulled out the bindle of coke and spun it onto the tabletop.

'In that case, we have a deal.'

Later, while the guard, blithely indifferent to the cocaine, was escorting them back to their cells, Dandi told Libano that he had acted like a genuine boss, a *vero capo*. Libano stared him right in the eye, holding his gaze with his will. Dandi wavered and looked away.

Libano went to sleep with a wry but worried smile playing across his thin lips.

II

PATRIZIA LIKED THE beach in winter. It matched her own sense of solitude. Her boredom. With Dandi in the slammer and her business practically running itself, she wasn't really needed in Rome. Ranocchia, whom she had finally decided to forgive, had found an old house on the coast between Terracina and Sperlonga and offered it for her use. It was cold out and it looked like rain. Patrizia was sitting by the fire leafing through a travel magazine. Ranocchia was just a shadow of his former self. He'd started using morphine to relieve the pain from his wounds, and by now he was sailing along on half a gram of smack a day. He kept his supply in a secretary desk along with a pearl necklace and the watch he'd stolen from his father before running away to live on the street. Even his dreams were drab now, not as fanciful and imaginative as they used to be.

'I'm in a room, and it's all painted black. I'm Ida Lupino, I'm sinewy and mannish. I'm wearing a grey dress. I'm chained to the wall; big iron rings grip my wrists tight. On the floor is a dog bowl full of water. The gangsters who've kidnapped me want to know where Johnny Ray is hiding. But I'm not going to tell them. This girl is ready to die, but not ready to give away my secrets...'

'Is that all?'

'A little patience, *cara*! I haven't dreamt the rest yet!'

Ranocchia had turned sad. The sunset was sad. The world was sad. Patrizia was having no fun. Patrizia felt empty inside, the way she used to back when she was just Cinzia, when she used to have to spell out the terms of the transaction with overeager men before she agreed to unhook her bra.

Ranocchia was grilling fish on the barbecue.

'What do you say about Morocco, Ranocchia?'

'Great idea. Even this time of year it's nice and warm. It'd do your heart good. I know a few boys in Casablanca. We could go together...'

'The furthest thing from my mind!'

'You could go with Dandi.'

'Not on your life!'

'Then with Libano.'

'Libano? You couldn't get him out of Trastevere, even if he was dead. He's afraid that the minute he leaves his territory, someone'll yank his chair right out from under his arse!'

'Fierolocchio?'

'He smells.'

'Ricotta?'

'Ugh!'

'Nembo Kid?'

'You want to tell Donatella about it?'

'Nero?'

'Oh, that'd be fun!'

'Then go with Freddo.'

'Freddo never looks me in the eye.'

'That's because he respects you. You're his friend's woman and he wants his friend to understand that he's steering clear!'

'No, you're wrong. Freddo feels contempt for me. He holds me and all the other girls in utter contempt.'

'Does he like men?'

'What are you talking about! He's searching for the love of his life...'

'Ah, I get it: he's a romantic! Never could figure them out, romantics. To love just one person at a time – sheer lunacy! To mate for all time. Eternal promises and all that other bullshit! There should be no limitations on love. That's how I see it.'

'There should be no such thing as love. That's how I see it.'

Ranocchia turned the pan-fried sea bream, breathed in the aroma, and nodded.

'They're almost ready. Patrizia, you wouldn't happen to be in love, would you?'

'Don't talk bullshit.'

'Once, when I was in the hospital, a cop came to visit me. A handsome hunk, the passionate type, with a smoulder, like Monty Clift with maybe just a hint of young James Bond, but less neurotic, more of the boy-next-door, if you know what I mean...If you ask me, if I talked to him, suggested he go to Morocco with you, he wouldn't think twice about it...'

'You talk too much, Ranocchia.'

They moved out to the patio. Ranocchia served the fish and popped the cork on a bottle of iced Bianchetto wine. In the hutch at the far end of the garden, the rabbit was quivering, in the throes of labour pains.

'She's about to have babies! I want to watch them come out!' Patrizia said.

'It's not much to see. They're little pink gargoyles, with their eyes closed and covered with disgusting slime...'

'I want to see them anyway.'

'Well, she'll be done in ten minutes or so. Just be patient, can't you?'

'I don't like being patient, Ranocchia.'

'That policeman, I can't remember his name...'

'Will you cut that out, for the last time?'

Ranocchia apologized and headed inside. Give us this day our daily junk. Patrizia sipped her wine. Ranocchia was making her feel uncomfortable. It had been a bad idea to come out here, to leave Rome. It had been a bad idea to go to a remote, isolated place with that half-crazed faggot. She'd never thought about the cop. Or maybe she had, when Zeta and Pigreco had told her that they'd gift-wrapped him, set him up, fixed him good. She'd had fun fantasizing about what the fallout would be if they shut down the bordello. Prison. Trial. Start over from scratch. She had enough money saved up that she had nothing to worry about.

Dandi stood back and let things play themselves out. But every now and then, a wave of jealousy would come over him. Are you still going out with strange men? What do they want you to do? Do you do it? Exactly what do you do?

Ranocchia wearily dragged himself out of the house and flopped down in his chair. His eyes were cloudy.

'Someday I'll paint your portrait, Patrizia.'

'You know how to paint?'

'I do all right. I finished a couple of years at the academy of art. I'll paint you the way you are. The way I see you. The way you don't dream you really are.'

'Oh, really? And how is that?'

'Geometric. Angular. Slavic. You don't have a typical Roman face. Roman faces are sweet and round, they tend to dissolve into a languid idyll, they inspire lust. You, on the other hand, make a man feel like outdoing himself. You're a woman of potential, a woman from the future, Patrizia. You don't see a lot of faces like yours around.'

Ranocchia was growing delirious from the effects of the smack. Patrizia ventured over to the rabbit hutch. Mama Rabbit was extruding her babies, one after another. Every time one popped out, she'd hasten to lick it off, gently. So that's motherhood. How disgusting. Ranocchia was right. Those little gargoyles were repulsive.

Ranocchia's voice was a soft, hallucinatory whisper. 'You're a woman on the threshold, Patrizia. You're here because you don't know what else to do. You feel like you're a prisoner and you yearn for freedom. But freedom is the most expensive thing there is on earth. Not even with all of Dandi's money would you be able to afford it. It will all amount to nothing. It's too much of a challenge for you. Too much for anyone, for that matter.'

'I'll have you ripped limb from limb, Ranocchia. You're one dead faggot.'

But Ranocchia hadn't heard a word she'd said. The heroin had put him under. He was snoring softly, his mouth wide open, arms crossed over his shrunken body. A noise from the rabbit hutch made Patrizia jump. Somehow, she couldn't see quite how, a dog, a sly-looking little mutt, had found its way into the hutch. Mama Rabbit was huffing threateningly. The dog paid her no mind. It crept closer to the rabbit kits, sniffed at them, and then gulped them down one after the other. Mama Rabbit emitted a faint lament. The dog continued to ignore her and then vanished into the night.

Patrizia went back inside and threw her things helter-skelter into a suitcase. The BMW stood waiting, under the reed lean-to roof. In an hour and a half she could be home. She could change. She could go out dancing. Alone. Or else she could call Alitalia and make reservations for the first flight out, wherever she chose to go. She didn't have to answer to anybody. She was free to do as she liked. The world was a dreary place. The world was filthy.

III

THE OLD MAN was the Old Man. The Old Man orders; God disposes. The Old Man was at the helm of an intelligence unit with a nondescript name whose power was understood by only a select few.

Surrounded by his mechanical toys – authentic antiques from eighteenth-century Austria, prototypes of modern automatons – the Old Man was battling his insomnia by playing at disordering the world.

The Old Man had had his eye on that gang of criminals for some time, and now they were beginning to make a name for themselves in the city. He'd issued the orders to exploit the bordello. The investment had proved profitable. Information was beginning to flow in. Mao had it wrong: power doesn't come from the barrel of a gun – it comes from information.

Later, he'd ordered Zeta and Pigreco to establish contact, making use of the time-honoured method. The Americans, who in their infinite conceit thought they were the first to ever come up with the idea – as if Sun Tzu, Von Clausewitz and the rest had never existed –called it a sting operation. Take a deviant, or a supposed deviant, make sure he deviates, catch him red-handed doing something deviant, and offer him a brutal alternative: either you start being a deviant how and when I tell you to, or I'll lock you away, slam the door and lose the key. It almost always worked. And now he had Libano and his boys where he wanted them. To do what with them? Why, to play with them, of course.

The Old Man was pleased with what Libano had to say about the street. He could sense a shared sensibility with that hoodlum. It was all about gambling and disorder. Wasn't Libano an inveterate gambler, after all? Sure, Libano was still nothing but a dilettante. For now, Libano cherished the dream of imposing order on chaos. Instead, what the game required was that the opposite take place: chaos must be imposed upon order. A world in disarray.

The Old Man nurtured a deep and abiding contempt for the so-called great men of the earth. He considered bankers, businessmen, politicians and crowned heads who fooled themselves into believing that they pulled the strings and ran the game to be nothing more than a troupe of buffoons. People incapable of grasping the larger interests at play. Mere hacks who struggled to gain laughably petty objectives: to conquer a state, to undermine a government, to uproot a subversive revolutionary weed.

There'd been a time when he too had been seduced by those siren songs. When they'd given him his first ministry badge, a shiver of pride had run down his spine. And then, when the Americans had chosen him as their trusted emissary, ushering him into the most exclusive, cosmic club of the twentieth century, he'd felt an infinite wave of joy surge through his being. Ah, the Americans! The guardians of liberty! The foot soldiers of democracy! *With God on My Side!* So simple, so straightforward, so amiably, intimately, innocently deep-down Fascist! So proud of the WASP traditions and their atavistic, inborn jutting jaws. But if you dug a little deeper into their pedigrees – alley-oop! Out popped Hispanics, Greeks, Armenians and Turkmen…The lower races, the benighted races…The Old Man didn't hate the Americans: he pitied them, as a father might pity an idiot son.

All this had happened long, long ago. Now the Old Man knew. In the vast sea of idiocy that he had used to reduce his people to mindless robots, Mao Tse-tung had included one sacrosanct truth: if there was great disorder under heaven, the situation was excellent. The only resource a superior could rely upon: work to disorder the world, in order to prepare an unending cavalcade of new chaos. If they could only have read his innermost thoughts, they would have discovered, to their great dismay, that this proponent of order was actually the most relentless anarchist of them all. Just like his favourite hero, Conrad's professor, wandering the streets with his secret cargo of hatred and death.

With a heartfelt sigh and a twinge of benign excitement tickling his ribs, the Old Man drank the rest of his whiskey, stopped the mechanism of his wind-up automaton, the chess player, and got to his feet, rising with some difficulty from his oversized black armchair. Tomorrow morning at nine thirty, he had an audience with His Honour, the minister. Progress report on anti-terrorism activity. At eleven fifteen, a meeting with his South African opposite number. One in the afternoon, lunch in Trastevere with the representative of the PLO, the Palestinian Liberation Organization. Make arrangements through Zeta for bordello access. Four thirty: confidential meeting with the delegate from Mossad. Make sure the historical enemies don't run into each other. Or make sure they do. He'd reserve his right to think that over. Eight forty: lodge meeting in the law offices of Counsellor Considinis. Long hours away from his beloved automatons awaited him.

Before year's end he would need to arrange a meeting with Libano.

IV

TALL, FAT AND balding, Saracca was a guy they used to send out to collect outstanding gambling debts, back when they worked with the gangsters from Marseilles. All Saracca needed to do was show up and swagger around, like the semi-moronic pirate that he was. Even the toughest card sharp tended to crap his pants at the sight. Peripherally sucked into investigations involving a few of the sort of kidnappings where the victim wound up fed to the hogs, after a preliminary investigation that acquitted him with such inexplicable generosity that it surprised even him, Saracca had found a new line of work as a fence and a loan shark. Lately, a friendship had blossomed with Scrocchiazeppi. Brought together by their shared love of horse racing, the two men had gone out on a few daytrips to the track at Agnano, where Trentadenari's cohorts in crime had lent a hand, making sure that certain old nags came in first, even though they barely possessed the standard equipment of four legs that one expects of a racehorse.

Saracca, in other words, was a good guy. Maybe he got drunk a little too often, but no one had ever had anything bad to say on his account. So everyone was left gobsmacked when Pajuca, one of the dope horses working the Villa Gordiani neighbourhood, reported back that for the past couple of weeks, Saracca had been bothering the dealers in the area. In fact, one girl they'd recently hired, Silvana – who could barely stand upright anymore and had been reduced to shooting up all around her tits, since every other vein in her body was played out – had had her jaw shattered by Saracca after he'd kicked her repeatedly in the face.

Scrocchiazeppi was sent ahead, tasked to summon Saracca to Franco's bar. He came back empty-handed and pissed off. Not only had Saracca refused to come with him, not only had he treated him, an old friend, rudely, but he had even started insulting him in front of the crowd, and in the end Scrocchiazeppi had been forced to withdraw in order to avoid even worse trouble. In any case, an excessively outrageous phrase had been uttered by Saracca:

'Tell those four arrogant midgets if they want to talk, they know where to find me!'

'He's gone completely loco!' Trentadenari commented. 'In any case, a challenge is a challenge!'

Bufalo was stamping his feet with impatience.

'Well, let's go, no? I'll go see Ziccone first thing and get two or three pistols...'

'Hold on. First we have to understand the lie of the land...' said Freddo.

'What do you want to understand? Things are clear: we've been insulted and now we take revenge. What more do you need?'

'Proof.'

'Proof? Proof of what?'

Since Libano had been in the slammer, Freddo had taken it upon himself to make sure the gang remained united. And he was concerned, he explained to the others, by that unexpected act of defiance on the part of a complete zero like Saracca. It worried him almost much as the arrest, still shrouded in mystery, of a substantial part of the gang. If you added two and two, the resulting four stank of foul weather and cop's breath, hot on the backs of their necks. It might be that Saracca was more than a harmless lunatic, as he was widely viewed. The two events – the act of defiance and the arrests – might be more than mere coincidence. They might be part of a single design. Before deciding to take any specific action, Freddo wanted to understand. Once it was clear, he could impose a penalty proportionate to the violation.

'Oh,' Bufalo marvelled, 'what's this? Have we turned into judges? This penalty...that penalty...the death penalty – enough said!'

In the end, even Bufalo fell into line. He trusted Freddo.

A few nights later, Freddo, Bufalo, Botola and Scrocchiazeppi tracked Saracca down in a gambling den in the Via dei Gelsomini. He was stinking drunk, and he welcomed them with a resounding belch. You could smell his stench from a long way off, and his beard was encrusted with nasty filth. With him were a couple of old acquaintances: the Bordini brothers. For an instant, it occurred to Freddo that behind the story of Angioletto and the unpaid shipment of cocaine – an enduring mystery if ever there was one – the answer might very well be none other than Saracca. There was that old rumour about the Bordini boys – a rumour that Botola had long tried to run to ground, without success. Still, when the four of them walked in, the Bordinis stepped aside after a quick nod hello to Botola. It was an elegant way of saying they had no dog in this fight. As for Saracca, Freddo asked him flat out to explain why he had offended them. Saracca responded with another belch and a nasty laugh.

'You want to know what I have against you all? Listen up and I'll tell you!'

Ever since they'd become a presence on the street, business was down for everyone. You were either with them or you were out of the picture. They had taken advantage of a particular situation, but their time wouldn't last. Rome wasn't about to let a bunch of raggedy-arsed newcomers like them rule the roost. The wind was shifting. There were more and more people like him who weren't afraid of their methods. No point in continuing to act like little Caesars: their fate was sealed. Soon, they'd go join those other pieces of shit in prison. Or maybe worse: end up in a shallow grave. Underground, where they'd sent that poor devil Terribile. Everyone in Rome knew that they'd done it. Only the judges seemed to have missed the point. But who gave a damn about judges? There were others who were ready to give them what they deserved!

'Oh, are we going to stand here listening to this idiot rave?'

Bufalo moved forward, threateningly. Saracca looked him up and down with enormous contempt through wine-reddened, blurry eyes, then he spat on him. Bufalo lunged at him. Under the impact, Saracca wobbled, folded over practically double, and collapsed onto the pool table. With Bufalo on top of him. Scrocchiazeppi did his best to separate them, and took a punch in the face from Bufalo for his trouble. Bufalo loosened his grip on Saracca and turned on his friend. Scrocchiazeppi was like a baby bird with both legs in the air, and with the violent fury that was driving him, Bufalo came close to putting Scrocchiazeppi into a coma. Freddo sounded the retreat.

A few minutes later, back in the car, Bufalo returned to the charge. Saracca had to die. And die now.

'That's not even open for discussion,' Freddo cut him off.

'Freddo, now you're busting my chops! If you're not up to it, I'll go do it myself. Alone!'

'Good thinking, Bufalo, good thinking. You go get your gun, hurry back to the bar, and shoot him down like a dog, ideally in front of the same witnesses who saw you having a fist fight with him an hour before...'

Bufalo sunk his head between his shoulders. Scrocchiazeppi, his cheek still aching from the blow, begged and implored Freddo to be lenient. Saracca had always been a good guy. Clearly he wasn't quite right in the head. He'd soon apologize for what he'd said. He'd ask forgiveness. Scrocchiazeppi would be in charge of the negotiations.

Freddo took his time before answering. While Saracca had been ranting and raving, he had realized that something wasn't quite right. It was just one more tiny signal to add to the others that he'd been gathering recently.

'For the moment, we're in a holding position. When Libano gets out, we'll decide.'

V

Nembo Kid, Libano and Ricotta were sprung in late March, with formal apologies from the court. Dandi, on the other hand, was screwed by an old conviction, nailed down, impervious to appeal: a violation of Article 80 of the traffic code, driving without a licence – practically an insult to an offender of his calibre. But driver's licences, passports and documents of all kinds would stop being a problem entirely, now that they had a deal with Zeta and Pigreco. The spies had come back to see them a few more times in Rebibbia. Nembo Kid had requested a little help for his old pal Turatello, who was having a hard time of things up in Milan. Zeta had suggested a name to turn to.

Nembo Kid and Donatella took a plane to Milan. Neither of them had ever flown before. At the Fiumicino boutique, Donatella bought her man new clothes, dressing him from head to foot. In designer clothes and a snugly knotted tie, Nembo Kid, who was tall and muscular, felt like an embalmed department store mannequin. But he fit in perfectly in the little piazza in front of the four-star hotel, which was teeming with smartly outfitted men with determined jawlines, a lot like Nero.

'Let Dandi be an example to you,' Donatella admonished him.

'Dandi's a fanatic.'

'You don't even know who we're going to pay a call on. At least dress up nice.'

'What do you mean, who "we're" going to pay a call on? You're not going anywhere. This isn't women's business, believe me.'

But Donatella, who was no longer the trusting soul she had been before what happened with the Colombian woman, followed him step by step through the city, in apartments, offices, restaurants, clubs and art galleries. Moving around Milan thrilled her at times, and depressed her at others. She saw shops offering boundless luxury, and it occurred to her that she could open something like that in Rome. She saw gleaming bars, and she made a chagrined mental comparison with the Full 80, which had once seemed like the top of the line but was actually, she could now see, a pathetic also-ran. She saw bony, highly toned women and noticed the ravenous hunger in their eyes as they mentally undressed the swaggering hunk walking at her side. She decided that it was time for her to start working out in a gym. She would try to rope in Patrizia as well.

She witnessed a furious shouting match between Nembo Kid and a middle-aged man with an unctuous manner, who kept calling him 'my dear friend' or '*carissimo*', and who claimed to be 'devastated' at the thought that he could 'make no further efforts' to resolve 'dear Francis's troubles with the law'. She saw Francis Turatello himself; actually it would be more accurate to say she caught a glimpse of him scurrying into the interview room at San Vittore with permits procured by the usual Zeta. An exuberant, overgrown boy, a bit of a pompous social climber, but handsome and, she could guess, an uncontrollable wildcat. Just like her own Nembo Kid, but with an extra dose of style. All things considered, she decided, it was better to hold on to what she had, walking freely on the street, in flesh and blood, than to yearn after her lost lover behind bars.

There was just one meeting from which she was excluded: a ceremony for men alone. Nembo came back late at night, grim-faced and furious. He told her nothing, and when she insisted on knowing more, he smacked her in the face. She wasn't the type to take that kind of treatment, and she responded by hurling a table lamp at him. It flew past his head and smashed against the wallpaper of the luxurious hotel suite. That was followed by screaming and tears, then savage lovemaking.

Just before falling asleep, while Nembo snored open-mouthed, his head resting on her breast, Donatella told herself that the life she'd chosen was the best of all possible lives.

In Rome, in the meantime, while Libano was trying to find the right words to explain to Freddo the whole story of the two police spics, a few of them met with Saracca in front of the porno film house on the Via Macerata.

He'd woken up from his binge, animal that he was, and now he was being all pious and holy. Kneeling at Bufalo's feet, he was begging for mercy. He'd been a lunatic to say all those things. He never meant them seriously. It was all on account of the wine, and a woman who wouldn't give him the time of day, and the racehorses that wouldn't come in the way he needed them. In other words, he had his excuses, or to put it the way the lawyers did: mitigating circumstances. He said he was willing to undergo any humiliation they cared to name: he'd crawl on all fours licking dog shit off the sidewalk the whole way to the Divino Amore sanctuary; he'd be glad to kill whoever they told him to, whenever they said; he'd give them his apartment, his wife, his children. Through a mask of tears, he was waving a wallet-sized photograph of two little kids with toothless grins, and sniffed and snorted worse than a lifelong coke-hound, and through his sobs emerged tattered snatches of ancient prayers.

What now? Bufalo thought with a mocking smile. Not only am I supposed to become a judge, but a saint too!'

'Okay, okay, we understand. Get up on your feet and let's just drop it,' Libano said.

Bufalo couldn't believe his ears. Are we really going to let this traitor go, just like that? Not even Saracca seemed able to believe it, and Scrocchiazeppi had to say it over and over again to him, until the idea seemed to penetrate his mind, and from tears of despair he moved on to tears of relief. In the end, just to get him out of their hair, they handed him over to Scrocchiazeppi, who was overjoyed at this unexpected turn. And since the two of them felt like spending a little time alone, Libano and Freddo dropped off Bufalo as well. He wouldn't stop grousing, incredulous about how it had turned out. They drove off to snort some coke in blessed peace on the beach at Castelporziano.

Not even when they were stretched out on the sand, faces turned to the icy sea breeze, did Libano find the courage to bring up the spies. They talked about this and they talked about that, but they never talked about the spies. They talked about the narcotics business, which was humming along nicely. About the gambling den, which was gone now, but which they'd be sure to start up again somewhere else. Freddo confided Nero's plans for laundering the proceeds from the bank robbery, and reported that contact had already been established with Secco. Libano insisted on the idea of buying the Climax Seven to give them a contractual base for their investments. Then Freddo lit a joint, took two deep drags, and while he was passing it over, Freddo said that Saracca needed to be eliminated at the earliest opportunity.

'He's nothing but a miserable loser!' Libano replied. 'Like the Gemito brothers! If you bark in his direction, he wets his pants. It would just be a waste of lead!'

'I told you before: it was a mistake to trust the Gemito boys. But Saracca is a whole different thing...'

'What thing, exactly?'

'To understand completely, you'd have had to be there that night in the bar, when he was raving deliriously. If you'd been there, you'd feel exactly the same way I do.'

'Fine, but I wasn't there. So tell me about it, why don't you?'

What had convinced Freddo were the eyes of the other guys present. Six or seven youngsters, all focused on the scene unfolding before them. Sorcio had already used a couple of them as ants before– kids who could be steered in this direction or that in the blink of an eye. Saracca was crazy, agreed. There was no one behind him, or even close to him. Fine. Still, when Saracca talked about them and Rome, and the fact that they were growing into a dictatorship of some kind, that everyone who was under their power was bound to rebel sooner or later... Well, Saracca had seen clearly on that point.

'Those guys were listening to what he had to say, and little by little he was bringing them around. You could see it in their eyes, Libano. They were on his side, they were with Saracca, and the only thing that was keeping them from moving was fear...'

'Fear's a good friend, Freddo,' Libano philosophized. The joint was working nicely, and the way that the far-off dots of the stars were starting to expand just made him want to laugh. He didn't know why, but he felt happy.

'That's right, fear. And that's exactly why we're going to have to ice Saracca. We want the others to taste that fear... Because if we don't, today it's Saracca, and tomorrow it'll be Jerk-Off or Coke-Snorter or Dick-in-the-Arse or whoever else... And we can't exactly forgive them all, can we?' Freddo said.

'All right then, let's take out Saracca. It'll hardly be the last time, no?'

'No,' Freddo shot back harshly. 'But afterwards, we need to tighten the reins.'

'Why should we do that? Business is booming...'

'There's a smell of loose ends in the air that I don't like, Libano. It's as if someone in our midst is already dreaming of being somewhere else...If it keeps up like this, we won't be able to go on controlling the street. We can't forgive everyone, but we can't murder the whole city of Rome just to prove our point, either!'

'Yeah, you're right. We need to take out Saracca.'

So, Libano thought, Freddo, on his own, had reached almost the same conclusions he had. If there was a time to speak, this was certainly it. But the joint had risen too powerfully into his head, and the stars were sparkling, almost intolerable to his sight. After Saracca there would be plenty of time for that conversation; and anyway, he just didn't feel like it. Nothing more to be said. And not even that night did Libano pour out his heart to his long-time friend.

VI

BEFORE ELIMINATING SARACCA, they waited for Nembo Kid to return and Dandi to be released from prison, because none of the gang members who'd been involved in the brawl on Via dei Gelsomini could take part. In fact, each of them was ordered to devise and implement a foolproof alibi.

When they told Dandi that the crew responsible for the hit would be made up of him, Ricotta, Fierolocchio and Nembo Kid, Dandi launched into a series of complaints. What the hell! He'd only just gotten out of that inferno of Rebibbia prison. Not even the time to take a nice forty-eight-hour holiday with Patrizia and they were already marching him back out onto the street! Why couldn't the Buffoni boys take care of it, or Trentadenari, or any of the new kids who were trying to make a name for themselves and were constantly buzzing around, eager to show off! Moreover, Nembo had brought him a gift from Milan, a baby puma named Alonzo. Ever since he'd heard the story about the lion that Epaminonda il Tebano had given to the politician, Dandi had got it into his head that owning a wild animal was somehow refined. Nembo accepted the gift of the oversized kitten from a banker's wife, one of those fur-coat-clad Milanese skinny bitches. Donatella had decided to feed it to the cougar once it was fully grown. Patrizia, with whom the puma cub had been left, raised hell when Alonzo lacerated a couple of love seats with his claws, unleashing panic among the girls. And so the puma wound up at Gina's house. When she saw it, she hugged it to her breast and burst into tears. Alonzo reminded her of the son she so desperately wanted but would never have.

'But I can't keep him in my place,' Dandi justified himself. 'There's no way...'

Because, ever since Professor Cervellone first put a copy of the *Protocols of Zion* in his hand, Dandi had turned into a book-hound. Not to read, of course. It was more a case of developing a yen for the rare and the antique. It was chic to fill the house with venerable tomes; even better if they had illuminated pages or some faded old nautical chart in Latin. So, because the puma chewed and chewed and chewed, and those books were worth a fortune, Dandi couldn't join the mission because he was too busy trying to find a new home for Alonzo!

When he heard the story, Bufalo snickered loudly.

'Dandi's turning middle class on us. Soon he'll be a faggot!'

Libano didn't feel like joking around. He took Dandi aside and, staring him in the eye, said to him: 'But if those other guys told you to do it – the two guys from Rebibbia – you'd be off like a shot, wouldn't you?'

Dandi gulped, visibly embarrassed.

'Anyway, it just means I'll go in your place.'

Dandi kowtowed and, without another word, went to withdraw the weapons.

To summon Saracca they used Scrocchiazeppi, who, even though he was in deep disagreement with the decision, went along with the general will. Scrocchiazeppi picked up Saracca along the way, taking care to avoid witnesses. As an excuse, he mentioned a nice little job with no complications. Poor Saracca let himself be led like a lamb to the slaughter without so much as a flicker of suspicion. Even when he saw Fierolocchio, Dandi, Nembo Kid and Ricotta standing in a row, smoking under the thirty-fifth bridge on the Laurentino, he walked towards them with a smile on his face.

Dandi fired the first shot, and Saracca fell to his knees with a look of disbelief: wait, what? Wasn't everything taken care of? Weren't we all friends again? Then, with a bullet each, the gangsters finished him off. They left the body there, under the bridge.

As for the others, Bufalo showed up at Trentadenari's front door whistling a tune and carrying a couple of hot pizzas and a bottle of ice-cold white. He stood thunderstruck when he realized that Vanessa had chosen that night of all nights to stick a pair of cuckold's horns on Sorcio's forehead. Trentadenari swung open the door with a pissed-off smirk. Behind him the living room/sex parlour reeked of marijuana smoke and the scent of a woman in heat. They finally decided to call Patrizia and have her send over a girl so Bufalo would have someone to share his pizzas with. No one knew what Libano got up to that night.

Freddo, on the other hand, tracked down Gigio in a little trattoria next door to the San Giovanni di Dio market. Word had gotten back to him that his little brother had found a girlfriend and he wanted to take a look at her. Roberta had curly blonde hair and was studying at the university. Her father had a job at City Hall. She told him that she was going to help Gigio pass his high school finals. Then she asked him what line of work he was in.

'Businessman,' Freddo replied, keeping it vague.

She didn't believe him, that was clear. All evening long, Roberta talked about herself, her projects, her life, speaking almost exclusively to Freddo. Gigio, a pale satellite of his brother, sat gazing at her with the adoring eyes of a dog, unaware that anything else was going on. The problem was that Freddo, the minute he'd laid eyes on her, had been lightning-struck by her impertinent blue eyes. As she reeled off one observation after another and smoked one cigarette after the other, what streamed through his mind were landscapes: green countryside, seascapes and other images he never thought formed part of his limited imagination. Something warm and taut seized him in the pit of his stomach and then sank lower down, deep into his crotch, every time she darted him a furtive smile or distractedly let her fingers brush his thigh in a fleeting caress. All the while, Gigio, affectionate and head-over-heels in love, eagerly pointed out how cool his brother was, how hip and together, how he'd solved family problems, how he'd built that huge mansion, practically with his own hands.

'But he doesn't live there; he's a loner!'

'Maybe,' Roberta insinuated flirtatiously, 'it's just that he hasn't found the right company to keep!'

'What are you talking about!' Gigio crowed eagerly. 'He can't keep the women off him, my big brother!'

'Sure,' Roberta went on, prodding, 'but what about the right woman?'

Freddo decided he'd had enough of this playacting. He paid the bill and begged off with some random excuse.

Before letting him go, Roberta held his hand a little too long between both of hers. Freddo found himself holding a small folded note with a tiny heart inset with a phone number.

Death of a Boss
1980

I

NOW FREDDO WAS living at the Pigneto, in a great big flat in the old apartment buildings erected for railroad workers, just a hop, skip and a jump away from the overpass crossing the old Via Casilina. Ziccone's construction crew had renovated the place for him, and if Freddo ever made up his mind to furnish the place, it really would look like a palace. But Freddo had no time to think about that kind of thing: he was happy with a sofa, a bed, a couple of chairs and a few table lamps picked up here and there.

Libano went to see him one evening in late June. Freddo was stretched out watching television with a young curly-headed blonde. Freddo introduced her as Roberta. She left after a few minutes, once Libano made it clear that the two men needed to talk alone.

Libano made himself comfortable. Streaming on the television screen was footage of the victims of the plane crash off Ustica. Libano was particularly struck by a legless corpse bobbing in the stunning blue waters of the Tyrrhenian Sea. Freddo switched off the set.

'If we're up for life without parole, what kind of sentence are they going to give those guys?'

'They said it was mechanical error.'

'Mechanical error, my ass…So who was she?'

'A girl.'

'Someone serious or just some girl?'

'Someone serious.'

Libano decided that the girl had flashed him a smile that promised nothing good, like a particularly sly whore. But he kept that thought to himself.

'We need to talk,' he said decisively.

'Trouble?'

Libano laid out one of the organizational charts that he periodically drew up to keep track of the gang's progress.

INVESTOR // HANDLER // RESULTS

Libano // Secco //

share Climax Seven;
share Sandy shop, Via dei Giubbonari;
share Cameo 700 shop, Via dei Coronari;
apartment Torretta (2);
Prenestina, office building (1);
villa and land, La Storta (1)

Dandi // Secco (via Libano) //

share Climax Seven;
share Sandy shop;
share Cameo 700 shop;
share Donna Chic boutique, Via dei Santi Quattro;
apartment Torretta (2);
Villa Olgiata (1)

Buffoni brothers // Ziccone //

loan sharking;
apartments Vitina (two, one per brother)

Fierolocchio // Ziccone //

loan sharking;
apartment Casalbruciato

Bufalo // Ziccone //

foundry La Malana (Grottarossa);
loan sharking;
share beauty shop Sabrina (Ostia);
foundry making a loss

Nembo Kid // Secco (via Libano) //   share Climax Seven;
                                       share Cameo 700;
                                       share Sandy;
                                       share Donna Chic;
                                       apartment Via della
                                       Bufalotta;
                                       apartments Via del Pellegrino
                                       (2);
                                       percentage of apartment
                                       (Donatella)

Botola // Secco (via Libano) //   share Climax;
                                       share Cameo;
                                       share Sandy;
                                       share Franco's bar;
                                       share Equal's carwash (Santa
                                       Maria Liberatrice);
                                       loan sharking;
                                       building in Via Bianchi;
                                       apartments in Via
                                       Dall'Ongaro (3)

Scrocchiazeppi // Secco (via Libano) // share Climax;
                                       share Cameo;
                                       share Sandy;
                                       share Franco's bar;
                                       loan sharking;
                                       apartments Lungotevere di
                                       Pietra Papa (3);
                                       Villa Olgiata

Trentadenari // Neapolitans //   apartment Via Como;
                                       ?

Sardo // Neapolitans   ?

Freddo // Secco //   money laundering;
                                       parents' apartment;
                                       Pigneto apartment

Nero // Secco //   money laundering;
                                       ?

Freddo handed back the sheet with a quizzical look.

'When what happened with Saracca was going down, you told me that there was a smell of loose ends in the air, that we needed to tighten the reins,' Libano said. 'Well, you were right!'

All you had to do was read the organizational chart, he explained, and you could see right away that there was a nasty split down the middle of the gang. The shit came in and went back out smooth as silk, business was humming along just fine, the operation was practically running on autopilot; everyone got the same share, and the shares were plentiful, generous for one and all. But things were different further down when you started looking at the category 'investments'.

Secco was moving the money in his own fashion. He had a bank CEO in his pocket and, after hours, he'd take over the man's office and do a little loan sharking for the clients whose loans were in arrears. When his victims failed to pay up, he quickly gobbled up their cars, homes, land and companies. The real deadbeats he left to the Buffoni brothers and certain gypsies that Secco relied on implicitly. There was nobody who really had nothing left to lose, Secco liked to say: in the end, you could always squeeze something out of anyone.

What with the steadily mounting flow of real estate holdings and financial liquidity, Dandi, Nembo, Botola, Libano and Scrocchiazeppi were growing to be an economic colossus. But the others? Bufalo was just making ends meet, guided by nothing more than gut instinct. Trentadenari was a mystery. Sardo, on the other hand, was of no particular concern because no matter what, once he got out of the insane asylum, his fate, short of some miracle, had already been sealed. But the rest of them? From Fierolocchio to the Buffoni boys and their various acolytes – the rest of them were a disaster! They squandered more money on women and drugs than they brought in at an evening's end. They were spending and bingeing without a thought for the future and it wouldn't be long before envy had seized them in its grip. They were travelling at two different speeds.

'I can smell bad shit getting ready to happen, Freddo. We've got to do something.'

'What do you have in mind?'

Libano laid out the proposal that he'd come up with during his long solitary evenings. The main problem was how to smooth out the differences. Otherwise, over the long term, this division between the rich and the poor would trigger hatred, feuds and vendettas. And one day they'd have a bloodbath on their hands.

'We can't touch the equal split. Every load of drugs we move, we each take our share and that's the way it is. But who says we can't do something about the investments?'

'Explain what you mean.'

No sooner said than done. The split would be paid out, but immediately afterwards, a substantial percentage – say, 70 or 75 per cent – would be collected by Libano and deposited with Secco for further investment. There would be another split of the profits from that investment, and the same clawback would be taken out of those profits. Here was an example: the shares of the Climax that were now in the hands of just a few would be redistributed to everyone. Everyone would have equal shares, in both income and outlay. And so on. It would be up to Secco to identify the most fruitful investments and cultivate his own personal specialty: moving money. Each new deal would be put on the floor for debate and discussion. If accepted, it would be managed according to those rules.

'So what are you saying? You want to put us on salary, Libano?'

'It's the only way to keep us united! Instead of letting everyone decide for themselves, we need to centralize operations...'

'What if someone wants to get out?'

'They can sell their shares, take the cash and piss it away however they see best. But in that case, the gang's obligations towards them are gone!'

'What do the others think about this?'

'You're the first, Freddo.'

'Why me of all people?'

'Because you and me think alike. We have the same head. Because we both think about the gang more than we do about ourselves. Because without us, the whole thing will fall apart...'

Freddo poured out two whiskeys and started rolling a joint. A couple of days ago he'd hooked up with Roberta, and now they were an item. He'd told her everything about his life. She had neither criticized nor supported him. She was fine with him just the way he was. He hadn't told Gigio yet, but his conscience was blistering him.

Libano was convinced of his proposal. Freddo told him it would never work.

'The others won't go for it. Nothing like this has ever been tried in Rome.'

'Sure, but there's never been a gang like ours, either...And yet here we are, and we're unstoppable!'

'As long as it lasts...'

'If we do it my way, it'll last forever.'

Freddo shook his head.

'And if we don't do it my way,' Libano prodded him, 'one of these days the whole castle of cards collapses...Bufalo, just as an example, starts to wonder why Dandi's living the high life while he's walking around town with patches on his pants. He ought to admit to himself that Dandi's a sly dog and he's an idiot, but it'll never occur to him. And since he's going to need to take it out on someone...'

'There could be another way forward,' Freddo said in an offhand voice. 'We could just shake hands and call it quits now...'

'That's not possible,' Libano retorted promptly.

And then he told him about the two spies.

'They know everything, and they're truly powerful. If we pull out now, they'll arse-rape us good!'

Freddo jumped to his feet and threw the whiskey glass against the wall. His fists clenched and eyes narrowed till they were angry slits. Libano had never seen him look so ravaged by anger.

'So now we're working for a boss! And what a boss! The Italian state! The filthy Italian state! Damn, Libano, you sold us out for a plate of beans!'

Libano tried to explain that that was not the way things were. There were no servants and no masters – only allies. Allies that were all the more valuable the greater the turnover their business was bringing in. The further they spread their reach, the greater their need of contacts, insurance and inside arrangements. Now it was no longer a matter of paying a crooked cop to get their hands on a rumpled copy of an arrest report. They were finally playing in the big leagues. And the arrangement with the two spies was a deal between peers. Just like with Uncle Carlo. I give something to you and you give something to me. They give us the office buildings, and we give them the street. That was all it was. What was the matter with that?

Freddo was gradually calming down. He returned to his seat and rolled another joint. But he lit it up and took a drag without offering it to his comrade first.

'Nice work, Libano! So you've put together a criminal gang, the Fascists, the Neapolitans, Cosa Nostra, and now spies for good measure… What'll you think of next?'

Caught off guard by Freddo's sarcasm, Libano waved his arms, snorting in exasperation. And with that gesture he seemed to be expressing two things, or at least that's what Freddo understood: that they could wrap their arms around the whole fucking world and take it for themselves; or that wondering 'what you'll think of next' was both stupid and pointless.

'If you come in on this,' Libano finally said, 'I'll turn this shack into a Ferrari!'

'Me?' Freddo laughed bitterly. 'It looks to me like you're getting a swelled head, Libano!'

Now it was Libano's turn to unleash a tirade of fury. Go on, Freddo, mock all you like! What the hell do you think? That he, Libano, had put together this whole complicated game so that he could wind up another penniless, shitty *borgataro*, just another two-bit street corner hoodlum? If he'd wanted to stay a miserable flea-bitten pauper for the rest of his life, he could have gone to work in a factory, or worse, finished school and gotten a pathetic office job, which, smart as he was, he would surely have found. But he wanted everything, he wanted nothing but the best, and this was finally the right time to take it! Stop now? Sheer idiocy! Stop now, and scrape by like any other freelance criminal from the outskirts of town! Stop now, and maybe take a bullet to the head from some freaked-out junkie as you walk out the door of a filthy down-at-the-heels gambling den! Freddo could have it, that brilliant future! Or had he lost his balls from hanging out with this new girl, Roberta? Was she the one who put those ideas in his head? Give up now? Retire now?

'Leave Roberta out of this,' Freddo said menacingly.

'Who wants anything to do with Roberta!' Libano shouted, and stormed out, slamming the door in a black temper. Freddo had lost his way? Fine: he'd take care of things on his own from now on.

IN MODENA, SCIALOJA had fallen into a state of lethargy. There were more Communists in Modena than in all the rest of Italy. There were more Ferraris in Modena than in all the rest of Italy. There were more junkies in Modena than in all the rest of Italy. Junkies on the Viale delle Rimembranze, junkies in front of the Teatro Storchi, junkies scattered the length of the ring road around the old city park, junkies hollow-cheeked and foul-smelling, hippie junkies with guitars and long beards, junkie chicks who'd give it away for twenty thousand lire, junkies drifting off into eternal sleep with a needle in their vein, sprawled out on a filthy piece of cardboard, just lying there in the morning crowd until the morgue wagon came to haul them away. Junkies, junkies, everywhere.

Scialoja dreamed about junkies at night. Drugs were the key to everything. Drugs were a money river that fed a crop of crime. Drugs were the perfect form of contemporary capital accumulation. Scialoja really owed the junkies of Modena a debt of gratitude. Because they were the ones who had opened his eyes to it. Now he knew what had become of the ransom from the baron's kidnapping. Libano's men had taken that money and used it to crowbar their way into the narcotics market, and now they controlled it. If you controlled the narcotics market, you controlled the city. And Libano's men controlled the city. Now he knew. But Rome was still off-limits.

Scialoja and Borgia hadn't exchanged a word since that unhappy morning when he'd turned his head away and said yes sir. Scialoja spent his days cleaning junkies off the streets of the opulent Red region of Emilia. In his lethargy, he hibernated and learned how to forget. He'd never be able to change the world. He'd never again lay eyes on that whore who drove him crazy. Scialoja was slithering into a beneficent narcosis. He devoured Langhirano prosciutto, *ciccioli fritti*, fried fatback, and *erbazzone*, a vegetable tart from the hills over Reggio Emilia. Between one emergency call and another, he got fat and catnapped. He'd bought an old second-hand streamlined Ducati. A colleague from Formiggine had souped-up the engine. He could make it down the Via Emilia from Modena to Bologna in seventeen minutes. To hell with the fog.

He lived in the police barracks. The piazza out front was lined with poplars. In the spring, the trees had started firing off their wind-borne seeds. The courtyard was carpeted with fluff. Scialoja woke up every morning with puffy eyes and a splitting headache. He'd met a girl. She'd actually picked him up as he was leaving a cinema. They were showing Louis Malle's *Atlantic City*. Her name was Marilena and she was a teacher in a voc-tech school. She said that she was a Christian Democrat. She said that anyone who'd been born in Modena or had lived there for more than six months wound up hating the Communists. She said that anyone who had enough brains to blow their nose either wound up in the parish church or would take to the mountains, like the partisans in the old days. She said that all you had to do was take a look around and you could see why the Red Brigades got started here, of all places.

On weekends they'd go dancing. They made love in her apartment, in the old centre of town. For years Marilena had gone to a fashionable psychoanalyst. She considered unnatural everything that struck him as imaginative. There was no thrill, no passion between them. Sex was turning into a form of calisthenics. Scialoja was beginning to give serious consideration to the idea of a fat, colourless future. He'd never change the world because the world didn't want to be changed. A submissive girlfriend, a steady routine at work: that was what destiny had decreed for him. So he might as well resign himself.

Scialoja was already dead inside when on 2 August his boss ordered him to put together a squad with three of his toughest men and two ambulances.

'A hot water heater must have blown up at the Bologna train station. It's a mess. General mobilization.'

Officially the theory of the boiler held up until nightfall, but there was no real doubt about what had happened by noon. In Scialoja's crew there was a non-commissioned officer who'd been in the army, where he'd served in an explosive ordnance disposal unit. He only had to take one look at the smoking crater before he shook his head and decreed:

'Hot water heater, my arse. This was a bomb.'

The station was gutted. Sirens wailed. Soldiers and volunteers, side by side with gauze masks over their noses, were digging through the rubble in search of signs of life. Some wept, most of them worked frantically, doing their best to postpone till later their appointment with their appalled rage. A television news crew pulled up. A crowd of horrified relatives stood lining the tracks. A miserable yet revealing word was beginning to circulate: massacre. The hands of the large clock overlooking the west platform were stopped at 10.25 – the hour at which Italy's heart had begun to bleed.

Scialoja decided he could stop for a cigarette. A busybody journalist was on him instantly. Scialoja told her to go to hell and raised the gauze mask over his face again. From deep beneath two shattered beams, which had miraculously landed one over the other to form a sort of natural cavity, came a faint lament. Scialoja rushed over. He saw a tiny hand covered with scratches. He gripped it, and then pulled. The beams remained in place. The little girl was in shock. But she was breathing. She looked up at him with huge stunned eyes and breathed. Scialoja took her in his arms and handed her to a nurse. The child was blonde, very blonde, and didn't understand Italian. A carabiniere officer in dress uniform called for him to halt.

'You! Hustle over to track one immediately. We need to organize a police escort for visiting authorities!'

Scialoja told him to go to hell just as he had the journalist and went back to work. He was torn and tattered, sweaty, foul-smelling. But he didn't even notice his exhaustion, he didn't feel his discomfort. He'd slept for too long. He was done hibernating. Like an animal, Scialoja followed the trail of an acrid mixture of dust and blood. He followed the deafening scent of death, in the absurd conviction that there were still victims to be rescued from the chemistry of decomposition, children to be restored to their mothers, shredded bodies to be reassembled. He rescued an old woman who was clutching a scorched rosary to her chest. He recovered a dismembered cadaver, recomposing the limbs in an act of pious mercy. He brushed shut the eyelids of an armless girl with bloodless pink lips. He kicked and chased off a stray dog that was nosing around curiously. In the darkness of night, he went on digging, hoping against all hope. The searchlights of the engineering corps illuminated the tortured, twisted steel, the lunar rocks of the ballast driven into the interior of the ravaged passenger cars, the shattered plate-glass windows of shops filled with debris, the scorched grass that the forensics technicians, with the cold light of their acetylene torches, were burning in search of traces of explosive.

At midnight, overwhelmed by pity, Scialoja stretched out on a track and lit his last cigarette. The night sky was clear and filled with stars. He felt a rough hand shake him.

'You're not allowed to be here. Show me your documents.'

Scialoja stood up and pulled his folded and creased identity card out of his pocket. The railroad cop scratched his head.

'My apologies, commissario. But I've been ordered to clear everyone out of this area.'

'What's up? Is President Pertini arriving?'

'I don't know, sir. That's what they told me to do and that's what I'm doing.'

Scialoja moved away a short distance, vanishing into the darkness. But he stuck around, his curiosity aroused. Three men showed up a few minutes later. Scialoja immediately recognized Zeta and Pigreco. With them was an elderly, corpulent man. Someone important, to judge from the respectful way the two spies treated him. Scialoja was too far away to be able to eavesdrop on their conversation. But there was no mistaking the general meaning. Zeta was waving his arms, making exaggerated gestures. The old man nodded his head, anything but convinced. Pigreco kept darting glances in all directions, looking worried. Zeta was doing his best to talk the old man into something. The old man wasn't going for it. Zeta was justifying himself. Zeta was in trouble. Scialoja thought how much fun it would be to step forward just then. Unholster his pistol and call out for them to freeze. Demand that these strangers identify themselves. Savour their alarm and annoyance. But facing off with them would be nothing more than a senseless act of bravado. The presence of men from the intelligence agencies on the site of the massacre was completely justified. They investigated: that's what they did. Still, he knew who these men were. He knew who protected them in Rome. Were they investigating to find out more or to keep others from finding out? Scialoja guessed at connections, conduits, detours and back channels down dark, dank, unhealthy alleyways. The enormity of the vista that opened out before his eyes was starting to make him tremble. Scialoja edged away and fled into the night. He wished he hadn't seen, but he had. His hibernation was over, the lethargy shaken off.

*

211

A few days later, while all the police forces of Europe were fielding a manhunt for a mysterious Bavarian Neo-Nazi group that the reports of the intelligence agencies had accused of the massacre, Scialoja put down his full confession, black ink on white paper, and mailed it to Judge Borgia. He was ready to return to Rome. He was ready to start up again from the point where his cowardice had brought him shuddering to a halt. He was ready to face the consequences. He trusted Borgia. It was only right for the other man to know everything. Scialoja mailed his letter and sat back to wait.

III

IT WASN'T LIBANO'S way to give up on an idea. There were no problems with Dandi, Nembo, Botola and Scrocchiazeppi because they were all on the same wavelength already. With the others, he had a series of one-on-one conversations, not as straightforward as he'd been with Freddo, skipping over the matter of the spies and doing his best to adapt the sermon to the psychology of each individual. Trentadenari stalled for time. Bufalo, after shaking his big head, took the whole month's split and went to hand it over to Secco. Fierolocchio and the Buffoni boys hemmed and hawed. Ricotta burst out laughing and told him to go to hell: it was his money and nobody else's, and he'd do what he wanted with it! Nero took the proposal seriously, and assured him that he'd want in on the real estate deal just as he soon as he'd ironed out 'certain wrinkles' in his business dealings in the autumn. Libano was starting to have a new appreciation for Nero – for his discretion, his decisive manner, his complete lack of arrogance. He asked him to put in a word for him with Freddo.

'I'll do my best. But Freddo isn't a guy who retraces his footsteps.'

The undecided ones also turned to Freddo, including Ricotta, who once again trotted out his obsessive idea of writing a letter to Sardo. And Freddo, loyal to his last nerve, told them that Libano was a real man, a guy with balls, but that everyone had to make up their own mind. Libano heard about it from Trentadenari, who had also guessed that the two bosses were having their disagreements:

212

'*Guaglio*,' he said in Neapolitan dialect, 'that guy is a true friend!'

Sure, they were friends, and they'd stay friends for the rest of their lives. Neither one was talking to the other, but they were both dying to. Neither one was willing to make the first overture. It was out of the question to reopen the argument, obviously. Still, the separation, after everything that they'd been through together, was hard on them both.

Freddo had finally confessed to Gigio about Roberta. His little brother had burst into tears in his arms, then he'd run away, but not before looking at him with the eyes of a helpless lamb. A despair that Freddo couldn't stand. He felt like an animal, plain and simple. He went to see Roberta, determined to tell her that they couldn't see each other again. They wound up in bed together. There was nothing to be done: fate had already chosen, for them all.

As for Libano, the harder he tried to keep a clear head when it came to business, the more he acted like a bastard towards the rest of the world. The spies had slipped a girl, a Cuban refugee, into his bed, and that had taken care of his abstinence issues. He'd never developed any fondness for her, and he didn't really give her the time of day: a few minutes for a fast fuck, and then he had places to go. Above all, no sharing of information. It was obvious that the young whore was there as an informant, so zipper open but lips sealed.

He'd caught the gambling fever again, and every night he lost heavily. It really seemed as if the cards themselves were missing the presence of a friend like Freddo.

At the end of July, at the Re di Picche, where it had all begun the night they made their plans to kidnap Baron Rosellini, he lost thirty-five million lire to Nicolino Gemito with a hand of three aces. But, since he hadn't liked the mocking grin with which his opponent had laid down a straight flush, he announced that he had no intention of paying.

'Ah, come on, Libano, it was just that kind of a night…They're things people say…'

'No, I'm not going to pay you. Not tonight, not ever!'

Because he was Libano, because he was Number One. Because no slimy weasel like Nicolino Gemito could tell him what to do and when to do it. Because if the Gemito brothers were still alive and on the street, they had him to thank for it – him and nobody else but him. His personal generosity. Therefore, they'd better not piss him off, or that generosity would soon be in damned short supply. And he'd better not hear a word from anyone in Rome about that unfortunate night, or he'd make sure that the gambling den was levelled, a fire the likes of which the city hadn't seen since Emperor Nero's time. Because he was Libano. He could do whatever he liked. One word from him was enough to open any and all doors. A crook of his finger and the Gemito brothers, their whores and their snot-nosed kids would all wind up laid out on slabs in the morgue, first thing.

If only, later that night, after his outburst, he'd had the good luck to bump into Freddo, perhaps Libano would have stopped to think. He might have patched things up with the Gemito brothers. He'd have even honoured the debt. If there was one thing that carried weight in Rome, it was Libano's word. But his noggin – after all that time running things, and keeping his mind focused, and calculating timing, moves and risks – had finally cracked. And there was no one to share with him the enormous weight of the whole huge contraption he'd assembled! Who dared to say a word to Libano? All the same, that's exactly what he needed to be told: stop right there!

If only he'd run into Freddo that night...

But Freddo had already been locked up at Regina Coeli for a week. He was driving with Nero when something as trivial as excess velocity on the Circonvallazione Clodia brought a motorway police car chasing after them, siren screaming. When the officers checked their identification cards, out came a series of priors, and the VW Golf was promptly and thoroughly searched. There was some dirty money in a briefcase slated to be handed over to Secco.

Judge Borgia rushed over to interview them that same evening. Freddo and Nero confessed to possession of marked notes; they claimed a Spaniard who was looking to unload the cash had given it to them. They were willing to plead guilty to receiving illegal goods, but were hauled up on armed robbery. Vasta, with his usual smile, guaranteed that they'd be out by September. Without solid evidence, the armed robbery charges would never stick.

In prison, they ran into Pischello, who'd been working out with weights. He'd beefed up, with a pair of shoulders a yard wide, and now he was eagerly expecting a special leave to attend his sister's wedding, who was getting married to a young journalist. The lower court had given him nine years. The defence strategy Bufalo had suggested seemed to have done him some good.

On 2 August, when word began to spread about the explosion at the Bologna train station, Nero reacted with a look of annoyance.

'So they finally did it!'

Freddo asked no questions. In order to be able to come see him on a regular basis, Roberta had signed an official statement of cohabitation. When her parents found out about it, they threw her out of the house. Patrizia offered to take her in. Freddo got a message to her: the instant she so much as tried to speak to his woman, she'd already be one dead whore.

They were punctually released on 14 September. While he was inside, Freddo had considered trying to write a letter to Libano, but then he hadn't been able to write two sentences that lined up to his satisfaction. But he'd made up his mind he'd go and see him.

He never had time.

They iced Libano the night of 15 September as he was leaving Franco's bar. The one who fired was riding pillion on the stolen motorcycle. A woman was driving; they found out later that it was a man with a wig. The first bullet hit Libano in the back. Stars ripped a hole in the dark, there was the foul smell of a puddle, and Libano understood he was a goner.

Before the death shot blew his carotid artery wide open, a tear ran down his cheek, half pain and half laughter. The last thing to go through his mind was his comrades: what would become of them without him?

PART TWO

Hubris, Dike, Oikos
1980–81

I

VENDETTA, THEY AGREED that same evening in Sorcio's shack. Merciless, absolute vendetta. But lucid, clear-eyed vendetta: the way that Libano had been lucid. Because all of them – including Bufalo, who was holding his big, old head in his hands; including Ricotta, for whom that day, along with the 2 November when Pasolini had been killed, was the worst day of his life – all of them were doing their best to think clearly and reason, just as Libano would have done if he were still alive. What's more, every one of them felt like they each had a little bit of Libano in them now. They spoke in low voices, with a barely controlled despair in their gestures – gestures that were almost hieratic in their rigidity. Even Nembo Kid, in his shiny black tracksuit, seemed a little less oafish than was customary for him. Even Trentadenari was sober and composed, suddenly having lost his impulse to banter and joke. And Scrocchiazeppi, who had served mass as a kid at the church in Via di Donna Olimpia, had brought an old rosary with him, and he sat telling the beads and muttering one senseless phrase after another – a death prayer that if the priest had heard it would have blasted Scrocchiazeppi straight to hell, *nunc et in aeternis*. And even the Buffoni brothers softly wept.

What was needed was an investigation. It was decided to assign Freddo to do it. But Freddo had already heard the news, and no one knew where he'd gone to brood over it.

Secco dropped by to express his condolences, with a couple of body-guards who waited outside the door. He put eyes, ears and information at their service – the least he could do, given their grief. Feccia, the one who had caused all that trouble during the kidnapping of Baron Rosellini, had been seen around town lately. And guess who was with him: Satana, that renegade!

'We'll see,' Nembo Kid cut him off.

Bufalo spat on the ground. That tip was certainly bogus. Secco probably had some grudge against Feccia and Satana, and was just looking for an excuse to get them out of the way. Secco never got his hands dirty. He didn't give a damn that Libano had been killed. That tub of lard had lire signs in his eyes, just like Scrooge McDuck. Not one of them agreed with him. Secco took Botola aside – the most reasonable member of the gang, after Dandi, he need hardly point out.

'Hey, Bo, there's a problem...'

'What kind of problem?'

'I mean to say...this might not be the right time but...as far as Libano's shares are concerned...the companies, I mean, our investments...'

Botola gave him a good, hard shove and went back to be with the others. Reasonable! He was no different than any of them. When it came to bloodshed, none of them were capable of thinking straight! As if there was anything anyone could do to bring Libano back to life, God rest his soul!

Secco squeezed into the BMW as one of his bodyguards courteously held the door open for him and the other hurried around to the driver's seat and slipped behind the wheel. Secco lit a cigar and allowed himself a relaxed smile. Well, he'd given it his best effort. No one would ever be able to accuse him of holding back. But so much the better. He'd tell them when the time was right. He'd choose his words carefully. If there was one thing Secco was good at, it was using words adroitly. Almost as good as he was with accounting. He practised the little speech he'd deliver to the others. Truth is, Libano lately just hadn't had his head screwed on straight. He was sending the whole operation hurtling straight to hell. Secco himself had been forced to step in to stave off disaster. It had been no easy matter to persuade him because, let's face it, there at the end, Libano's brain was really starting to misfire! In any case, they'd managed to work out an agreement...Secco could just see their astonished faces. He'd save the biggest bang for the finale: the simple fact was this – Libano had died penniless. Everything he'd had, from his shares to his bank accounts, everything, everything, everything, every last lira was now mine. Secco wasn't kidding himself. He wasn't powerful enough yet to be able to do without them. This wasn't the time to act greedy. He wanted them to know, and appreciate. He'd make a firm, straightforward speech: here are the accounting books. Go ahead and look them over. Everything that you see on these pages will be redistributed down to the last lira. Of course, minus my usual 10 per cent commission.

Secco prided himself on understanding the way men think. Secco was certain that if Libano were still alive, he would have asked him the one question to which there could be no answer:

'And what do you have to say about everything that's not written in the books?'

But Libano was gone now. And none of the others, at least for the moment, could have possibly formulated such a question. No one would ever know that half of Libano's cash had never even been entered into those account books.

'Stop here, I've got a thirst!'

Secco walked into Harry's Bar, mopping the sweat off his brow with a handkerchief. A maître d', or whatever he was, let a shade of worry darken his face, eyebrows twitching ever so slightly. Secco made a mental note: buy this shithole, prepare a reinforced concrete overcoat for that piece-of-shit busboy.

Freddo, in the meantime, had driven Nero up to the same place in Castelporziano where, in the spring, he and Libano had exchanged their first words of truth. He and Nero smoked one joint after another and drank from a bottle of champagne. But neither the hash nor the alcohol were revving him up. That cold lucidity, under those stars, was horrifying and nightmarish.

'A couple of years ago there was a poetry festival here,' Nero said. 'A hippie thing.'

'Oh yeah? What do you know about it?'

'I went to it.'

'I don't give a fuck about that, Nero.'

At any other time, Nero would have complied and remained silent. But there was something unhealthy about Freddo's black mood. Freddo felt guilty. He needed to make it clear to him that Libano had constructed his own fate for himself. That Libano had been a real man, even in the hour of his death.

'I had an affair with a leftist chick. A Jewess to boot, can you imagine? She knew all about karma, even if she hadn't really understood a thing. Deep down, we're not even all that different...A sweet fuck, in any case...'

'I don't feel like talking right now.'

'The freaks were all smoking dope and fucking. Up to that point, she said they had a pretty good time. Deep down, though, there's something sad about them. Unless they drop dead first, Papa's going to find them a nice job and...how do they put it? They'll get their head screwed on straight. There's the difference. We're going all the way to the end of the line. We're not going to die in our beds. We're going to die the way Libano did. But there's ways to die and ways to die. Libano got it wrong!'

'Leave me alone, Nero.'

Nero sighed.

'Libano was asking for it, Freddo.'

Freddo was about to lose his temper, then he saw the sad smile on Nero's thin lips and let it go.

'It was the Gemito brothers. For a miserable gambling debt; chump change. Libano was losing his mind, Freddo...'

Freddo grabbed a handful of wet sand and hurled it towards the sea. The wind tossed it back into his face. Freddo felt like sobbing.

'The warrior's tears pierce the stars,' murmured Nero, as if he'd read his mind, 'and they return to earth as drops of blood.'

Dandi arrived at the shack at two in the morning. He embraced them all, one by one, and told them that everything had been cleaned up at Libano's. The traces that could have interested the denizens of cop-land had all been made to vanish. Nembo Kid launched him a silent semaphore of glances, and Dandi nodded imperceptibly: Zeta and Pigreco had been duly informed.

II

THE OLD MAN dismissed Zeta with two dry phrases, handed the phone back to the maître d', and expressed his fervent apologies to Comrade Solomonov.

'Some problem?' the Russian asked affably.

'Hubris,' the Old Man sighed.

'Sorry?'

'Folly. The folly that the gods put into the head of those they wish to destroy. It's a story as old as mankind itself. Nothing serious, in any case. Shall we order?'

'With pleasure, *tovarishch!*'

Deep down, though, the Old Man was furious with Libano. He wouldn't tolerate defeats, much less disappointments. The agreement was off. With all his charisma, Libano hadn't been capable of crushing underfoot a few raggedy-arsed card players like the Gemito brothers. The others were of no interest whatsoever. So much wasted time. How unseemly.

The KGB resident, an Armenian with tiny, cunning eyes, had murmured a question that he hadn't been able to catch.

'Yes, of course,' he replied, as mechanically as one of his automatons.

The Russian stared at him in astonishment.

'Really, you already have a clear picture of who was behind the train station bombing?'

No, certainly not. Or yes, depending on your point of view. He shouldn't act is if he were too sure of himself. That could be an error. Or perhaps it was an advantage. Seeing how excited the Russian was, perhaps he should let him believe in yet another mystery cover-up on the part of the rotten-and-corrupt-pro-Yankee-Italian-democracy. The fact was that he was lost in thought. Hubris. Typical sin of human beings. The gods were immune to it. That's why he would never slip and fall.

'Well, whatever you may or may not know, I can assure you we had nothing to do with that operation!'

He nodded. Once he'd struck a deal with the Armenian, he'd evaluate the situation calmly and carefully. Perhaps, all things considered, there were still a couple of subjects he could salvage out of the wreckage. That would depend on the outcome of the all too foreseeable gang war that was about to be unleashed. Still, what an annoying waste: of time and energy!

Judge Borgia only heard about it twenty-fours after it happened. Until that moment everyone had underestimated the murder: how ironic, for someone as ambitious as Libano had been! The fact was, yesterday, a three-toed sloth of a colleague had had the night shift and he wasn't looking for trouble or excitement. That death in the Testaccio quarter lit up no synapses. The young lieutenant from Friuli, who was commanding the squadron of armed judicial police, was no wider awake. Borgia's eye happened to catch the news in a copy of that morning's *Il Messaggero* during an interval between hearings. He rushed right over to the district attorney of the Italian Republic and demanded men, resources, wiretaps, warrants – and free rein.

'There's a dangerous gang operating in Rome. Libano was one of the leaders, possibly *the* leader. Seeing that they basically rubbed him out on his own doorstep, it's one of two things: either someone's settling scores, or there's a rival gang on the rise!'

The district attorney, staring at him over his thick jurist lenses, demanded 'evidence – solid evidence'. Borgia, astonished, reminded him that this was precisely the job of the prosecuting magistrate: to seek out evidence. The district attorney offered him a cigarette and a very Neapolitan smile.

'In your opinion, what should we do?'

'I have a list of names. Some of them are definitely linked to Libano; others might be. Let's carpet-bomb them and search every address. We'll assign two or three men to tail each of them, day and night, and you'll see...'

'Sure, two or three men! Why don't we ask the FBI to lend us a few! If you ask me, there isn't much here!'

'But this is Mafia, Mr District Attorney!'

'Mafia, Mafia...in Rome! With all the problems we're having with terrorism, this one comes talking to me about the Mafia!'

'Oh, speaking of terrorism: did you know that Freddo and Nero were arrested together? A member of the gang and a terrorist...'

'Terrorist terrorist?'

'An extremist suspected of ties with terrorist fringe groups,' Borgia conceded.

'What sort of fringe groups?'

'Nazi-Fascists.'

'Ah, okay. Terrorists, whether Red or Black, are a danger to the stability of the state, but if you want to know the way I look at it...Fascism is dead and buried! And the Red Brigades are a hundred times bigger sons of bitches! In any case, that's our number one priority: to defend the stability of the state!'

'Libano was a gang boss. I'm afraid there's a bloodbath coming down the pike!'

The district attorney shrugged dismissively.

'Let's speak frankly: if a few miserable thugs feel like shooting each other in the streets...'

Borgia went back to his office in the throes of a dull rage. They were underestimating the threat. They were indifferent. Investigating magistrates were like bulls: they only charged when they saw red – especially with hammer and sickle. The rest meant nothing to them. He impulsively seized the receiver and dialled a number he should have called long ago, kicking himself for being an idiot. Why hadn't he done this before?

Three days later, Scialoja walked into the office. He came in with a cautious expression on his face, looking around warily. Borgia noticed that he was pale, puffy and demoralized, and he stifled a nasty snicker. Was he expecting a pair of carabinieri loaded for bear with an arrest warrant and a pair of handcuffs? Without inviting him to take a seat, Borgia tossed him a crumpled envelope. Scialoja recognized his own handwriting and shot him a worried glance.

'You can tear up that crap, commissario.'

'What are you saying?'

'Your girlfriend, Sandra Belli – the grand jury decided not to proceed. Lack of compelling evidence. The prosecution can't appeal. The intelligence agencies can't hassle you anymore.'

'I'm free!'

'That's right. Free and clear, dear heart!'

Scialoja fell from his state of ecstasy into a black fury when Borgia, sniggering under the threadbare moustache that he had stubbornly decided to cultivate to placate a whim of his wife's, informed him that he'd known Belli's case had been archived for at least a good month now.

'And you left me there stewing away all this time!'

Borgia said nothing. Scialoja needed to come to it on his own. He had to understand that he had no right to dump those damned conflicts of conscience of his on his judge's head. And at the very least, Scialoja owed him a little payback for the world of shit he'd put Borgia through during the days after he'd first read his confession. Days filled with doubts and nightmares. Days he'd much rather forget entirely, spent struggling with the thorn bush of clashing loyalties, to the state and the judiciary – loyalties that demanded that he indict Scialoja forthwith. And then there was the deep, personal conviction that Belli was nothing but a pretty idiot who was playing a game much bigger than herself; the spies were two creepy sons of bitches; and Scialoja was a brilliant mind with a single, cumbersome shortcoming – too much testosterone in his bloodstream. In the end, Borgia made up his mind to phone the colleague who was in charge of the investigation. To justify the acquittal of the suspected Red Brigades terrorist, his fellow prosecutor had pointed to the intrinsic weakness of the investigators' case. In times like these when, as far as Communist terrorists were concerned, suspicion was tantamount to cold certainty, it was clear to Borgia that he had every right to theorize that a certain influence on the decision had come from the presence of a thoroughbred racehorse of a lawyer and the pressure exerted by a powerful and well-to-do family with excellent contacts in the Vatican.

Whatever the case, now that Belli was out of harm's way, his first thought was to call Scialoja. Then he changed his mind. The policeman had in any case made a mistake. Was it an unforgivable mistake? Did he still need him? As magistrates liked to say in a jargon all their own, Borgia 'had put the matter in abeyance'. But it was Libano's death that had unknotted his lingering doubts. And now here they were, face to face. Shoulder to shoulder. Scialoja tried to say how sorry he was. Borgia stopped him with a single brusque gesture, thrusting into his hands a pink file containing the documentation concerning the killing of Libano.

226

III

CRAVATTARO LIVED IN a mansion on the Via Ardeatina: 17,000 square feet on three floors and a hundred acres of grounds. It had taken him less than eight months to pry it out of the clutches of a once-wealthy Jewish furrier, incapable of meeting interest payments of 275 per cent at thirty days. Newly installed in his palatial estate, he'd had a plaque engraved on the front gates: 'Villa Candy', named after the Italian brand of washing machines that had given him his start. A memento of the days when, before managing to claw his way up into the circles that matter, he'd been a washing machine salesman out in the old section of Monteverde. That's just the way Cravattaro was: a sentimental old softy. Two days after Libano's murder, he invited Dandi and Nembo Kid to a party at Villa Candy.

'Half of the Rome that counts is here,' he said, welcoming them at the door, 'and the ones who didn't show up can eat their hearts out!'

Dandi and Nembo Kid were in no mood for this. Libano's death still smarted and all that hilarity was an annoyance.

Wandering freely through the crowd of actresses, real estate developers, councilmen, provosts, lawyers, tax accountants, even a couple of judges – all the men trailing the requisite entourage of trophy sluts – was the guest of honour, the Maestro. He'd just become the proud father of a baby boy. He formed the centre of a small knot of enthusiasts, proudly waving a snapshot of the new mother, tired but happy. The newborn's face was purple and clenched.

'Danilo's the name. Like my father. Did you know that my father, down in Sicily, was so poor that there were weeks at a time when all we ate was fried prickly pears? It's the truth, I swear it! You want to know how to make them? You take prickly pear rinds – yes, that's right, the ones with thorns – and you parboil them, so the thorns fall off. Then you slice them into thin, thin ribbons, and then you roll them in flour and egg – you bread them, in other words. And after you fry them up, you put a sauce made of olive oil, vinegar, sugar, capers and, if you have them, sardines. But my father was so poor that we could only dream of sardines! Dandi, Nembo! My friends! Come, come see...'

Uncle Carlo arrived a little before midnight, guarded by an entourage of three gunsels dressed in dark suits. Cravattaro eagerly offered him the use of his own private study.

Dandi and Nembo Kid were ushered into a vast room with a mahogany writing desk and matching bookcases, cluttered with Caesar busts on pedestals, Persian carpets, canvases by various artists of the Neapolitan school, followers of Salvator Rosa, mirrors with solid-gold frames and antique folio editions with uncut pages, scattered here and there, perched on austere lecterns. Dandi, who'd been making progress in his aesthetic training, turned up his nose. Taken alone, they were all fine pieces, worth real money; but heaped up like that, at random, in that relatively confined space, they unmistakably revealed Cravattaro's lack of any true refinement – a gauche millionaire with the soul of a two-bit ghetto fence, a hanger-on for a gang of burglars. Uncle Carlo appreciated Dandi's sneer of distaste every bit as much as his tasteful attire. The boy was learning fast. As long as the life of a gentleman didn't sap his rude vigour! Nembo Kid, on the other hand, was born a thug and was bound to die a thug.

Uncle Carlo embraced the Maestro and offered his felicitations for the birth of a bouncing baby caruso, using the Sicilian term for boy.

'My father was an illiterate. I made it no farther than year three. My son Danilo will go to university in America, and someday he'll be an important man!'

Then Uncle Carlo expressed his condolences for Libano. Cravattaro uncorked a bottle of Krug Millésimé champagne and they all drank to the memory of their late friend. The Maestro said that they were pleased with the way business was coming along.

'But now we have other things to think about. We have a chance to make some investments in Sardinia. First-rate land, extremely profitable. A complicated configuration of holdings. We need fresh capital to support the operation. Uncle Carlo thinks we should bring you in on this deal. At first you'll be investing at your own risk, but in no more than six or seven months, the returns should begin to cover the principal. And cover it amply!'

'How much principal?' Dandi asked.

The Maestro named a figure. Dandi said that the sum was feasible. The Maestro said that an on-site inspection would be advisable. They could leave for the island the very next day.

'We can't leave Rome right now,' Nembo Kid murmured. 'Libano's death must be avenged!'

Uncle Carlo nodded.

'Vendetta is a noble sentiment. That's your concern – that's *cosa vostra*. The land in Sardinia is an important opportunity. It matters to me. And it's both your concern and our concern – *cosa vostra e cosa nostra*. Try to pay attention to both things. And pay close and careful attention!' he concluded, looking Dandi right in the eye.

For the others, though, vendetta was the only thing. The way Freddo saw it, vendetta should be the glue that Libano had been searching for with such tenacity. They should act, think, live and breathe for vendetta, as if they were all part of a single organism.

Before ten days were up, they had a complete picture of the situation.

The decision to eliminate Libano had been made at a meeting at the Re di Picche. All four of the Gemito brothers were present. They'd drawn lots to decide who would do the actual killing. One of the killers – the one disguised as a woman – was 'almost certainly' Nicolino Gemito. That identification rested on the physical description and the immediate motive: he was the one demanding money from poor dead Libano. The other man in the death squad must have been Saverio Solfatara, the crazy Sicilian. The description fitted him and there was one more unsettling detail that couldn't be overlooked: Solfatara was currently an inmate at the Castiglione delle Stiviere insane asylum. Officially declared insane, or partially insane, just like Sardo. But during the days in September that interested them – this information had been supplied by a new contact of Trentadenari's, a clerk in the Hall of Justice with a bad coke habit – Crazy Saverio had been given a fifteen-day leave for serious family matters. Now that they'd managed to identify the actual operative team, the death sentence still applied without distinction to the entire Gemito clan and all their hangers-on.

The first and most serious problem was how to track them down, the filthy traitors. The gambling dens that Libano, in his excessive, suicidal generosity, had given them to run were all shuttered. Their apartments were deserted, as were the love nests where they housed their various mistresses. The Gemitos themselves seemed to have vanished into thin air. Still, sooner or later, one of them would have to surface for air.

Nembo Kid suggested extreme measures.

'They might be gone, but their kids are still around. Why don't we grab a few of the little ones and see if they don't come out of their hidey-holes, the stinking rats!'

Bufalo scratched his big woolly head. Grab the kids – is that something Libano would have liked, an idea he would have endorsed? He wasn't comfortable with it, but he was just one vote. If the others voted for it…Nembo Kid was pushing for the idea, and Botola was with him. Vittorio Gemito, for instance, the youngest and the least fearsome of the four, had twin boys who regularly went swimming at a pool in Trastevere. They need only wait outside for them and shove them into a car, and then get word to whom it concerned that 'we're holding your tykes'.

'What if something goes wrong?' Fierolocchio butted in. 'What do we do then? Shoot them? Little kids?'

'They're all the same blood,' Nembo Kid said, cutting the discussion short. Every eye in the room swivelled to Freddo.

'It's not a good idea. Even if we do grab the little kids, the rats aren't going to budge out of hiding. We'd just be wasting energy and effort. The best thing is to bide our time…'

Nero, who wasn't at the meeting, instinctively took Freddo's side. There were sacrosanct codes of behaviour: leave women and children out of the fighting.

It was a time to wait, a time for patience, therefore. In the meantime, business had to be tended to. That's what Libano would have said. Freddo assigned Trentadenari and Dandi to handle regular operations. The others split up into small working teams. Anyone who had a sighting of one of the Gemito boys or the crazy Sicilian had full authorization to proceed.

IV

IT TOOK SCIALOJA two weeks to rule out the theory that someone was settling scores inside the gang. Fifteen days of stake-outs, informants and the fine craft of thinking things through. In the end, the story of the gambling debt and the Gemitos bobbed to the surface, and it looked obvious even to the district attorney that the hail of lead had flown from that direction. What they lacked, as usual, were witnesses, and the persons of interest were impossible to find.

Borgia was dreading the inevitable bloodbath that would break out any minute now. Scialoja was looking beyond. Of course, they were going to try to take revenge. But this wasn't Calabria or Palermo. Vendettas didn't last in Rome. Here tragedy had only limited room to manoeuvre. This was the Eternal City of the eternal human comedy. Sooner or later Libano's orphans were going to have to get back to work. Maybe some of them were already thinking in that direction, and were nurturing their vendetta with a hint of detachment.

By now, Scialoja felt as if he knew them. If there was a heart driving the quest for revenge, it could only belong to Freddo. What about Dandi? How far down that path would Dandi follow him? Dandi, who was grooming himself to be boss? Scialoja dreamed of pitting the two men against each other. He also wondered what had become of Libano's money, as Libano seemed to have died more or less penniless.

'Maybe he stripped himself naked like St Francis of Assisi,' Borgia said ironically.

'I'd like to find the poor man he enriched with his cloak…'

What really had happened to Libano's treasury? And just how did the intelligence agencies fit into all this? How to explain the link between Freddo and Nero? From whatever angle you lined up all the elements at play, the game was interwoven with a number of unpredictable wild cards. One thing was clear: Libano's death had derailed operations. It was time to hit them, and it was time to hit them hard. Right now.

Scialoja returned to the charge with the idea of a raid on the bordello. Borgia 'took it under advisement' with a mocking grin and an exhortation not to let his hormones push him off track. Scialoja took it with a certain bonhomie. In the end, Borgia was sure to let him have his way.

In the meantime, tragedy was beginning to be tinged with slapstick comedy, if not full-blown farce. What was this? Suddenly the Gemito brothers had become invulnerable? What, had old man Satan in person extended a leathery wing of protection over that clan of slap-happy gangsters?

*

Ricotta also dreamed about Satan. He was having a one-to-one with Libano, and at their feet lay Rome, the world's own head, *caput mundi*, eternal and immortal, and Old Nick spread his wings and let out a belly laugh.

'Hey, Libano, how do you like them apples?'

As if to say: you'd like things to go differently, but the fact is...

The first tip, a month after the funeral, came from Sciancato, a junkie that Sorcio used as a smack taster. If he overdosed – something that had already happened twice – then the shit was too pure, and they'd have to recalibrate the percentage of the cut.

'They're looking for coke for a party in Grottaferrata. They're all going to be there tonight.'

That afternoon, Freddo and Nero conducted an on-site inspection. The villa was isolated, surrounded by a fence, with a remote-controlled gate and closed-circuit surveillance cameras. Behind the fence you could hear dogs barking. Impossible to get inside. Across the street was a construction site. Freddo decided that they'd lay in ambush in a couple of cars by the construction hoardings. Headlights off. Catch them on their way out. They knew that Nicolino drove a fire-engine-red two-door coupe.

The crews of the two cars were: Freddo, Nero, the Buffoni boys and Bufalo in one car; Ricotta, Nembo Kid, Fierolocchio, Botola and Scrocchiazeppi in the other.

The first car they saw emerge from the gate, they laid down a hail of fire, peppering bodywork and car windows with bullets. They shouted and danced, firing sub-machine guns and revolvers in a transport of glee, Bufalo with tears running down his cheeks and a ninja sash around his forehead, all of them so carried away, so intoxicated by bloodlust, that it was not until Nero – the only one present who had kept his cool – actually tore the MAB pistol out of Nembo Kid's hands, that they realized that the occupants of the Volkswagen were not the hated brothers at all, but an unfortunate couple – a young man and woman who had nothing to do with their vendetta and whom nothing more than sheer filthy bad luck had guided into their line of fire.

The young couple miraculously survived. Ten days later, so did Pino Gemito, when Botola and Ricotta had him in their sights on the Via

Laurentina, after a long and patient stakeout. Blame it on Ricotta's Beretta, which chose the worst possible moment to go on strike, and on the target's agility: Pino Gemito got home that day with his skin intact after spinning a spectacular 180-degree turn befitting a professional racer.

Forty-eight hours later, in Vigna Murata, Nembo Kid, Botola and Dandi managed only to wound Vittorio Gemito in the arm. Botola fired too soon, and from too far away.

Too many bullets wasted, with insufficient results. Time was passing and nothing was getting done. The vendetta was in danger of withering on the vine. Bufalo was starting to be oppressed by a *basso continuo* of splitting headaches. There were nights when he felt like grabbing his gun and emptying it into the face of the first person he passed on the street, just to prove that he hadn't turned into a complete coward. But something had to go right one of these times!

Freddo was tense and preoccupied. The street was turning on him! The Maestro had sent word that Uncle Carlo's enthusiasm was starting to cool. Sardo was bombarding him with offensive letters: without Libano they were nothing but a herd of mental defectives. Luckily Sardo would be out soon and back in their midst. Then there'd be a change in tune!

But then other urgent business got in the way. The vendetta was withering away visibly by now.

On 23 November, an earthquake swept away half of southern Italy. Trentadenari was dry-washing his hands in hungry anticipation. The reconstruction pie was appetizing, to say the least. The dead – may they rest in peace – were dead, but there was a river of money to divvy up for at least twenty years, politicos permitting. Trentadenari checked in with Dandi, Nembo and Secco and then headed south on a reconnaissance tour. It would be helpful to get in touch with a few wise guys from the families with a well-established presence. A kilo of coke might be a nice way of paying one's respects.

Cutolo's time was over. He said he'd 'chosen to return' behind bars. Actually, they'd caught him, and his sister Rosetta, who had taken over for him and was running the family business, as well as quickly becoming a lightning rod for the collective hatred of all the old and the new Camorra.

A few days later, Surtano, a young man from a good family who'd gambled away his inheritance back in the days of the actor Bontempi, sold out Tommaso Gemito in exchange for liquidation of a forty-million lire debt. This pipsqueak Surtano played cards in a gambling den up in Monte Mario every Friday, until well past four in the morning. This time they pulled out all the stops: three cars, sub-machine guns and hand grenades. They left Tommaso for dead in a pool of blood.

Not even this deployment of force was sufficient. It was fate. On the evening news they reported that 'the notorious leader of an underworld clan in the capital' had 'miraculously survived an ambush probably laid by members of a rival gang.'

One December evening, Dandi invited them all to come see his new apartment in Campo de' Fiori. Patrizia had hired a very popular interior decorator. The place was brimming over with Guttuso hookers, Bukhara carpets, oversized metaphysical heads and vintage books. Bufalo wandered around, respectful but a little stumped by the display of luxury. Little Alonzo, who was growing up fat, happy and snarly, now occupied a small cage with all modern conveniences.

Freddo finally made it out the door at midnight. Dandi had just raised a toast to the memory of John Lennon. If he'd stayed in that apartment even one minute longer, he knew he'd take Dandi's whole collection of canvases by famous artists and smash it right over his head. It couldn't go on like this. Everything was shrivelling up and dying in his hands. Freddo could feel the burden of failure, the crushing pressure of isolation, the icy caress of indifference. It was as if they'd already forgotten Libano. It wasn't the street that had turned on them; if anything, they had turned their backs on the street.

That night, a small squad of cops under Scialoja's command raided the bordello on Piazza dei Mercanti. Patrizia wasn't there. They arrested her the following morning as she emerged, festooned with shopping bags, from the Nazareno Gabrielli boutique. With a contemptuous smile, she asked the officer, as he was reading her her rights, if he wouldn't mind holding one of her heavier bags.

V

THE MATRON ORDERED her to strip down. Patrizia took off her Basile skirt suit and stood there in her underwear. The matron lost her patience.

'Strip down, I said. Everything.'

Now Patrizia was stark naked. The matron told her to bend over and grab her ankles. Patrizia complied. The matron slipped on a pair of gloves and proceeded with a cavity search. Patrizia closed her eyes and decided that, all things considered, it wasn't all that different from working with her regular clientele. The matron did her duty: conscientiously, but without overdoing it.

'She's clean,' she said finally, to someone who must have been watching through the one-way glass, adding, 'you can get dressed now, ma'am,' in a courteous tone of voice.

Patrizia opened her eyes again and thanked her with a quick curt nod of the head. Her customers never called her ma'am.

They assigned her a blanket and put her in a cell with a couple of junkie chicks and a bottle blonde covered with a dense welter of tattoos. She walked in without a word to anyone and went straight to the bed that would be hers: an old, stiff bedframe screwed to the floor, just a few steps away from the microscopic cubicle that served as a bathroom. The cell reeked of dirty linen, coffee grounds and curdled milk. The junkies were whining in low voices. Patrizia stretched out on the bed, turned her face to the wall and fell asleep.

The rough grab of a hand shoved between her thighs woke her up again. Patrizia shoved the intruder away and sat bolt upright. The smile of the bottle blonde revealed rotten teeth and a strong gust of garlic.

'Try it again and I'll claw your eyes out.'

The fake blonde laughed. A small jagged shard of glass had suddenly appeared in her hand. Patrizia let fly with a kick. The fake blonde lost her balance. The shard of glass flew across the cell. Patrizia lunged for it. The fake blonde was struggling to her feet. Patrizia knew it would be easy to grab her from behind. Yank her head back and cut her throat from ear to ear. She felt a deep urge to do exactly that. The two junkies had their arms wrapped around each other, quaking with fear. The fake blonde spat on the ground.

'You're a dead woman. Just tell me your name, so I'll know what to call you after I've killed you.'

Patrizia told her. The fake blonde turned pale. She spat on the floor again and then held her head in her hands.

'Fuck, Dandi's woman!'

'Does that change things?' Patrizia asked, brandishing the jagged piece of glass. The fake blonde begged forgiveness.

'I didn't know! Christ on a cross, I swear I had no idea who you were. This place plays funny tricks on you, Patrizia. I can call you Patrizia, right? Forgive me, forgive me! Look out for those two.' She nodded her head at the other two junkies. 'They're the warden's spies. You just got here, right? Well, you should ask to be put in solitary confinement. In fact, now that I think about it, you shouldn't be here at all. You need to be in solitary confinement! They put you here because they were hoping that—'

'Shut up, I want to get some sleep.'

Patrizia went back to her bed. She turned her face to the wall again. But sleep wouldn't come. She was still clutching the jagged piece of glass as if it were one of her plush toys. She couldn't get to sleep without them. If only there was a man lying beside her…Even Dandi. She needed to just turn over and not think about it. Hold tight to her teddy bear and stop thinking. Behind her, the junkie chicks were chatting quietly. The fake blonde was snoring.

In the corridor outside, the guards were pacing back and forth. Every so often a guard would open the peephole and look into the cell. Her sadistic neighbours were banging on their bars, for no reason other than to wake up the sleeping prisoners. A little before dawn they brought in a newbie. Another junkie chick. Completely stoned. Practically a little girl, with a sweet round face and stark, staring eyes. Unbelievably, they'd let her keep her jewellery. The newbie was sobbing and kicking. She grabbed hold of a guard, begging him not to leave her, screaming for them to call her father. The guard roughly shoved her away and slammed the door. The junkie went on crying. The fake blonde made her move. Patrizia stopped her cold with a quick, hard glance. Then she went over to the new girl and started stroking her hair. The girl stopped screaming. Now her whole body was trembling. She smelled of rancid sweat and cheap perfume. She slowly calmed down. Patrizia escorted the girl to her own bed and waited until she'd fallen asleep. The fake blonde and the two others stared at her in disbelief. Patrizia asked for a cigarette. The fake blonde rushed over to offer a rumpled pack of Marlboros.

'What's your name?'

'Ines. Ines Rapino. But everyone calls me Ines del Trullo.'

'Well, listen carefully, Ines: you see this one, the new prisoner?'

'Yes.'

'If anything happens to her, I'll cut your throat. Have I made myself clear?'

In the morning, the warden told Patrizia that she would be placed in isolated confinement. He asked whether she'd been molested by the other convicts. Patrizia flashed her most seductive smile, crossed her legs, and told him that she'd been perfectly comfortable with her new circle of girlfriends. The warden dismissed her, nonplussed by her chilly calm.

They kept her on ice for a while and then, the instant the regulation forty-eight-hour time period was up, she found herself meeting with the judge and Vasta in the conference room. The cop, Scialoja, was there too. Pale as a corpse. Patrizia thought it would be fun to walk right up to him. Ask him, in the tone of a grand matron, *'Ciao, caro, come stai?* Have those nasty love bites and scratch marks I left all over you the last time we fucked healed up?' Then, just to complete the effect, a big fat kiss on the lips. But there was a mirror in the conference room. Patrizia noticed the grease stains on her jacket, her rumpled skirt, the runs in her tights. Her hair was a mess. She needed a nice long shower and a good spray of deodorant. She was on the verge of looking like a pathetic, threadbare streetwalker. She just shook Vasta's hand and sat down next to the lawyer with a sigh. She was obviously a wreck.

Scialoja felt sorry for her, along with a hint of remorse. He was using her to get at Dandi and the others. He'd always been using her. That had been his plan from the very beginning. But what about now?

Borgia cleared his throat.

'Let me advise you that you have the right not to respond.'

'I'll respond,' she said in a low voice, before Vasta could get out a word. 'I don't have anything to hide…'

'We'll see about that,' replied the judge.

Borgia was tough, but courteous. Unyielding, but with a hint of irony. Immune to any form of seduction, much less now that Patrizia was reduced to a shadow of her former self after her first two days in lock-up. The judge was asking her about the bordello, but it was obvious that the last thing on his mind was sex. All of them were there in some sort of sarcastic fiction. By proxy. Borgia because the cop was behind him. Patrizia because she was Dandi's woman. Vasta because he was Dandi's eyes and ears.

Vasta objected, discoursed, hindered: indifferent, just like the others, about what happened to Patrizia. Borgia took a good solid hour to lead up to the question that mattered most to him.

'You are the owner of a building used as a whorehouse. The investigating magistrate is interested in knowing how you came into possession of that building. Where did you get the money? Who gave it to you?'

'A girl has plenty of resources.'

'I have no doubt, Signorina Vallesi. The thing is, though, that even if we reckon – generously – a dozen daily services of the kind that is customary in these cases...'

'Are you talking about turning tricks?'

'In other words, you know what I'm talking about! I mean to say, even if you had all the...work that was humanly possible for a person to do, that still wouldn't account for the initial investment...'

Vasta lodged an objection: the prosecuting magistrate's questions were outside the bounds of inquiry indicated by the charges. Once again, he felt it was his duty to advise his client to remain silent. Patrizia ignored him.

'Let's just say that I had a little help from my friends.'

'Which friends?'

'Generous friends.'

'Friends like Dandi? Like Libano? Like Freddo? Like Secco? Like the secret agents from the intelligence agencies who regularly frequented Piazza dei Mercanti?'

Vasta raised his voice. Patrizia silenced him with a brusque gesture.

'Secret agents from the intelligence agencies? And what if they were? When I go to bed with someone, it's not like I ask to see their badge. As far as that goes, I've gone to bed with politicians, journalists, football players, writers…even cops!' she concluded with a sarcastic smile.

Vasta waved the papers he had in front of him, slammed a fist down on the table, started in on one of the theatrical productions that had made him so well known at the Hall of Justice. Now this was going too far! They were violating with reckless abandon certain core constitutional principles, not only those of his client! He felt obliged to remind the prosecution that the Merlin law does not punish those who frequent houses of ill repute, nor the women who freely engage in prostitution there. The law punishes only those who batten illicitly off the prostitution of others. Which, in the case in point, was not at issue. Therefore…

'All right, let's go take a little walk, and maybe we can get our tempers back under control!' Borgia snapped. He locked arms with Vasta and, indifferent to his objections, dragged him out of the interview room. Scialoja and Patrizia remained behind. She crossed her legs.

'I'm sorry,' he murmured.

'Give me a cigarette.'

'You're out of luck. I've started smoking these,' he replied, pulling a pack of Tuscan cigars out of his pocket.

'I'll make do. Give me one of those.'

Scialoja lit a cigar and handed it to her. She took a couple of puffs, turned red in the face, choked back a coughing fit and swallowed the smoke, clenched her fists, and then took another drag.

'I can get you out of here, tomorrow if you like,' he insinuated.

'Bullshit. Your judge won't let me go that easy.'

'Trust me. I promised you I'd shut down your bordello. I did what I said, didn't I?'

'What would I have to do?'

'Talk.'

'About what? The weather? Football? The things men like to have the girls of Piazza dei Mercanti do to them?'

'We could start with the room equipped with hidden microphones and one-way mirrors…'

'There are guys who like to watch, and there are guys who like to listen…'

'Sure, with a couple of spies like Zeta and Pigreco in circulation! This is serious business, Patrizia. You can't even begin to imagine...'

'No, you're the one who can't even imagine, my darling young turd!'

'Talk to me about the organization. About the boys. About Dandi. About the vendetta for Libano's murder. This is your chance to get rid of them all. All of them at once, Patrizia!'

'And who told you I want to get rid of them?'

'One time you told me that if I could shut this place down, you'd marry me...'

'I must have been drunk!'

'Or maybe you were just telling the truth.'

'I always tell the truth.'

She crushed the cigar under her heel and stood up. He got up too. They were standing close together. The smell of tobacco barely sufficed to conceal the smell of her weary exhaustion. Scialoja could tell she was weakened, but not resigned. He reached out a hand to caress her. She grabbed his wrist. A powerful grip. Her fingernails dug into his skin. With her left hand, Patrizia let fly a violent slap in the face. Scialoja recoiled. She began pounding on the door of the little room.

'Guard! I want to go back to my cell! Guard! Guard! Guard!'

Scialoja sat back down, stunned. Someone opened the door. Vasta and Borgia were walking slowly down the hall towards them. Patrizia turned to look at him and dedicated to him, and to him alone, her nastiest laugh.

VI

WHEN DANDI, EYES bulging out of his head, went to tell them face to face that they were a couple of overgrown babies, a couple of dickheads, a couple of arseholes, Zeta and Pigreco took the verbal assault with a shrug.

'What can we do about it? That cop is crazy!'

'We did our best to dissuade him, but he's completely out of control!'

'Protection my arse! Our deal is off, you two!'

'Do as you think best.'

'Right, as you think best.'

If he'd figured he had them over a barrel, or at least hoped to chip away at their emotions, Dandi had figured wrong.

Not to say that Zeta and Pigreco themselves hadn't experienced a certain discomfort where the sun didn't shine. Still, the truth was that the Old Man had issued orders: cut off, root and branch. Libano's murder had come as a disappointment to him. It would seem that now Freddo had seized the reins of the gang, but Freddo was a stray mutt, a feral street dog fixated on revenge. Certain sophisticated alchemistic formulae that were essential to keeping the great game turning seemed to have eluded him. Freddo was a waste of time. Maybe, further down the road, it might be possible to do something with Nembo Kid and Dandi. Too bad about the bordello: that was a write-off. They'd have to start over somewhere else. The important thing was to make sure that Patrizia didn't let slip any unfortunate indiscretions. The Old Man felt sure that the whore would keep her mouth shut. He had a hunch she'd tough it out. And she'd get her reward at the proper time. The great game was all a question of seizing the moment. There were times when the Old Man thought that it must all be written down in a big book somewhere, in the possession of who knows what deity, who knows where. Everything, down to the last detail. Even the death of Libano. Even the relentless itch of some idealistic cop. Everything, and especially the fact that there were individuals destined never to seize that perfect moment. Whatever the case, the order was clear: retrench. Cut off, root and branch, and retrench.

Dandi didn't have a lot more luck with the boys. Freddo, Nero and the others couldn't care less about Patrizia's fate. In fact, Freddo threw her familiarity with the spies in Dandi's face.

'But they were Libano's friends,' Dandi tried to justify himself.

'This isn't the first time we've found out that Libano trusted the wrong sort of people.'

'It was a mistake, Freddo. It could happen to anyone.'

'It wasn't a mistake. Those two are a con game. Politics is a con game. All it would take is one cop with a pair of balls and we'd be flat-arsed on the sidewalk. And then where would your protectors be, eh?'

No, with Freddo it was full speed ahead. He had only one thing in mind: revenge. Revenge and nothing else. But the whole topic of the cop with balls had left its mark. This Scialoja: just what were he and Borgia up to? What game were they playing? They'd got it into their heads that they could save Rome! You couldn't get close to them the way you could the coke-snorting clerks in the Hall of Justice. You couldn't pay them off the way you could good old Fabio Santini. These were a different kind of men. In a word, men with a pair of balls on them. Freddo was right. Dandi had sensed a certain hint of admiration in his voice. But admiring your enemy was just a kind of twisted way of admitting that you had a shortcoming of your own.

The logic struck Dandi as unmistakable, plain as day. Scialoja had shut down the bordello. The bordello was under Dandi. Scialoja beats Dandi one-nothing. Scialoja snickers. Dandi eats his heart out. Scialoja's up. Dandi's down. It was a simply matter of pride and honour, in other words. Dandi wondered whether it was time to think of getting physical. He mentioned the thought to Uncle Carlo, one night when he and the Maestro were roasting a kid goat in the garden of the new villa in Zagarolo that Uncle Carlo had purchased for cash, passing himself off as a wealthy retired engineer. Uncle Carlo issued an ironclad preamble: this was Dandi's business and he couldn't and didn't want to interfere. But he was in an especially good mood because he'd just taken part in person in the killing of certain pieces of shit from Porta Nuova in Palermo, and so he was willing to offer a little advice, free of charge. Just to make it clear to him – it was time he started to learn, the way a man of honour thinks about things.

'*Primo: storia di pulle è.* It's a big hot mess, with whores. *E gli uomini d'onore con le pulle non si devono mischiare, tranne che per ficcarisilli.* The only thing men of honour should do with whores is fuck them. *Sgubbàricci picciuli è cosa da infami.* Making money off whores is disgraceful. *E noi non siamo infami, siamo persone oneste!* We're upright citizens, after all.'

'You can take them to bed,' the Maestro translated, noticing Dandi's quizzical glance, 'but you can't exploit them.'

The Sicilian went on: '*Secondo: alle migne non si spara.* You don't shoot cops. *E non perché non se lo meritano, perché cornuti e sbirri sono, e cornuti e sbirri restano, ma perché una migna morta porta più danno che una viva*...Not because they don't deserve it, cuckold flatfeet that they are, but because a dead cop's a lot worse trouble than a live one.'

'You can't shoot at a cop unless you have broad shoulders and plenty of protection where it counts,' the Maestro summarized.

'Giusto!' went on Uncle Carlo. '*Right! È un cacamento di minchia di quelli allucinanti.* It's a tremendous pain in the arse. *Macari, è megghiu accattarisillo che astutarici la luce.* Maybe it's better to buy him than to put out his lights...'

'You could try to bribe him, maybe,' the Maestro suggested.

'Out of the question. He's a clean cop,' Dandi explained. Uncle Carlo nodded.

'*In tal caso...ragionamento da cristiano buono, da persona seria è: mettere tragedia 'n capu 'a migna, tipo che voleva soldi dalla buttana, e cunsumaricci famigghia e travagghiu. Accussì si leva 'u viziu e ci va a cacare la minchia in Sardegna!*' The right thing for a good Christian to do, Uncle Carlo implied in thick dialect, was to ruin the cop, defame him, frame him, deprive him of family and profession.

'Smear him with shit,' the Maestro translated.

'He's thick as thieves with the magistrate...' Dandi complained. To Uncle Carlo, who was enjoying the roast kid goat and the Rosso Grave dell'Etna with a shrug, the matter was settled. But Dandi wouldn't give in.

'It's a matter of principle with me!'

Uncle Carlo grew irritated.

'*Ma chistu cchi voli?* What does this one want? The Trojan war?'

The conversation was taking an ugly turn. The Maestro intervened. Rome wasn't Sicily. There were other variants that needed to be taken into account.

'What the fuck are you talking about?'

'Dandi's specific gravity within his organization. Unless he does something, he'll look like a dickhead.'

'Aahh! A matter of saving face! That's something I understand!'

Uncle Carlo re-examined the matter. Perhaps it was possible to offer a little satisfaction. This matter absolutely could not interfere with business.

'Shooting is out of the question. We're Christians, you have to keep that in mind. It doesn't matter that we get into the business, that we're...how do you say it up here...pimps. Real Christians, they leave this kind of talk for the con artists, people that talk as if they were holier than thou, but are only good to clean the cells of the good people in the world. And for as long as the world has existed, a smart man has nothing to do with these things, with these tragedies. It's women's business, and woman are good for one thing and one thing only – on their back, spread-eagled, or else cooking at the stove! But tell me: who's the owner of the bordello? You?'

'No. Patrizia's the owner.'

'Do you have your own money invested?'

'No. The initial debt has been repaid in full.'

'*E a te che minchia te ne fotte! Tanto, lo sappiamo bene, pigghia e si 'nni grapi 'n'autra, che le buttane c'hanno lo sticchio freddo e basta!*'

This time, no translation was needed. It had been a concentrate of vitriol and arrogance. Clearly, there was only one way forward – he had to dump Patrizia. Dandi heaved a sigh of relief. The authoritative advice of Uncle Carlo relieved him of all responsibility. Patrizia would understand. She was a smart woman. All the same, a dull, worrisome background hum kept echoing in his ears. Intelligent as she might be, Patrizia was still a woman. He'd need to talk to her. But Vasta had forbidden any and all contact. Soon they'd be questioned. As long as they both said as little as possible, the whole thing would just deflate and go away. Only one warning: don't overdo it with the sarcasm. This time, after all, they were just witnesses.

The lawyer had been right, down to the last detail. Borgia was depressed. Scialoja was doing everything he could think of, but drawing a line between the whorehouse and the gang was something that even Torquemada couldn't have pulled off.

Nero was questioned, and he inflicted on his questioners a philippic on the physiological needs of the warrior and the Kundalini technique of semen retention.

Bufalo grunted out a dispiriting sequence of I-don't-remembers and I-have-a-headaches, assisted by a tame physician and equipped with a stack of certificates stamped by an excessive number of medical luminaries.

Secco suggested that he might have been helping a girlfriend who was in trouble, at the request of another friend who was a friend, in turn, of another friend. And in any case, his intervention had been limited to a guarantee for a third party. After all, what could he do if the name of Secco was respected throughout Rome, if every day crowds of poor unfortunates turned to him for help....

Fierolocchio boasted that he could do it six times without stopping, and then hastened to add: but strictly as a paying customer, eh, strictly as a customer!

Freddo considered the mere association of his name to a house of prostitution as a mortal affront. Scialoja prodded him: did he know that there were spies operating in Piazza dei Mercanti? What would Libano have said about this tawdry scene? When he heard the name of his dead friend being taken in vain, Freddo had a hard time regaining control of himself. Scialoja felt he'd come close to Freddo's heart. Faithfulness and loyalty meant everything to him. Scialoja desperately tried to leap into the opening.

'People like that use you, then they dump you. If you're lucky, you wind up sitting in a jail cell, otherwise you're likely to come in handy as a target for a little shooting practice... They make promise after promise, but they're only really good at taking...'

Freddo stared at him with his intense gaze, brow furrowed. Once he'd been a clean, straight youngster, thought Scialoja. I wonder what twisted him. I wonder if he could ever turn back. In the end, Freddo managed to pass it off with a shrug of the shoulders. The magic moment was over. Or maybe it had come too early.

Of course, Scialoja interviewed Dandi. And Dandi, triple Judas that he was, confessed to an 'occasional frequentation of said Vallesi, Cinzia', and begged and implored: please keep this fact, this relationship, hidden from my beloved and devoted spouse. It would just kill her, poor little lamb... There was no mistaking the fact that Freddo and Dandi were two very different individuals. That a split was sure to develop soon. But what about Patrizia? Which side was Patrizia on?

'They sold you out,' Scialoja informed her, handing her Dandi's transcript.

She sketched an obscene Your Honour the judge on the back of the photocopy, with distinctive protuberances and moustache, folded it into a paper airplane, and flew it right into his face.

'You're going to pay the price, and the rest of them are going to get away scot-free,' Scialoja kept prodding.

Patrizia asked to be taken back to her cell.

They saved the spies for last. In the bordello they'd found a room that had been soundproofed and peppered with bugs. From the room next door, it was possible to watch without being seen, listen without being heard. In a broom cupboard, to which the proprietress claimed to have misplaced the key, they found reels of Super 8 film and a cardboard box filled with audio cassettes. Scialoja was certain that Zeta and Pigreco had used the bordello as a base for the collection of top-secret information. Borgia hemmed and hawed: they were sure to claim a defence of insatiable perversion, or else just peeping toms. Whatever the case, they'd have to wait for the film to be developed and the tapes to be transcribed.

Confronted with the findings, the two secret agents feigned a polite astonishment.

'They were spying on us!'

'Incredible!'

'A person thinks he's going to spend a relaxing afternoon in a first-class establishment...'

'Because let me assure you, my dear colleague, that *was* a first-class establishment...'

'There were some girls there...'

'But you must be aware of that yourself, right?'

'In any case, you go there expecting to enjoy yourself and the next thing you know, you're starring in a porno film!'

Even though he could feel flames of anger fanning inside him, Scialoja feigned courteous indifference. Smiling, even gentlemanly, he ushered them out of the interview room without even bothering to note down the last piece of arrant bullshit they'd foisted off on him. The better plan was to await further developments and put off any serious questions to the next opportunity. Such as: what were you doing in Bologna? Who's the fat old man at whose slightest gesture you were trembling like a couple of piker bastards on their first detail? What does it feel like to represent the filthy face of the Italian state?

The expert's report came in on the material confiscated in Piazza dei Mercanti.

Due to 'a regrettable mishap in the processing lab, attributable to neglect on the part of the cleaning staff', most of the Super 8 film reels had been damaged, beyond any hope of retrieval, corroded by a flow of acid that, according to the expert's account, made the eruption of Vesuvius that buried Pompeii look like a popgun. Only two reels had been saved, and they were in poor condition, too. The contents: 'pornographic films depicting starlets, including a fairly well-known character actress, engaged in sexual congress with numerous partners of both sexes and other practices contrary to nature.' As for the audio cassettes, some of them were no more than a tangle of incomprehensible background noises, while others were 'home-made compilations of popular music'. In conclusion, 'the audio material recovered was insignificant in terms of this investigation. The audio-visual material can be presumed to have served to excite the sexual appetites of the establishment's clients, as indicated by the six projectors now under court-ordered confiscation.'

Scialoja and Borgia looked heavenward, arms spread, feeling defeated. The enemy had a thousand faces. The enemy was snickering at their pathetic efforts. The bad guys were more powerful than the good guys.

'The thought of that poor woman...' Scialoja ventured. 'She's going to pay for the rest of them...'

'Well?'

'Does it strike you as fair? I mean to say, perhaps you could reconsider her indictment...'

'Are you asking me to set her free?'

'After all—'

'One more word and I'll ship you back to Modena!'

Borgia was certainly capable of carrying out his threat. Scialoja felt more and more beaten down by his own failures. The smug smiles that Zeta and Pigreco had flashed him weren't sitting well. He started digging through old documents on Nero. He ordered top-secret documents from Bologna. He started prying into matters that didn't concern him. He was looking for something he still couldn't seem to envision properly. Material for a new report, and sooner or later he'd track it down.

Once the waters had calmed down sufficiently, Dandi managed to obtain permission for a prison visit. He showed up at Rebibbia with a big bouquet of roses, which he was obliged to leave at the guard's front office. He was searched. He was escorted to the visiting room. There, instead of Patrizia, he found that big old bull dyke Ines del Trullo.

'Patrizia sends her regrets, but she doesn't feel at all well today. I'm so sorry, Dandi...'

Dandi went back and picked up his flowers and stormed furiously out the front gate of the prison. Fuck Freddo. Fuck Patrizia. Dandi phoned Zeta and Pigreco: is there anything, even the tiniest little thing, that we can do to that bastard cop? Zeta said he'd give it some thought.

In late January, Botola just happened to run into Saverio Solfatara. The crazy Sicilian, the one who shot Libano, had just slipped into a betting shop in the Prati section of Rome. Botola made a fast phone call to Franco's bar. Aldo Buffoni answered the phone. The news spread fast. Preparations were set in motion for an ambush.

Freddo grabbed a handgun and a visored cap and took off, alone, on his motorcycle. He was at the betting shop twenty minutes later, running red lights from one side of Rome to the other. He walked in with the hat pulled down low over his eyes, safety off, pistol cocked and ready in his trench coat pocket. He walked up behind the Sicilian and fired three shots into him, in full view of everyone in the place. Then he walked out of the place, at a leisurely pace, and got back on his bike. When he got back to Franco's bar, they were still arguing over who ought to go out on the job.

'Take it back to the store room,' he ordered, handing the pistol to Dandi.

Nero gave him a hug. Dandi avoided his gaze.

Rivers of Blood
Winter–Spring 1981

I

As soon as he was released on special leave, Sardo summoned them to his sister's apartment, a small penthouse apartment with a view of St Peter's cathedral, redolent with good smells: roast pork and amatriciana sauce. Freddo, Dandi and Nembo Kid went to pay the call. Sardo was even more a raging oaf than usual. He listed his grievances while Ricciolodoro and Barbarella could be heard enjoying themselves in the bedroom and a tabby cat with one glass eye stood guard, arching its back.

'What the hell has got into your heads?' Sardo began. 'You're buying this and shipping that, and seeing this one and then seeing that one, shooting, organizing, building...What the hell has come over you all? You've made billions, but in the two years I spent in the booby hatch, all I've ever seen is crumbs. In Naples everyone's furious about the whole earthquake thing, and now I have to find out from Don Rafaele in person that that bastard Trentadenari turned to the old families for the operation. And what's all this about working with the Mafia? And all these shops, hotels, restaurants and *buticche* –' using the Italian pronunciation of boutiques – 'in the centre of town? And the fifty kilos of narcotics? Do you guys realize that my last month at Castiglione, poor Ricciolodoro was forced to choke down the food there?'

'We always paid what was due, and on time,' Dandi objected.

'I never saw my double share...'

'Why, were you supposed to be paid double?'

'Of course I was. I'm the boss, and don't you forget it, you little piece of shit...'

'Hey, Mario, look, your end has been set aside and it's waiting for you,' Nembo Kid butted in.

'Bullshit! Till now, there's been nothing but talk. I've seen nothing! Ah, but now you'll be dancing to a new tune, all you good old boys! You just remember that in Rome, not a leaf on a tree dares to flutter without Sardo's say-so! And anyone who doesn't want to sing with the choir – pow, pow! What do you say, Freddo? Cat got your tongue?'

'It'll all work out, Mario, don't worry.'

Sardo poured himself a drink, making a big show of offering nothing to the others. They'd even had to go get chairs for themselves.

'Libano didn't understand a thing. He wanted to do everything on his own, and look at what happened to him. But now you're going to be dancing to the tune I play, my fine young dickheads! I expect a double share from now on, plus special compensation for the shitty two years I just spent in the asylum. Tomorrow we're all going to get together at that Judas Trentadenari's house, and if he doesn't have a full and believable explanation, I'll take care of him myself. Tomorrow we're going to settle our accounts. What the hell, the mice have been playing and they've even gotten carried away with themselves, but Big Daddy Tomcat is back in town! In the meantime, I need a hundred million lire, right away. And a kilo of coke for certain friends of mine. You guys still here? *Raus*, get going!'

Dandi looked at Nembo, and Nembo looked at Freddo. There were people who learned how to live behind bars, and there were others who were never quite right after their stint. Sardo was gleefully gambling away every opportunity he might have to remain standing for a few more years of life.

'Did you say a hundred?' asked Freddo, his voice silky with false courtesy. 'You'll have it tomorrow.'

They held the go/no-go meeting at Trentadenari's house. No question, Sardo hadn't really picked the best moment to leave the safety and comfort of his loony bin. After the exploit in the betting shop, a general sense of confidence had started to circulate once again. They were starting to feel invincible and, more important still, united. Freddo asked Trentadenari to give the books a once-over. The Neapolitan, who'd been keeping the books ever since Libano's death, said that everything was in order.

250

'He was paid every last lira we owed him. He even got his share of deals that he never dreamed of in his lifetime. That guy's brain is fried completely!'

As for Sardo's demand for a double share, not even Libano, whose unquestioned authority was acknowledged by one and all, had ever dreamed of such a thing. In other words, there was no reason to hesitate. Perhaps if Sardo had approached things in a less high-handed manner, there could have been a little more room to negotiate. As matters stood, however, there was no reason to put off the decision any longer.

Freddo devised the plan. Judge Borgia knew too much. The minute the thing was done, he'd come looking for them. So Sardo had to vanish, literally, into thin air.

'The Sicilians dissolve corpses in acid,' Nembo Kid informed them.

'There's no time for that,' Freddo cut him off. 'We're going to have to dig a hole and dump him in it.'

Ricotta volunteered. He knew just the place – a quarry on the Via Salaria, where just three or four days from now, the city government was planning to do some blasting.

They made an appointment to meet at the Pyramid.

'We're going to take care of this piece of work at Sorcio's shack. We're all going to be there at the appointment. We'll need three cars and two motorcycles. The Buffoni boys can take care of that. Now, we're going to need alibis. Wives, lovers, girlfriends, gamblers, you name it…Just make sure you've got it tied down tight. That's it, let's get cracking!'

'What about Ricciolodoro?' asked Bufalo.

'He's small fry,' Dandi snorted. 'Let's forget about him…'

'No,' Freddo said. 'He saw us today. He knows too much. He's coming to Sorcio's, too.'

'That means I'm going to have to dig a double-wide grave,' Ricotta concluded in a resigned voice.

Bufalo laughed.

ROBERTA'S SLENDER, SWEET-SMELLING fingers ran over the taut hollows of Freddo's face.

'You're changing.'

'What do you mean?'

'You're becoming…more of a man.'

'Why, I wasn't enough for you?' He tried to make it into a joke. Roberta gave him a stern glance, with a hint of tenderness.

'Humour isn't your strong suit, sweetheart.'

'You're right, forgive me…'

Freddo was blushing. She smiled. An afternoon of lovemaking, the first moment of peace after those hellish months. Almost as if Saverio Solfatara's blood, finally spilled, had somehow placated Libano's unquiet ghost. Now Roberta was examining her small breasts, reflected in the large mirror that hung facing the bed. Ever since she'd moved in, the place in Pigneto almost seemed like a real home. With furniture, electric appliances, a huge bathroom, always sparkling clean. Nothing like the palatial apartment of that fanatic Dandi, but still, a home; sometimes even cosy, sometimes warm.

'Am I putting on weight?'

'What are you talking about!'

'I'd like to gain a little weight.'

'But you look great just the way you are…'

'You don't understand. I want to have a baby.'

'With the life I lead? That's out of the question!'

'So you don't want to leave anything behind when you're gone, eh?'

It wasn't the first time they'd discussed the topic. Roberta was never pushy about it. Even when she wanted to let him know that something wasn't right, even something important, she always managed to put it in that gentle way of hers.

'The other day, I read about a woman terrorist giving birth to twins, in prison. She and her lover were arrested three years ago. The only way they could make love was during their trial. You know how they put all the defendants in those trials in one big cage? So their comrades made a circle around them, and now they have kids of their own…'

'Right under the judge's nose! Not bad, I've got to say...'

'Keep running, my love. One day, even you will have to stop. And you know what you'll find waiting for you at the end of your road?'

'A couple of hollow-point bullets?'

'No. You'll find *me*...'

Sometimes he thought about it too. Retiring. Taking a different path before everything came tumbling down. But not even Puma had managed to get out entirely. He was still always around working his little hustles, one foot in and one foot out...And sooner or later wasn't the cheque going to come due? And in that case, wasn't it best to just keep going until they brought the curtain down?

Freddo jumped out of bed and went to take a shower. Roberta stayed under the covers and smoked a cigarette. She watched him dress carefully: white shirt, jeans, light jumper, leather jacket. This strange, kind, taciturn boy who'd stolen my heart away. This killer.

'If they ask you,' Freddo murmured, grabbing an assortment box of chocolates, 'tell them that we spent the whole day together.'

'Who are those for?'

Freddo lifted the top and laid his Smith & Wesson .357 Magnum in the box.

'For a friend.'

At the Pyramid, Sardo and Ricciolodoro found Freddo, the Buffoni boys and Fierolocchio waiting for them. Botola, Bufalo and Scrocchiazeppi aboard a VW Golf, and Dandi and Nembo Kid on a motorcycle, were waiting in concealment on the Viale Giotto side of the piazza. They watched, unseen. Freddo said that the cops were tailing them and that the handover of cash and narcotics would take place in a safe location. To quell suspicions and avoid wasted time, everyone opened their jacket, making it clear they were unarmed. Sardo spat on the ground and said that they'd follow them in the armour-plated Lancia.

'You go sign the parole register and wait for me at home,' he ordered Ricciolodoro.

Freddo and Fierolocchio exchanged a knowing glance. Sardo thought he was pretty damned clever: to avoid surprises, he'd brought along a witness.

'Let's go.'

Ricciolodoro climbed into his aubergine Mini and put it in reverse. Dandi and Nembo Kid let him pull out and gave him a hundred yards or so head start, then started after him. Botola, Bufalo and Scrocchiazeppi headed straight for Sorcio's shack, where Ricotta was waiting impatiently.

When he saw him standing there, big, strong and uncomfortable, Sardo flashed him a dismissive sneer.

'Ah, so you're stuck with these guys too! What a shitty way for you to wind up!'

'Not half as bad as you're about to wind up, Sardo!'

Freddo, who had hung back on the pretext of getting his jacket, was just pulling something out of a box of chocolates. Maybe then it dawned on Sardo that he'd walked into a trap. Or maybe he never even had time.

At almost the same instant, on the other side of town, Ricciolodoro scribbled his signature in the parole ledger and waved a farewell to the desk sergeant in the police station.

III

JUDICIAL REPORT ON THE MURDER OF PUDDU, NATALE MARIO,
AKA 'MARIO THE SARDINIAN', AKA 'SARDO' AND MAGNANTI,
FLAVIO, AKA 'RICCIOLODORO'
*(drafted by Commissario Nicola Scialoja, judicial police,
17 February 1981)*

From the investigation conducted into the events in question, the following facts have emerged:

Around 1800 hours on 7 February 1981, in Via dei Campani, immediately after leaving the local police station where he had signed his parole ledger as required by the conditions of his release, the well-known ex-convict MAGNANTI, FLAVIO, AKA 'Ricciolodoro', was struck down by five bullets from a .38 special revolver fired by two or three individuals, who then made good their escape aboard a high-performance Kawasaki motorcycle. Although medical care arrived immediately, MAGNANTI was dead on arrival at the Policlinico Umberto I.

From the preliminary investigations, it would appear that MAGNANTI had family ties with PUDDU, NATALE MARIO, AKA 'Mario the Sardinian', AKA 'Sardo', having married Puddu's sister MAGNANTI, BARBARELLA.

On the night of that same day, 7 February 1981, approximately two hours after the documented murder of MAGNANTI, relatives of Puddu appeared at the San Paolo police station, stating that they were concerned because their relative had been out of touch for several hours.

PUDDU, an inmate of the judicial psychiatric hospital of Castiglione delle Stiviere, had been authorized to take six months of probationary leave beginning 4 February 1981.

It was ascertained that on the evening of 6 February 1981, PUDDU, while accompanied by MAGNANTI, had received a visit from three individuals, Roman ex-convicts known as DANDI, FREDDO and NEMBO KID.

An appointment had been made for the following day, by PUDDU and MAGNANTI, to meet with the above-mentioned DANDI, FREDDO and NEMBO KID.

In fact, on the afternoon of 7 February 1981, PUDDU and MAGNANTI left the house, telling their relatives that they were going to see some friends. PUDDU had further stated that he expected to receive a substantial sum of money from these friends.

On the night of the 7/early morning of the 8 of February, MAGNANTI, BARBARELLA went to see the above-mentioned DANDI, asking him what he knew about her missing brother and accusing him of the murder of her husband. The above-mentioned DANDI, according to the woman, 'could not have been more astonished' but was 'obviously putting on a show'.

Staff from this division undertook preliminary interviews with the above-mentioned Dandi and his wife, who stated that her husband was at home all afternoon, suffering from a bad case of kidney stones. A doctor's certificate was displayed, dating from the night prior to the murder of MAGNANTI, and it did in fact appear that the above-mentioned DANDI had been prescribed three days of bed rest on account of his renal colic.

An interview was also held with the above-mentioned Freddo, who stated that he had spent the afternoon and the evening with De Santis, Roberta, who cohabits with him. The signorina in question confirmed that version of events.

As for Nembo Kid, he appeared to have been in the company of a certain Morai, Donatella, with whom he cohabits, for the entire duration of the afternoon and evening.

As of this writing (17 February) no trace has been found of the missing Puddu, Natale Mario.

The author of this report is of the opinion that Puddu was the victim of a murder followed by concealment of the corpus delicti, and that both events (murder of Puddu and murder of Magnanti) are closely interlinked. The motives for the double homicide should be sought in the relationships that the deceased Puddu had with major figures in the Roman underworld, among them Libano, murdered by unknown killers last September, Nembo Kid, Dandi, Freddo, Bufalo and others. To our knowledge, all these men are part of a well-armed, vast, deep-rooted criminal conspiracy engaged in arms and narcotics trafficking. The motive for Puddu's murder probably involved a gangland feud, a settling of scores, while Magnanti was killed only to eliminate an inconvenient witness to recent events.

To complete this report, we should point out that the alibis supplied by the three suspects seems anything but convincing. They are based on the conniving statements of girlfriends and lovers, and should be dismissed out of hand for the barefaced tissues of falsehoods that they probably are.

There were many other observations in Scialoja's original report. For instance, the fact that Mario the Sardinian meant Cutolo, and Cutolo meant Camorra. That the 'vast, deep-rooted organization' was not only involved in arms trafficking and narcotics distribution, but also had regular dealings with the bastards in the Italian intelligence agencies. That right-wing extremists were involved as well. That Libano had created a many-headed monster whose power was still impossible to test or measure. Borgia had talked him into drafting a more digestible version.

'I know my chickens. It's not a good idea to lay down all your cards on a single turn. Let's stick with the two homicides. That'll be more than enough for the district attorney!'

That proved to have been a tragic miscalculation, poor Borgia. The district attorney read the report, shook his head, offered a cigarette, and then unfurled the smile of a sympathetic older brother.

'I know this will come as a disappointment, but you won't go far with this kind of stuff...'

What evidence there was remained largely circumstantial. There were no witnesses. And what could be said in the face of those alibis? It's easy to say: gangsters' molls are unreliable by definition. But just try telling that to a jury of their peers! Moreover, those women, with no criminal records, were uninvolved in the crime spree as far as could be determined. Take Dandi's wife – a pious, church-going woman, a woman dispensing charity on a regular basis, moreover a personal friend of the Monsignor...No, no, my good Borgia. I'm sorry, no arrest warrants. Not these days, with the civil libertarians accusing us of trying to establish a police state...No, he needed to take the old platitude as an article of faith: better to let a hundred guilty men go free than land one innocent man wrongly in prison...

Fabio Santini, who by some mysterious machinations had managed to gain several steps up in rank and a new position at the Hall of Justice, let Trentadenari know that Judge Borgia was fit to be tied, carpet-chewing mad.

As Borgia stormed out of the district attorney's office, he had been heard to mutter through clenched teeth a series of colourful curses, and one phrase, more clearly enunciated than the others, had been overheard by those present:

'Civil libertarians, my arse! If these were Communists, it would be up against the wall for the lot of them, forget about any reliable alibis!'

They themselves, for that matter, hadn't expected such a bland reaction from the state. They quickly abandoned their hiding places and poured out into the streets to accept the enthusiastic plaudits of the Rome that counted in the negative sense. They knew that what awaited them now would be nothing more than a series of cannonades firing blanks: routine interrogations, Vasta's stern frown, Borgia's black mood,

Scialoja's spiteful nonchalance. That was it, nothing more. The fear of bombs had lodged them in a sort of protected niche. High up on the food chain, they were far too fearful for the safety of their own reverend arses to worry about the pools of blood in the streets. Sort of like what happened at the Forlanini Hospital – an episode described by Vanessa at Trentadenari's celebration dinner – when packs of wild dogs were terrorizing the wards. As long as the dogs were only attacking the sick or their relatives, no one gave a damn. Then one evening a three-legged calico pup dared to bite the health care commissioner; in twenty-four hours, every one of the mangy beasts had been exterminated.

'What does it mean? That we should be good, or we'll wind up like the dogs?' asked Bufalo, trying to puzzle out the meaning of a parable.

'Or that we should become commissioners,' Dandi glossed the story. In short, it was a time when everything seemed to be running smoothly. But it ended far too soon.

In mid-March, Surtano gave Scrocchiazeppi a solid tip on Nicolino Gemito: the turncoat had moved bags and baggage to a penthouse on Fleming Hill. They trooped out in the afternoon, two days after the tip came in. Freddo and Botola, in a Mercedes that Sorcio had stolen, were waiting five hundred yards away for the escape manoeuvre. Dandi, with a MAB assault rifle, was covering the operation on a Kawasaki. Bufalo and Ricotta had parked Bufalo's Citröen DS on a nearby parallel road and were waiting outside the street door. They were the death squad.

Nicolino Gemito, his brother Vittorio, and two women got home around six. Bufalo and Ricotta waited for them to open the street door and go in, and then they made their move. They shoved the women aside and galloped up the stairs, in pursuit of the men. Bufalo laid Nicolino out dead with his first shot. Ricotta kneecapped Vittorio, who was unsuccessfully trying to return fire. The women were screaming. Bufalo and Ricotta fired a few more shots and then headed back downstairs for the front door.

By pure coincidence, a police car heading back to the station at the end of the shift just happened to be passing by. Police officers Bernardi and Dazieri had chosen that street precisely because it was quiet and there was never much traffic.

The sharp crack of gunfire, screaming women, the sound of breaking glass: the officers swerved their Alfetta around to block the street and, guns levelled, rushed to the building at number 90. Out of the corner of his eye, Officer Bernardi saw a big motorcycle make a sharp turn and roar away at top speed.

'Look out!'

Bufalo and Ricotta came running towards them. Bernardi called out to them to halt. The two men fired. The officers returned fire. Ricotta, shot in one arm, dropped his gun and screamed in pain. Bufalo grabbed him and helped him hobble along. The officers drew closer. Bufalo tried to clear a path, firing indiscriminately, the Colt red-hot in his hands. The officers dived for cover behind the Alfetta. If he'd been alone, Bufalo might have made it out of there, but Ricotta could barely stay on his feet, and blood was pumping out of his arm. In the meantime, the officers were taking aim from their hiding place. Bufalo felt a bullet graze his leg, and he looked around wildly. Where was that arsehole Dandi? Why didn't he take the cops from behind? What about the others? Too far away to come to his aid! Another shot went whistling past. It was a good thing that the cops were no marksmen, but this couldn't go on forever. Ricotta was as heavy as a side of beef, and he had started to whine. There was an apartment building door, two or three yards away. Bufalo dived through it with the strength of sheer desperation.

Officer Dazieri sounded the alarm via radio. Bernardi hauled a terrified concierge out from the front desk.

'Where did they go?'

'Up...up the stairs...'

'Are there any other exits?'

'No.'

When Freddo's Mercedes rolled downhill, the street was crawling with uniforms. There was even a shift commander with a megaphone.

'Go,' Freddo ordered. 'Something went wrong. Go, go, go!'

They were caught in a trap. The old woman that they'd physically hauled out of the fifth-floor apartment was snivelling and clutching at her rosary. The place stank of cats. Bufalo was getting more and more worked up.

'I'm not going to let them take me alive!'

259

'Don't talk bullshit, Bufalo. Hand me the phone.'

Stretched out on the sofa, his arm bandaged, Ricotta was rapidly recovering. He called Vasta.

'What should I do? Should I demand a car and fifty million lire and tell them that if I don't get what I'm asking, I'll kill the old woman? Eh? What should I do, Counsellor?'

'Surrender.'

'What do you mean surrender?'

'You heard me. This isn't some American gangster film. Surrender, then we'll do what we can.'

'What'd he say? What's the lawyer say? What the fuck are we supposed to do now, Ricotta?'

Ricotta ignored him and dialled another number.

'Trentadenari? It's Ricotta. Eh, so-so…Let's just say that I'll see you in thirty years or more…'

Violent pounding on the door. The old woman wailing.

'We're coming out, don't shoot!' shouted Ricotta, struggling to his feet.

He felt like laughing. It was over. Still, they'd had some fun. Nicolino was a goner, and this time there were no two ways about it. Anyway, it had been a thrilling adventure. With a magician of the legal code like Vasta, there was still hope. Still, if he ever managed to get his hands on him, Dandi was a dead man.

'Come on, Bufalo, let's go!'

Bufalo dropped his pistol and followed him, hands held high.

IV

ROME, CALIBRE 9. *The Capital in the Grip of Crime. Dodge City Shootout on Fleming Hill.*

The press was running wild with the story. Suddenly the whole city was in a spaghetti western starring Maurizio Merli.

The district attorney claimed credit for having been the first, amidst a general atmosphere of scepticism, to identify 'an unsettling qualitative leap forward on the part of the traditional Roman underworld'. The old mob bosses were being swept away by the shockwave of a 'new genera-tion of ruthless gangsters'. Still, the police, even as they were being put to the test by the emergency of the terrorist threat, 'were not caught completely off guard' and were able to face up to the criminal offensive. That said, before using words like 'gang war' or, even worse, 'Mafia', as so many were already starting to do, no matter how reckless that might appear, it would be wise to think not once, not twice, but a hundred times.

Borgia had dusted off Scialoja's original report. That word – Mafia – had been uttered by him, loud and clear, in front of a crowd of excited journalists. The district attorney's ambitious self-regard only bothered him to a certain extent. What mattered now was results. Results, and a change in the climate. People needed to understand that terrorism wasn't the only thing in the world we live in. Terrorism passed. The Mafia was always with us. That was the point of departure.

The legal battle promised to be brutal. Bufalo and Ricotta knew their hopes were dim at best. But what mattered most was to ensure that the behind-the-scenes manoeuvrings not emerge. It was up to Vasta to limit the damage.

The lawyer had a brilliant hunch. The thing to do now was diver-sify his litigation strategies. One of the two of them would have to pass himself off as crazy. Naturally, the ideal candidate was Bufalo, who already had a past history of apparently irrational explosions of violence. As for Ricotta, he'd play the role of his partner's willing victim. Therefore, to ensure the strategy would be successful, it was necessary to eliminate any possible suspicions of collusion. Vasta took himself off Ricotta's case and handed it over to a colleague.

'That way, if things go the way they ought to, Bufalo will get off with ten years in a criminal insane asylum!'

'What about me?'

'Less than twenty-six or twenty-seven years, don't even get your hopes up. Anyway, it's not life without parole, so that's something, eh!'

And so Bufalo, with the help of Pischello, who had embraced him warmly like a little brother the minute he spotted him in the exercise yard, wrote a letter and made sure it reached Borgia.

Dear Judge,

I killed Nicolino Gemito because that filthy bastard murdered my friend and brother Libano. Since Libano was killed, my life had become a living hell. At first I'd see him in my dreams at night, white as a sheet, calling my name and begging me, and I'd break out in a sweat and try to tell him: *you're dead, rest in peace, what can I do for you?* But he wouldn't stop, and he told me that his soul would never find peace until the miserable renegade had paid for his crime.

Then the voices started…I would hear them at all hours of the day and night, here, inside my brain. It was Libano, shouting one word over and over: 'Vendetta! Vendetta!' I'd lost the pleasure of sleep, of my friends, all the joy of life was gone…Then, since I didn't seem able to make up my mind, he started appearing before me. The first time he came right out of the television. They were showing a film, and suddenly there he was, with his face blown open, all covered with blood and brain matter. And again, that word, *vendetta, vendetta*…I was reduced to a human ghost, Judge, Your Honour. You can't begin to imagine…I'd see Libano at the bar, in the marketplace, at the cinema, in my car, on the street…He was sad and furious, a tormented soul. Could I remain indifferent to his cry of pain? I might as well have just murdered him a second time!

Then, that damned afternoon, I was out and about with my poor friend Ricotta. He was doing his best to cheer me up. You need to go see a doctor, he told me. You need to get some professional help…That afternoon I saw them before me, him and his brother, and behind them I saw Libano. He was staring at me with an indignant expression. He seemed to be saying to me: *What? I'm in this torment and they're still on the face of the earth?* So I grabbed Ricotta and we followed them, and what happened after that is what you know. I'm sorry, but this is the truth!

Ricotta, appearing voluntarily with his new defence lawyer, confirmed that version of events. That damned afternoon, when he had laid eyes on the Gemitos, Bufalo flew straight at them like a madman. Just like a madman. And he, Ricotta, had gone after him, doing his best to talk him out of whatever it was he had in mind to do. But it was too late by that point: Bufalo had already started shooting, the Gemito boys were returning fire…What alternatives did he have? He too had fired his gun, and now he was willing to pay for what he'd done.

Borgia ran into Vasta at the bar and complimented him on his adroit defensive approach. The lawyer minimized: he'd long ago broken off all contact with Ricotta, and as for Bufalo, he was only a pathetic nutcase.

Borgia laughed heartily, indicted them both for premeditated homicide, and forwarded the proceedings to the investigating judge. Vasta requested the intervention of an expert witness. The judge appointed two experts.

Now it was time to move against the ones outside.

V

PATRIZIA DRANK IN the warm spring wind. A burst of laughter carried over to her from the female terrorists' wing. She followed the voices through the flowering garden of the women's section of Rebibbia. An old lifer, a peasant woman who thirty years earlier had hacked her violent, abusive husband to death with a pruning hook, lifted her head from her budding miniature roses and flashed her a toothless smile. Patrizia returned the greeting. The woman had never applied for release because she wouldn't know where to go in the outside world. By now, prison was her life. Would the same thing happen to Patrizia? At first, she'd made plans for the future. They were muddled, confused plans. Go away, stay, start over, renounce. Then she'd forgotten about plans. Prison could be comfortable, in its own way.

Palma, another inmate, had given Patrizia a copy of *I Ching*. 'This is funny, Patrizia. It says you picked the wrong path in life.'

'Tell me something I don't know!'

'It says you should have been a schoolteacher. Or a nun.'

She no longer answered them when they questioned her. She knew that her attitude was only making the situation worse, but the truth was she no longer had anything to say to anyone. Not even to Dandi. Not even to that animal of a cop who kept staring at her with his dark, slightly crazed eyes, still wondering: Who are you, Patrizia, what's inside of you?

Was it really that hard to figure out that there was nothing left to discover; nothing but a void made up of anger and resignation? Patrizia went on walking, caressed by the impetuous May sunshine. She crossed unimpeded into the confines of the female terrorists' territory, even though she was strictly forbidden to do so. But the guards were all too happy to turn not one but both blind eyes to anything Dandi's woman wanted to do. The guards didn't know, or pretended not to know, that for months she had refused to see him on visiting days.

The terrorists sunbathed in bikinis. The famous sunshine of Rebibbia. There was the scent of roses in the air and the odour of suntan oil. The female terrorists read deadly boring books with incomprehensible titles and snickered at the life sentences without parole that the tenacious judges kept piling on their slender bourgeois backs.

Palma broke away from the small knot of women and came towards her with a smile on her face. Palma came from a well-to-do Sicilian family, was twenty-four years old, and had been found guilty of two homicides. The first time that Patrizia had ventured into the garden of the 'special wing', Palma had vouched for her with her comrades. It was an instinctive trust: she hadn't done anything to deserve it. It had been mere curiosity that pushed her to venture across the forbidden threshold. Curiosity, and a fierce desire to break out of the company of ordinary prisoners. The group, however, had never broken ranks, and had continued to hold her at arm's length. Palma was the only one who didn't treat her as if she had some contagious disease. She'd never tried to use her as a courier or, as the terrorists put it, a 'runner'. Palma was the closest thing to a friend she'd ever had.

One time Patrizia had tried to provoke her.

'You say you want a revolution, everyone equal, but you consider me a piece of shit because I'm not part of your group!'

Palma had ventured into a lengthy disquisition on the relationship between bourgeoisie, avant-garde and sub-proletariat. Patrizia finally lost her patience.

'The truth is, you're a stand-up gal, and the other women in there are a crowd of bitches!'

Patrizia pulled her pack of Marlboros out of her jeans pocket, tapped out a smoke for herself, and handed the rest to Palma.

'But now you're out of smokes.'

'It's not a problem. But smoke them all for yourself, eh? Don't let those bitches get so much as a whiff!'

Palma laughed. She had long black hair and a serene expression. The type that was sweet and aggressive at the same time, which drove men crazy. They lit their cigarettes. Palma was writing her university thesis; she was studying psychology. Topic: the historic evolution of the model of the criminal woman.

Patrizia stretched out on the grass. Palma asked her to talk about dreams.

'My dreams?' Patrizia snapped out in annoyance.

'Your dreams, other women's dreams... Whatever you prefer.'

'Whores always have the same dreams: a house with a big television set, two children, a man who doesn't beat her every day, maybe just on weekends. They dream of being addressed as 'signora' when they go food shopping. Fine clothing, some jewellery, at least one car, maybe two... They dream of being just like you and your girlfriends, and this idea of a revolution, they really don't get it!'

'What about you?'

'What do you mean?'

'Do you get it?'

'We already discussed that, didn't we?'

'Tell me something else.'

'Ines del Trullo always makes my bed and cooks for the whole cell. She sets aside the choicest morsels for me. She's in for an old series of concurrent sentences, and she hopes that when she gets out, I'll take her in and give her a job.'

'Will you?'

'Not on your life! Ines is a bitch. Do you remember that girl I told you about, the one they tossed in the cell the night I was arrested?'

'What's her name...'

'Adele.'

'Right, Adele. So?'

'Ever since she first laid eyes on her, Ines has been trying to get into her pants. And now she's finally done it!'

Palma snickered to cover her embarrassment. A terrorist and a moralist!

'But she played dirty to do it,' Patrizia went on. 'She procured a couple of doses of heroin for her...'

'Here? In prison?'

'Where the hell do you live: on the face of the moon? Of course here, in prison. Open your eyes, sister! Anyway, the minute I found out about it, I went to see Adele and I told her that if I caught her doing it again, I'd arrange for her to be transferred to a cell with Matrona...'

'And who is this Matrona?'

'A monster who weighs 265 pounds, stinks like a sewer, and likes to force young girls to lick her feet...'

'Oh, Madonna!'

'Right. And I hit Ines so hard her face is all swollen up...'

'But why?'

'Because I don't like her, that's why. Do I have to have a reason?'

Palma burst out laughing. Patrizia told her to go to hell. Palma apologized.

'Still, it's a funny thing...Isn't your man, Dandi, the one who sells shit all over Rome?'

'So what?'

'So what, so what – that just makes me laugh! Out in the street, he's making money off junkies, and here in prison you're denying him his basic material!'

Patrizia went back to her cell in a bleak mood. Palma didn't understand. As far as that went, even she didn't understand all that well why she did certain things. She felt like it, and she did it. She could, so that was that. And the thing that drove her crazy most of all was the fact that the reason she could afford to do whatever she wanted was that she was Dandi's woman.

Ines came to meet her, waving a crumpled piece of paper.

'Mail call! Mail call for the beautiful Patrizia!'

'Give it here!'

It was a letter from Ranocchia. Patrizia lay down on her bed and did her best to decipher the old faggot's crabbed, scratchy handwriting.

I'm writing to you from the airport in Casablanca, Morocco. Wasn't Morocco where you wanted to go, the last time we saw each other, that night of the rabbits? I'm Ingrid, the divine Ingrid with my impeccable skirt suits and my glistening eyes, like a wounded puppy. The little prop plane is warming up its ridiculous motors. The man I love has just kissed me and, according to the script, now he should hand me over to the man I don't love but who desperately needs me. For this dream – which, by the way, unlike the original, is in Technicolour, not black and white – I have a different, happier ending planned. This time, Rick will be taking off with me. The big-hearted, charming, fascinating Rick. Not that parboiled octopus Victor Laszlo. I don't give a fuck about Victor Laszlo. Let him go take it up the arse somewhere else, little faggot that he is, him and his operetta revolution. Rick, Rick, oh, Rick! Can't you hear the sirens wailing? Don't you hear the roar of the engines? Let Laszlo talk his way out of trouble with the Nazis! You and me can fly out of here together. You and me can escape. You and me can be happy.

We'll never see each other again, Patrizia. I'll never hear your sweet lips utter those words of contempt that I used to adore. Even the silences filled with emptiness were perfectly suited to your hard, Slavic oval. I'll miss you, but destiny has decided for me, and when destiny decides, there's nothing you can do about it! Nothing, you understand? Oops, they're calling my flight. It's Rick. He's already on-board. The pilot's waving for me to get on-board. I have to hurry. I have to run. But before *The End* appears on the screen, I want to give you a piece of advice. You should run away too, Patrizia. You should run away with your Rick. Whoever that may be. Wherever he wants to take you, follow him. Follow him and don't look back. Seize the fleeting moment. Don't let this miserable world screw you. To hell with the world. Fuck them all. And every once in a while, think a special thought of your devoted Ranocchia.

Patrizia let a renegade smile appear on her face. Crazy old thing! Crazy, kind old faggot! She'd miss him! At least she hoped he'd be happy.

Patrizia slipped into a light slumber. And she dreamed. Something that hadn't happened to her since she was a little girl. She dreamed something of which she later had nothing more than a muddled memory: images in motion, warm hues, water burbling gently by, soft animal muzzles.

Rien ne va plus
1981

I

EVERY TEN TO fifteen days, Sorcio went over to Trentadenari's or Freddo's place to sample narcotics. If it was coke, he licked it off his fingertips. The smack he shot up in very small amounts, to avoid the danger of overdose. As a narcotics taster, there was no one who could even come close to him. His evaluations of the degree of purity and the cutting compounds could hold their own against any chemical analysis. Depending on the quality of the shit, they would decide on the percentage of the cut for distribution, how much to step on the pure original, what price to set for wholesalers and retailers, and what the profit forecast would be. Never once had the entire shipment not been safely placed prior to the next sampling session. Sorcio was due a miserably slim share of the net profit, and he inevitably took that share in more drugs. Sorcio was operating on a daily regime of a gram, maybe 1.2 grams. The temptation to take advantage of all that manna from heaven was enormous, but Sorcio knew that his very survival depended on his commercial ethics.

Once Vanessa dumped him and hooked up with Trentadenari, Sorcio's standing within the gang had plummeted. Truth be told, he wasn't even really in the gang at all. Aside from the tasting sessions, no one ever reached out to him, except for the occasional two-bit deal, like stealing a motorcycle or souping up a car. Even then, they were careful not to let him know what they were planning to do with the machines. He was barely one step up from the lowest junkie on the totem pole. He couldn't afford even the smallest violation of the code. So the minute he figured out what Aldo Buffoni was up to, he hastened to make a report to Trentadenari.

Vanessa was there too, that night: languid and saccharine-sweet. But under the cooing, there was no missing the contempt she felt for him. Anyone else, in his place, would have settled matters with Aldo directly, one on one, man to man. But he wasn't even a man. If he had been, he'd never have lost Vanessa in the first place. And he certainly wouldn't have come to sob on the shoulder of the man who'd stolen her away from him. He was Sorcio – not a man, but a mouse. So he spilled the whole story to Trentadenari, and Trentadenari dismissed him with a pat on the back, and then hurried to tell Freddo. And now Freddo wanted to talk to him. Sorcio wished he could run away, a thousand miles away from all that filth, from that profoundly wrong life. But you couldn't go far with empty pockets and a monkey in your head, and anywhere he went, they would track him down. And so, after an exploratory phone call, he went to see Freddo one Saturday afternoon.

Freddo asked him to speak softly, because that morning Roberta had woken up feeling sick, and now she was trying to get some sleep. To build up his nerve, Sorcio had shot up twice in the course of an hour. His legs were unsteady and he was slurring his words. He smelled just as bad as back in the old days. Freddo opened the window. The winter chill made them both shiver. Sorcio felt like vomiting, and more than stating the facts, he conveyed them. It took Freddo a few minutes to understand. His questions kept drilling down on one basic point: but was he sure, 100 per cent sure, about this thing? Once the pressure became intolerable, Sorcio burst into tears.

Roberta, her face pale, her hair a mess, appeared in the doorway in pyjamas. Freddo reassured her, took her by the arm, led her back to bed. Sorcio's throat was dry. Freddo came back and slammed him against the wall. He pulled a revolver out of a drawer and span the cylinder. Then he pushed the muzzle against his forehead and told him to tell the story again, from start to finish, from the first time that ant in Torpignattara confided in him, up to when he went back over the accounts. And Sorcio repeated everything, in a faint voice.

'Aldo makes the horses give him shit without paying, then he steps on it with baby laxative, sells it below market price, and pockets the cash.

This has been going on for six or seven months. The horses are all afraid of him because one of them got his head cracked open when he tried to say something. So far, with this system, he's run through a good solid kilo of shit.'

Freddo put away the gun and, suddenly courteous and kind, asked him if he wanted to take a shower. Sorcio had a panicky eruption of paranoia.

'You're planning to kill me! You're planning to kill me! Kill me right away! Just do it now. Sweet God almighty, just kill me now! Jesus Christ, kill me now...'

A thin whiny voice came out of his mouth, unrecognizable, like a cornered animal. Roberta objected, her voice muffled, from the other room. Freddo slapped him in the face, then poured a glass of whiskey down his throat and politely showed him to the door.

Sorcio stood there in the street for a solid hour, shaking and repeating over and over: 'I'm alive, I'm still here.'

That night he shot up one last time, and as his jangled nerves calmed down, he swore that he was done once and for all with that life. He swore that this was his last dose, that tomorrow was another day. He swore every last thing he could possibly swear until a leaden sleep sucked him under.

Once Roberta started feeling better, three or four days after the meeting with Sorcio, Freddo took her out to a seafood restaurant in Trastevere, a place run by Calabrians, limping along on debt. He'd heard that Dandi had his eyes on it.

He'd invited Aldo Buffoni along too. Aldo brought a skinny, spacy chick in a long skirt with beads in her hair. Her name was Dorotea and she was studying art, but only, she said, to improve her karma. She and Roberta seemed to hit it off, and soon the two girls were deep in conversation.

Freddo studied Aldo. He was on edge, barely touched his *spaghetti allo scoglio*, guzzled half the bottle of white wine and, between one glass and the next, went to the bathroom three or four times. They ordered grilled swordfish. Aldo caused a scene with the waiter, whom he accused of giving him a threatening look. Someone complained at a nearby table. Dorotea and Roberta, rapt in their chitchat, seemed indifferent to whatever was going on. When Aldo got up yet again, Freddo followed him into the bathroom.

'Hey, Freddo, look out or they'll take us for a couple of faggots!' said Aldo while he was pissing.

Freddo smiled, went around behind him, and knocked him to the floor with one sharp blow of the knee to his spine. Then he seized Aldo's neck in an iron grip and shoved his head into the toilet bowl.

'Why would you do this to me, Aldo? Why you, of all people?'

Aldo was flailing his arms like a lunatic. Freddo loosened his grip and pulled him to his feet.

'What, have you lost your mind?'

'Why would you do such a thing to me?'

'I didn't do anything...'

'Look, I know everything. Don't try to bullshit me, Aldo, because if there's one person on earth who can still save your arse, it's me...'

'You've lost your mind...'

Freddo hauled back and punched him. Aldo keeled over and hit the floor. Freddo grabbed his head and started pounding it against the porcelain tiles.

'Unless you do exactly what I tell you, you're fucked, you hear me? Fucked.'

Someone knocked on the door. Freddo yelled out that his friend wasn't feeling well, but that he was taking care of him. Aldo started sobbing. Freddo soaked a wet towel and did his best to wipe off the tears and bloody cuts. He helped him to his feet and set him down on the can.

Aldo started whining. 'I don't know what came over me...Around here, everyone's looking out for themselves...Really, Freddo, I don't know what came over me...'

'Listen to me, Aldo. Now you get twenty million lire together and go deposit it in the general fund...'

'I don't have a lira to my name, Freddo!'

'I'll help you, don't worry! For six months your share is nothing. That whole time, you stick to your routine: you pick up the shit, you sell it in your zone, and you don't collect a dime. Stay on the straight and narrow, and everything will take care of itself...'

'What about the others?'

'Leave them to me. But don't fuck up, eh? Not even a lira short, not even a gram short on the scale...'

They emerged from the toilet with Freddo supporting him, one of his arms wrapped over his shoulder. Aldo had stopped sobbing by now, but there were unmistakable marks on his face, and he was pale as a sheet. All the diners at the other tables glared at them angrily.

Freddo paid the bill and left with Roberta. In the car, she burst out sobbing. Freddo moved closer and took her in his arms.

'I just had an abortion.'

'You never said a thing to me about it...'

'Why? What does it matter to you? You never even noticed. I only told that girl, Dorotea...She understood me...'

Freddo didn't know what to say. Back home, she told him that for the next few days they'd sleep separately. Freddo sat down to watch an old video cassette of *Mamma Roma*.

In the middle of the night, Roberta came to him.

'Please, whatever you do, don't hurt him!'

At dawn, Freddo called Nero. The phone rang and rang but no one picked up.

II

DISAPPEAR. THAT WAS what Zeta suggested. After the bomb in the Bologna train station, there was an unmistakable crackdown on the right. There were certain nosy judges who started asking questions about Pidocchio's mysterious death. Nero loaded a suitcase full of cash and a duffel bag full of weapons into the back of the Audi. Zeta procured a set of documents. The plan was a six- or seven-month stay in the Canton Ticino. As he approached the border crossing, Nero hummed the anarchist ballard '*Addio lugano bella*' under his breath. He had a sneaking fondness for the anarchists, especially those among them who had, patiently, day by day, built a destiny of rejection and defeat. Warriors, in their own way.

He wasn't leaving much behind him: just his entire world. But it was only a temporary departure. He'd write a letter to Freddo. Maybe he'd invite him to come up and stay a while in his provisional place of exile. He felt bad for Bufalo, a purebred fighter. But he honestly had to recognize that, in military terms, the operation had been a disaster. Too many seat-of-the-pants ambushes. There'd been a clear drop in quality. They'd gone bloodthirsty and just stopped thinking entirely. The Sioux never killed too many buffalo: mass extermination was something Stalinists – or palefaces – liked to do.

What now? A roadblock? The carabiniere waved him to a stop. Nero pulled over smoothly to the side of the road and held out his brand-new passport.

'Olivier Benson, eh?'

'*Oui.*'

'I'm going to have to search the car. I'm sorry, Monsieur Benson. Or would you rather I call you...'

When he heard the sound of his own real name, Nero understood that they'd sold him out. Zeta, that dishonourable bastard. Freddo had been right: he never should have trusted them.

He was about to put up his hands, but the carabiniere must have misinterpreted the move, or perhaps he'd received orders. A ragged burst of fire exploded from the muzzle of the sub-machine gun. Nero felt the lead biting into his legs and he curled up, shouting:

'Don't shoot! I'm unarmed!'

The carabiniere fired again. After all, he was just doing his duty, thought Nero as he lost consciousness; you can't argue with orders.

When he was told that Nero had survived, the Old Man flew into such a rage that, without thinking, he snapped an arm off his Dancing Girl of Düsseldorf, a model inspired by Hoffman's *Coppélia* of short stories. Once he realized what his unbridled fury had caused him to do, he felt both a stabbing jolt of remorse and a violent urge to have Zeta fed to the hogs.

'You realize what consequences you might face if that man were to...'

Zeta caught his breath. The Old Man was starting to take things a little too far. Instead of insulting him, maybe he should be worrying about the consequences *he* might face. All the same, he decided to reassure him.

'Nero won't talk. He's a loyal man. Perhaps this...regrettable incident will just cost us a pile of cash.'

'An opinion that comes to us from acknowledged heights of sage wisdom!' the Old Man retorted sarcastically.

Zeta had had his fill. He snapped a sharp military salute and turned on his heel.

Now what? The Old Man ordered his secretary to find him the finest expert in restoration of wooden statues in Rome. No, the finest in Italy. Wait, now that he thought about it, he could turn to the Czech Communists; after all, the Dancing Girl had been designed and carved in Bohemia. And even though things tended to change in a hundred and twenty-five years, and even if every variation tended inevitably to be a deterioration, some lingering trace of the age-old talent must still have survived...

Now what was to be done? Get rid of Zeta? And plunge into the thankless task of training up another useful idiot? There were only two paths forward: either a lightning operation inside the penitentiary where Nero was being held, or renew his trust of that degenerate progeny of Nietzsche. He'd think it over.

Why was his secretary taking so long? The sad gaze of the mutilated Dancing Girl was a vision that was breaking his heart.

III

WHEN THEY REACHED out to ask him to help procure a first-class expert witness, Mazzocchio, his nose still out of joint after what had happened with Professor Cervellone, played hard to get. If only they'd listened to him when the time was right! If only they hadn't been so arrogant! If only they'd had a little confidence in him! Still, Mazzocchio hesitated. Conditions weren't as favourable as they'd been two years ago. After hammering away relentlessly on his theories about the 'coalition of deviants', the professor had finally found someone who took him seriously: the investigating judges. And they'd thrown him in prison on charges of being one of the secret masterminds behind the right wing's bomb-planting strategy of terror. Still, in the end, after lengthy negotiation, and after extracting the promise of four or five ounces of cocaine, Mazzocchio coughed up a name.

So they placed themselves in the presumably capable hands of Professor Cortina, a piece of work with a booming voice and brusque manners who demanded an eighty-million-lire retainer, payable under the counter, in advance.

'The judge has appointed two of my colleagues. Fine professionals, tough opponents. I make no promises.'

Here's what we'll do; we'll see how it turns out. Freddo didn't feel his confidence gelling, so appointed Trentadenari to explore other options.

The most urgent problem at this point, however, was Dandi. Bufalo hadn't expressed his opinion, but Ricotta, from lock-up, was not being shy about calling down exemplary punishment.

'If that piece of shit hadn't been crapping his pants in fear, they'd never have caught us. As safe a bet as death itself!'

Fierolocchio, Scrocchiazeppi and the Buffoni brothers made no secret of where they stood. Dandi had behaved like a traitor. Whether it was fear or something else didn't much matter. Two of their comrades had fallen into the cops' hands and it was his fault. He needed to be punished.

Proposals ranged from expulsion from the gang to a bullet in the back of the head. But Dandi wasn't just an ordinary gang member. Nembo Kid and Botola made it clear that whoever laid a hand on Dandi might as well do the same to them.

Freddo had never felt so desperately alone. More than anything else, what he missed was Libano's wisdom and Nero's encouragement. Fierolocchio and the Buffoni boys were part of his past. Dandi was the present. Dandi had fucked up, no question. But taking him down would mean starting a war.

Trentadenari organized a reconciliation dinner. They all agreed to attend unarmed. They spoke over each other, trying to drown each other out. Harsh and determined were the voices of the accusers; arrogant and occasionally sarcastic were the voices of Dandi and his people.

'You just chickened out!'

'There wasn't time to intervene!'

'The ambush was poorly organized.'

'It was just a piece of bad luck.'

'It would have been easier to shoot than run away!'

Even in the Neapolitan's living room, even in the seating arrangement around the table, it was clear that they were becoming two separate things. With Freddo in the middle, mourning the dead.

They finally reached a compromise. Trentadenari was the mediator. Dandi would be responsible for all legal fees, expert witness included, and for however long the two men might remain under detention, the percentage and share due to them both would come out of Dandi's end. It sounded like an admission of guilt, but it also warded off far more dire consequences. They parted ways, saying their farewells in an atmosphere charged with tension: a perfunctory handshake, fleeting nods of the head, sidelong glances.

Dandi was well aware that something was broken, possibly for good. But unlike Freddo, he couldn't care less. So he hadn't shot a couple of cops in the back. There were things you could do and then there were things you couldn't. That was the lesson Uncle Carlo had taught him. Even Libano himself wouldn't have done any different. Rules. The rules of the game. You don't shoot cops in the back. As long as it was Nicolino Gemito, okay…But a couple of cops! If he'd pulled the trigger, in a couple of hours he would have had every uniformed cop in Italy gunning for him. He'd have been hotter than the Red Brigades!

Now the thing was to think about the future! About business! The problem with Freddo and the other guys was they kept living in their memories, in the past. And then this whole vendetta thing…When were they going to be done with it? Did they really think there was such a thing as an 'up there', some cloud that Libano was perched on, looking down on them and showering them with benedictions? Libano…Who could claim to have known him better than Dandi had? The things they'd been through together! And now he was nothing more than a side of rotting beef. No better or worse than Sardo, Ricciolodoro and that other guy…Terribile. They'd all been so scared of Terribile! And now he was spending his days hanging out with the worms…

Sure, Dandi could have fired, but he'd deliberately refrained from doing so. He would shoot when the time came, but only when he knew the time was right. Uncle Carlo had put it nicely: vendetta was noble, but business was important. If possible, the thing to do was tend to them both. If not, the dead could rest in peace.

'THE GREATER HORN of flame began to flail/And murmur like fire the wind beats, and to ply/Its tip which, as it vibrated here and there/Like a tongue in speech, flung out a voice to say:/"When..."

Protected by the massive bulk of his colleague Bulgarelli, Scialoja had managed to wedge himself in at the foot of Bologna's two towers. Standing minuscule, high atop the minaret, crowned by a Moorish moon, his voice enormously amplified by a formidable battery of powerful speakers, Carmelo Bene was declaiming Canto 26 of Dante's *Inferno*, dominating the immense crowd like an ancient deity, solitary and truculent.

'Not fondness for my son, nor any claim/Of reverence for my father, nor love I owed/Penelope, to please her, could overcome/My longing for experience of the world,/Of human vices and virtue...'

Bulgarelli had filled him in on the controversy that had preceded the first anniversary of the massacre. When the decision was made to hold a demonstration entitled 'Stop Terror Now!' and to transform grief into commemoration and mourning into celebration, there had been indignant objections. Many people would have preferred a more sober observation, perhaps the usual political boilerplate, the stem-winders spouted out by whatever politician happened to be in line. The idea of commemorating the tragedy with singing and dancing struck some as a desecration. Respectable citizens had thundered against the ludicrous idea of turning over the city to acrobats and strolling musicians. Bulgarelli had explained that 'Stop Terror Now!' meant affirming life with a mighty shout, talking against the darkness of death. It meant: we're here, in spite of everything, we're alive, and we won't forget. Bologna was there, the whole city, the sea at high tide. The great wizard high atop the tower was lending his voice to the collective defiance of grief.

"'O brothers who have reached the west," I began,/"Through a hundred thousand perils, surviving all:/So little is the vigil we see remain/Still for our senses, that you should not choose/To deny it the experience..."'

It was memory that had brought him back to Bologna, one year later. Memory, yes, as well as a new consciousness that he was making headway. Scialoja had become increasingly mistrustful of coincidences.

Nero's capture was the final blow. Scialoja couldn't imagine it, an operative as tough and experienced as Nero, letting himself be shot down like
an ungainly grouse by a carabinieri patrol team during a random document check at a roadblock. Nero was close-mouthed, saying nothing
except to confirm the official version: I was in the middle of an escape
attempt, they took me by surprise, I had a weapon, they beat me to the
draw, so now here I am.

Scialoja didn't believe him. It was a Fascist bomb. Nero was a Fascist.
Nero couldn't have planted the bomb because on 2 August 1980 he was
in prison. But Nero was a member of the organization that he and Borgia
were fighting. Zeta and Pigreco were protecting the organization. Zeta
and Pigreco were at the train station a few hours after the bomb went
off. The protection formed part of a larger exchange of favours. That
was what they needed to focus on. Favours. But what favours? To what
lengths were they willing to go? It might be handy for Zeta and Pigreco
to have people available who were ready to go to any lengths.

'Consider well your seed:/You were not born to live as a mere brute
does,/But for the pursuit of knowledge and the good...'

Scialoja had discussed his theory with Borgia. Borgia had put him
in contact with a prosecuting magistrate in Bologna. Bulgarelli was the
magistrate's trusted associate. Bulgarelli had listened very carefully to
what Scialoja had to say. Nero had done something or knew something.
Zeta and Pigreco decided to seal his lips once and for all. But what had
Nero done? What did Nero know? Something very, very serious, if they
really had decided to get rid of him. Scialoja couldn't imagine anything
worse than the train station bombing. But Bulgarelli had opened his eyes
to vast new horizons. In Bologna they had been investigating the links
between intelligence services, right-wing neo-Fascists and organized
crime. In Bologna they took certain things very seriously indeed. They
considered his contribution to be 'an invaluable piece of new investigative
intelligence'. Why were they so distracted in Rome? Was it just distraction, or something more? In Bologna, you could sense a certain optimism
in the air. There were whisperings – cautious, quiet whisperings – that
a big fish from the extreme right wing was about to turn informant,
bowed under by hard time in prison. In Bologna they didn't think that
the intelligence agencies had planted the bomb. More likely they'd gotten

involved afterwards. To protect, misinform, cut off, root and branch. And when Scialoja asked why, Bulgarelli had dragged him out into the street. Look at these people, he'd said. Look at this city. The Red capital of Italy. If they can bend Bologna to their will, they can bend Italy. It was all here, then: stand or fall. Stop the Reds. By any means possible.

'Then all of my companions grew so keen/To journey, spurred by this little speech I'd made,/I would have found them difficult to restrain./Turning our stern towards the morning light,/We made wings of our oars, in an insane/Flight.'

Carmelo Bene was shouting. His voice was piercing the stars. The piazza fell silent, the streets all around fell silent. Two hundred thousand anonymous faces giving in willingly to dizzying vertigo, hearts on fire, revisiting Ulysses' last voyage like the officiants of an ancient rite. Carmelo Bene was singing for Bologna. Carmelo Bene was singing for the world of the living. Carmelo Bene was singing for him. There was nothing to understand. There were just certain things you had to experience.

Scialoja felt a hand grip his arm. Bulgarelli's eyes filled with tears. They hadn't succeeded in beating Bologna to its knees. The train station had been rebuilt. High up there, the moon was rivalled only by the searchlights slicing across the towers crowded with prominent officials eager to congratulate the actor. Scialoja and Borgia weren't the only ones who glimpsed links, guessed at connections. Even if evidence vanished, even if certainties crumbled, it was their duty to move forward.

V

PROFESSOR CORTINA REPORTED that Bufalo's evaluation was going badly.

'Your friend was too smart for his own good on those tests, and my colleagues spotted what he was doing. Now it's been put down, black ink on white paper, a fine, unmistakable "simulated mental illness". We need a dramatic plot twist here. The problem is, we don't have a single scrap of documentation. And apparently the young man has an iron constitution!'

The phrase 'iron constitution' gave Trentadenari a sudden inspiration. He checked it out with Vanessa and a few days later went to see Cortina with a thick file under his arm.

'Professor, in your opinion, can this stuff be useful at all?'

The professor rapidly skimmed the documentation.

'You wait until now to tell me about these things?'

'I don't know, I guess we forgot…'

'What, and you guess he forgot too?'

'He was the first to forget, professor…We know he's not quite right in the head, don't we?'

They exchanged an eloquent gaze. The professor demanded another fifteen million lire and ushered Trentadenari out of the office with a winning smile.

'With the bomb we're about to drop on them, we're stitched up cosier than a cow's belly!'

The next day, Cortina presented the documents to his fellow experts. Bufalo, born prematurely, was the victim in childbirth of a transient hypoxia with resultant neurological trauma. The functionality of a number of cerebral areas was gravely compromised. At age fifteen, in the wake of emerging behavioural oddities, he had been expelled from school and hospitalized for tests and observation in a well-known clinic in Rome. The file, dutifully made available in the spirit of collegiality, documented the presence of neocortical epileptic foci and multiple malacic lesions in the cortical zone. Bufalo was certainly, absolutely unwell. The experts acknowledged the evidence of the facts. Cortina was a luminary whose competence was not open to debate. The documentation was perfectly in compliance, complete with stamps, dates and signatures.

All credit is due to my brilliant hunch, Trentadenari explained to the others, and of course Vanessa's enterprising flair: she'd pilfered the documentation of some poor loser who'd died a good ten years back and had assembled the montage with the assistance of a young, newly minted doctor with a pair of floury white nostrils. The whole operation had cost a tidy sum. But what did that matter – Dandi was paying!

Dandi was paying, and happily, because there was plenty of money. The Sardinian land deal was proceeding swimmingly. The Maestro paid punctually, and the initial capital investment was beginning to yield nice returns, with extras that, by common agreement, he and Nembo Kid decided not to share with the others. As Uncle Carlo liked to put it, this was *cosa loro*, their thing, and *solo loro*, theirs alone. Uncle Carlo had appreciated Dandi's behaviour in the aftermath of Nicolino Gemito's murder, and he was not shy about letting him know.

'The lesson I taught you about flatfoots was a good thing. You're out on the street, free and unfettered, and for the others? It's just another occupational hazard!'

The Old Man, too, had been impressed with his tactical instincts, and he'd conveyed that sentiment through Zeta and Pigreco. The spies offered to arrange for 'a little something' to befall the commissario. Dandi, the new Dandi, let the offer drop. Things were going famously. Investigations languished and cases were dropped one after another. No point in poking the sleeping guard dog with a stick. After all, the policeman forced him to think about Patrizia. That remained an open question, and if he was going to play his cards, he'd do so with cunning and sensitivity. He'd stopped pestering her for that prison conversation she stubbornly continued to refuse him. She was certainly offended, and he could hardly blame her. He'd have to come up with a strategy to make his way back.

Vasta had reconciled him to waiting for the terms of preventive incarceration to expire: that meant waiting patiently for just a few short months. And Dandi was discovering the value of patience, the pleasure of toying with time. Uncle Carlo's words had paved a superhighway through his mind. You could learn everything from the Mafia's men of honour. So Dandi studied. He regularly forwarded a share of the profits from the real estate deal to Secco, and that channel too was showing very promising results. Therefore, in the autumn, when Gina started demanding money, Dandi handed her thirty million lire without blinking an eye. Maybe his wife had found a boyfriend; maybe they could even start discussing the idea of divorce. Perhaps Patrizia, newly sprung from prison, might find a nice coming-out present waiting for her: a handsome offer of marriage.

Then, one morning when he was dropping by the old apartment to pick up a Futurist canvas that he thought would look nice hanging in the boudoir of the new place, he found himself face to face with none other than Don Dante. The prison chaplain had advanced his career: now he was a parish priest on the Via del Corso, with venerable aristocrats, actors and politicians among his flock. All beaming smiles, Don Dante told him that he had just administered holy communion to 'your priceless wife Gina, that creature of most pious sentiment'. And he thanked him, in the bishop's name as well, for his exceedingly Catholic generosity.

Dandi opened his mouth in a creditable impersonation of a newly gaffed tuna fish. The priest assured him up and down that whatever problem might present itself, he was sure to find in the priest and the cassock he wore 'the staunchest ally imaginable'.

Dandi questioned Gina. Of the original thirty million, she'd donated ten million for masses for the recovery of the Pope, wounded just a few months ago by that criminal lunatic of a Turk. The rest of the money had been put to good work: pious charity on behalf of the poorer parishioners, a tangible sign of jubilation for the miraculous salvation of the Holy Father and a dutiful tribute to the Almighty for His intervention, which had surely proven decisive. Dandi was blind with fury. What was she thinking, to waste money that way? Why couldn't she be like all the other wives and buy a nice fur coat, or take a nice expensive holiday somewhere?

'I'm doing it for you too, for your soul, cursed to hell!' was her grim-faced response.

Dandi didn't know what to say, and decided to just leave well enough alone. After all, if she wanted to become a nun...As long as she got out from underfoot, that living corpse of a woman!

In that period, Trentadenari took a little trip to Naples, where he met with Baffo di Ghisa. They were cousins. Baffo, like him, was a guy who was happy to change sides early and often. First he was allied with the Giuliano clan of Forcella, then he went over to the Cutolo clan, and then, after a quick excursion through the ranks of the Mariano clan, he'd returned as an ally of Professor Cutolo. Finally, in the aftermath of a bloodbath that ended with five corpses sprawled out in the Via Toledo, he went into hiding in Uruguay, a notoriously open-armed country with no extradition treaty. Now he was living the life of a wealthy landowner, surrounded by beautiful *chicas* in a fairytale *fazenda*, returning to Italy two or three times a year with a few kilos of coke to put into circulation, just to keep from losing his touch.

Trentadenari told him all the latest developments, and when they got to the touchy subject of the expert witnesses, Baffo recommended he drop his contacts with Professor Cervellone and all his ilk.

'First of all: all these *professors* are spies…'

'What do you mean, spies?'

'That's right, spies – secret agents, spooks, whatever you call them in Rome. They gather up secrets and sell them to the highest bidder.'

'What on earth are you saying?'

'Eh, I'm just telling you…Second thing: either they kill Cervellone in prison, or when he gets out, the *cumparielli* – the Mafia – will take care of him…'

'But why?'

'Because he's playing both sides against the middle, that's why!'

And so one fine morning, Trentadenari took Freddo to an office over near the building housing the Italian parliament. There he met a well-mannered and elegant gentleman in his early fifties who claimed to be a 'long-time friend' of the investigating judge, the one who held Bufalo's fate in his hands. For twenty million lire, the outcome of the trial was guaranteed. Freddo would have been all too happy to walk away from there – everything about that man, from the scent of the sacristy to the unctuous smile, radiated falsehood – but Trentadenari was so sure he knew what he was doing that in the end, the bundle of cash changed hands.

Baffo di Ghisa's prophesy, in the meantime, was taking shape. First they slaughtered one of Cervellone's assistants with a spray of sub-machine gunfire. Prison radio, which attributed the attack to the Neapolitans (though who could say whether members of the old-school or the new-school family), spread the rumour that the professor was curled up in his cell, ready to squeal on them all. That was probably a fabrication, but Cervellone had pulled one too many, no matter what the truth of the matter might be. And so, a short while later, when the Court of Cassation overturned all the warrants for his arrest and he was set free, the *cumparielli*, always one step ahead of the law, seized him and beheaded him, just like St John the Baptist at the court of Herod the Butcher.

Patrizia was released from prison in late October. A few days before getting out, she'd saved the life of Palma, the female terrorist. Word had started to circulate that Palma's boyfriend was on the verge of turning informant. That betrayal demanded punishment. The Red prisoners isolated her. Palma could easily have asked to be transferred but she chose not to. She threw down the gauntlet: she was ready to face trial before a 'people's tribunal'. Her sister terrorists took her at her word, met in council, and sentenced her to death. They considered her to be a creature of her man, dancing to his tune. They feared she might turn traitor. They ganged up on her during the afternoon exercise hour in the yard, six of them tackling her alone. Two pinned down her arms, two held her legs, and two of them tugged on the rope wrapped around her throat that they'd patiently plaited from strips of a pair of blue jeans ripped to shreds.

Patrizia had sensed it coming. She charged, bellowing, down on the knot of prisoners. Palma was already emitting death rattles. Patrizia began raining down kicks, scratches, savage bites, grabbing handfuls of the hair of a petite ferocious woman, twisting tits, kneeing arses, plunging thumbs into eye sockets. The racket finally woke up a guard or two. Patrizia was physically hanging off one of the two executioners, her fingernails digging deep into her throat.

None of it seemed to have any effect: she and her accomplice continued hauling on the noose, and Palma turned blue in the face, her legs shaking with an uncontrollable tremor. Even under a hail of billy clubs, the two women held tough. There was no missing the point: they were determined to eliminate Palma! It took six rank-and-file guards and two brutal and brawny non-commissioned officers to get her out of the women's clutches. They rushed her to the intensive care unit at the Policlinico.

The day Patrizia received notification of her release, Palma, now out of danger, returned to the prison infirmary. Patrizia went to visit. Palma was wearing an orthopaedic collar and when she saw her, she limited herself to a chilly little greeting. From her revolutionary point of view, the trial had been just, the sentence equitable. She almost resented the fact that Patrizia had saved her life. Patrizia flew into a rage.

285

'You're twenty-four years old! You're pretty, you have an education, and you still waste yourself on these pieces of shit. I told you they were pieces of shit, didn't I? You should do like your man: rat them all out, fuck them, comrade sister!'

'Fuck you, you hoodlum bitch!'

A wave of pity swept over Patrizia. She might very well have murdered two men, this Palma, but in here, surrounded by all these wolves, she still looked like a little girl to Patrizia.

'I left a carton of cigarettes with the head nurse here. I spread word that you're under Dandi's protection. Maybe they'll give you a single cell. More than that, I couldn't do...'

Palma sighed, then a faint smile twisted her chapped lips.

'Well, I'd better be going,' Patrizia said brusquely. 'Seeing as I'm free to go, I don't think I'd better hang around. You know how it is – they might get the idea that I'm tempted to stay and send me the bill!'

Palma laughed. Patrizia was already out the door when her prison sister called her name.

'Patri...'

'Aah, you can talk again! *Evviva!*'

'Don't waste your life!'

Outside the main gate was Dandi, standing next to his new Porsche, holding a basket of orchids. Patrizia strode towards him beaming, planted a kiss on his lips, and then suddenly hauled off and smacked him in the face with a tremendous roundhouse punch that left him reeling. She darted rapidly behind the wheel, put the car in gear, stomped on the accelerator and roared off, clipping Dandi in her getaway, who was left to curse all the saints known and even a few unknown, saints that resided only among his own personal set of Madonnas.

VI

SCIALOJA WAS SLEEPING with his arms hugging his pillow. Patrizia, awake, was watching over him. Her gaze was running over the curve of his nose, caressing his broad, muscular chest, descending the length of his legs, and following the silhouette of an arm marked by the tiny wounds of their lovemaking at play. Love! Patrizia slipped out of bed, drew the covers over him, and went into the bathroom to light a cigarette.

She was ashen in the light of the vanity bulbs surrounding the mirror. She looked downcast and unsettled, and she began to feel out of place again. When had she really ever felt any different? Maybe only in prison. In prison you didn't have to answer to anyone about how you used your time. Only to yourself. Maybe that's all I'm looking for after all, she thought. Maybe it's just boredom.

Patrizia slipped on a heavy robe, pocketed cigarettes and a lighter, and headed for the French doors that led onto the little terrace of their suite at the Marina Grande Hotel. As she went by the bed, she saw he was still asleep. A vague smile flickered on his lips. Patrizia opened the French doors and gently closed them behind her. A gust of icy wind made her shiver. There was a slender crescent moon, riding high in the sky. The sea was crashing stormily against a bulwark made up of what seemed like a fragile barrier of rocky shoals. At the centre of the vast expanse of darkness, she could just guess at the lights of Capri.

She had told him: I've always wanted to see Capri. He'd rushed down to the waterfront to reserve a boat. At the last second, with a flimsy excuse, she'd cancelled the excursion. Oh, she'd been to Capri before, more times than she could remember. With men and women whose faces she'd long since banished from her memory. But she couldn't forget their laughter. The salacious wisecracks. The endless mockery. The cash transactions. She hadn't been unhappy then, exactly, but she hadn't been happy either. For that matter, she was neither one thing nor the other right now.

Patrizia lit a second cigarette with the smouldering butt of the first, then flicked it out into space. She tried to follow the trail all the way down to the sand beneath her, but the glowing cinder died out halfway to the ground. She heard the sound of the French doors opening, and then he was behind her. Instinctively she laid her head against his chest. Scialoja wrapped his arms around her, kissing her neck.

'Come inside, it's as cold as a witch's tit out here!'

He was bare-chested, the macho man. With a smile, Patrizia let him steer her back into the room.

'Penny for your thoughts?' he asked, pulling two small bottles of champagne out of the mini bar.

'I have none.'

'You want to talk?'

'Later,' she murmured.

That was the word most often on her lips these days. Later.

She had stopped him dead as he left the police station, cutting off his path with the front fender of Dandi's Porsche.

'Let's go to your place,' she'd suggested. 'I want to see where you live.'

Once inside the small studio apartment near the university, she'd wrinkled her nose. The half-empty refrigerator had filled her with sadness. She stopped him when he tried to take a shower.

'I want you just as dirty as I am. I want you to know what prison tastes like.'

They had made love like a man and a woman. He had slowly and leisurely kissed her neck and breasts. They'd gripped each other tightly and furiously.

'Talk to me about yourself,' he suggested.

'Later.'

'Are we going to be together, at least for a little while?'

'Later.'

'I have lots of things to tell you...'

'Later.'

That morning she had taken him to Positano. He'd turned pale when he laid eyes on the Porsche. But he'd followed her lead. He'd rid himself of all obligations with a single phone call. Now he was with her. And he was happy.

'Here's to impossible love affairs,' he toasted.

Patrizia emptied her champagne glass in a single gulp.

'Come here,' she ordered.

He threw himself at her feet. She clawed his cheek. He groaned in pleasure. She wrapped her hands around his neck and throttled him. He up-ended her as if she were a little girl, a basketful of goose down. Patrizia, eyes open, stared at the ceiling. Since that night in prison, she hadn't dreamt again. Palma told her: don't waste your life. Ranocchia said: fuck them all. Patrizia was trying to be a woman – his woman. She closed her eyes. He whispered sweet nothings to her; he whispered insults. Patrizia opened her eyes. Her line of sight was filled by a face twisted by the tension of pleasure, veins standing out, drops of sweat glistening on muscles straining to delay the impending orgasm. She shoved him away with a shudder of horror. He didn't understand. And how could he have? She'd glimpsed another man. One of many.

'Let's do it from behind,' she said, soothing him in a low, hoarse voice. Scialoja grabbed her by both breasts and slid into her. Patrizia closed her eyes again.

'Please come now,' she whispered. 'Let's come together…my love…'

Just before dawn, Patrizia wrote a brief note of farewell, grabbed the travel bag she'd packed the night before, settled the bill, and reminded the manager, an old friend of Ranocchia's, to keep his mouth shut. Waiting for her in the garage was Dandi's Porsche.

When Scialoja woke up, he understood immediately. To stifle his sobs, he plunged under the spray of an ice-cold shower. He found the note while stuffing his things hastily into his duffel bag. On it was written a word – *weapons* – and an address.

VII

THEY WERE HAVING dinner in their usual restaurant when Uncle Carlo asked Dandi and Nembo Kid if they would be willing to 'do him a favour'.

Dandi said yes immediately, sight unseen. Uncle Carlo liked that boy more and more every time he saw him. Nembo Kid, spraying lobster juice in all directions, asked what kind of favour he had in mind. Uncle Carlo, disgusted, yielded the floor to the Maestro.

'We have a problem with Cravattaro.'

'What kind of problem?'

'Lately he's been under a certain amount of stress…He's not behaving as well as he used to…He's not sticking to our arrangements…'

Uncle Carlo approved that statement with a broad smile. Dandi understood immediately that Cravattaro's fate was sealed.

'Why us in particular?'

'Everyone's the master of their own house,' Uncle Carlo pointed out, still smiling. 'And when you're at someone else's house, it's not like you just get up and pour yourself a drink. You let the master of the house serve you. Isn't that right?'

Uncle Carlo knew perfectly well that Cravattaro was an old friend. Entrusting the job to the two of them was a mark of respect, but also a test.

Dandi and Nembo Kid gave their word and, three nights after the dinner, with Botola along on the job, they shot Cravattaro as he left Villa Candy.

This was a sudden and unorthodox development. Cravattaro had been a member of the underworld in good standing for twenty years. He was considered untouchable. The reports of his death in the newspapers speculated on the violent end of a 'skilful and ruthless businessman' who, after 'early beginnings shrouded in some mystery', lived in luxury, moving freely in – and enjoying the respect of – Rome's high society.

Borgia speculated it might have been something personal, someone sleeping with someone else's wife, or, at the very most, an act of vengeance by some debtor pushed to the end of his rope. It never seemed to occur to anyone that they might have had anything to do with it. There'd never been such a clean job of murder.

Only Freddo understood instantly what had happened. He'd recognized the style. In that period, he'd been thrown in the slammer for an unserved sentence dating back to 1976. He got word to his comrades through Roberta, and the ones still on the outside summoned Dandi to account for his deeds. Dandi lied shamelessly: while someone was shooting Cravattaro, poor old thing, he was enjoying the Franco Califano concert with a brand-new girlfriend. He'd even managed to get a couple of autographs. What, was the Caliph a suspect now, too?

The whole thing just stuck in Scrocchiazeppi and Fierolocchio's throats.

'It was definitely them.'

'Obviously. I wonder what kind of a quarrel they had with that unlucky bastard!'

'Those guys are freelancers, running a gang on their own!'

'I'd like to go back over the accounts and see if everything adds up!'

'Trentadenari's in charge of accounting…'

'What, you trust him?'

This time, they couldn't let things slide. Freddo sensed that a crucial turning point was fast approaching. He told the others that measures would be taken. They couldn't keep putting the issue off.

But the issue was in fact put off.

It was just before Christmas when the anti-terrorism squad placed judicial seals on the store room in the ministry cellar.

The Smell of Blood
January–April 1982

I

AT THE PRESS conference the chief of police explained that the political branch of the police department had stumbled upon the weapons by pure chance. An old report identified the custodian Brugli as a left-wing extremist. A zealous bureaucrat had had the brilliant notion of a routine check-up, one of a constant round of watered-down searches and interviews. But the minute the unfortunate Brugli saw four big, strong officers in combat gear, he spilled the beans.

'This is all Ziccone's fault!'

So it was Ziccone this and Ziccone that, and weeping and wailing and banging heads against walls. In the end, Brugli led the cops down into the cellar. At the sight of that formidable armoury, the policemen had a hard time believing their own eyes.

A couple of reporters dared to ask whether there might not be the fingerprints of a police informant behind that brilliant piece of sleuthing. While the chief of police manifested, *Urbi et Orbi*, his indignation at the very idea, Scialoja scampered out of the room, suppressing a faint smile of contempt. He'd arranged with his superior officers to stay out of the picture entirely. The chief of police was incredulous. In all his years on the force, he'd seen policemen much less promising than Scialoja cut each others' throats for a tiny squib on the local crime pages, and now that Scialoja had a shot at the front page...But Scialoja was unyielding. It was all part of a larger strategy, he'd explained; and in any case, he wanted to avoid burning his source. The chief of police had shrugged at that response: if that's the way he wanted it!

Borgia hadn't wasted more than a throwaway line.

'I see that your relations with La Vallesi are developing wonderfully well, commissario.'

Scialoja responded with nothing but a bitter smile. Borgia revealed a twinge of human feeling and desisted from his mockery.

Of course, the tip-off had been Patrizia's farewell gift. Scialoja had looked for her everywhere. She just didn't want to be found. Scialoja couldn't resign himself to the idea of a love affair without a future. He'd go on looking for her. He had to find her. He had to walk away.

They'd made love like a man and a woman. She'd let herself go, heart and soul. But is that what had really happened? Now he was starting to understand certain extended silences, certain vague smiles, her eternal procrastination. He'd held her in his hands, and then he'd let her go! He hadn't been capable of tying her to him. Was there anyone capable of tying her down?

Scialoja struggled to suppress the turmoil warring in his heart, a basso continuo in his everyday life, from bleary awakening to nights of tossing and turning. He had to use cold reason. Forget about her. Focus on his investigation.

Scialoja hurried into the office by the early dawn light and pulled the door shut behind him as he left in late-night darkness. And the night was black. The night was hard.

In the meantime, the whole gang was in the middle of a complete shit storm. That pig Brugli (teach them to trust a Red!) hadn't even been offered a chair in the UCIGOS director's office before he'd already spilled the complete list of names.

In the middle of the night, handcuffs snapped on the wrists of Ziccone to start with, but also Trentadenari, Scrocchiazeppi and Nembo Kid, while Bufalo, who already had plenty of trouble of his own, and Freddo, on the brink of release, were served with shiny new incarceration orders.

The idiot porter named those names and no others. Just why a number of regular customers of the ministry's basement armoury should have been missing from the catalogue – among them Nero, Fierolocchio and Dandi himself – would remain a stubborn mystery.

The fact remained that Borgia rubbed his hands eagerly and immediately issued an indictment for weapons possession, plus Article 416 of the criminal code: racketeering and criminal conspiracy.

'It's starting to look like you have a fixation,' Vasta said in jest. 'Every time one of my clients is unjustly accused of something, out comes a racketeering charge...Are you still chasing after your imaginary "gang", Dottore Borgia?'

'I'm curious to see just how you'll wriggle out of it this time. We have a nice solid case!'

'In the end, as always, I'll be successful in proving my clients had nothing whatsoever to do with these matters.'

That much was due to his lawyerly art, and certainly all that he was going to give that oaf of a prosecuting magistrate. But when meeting with his clients, Vasta stripped off his mask of amiable equanimity and unfurled the furrowed brow and grim scowl suitable to the world of pain that faced them.

'Brugli's conspiracy testimony is rock solid. We're just lucky that Ziccone acted like a man, or we'd really be up to our neck in shit. We need to find some way to reframe the facts...'

'The real problem is that there are hot pistols in that room,' Freddo pointed out.

Vasta went all stiff and professional.

'Those are matters that do not concern me in any way.'

Freddo's jaw dropped. He'd long since dropped all playacting with his lawyer. He thought things were abundantly clear between the two of them.

'What's going on, counsellor? Are you pulling in your oars?'

'There are certain things you'd do better not to share, even with your lawyer,' he cut in brusquely, gathering up his notebook and bag. 'We'll talk in the next few days.'

Things were out of control if even Vasta was looking for the exit. In any case, the problem of the weapons wasn't just going to take care of itself. In the store room there was the pistol that had killed Tigame, the one used on Saracca, the sub-machine guns that cut short Terribile's reign, a couple of revolvers that were fired on Sardo and, most important of all, the Tanfoglio that Nero had used to eliminate Pidocchio.

Who was still outside and free to move around? Dandi, Fierolocchio, the Buffoni boys, Botola...And even Sorcio, who counted for nothing, the poor cuckold. It was up to them to solve the problem.

Vanessa smuggled the message out of the prison. In the scrap of paper that Nurse Vanessa hid where guards didn't search, Freddo had jotted down: *Hey Dandi-lookout-Tanf-Pidocchio-Nero.*

Dandi got down to work. If for no other reason than that the case affected him personally. Brugli, who at one time or another had seen them all at the ministry, could suddenly decide to get talkative. The danger of a tidal wave of arrests was real. The consequences could prove disastrous.

First, preventive measure: everybody off the streets and into hiding. Some holed up in hotels with false IDs; others, like Fierolocchio, went to lie low with relatives in the Marche. Sorcio remained behind to oversee the drug trade, under armed threat; once the typhoon had blown over, he'd be required to account for every last cent, or he'd be done for. The general fund was entrusted to Donatella, who was thus in charge of seeing to the needs of those in prison: double share for Bufalo and Ricotta, who never got tired of busting chops.

Dandi asked Zeta and Pigreco for help. The spies shrugged: it was none of their business.

'Ah, so that's how it is? When *you* need a favour, it's all friendly back-slapping…But now what kind of friends are you?'

'It's not our fault you guys got yourselves arrested. You've only got yourselves to blame.'

'Well, I know that Nero used the store room just like the rest of us…'

'So? Why should I give a flying fuck about Nero?'

'The gun that killed Pidocchio was in that room too!'

Zeta flew into a rage, but what could he really do? They had him firmly by the balls! If word got back to the Old Man, he and his partner were fucked. At the very least, he'd lock them both up inside one of his mechanical toys.

Zeta hurried to see Uncle Carlo. The Sicilian was tangled up in the Pidocchio case too, so the best idea was to report to him and try to come up with a solution together. Uncle Carlo, without getting bent out of shape, told him he'd think it over, and then invited Dandi to dinner.

'One time, in Palermo, they arrested two gunmen, a couple of gunsels. There were three eyewitnesses, and they'd all seen the gunmen standing

296

over the dead body with the rifle still smoking. They had an expert evaluation performed, and it turned out the rifle was, what's the word – *fasano*.'

'What's "*fasano*" mean?'

'It means it was *favuso* – fake. It wouldn't shoot. It was nothing more than a piece of carved wood. It never had fired and it never would. The two gunmen were released with a formal apology.'

'I understand, Uncle Carlo. But what did they do about the witnesses? Bang bang?'

'Naw. They'd misidentified the suspects, so they said they were very, very sorry!'

Not much more to be said. Before bidding Dandi farewell, Uncle Carlo chided him affectionately for the stubble on his face.

'These have been tough days, Uncle.'

'Eh, my son, you'll have plenty of stale bread to sink your teeth into in the days to come!'

II

DANDI SAW THE Porsche parked in front of his apartment building, looked up, saw the lights on in the windows of his apartment, and understood that Patrizia had come back. He ran up the stairs, taking them four at a time, panting with the effort because lately he'd put on a few pounds. Inga, the Austrian girl that he'd been squirming around for the past month or so, promising her a brilliant career in the world of nightclubs, was chasing after him, cursing as she teetered on her stiletto heels.

Patrizia was sitting on the sofa, beneath the canvas by Tamburi, with a glass in one hand and her legs crossed. She was a blonde now. From the instant he entered the room, his voice boomed, almost a shout.

'How the fuck did you get in here?'

'With my keys,' she replied, unruffled.

'Who's that?'

Inga had taken up a stance in the middle of the living room, arms akimbo, brow furrowed. Patrizia looked the six-foot whore up and down, ran her disgusted gaze over the jacket that could barely contain a buxom FF cup, dismissed the heavy make-up, sniffed with distaste at her powerful perfume, and finally flashed an insincere smile.

'Get rid of this slut. We need to talk.'

'Who are you calling slut?'

Dandi stopped the Austrian girlfriend, spun her around, and managed to get rid of her with a series of whispered sweet nothings and a pretty substantial cheque. When he came back to the living room, Patrizia was peacefully enjoying a cigarette. Dandi had decided to take a hardline approach.

'You mind telling me where you've been all these months?'

'At the hairdresser. Doesn't it show?'

Dandi took a step towards her, arm raised. That woman had always been able to get under his skin.

'If you so much as lay a finger on me, you'll never see me again.'

Dandi spread both arms wide and plastered a diplomatic smile on his face. After all, she'd come back. After all, the minute he'd laid eyes on her, he hadn't been able to think of anything but that one thing: *ficcarisilli*, as Uncle Carlo would have put it: to fuck her good and hard.

'Fine, fine. Can I sit down, at least?'

God, she smelled good. Dandi could feel a fire start to burn deep inside him. He tried to make a clumsy pass. Patrizia blocked it.

'Well, why the hell did you even come back, goddamn it?'

'I've lost my home. I want a new apartment.' Patrizia stood up, looked around, and seemed to like what she was seeing. 'I'll take this one!'

'You already have the keys. You can come and go as you please...'

'I'm talking about property ownership, darling. Four walls. Deed of trust. Land registry. You follow the concept?'

Patrizia kicked off first one shoe, then the other. She delicately massaged her heel and then, with a sudden gesture, she unbuttoned her jacket. Underneath she was wearing a demi cup bra. Flame red. Dandi sighed.

'You want the apartment? It's all yours!'

Patrizia smiled and walked over to him. Dandi reached out a hand and laid it on her breast. She pulled away.

'Now that I think about it, darling, an apartment's very nice to live in, but in terms of work...'

'What do you mean, work?'

'Earning a living, that's what I'm talking about.'

'You want to start the bordello back up?'

'No more bordello. No more fucking spies. No more guys with loose pistols. A discreet, classy little house. Mine, and mine alone.'

'Let's not exaggerate now, eh!'

Patrizia took off her skirt. She was wearing minuscule panties, the same colour as the bra. She went and stood in front of him. She seized his curly-locked head and plunged it between her legs. She started undulating slowly.

'It's all or nothing!'

Inebriated by the smell of her, Dandi wavered between desire and rational thought. He was fighting to become a *capo*. And becoming a *capo* meant being able to afford the whims of a *capo*. Dandi knew that he'd never find another woman like Patrizia even if they made him the eighth king of fucking Rome. Dandi made up his mind. Fuck Uncle Carlo, fuck the guys, and fuck his scruples. Patrizia and him were made for each other. That was something he could feel inside. So Patrizia wanted an apartment? Two apartments? He'd buy her a whole apartment building. A street. A city. That's what money was for, anyway. To live. That's what life was.

'All,' he moaned, trying to make his way between the folds of the red fabric. 'I want it all.'

Patrizia delicately shoved his hands aside and placed one of her long legs on his chest.

'I still haven't heard you making a phone call to your notary, Dandi, *bello*!'

In the middle of the night, once everything had returned to the way it was in the old days, including Patrizia's demand that he take a shower first before they had sex, when Dandi lay snoring, played out, his cock chafed red with overuse, she turned on all the lights and yanked him out of bed.

'What the fuck else could there be now?'

'That animal,' Patrizia spoke imperiously, pointing at Alonzo, who was pacing hungrily in the cage that was by now far too small for his adolescent lion frame. 'I want it gone, immediately!'

III

ZETA WAS IN charge of relations with the expert witnesses appointed by the investigating judge. One of the ballistics experts had long been on the intelligence agency's payroll, so he had no choice about co-operating. In part because, like it or not, he was bound to make a tidy sum. The other expert, a Lombard with a straightforward manner, was a tough customer. Too honest to talk to. Either kill him – a counterproductive and expensive approach – or find another solution.

Borgia had demanded a comparative analysis, exhuming the shells and bullets from the last five years of shootings. The friendly expert talked his colleague into splitting up their responsibilities. While the Lombard laboured away peacefully on the weapons of no particular interest, the other expert – with acids, sledgehammers and corrosive compounds – was busy neutralizing the hot weapons. Riflings, striations and barrels were all sanded, scraped, punched and ravaged. Any comparison with previous homicides became impossible. It was a brilliant way of limiting the damage and it only cost ninety million lire.

Botola and Fierolocchio took care of the rest of it. When Brugli, as a reward for singing, was let out on bail, they went to pay a call on him, offering him chump change to retract his testimony. There was no need to even mention the alternative – a bullet to the head, or a plunge to the bottom of the muddy Tiber waters. As evidence of his good will, Brugli handed over a duffel bag with three semi-automatic pistols and a machine rifle that, for reasons unknown even to him, had eluded the investigators.

Bright and early the next morning, Brugli was waiting in Borgia's office, complete with lawyer and petition. Ziccone had nothing to do with any of what happened, and his only crime was that of having intro-duced Brugli to Bufalo. Now Bufalo, a terrifying individual, mad, bad and practically insane, came and went as he pleased and sometimes brought a friend with him; and no, Ziccone had no idea who the friends were. Brugli – terrorized by the police search of the premises, thrown into a state of panic by the violent methods and cowing tactics of the anti-ter-rorism officers, who were flagrantly indifferent to his civil rights – had been practically coerced into reeling off the first names that came into his mind.

'I read those names in the newspapers, Judge, Your Honour, and that's why I accused them. But I swear to you on the heads of my children that I've never seen them as long as I've lived!'

When Bufalo learned that he'd been chosen as the scapegoat and fall guy, he shattered the television set, ripped the toilet out of the floor, and even managed to bend two of his window bars. To calm down the Incredible Hulk in action, it took a special assault squad, and Bufalo wound up in the infirmary with two broken ribs.

Freddo went to see him with Pischello and explained that the reason they'd picked him was that he was already indicted for the Fleming Hill murders.

'And if things go the way we're hoping with the expert witnesses, you'll get off with mental infirmity for the weapons too!'

Bufalo couldn't hear the words that Freddo was trying to foist off on him, and if it hadn't been for Pischello's soothing words – the kid seemed to have some kind of magic effect on his nerves – he would have eaten Freddo alive right then and there. In the end, they managed to talk him into it. But deep down, his rancour kept rising, like yeasty dough.

In spite of Borgia's best shots, Trentadenari, Nembo Kid, Ziccone and Scrocchiazeppi were ordered to be released. When Vasta showed up with his bill, it was all Trentadenari could do to keep from slapping him in the face.

'Hey, you realize we did it all ourselves, right?'

'That's not quite accurate,' the member of the bar insisted in an icy voice. 'The idea of revising the facts worked beautifully, and that was *my* idea!'

Freddo, on the other hand, remained in prison. Borgia had managed to come up with a new warrant: this time on charges of having suborned and intimidated poor Brugli. No one had any doubts that the whole thing would soon be resolved. But in the meantime, still sitting in his cell, Freddo missed the party in honour of Beato Porco.

Beato Porco – literally the 'blessed pig' – was a tall, hairy oaf, almost more gorilla than human being, and had worked with Feccia back in the days of Baron Rosellini. Word was that he was the one the kidnap victim caught a glimpse of, thus signing his own death sentence.

Feccia's men were not doing well at all: the five hundred million lire they'd cashed in for the kidnapping had all been quickly squandered in ultimate gangland style – on women, trips, cocaine and champagne. A couple of them had been shot and left for dead on the street during a drug-fuelled armed robbery. Others were scattered across the landscape, some in prison, others OD'd on heroin.

Feccia himself was barely scraping by on a shakedown racket in the north-east section of Rome, but he couldn't venture any closer in than that, given the fact that an embargo had been imposed on him after the miserable impression he'd made with the unfortunate baron. After a period of in-again out-again in Rome's five-star Hotel Regina, he'd clearly lost his mind. First he went to Trentadenari, immediately after his release from prison, and beat the shit out of him for no apparent reason. After, he demanded fifteen million lire just like that, because he wanted it, threatening that if he weren't paid, he'd report them for the kidnapping.

To Dandi and the rest, fifteen miserable million just tickled. They could easily have tossed him what amounted to a tip and been rid of him without trouble, but Beato Porco had pushed his arrogance a little too far this time, so they told him to go to hell after beating him black and blue.

Beato Porco had sworn to get even, and since he was a lone operator, out of control, and a coward, he'd decided to take it out on the women. First thing, he showed up at Patrizia's new house, with that idiot Fierolocchio as his involuntary accomplice after he'd foolishly dropped the correct address in conversation. And when Patrizia made it abundantly clear to him that nothing was going to happen, he tried to bend her over a table and screw her, only to discover that Patrizia was a past master of the claw-and-talon art of face-scratching. That was the end of that. But Beato Porco decided to shift his aim to Barbarella, Ricciolodoro's widow. Patrizia had taken Barbarella under her benevolent wing, but Barbarella was nowhere near as good at defending herself as Patrizia was. The result was a full-blown rape, and the poor woman still bore the signs of Beato Porco's bestiality on her face.

Even then they would have let him go as more trouble than he was worth: because Beato Porco rated lower on the scale than fly-dirt, lower than Tigame, lower than Saracca – not even nothing, less than nothing is what he was.

But ever since Nembo Kid got out of jail, he seemed to have become a loose cannon. Maybe it was because of his problems with Donatella and her irrational jealousy; or perhaps because of a shipment of 'Bolivian Pink' that went straight up his nose without passing through the street or the general fund. Or possibly his short stay in a prison cell had simply knocked a screw loose somewhere. Whatever the explanation, Nembo was spoiling for a fight. Maybe he missed having a physical enemy and was just hungry for the smell of blood.

'I'm going to murder Beato Porco!'

Dandi wanted nothing to do with it. From prison, Bufalo sent word that if he was so keen on firing his rifle, then maybe he could figure out how to break him out of jail – Prima Linea style. Why was it that the commies managed to do certain things but every time *they* tried, it always went wrong?

Freddo voted against the execution. They could somehow recover from the seizure of the weapons, but they still had a problem: how to replace their arsenal. Putting sub-machine guns, pistols and rifles in another store room somewhere was too risky. Everybody was going to have to look after their own weapons. Keeping them at home was out of the question. They'd have to find secure hiding places and reliable people to run the risk for them. And another thing: time to stop trading and lending out pistols. Time to stop recycling weapons. The ideal thing was just to get rid of a hot weapon immediately after use. It was like in a football championship: the only way to win was with a deep bench. They needed to have a much larger assortment of weapons than they were accustomed to keeping. Moral of the story: instead of wasting time on bullshit, they needed to procure weapons and find a way to keep them out of sight.

Trentadenari subscribed to this approach, but Nembo Kid took a hard line, in terms of the gang's good name – because Beato Porco had insulted their women's good names, and that was intolerable – and as a personal point of pride.

'I've made up my mind to kill him and that's what I'm going to do! If you're not with me, I'll do it all on my own.'

In the end, just two of the gang – Scrocchiazeppi and Botola – decided to go in on it.

Patrizia refused to make her place available. So they turned to Barbarella, who wasted no time throwing a notable party with certain female friends of hers. She got word out that, sure, Beato Porco might have been a little rough on her, but what a macho man! How potent! So when Scrocchiazeppi showed up bearing an olive branch, Porco was eager for a chance to attend an orgy free of charge. Anyone else, in his place, would have caught the first flight to Rio. But he was already flying high, on a regular diet of speedballs – three parts coke to one part smack, intravenous, like that American actor, the fat one, who'd killed himself on the stuff just a few days ago. One kind of white powder to sail straight up into the stratosphere, and the other for a nice smooth re-entry and glide path. He was so fucked up that his only reaction to the invitation was: they're afraid of me! They're trying to placate me!

Barbarella had arranged things in style: the finest girls; the purest dope; the iciest, bubbliest champagne. Beato Porco was allowed to reach the verge of the most beautiful orgasm of his life, then Scrocchiazeppi hauled him by main force off the redhead and told him that they needed him for a special little job.

Beato Porco, still half naked, trotted along behind him, all trusting and contented. They climbed into a Fiat Panda. Botola was in the back seat, keeping up a steady patter of jokes, buddy buddy. Nembo Kid was waiting for them at Fregene. Beato Porco walked right over to him, hand extended in friendship. Nembo fired the first shot through the pocket of his trench coat and Beato Porco went down, one kneecap shattered. Botola immediately ran a length of piano wire around his wrists and ankles. Scrocchiazeppi shot him in the other kneecap.

While the big ugly worm slithered along on the ground, coughing and begging for mercy, they snorted two or three lines, discussing the latest exploits of Falcão. Beato Porco had almost made it over to the Fiat Panda by this point. Where did he think he was going, the poor sucker? They got him back on his feet, so to speak, careful to avoid getting blood on themselves, and tied him to the trunk of a tree. Scrocchiazeppi turned on the stereo and popped in a disco cassette. Nembo Kid felt like having a little fun with knives. Every slice of flesh had its own justification:

'This one's for Patrizia, and the way you insulted her. This is for Donatella, and how hard she took it. This is for Barbarella, and the way you slapped her around, you pig. This one's because I don't like you and never have. And this one's just because.'

Then the knife was handed to Scrocchiazeppi, who finally handed it to Botola. But Botola refused it: someone needed to keep a lookout, in case of unexpected arrivals.

After a while they were sick of it. Beato Porco's head was lolling, and rivulets of blood were streaming from holes all over his body. You couldn't tell if he was dead already or still hanging on. Just to make sure, they unloaded three bullets each into him, then carried his body to the car and lit a nice bright bonfire.

Botola drove them home in Nembo's Audi. He drove very carefully and felt a lingering sense of disgust.

The partially charred corpse was found the next day. Scialoja summoned Freddo on the pretext of an informal conversation. Without lawyers.

'A fine mess you made of that poor bastard!'

'This time I have an absolutely bomb-proof alibi!' Freddo chuckled.

'There are masterminds and there are foot soldiers.'

'If you say so...'

'Still, there's something odd about it, you know? In all these years, I think I've learned a lot of things about you...For example, you're a person – I don't want to say a respectable person – and perhaps if you'd made different choices in your life by now...But I just can't see you spending three hours torturing some poor lout strung out on drugs...'

'I was locked up in here!'

'That's exactly the point! You're in here, but the others are out on the street. You're a boss...'

'What are you talking about?'

'Come on now! You're a boss, just like Libano was a boss...When Libano was alive, something so...absurd could never have happened...'

'Quit busting my balls! You've already sung me that refrain, cop! If you're charging me with something, I want my lawyer,' Freddo protested.

Scialoja smiled. 'They're going crazy out there. It happens sometimes, you know that? It's like they're drunk. Sooner or later you're all going to wind up killing each other...'

'Boss!' Freddo shouted, leaping to his feet. 'Boss! I want out! I want to go back to my cell!'

The maresciallo hurried into the conference room. Scialoja halted him with a brusque gesture.

'Just remember that whoever's out on the street is in charge. And whoever's behind bars is soon forgotten!'

Freddo went back to his cell, tormented by flights of the blackest Madonnas. Yes, that son of a bitch had sharp eyesight. And he always tried to divide them. As if there were any need of his help! That whole thing with Beato Porco was a ridiculous shit-storm. Worse. They'd behaved like those sadistic kids who thought it was fun to stick a fire-cracker up a cat's arsehole. Childish. Childish and tragic. So they wanted to kill Beato Porco? A bullet in the head and you're done! What was the point of savaging the poor idiot?

What that execution reminded Uncle Carlo of, on the other hand, was the good old days of their campaign against the Palermo Mafia. *Viddani*, they called them in Palermo: crude, unlettered peasants, strictly useful as cannon fodder. They systematically excluded them from all the important decisions, until the *viddani* finally decided to take matters into their own hands. To do nothing more dramatic than shoot their Palermo rivals wouldn't have been enough. Useful, but inadequate. Ripping out fingernails, burning nipples, shoving their own severed ball sacks into their mouths – now that meant treating them the way they do with barnyard animals. Spread a little terror. Push that terror right into the baroque drawing rooms of their understated, sophisticated clubs. The one language that could be understood.

The Maestro was astonished.

'They're as powerful as they are, and they still unleash these bloodbaths!'

'There's one thing, Maestro: where I come from we say, "*Cu nasci tunnu, nun po moriri quatratu*." If you're born round, you can't die square. Blood is blood. I don't know if you get my point. If people wise up, that's a good thing. It's a satisfaction, and the cock flies free!'

A week before carnival, in a forty-eight hour period, three junkies were found in the Tufello district, foaming at the mouth, syringes still dangling

306

from their veins. Two of the junkies died, the third miraculously recovered from his overdose. The press had a field day with the lethal heroin. The police assumed the mask of honest repressors, and five or six busy little ants suddenly found themselves tossed into cells at Rebibbia. The gang sent for the local supervisor, Bonalana, and he expressed helpless astonishment. The three victims? Old acquaintances, but none of them had bought from him for a while now. Word was that they'd fallen into the hands of one of those priests who try to earn their one-way ticket to heaven by saving junkie souls and getting them off the stuff. Apparently, though, that wasn't why they'd stopped coming around. Someone else was trying to horn in on the market. Bonalana seemed to be on the up and up.

The decision was made to undertake an investigation. Trentadenari was put in charge, since he was the puppet master in charge of distribution and pushers. In just two days, thanks to a tip from the surviving junkie, the identity of the interloper was made clear.

'Can you guess who this stinker is? Satana! And he's selling thirty per cent below our price!'

If Freddo hadn't been in jail, things would have turned out differently. Afterwards, they'd have all the time they needed to regret their actions. That Satana had to pay for what he'd done was a foregone conclusion. But that wasn't the main thing: sooner or later they'd manage to rub him out. So, before making any moves, the smart thing to do would have been to put their brains into gear. The serious problem was the fact that junkies were dying. Only an idiot pays no attention when junkies start dropping off. It had nothing to do with humanitarian impulses; it was about market forces. Every dead junkie was one less source of profit. Those two miserable losers had died because they'd changed supplier. That was why junkies dropped dead in the street: they changed type of narcotics without paying any attention to the proper dosage. It happened because junkies didn't think. Junkies were animals. Someone had to do their thinking for them.

Sorcio, the official junk-tester, had informed them that Satana's smack was exceptionally pure. Evidently there were supply channels they knew nothing about. Before killing Satana, good sense dictated that they identify the supplier. Find out whether Satana had partners, hidden or

307

overt. Make him talk. That was how Freddo would have insisted on doing things, if he hadn't had his hands tied, if he wasn't stuck in a prison cell.

Instead, in the outside world this was a moment of excitement, and the scent of blood was in the air. Nembo Kid was dragging them headlong, and Dandi was giving him free rein. Had Satana fallen into their hands? Then they should rub him out! After all, they had that old account to settle with him from the Libano days. Satana would have been a thousand times wiser to have just stayed back in Rieti, or wherever the hell. They knew he hung around a gambling den in the Tufello district. So they went there on Fat Thursday night and shot him to pieces with sub-machine guns and revolvers. A touch of class suggested by Nembo: the three members of the team – Nembo himself, Scrocchiazeppi and Fierolocchio – all wore masks. All the eyewitnesses could tell the police was this: an Audi pulled up, Goofy, Pluto and Donald Duck got out, and then they mowed down Satana. Amen.

IV

AFTER THE RECENT bloodbaths, whatever it was that Nembo Kid was carrying inside of him turned into a full-fledged frenzy. He'd started spouting weird rambling rants: about the friends from Milan and the friends in Rome, who just weren't up to his standards; about giving a serious arse-fucking to this guy or that; about the idea that real men had no obligations and answered to no one. He was overdoing it with the coke. Sometimes he'd lose control over the tiniest things. One night he threw a fit over some guy in a bar who happened to jostle his elbow. He waited for the guy to finish his drink, then he confronted him, and he would have kicked his head off his shoulders if Trentadenari hadn't intervened.

The guy came back with two friends and an ancient pre-war Luger. Nembo Kid was with Dandi. The Luger jammed at just the right moment, and that was the end of that. Nembo Kid wanted to organize a punitive beatdown. Dandi snarled that Nembo needed to remember that he was the one who had started it.

'I've had enough of your bullshit!'

Even Donatella was having a hard time recognizing him. He kept asking for the weirdest things in bed, and when they were done having sex, he seemed dissatisfied and gloomy.

When Uncle Carlo sent him to Milan, everyone heaved a sigh of relief.

Milan. This time was quite different from the last trip north. First of all, Donatella wasn't with him, and that was intolerable. Also, the Maestro had been categorical: no contacts, no meetings, especially not with old friends. Forget certain addresses and certain meetings. Make use of false identification papers. Stay places for the shortest possible period of time. Contact Tedesco immediately: he had the instructions for the operative phase of the mission. Most important of all: no cocaine, and no impulsive behaviour. They'd taken him for a fucking monk! Then why hadn't they sent Dandi?

Anyway, there was no arguing with Uncle Carlo's advice. Nembo Kid wasn't interested in seeing Uncle Carlo's smile. So, no cocaine. The first day he just stayed shut up in his hotel room. When you cut out drugs, cold turkey reality changes pace. The very flow of life itself goes galloping by at an insane speed one minute and then slows to a liquid ooze the minute after that. Your head is gripped in an iron band and your heart leaves your chest and goes pumping through the air on its own account. Nembo Kid consoled himself with the thought that he was doing without, strictly as a temporary necessity.

The second day he went out to take a walk around the centre of the city. Delirious Milan, under a steady drizzle and the stench of car exhaust. He saw buildings teeter dangerously, looking like they were about to topple over onto him. From the trees, the few, miserable, stunted, traitorous Milanese trees, hooked fingers reached out, eager to clutch at him. Every glance concealed a trap.

That night, back at the hotel, he decided he wasn't going to go far like that. He called the Maestro.

'I'm not going to make it without dope.'

'Have you tried calling Tedesco?'

Tedesco was diminutive and dark, and he owed his nickname – the German – to a collaborationist aunt of his who'd been shaved bald by the Italian partisans in 1945. Tedesco gave him the instructions and two bottles of Valium. One contained the sedative, the other was full of cocaine. He snorted greedily and his off-kilter world started spinning on its proper axis again.

The appointment was for the next day. That afternoon, Nembo Kid laid waste to a lingerie shop in Milan's Galleria. He paid with a legitimate credit card and had the packages sent to his hotel. One thing Uncle Carlo hadn't said was: no women. The desk clerk put him in touch with an escort agency. Milan was a hi-tech, advanced city.

The girl they sent over had almond-shaped eyes: a delightful little morsel, maybe just a bit skinny, small-titted, and stand-offish at first. But the cash and the coke melted her reserve, and Nembo Kid indulged in certain thrills that he could never have confessed to Donatella. When they were done, a decidedly satisfied Nembo gave her a silk negligee. Then he called the Maestro.

'Thanks. It's much better now. It's for tomorrow.'

'Do a good job. This is important to Uncle Carlo.'

Tedesco was riding a Suzuki racing bike. Nembo Kid admired the streamlining of the vehicle and certain details of the bodywork that filled him with enthusiasm. It was a damned fine bike. When they were done, he'd propose a trade. But there was plenty of time for that. Tedesco had a Browning semi-automatic and a long barrel revolver. Nembo Kid selected the revolver. They put on their helmets, zipped up their leather jackets and roared away. Their destination was a little piazzetta on the edge of the business district. Tedesco let the engine idle quietly. He pointed out a small, discreet street door – nondescript, really – manned by a doorman with gold-braid epaulettes.

'Banchiere – the Banker – is a man of strict routines. Every morning at eight on the dot he emerges from that front door and climbs into his chauffeured vehicle. The car will be here any minute. It always parks right out front. We have to take him down as he crosses the street to reach his car. It's a matter of forty, maybe fifty steps. We won't have much time.'

'It's all under control.'

The bulletproof Lancia Thema pulled up on the far side of the street at 7.55 a.m. At one minute to eight, the street door swung open and the doorman snapped to attention. Tedesco revved the accelerator. Nembo Kid wrapped his hand around the revolver and snapped off the safety.

310

Banchiere strode past the doorman, ignoring his salute. He was a short man with an arrogant posture.

Tedesco took off, heading straight for him. Nembo Kid shifted around on his seat, in search of the proper position, then extended his arm. When the motorcycle was so close that he could practically touch his target, he squeezed off two shots in rapid succession. Banchiere twisted, spiralling, as he fell to the pavement. A second later he was back on his feet, one hand clutching his belly. He stumbled, trying to make his way back to the door. Someone nearby shouted. Tedesco swerved the Suzuki around. Nembo Kid took careful aim. He had to finish him off now. The coke that he'd snorted at dawn gave him a perfect clarity of mind. Not even the slightest tremor shook his arm.

'Halt!'

Who'd just shouted? Where was he? It was a man in uniform. In the middle of the street. Back arched, legs straddling, levelling a sub-machine gun with both hands. Nembo Kid hesitated. A tremendous impact knocked him off the bike. His gun had flown out of his hand. Out of the corner of his eye he saw Tedesco fly into the air. The bike was tumbling onto him, out of control. He crawled, groping for his gun. There was a fire in his chest that was eating him up. He tried to brace himself on his elbows. The second burst of bullets pinned him down for good, without even giving him time to formulate one last thought.

V

AT THE AUCTION house, bids were being taken for the little mechanical theatre with the scene of the meeting between Tamino and Pamina. The Old Man was indifferent to the divine notes of *The Magic Flute* that so clearly delighted the entire crowd of onlookers clustered on the parterre. But the serious collectors, seated on the red velvet chairs, were battling for possession of that exquisite jewel that had once brightened the child-hood of the Grand Duke of the Palatinate, and they couldn't care less about Mozart. Mayer raised his paddle. The Old Man bid higher. Mayer raised his paddle again. The Old Man raised his twice, angrily. A tense 'o-o-oh' filled the air in the room.

'Long-distance call for you, sir.'

'Italy?'

'Yes, sir.'

'I'll call back.'

'They say it's very important, sir.'

'Shut up!'

The director of the auction house withdrew with a bow. That elderly Italian really could be prickly sometimes. You never knew: sometimes he was so impeccably polite.

The director went back to the phone and regretted to inform that, at the moment, the party in question was unavailable. Zeta, calling from Rome, begged him to try again.

Finally the Old Man took the call.

'I hope that whatever you have to tell me is *truly* of the greatest urgency!'

'At eight o'clock this morning Banchiere was wounded in a terrorist attack.'

'Which matters why?'

'The would-be assassin was killed by a security guard who just happened to be in the area. The unsuccessful killer was a certain…Nembo Kid. Does the name mean anything to you?'

'Have you been taking comedy classes lately? Issue an official comment: the cowardly attack…the focus of law enforcement…the disturbing presence of a well-known member of Rome's criminal under-world…The usual thing, in other words.'

'Anything else?'

'Don't you dare bust my balls again, Zeta.'

On his way back to the auction room, he ran into Mayer with the toy theatre under his arm. They exchanged a friendly nod.

'Sorry. This time the winner is me!' The American smiled.

'Next time I'll be luckier!' the Old Man courteously replied.

Later, alone in the presidential suite, he jotted in his notebook: *28 April. We live in a degenerate time. Even the Mafia is only a shadow of its former self. Still, every cloud has a silver lining. Another tile has been added to the mosaic of confusion.*

VI

No ordinary torpedo, but one of the heads of the Roman under-world flies to Milan to riddle with bullets a big gun of the world of finance. The murder was authorized and planned out in Rome. The presence of a gangland boss of Nembo Kid's stature served a two-fold role: it reassured the clients who have commissioned the murder that it will turn out as expected, and it placed the seal of permanency on an alliance between twin powers. Milan represented the power of money, while Rome was the Palazzo, the power of the state. Banchiere's accounts were in the red. His bank was taking orders from the Vatican. The subterranean river that flowed in both directions between Rome and Milan was a river of blood and money. Study, investigate, decipher, understand, and strike a blow. Borgia and Scialoja came back from Milan loaded with new hope and information.

In the days that followed, Scialoja worked in the utmost secrecy on a new report concerning the killing of Nembo Kid. He left nothing out. The gang. The spies. The drug trafficking. From the hotel's switchboard it emerged that Nembo, from Milan, had been in contact with a subject they'd never heard anything about before. He called him 'the Maestro'. Scialoja did a little digging. This Maestro had begun his career as a two-bit ex-con and then, at a certain point, he'd made the great leap forward. Real estate holdings. Farmland. Financial investments. Real estate investments in Sardinia conducted through a small bank that had only two branch offices: one in Milan, obviously, and the other in Palermo. Scialoja looked for a conduit with his Sicilian colleagues. He ran up against a brick wall of mistrust. He asked Borgia for help. It took two weeks, but finally a call came through from Palermo. They apol-ogized for the delay, but explained that first it had been necessary to 'acquire information'.

'The bastards subjected me to a full-bore anti-Mafia test and certi-fication but finally decided I was clean,' Borgia complained. 'Still, the information is juicy: your Maestro is Uncle Carlo's right-hand man.'

'And just who would this Uncle Carlo be?'

'Uncle Carlo? In a word, Mafia.'

Scialoja included that piece of information in the report. In the

313

meantime, as he read through the preliminary results concerning the weapons found in the cellar at the ministry, he cursed the entire tribe of expert witnesses. Between one dissertation and another on the epistemology of ballistics, the good professors had managed to sink the entire ship of evidence. There had emerged, in connection with certain identifying imprints that necessarily had to be demolished, a contaminating greasy material that produced the so-called technical phenomenon of 'tropicalization'. The whole idea of a tropical shell casing made his colleagues on the forensics team fall down laughing. One witty soul hung a sketch on the wall of Borgia's office depicting a revolver stretched out on a lounge chair on an atoll sipping an umbrella drink.

When push came to shove, though, there wasn't much that could be done. There it was in black and white: the pistols that were in good condition had never been fired, and were therefore useless in terms of ballistics matching. And the ones that had been fired were in such bad shape that it was impossible to extract any usable information from them. But in any case, it hadn't been possible to pull off a complete miracle: they had confiscated certain Winchester shells that a special modification had rendered especially rare. They happened to correspond to the bullets found in Pidocchio's corpse. Scialoja lingered over the circumstance. Pidocchio – another murder left unsolved despite torrents of newsprint and glossy magazine pages devoted to the scandal rag that the victim had published, his links to the powerful and (remarkable coincidence worth noting) with 'certain milieus of the intelligence agencies'. It was a safe bet that the Pidocchio murder was their doing as well. It was a safe bet that he too was a victim of the usual 'exchange of favours'. There were no certainties, but in the end what emerged was a three-hundred-page volume. And the writing wasn't all that bad, either, Borgia ribbed him.

'It can always be archived, for future memory,' Scialoja retorted glumly.

This time he'd pulled no punches. A venomous reaction of some sort was inevitable. A week after he handed in his report, Scialoja got a phone call from Ranocchia. They met in a car park in the Prenestino quarter, surrounded by gypsy caravans and junkies coming and going, in an arsonist's idea of a sunset. They shook hands.

'Well,' asked Scialoja, 'what's this sensational news?'

Ranocchia handed him a plastic bag full of coke.

'Your friends Zeta and Pigreco send this with their greetings.'

Scialoja shot him a quizzical look. Ranocchia gestured for him to check it out himself. Scialoja opened the bag, stuck a finger into the little cascade of white crystals, took a taste. A sly smile crossed Ranocchia's face.

'Peruvian White. Three ounces. Moderate quality: seeing that the delivery came free of charge, Dandi overdid it with the amphetamine.'

'What's this supposed to mean?'

'I call and you come running, because you're hoping to find out something about Patrizia...'

'Don't talk nonsense, Ranocchia.'

'No, listen to what I have to say. They know everything. Those two always know everything. For real...'

Scialoja lit a cigarette. Something told him he could trust Ranocchia.

'So Patrizia decided to let the cat out of the bag, eh?'

'It was that guy at the hotel, the man in Positano. Okay, he wasn't exactly Richard the Lionheart, and he wasn't a friend, for that matter...Plus, in my small way, as you may remember, I'd guessed a thing or two...'

The rictus on his face, a grimacing grin, meant to be languid and conniving at the same time, made Ranocchia still more repulsive. It wasn't even clear how he managed to stay on his feet. He reeked of flop sweat and a cloying perfume.

'How does Patrizia fit into this story?'

'She doesn't know a thing. In her fashion, Patrizia is a stand-up gal. Or a lie-down gal, take your pick...'

'Where is she now?'

'Are you sure you want to know?'

'Yes.'

'She's back being Dandi's girlfriend. But don't take it to heart, commissario! Just think of Scarlett O'Hara. It's never clear which one she likes best – that cigar store Indian Ashley or that shameless son of a bitch Rhett...Anyway, those two backstabbing spies have a plan. Cop stuff. You and me meet, I pretend to be having what looks like a heart attack, you're a good Samaritan, you offer to drive me to the hospital, I get in your car, along the way I plant this nice fat baggie filled with dope, then I feel a little better, we say our farewells: thanks for the ride, cop; why, don't even mention it, my faggot friend. You drive off and finish your rounds. When you get home, there's a police car waiting. A random check. You laugh heartily: oh, please, we're all colleagues here, after all…But the lead officer is stone-faced. We've received a tip-off…See how it works? Listen, I don't know why, but those two really have it in for you…'

Scialoja handed him a cigarette. Ranocchia thanked him. He took a couple of drags and coughed. He stubbed out the cigarette angrily. He lost his balance. Scialoja hurried to catch him. Ranocchia smiled at him through his rotten teeth.

'I didn't even really have to pretend, as you can see…'

'Why are you helping me?'

'What do you want me to say? For Patrizia; because I'm sick and tired of it all; because you're a handsome hunk; because every time I cough these days, I'm spitting up chunks of lung, and my doctor tells me there's something wrong with my blood but he can't quite figure out what it is; because I just like adventure films and in this phase of my existence I'm feeling a lot like the divine Marlene in *Shanghai Express*…You get the reference?

Scialoja tried to delve down to the elusive reality of that stubborn gaze. Ranocchia's eyes were just like Patrizia's: they were always some-where else – they were there with you, but it was as if they weren't anywhere at all.

'Are you willing to file a complaint against them?'

'No disrespect intended, but go fuck yourself, commissario. The law makes me sick.'

'They'll figure it out. You're running a tremendous risk.'

'I don't give a damn about that. I'm having too much fun.'

An idea occurred to Scialoja. It was risky, no doubt, but as his saviour had just said, too much fun.

'Give me back the baggie.'

'What are you going to do with it?'

'Come on, just give me the baggie!'

Scialoja explained his plan.

'You call the two of them in an hour and a half. Just tell them there was a change of plans. That we went to my house. Got it?'

Ranocchia enjoyed a hearty laugh.

'Well, now I can die a happy man. I finally found a bigger malcontent than me. Too bad you don't like guys, dottore!'

Scialoja returned home. Along the way, he bought a kilogram of coarse salt at the tobacco shop in Piazza Bologna. He made himself a sandwich with a half-can of tuna that was turning rancid in the refrigerator, popped open his last beer, and sat down to watch tennis on TV. Tennis was the stupidest sport on earth. The television set was the stupidest electric appliance on earth. Put the two of them together, and you had the most effective antidote against anxiety.

Zeta and Pigreco kicked down the front door a few minutes before midnight. They'd brought along a squad of oversized lunkheads in full combat regalia. Scialoja greeted them with a sarcastic smile and told them how sorry he was not to be able to offer anything better than tap water. Zeta informed him that he had the right to have a lawyer of his choosing present. Scialoja shrugged. The search only lasted a few seconds: Pigreco went straight to the bedroom, fished out the baggie, and shouted: 'Bingo!'

Zeta pretended to examine the evidence with a critical air. He pretended an exaggerated astonishment. It looked like a scene from *Police Story*.

'Michael Douglas is a little more stylish,' Scialoja needled them.

'You want to know what the most disgusting thing on earth is, commissario?' hissed Zeta in feigned indignation. 'A crooked cop!'

'Truer words were never spoken,' Scialoja agreed, staring him right in the eye.

Anyone else might have understood. But the two of them were too thrilled with themselves to be able to afford the luxury of rational thought. They gift-wrapped him and marched him in to the logistics unit, where a *maresciallo* from the scientific analysis group was waiting for them. They handed the baggie full of drugs over to him. Zeta called the assistant district attorney who was on duty at that time of the night. Scialoja declined to call a lawyer, and lit a cigarette. Zeta smacked the cigarette out of his hand. The assistant district attorney on duty introduced himself to Borgia. They'd tumbled Borgia out of bed in the middle of the night: professional courtesy. After all, Scialoja was his cop. Borgia pitched a tantrum with the spies, who listened, imperturbable.

'So you have nothing to say for yourself?' he shouted at Scialoja, who had managed to get his cigarette lit and was finally smoking in peace.

'I wish to avail myself of my right not to answer that question. I prefer to wait for the findings from the crime lab...'

Borgia caught his colleague's ironic glance, and it dawned on him. It dawned on Zeta, too. Judge and spy both rushed out of the room together. Just then the *maresciallo*, in a white lab coat, emerged from the laboratory looking annoyed. He didn't recognize Borgia, or pretended not to recognize him, and he pointed his forefinger right in Zeta's face.

'That's nice! You haul me out of bed, you make me turn on my lab equipment, and all for three ounces of sodium chloride. That someone ran through a blender, by the way...Nice prank you pulled!'

Zeta grabbed him by the arm and shoved him into the laboratory. He closed the door behind him, ignoring Borgia's objections.

'Did you look carefully?'

'Are you taking the piss?'

'Can't we retest it?'

'I'll tell you what that salt's good for: we can make a nice *spaghetti all'amatriciana* with it!'

'Is there really nothing we can do?'

The *maresciallo* looked the spy up and down. He considered his outfit, dressed for the cop gala prom: the snazzy jacket, the gleaming brand-name loafers, the jeans that highlighted his junk. He breathed in the scent of cologne, pitied him the buzz cut. He laughed heartily and reached out to slap him on the shoulder.

'Hey, what's-your-face, how much do they give you spies in special supplemental pay? Three million lire extra a month? You know what I'd give you? Three million kicks in the you-know-what!'

Scialoja was released with a formal apology. Borgia asked him why he hadn't cleared up the misunderstanding immediately.

'I didn't want to miss the look on Zeta's face when the lab results came back.'

'Could you draw up a short report on this?'

'Oh, everyone can make mistakes.'

Borgia cursed under his breath. There were times when he felt like nailing Scialoja to the wall.

'I would love to know who saved your arse this time. Perhaps it was your old friend: Vallesi, Cinzia?'

'Negatory, Judge, Your Honour. Let's just say that I have a debt of gratitude with the gay community!'

Si vis pacem, para bellum
1982–83

I

ROBERTA WAS WAITING for him at the front gate. Freddo, with the sun in his eyes, took a few uncertain steps. They kissed gently. She tasted of fruit, something warm and good. Freddo gulped down something else, wet and salty, and tried to slip his tongue between her teeth.

'Not now.'

This was the first time that Roberta had resisted his will. Freddo followed her to the car without speaking. Roberta got in behind the wheel of her old Mini and pulled onto the road cautiously.

'This has been exhausting,' she said.

'Well, now it's over.'

'Over till when? Until the next time they catch you?'

Freddo fiddled with the knob on the radio. Everyone was talking about the excellent cadavers that had littered the streets in recent days. Everywhere you turned, there was someone despising Nembo Kid and deploring the death of comrade Pio La Torre, shot down in Palermo. If he'd had a telephone handy, he'd have called into the station to let off some steam. What the hell are you wailing about, you pieces of shit? Don't you know how the world works?

'Have you heard a word of what I've been saying?'

Roberta had a stern expression on her face. Freddo had expected a different kind of welcome. He curled up into a ball, like a hedgehog.

'You have enough set aside to retire. Let's leave this town. Go somewhere. I can't stand living this way anymore!'

He was tempted to confess that he was sick of it too. Sooner or later he'd have to serve out some sentence that had been upheld on the last appeal available. If they stuck to the smaller charges, four or five years. But if he decided to call it quits, how long could it last? The idea of the two of them, maybe in some foreign country, penniless, cut off from the street, friendless...

'Drop me off here. I'll come home later.'

She slammed on the brakes. Freddo tried to work a mild smile onto his face, but what came out looked more like a twisted leer. Roberta roared away. It was going to be tough, the next few days.

'Freddo, my friend!'

Dandi was home. With him was his interior decorator: a queer in his early sixties with tinted hair and hippy-style bead necklaces.

'I strongly advise against hanging a Mafai near a Vespignani... What I'd like to see here is a Masson. How does that strike you, sir?'

'Ah, sure, sounds fine. Let's talk it over another day, maestro. Right now, a friend of mine's here, and I haven't seen him for a long time...'

The interior decorator accepted the cheque with six zeroes, emblazoned with the swoops and flourishes of Dandi's signature, and ushered himself out with a courtly bow.

'What do you think, Freddo?'

'You've put on some weight.'

'I meant, what do you think about my home?'

Ah, the museum! With all his possessions neatly arrayed, the walls cluttered with canvases, a smell midway between wax and incense, spotlights hidden behind the curtains, and tunes piped in like what Trentadenari played in his sex parlour...

'Downstairs, I've had a billiards room put in. Care for a game?'

'Downstairs' was a spacious cellar equipped as a kitchen/dining room, for banquets, parties and entertaining of whatever kind. Freddo chalked his cue and noticed the desolate, empty cage.

'What's up with that?'

'That? Oh, that... Poor Alonzo! He just got to be too big. He was starting to cause trouble. So anyway, I had to have him put down...'

In that requiem you could read the sum of Dandi: hypocrisy and violence. Freddo took a half-hearted shot and lit a cigarette. He stared at his comrade in arms. There was something in the air reminiscent of the last dinner with Libano. But there was none of the old camaraderie with Dandi. It was up to him to justify himself.

'Well, anyway, things are moving along fine. Now you're back out, at this point...'

He was putting a brave face on it, but he reeked of awkwardness. Freddo crushed out his cigarette butt in an ashtray with a blue rooster. Dandi's face darkened.

'Hey, take it easy there, if you don't mind. That's an original piece. Grottaglie ceramics...It was a gift from Pugliese. In here, my good man, everything is first class!'

'Ah, you call this first class?'

'Why, do you have something to criticize? It's time to rise to a higher level!'

'And just when was the last time you rose to a higher level? When you sliced and diced Beato Porco? Or maybe the time you rubbed out Satana and forgot to ask him who was supplying him with dope before he checked out? You know what I hear on prison radio? That one night, since you all were out and about with nothing better to do, you lit a bum on fire...'

'That's pure bullshit!' Dandi snapped. 'I don't know anything about that!'

'Of course not! The very idea! You don't get your hands dirty anymore...'

Freddo was spitting venom. Dandi tried to lay on the molasses.

'Fine, fine, Freddo. Let's just say that the boys have overdone it a little. Take Nembo Kid: we couldn't control him anymore, poor old buddy. And the others started following his lead, after a while. What was I supposed to do? Anyway, he wound up the way he wound up...'

'And you don't know anything about that either, do you?'

'But I'm telling you—'

'Nothing about nothing! Nembo ups and heads for Milan, checks into a five-star hotel with a diplomatic passport, tries to shoot a shark in the world of high finance in the head, and you're shocked – shocked and taken by surprise!'

Things were going downhill fast. Prison hadn't been good for Freddo, that much was clear. There was no point dodging the question any longer. Dandi decided to lay his cards on the table.

FREDDO EXPLAINED TO his faithful followers that Dandi had decided to pull a Libano.

'He's got contacts and deals going that he doesn't want to share with the rest of us, but since he's not looking to have any of us bust his balls, either, he wants us to keep working together on the narcotics and contributing to the general fund for prison inmates and their families. The rest of it, dissolved.'

'The investments dissolved too?' Fierolocchio asked.

'Everything.'

'To me, more than pulling a Libano, it looks like he wants to pull a Sardo!' one of the Buffoni boys observed.

'No,' Freddo corrected him. 'Sardo wanted to be in charge; Dandi's just going out on his own. It's different.'

'So who's to guarantee that one fine day he doesn't decide to play a little prank on us?' asked Scrocchiazeppi.

'Like the ones you had so much fun pulling with Botola and Nembo?' Freddo glared at him; he was suspicious of Scrocchiazeppi after what happened with Beato Porco.

Scrocchiazeppi bowed his head.

'Freddo, what can I tell you...I don't know what came over me...I just kind of got derailed there...But I'm with you!'

'So are we!' cried the Buffonis.

'Obviously!' said Fierolocchio.

'And Bufalo and Ricotta are on our side. They haven't gotten over what happened!' Scrocchiazeppi added emphatically.

'So he's got Botola.'

'Botola and no one else...'

'Well, maybe Trentadenari too, to move the dope...'

'And Secco, to handle the money.'

'Secco's not in the gang. He just helps out when we need him.'

'What are you talking about! He's got everything wired the way he likes it...'

'What about Trentadenari? Are we sure he's on the other side?'

'Nobody knows what side Trentadenari's on! He spins around like a merry-go-round...'

'So what are we waiting for? We'll just arrange a meeting and...'

Freddo poured water on the flames. It wouldn't do any of them good to start a war. Dandi hadn't issued a challenge. And his offer, all things considered, was fair and reasonable. Scrocchiazeppi was indignant.

'Reasonable? What the hell? You want to just let that piece of shit walk away?'

'All I'm saying is that a war isn't in anybody's interest. Not now, anyway...'

'Then when?'

Any moment could be the right one, but there might also never be a right moment. In other words, Freddo explained, there'd never been a problem with the narcotics business. The mechanism worked and the money poured in reliably. What good did it do to argue? The general fund needed to be kept in place, too. So far Dandi and Botola had always reliably paid their dues to the sinking fund for unexpected expenses.

'Then what are you trying to tell us? That nothing's happened at all?'

No. What had happened was exactly what Libano said would happen, God rest his soul. What happened was that they had gone their separate ways, but as long as everyone was meeting their obligations, there was no reason to fight. Business partners, and nothing more.

'We can sell together, buy together, shoot together, even invest together, but nothing in the Bible says we have to go to bed together!'

Those had been Dandi's last words. Loyalty to the gang had become loyalty between gangs: on the one hand, Dandi's group; on the other hand, their group. Recruitment season was open, of course. For now, they had the advantage of numbers, but you could never say. Therefore: let them deal in peace with all the Mafiosi and spies they wanted, as long as they respected the rules, no problem. Otherwise, they'd wind up like Sardo.

Bufalo and Ricotta, duly informed of events in prison, complied with the new configuration. Trentadenari sent word that he didn't want to take sides. He was, and would always remain, friends with them all. As for Secco, he paid a call on Freddo and told him that even Bufalo had given him a little money to take care of.

'Only you and Scrocchiazeppi and Fierolocchio and the Buffonis still don't trust me…But your friends are penniless, and the more they make, the more they spend…You, on the other hand, if you chose to…'

Freddo told him to go to hell, and Secco, behind his humble smile, decided he'd make him pay for that someday. He told Dandi that they were scheming against him, but it did him no good: Dandi said that, quite frankly, he couldn't care less what those miserable beggars were trying to do.

At the end of all that, Freddo managed to patch things up with Roberta, who was just too much in love with him to risk losing him. And when, after they'd made love, she asked him for what seemed like the thousandth time why he was doing all this, he finally managed to come up with a sincere answer:

'Because it's the only way I feel free.'

III

WHAT WITH ONE exchange of cash after another, Climax Seven had officially become the joint property of Dandi and Botola, and Secco even had a minority share. With the new agreement, an unstated division of responsibilities had come into play. Freddo and his men kept an iron grip on the drug peddling, and did relentless nit-picking on Trentadenari's accounts. Dandi had signed a contract with a guy from Lecce he'd met through compatriots of his who were peddling hashish, and that had allowed them to get a foothold in the video poker business, which was starting to look like the goldmine of the century. Then they'd hooked up with Nercio, a hotheaded Sicilian who was starting to become a force to be reckoned with in the Primavalle zone. Nercio had cut into the heroin business and the floating poker games with weapons and cash and, showing proper respect to Freddo, he'd aligned himself with Trentadenari: a friend to everyone, a partner flying all flags.

In the meantime, they were making the rounds, from an orgy in celebration of Italy's World Cup victory in Spain to a cosy little private dinner that Uncle Carlo held to properly celebrate the bloodbath that ended the career of 'that complete cuckold shitbag, General Dalla Chiesa'. It was an event that seemed to greatly console the Maestro, because for the past year or so things hadn't been going all that well, especially in Milan, where a couple of investigating judges were sticking their noses into certain lists that were meant to stay secret, and in Palermo, where the stinkers in the district attorney's office had somehow got it into their heads that the information that one of them had should be shared with the other.

During one of the evening entertainments, Vasta – who officially remained ignorant of the Sicilian's true identity – stated that sooner or later the country's judges, notoriously a band of die-hard Reds, were going to pay for their insane perversity, and for the way they had it in for the nation's most prominent citizens. They just needed to be patient, and time would put them in their place. Uncle Carlo had smiled at the thought. Vasta hastened to point out that he was speaking in purely theoretical terms.

'I mean to say: there are laws and there are civil rights… These judges can't just go on trampling the rights of the defence… That kind of thing…'

Uncle Carlo, still in high spirits, just nodded meaningfully.

Everyone already seemed to have forgotten about poor Nembo Kid. Only Donatella wept day and night over his memory. She'd turned skinny and hard-faced, just a shadow of the Junoesque matron she had once been. Patrizia had the unfortunate idea of inviting her to a little evening's entertainment with a couple of wealthy Arabs. Donatella scratched Patrizia's face, smashed two valuable paintings, and then threw herself headlong on the couch in tears.

'Do you want to tell me when you're going to get over it?' Patrizia asked her, doing her best to stop the bleeding.

Donatella had turned on the waterworks. He was my man! He was a beast, he was even starting to get into S&M, but still, he was my man! When we were together, we were like a couple of ferocious tigers. I miss everything about him! The hitting, the kissing, and even the tantrums I had to throw when he took some slut to bed! But he was my man! There'll never be another one like him!

Patrizia stroked her hair: it was straw-like, filthy and damp. This was certainly what you'd call passion! What a strange thing! She was reminded of the cop's kind exaltation. She thought of Dandi at his craziest. Men among men, so similar one to the other. And for her, there was nothing but the eternal allowing of herself to be taken. She wondered where passion resided, in what part of the body. Not between the legs, not in the head, not in the heart. Somewhere else, of that she was certain. Maybe in a gland that some had and others didn't.

'You'll find another man,' she said, to console her. 'Better than him!'

And she envied her, from the bottom of her heart. She'd never felt that gland deep inside her.

IV

AT FIRST, THE Old Man had decided to drop the matter. The Scialoja problem, in the final analysis, was the exclusive concern of Zeta and Pigreco. Then he'd thought it over again, and he'd given orders to have the cop brought in to see him. He'd changed his mind because it was a quiet period. And if there was one thing the Old Man detested, it was peace and quiet, however relative.

The Red Brigades terrorists were melting away like snow under bright sunshine. All it had taken was a little hard time behind bars to break their will. A little well-calibrated infiltration had done the rest. The speed with which they'd surrendered their weapons was emblematic. The problem with Reds never changed: a disconsolate lack of anything resembling balls. Aside from Stalin – the only leftist who had ever really thrown a scare into them. The Old Man admired Stalin. Though he still nurtured a preference for the pint-sized and demoniacal Lavrenti Beria. In any case, left-wing terrorism had served its historical purpose. Tender-hearted sociologists were already starting to scheme for a 'rehabilitation of the generation of the armed struggle'. In other words, what a crashing bore. The Old Man, without tables on which he could display his magical card-cheating skills, felt like a Raphael without his palette and paintbrush, a Thomas Mann suffering from writer's block. And so the Old Man had the cop brought to see him in a decoy office with a desk scattered with fake dossiers and dead telephones, and there he handed Scialoja the original of the report drawn up after the killing of Nembo Kid.

Scialoja took in with an ironic cocked eyebrow the broad picture window that featured the giant dome of St Peter's, the demeanour

– apparently idle and indifferent but actually keenly alert – of Zeta and Pigreco, and the Old Man himself, impenetrable and massive, staring at him through half-lidded eyes, his fat, stubby fingers playing with a tiny lead pencil.

Scialoja pulled the bag of cocaine out of one pocket and set it down carefully on the desk. The Old Man furrowed his brow.

'It's all still there. It might have gotten a little damp...'

The Old Man imperceptibly nodded his head in Zeta's direction. The agent hastened to pocket the coke.

'That's the coke we bought out of the special fund, you remember, sir?' Pigreco felt obliged to point out.

'Dandi gave it to you,' Scialoja snickered wryly.

The Old Man cut off Zeta's objection before he could get a word out.

'Leave us alone.'

The two spies went packing, leaving behind them a wake of resentment. Scialoja crossed his legs.

'I see you like to surround yourself with trustworthy individuals.'

The Old Man pulled a large wooden box towards him, extracted a pair of fat cigars, and offered one to Scialoja.

'Thanks. I prefer my little Tuscans.'

'That's no good. Come on, have one. It's an authentic Cohiba. It may very well be a cliché to say that Cuban cigars are the best in the world, but we shouldn't turn up our noses at clichés...'

Scialoja gave in. He lit the cigar. It was strong and velvety, with a scent of forests and old brandy.

'Excellent. Don't tell me that Fidel sends them to you personally?'

'Touché.' The Old Man cackled with a grimacing grin that, for some reason, reminded Scialoja of the horrid Ranocchia.

'Those two pulled one over on you,' Scialoja went on.

'Bah!' the Old Man grunted. 'That's of no concern to me. That's standard operating procedure. If there's one thing I hate, it's trustworthy individuals. Trustworthy people are loyal and therefore utterly lacking in imagination. If I had surrounded myself with *trustworthy* individuals, by now I'd have long ago been dead and buried...'

'And just where are you instead? At the helm of the ship? In the control room? On the topmost branch of the sequoia? Where the hell are you?'

The Old Man spread his arms. 'In an office that doesn't exist, in a building that doesn't exist, engaged in a conversation that doesn't exist…Does the answer meet with your satisfaction?'

Scialoja leafed through his report. It was full of underlinings, notes in the margin, exclamation points.

'These papers exist, though, after all. And sooner or later someone's going to be called to account for them!'

'Maybe so, maybe not…You know, when you say "sooner or later" you remind me of an old poem by Corneille: *La Marquise*. This "marquise" is a courtesan. You know the kind of woman I'm talking about, don't you. You have a little experience with such things, if I'm not mistaken?'

'Touché!'

The Old Man appreciated the touch of style. He was starting to enjoy himself.

'Fine,' he conceded. 'But now let's talk about us. All right, so, Marquise is beautiful and young, and Corneille, at the height of his glory, is drooling after her. But he's so ugly and wrinkly and old! In short, Marquise laughs in his face. The poet decides to take revenge. He writes a poem: take care, Marquise – you think you can be funny today because you're fresh and lovely, but don't forget that one day you too will age, and when that happens, the same wrinkles of mine that you sneer at will begin to appear on your lovely face. And so on and so forth…In any case, quite the poetic curse, don't you think? But wait, listen to what comes next. Three centuries later – or maybe four; dates aren't my forte – a wit named Tristan Bernard takes up Corneille's poem again and adds Marquise's response: that's all well and good, my aged Corneille, it may well be that things go just as you've said, but *in the meantime* I'm twenty-six years old and I couldn't care less about you! Very clear, isn't it?'

Scialoja had clearly grasped the sense, but he decided to toy with the Old Man.

'No. The meaning is somewhat obscure to me,' he murmured, relighting his cigar.

The Old Man put on a disgusted expression.

'Come along! It's all dependent on the expression *in the meantime*, which in French, of course, is *cependant*…Maybe someday a court will decide to delve seriously into certain matters, maybe it will even go to trial, with verdicts, perhaps prison terms, but in the meantime – *cependant* – I'll surely be dead by then…And in the meantime – *cependant* – what needed to be done will have been done…'

'And what is it that needed to be done? A choice bit of mass murder? A few cute bombs? Bubbly bloodbaths?'

The Old Man's face darkened.

'The day will come when you think back fondly on these times you now consider so grim.'

'I'll feel nostalgia for Moro? Pidocchio? Bologna?'

'Wait and see. It's your good luck to live in close contact with the last real men. Men who have passion and identity. Alas, all this will prove short-lived! Today is dying and tomorrow will be the exclusive dominion of bankers and technocrats. Ah, of course, I forget to add: of youngsters lobotomized by television!'

Scialoja stubbed out his cigar.

'You asked me to come see you but I'm not hearing anything I haven't already heard before.'

'Maybe so. But that's your problem, not mine. You insist on seeking a pattern, a design, where there is none; a plot where no plot exists. You need to give up this absurd ambition. The violin and the calendar lie side by side on the anatomist's gurney, and nothing links them but chance. This is no longer the century of Hegel. This is the century of Magritte!'

Scialoja had heard enough. The Old Man sank back into his ample armchair and closed his eyes. His voice dwindled to an almost indistinguishable murmur.

'I give you my word of honour that the structure you're referring to had not the slightest involvement in the Bologna train station bombing.'

'Your word of honour?'

'I understand that the thing may strike you as perplexing, but what I tell you is true. Let me assure you! And I further assure you that sooner or later, as you like to say, the law will catch up with whoever planted that horrible bomb…'

'What about the masterminds?'

'Those are often the same people as those who committed the actual crime.'

'And are you willing to swear this on your word of honour, as well?'

'Now you're asking too much!' The Old Man laughed, banging his hand down hard on his desk.

Scialoja was already heading out the door when the Old Man called after him. There was a note of courteous concern in his voice.

'Shall I have Zeta and Pigreco give you a ride?'

'No thanks! You know what they say: better alone—'

'Than in bad company. I get it. But I guarantee that you'll have no more trouble from that direction. And I'd be pleased to have another chat with you sometime, commissario.'

'Well, since this office doesn't even exist, I'll have to rely on you to look me up!'

'I'll be sure to, you can rely on it!'

'What is this, a recruitment offer?'

'Heaven's, no! I wouldn't have any idea what to do with someone like you!'

'Thanks.'

'Why, don't mention it!'

Scialoja closed the door behind him. Halfway down the empty hallway, lined with freshly painted doors, all firmly shut, he remembered that there was one more thing he wanted to say to the Old Man. He retraced his steps and walked in without knocking. The Old Man was playing a carillon, an antique toy with two ladies dancing gracefully. The cop's sudden entry had caught him by surprise. Scialoja saw him look up in panic and slam shut the lid of the mechanical box: a child caught red-handed in the midst of a forbidden pastime.

'I'd be very sorry if poor Ranocchia were to meet with some…accident.'

The Old Man relaxed.

'You have no cause for concern,' he said briskly, with a wicked little smile.

V

THESE MEETINGS WITH Scialoja were turning into a routine, thought Freddo. He was working to split them up, and he didn't seem to know that it was all pointless. Because they had already split up. They'd already

332

taken care of it some time ago. They'd torn each other apart.

'What can you tell me about Terenzio Gemito?'

What could he tell him? Nicolino Gemito had a young nephew, Terenzio. He was a guy who minded his own business and kept his hands off what belonged to others. He had nothing to do with Libano's murder. To make that fact completely clear, there'd even been a meeting with Dandi and Freddo in front of the trattoria Agustarello in Testaccio. It was not like they'd suddenly become best friends, but they parted as they had met: at peace.

'Nothing, commissa—'

'Last night, someone shot him as he was returning home.'

'I'm sorry, but I—'

'He's dead. Six shots from a .38 calibre gun. There's a witness. He says that Gemito was approached by a single man. The killer is described as a short, powerful individual, with a roundish face...'

'Why are you telling me these things? I'm no damned informant!'

'Look here...'

Freddo found an artist's sketch in his hands, done in charcoal on paper, an identikit, and he had to summon all his strength of mind to keep from leaping out of his chair. Either that was Botola or it was his twin brother. And he happened to know that Botola was an only child.

'Who's that?' he sighed, in a bored voice, handing back the sheet of paper.

'There's no point in you rushing to alert your friend Botola,' the police detective murmured with a weary smile. 'Sooner or later we're going to nail him for this. This and the other things he's done. We're going to nail you all. Don't kid yourself. If I were you, I'd try to cover my arse while there's still time...'

It was an invitation, an offer to turn state's witness. Freddo lit a cigarette and blew a plume of smoke right in the jackal's face.

'Can I go now? If not, you'd better call my lawyer...'

They let him go without further comment. As he was leaving the police station, he ran into Judge Borgia. Borgia walked right past him, pretending he hadn't even seen Freddo.

So the whole thing had been orchestrated. They were just trying to get under his skin.

That night Freddo showed up at the Climax Seven. There was a big birthday party for a Christian Democrat politico who was screwing some show business slut or other. Guest of honour: a famous singer. The bouncer, who was new on the job, didn't want to let him in at first, on account of his leather jacket and jeans, apparel that threatened to lower the tone of the event. Dandi took care of the situation and steered Freddo to his office. The desk was littered with oyster shells. Floating in the air was the unmistakable scent of Patrizia, a blend of overstated floral essences and pure unadulterated sex. Stiff and wary, Dandi and Freddo seemed, rather than old comrades in arms, like the Arabs and the Jews at the negotiating table.

Freddo had written a little speech, flat and smooth, in his head. The agreement could hold if they both respected the borders. The fundamental issue was an agreement that all shared business be run by consensus. The Gemito brothers were common property, and if anyone was going to move against one of them, everyone had to come to a prior agreement on it. Therefore, whoever had eliminated that sorry bastard – who, by the way, important point, had never lifted a finger against them – had broken the rules.

'And look, Dandi, let me tell you that the fact that we haven't already taken steps against Botola is only out of respect for you...'

Dandi snorted, rummaged through the papers that were cluttering the desktop, and tossed a sheaf of photographs in Freddo's face. There were shots of Botola and the Maestro in tuxedos. Botola and Dandi with champagne glasses in hand. Botola with Patrizia in an evening gown. Dandi, the Maestro and some fat guy with a crew cut and foxy, unsettling eyes.

'Who's that?'

'They call him the Old Man. He's a guy who gives orders. But he's not part of the common cause.'

'Okay, you've shown me the pictures, Dandi. Now what? What do you have to say about Botola?'

'Here's what I have to say, Freddo. First: last night here at the Climax we had the American ambassador. You know 'The Star Spangled Banner'? Ta-ta-ta-ta-tatta... Second: we were all here. Everyone, from seven at night till four in the morning. Botola in the front row. If I'd known that something was going to happen, I'd have invited you too…Third: if Borgia tries to bust our balls, Botola has an alibi with minimum three hundred and fifty guests. A real alibi, Freddo, my man, not like in the old days. And fourth: look out, because with all your suspicions, I'm starting to wonder if you're not going just a little paranoid on me…'

Without a shadow of a doubt, Botola was innocent. Same for Dandi, same for all the others. The fact remained that, thanks to this lovely turn of events, sooner or later they'd pin a murder on them that, for once, they'd had nothing to do with.

An investigation was set afoot. It emerged that the late Terenzio Gemito had failed to pay for a delivery of poor quality cocaine, and the one he'd stiffed on the deal was a horse from the Acilia zone, Er Zaraffa. A devious conniver, short and chubby. Looked just like Botola. Trentadenari, who was in charge of the zone, came around all cheery and offered him a drink at the bar by the Mercati Generali.

'Now then, just what happened with Gemito?'

'You're not mad about it, are you?'

'No-o-o! Whoever killed him did us a favour!'

'It was me! He wouldn't pay! He was doing you harm! He needed to be punished! Modestly speaking, when I make my mind up…'

With this proud claim of responsibility, Er Zaraffa had laid the foundations for his induction into the gang; at the same time, he had signed his own death sentence. No one could be allowed to go around meting out justice in the name of and on the behalf of the gang without permission.

Trentadenari invited the condemned man to a meeting with the big bosses, who wanted to thank him in person for his initiative. They agreed to meet in front of Franco's bar. Er Zaraffa had dressed up in jacket and tie for the occasion. A stolen Alfetta pulled up, and Er Zaraffa was told to hop into the front passenger seat. Freddo was at the wheel. Seated in the back were Scrocchiazeppi and Trentadenari. The Neapolitan had insisted on being part of the crew. Even someone less cunning than Trentadenari would have understood that a settling of scores in grand style was in the offing. And his problem, in fact, was entirely one of accounts.

The accounts that he'd managed to palm off on Freddo had been skilfully doctored by a CPA who was a friend of Fabio Santini. But a more thorough examination was bound to bring to light the systematic commission on the overall revenue from coke turnover that Trentadenari had been shovelling into his pocket ever since Libano's death. Trentadenari considered these appropriations to be fair compensation for his invaluable efforts in overseeing the narcotics distribution and the general fund. The others might have had a different opinion. Therefore, the best thing to do was to put on a show of vigour and zeal, overwhelm any potential lingering doubts.

They were driving north, heading for Femmina Morta, on a relatively deserted road, made even safer and emptier by the chilly winter afternoon. They'd told Er Zaraffa that his merciless action had made such a big impression on them all that they'd decided to introduce him to a wanted fugitive. The idiot kept running his mouth the whole time, passing himself off as such a cold-blooded criminal that before long, he was sure to become a major player. At a certain point along the way a Fiat Panda, coming from the opposite direction, flashed its brights.

'Hey, look, it's Botola!' Trentadenari called out.

'Botola!' Er Zaraffa exclaimed. 'Say, Freddo, don't you think we look alike, Botola and me? Two peas in a pod, right? Just think!'

Freddo pulled over. Botola asked where they were going. Freddo shrugged. Botola decided to join them and form a convoy.

'This looks good,' said Trentadenari, a few miles further down the road.

'Good for what?' asked Er Zaraffa, suspicion aroused. Trentadenari, lightning quick, slipped a thin rope that he'd brought especially around Er Zaraffa's neck. He started kicking and struggling. He thrust out an elbow and broke the window. The rain of shards wounded Scrocchiazeppi, whose face darkened with anger.

'I'll take care of it, you fuck-up!'

He lunged at Zaraffa, who was coughing and flailing in desperation, and sawed his throat open, Arab-style. Er Zaraffa flopped over with a gurgling sound. Just to make sure, Scrocchiazeppi plunged the blade into his chest before pulling it out.

'What a mess! I'm all covered with blood!'

Freddo pointed out it might have been easier just to fire a bullet into his head. Scrocchiazeppi retorted that when it's time to kill a traitor, one way's as good as another. Botola pulled up after it was all over, surveyed the gory scene, and pointed out the incredible resemblance to the dead man.

'You see? He spoke the truth!' Trentadenari laughed.

Scrocchiazeppi took Freddo aside.

'Let's take care of him.'

'Take care of who?'

'Botola.'

'Now?'

'Now, tomorrow, what the fuck's the difference? In any case, you know how it's going to end...'

Freddo grabbed him by the shoulders. Scrocchiazeppi was matted with sweat, his eyes dialled down to pinheads. He reeked of acrid sweat and a sickly sweet scent. A small, feral creature. Keeping the situation under control was getting harder and harder every day.

'How much did you snort, eh? How much coke did you snort?'

'Fuck you, Freddo! Let's get rid of him, before they wipe us all out – him and that serpent Dandi!'

'No.'

'Why not?'

'Because the day we decide to do it, we're going to have to take them both out together. Botola and Dandi. Otherwise, there's no point!'

Scrocchiazeppi lowered his head. Seeing that the Alfetta was useless all covered with gore and blood, they asked Botola to give them a ride back to Rome.

Not long after that, someone tossed a bomb through a picture window and devastated Secco's supermarket in Via Oderisi da Gubbio. Secco, terrified, asked Dandi for protection. It emerged that for the past few weeks, Secco had been the target of a steady barrage of threatening phone calls. Dandi gave him the use of a super-secure penthouse apartment and four professional cut-throats recruited from the ranks of the Laurentino horses.

Freddo sent word that it would be smart to investigate the source of the bomb. That it wasn't a good idea to rely on Secco's word.

'Go find out what kind of trouble he's in, and with who. Be on the lookout, Dandi. Secco is a fucking eel.'

Dandi reacted with a shrug of the shoulders.

'I already told you, Freddo. You're getting to be paranoid. Above all, you're starting to see enemies everywhere and you don't even realize when it's your own friends who are ripping you off...'

'What are you talking about?'

'The fact that one of these days, you ought to go have a chat with Sorcio.'

Turncoats
1983

I

FREDDO HAD TAKEN Aldo Buffoni to Castelporziano, out where he and Libano had talked that night – the exact same place where he'd gone with Nero to digest his grief over the murder of his friend. He'd chosen it because it was a sacred place for him. Aldo, who was dating a Brazilian showgirl, had his hair gassed back and was dressed to the nines. We'll go for a nice drive, Freddo had told him, to persuade him to come along willingly; a quiet chat, just like in the old days.

Freddo parked behind the dunes and headed out to the beach. In the dim light of sunset, a new quarter moon was casting its light ahead of their arrival. The Tyrrhenian Sea was a flat expanse, with a few fishing trawlers just visible on the horizon.

'All right, Freddo, what did you want to talk about?'

Aldo was eager to head back to Rome, where he'd already planned a hot date with his girl Filly. Freddo lit a joint and offered it after taking a couple of drags. Aldo declined the offer with a smirk of disgust.

'Try some of this: it'll put some colour in your cheeks!'

From the fob pocket of his vest, Aldo extracted a snuffbox full of coke and a tiny silver spoon. He tapped out a small heap of coke and snorted hungrily.

'This is some classy equipment, Freddo! If I told you what they charge you at Bulgari for a fine little snuffbox and spoon like this...'

The two silver objects went from Aldo's hands to Freddo's.

'Where'd you get the coke, Aldo?'

'Aw, what do you care, Freddo! It's all shit that belongs to us, no?

All the coke in Rome is our coke…What, nobody told you?'

Freddo lifted the lid, stood there for a second contemplating the vivid pink hue of the granules, then, with a sharp twist of the wrist, he dumped the whole pile of coke into the sand.

'What, have you lost your mind?'

Freddo sighed, staring at him sad-eyed.

'I had a talk with Sorcio…'

'That fucker!'

'He told me everything.'

'It's all bullshit!'

'Is the kilo you ripped off a couple of weeks ago bullshit, Aldo? What about the way you stiffed the Calabrians?'

It was starting to dawn on Aldo. He looked around in panic. The car wasn't far away, but Freddo had the keys. And he was unarmed. He raised his hands in a sign of surrender.

'I'll explain everything, Freddo.'

Freddo held up a hand, calmly, to stop him.

'What popped into your head, Aldo? I've already saved your arse once…'

'I'll pay it all back to you, down to the last lira, I swear it…'

'The problem – the real problem – is that this time everyone knows about it…Dandi…'

'He's a snake, don't trust him!'

'So who'm I supposed to trust, Aldo? Friends like you?'

He'd said it softly, with all the pain he was feeling inside.

Aldo fell to his face on the sand and crawled over to Freddo's feet. Did he remember when they were kids? When they stole blocks of tickets for the Roma vs Lazio derby and went out and sold them right under the noses of the officially sanctioned scalpers, and kept two tickets for them-selves, and went off to root for Roma under the waving banners on the stadium's curve…eh? Did he remember Cudicini and that other guy, what was his name anyway, the Spaniard, a game little rooster if ever there was one, tough in spite of his size…Ah, sure, Del Sol was his name. Cudicini 'the Black Spider' and Del Sol…And how them and Carlo would go out at night to the gambling den run by Mastro Pepe, down behind the Parco Ramazzini, but they didn't want to let them in because they said they were too little, just kids, and how they made so much noise and uproar that in the end they let them in through the front doors of that temple of gambling, and they thanked them kindly and paid them back by scooping up the change that fell on the ground underneath the zecchinetta tables, and the grown-ups watched them and did nothing to interfere, and then at night back home they caught it good, smacks and slaps and kicks in the arse...No question back then they were a couple of sons of bitches, weren't they, eh, Freddo, don't you remember, Freddo, my friend?

Freddo heard him but wasn't listening. He wished he was a thousand miles away and yet he wanted to be right there where he was standing, wanted to finish the job he'd set out to do, do the right thing, the thing that had been decided so long ago, years and years ago, before any of them could even say: there, I've made my choice...And in the meantime Aldo had moved on to when they'd been sent out to Vitinia, eh, Freddo...'Fre, you remember those shakedowns for pastry snacks? Sure, of course you do, back in year nine, my God, how did we ever even make it to year nine...Oh, we'd almost finished middle school, when we used to hang around the front door and make all the little kids hand over their pastry snacks and then we'd sell them back off, with that hall monitor, what was his name? Cotecchia...Help me, Freddo...'

'I can't help you this time, Aldo...'

Now Aldo was sobbing. Sure, sure, there must be a way! Wait, he'd just had it, the idea, an idea that could save them all, everything, a human life, fuck, the precious human life of a friend, and his reputation, sure, Freddo's reputation, he was a boss and, of course, he, Aldo, understood clearly that Freddo had his considerations, otherwise...

'Take me home, Freddo. I've got a pile of cash set aside. I'll grab Filly and we'll get tickets for Brazil tonight, right away. We'll fly out of here and no one will ever hear another word about us.'

'No one will ever see you around here again, my friend.'

'Thanks, Freddo, thanks. You're more than a brother to me. Come here, let me give you a hug, Freddo, brother of mine!'

The two men embraced. Freddo shot him through the pocket of his trench coat, with the .357 with a silencer that he'd assembled before picking up Aldo. Arms wrapped around his shoulders, Aldo jerked in shock. Freddo fired again. Aldo slipped down onto the sand.

Freddo made the mistake of looking him in the face. His eyes were filled with tears and astonishment. He saw the lamb's head again, hurled the gun as far away as he could, let the sea swallow it up, goddamned pistol, goddamned life. He felt filthier than a turncoat.

The cost of the funeral came out of the general fund. There was no point talking about the thing among themselves. Dandi and Botola could not have cared less. Trentadenari, as usual, took no particular position; given the turn of events, though, he stopped skimming off the top for a while. Bufalo and Ricotta, for their part, had sent word that one less partner was the last thing they were going to worry about. Scrocchiazeppi and Fierolocchio, who had been there from the very start, showed up with a bottle of whiskey and tense smiles. They understood how hard this had been for Freddo. But, after all, he'd been the one to offer the guarantee; it was his trust that had been betrayed, so it necessarily fell to him to mete out the punishment.

The question of Carlo Buffoni still remained open. He'd always been a stand-up guy, but at the same time you could hardly ask him to continue doing business with the murderers of his twin brother.

Freddo went to see him two days after the funeral and had a little talk, made things as clear as could be.

'Dandi is already starting to look daggers at you. You ought to just take your share and retire. If you want, I'll bring you the money tomorrow.'

Carlo spat in his face and called him a Judas. Freddo took it.

Two days later Carlo picked up what he was owed and bought his wife and his sister-in-law, the widow, a couple of beautician licences in Giardinetti.

II

Bufalo's psychiatric evaluation had been going on for two years now, and they still weren't any closer to a final conclusion. When Trentadenari asked him for reassurances, Professor Cortina offered nothing but panic.

'I've got one of the expert witnesses in the palm of my hand, but the

342

other one is a hard nut to crack – too hard.'

'So what are you telling me?'

'If everything works out, we're looking at a declaration of partial mental infirmity...'

'Which would mean?'

'Twenty years' imprisonment and another five or so in a criminal asylum...Minimum.'

'Professor, Bufalo could flip out and kill us all!'

'What am I supposed to do about it? My colleague won't come around...'

'Do you need money to pay him off?'

'Heavens, no! He's immune to bribes.'

'Well? What's the problem?'

'He's afraid!'

'Afraid of what?'

'Of winding up like Cervellone!'

'Aw, that's ancient history! We're different people now...'

'Would you care to explain that yourself to my colleague?'

They'd hit a blind alley. Trentadenari and Freddo paid a call on the judge's 'long-time friend', the guy who had taken twenty million lire and now seemed to be unreachable by phone. In order to obtain an audience, they kicked down the door to his office and, to make the point of how pissed off they were, hung him on the wall coat rack for fifteen minutes and took turns smacking him around and spitting in his face, just to show how much they cared.

It turned out that the guy was nothing but a middleman. If they wanted to be certain they were getting what they were paying for, they needed to talk directly to the person of interest: a 'terribly powerful officer of the court' who was the 'linchpin of the case'.

No sooner said than done: Freddo and Trentadenari bunged the 'long-time friend' into their car and escorted him to Piazzale Clodio, site of the Hall of Justice. As they walked in the front entrance, they ran into Judge Borgia with his police escort. All of them, trembling judicial underling included, had their documents examined and recorded.

The 'terribly powerful officer of the court' proved to be a senior clerk of the court. One glance at the authentic canvases and thick carpets that adorned the enormous and well-appointed office in which they were given audience, and Freddo couldn't help but compare it in his mind to the monastic poverty of Borgia's tiny cubbyhole. If influence and power could be measured by sheer ostentation, then they were talking to the right man, no two ways about it. These were odd thoughts, given the time and the occasion, but Freddo let them lull him, ignoring the negotiations that Trentadenari was conducting with a wreath of smiles and a chain of handshakes.

When they left the office, they carried with them a list of demands that they immediately turned over to Dandi. Dandi didn't take it well.

'Whoa! A Rolex...a marble bust of an ancient Roman senator...two or three fur coats...a leather desk blotter...an antique vanity table...What the hell has popped into this guy's head? And who's to tell us this isn't some rip-off?'

In the meantime, though, there was nothing to be done. As long as they had a deal, they had to pay.

Moreover, they had plenty to worry about at the same time: in particular, the attack on Secco. It had emerged that the bomb had been constructed with an explosive consisting of dynamite and blasting powder. At Trentadenari's behest, Fabio Santini, who had proved he was capable of earning the vigorish he'd been given, managed to get his hands on certain police reports that stated the blasting powder might well come from a stock of explosives stolen a few weeks back from a local quarry. Now, the quarry in question happened to be located in the zone where Nercio was in charge of the distribution of narcotics. Dandi asked Nercio to ask around and see what he could find out.

After a while, Nercio sent for him. Dandi liked Nercio. He was younger than him, determined, and a man of few words. A Freddo from the early days, before the paranoid obsessions started swirling through his mind. Nercio informed him that the reported theft was bogus, and that the owner of the quarry was selling the explosives out the back door. Just about everybody was using his explosives: Red terrorists on the left, Black terrorists on the right, sharks and minnows alike.

The police report happened to coincide with a purchase made by the Bordini brothers. When Secco received the information, he sat open-mouthed in astonishment. He'd never had a thing to do with the Bordini boys, except the occasional *buongiorno* and *buonasera*. It was inconceivable that they'd been responsible for an attack, much less a payback, either of which would have been equally unwarranted. Either the Bordini boys had lost their minds, or else Nercio's tip was a lie.

Dandi, who knew Secco far too well, and who put little or no credence in his show of wide-eyed disbelief, informed the others. The reappearance on the local stage of two old acquaintances like the Bordini brothers – already suspects some time ago in the murder of Puma's brother-in-law, that same Angioletto whose death remained an unsolved mystery – transformed the case into a larger question, one that affected the whole gang. The decision was made: track down the Bordinis. Once they'd been brought in, they'd have quite a bit of explaining to do!

Dispatches were sent out to the ants, they made the rounds of gambling dens, nightclubs and taverns, but the days turned into weeks, with still no trace of the two brothers. Finally, one night a mobile squad patrol car found them. They were stretched out at the foot of the Albero dei Pippatori, the Coke Snorter's Oak – a huge tree that served as a landmark for the coke-hounds and streetwalkers of the Agro dell'Acquedotto Felice. Both of them dead as a doornail, each with a revolver in his hand. The setting suggested a country duel, a cudgel fight. And even though the very idea that the Bordini boys had shot each other to death brought a smile to the lips of the finest minds in cop-dom, the case was still quickly filed away and forgotten.

III

ROBERTA HAD HEARD about Aldo. An icy abyss opened up between her and Freddo.

For some time after that night two years ago, the very night that had saved Aldo's life, Roberta and Dorotea had met up regularly. Dorotea and Aldo had split up almost immediately. The young woman had resumed her art studies, and she'd even made a stab at painting a portrait of Freddo. It was one of those modern things, and at first he'd just laughed at it. Then, once he'd had time to reflect on that twisted face with its alien features, a creeping sense of disquiet had seized him.

'Is that really the way you see me?' he'd asked Dorotea.

'I see a person who's not happy.'

Then and there he'd chuckled at the thought: me, unhappy? I'm the King of Rome, what are you talking about! But now, in the aftermath of what had happened with Aldo, those words came back to him. The truth was that it had left a rock in his heart that wouldn't melt away. A thousand times he had relived that scene of the two of them hugging, and if he'd still believed in anything, he would have petitioned for just one last grace, one final favour: to be able to go back in time to that cursed moment. To be able to rewrite the end. More than anything else, what tormented him most was one question: why hadn't he just let Aldo go?

In the meantime, Nero had been released from prison. On parole – conditional release for health reasons. The firefight with the carabinieri had left him with a legacy of five lead fragments that, after a lengthy peregrination, had settled into a soft area of the brain. He had difficulties maintaining his balance, he was oppressed by a ferocious headache that he was barely able to hold at bay with massive doses of analgesics. Freddo found him skinny and combative.

'But I'm alive, I'm still alive, comrade, and that's the thing that matters!'

Nero had made a deal directly with the Old Man: protection in exchange for silence and no more tricks. His life insurance policy took the form of a document now in the hands of a trustworthy person; in case of his death by violent or mysterious means, that document would be sent to the appropriate recipients.

'Aren't you afraid they'll find it first?'

'It wouldn't be to their advantage. I know how to stick to a deal, and they know that.'

As for his legal situation, he'd confessed to a couple of armed robberies and other small-time offences, like fencing, money laundering, illegal possession of weapons. He figured he could get off with three or four years, total, and stay out on bail or parole as long as possible.

'And you? How's it going with you?'

Freddo opened his heart. Nero listened in concern, his face sharpened now and again by a stirring of pain.

'I'd have done the same thing. Or maybe I wouldn't have, now that I think about it.'

346

'Tell me what you mean.'

'We all talk about traitors and informants, Judases and so on…But perhaps there's a certain degree of beauty even in betrayal…'

'I'd never betray you, Nero…'

'How do you know that? When your life depends on five tiny particles of lead that lie fast asleep – or that pretend to sleep in your brain – when yawning or even spitting could send you straight into the afterlife without warning, suddenly, while you're fucking, or just kicking back in your bed…Well, comrade, let me assure you that you start to look at things differently!'

'Are you telling me that you don't believe in anything anymore?'

'Quite the contrary! I used to not believe in anything. You remember all that talk about the Idea? The Idea this, the Idea that…All so much bullshit! Now I believe in lots of things, Freddo. You want to know the most important thing of all? Being here, right now, talking to you…'

Nero brewed some hashish tea and told him that, in consideration of his precarious state of health, he was authorized to legally possess a certain quantity of drugs 'for therapeutic purposes'.

'With a medical prescription, Freddo! Of course, we run the prescriptions through a friend of Vanessa's, which means we procure a bit of fresh, legal dope to sell. Not much, just enough to keep my hand in…'

Freddo laughed. Welcome back, the good old Nero he used to know!

A police inspection came rolling through, and Freddo hid out in a bathroom. Once the police had moved on, Nero told him that he'd recommended to Dandi and Secco that they invest in computers.

'In what?'

'Electronics. The business of the future. Just think of what a network of computers would do for betting and video poker…You know that Dandi got into that business with the Pugliese, don't you?'

'I don't like Dandi, and I don't like Secco…'

'I understand you, Freddo. Still, you have to make up your mind: whose side are you on?'

'What do you mean, whose side am I on! I'm on my side, Nero…'

'You're not happy being on your side; you're not happy with yourself, comrade.'

Freddo, stricken, looked away.

IV

NOW THAT THE question of the Bordini brothers had been taken care of, Secco was once again doing business in the light of day. Dandi found him in a bank manager's office where the fat man, outside of banking hours, was loan sharking the debtors who'd fallen into arrears, only to fall into much worse hands at 300 per cent annual interest.

'Dandi, my friend! What can I do for you?'

'You know what your problem is, Secco? You're conceited!'

'What are you saying?'

'You think everyone else is an idiot. You think you're the smartest man in Rome, don't you?'

Secco tried to lodge an objection. Dandi, with icy fury, swept a small pile of cash and post-dated cheques off the surface of the desk. Secco started trembling. Dandi sat down on the desktop and lit a Cuban cigar. He'd started smoking them after seeing a film starring Paul Newman. He'd even joined a Havana cigar fan club.

'Now let me tell you just how things went down with the Bordinis...'

After the 'duel', Botola and Nercio had been sent to do a little further investigation. The judges might fall for the fairytale of a couple of brothers shooting each other to death, but it would never fool people who know something about the street. All they had to do was ask a few questions, contact the right people, the ones who no longer had anything to fear from the Bordinis, now that they were both dead.

'So I asked myself: how could it be that, the minute word gets out that we're looking for the Bordini brothers, they go and have the brilliant idea of shooting each other dead? What a remarkable sense of timing they had! They'd managed to avoid so many annoyances., so many awkward questions, because if we had managed to lay our hands on them, those Bordini boys, we know very well how to make them talk. So at that point I ask myself: who did kill them? And it's clear: somebody with a strong interest in keeping them from talking. But why? After all, what could they have been about to say...?'

Secco stirred uncomfortably in his chair. Dandi tapped a dusting of cigar ashes onto Secco's waistcoat, calmly pulled a revolver out of his pocket, and scratched Secco's forehead with the front sight.

'Botola and Nercio are right outside. If you're thinking of calling any of your friends, you'll be a dead fatty in ten seconds flat!'

Secco flopped back in his seat, his face a mask of sweat. Dandi took a long drag of smoke.

'All right, listen up good. You, the Bordinis and poor Angioletto find a supply route for coke that we don't know about. And you start doing a little dealing on your own. Angioletto pulls a con and you rub him out. You replace him with Satana. We catch on and so long Satana. No big loss. You keep on dealing. Until one fine day you try to con the Bordinis, and they plant the bomb. We find out about it and you kill the Bordinis…Simple, no?'

'Dandi…'

'And you know where you got the money to start with? From Libano's treasury, poor old friend! That's where it came from.'

'Dandi, I…I've always had plenty of money…It's my specialty, right?'

'But never this much, and never all at once, my little mama's boy. You ripped us off, Secco. You pulled a con job on us. Now you tell me what I'm supposed to do…'

'Dandi…'

'Dandi, Dandi, *Dandi*…What I don't understand,' roared Dandi, grabbing him by the lapel, 'what I just can't figure out, is why you would try to undercut our market? How much could you make off a deal like this? Peanuts…Everybody knows we control the market…We've made you rich. But if you had a supply route of your own, why didn't you just tell us about it? We could have worked together…Now, you tell me, Secco, what do I have to do? What do I have to do to you?'

Secco understood that to go on denying was pointless. He threw his arms open and put on his usual oily little smile.

'Someone as good as I am at moving money – where are you going to find him?'

Dandi snapped off the safety and placed the muzzle against Secco's temple.

'Bullshit. Come up with something better.'

'We aren't all equal.'

'Who?'

'Men.'

'What are you saying?'

'I can't work under someone like Freddo.'

'I'm not Freddo...'

'That's why we're here talking...'

Slowly, Dandi lowered the muzzle. Secco wiped his forehead with an embroidered handkerchief. He had men and he had resources. And a Chinese supply channel that no one else knew anything about. Sure, he'd made a mistake by not confiding in Dandi, not trusting him, but it had all been Freddo's fault – Freddo and his comrades, Scrocchiazeppi, the Buffoni boys, Ricotta, Fierolocchio...Street thugs, two-bit cut-throats...One day or another, they'd all, inexorably, take the fall. People who were as greedy as they were stupid.

If only Libano were still there, things would have turned out differently. Even if Dandi himself hadn't been so 'loyal' to a bond that no longer existed, things would have turned out differently. Men weren't the same; men weren't all equal. A band of desperadoes couldn't control the whole city of Rome. The important thing was to work through alliances, shoot only when you had to, live and let live, let others have their territory...

'None of this is new to me,' Dandi cut in.

In the meantime, however, the pistol had slipped back into his pocket and Dandi had made himself comfortable in an office chair. There was a spark of interest glittering in his eyes. Secco pushed his advantage a little further.

'You haven't said anything about this to the others, have you? I mean this whole issue – you haven't talked about it, that's right, isn't it...?'

Dandi nodded, vaguely surprised at the question.

'That means,' Secco said triumphantly, 'that you think the same way I do...'

'Tell me about this Chinese supply route,' said Dandi, leaning back and crossing his legs.

Other Turncoats
1983

I

THE NIGHT THAT Gigio overdosed, Freddo was watching Falcão and
the others players celebrating the Scudetto, the Italian national football championship, on television. It emerged that the guy who found
Gigio with a needle still in his vein was Bazzica, one of Trentadenari's
horses. Anyone else, in Bazzica's place, would have looked the other way
and minded his own business. All the more so, given the fact that the
boy's illustrious family ties were well known in the trade, and everyone
knew that Freddo had issued a prohibition against selling him shit of any
kind. But Bazzica, who must have had something approaching human
sentiment deep down in his black soul, leaned over the body that lay
half-seated in a boxer's stance between two piles of tyres that served as
the gateway to an abandoned junkyard, and he realized that Gigio was
still breathing. He was in that grey no-man's land where the Via Cassia
stopped being hinterland – *borgo* – and turned into open countryside.

Bazzica got word to Vanessa, and in less than an hour, Gigio had
been taken to the clinic of Villa del Mirto. Still, no one had the courage
to inform Freddo that his only brother had one foot in the grave and the
other looked like following it. That would take someone with real balls.
So Nero went to do the job.

Freddo saw his face framed in the orange, surreal light of the video
intercom, with a tense expression, as he told him softly, 'Come downstairs, we have someplace to go.'

Freddo went with him, no questions asked. Nero explained the situation to him in a few words. Freddo felt a stab of ancient pain.

'I need to call my father,' he murmured.

'That's already taken care of,' Nero reassured him.

The clinic was in the Parioli district, immersed in a forest of flowering magnolias. Outside the door of Gigio's room stood his father and his mother. Nero and Vanessa hung back a few steps. Freddo strode decisively towards the hospital room. His mother was holding a handkerchief in her fingers. Her eyes were red. His father was blocking the way.

'I want to see him,' said Freddo.

His father was standing between him and the door: a small man with drawn features, grey hair and a fierce, sorrowful glare.

'Please, let me by.'

His mother touched his arm. His father barely stepped aside.

In the dim blue half-light, Gigio's eyes were closed, his face stamped with a grim, resigned expression. Freddo hadn't seen him since that time with Roberta. They had been long years of silence and hostility.

Freddo delicately ran two fingers over that lamb-faced forehead, the narrow nose, caressed the several days' growth of whiskers, touched the sweat-matted hair. He wept. Vanessa stuck her head in at the door.

'Doctor Spadaro wants to talk to you.'

Outside, Nero was leaning against a wall covered with portraits of priests of all races, smoking a cigarette. Freddo's father and mother took turns holding each other up.

Vanessa led Freddo to the clinic's administrative offices. Dr Spadaro was a ruddy-cheeked gentleman of about fifty, with small, bloodshot eyes.

'Your brother's out of danger. I found no needle marks, so I am assuming he is not a drug addict. Evidently, he just wanted to sample the thrill of heroin and he had a bad experience. This time he'll recover. I'd keep him under observation for three or four days, then he can go home.'

Freddo thanked him and told him that he'd take care of all the expenses. Spadaro sniffed loudly.

'In consideration of a number of factors that Signorina Vanessa has explained to me, we thought it best not to inform the authorities...'

As they were walking back, Vanessa explained that the doctor was snorting half a gram daily.

'How much does he want?'

'Fifteen million lire for the hospitalization and his silence. And a little coke now and then.'

'Fine. Tell Trentadenari that I want to see all the horses and ants. Tomorrow at eleven, at his place.'

'And your brother?'

'What about my brother?'

'When he comes to, is there anything I should tell him?'

'No.'

His parents were still standing outside the door of Gigio's room. Nero was sitting in a chair, leafing distractedly through an illustrated weekly. Freddo avoided his father and went straight to his mother.

'He's okay,' he told her, looking her straight in the eye.

His mother threw herself into his arms. Freddo hugged her tight. She began to sob. Freddo clenched his fists. He wished he could console her. He wished...

'Come on, let's go.' Nero rested a hand on his shoulder.

Freddo pulled out of the embrace with difficulty and followed Nero down the hall to the front door.

'Want to take a walk?' Nero suggested.

'I just want to be by myself.'

'That seems right.'

'Nero...'

'Yes?'

'Thanks.'

'You would have done the same thing for me. Sleep on it, and don't do anything stupid.'

The streets were thronged with delirious football fans celebrating. Forty years they'd waited for it, this Scudetto. Forty years writhing under the heel of those bastards from up north. Thieves, sleazebags, sell-outs. They'd even dared to spit on that one victory forty years ago. They said that it had been a decision handed down by Thunder Jaws. Thieves.

The triumphant fans splashed into the city's fountains, waved their banners, shattered shop windows. They were weeping with joy; diehard fans loved to suffer almost as much as they loved to win.

Freddo was a Roma fan too. And in that victory he'd long yearned after was a sense of redemption. But now he was thousands of miles away from it all. Gigio's lamb face kept coming back to torment him.

He caught a late-night bus. He hadn't set foot on a public conveyance of any kind since high school. They were strictly for losers. But that night the rumble of the engine, the rattling and clinking of the windows at each stop – it all somehow reassured him. It was like coming back home after a long time away. Coming home and finding that nothing had changed. As if nothing bad had happened. For a short time it was just him and the driver, alone on the bus. Then a drunk got on and stood right next to him.

'The other night, St Gaspar appeared before me. Or was it St Vincent? Say, what do you think – was it the saint or a hallucination?'

Freddo rummaged through his pockets and offered him some money. The drunk refused, indignant.

Two young football fans boarded the bus, their eyes frantic, cans of beer in their hands. The drunk went on raving. The two kids started insulting him. The drunk ignored them, lost in his delirium. First one shove, then another. The drunk tripped and fell, landing heavily between two seats. The young men piled on him.

'Leave him alone,' said Freddo.

The two kids swung around, disbelief on their faces, and burst into raucous laughter. Then they went back to work on the drunk, who was trying to get back on his feet. Freddo lunged at them. He grabbed the first guy by the shoulders, spun him around and slammed him against the ticket machine. He dropped the other one to the floor with a boot right between the legs.

'Now stop the bus and open the doors,' he told the driver.

The driver, who had watched the whole scene in his rearview mirror, hastened to comply. Freddo hurled the two thugs out into the street.

'You can go now.'

The bus started up again. Freddo helped the drunk to his feet and slipped all the cash he had on him into his pocket. Then he asked the driver to stop again. He'd had enough.

The next morning, at Trentadenari's place, he was the same old Freddo as ever.

'Pieces of shit. You're all so many pieces of shit. You don't even have the courage to call things for what they are. If it hadn't been for Nero…Nero, who has five chunks of lead in his brain…Pieces of shit.'

Fierolocchio, Trentadenari and Scrocchiazeppi took the tongue-lashing, heads bowed. Ants and horses were trembling in terror. Even Botola seemed genuinely chagrined. Only Dandi sat stroking his brand-new moustache – a whim of Patrizia's – in total indifference.

'Well? It turned out okay, didn't it? Next time your brother will be a little more careful!'

'There's not going to be a next time. Anyone who sells so much as a gram to Gigio is dead when I catch him. Now I want to know who gave him that shit!'

II

AT THE BEGINNING of the summer, Bufalo was suddenly assigned to the mental institution of Montelupo Fiorentino. The experts had decided to subject him to another session of psychiatric observation 'in pharma-cologically-assisted therapy'. The very evening he arrived, Conte Ugolino – a colossus from Viareggio about whom it was whispered that he had practically chewed the flesh off an unfair competitor in the coke-traf-ficking business – explained the meaning of that obscure phraseology.

'They stuff you so full of pills that you don't know your own name, and then they watch to see what effect it has on you!'

'And then?'

'If you're the same as ever, no problem. But if you go all calm on them, then they put in your file "mentally sound" and then you're royally fucked!'

'Then I just won't take the pills!'

'If only it was that simple! These guys have shit that they put in your food, in the water, and you can't even taste it or smell it…'

'Then I'm fucked!'

'What are you talking about, Roman! Stick your fingers down your throat after meals and only keep down food from the snack bar, and you're the one who fucks them!'

At first, Bufalo hadn't taken the transfer well. It was one thing to play the crazy card to avoid a life sentence without parole; it was quite another to wind up in the middle of a bunch of real crazies. But it wasn't long before he realized that there weren't many real crazies in there at all, and almost all the inmates were charged with ridiculous crimes: a Neapolitan ex-cop who had the unfortunate habit of jerking off onto fresh graves because voices told him to; a wino who had been incarcerated for six years now for stealing a case of Stravecchio Branca brandy and would probably spend the rest of his life in there, because he had no family; a junkie who had robbed a friend only to return the loot to him the next day – and maybe it was that odd twist on the crime that had caused him to be sent there.

All of the other permanent guests of that ancient and austere building were no crazier than Bufalo was, and they were all hoping to be certified mentally infirm more or less as if it meant passing their final exams. But they hadn't been coached very well. They were text-book lunatics, all grimaces, shouts and dicks in the wind, doing their best to scandalize the arrogant, mocking male nurses. Even the greenest expert in the world would have spotted the masquerade for what it was. Better to steer clear of the others, Bufalo thought, and not get lost in the mass of prisoners. In that case, though, who was he going to pass the time of day with? After all, that was his main problem.

Aside from Conte Ugolino, who really was a good enough guy, as long as you didn't piss him off – he was capable of lifting Bufalo into the air with just one arm – the only one with his head screwed on straight in there seemed to be Turi Funciazza. The Sicilian, a smart boy who didn't say much and a specialist in the extortion game, was one of the most respected enforcers working for the clan of Piazza del Gesù. Arrested after a gangland slaying on behalf of the Corleonese allies, betrayed by a turncoat whose two cousins and three nephews had already been liquidated, literally, in muriatic acid, Turi was courteous but reserved, distant and, according to Bufalo, vaguely arrogant. Before his sentencing, he'd never set foot off the island of Sicily, or really out of the province of Palermo, and underneath his well-mannered front you could see what he thought: anything that wasn't Cosa Nostra was either the government or else simply didn't exist.

Bufalo, who was used to the respect and terror of his underlings back home, did his best to put on a tough front, but the Sicilian did nothing but shrug with a faint smile of indifference:

'It takes five hundred years to become the way we are, friend.'

Five hundred years because, Turi explained, that's how long Cosa Nostra had existed. It all started when three noble brothers – Osso, Mastosso and Carcagnosso – killed the brother of the king of Spain in a duel for having offended their honour.

'But that coward with a crown sentenced them to death, and Osso, Mastosso and Carcagnosso ('Bone', 'Masterbone' and 'Heelbone') were forced to flee for their lives. And Osso landed in Favignana and there he founded what you call the Mafia; and Mastosso, in Naples, what you call the Camorra; and Carcagnosso established the first 'Ndrina in Calabria. But plenty of water has passed under the bridge since then! So, you can talk and talk, Roman, but you and people like you will find yourselves eating hard, stale bread...'

When the name Dandi was mentioned, Turi reacted oddly, and two days later he was back, with a nice open smile and a warm, firm handshake. He'd gathered information from the 'family'. Bufalo could be considered a trusted person.

'Friend, you should have told me from the very beginning that you were in Dandi's gang! He's a man that Uncle Carlo holds in the highest esteem!'

And so Bufalo won respect and recognition because he was a friend of Dandi's! Dandi, who would gladly have put him face to face with an angry Conte Ugolino, just to see if the Tuscan really did like to dine on human flesh! Dandi, the turncoat who had ruined his life!

Turi Funciazza's revelation forced Bufalo to check his brain out of the left luggage where he'd abandoned it, and as he emerged from the mental sloth that had come over him during the long months of straining to pass for a lunatic, one thing was clear: Dandi was out in the world doing business with the Mafia, while Bufalo was rotting away in an asylum for the criminally insane. Dandi was making billions, while Bufalo was relying on the charity of his comrades. Dandi was on his way up, while Bufalo was heading nowhere but down. Dandi was winning, while Bufalo was losing. Bufalo took revenge for Libano and paid the price. Dandi said to hell with the vendetta and got off scot-free. There was only one possible conclusion to be drawn: Dandi was a slick con artist, while Bufalo was a miserable piece of shit. Dandi was smart to think only about the future, while Bufalo's mistake was to dwell on the past.

The holiday in Montelupo lasted fifteen days. By bribing a non-commissioned officer in the registry, Bufalo found out that the final report 'simply confirmed the findings of the preceding observation'. All pointless, in other words.

The night before his return to Rome, Bufalo asked Turi how a man of honour would behave towards a rival who failed to respect boundaries but who was also too powerful to be attacked face to face.

'With cunning and humility, brother. With smiles and poison,' came the reply.

III

AFTER THE MEETING in the 'office-that-never-was', Scialoja gathered a little information on the Old Man. The sources seemed to vary widely. The Old Man was a special intermediary in the parallel diplomatic channels that served as a covert conduit between Italy and the United States. He was a champion of visceral anti-Communism. He was a moderate who helped to temper the views of the harshest extremists with his calm wisdom. He was trusted behind the Iron Curtain. No, the Old Man was nothing but an old relic, destined for the junkyard, a holdover from a bygone era, a trick of blue smoke and mirrors, a straw man they relegated to an incidental office, starved of funds and staff. Rubbish. Never so much as in the case of the Old Man was there such a sharp discrepancy between the ostensible position and the actual power wielded: seemingly mediocre and strictly peripheral, yet also limitless. The Old Man was nothing but a scarecrow staked out in the field at times of crisis. The Old Man lay at the crossroads of the secret history of the past quarter century...

From certain recurrent details, variously writ large or twisted almost beyond recognition in one case after another, as in some popular folk tale, Scialoja gathered that the most prolific source of rumours about the Old Man was none other than the Old Man himself. It was he who fed the flames of unsettling mysteries, bizarre gossip, awe veined with genuine fear, or even the ironic snicker – all or some or just one of these were sure to be elicited whenever Scialoja mentioned his name in conversation. The Old Man was an anarchist. The Old Man was having his fun. The Old Man, in his way, had offered a deal: we'll give you a little something, or even someone, and you'll be able to make a meal of it, but don't ask about the larger game because it's not something you could swallow, much less digest.

The various investigations that sprang from Scialoja's report were hobbling along. No one had the courage to cut those investigations off entirely – times had changed. But between the occasional, infrequent deposition, a distracted re-reading of the documentation, an article or two in the leftist press – quickly read and forgotten – the plot was fading out, trickling away down the thousand rivulets of the perverse jostling and interplay of jurisdictions. The only remaining option was to focus, once again, on the murders and the weapons. The Old Man had made it clear to him that someone would pay the price. Specifically, whoever was stubborn enough to keep tracking down leads. Or those who hadn't been smart enough to get rid of their balaclavas and don a double-breasted suit. But was the Old Man capable of honouring his agreements? Zeta and Pigreco seemed to have vanished into thin air. Officially on an over-seas mission, Scialoja had read somewhere. But Ranocchia had been left alone. Scialoja had gone over to look for him one night at the Baths of Diocletian. He looked like a ghost, but was still selling his arse.

'It's the law of desire, my big, strapping young man!'

As they downed a whiskey together (Ranocchia had insisted the drinks were his treat), in a grim little dive by the train station, Scialoja wondered inwardly whether there was anyone on earth desperate enough to take the man to bed.

'Patrizia asked me to say hello to you.'

'Is that all?'

'What were you hoping for? A declaration of undying love on bended knee? Go see her and find out how far you can get. God, you men are just intolerable! You always have to have everything explained to you, from A to Z. You never leave the slightest room for imagination or mystery!'

So now Patrizia wanted to see him. But Scialoja didn't go. He didn't even ask Ranocchia how he could find her. He didn't so much as lift a finger to track her down. The wound from Positano still smarted, but it was a dull, aching pain that came and went, well on its way to healing, he hoped.

Scialoja was in the middle of interrogating a lunatic from Cinecittà, a derelict who had raped, strangled and burned a fourteen-year-old girl, when Patrizia finally phoned him at the police station. Ranocchia was dead.

Scialoja cursed the Old Man, moved heaven and earth to lay his hands on the medical examiner's report, and had a hard time resigning himself to the unmistakable facts. In the end, he was forced to give in. There really was no mystery. Ranocchia had gone home, grabbed a belt and hanged himself from a roof beam. He'd just made up his mind to end it all: nothing more, nothing less. When they autopsied him, they'd found more diseases than you'd expect in a leper colony. All that could really be offered as a requiem was that the man had decided to quit the stage with some style once it became clear to him that his ugly, failing body had stopped responding to even the most basic commands.

Scialoja saw Patrizia again at the funeral. Under a driving rain, a small eight-piece band was escorting the coffin, banging away at various jazz pieces as it straggled along behind the velvet-canopied horse-drawn hearse. Scialoja recognized 'When the Saints Go Marching In'. By the time they'd reached the front entrance of the Prima Porta church, they'd begun a languid, heartbreaking version of 'Sophisticated Lady'. *Play that piece for me*, Ranocchia had written in the last letter he wrote, left marked for Patrizia's attention. Deep down I've always felt – as he put it in Italian – like a *signora sofisticata*.

Aside from the members of the little orchestra, they were the only two people attending. The only people who could boast, as it were, a friendship with Ranocchia. They waited in silence for the coffin to be closed. By now the rain had stopped falling.

Patrizia paid the musicians and then locked arms with him.

'You're looking well,' she said.

'I wish I could say the same for you. You're overweight, you have too much make-up on, and you're loaded down with garish jewellery. You're well on your way to turning into one of those Mafia matrons...'

'That's not very nice. You're still angry at me over what happened in Positano...'

'Why? Did something happen in Positano?'

They walked along side by side until they reached her Maserati, still arm in arm. Patrizia let go with one of her deep-throated peals of laughter.

'Ranocchia liked jewellery. He said that when I wore jewellery I looked like Cleopatra.'

'Cleopatra died a nasty death.'

'Well, that isn't going to happen to me.'

She suddenly grabbed his head in her hands and tried to force his lips open. He shook his head and gently pushed her away. No syncopated racing of his heartbeat, no sudden bubbling up of desire, no stabbing daggers in his lower belly. Scialoja felt as chilly as the rain that was starting to drum down again on the roof of the luxurious Maserati.

'Have I really become so unappetizing?' she flirted.

'Things change.'

'Fuck you, I want some sex.'

'What happened? Did Dandi give you a day pass?'

She laughed. Her eyes turned languid, then filled with despair, and then finally overflowed with pride and malice. She threw herself upon him furiously, indifferent to the rain. She bit deeply into one of his ears.

'Freddo wants to kill Sorcio,' she murmured. Then she got into the car and pulled away, tyres screeching.

Later, Scialoja realized that Patrizia had slid a pair of keys into his pocket.

IV

HOWEVER MANY TIMES Freddo tried, once Gigio was out of the hospital, he refused to meet with him. Freddo had no alternative but to send a little money to his mother and ask her to talk his brother into taking a short trip abroad. In the end, Gigio had given in, and now he was safe in London: rebuilding his life far away from all the filth, Freddo hoped.

But in the meantime, the jackal who had sold him the dose in the first place continued to elude the searchers. All appeals and bounties proved useless; all threats and blandishments were in vain. No help from the others. This was a personal family matter, and it wasn't all that hard to figure out that, deep down, they all agreed with Dandi: a junkie, whether habitual or occasional, was looking for trouble. Isn't that how Freddo had always seen it himself, before what happened to Gigio? Still, somebody had to pay.

His mother had told him that when Gigio was shooting up, he never had a lira. When he left the clinic, his brother no longer had the motor scooter that Freddo had given him one night so many years ago. No doubt he'd traded the bike for a dose. But Freddo spread the word that someone had stolen something that belonged to him. It wasn't the kind of thing anyone would take lightly.

Before the week was up, a two-bit thief from Centocelle came to see Freddo. Terrified, the kid swore up and down that he'd had no way of knowing; if he'd ever even imagined…But the bike had seemed pretty clean, and he was glad to tell him that he'd bought it from Zoppo, a fence who was fairly well respected in the network.

Freddo thanked the kid and said that if his information proved to be true, he could keep the motor scooter. Zoppo, in his turn, came around: the motor scooter, he informed Freddo, hadn't appeared to be stolen, and when Sorcio brought it around he hadn't had the slightest suspicion that…Okay, that's fine, you can go.

So it had been Sorcio. And now he had to pay. The evidence? What need was there for evidence? It was all so clear, such a straight, bright line…

When he saw him heave into view outside of Franco's bar, Sorcio immediately understood that Freddo was on to him. His legs turned rubbery, and the smile died on his lips. The place was buzzing with people, and Freddo had no wish to cause himself trouble by shooting the kid in front of witnesses.

'Come with me,' he said.

Sorcio followed him obediently, quaking with an uncontrollable tremor. Freddo took him to his VW Golf, poked his gun into Sorcio's side, and told him very clearly:

'Now let's go find you a nice place to die.'

At that point, he was no longer a man but a machine. Still, there had to be, somewhere up there, an out-of-work archangel willing to stretch out his great big wings over miserable losers like Sorcio. Already the feral little animal had survived that first time, when he'd stolen Libano's duffel bag. And Freddo himself, the second time, had decided to spare his life for the story of poor Aldo Buffoni. Yes, they really should change his name; old Sorcio, from that afternoon on, would be known as 'Somebody Up There Likes Me'. Because Freddo had just turned off onto the highway for Fiumicino when they were stopped by an unmarked mobile squad Fiat Uno.

Sorcio, who couldn't believe his eyes, started screeching, 'Look out, he's armed!'

In the hands of the assembled cops, standard issue Berettas suddenly appeared. Freddo, who knew how to lose with a smile, handed over his 9-millimetre handgun – an unregistered gun with the serial number filed off. And so it was that the would-be killer and his narrowly saved victim found themselves at Regina Coeli, each of them mulling over the power of celestial forces.

Neither Freddo nor Sorcio knew that the archangel responsible for the miracle was named Scialoja. He'd taken his sweet time to identify Sorcio – small fry if there ever was one, as nobody knew his name – but in the end, the idea of putting a couple of trusted cops on his tail turned out to yield abundant fruit. Scialoja was rubbing his hands in glee. Leaving aside the arrest itself, if he could only work this Sorcio properly...

Freddo's arrest came as dismaying news to Scrocchiazeppi and Fierolocchio, who were and always would be genuine friends. It was also a cause for dismay to Trentadenari, but in his case, friendship had nothing to do with it, only regret for the temporary loss of Sorcio. It wasn't going to be easy to replace a dope sampler of Sorcio's calibre. As for Dandi, he saw it as yet another confirmation that his strategy of withdrawing from his commitments had been the right one. If even Freddo – the only one left who, in terms of guts and brains, could still pose a challenge – took his eye off the ball to go chasing off after his junkie brother's ravings, well, then it was clear once and for all that he and the rest of them were living on two different planets. Now that his agreement with Secco guaranteed him men and alternative narcotics channels, the remaining problem was one of jettisoning dead weight. Dandi would have to choose the right moment. But he felt wary about unleashing wholesale warfare. If he wanted to strike, he'd have to do so in a scientific manner, and once and for all. But with Freddo, Bufalo and Ricotta behind bars, there was a real risk of leaving behind dangerous resentments and grudges. Freddo was an adversary deserving of respect. Bufalo was someone you'd want to keep an eye on. But then again, the network of dealers was entirely in Trentadenari's hands. Now he was a guy you could reason with. It wasn't necessarily the case that a hail of lead would be the last word in this argument. This wouldn't be the first or the last time in gangland history that members of a mob had amicably agreed to go their separate ways. For the time being, things would have to move along the usual tracks. The Chinese supply network had been made common property, even if Dandi had reserved for himself exclusive control over the shipments. Which meant, for instance, that he took delivery of three kilos and told his comrades that he'd received two. He deposited his share of two kilos into the general fund; he split the rest down the middle with Secco.

Secco was a genuine power all to himself. Not only was he good at moving money – everyone already knew that, anyway – but he was also incredibly skilful at maintaining an array of contacts. Little by little, as the agreement came into being, Dandi was amazed to see with his own eyes just how many people Secco was capable of controlling: officials, policeman, builders, bank managers, even two or three judges. Many of them were on his payroll; others were being blackmailed for their sexual peccadilloes or else they were paying back in kind Secco's incredibly high loan-sharking rates.

The politicians were another matter entirely. Secco greased them freely and abundantly, he took them to dinner, he procured willing and generous girls to entertain them, thus creating a robust network of vested interests and subtle complicity that, at the right time, skilled fishermen that he was, Secco would certainly hook and reel in. He was a known quantity even to an old fox like Uncle Carlo. Dandi had gone with him to do an on-site inspection of certain real estate on the Sabaudia waterfront that interested Uncle Carlo's Milanese partners. The Maestro was there too.

Uncle Carlo had been quite critical of the brand-new saffron-yellow Ferrari that Dandi had just picked up three days ago from the showroom.

'It's too flashy.'

'But Uncle Carlo, after all, money's there to be enjoyed, no?'

'Son, take care, don't let your mind get fucked up.'

Dandi would happily have answered back, but Uncle Carlo had already moved on to other subjects. That morning he was in a particularly good mood: in Palermo they had just blown up the vehicle of another filthy investigating magistrate who had taken it into his head to co-ordinate the work of the other prosecuting magistrates with an array of modern methods. They called it a 'pool', that group of dickheads. And modern operator that he was, Uncle Carlo had put himself at their service. The topic of Secco came up at the end of the day.

'An interesting element,' the Maestro had warned, 'but don't give him too much rope.'

'The situation is perfectly under control!'

'We'll see about that.'

What was the Maestro worried about? Dandi knew perfectly well for himself that Secco was two-faced, treacherous, deceitful by vocation. The days of Libano and Freddo were gone forever. Loyalty, nowadays, was a market commodity: you simply had to renegotiate the price on a daily basis.

If Dandi expected to be able to run the operation, he'd have to rely on his ability to manipulate men. Secco, with all his money and his diabolical skill at negotiating with the powerful, didn't know the first thing about how to think on the street. His own men, the ones who were growing fat thanks to his brilliant ideas, at the very most respected him, but they'd certainly never love him. Little by little, Dandi would draw them over to his side. Secco wouldn't even notice what was happening. Secco was a man alone. Secco could order a killing, but he'd never have the courage to face off with an enemy, eye to eye. Secco had neither the build nor the guts of a real leader. And if some day Secco started busting his chops, Dandi always had that bullet ready for him that he hadn't fired that night long ago...

IN HIS FIRST interrogation after his arrest, Freddo said that he'd offered to give Sorcio a ride. Sorcio was someone he'd known from back in the day when Libano was still around. Obviously he had no idea that the kid was packing a gun, much less an unauthorized one. Otherwise, given his own priors and the well-known 'attention' being lavished on him by the authorities, he would certainly not only have avoided putting his vehicle at Sorcio's disposal, he would also, he added with a considerable display of irony, have withheld his 'friendship'.

Sorcio had confided to Scialoja that Freddo wanted to kill him. But in the presence of the prosecuting magistrate, he'd retreated into a stubborn silence. In solitary confinement, where he'd been held for four days and four nights, he'd gone cold turkey and worked through his withdrawal symptoms. Once his nerves had calmed down, he'd asked to meet with the judge, and had begged him to put him in a cell with one of his comrades.

'They'll either think that I've ratted them out, or that I'm planning to turn state's witness...'

Scialoja had mischievously suggested they put him in a cell with Freddo. Sorcio had gone into a series of fainting spells at the thought, and they'd been forced to rush him to the infirmary. Another investigation threatened to die before it could get started, Borgia commented. But Scialoja insisted: we need to focus on Sorcio. This was a remarkable situation. That a criminal of Freddo's stature would give a ride to a complete zero like Sorcio and be unaware that his passenger was packing a handgun was pure science fiction. And why would Sorcio even be carrying a weapon in the first place? Sorcio was a two-bit junkie, with a minor rap sheet mostly featuring charges of burglary and drug dealing. The fact alone that he was a passenger in Freddo's car was suspicious in and of itself. No question. Sorcio had told the truth: Freddo had been planning to murder him. The 'chance' traffic stop had saved Sorcio's arse. Now they needed to find out why Freddo had it in for Sorcio. What possible link could there be between one of the top bosses in Rome and that miserable loser? What was the reason for the vendetta?

'But he won't talk!' Borgia protested in an exasperated voice. 'I can't very well torture him!'

'Sorcio's crapping himself in fear. Let's put him back out on the street.'

'Let him out? Out is right, but out of your mind is what I'm thinking, Scialoja!'

'Listen: this is a golden opportunity. Trust me on this one!'

A week after being arrested, Sorcio was released, officially for considerations of health. From the moment he walked out the front door of the Hotel Regina, he had a couple of veteran cops on his tail 24–7. Scialoja had had another idea: to keep the operation top secret, aside from the veteran cops themselves. That was why Fabio Santini never managed to warn Trentadenari that Sorcio was under surveillance.

But Sorcio, at first, was a huge disappointment. The operatives reported that the subject stayed at home all day, windows and doors shut tight. Once, taking advantage of the subject's very short outing one afternoon, one of the two cops managed to sneak inside. His eyes met with an incredible scene of filth and neglect: Sorcio was practically wallowing in his own shit.

Borgia was stalling. Scialoja was pushing. He was willing to release Freddo too and wait and see what happened.

Sorcio, meanwhile, had figured out that someone had been in the apartment from a series of minuscule signs. And his paranoia proliferated accordingly. He saw Freddo everywhere he turned. He trembled in warm sunlight. If he'd had a normal quantity of blood in his veins, he'd have put a bullet in his own head. Anything, anything, as long as it helped him to put an end to the anguish that was devastating his life.

Trentadenari, worried by his silence, was forced to hoist his arse up off his chair. The Neapolitan did his best to be reassuring: no one had it in for him, and as long as Freddo was behind bars, he could lead a normal life.

'What about when he gets out?'

'When he gets out we'll talk. Freddo can't go on doing whatever the fuck he wants forever!'

But Sorcio was still using delaying tactics. Trentadenari played the smack card.

'Hundred grams. Purest shit. Eighty to sell and twenty all for you!'

Once Sorcio was alone, he sat staring at the little package the Neapolitan had left him, tempted to flush it down the toilet. Tempted, but in the end, his eager yen won out, and after a nice, warm shot, he felt at peace with the world.

The two cops sprang into action when they saw him emerge all clean-shaven and freshly showered. They rushed at him, shouting, 'Freeze, police!'

But the instant Sorcio saw them coming at him, he fainted and sprawled headlong. They dragged him inside and found the paper with the dope unfolded on a nasty rickety kitchen table. Sorcio regained his senses, understood the situation he was now in, and suddenly the foul beast that had dug its claws into his throat for so long flapped its wings and flew away. He asked to be taken to see Judge Borgia.

'I intend to make a full and complete confession. For a number of years now I have been a member of a vast and wide-ranging criminal organization...'

PART THREE

PART THREE

Everyone Behind Bars
1984

I

SORCIO DICTATED AND Scialoja took shorthand.

Nerves, sheer will and hope gave the kid a strength that he'd never even remotely dreamed he possessed. For the first time after so many years, he thought he had glimpsed a way out. He could leave both the monkey and the paranoia behind him. And if someone called that treason, so be it. What obligation did he have to Freddo and the others? He felt no pity for them. The first name he offered up was that of Fabio Santini.

'We can stay here until tomorrow, but unless you stop the spy, it's all pointless.'

They suspended the interrogation, ordered a panini and beer for the kid, and locked themselves into the director's office. Borgia wanted to frogmarch the corrupt officer directly into a cell in the military prison of Forte Boccea. Scialoja was opposed.

'All we have against him is Sorcio's word. It all needs to be checked out. All he needs to do is claim that he's the victim of some sort of payback from an underworld criminal and he gets off scot-free. If we arrest him now, he will fuck up our investigation for good.'

'Even if he stays out, he'll fuck up our investigation.'

'That depends...'

Scialoja laid out his plan. The magistrate recoiled in horror.

'But that's illegal!'

'Then you go back downstairs and resume the interrogation. You and I never talked about this. If everything works out, the Santini problem is resolved in the next three hours.'

'But what if nothing works out?'

Scialoja had no reply.

As he was walking down the filthy staircase that led to the secure interview rooms, Borgia told himself that the idealistic young judge that he once was would have told Scialoja to go to hell. Worse: he would have filed a criminal complaint against him.

Now, with his silence, he was tacitly giving him free rein. And this wasn't the first time he was covering up for that hothead. Did he feel guilty? Not in the slightest. He was dealing with deeply unscrupulous people. Murderers protected by an invisible and insidious network of conspirators. Civil liberties, at a certain point, could slide into the domain of complicity.

Scialoja handed Fabio Santini his service orders, properly signed and stamped.

'Salerno? What am I going to go do in Salerno, commissario?'

'Don't you know how to read, Santini? You're going to pick up a Red Brigade's terrorist who's turned state's witness and bring him back to Rebibbia. Before tomorrow morning.'

'But this falls within the jurisdiction of the anti-terrorism squad!'

'They're short on men and asked us to help them out.'

'And you picked me out of the whole staff?'

'I needed a trustworthy man!' said Scialoja, cutting the conversation short with a broad smile.

Outside the station, in an unmarked car, there were two weathered old veterans from the mobile squad. It was their responsibility to make sure that Santini really did leave on his unlikely mission. The cops down in Salerno had orders to delay things. While the corrupt cop was collecting his Autostrada toll card and heading south from Rome, two other officers were discreetly letting themselves into Santini's fourth-floor apartment in a building in the Garbatella.

Two hours later, Scialoja received a phone call. Borgia saw him hang up the receiver with the smile of an evil cop on his face.

'Out in Garbatella we found half an ounce of cocaine and a pistol stolen two months ago from the armoury of the Casilino police station. My men are still going over the premises.'

With a sigh of relief, Borgia signed both the arrest warrant and the search warrant. Santini was shipped straight to a cell at Forte Boccea, arriving with a black eye and a swollen nose. The two weathered veterans from the mobile squad wrote in their report that the arrestee, in a frenzy of desperation, had repeatedly pounded his head against a bulletproof window.

Once again, Sorcio was dictating, and Scialoja was taking shorthand.

'So you've arrested Santini? Then go get the dope and bring it here. It all starts with the hundred grams that you found on me when you stopped the car. Brown sugar from Thailand.'

How could he be so sure? They were free to ask around: there wasn't a more sensitive nose or discerning vein than Sorcio's in all of Rome! The supplier? A small businessman from Terni, known as Barbetta. He did business with Bangkok, legitimate deals; but at least twice a year, along with the cotton and rice destined for the communal tables of freaks and longhairs, he brought back two or three kilos of smack. A good six ounces – 150 grams – of it he distributed directly to his close circle of friends – smackheads, all of them. The rest, Trentadenari bought whole-sale. Trentadenari never kept the shit at his own place, but relied on Maurone, a tyre shop owner with a warehouse at Quadraro. The shit was hidden inside a furred-out wooden partition concealed behind a chart showing the odds on the Tris football lottery.

A machine gun, that's what Sorcio had turned into. Scialoja sent a team to Terni and three leatherheads from the special anti-robbery squad – all of them such tough cops you couldn't scratch them with a diamond – to get Maurone at the Quadraro. When Barbetta saw his house surrounded by police officers, he tried to make his escape over the rooftops. But a loose terracotta tile had a vote, and after Barbetta hit the ground, he wound up in the hospital with a femur shattered into tiny pieces and a police guard around the clock. In his boudoir they found, along with a skeletal-looking junkie chick, the long-sought 150 grams of brown sugar.

Maurone, a jailbird out on parole, greeted the cops with a tough-guy sneer. The team put on a little song and dance at first to keep from showing their hand, to conceal the fact that they had a detailed tip-off. Finally, 'by pure chance', the hidey-hole was uncovered. Inside it they found the heroin, and right next to the heroin, a little coke, and just to make things tidy, a Beretta semi-automatic and a box of Lapua bullets. And so Maurone, too, his sneer fading at the prospect of a lengthy stay as a guest of the state, wound up handcuffed and checked-in at the Hotel Roma.

Meanwhile, Sorcio dictated and dictated. Scialoja took it all down, and Borgia took notes on the most salient passages, sketching diagrams, breaking in to highlight details that might have appeared insignificant but that at trial could well prove decisive.

Finally, around midnight on the second day, Sorcio collapsed in exhaustion. They'd filled more than a hundred pages of deposition. Scialoja ordered a carafe of coffee and a tray of warm buns. But Sorcio was out, sunk deep in a comatose slumber. Borgia found himself wondering how many years it had been since that poor soul had been able to sleep so soundly. Scialoja, more pragmatically, reminded him that in the last few minutes, Sorcio had started circling back, getting tangled up and repeating the same statements.

'He's squeezed dry. No point continuing.'

Sorcio was transferred to a special wing of Rebibbia prison, to keep company with turncoat terrorists. Before climbing into the armour-plated unmarked Alfetta, Sorcio stopped to look Borgia right in the eye.

'I'm relying on you, judge.'

Borgia extended his hand but avoided his gaze. He knew there wasn't much he could do for Sorcio, and for that matter, in all honesty, he'd been sparing in his promises. Maybe, if the government ever decided to approve that law on the *pentiti*, or co-operating witnesses, that they'd been debating for years... They'd moved quickly to approve it in terrorism cases, but terrorism was nothing but trouble for politicians. When it came to the Mafia, on the other hand, everybody inexplicably started moving as slowly as dead lice...

The Alfetta peeled out, tyres screeching. Scialoja, who had been watching the whole pantomime, laid a hand on Borgia's shoulder.

'What now?'

'Now we inform the district attorney and we start issuing warrants.'

Scialoja's assault teams went into action at the rottenest time of the night, when anyone's guard was lowered and the muffled thud of weapons pounding against your front door was enough to make the most hardened criminal curse the day he chose the gangland life.

They arrested Fierolocchio – who had finally found a steady girl-friend, after all his years of sexual escapades – as he lay snuggled against his fiancée, a bejewelled and buxom brunette who owned a restaurant in Fiumicino.

'Where are these men taking you, my love?'

As she went melodramatic on them, wringing her ruby-studded hands together, her man was desperately trying to cover his junk, hopping around barefoot in search of a shirt and boxer shorts, with a litany of curses showering down on the ancestors of the cops who'd come to collect him. Quite a show!

Scrocchiazeppi, who was sleeping with a pistol under his head, raised his hands high when they kicked open the door and declared himself a political prisoner. The team captain burst out laughing and kicked him hard in the arse. Scrocchiazeppi lowered his hands and shrugged. He'd never really had much of a sense of humour.

At Trentadenari's place there was a pretty young girl with a naïve, frightened look on her face. The Neapolitan told them that she was his personal nurse, summoned urgently to treat a case of colic. The police asked for her ID, took down the details, and then let her go. After all, in his long deposition, Sorcio had made no mention of anyone called Vanessa.

Trentadenari offered them a drink, which the cops refused. He dropped Fabio Santini's name, and they informed him that Officer Santini had already been reassigned to the brig at Forte Boccea. Then he tried to offer a bribe, and got in return some sharp straight-armed smacks. Finally resigned to his fate, he packed a briefcase full of medical certificates and went along peacefully.

Botola, who still lived with his mama, tried to hide in a clothes cupboard, but a sneeze gave him away.

Carlo Buffoni, when the police crowbarred open the roll-up metal shutter over the front of his family store, vigorously objected with every last breath in his body. Not only had it been months since he'd had anything to do with that world, poor thing that he was, but even mentioning his name in the same breath as those bastards who'd murdered his twin brother was actually and deeply offensive! It was an admission that was as significant as it was dangerous, though then and there it was largely overlooked. The cops were implacable, and they'd been given one simple order: throw them all behind bars. And so they carted him off to join the rest of them, and no trace remained on any official report of the incriminating phrase.

Dandi alone managed to escape the round-up. According to Sorcio, Dandi had a pied-à-terre just a short walk from the Rome trade fair. Officially the place belonged to Patrizia, but he came and went as he pleased. No armour-plated doors, no particular obstacles to entry. Ever since she'd spent time behind bars, Patrizia had taken a dislike to chains and bolts. For that matter, in the city of Rome the lunatic had not yet been born who would think of annoying the boss's woman. Scialoja got in thanks to the keys that she'd slipped into his pocket at Ranocchia's funeral. No matter how much personal danger he might be in right now, he couldn't help but take an admiring look around. White everywhere, with just a few pieces of designer furniture.

Scialoja turned off all the lights, lit a cigarette and got comfortable on a couch facing the front door. She'd certainly made her way in the world, his little turtledove, since the days of Porta Maggiore. And yet, he'd bet his life that somewhere in here she still had her little treasure chest tucked away, with the objects that embodied her poor, ordinary dreams of conquest: the coins, the rings, the photo of Raquel Welch, the Bulgari jewellery catalogue, the pamphlet promising the trip of your dreams to a tropical paradise...

In any case, while his men were rounding up the bosses, Scialoja had decided to capture Dandi on his own. Borgia would have called that a stupid stunt. And perhaps it was. But it also had something to do with breaking chains, abandoning old legacies, perverse games that you either put a halt to once and for all or they would drag you down into who knows what abyss. An obligatory choice. An instinct for self-preservation. Scialoja had discovered that he had actually been endowed with a fair supply of that commodity the time he bought from a circus property master a vial of Afghan hashish oil. After his first drag, he felt as if he'd been split in two. After the second puff, he'd had the sensation that his heart was wandering around the room on its own. There never was a third puff, because he'd flushed the dope down the toilet. He was sixteen years old. Since then, he'd never again smoked a real, full-fledged joint. Instinct for self-preservation.

To justify this radical move, Scialoja had explained to his colleagues that, given the fact that Dandi was an extremely dangerous individual, it was best to proceed in a relaxed manner, without excess ruckus or any sudden moves. But as he was sliding into the uneasy sloth of waiting, he found himself caressing the handle of his police-issue Beretta with a reassuring, even affectionate, sensation. No question: Dandi would be armed. What if he put up resistance?

Scialoja clicked off the safety. He might be forced to put him down. The prospect of killing the man, he realized with a shiver, didn't bother him all that much. On the other hand, there was no guarantee that Dandi, that particular night, should decide to make use of his *buen retiro*, his pleasant retreat. In that case, when dawn came, he'd resort to more conventional methods. He'd just have wasted a little time, that's all. What a hypocritical solution! He lit a cigarette, another, and another still. What if Dandi came back with Patrizia? He put that thought out of his mind with yet another cigarette.

When Dandi finally did show up, well after three in the morning, he found Scialoja waiting for him, wide-awake, nursing a grudge, pistol levelled. Dandi was wearing a black jacket and heavy leather work boots. He'd put on even more weight and he was starting to lose his hair. He instinctively looked around for a way out. Scialoja did nothing more than lift the barrel, aiming directly at his forehead. Dandi spread his arms.

'Turn around and put your hands up.'

Dandi obeyed. Scialoja searched him, the muzzle of his pistol pressed against the back of his neck. Dandi smelled of cologne and a vague hint of sweat. He was clean. His tone of voice was mocking.

'What did you think, that I still go around packing artillery?'

Scialoja informed him that he was under arrest. He had the right to contact his lawyer. He had the right to make a phone call to his family. He was about to read him the arrest warrant when Dandi burst out in a belly laugh.

'Did you need this whole show of force? Ah, I get it...It's for Patrizia, isn't it?'

Scialoja took a step back, as if appalled by the unmistakable face that had just been put on things. Dandi took advantage of the opportunity to lower his hands. Scialoja jerked the gun in his direction. Dandi smiled.

'You wouldn't think of shooting an unarmed man, would you?'

'And you of all people ask me that!'

'What's that got to do with anything? Fuck, you're the law! There are things you just can't do. There are things you can't even think, such as: I'll go ahead and kill Dandi and then I'll fuck his woman…Because that's what this is all about, isn't it?'

'Keep back!'

'Who's moving? I'm just trying to tell you, before you go off on me, that there's a way to settle matters, and this isn't one of them. You want Patrizia? Be my guest, my handsome young man! I'm out of here, and when Patrizia comes home, she's all yours! Then we're even, we can call it quits. What do you say, eh?'

'You're an animal, Dandi!'

'What do you think – that you're better than me? You're out of your mind, friend!'

Dandi went on talking and kept on walking forward, one step after another. And the commissario kept walking backwards, one step after another. Until suddenly he found himself pressed against the sofa, lost his balance, tried to brace himself with his left hand, and Dandi lunged.

A fast, sharp knee to the groin and Scialoja bent over double in pain. An uppercut to the chin and his head shot back and the pistol fell out of his fingers. Scialoja tried to react, but it was as if his will had simply stopped working. The effect of the series of blows, no doubt, or else a subtler enchantment, a jerk on that chain he'd been unable to shatter. Dandi was quickly on top of him, rummaging through his pockets. He found the handcuffs and clapped them on Scialoja's wrists. As he was getting back up, Dandi took a second to let fly with a sharp little kick to his ribs. Almost a love tap. Dandi picked up the gun.

'You know,' he resumed, putting the barrel of the gun against Scialoja's temple, 'you know how easy it would be for me to shoot you right now? Eh, dotto? I saw some guy walking around in my house, so I shot him. Legitimate defence, no? How was I supposed to know that he was a cop? And on a warrant, too, when everyone knows that at the very least when there's a warrant out for Dandi the mobile squad comes galloping in on horseback with trumpets playing a fanfare. Yet this guy comes all alone into the wolf's lair…Eh, yes, it would be great, but I just can't do it!'

Dandi stood up, clicked on the safety, snapped the clip out of the butt of the semi-automatic. His tone of voice expressed authentic regret.

'I just can't do it! That friend of mine has a point: shoot cops and all you have to show for it is a world of misery…Not me. I'm walking out of this whole thing as clean as a choirboy, with Patrizia at my side! Well, so long, you little piece of shit. Dandi's grabbing his hat and waving as he goes. First, though, allow me a small satisfaction…'

The boot caught him at an angle, right on a line with his carotid artery. Scialoja tasted the bitter flavour of vomit and blood, rolled his eyes, just managed to glimpse a flash of the other man's smile, and then darkness descended.

A fruity fragrance brought him to, with a bittersweet undertone of cinnamon. Patrizia was leaning over him. Scialoja realized that morning light was filtering in through the windows. How long had he been lying there, passed out?

'Get these handcuffs off me.'

He tried to wriggle free, but a brutal stab of pain to his ribs dropped him to the floor again. Scialoja closed his eyes. His head hurt.

'Patrizia…'

'Later.'

He opened his eyes again. Patrizia delicately lifted his arms and pulled his shirt over his handcuffed wrists. Her fingers moved warm and rapid over his back muscles. They lingered for a moment in the hollows of his armpits.

'You've lost weight.'

'So have you.'

'I took your advice. I don't like playing at being a gangster's moll.'

'But you are a gangster's moll. And you should go back to dark hair. Being a blonde makes you look vulgar.'

'Take it easy. I have the keys to your handcuffs right here.'

KEEP CALM. WAIT for the storm to pass. Time was on their side.

To hear Vasta tell it, the devil wasn't as black as he was painted. Sure, they were looking at a stormy sea of criminal charges, and this time they were certainly going to have to do some time. But not much time; measurable in minutes, practically. The most specific charges, to be clear. The prosecution had left those charges bobbing in the larger ocean of criminal conspiracy. And what Vasta planned to do was patiently single them out, extract them from that context, analyze them, and then club them to death one at a time.

A dedicated adept of the old Latin maxim *divide et impera* – divide and conquer – Vasta appointed himself defence counsel for Bufalo, Freddo, Scrocchiazeppi and Fierolocchio, and then assigned the others, assorted according to rank, degree and affiliation, to a host of legal colleagues, variously warlike and competent. As for Dandi, as long as he was still a fox on the run, there was no point worrying about him. They could decide about that when the time came.

For a solid month, the non-commissioned officers of the correctional staff saw the hallways overrun by a brigade of legal professionals dressed in Loden overcoats and checked double-breasted suits, toting leather attaché cases. The gang members were all there for the lengthy sessions of questioning with Borgia, and they all emerged afterwards with jaws set grimly but a faint smile on their lips. The judge was indulging a pipe dream if he thought he could build up his case by tricking the gang into contradicting each other; none of them were turncoats or informers. Leaving aside Sorcio, of course, but that was another matter.

The gang members did their level best to follow Vasta's legal advice, but it was no easy thing. Stay buttoned up, Vasta had told them. Avoid sarcasm and, worst case, invoke their patron saint, St Denial. But with a steady diet of the increasingly grim and determined prosecuting magistrate, human nature won out. They started firing off wisecracks that were sarcastic enough to undermine the six-foot-thick walls of Rebibbia.

Freddo justified house and cars with an unexpected inheritance from an uncle in America.

Bufalo proclaimed his opposition, for reasons of religious conscience, to the consumption of any and all false drugs, including tobacco, and demanded that this declaration be entered into the official transcript of the deposition, even as he blew a puff of smoke from his dozenth Marlboro of the morning into the prosecuting magistrate's face.

Fierolocchio explained that the reason he had a revolver at home with the serial number filed off was because 'you just never know with all the hoodlums out in the street these days...'

While Botola, who'd been arrested with two hundred million lire in cash, called on 'his mama's pension' as a rational explanation, and so on and so forth.

When Borgia, presented with Bufalo reciting the Lord's Prayer with an expression of transcendent emotion on his face, finally lost his temper and meant it, Vasta was forced to weigh in at last. From that moment forward, to avoid unexpected collisions, it was a succession of 'I choose to avail myself of my right not to answer that question', and the pace of the depositions began to flag.

The more time that went by, the clearer the general outlines of the matter became. Vasta made no secret of his optimism. The time came to move on to the second act: the sacrifice of the pawns that would lead to checkmate.

The lawyers representing the small fry, at Vasta's suggestion, requested a face-to-face meeting with their clients' accuser – namely Sorcio. All of the horses and ants lit into the turncoat witness. Every single gram of the dope that the police had confiscated and all the shit that they'd sold, snorted or fired into their veins – all of it – had first passed through Sorcio's own hands. He was the central engine driving the whole operation. The others confessed to small-scale dope peddling and threw a monkey wrench into the prosecution's central mechanism.

One week after the last face-to-face confrontation, Trentadenari demanded to be questioned. He confessed to purchasing the shipment of brown sugar, and cheerfully sold out Barbetta, hastening to add that Sorcio was his trusted long-time retailer. He'd done everything on his own. He was, he added with his customary courtesy, a self-made businessman. If there was any criminal conspiracy here, it was strictly between him and Sorcio. He couldn't even bring himself to place the blame entirely on him, the poor kid, so alone in the world, so beat-up and worn-down that he had a procession of junkies trooping through his apartment testing his dope. He'd shoot the junkies up right then and there. Even underage kids, Judge, Your Honour.

As for him, Trentadenari? He'd learned his lesson: drugs were bad, and drugs were bad for you. His hopes for the future? To repay his debt to society and try to rebuild a life of some kind. Needless to say, Barbetta, confronted with the evidence against him, made a 'wide-ranging and detailed confession'. Sure, he'd couriered a kilo of smack from Thailand. Sure, he'd sold part of it to Trentadenari. But he didn't know anything more about it than that. This Sorcio? Never heard of him, never seen him. I swear on everything I hold most dear in my life.

Documents in hand, Vasta went to call on the district attorney. The preliminary judicial investigation, as far as the Trentadenari-Barbetta-Sorcio triangulation was concerned, could be considered complete. This was a single case of narcotics distribution, however vast the scale. His request: summary trial, immediate proceedings. And for those who had entered guilty pleas: house arrest.

The district attorney sent for Borgia.

'Vasta has a point. We can already cut a plea bargain on these charges. For the rest of it, the theory and evidence are a little weak. Your state's witness has nothing but hearsay on the murders. The defendants are refusing to respond. It doesn't look promising.'

Borgia unleashed the finest guns of his dialectical arsenal. He reviewed all the murders and mayhem of the past several years. He emphasized the furious quest for solid evidence that was yielding, he recklessly claimed, 'unhoped-for results'. In the end, he managed to snatch only a brief, last-minute delay.

That night, he showed up at Scialoja's place. The commissario invited him in with an embarrassed smile. Ever since Dandi had beat it on the run, the two men practically hadn't exchanged a word. The report on the failed arrest attempt had sailed right out the fifth-floor window of the Hall of Justice. Scialoja blamed Dandi's escape on a well-timed tip-off. As for the abrasions, lacerations and contusions, those were the result of an unfortunate mishap: he'd had a high-speed tyre blowout.

Borgia was starting to get tired of the policeman's mood swings, but deep down he envied him his reckless ruthlessness. Provided, however, that he produced results. In any case, Borgia wasn't willing to let anyone give him the run-around. Still, they were both in the same boat at this point. He'd have to resign himself to the situation. He had to take Scialoja for what he was, with his twisted cop ethics and his recurrent hormonal tempests. Anyway, that night he was in need of a friend. A true friend.

Borgia pulled a bottle of fine grappa out of his briefcase and swore that he wouldn't strike camp until they'd tipped out the last drop.

'What I can't stand is the feeling that we've sold poor Sorcio down the river!'

'Don't take it so hard,' Scialoja consoled him. 'The kid isn't exactly a choirboy. Plus I'm pretty sure he hasn't told us everything he knows...'

'Just how do you know that?'

'That's always the way it is with state's witnesses. They let their friends off easy and stick it to their enemies. We just have to write it off as the cost of doing business and keep our fingers crossed.'

'The weight of experience versus the daring of ruthlessness?' Borgia retorted, with a hint of offended sarcasm.

Scialoja let it drop. The time always came, sooner or later, when an investigating magistrate – even the best of them – suddenly remembered that he was also Your Honour, the judge.

III

No, SORCIO DEFINITELY hadn't told them everything he knew. He'd remained silent about Baron Rosellini; mainly out of self-interest because, even if it was only for a couple of phone calls from Florence, he still ran the risk of facing charges of complicity in kidnapping and murder. He was also silent about Vanessa, because of the long-standing love that won out at the last minute over his instinct for vendetta. He stayed silent about Nercio, silent about Uncle Carlo and the Maestro, silent about Secco, and even about Nero – because a zero like him knew nothing about such things, and it had been a very good idea to have kept him on the margins, that infamous turncoat.

Dandi was hiding out in the Circeo. One of Secco's friends, a Neapolitan builder with ties to the Casalesi clan, rented a two-storey residential suite overlooking the beach of Sabaudia for the year. Secco and Nercio kept him constantly informed about the new developments of the investigation. Still, the isolation was a tremendous pain in the arse. From the glass doors opening out onto the terrace he could see the villas of the Communist intellectuals. They stood empty all through the week, but on the weekends they were teeming with well-known faces. One night when they were celebrating whatever literary prize they'd just collected, Dandi showed up with a magnum of champagne. He told them he was an industrialist who admired them deeply. Culture was all important. Once they'd gotten over the awkwardness of the moment, they pulled out the champagne glasses and invited him to join them in a toast. Dandi cornered a famous film director and confided in him that films had always been his dream. The director considered, with a vague sense of disgust, the spruced-up bumpkin and politely enquired as to the kind of parts he generally preferred.

'I'm not an actor. I want to be a producer, make films of my own.'

'That takes billions of lire, my dear boy.'

'Money's not a problem.'

'Just what sort of film would you have in mind?'

'A story about organized crime, gangland, the underworld.'

'Strictly for Americans,' the director sniffed dismissively.

'Well then,' fumed Dandi as he returned to Trentadenari's beach house, 'I'll just fly to America and buy up Hollywood!'

It had been a reckless act of bravado, true, but the solitude was really starting to get him down. When Zeta procured him a set of safe ID papers, he recommended leaving the country. Why, sure! So I can wind up getting shot just like Nero! No, Dandi wasn't going to run. He waited a month, and then one morning he showed up at Patrizia's.

'Have you lost your mind? You realize they're looking for you? There's a new raid or a search every day...'

'Close your eyes!'

Patrizia did as she was told. Dandi went around behind her, and she felt something cold slide around her neck.

'You can look now.'

'Beautiful,' she conceded, admiring the string of pearls. 'But how did you do it?'

Dandi flashed his biggest smile, the one he reserved for special occasions.

'Details. Get undressed. I'm about to explode.'

'Shower first.'

'Like our first time, you remember?'

Patrizia couldn't repress a soft-hearted smile. She had to admit, in spite of herself, that she'd missed him.

Dandi came back from the bathroom dripping wet, nude and ready for action. Patrizia stretched out on the black sheets, spread her legs and closed her eyes. Dandi threw himself on her, moaning.

They stayed in bed for three hours. When they were done, Dandi tore himself away with an endless kiss. He didn't know when he'd return, if ever, but after that roll in the hay he felt like Superman after doffing his Clark Kent disguise.

That afternoon he dropped by Vasta's office and signed the form retaining him as counsel. At seven o'clock he was in the Maestro's villa. Uncle Carlo blessed him from the venerable pedestal of his fourteen years on the run from the law.

'Stay out of sight, trust no one, and if you smell something wrong, remember: better to do your time than take a sudden bullet.'

Dandi asked how little Danilo was doing. The Maestro's face lit up.

'He's not even five years old and he's already learning to read! I hired an American nanny for him because nowadays, if you don't speak English, you're less than nothing. My son is a child prodigy, I can just tell!'

Uncle Carlo coughed discreetly. The time had come to talk about serious matters. There was a first profit report from the Sardinian real estate deal: two hundred million lire.

'Do you want the money or should we reinvest, Dandi?'

'Half and half. I need a little cash for my lawyers.'

'I understand,' Uncle Carlo sighed. 'Lawyers are just like whores. They suck you dry, cock and soul!'

The Maestro reported that there were two kilos of dope to move out. Dandi asked for a week to get his network back up and running, after the damage done by the arrests. The Maestro offered to send for a dozen or so made men from the Palermo area. Dandi wasn't convinced.

'What do they know about the way Rome works? The minute they set foot on the streets here, the police'll pick them up.'

Uncle Carlo approved. He'd give him a week, but not one day more. Leaving the market untended for too long could whet unwelcome appetites.

'I can do it,' Dandi promised.

'I have no doubt about that,' said Uncle Carlo.

Secco, Nero, Nercio and Vanessa were waiting for him at Villa Candy. Nice touch of class on Secco's part: the purchase of the late Cravattaro's estate. Nero reported on the gambling and video poker sectors: everything was stable, the gambling dens were producing as usual and the revenue collectors were contributing on time. Secco laid out the general situation: Sorcio's revelations had flamed out the entire drug-dealing network in the central and southern zones, from Trastevere–Testaccio to Palocco, Infernetto, Ardeatino, all the way out to Ostia. But the northern Rome–Flaminio region was virtually intact.

'Sure, on paper,' Vanessa put in. 'But the dealers are shitting their pants and the junk is just mouldering on the shelf!'

'We've got to persuade them to start selling again,' Dandi pointed out.

'I'll take care of it,' Nercio assured him.

'You think you can do it?'

'Guaranteed. We can start out by asking nicely, and if that doesn't work, we'll step it up to the rough stuff.'

'And we can double the price,' Secco suggested. 'There hasn't been a shot available on the streets of Rome for forty days now. The junkies are losing their minds out there.'

Dandi thought back to the old days and Libano's words of wisdom.

'No. Let's give them all they want, and at half-price. For a whole week it's going to be Pleasure Island around here. We need to win them all back. All together, all at once. Then we'll hike the price, a little at a time.'

'That means we'll lose money,' Secco pointed out in dismay.

'No, not if we're moving lots of product at a steady rate.'

'So who's got all this product to sell? The supply channels have all dried up...'

'That's my concern,' Dandi said, hard-nosed, staring him right in the eye.

Nercio smiled. 'I'm with you, Dandi.'

'So am I,' said Nero.

Secco wasn't giving in.

'What's the point? We're just going to flood the market. What's the rush?'

'We need cash, Secco,' Nero, who had figured it out intuitively, explained calmly. 'The guys behind bars are pissed off, but good.'

'Ah, the guys behind bars!' Secco echoed him scornfully.

'Trentadenari hasn't seen a lira yet,' Vanessa chimed in.

Dandi stared at Nero. Nero tilted his head in Secco's direction. Secco, seized by a sudden urge to do some accounting, pulled out his pocket calculator and started pecking away furiously at the keypad.

'Better leave us alone, Vanessa,' Dandi ordered in a relaxed voice.

She walked out of the room, swinging her hips. Dandi tore the calculator out of Secco's hands and fastballed it against the wall, shattering it.

'Don't tell me you haven't paid the guys in the slammer.'

'Dandi, there've been some problems...'

'Don't tell me you haven't given the families their share.'

'Come on, Dandi...'

Dandi let fly with a punch. Secco grabbed at thin air, doing his best to stay upright. Dandi hit him again. Secco sprawled to the floor.

'Dandi, that's enough!' said Nero.

Dandi managed to regain control.

'When one of our guys winds up behind bars, certain obligations come into play, Secco. Imperative obligations. Tomorrow morning I want you to send out those payments and distribute the shares. Is that clear?'

With help from Nero and Nercio, Secco got laboriously to his feet. His eyes were glittering with a flash of pure hatred. But innate caution won out. There was no point in insisting. Secco shrank, becoming humble and courteous.

'You're right, it's all my fault. I thought that until you got back it might be best just to leave things the way they were. It was all a matter of respect, Dandi, believe me...'

Nero suffocated a giggle that was a mixture of indignation and outright admiration. How about that, Secco! The Lord High Rector of the Institute of Higher Snakishness!

'Bullshit! I'll tell you exactly what you thought. You thought: those guys are behind bars and we're out on the street. Fuck 'em! You decided to unleash a war at the worst possible time, Secco. Just when we're at our weakest, when we most need to stay united. And what if Bufalo decides he's had enough and it's time to let the cat out of the bag? What if Freddo turns state's witness? None of that ever occurred to you, eh? What about Botola? He's one of ours. You never thought about Botola?'

'Okay, Dandi, I've learned my lesson,' said Secco, genuflecting and then extending his hand. 'Friends again?'

Dandi ignored the overture.

'I'm heading back to the beach,' he said, addressing the other two. 'I'm relying on you.' Before turning to go, he spat on the floor.

Secco closed his eyes. It might cost him his house, all the money in his bank accounts, his shop, the clubs, everything that he'd built up over the years – but one day or another he was going to make Dandi pay.

Solitude, *Disamistade*
1984

I

'WE'RE THE KIDS of today/the souls of the city/sitting in empty cinemas/sitting in some bar/we walk alone/through the darkest night/even if tomorrow/kind of scares us...'

The warden was granting them two extra hours of television. It was the first time that Freddo had ventured out into the larger prison population since Borgia repealed his restrictions on fraternization. The inmates had turned out en masse for the final night of the San Remo music festival. There wasn't a single empty seat. The other guys were all in the front row. Bufalo was chatting idly with Pischello. Trentadenari and Botola were sharing a cigarette. Scrocchiazeppi and Fierolocchio were raising a ruckus, lampooning the performers and whistling derisively. Freddo remained standing at the far end of the rec room, captivated by the images that streamed past on the television screen.

'Until something changes/until someone gives us/a promised land/a different world/where our thoughts can grow/we'll never stop/we'll never get tired of searching/for our path...'

The singer was baby-faced and young, and he had a heavy Roman accent. He tore the notes out of the guitar with a terrifying burst of energy. The beat of the song, a melancholy thrum charged with suppressed violence, pierced Freddo's heart.

His desire for Roberta had become excruciating since he'd been in there. She refused to answer his letters and she hadn't yet requested a visitation permit.

'We're the kids of today/gypsies by profession...'

The kid on the TV screen seemed to be staring at him with an expression of scowling contempt. I have my guitar and my anger and my cunning, he was saying, and what do you have? You, who think you're the King of Rome, what do you have?

'A promised land/a different world/where our thoughts can grow...'

'Oh look, it's Freddo! Hey, Freddo, come on over here!'

Fierolocchio had spotted him and now he was waving his arms, emitting shrill, sharp whistles like a goatherd. Freddo waved hello.

'Hey, Freddo, let me free up a chair for you!'

Fierolocchio turned and said something to a Moroccan inmate sitting next to him. The North African vigorously shook his head no. Fierolocchio gave him a good hard shove. The Moroccan fell over against Scrocchiazeppi. The two men lifted him bodily by legs and arms and hurled him headlong into the seats behind. Someone objected. Fierolocchio swung around and bellowed a succession of insults. Silence ensued. The Moroccan got to his feet, frightened and hurt. The guards looked on without intervening. Even the guards lacked the balls to take on the lords of the prison.

'Well?' shouted Scrocchiazeppi, lifting the newly conquered chair high over his head.

Freddo started forward, strolling lazily. The young Roman onscreen bowed to the thunderous applause of the audience.

'Eros Ramazzotti! *Terra promessa!*' shouted the host of the show.

Freddo exchanged a quick nod hello with Botola and Trentadenari, and when he was standing in front of Bufalo, he extended his hand. Pischello had got to his feet in a sign of respect. Bufalo didn't move. He limited himself to a curt nod, cocking an amused glance at him.

'So you got tired of playing Sleeping Beauty!'

Freddo pushed his open palm right under Bufalo's nose. Bufalo finally made up his mind to shake his hand. Finally Freddo took a seat between Scrocchiazeppi and Fierolocchio.

'What's up with Bufalo?' he asked with a sigh.

'It chaps his arse being in here,' Scrocchiazeppi said in a loud voice.

'Thanks for the news!' Fierolocchio retorted.

'It chaps his arse that we're all in here and Dandi isn't,' Scrocchiazeppi clarified.

'I don't like it.'

'You know what Bufalo's like. He'll get over it.'

Now there was a female singer on stage, immersed in an extravaganza of carnations. She had a round face and the voice of a cat in heat.

Freddo stopped watching the show. Bufalo had it in for Dandi, for him, for everyone in the world. Bufalo was turning into a serious problem. At the exact moment when it was most important for them to remain united…But what did it matter? Had they ever really been united? Sure, maybe once, when Libano was still alive, poor old friend…What were the words that boy had sung? A promised land, a different world…

Freddo felt something poke him at the nape of his neck and he turned to look to his left. Bufalo was staring at him with a mocking smile. With the forefinger and thumb of his left hand, he was making the sign of the pistol.

II

DANDI WAS BLACK with rage. All the appeals had been rejected. Everyone was staying behind bars.

'They call it the Tribunal of Liberty, as if! Liberty, my arse! It's a firing squad is what it is!'

Vasta did his best to calm him down.

'You know what they say? Dog doesn't bite dog…They're all people from Rome, you have to understand. They weren't willing to go against the wishes of the district attorney's office. I've already prepared my briefs for the Court of Cassation. You'll see, they'll play a different tune there – a very different tune!'

'Maybe so. In the meantime, we keep paying. And as long as we're paying, you'd better do your best to earn your cut!'

But Borgia must have laid it down ugly, because it was not like things went any better with the Court of Cassation. Quite the opposite. To read the decision – fourteen closely typed pages of sarcasm and backhanded slaps at Vasta, the bar in general and all of them – it really seemed like there was no more hope: 'Highly reliable statements…' 'Testimony and collaboration with the forces of law and order attained only after a profound spiritual struggle...' 'Elevated probative value of the evidence obtained...' 'Solid external corroboration of the evidence provided by the state's witness...'

Dandi was so furious he couldn't sit still.

'Now what, the turncoats are going to be canonized as saints?'

Once again, it was up to Vasta to restore calm and confidence. Certainly, he opined, it was daunting to be faced with a juridical reversal as sudden as it was unfortunate. In all probability, the recent developments in the realm of terrorism and the sudden worsening of conditions with respect to the Sicilian Mafia had no doubt hardened jurisprudential hearts and minds. The verdict was quite simply deplorable: they were paying the price of a deteriorating climate of political polarization. Those judges had performed a poor service to the greater cause of justice, but rest assured, this was no more than a transitory phase. The thing now was to be prudent and patient. That might entail further delay, but in the end, judicial logic was bound to prevail. And on that terrain, Borgia would meet with yet another bitter defeat.

Dandi didn't want to be reasonable. If Vasta had suddenly started spouting legal Latin, it could only mean that things were really going to hell in a handbasket. It was time to look for other solutions. All of this whore-wrangling language, to Dandi's eyes and ears, could mean only one thing: Vasta's time was over. He'd become obsolete. The lawyer, from behind his coke-bottle lenses, stared at him with his small, icy, gelatinous eyes.

'You want to get a new lawyer? Be my guest. There are more lawyers in Rome than there are judges in all of Italy...'

Dandi reached out to Zeta and Pigreco. The two agents stalled for time and asked the Old Man for instructions.

The Old Man, for once, seemed unsure what to do. It seemed clear that the general situation was starting to settle down and return to normal. The Communists had been shoved back into their role as the opposition party and, even if they were throwing their weight around, their influence was in sharp decline. The sun was ineluctably setting on the party. No more than a few more years and hammer-and-sickle flags would be up for sale at the flea market of Porta Portese. Terrorism, both Red and Black, had swirled into a spiral of self-destruction from which there would be no return. What with terrorists turning state's witness and informants, and with others rejecting the armed struggle or under arrest, the generation of 1970 had been wiped out, to all intents and purposes. As for the Mafia, it had never really constituted a problem. The Mafia was more than an institution: it was a historical necessity. One way or another, it had always been possible to find a *modus vivendi*, and that would continue to be true. Italy was sailing peacefully on towards the dawn of the Nineties, gently lulled by the age-old comedic rhythms of the stylized minuet of endlessly warring powers. Sure, the ship sails on, and if the ship sails on, what need did we have for pirates? If you thought it through objectively, it was time, once and for all, to be rid of that ramshackle band of tidied-up gangsters. But that was only one of the horns of the dilemma; the most obvious one, the least interesting one. If there was one thing the Old Man found repugnant, it was thinking things through objectively. The coiled serpent against a blood-stained red field had always been his favourite heraldic device. The *ouroboros* – the serpent eating its own tail – was the symbol that had always kindled his dreams. The chorus from Verdi's *Falstaff*: '*tutto nel mondo è burla...tutti gabbati!*' – everything in the world was a jest, we were all figures of fun – was the highest manifestation of wisdom ever conceived by the human mind. Yes, everything was a jest, everyone was a figure of fun. Keep pulling the strings of the game. Keep one's allies in play, even the most inconvenient ones. Because you never could tell what might happen tomorrow, and a few extra pirates in your back pocket might always prove to be useful. But it was also, for the Old Man, a love of the art: to preserve, for future memory, that powerful gusting, unreasoning wind, that force with allegiance to no one that constituted the most solid foundation of power. A unique power, without origin or outcome. The most perfect, fully achieved form of anarchy imaginable.

It was the Old Man's own invention, but there would be no bequest, no legacy for posterity. Once the Old Man was dead, the system would die with him. Eternity was the one enemy he'd never be able to defeat. The wrinkles on his face were proliferating. He too would wind up like the beautiful Helen in Lucian's dialogues: an empty skull, no longer of interest even to worms. In the meantime, the important thing was to go on playing the game. He needed to help and protect Dandi, with an eye to his own self-interest. The prices of automatons on the collectibles marketplace had risen to dizzying heights. He had recently managed to acquire a perfectly functioning model of the bookwheel reading machine that Agostino Ramelli designed in 1598 and which a remarkable Polish artist had constructed almost four centuries later. Not an original and, come to think of it, strictly an amuse-bouche with respect to the main course constituted by the other pieces in his collection. But the sheer beauty of that contraption made of wood and screws, and the way it presented you – spinning like a water-wheel – with a succession of two hundred antique tomes at a simple touch of your foot on the pedal! Fine, fine, he'd bought it on a whim. But what a grim thing life is without whims! In any case, his funds had run dry. Therefore, if Dandi was looking for help, Dandi would have to pay.

III

WHEN RICOTTA ARRIVED at Regina Coeli prison in mid-March, the situation he found was terrible. Scrocchiazeppi and Fierolocchio formed one group, and Botola was having nothing to do with them. Bufalo wouldn't talk to anyone but Pischello. Freddo spent almost all his time in the seclusion of his cell, counting the crab lice crawling on the walls. Everywhere Ricotta looked: long faces, grumbling, disgruntled wisecracks. Ricotta really was a goodhearted kid. To see them all so depressed, angry and demoralized caused him genuine pain. He spoke with Bufalo and he spoke with Freddo, and then he talked to Bufalo again, and then went back to Botola and Freddo, and in the end, through much conniving with a tractable *maresciallo*, he managed to get them all seated around a table.

'Listen, comrades, what's come over you? The guys out on the street have everything back under control. Rome is ours again, the way it used to be. We receive our share regularly, and for the two of us, me and Bufalo, since we've been in here for the longest time, there's a double share. You want to tell me what the fuck's not to your satisfaction?'

'I want to see Dandi in here. Like all the others,' Bufalo roared.

'It's an obsession with you!' Botola snapped. 'Would you get it through

394

your head once and for all that having Dandi out on the street is the best thing that could happen for all of us? If they catch him, who's left? Trentadenari? Nero? They can't do it on their own, they don't have the balls...'

'At least Trentadenari's done his time,' Bufalo muttered. 'And Vasta even managed to get him out of jail!'

'Bufalo, cut this shit out! You've busted our balls enough now about Dandi!'

'You've got a nerve to lecture me, you kiss-arse!'

Botola leapt to his feet. Bufalo spat on the floor.

'What, you looking for a fight?'

Fierolocchio and Scrocchiazeppi didn't want to get involved. Ricotta got between the two men and begged Botola's pardon in Bufalo's name. Then he shot a despairing glance at Freddo. Freddo shook his head, stood up and left the meeting without saying a single word.

Ricotta never stopped trying to get his fellow gang members to make peace. But they soon convinced him that he was wasting his time. Ricotta, who couldn't stand solitude and silence, made friends with Tonchino – his name was the Italian spelling of Tonkin, as in the Tonkin Gulf Resolution – an almond-eyed Red Brigades terrorist of the first generation.

That was odd, because they all felt a mixture of pity and contempt towards terrorists, especially Red terrorists. But Tonchino was different. He was an open-hearted guy, Tonchino. He played strange songs on his guitar and read mountains of books. He had two mandatory life sentences on his back, and twenty or so charges still pending. He was dirt poor, so poverty-stricken that Ricotta, stirred to pity, regularly slipped him a portion of his monthly split, without a word to the others.

One day Ricotta caught him copying something out of a book.

'What now? Some new proclamation of the armed struggle?'

'Poetry,' the other prisoner replied brusquely.

'Poetry?'

'That's right, Rico, poetry! Even Mao wrote verse!'

'Oh really? Ah, I get it: since things didn't work out too well for you with the machine gun, now you're going to stage a revolution with poetry!'

Tonchino laughed and threw him the book.

'Here, why don't you get yourself a little culture!'

Ricotta glanced at the title and his face lit up.

'Ah, Pasolini! I knew him. Cool!'

'Did you know he was a Communist?'

'As far as that goes, he was a faggot too. But everyone's entitled to their tastes, no? And what does that have to do with the revolution?'

'I don't know either,' Tonchino replied, lost in thought. 'All I know is that in here, they do their best to erase my basic nature as a human being. Poetry helps me to remember that I exist. That I'm still here...'

Ricotta let out a rude sound of derision. My basic nature as a human being! Still, all in all, the Red Brigades might yet turn out to be useful.

'Listen, you know all about poetry. Do me a favour: write me a letter!'

Tonchino softened and turned kind.

'You have a girlfriend?'

'I wish I did! But just maybe, if you give me a hand, I'll find one...'

He'd been thinking about Donatella for a while now. Good-looking woman, all fire and passion. Nembo Kid had played a rotten trick on her, getting himself riddled with lead like a wild turkey up there in Milan. Maybe she was sick of being a widow by now. You never know, sometimes a couple of the right words, dropped at the right moment...

'All right, let's get started. What do you want me to write?'

'Well...No, wait, I know: in here, behind bars, life sucks, but if I think about you I get a stiffy between my legs like a fifteen-year-old boy. What do you say? Is that a little to strong for a first letter?'

'Let me work, you hooligan!' Tonchino laughed.

When Donatella read the first letter, she flew into a rage. How dare he! Ricotta was nothing but an animal, and no self-respecting woman could get within ten feet of him, what with the sheer fear and the rancid stench! But Ricotta wasn't the kind of guy who gave up that easy, and letters came one after the other, and Tonchino was a proper poet. He kept pushing and pushing, knocking and knocking at her door, until finally Donatella gave in and requested an inmate visit.

When she got there, Ricotta wasn't quite as horrible as she'd remembered; in fact, he was almost civilized now, and even charmingly clumsy in the rough shyness of his first advances. Anyway, between the letters and a pilfered kiss, before two months were out, they'd become affianced.

Ricotta, in an impulse of sincere gratitude, let Tonchino have his entire month's share. The Red Brigades terrorist thanked him and invited him to dine together that night. Unexpectedly, by mid-afternoon, Tonchino had packed his duffel bag and was loaded onto a paddy wagon. Destination unknown. Ricotta was knocked for a loop.

One week later, the news headlined every newspaper in the country: Tonchino had turned state's witness and his confessions had brought down the entire network of the Turinese diehards.

'I'll just bet that I put the idea into his head myself,' Ricotta muttered to himself.

But he could hardly blame him. After all, he owed him Donatella.

IV

WHEN ZETA AND Pigreco brought the Old Man's proposal to him, Dandi immediately took umbrage.

'All right, help me understand this discussion: your boss needs certain papers, and since these papers are being held in a place you can't get to, the Old Man organizes a little armed robbery...'

'Let's call it a recovery of property, if you don't mind,' Zeta retorted, stung to the quick.

'Sorry, comrade, I never was good in Italian at school...So where was I? Ah, that's right, the recovery of property...So you put together a group of guys and you organize this recovery of property. The understanding is clear: we give you the money, you give us the papers. Only just as things are sailing along nicely, the head of this property recovery team decides to hold on to the documents and play a trick or two on you guys...'

'You've got the main point,' Zeta conceded.

'Yes, you certainly have!' Pigreco confirmed.

'So now what you need is yours truly. For the recovery of the recovery...'

'Exactly.'

'And just who is this individual we need to recover the recovery from?'

'He's called Larinese.'

'Think of that!'

'Do you know him?'

'A lifetime ago. We were in boarding school together.'

'Well: yes or no?'

Dandi lit a cigarette and sat, perplexed.

'What I'm wondering is this: if this guy is such a problem for you, why don't you take care of him yourselves?'

'That's not something you need to know.'

Dandi chomped down on his gum before spitting it out in a sign of the greatest possible contempt. He had a burning desire to tell them all to go fuck themselves. Even better, with a noble curled-lip dismissal along the lines of: 'Dandi doesn't betray his long-time comrades.'

Actually, he didn't give much of a damn about Larinese. A son of a bitch, a gangster operating strictly on the sidelines of the big time. Larinese had had his opportunities but he hadn't known how to take advantage of them. If anything, it chapped Dandi's arse that the Old Man and his underlings continued to treat him like the street thug that he once was but no longer wanted to be. A pawn that sooner or later they'd have to sacrifice. He didn't want to report to anyone anymore. He wanted to make a clean break with this and all the other claptrap. Only the Old Man could help him.

'That's fine. We'll talk again once the job is done.'

He'd had no real choice but to accept. Still, he was reluctant to pull this job, almost hoping deep down that something would go wrong at the last moment. The job in and of itself was not particularly challenging. Larinese took no particular precautions, and never seemed to be without the attaché case that presumably contained the documents that were of such intense interest to the Old Man.

Dandi had only to get out his old balaclava, procure a firearm with the serial number filed off, steal a car, and wait for Larinese to be done enjoying himself with his girlfriend – a Polish woman he went to see every Friday afternoon in Torvajanica – fire a couple of shots at the oversized target, and complete the 'recovery of the recovery'. Then he disassembled the pistol and threw the pieces into the waves.

Perhaps Larinese would recover, but when he left him it had sounded to him as if the man was in his death throes. Dandi hadn't shot to kill; he'd almost fired at random, without really taking aim.

He delivered the attaché case to Zeta with a sneering grin. He'd gotten no thrill from the killing. If anything, he felt a hint of fear, the dread of stumbling into a roadblock, the helpless fury of having been downgraded to paid assassin. Him, Dandi!

That night, back in his hideout in Sabaudia, he learned from the evening news that Larinese hadn't made it after all. For the first time in many years, Dandi felt like a piece of shit, and he drank himself under the table.

In the days that followed, Zeta and Pigreco gave him a pamphlet to read, and a week later he was summoned to an apartment building across from Villa Balestra. He was ushered into a dark room and bombarded with idiotic questions by a flock of hooded men. Dandi recited from memory the formulas and spells that he'd learned from the pamphlet, while polite titters underscored his grossest grammatical errors. Then he'd sworn undying loyalty three times to a certain renowned architect and in the end the lights switched on, the hosts doffed their hoods, and a cheerful round of applause festively announced the successful initiation of the new adept.

Dandi looked around, disappointed and somewhat annoyed at the clownish mess that he considered that ceremony to have been. Zeta and Pigreco introduced him to his new brothers: a politico, an actor, a university professor, a physician, and Miglianico and Grattantini, a couple of lawyers, familiar faces in the Hall of Justice. He'd once heard Vasta describe them as 'overpaid fender-bender specialists'. Dandi began to wonder whether he'd just committed a tragic error. Zeta handed him a drink in a paper cup. Dandi sneered in disgust at the cheap bilge in the cup, a poor Moscato. He'd murdered Larinese for this rip-off?

Miglianico locked arms with him. 'A frugal ceremony in the spirit of the brotherhood…'

'It wasn't cheap for me, let me tell you!'

'I met a friend of yours some time ago. Nembo Kid. He too was inducted as a brother…'

'And he came to a damned shitty end!'

'Oh, things'll go much better for you, don't think twice about it.'

Dandi scratched his head. The lawyer laughed and slapped him on the back.

'Trust me. It'll all turn out!'

Dandi sent word to those behind bars that he was changing lawyers. Bufalo and Freddo remained loyal to Vasta. All the others followed him to the new legal counsel.

Ten days after the ceremony with the hooded brothers, the investigating judge assigned Trentadenari to house arrest. True enough, the stroke of genius was the fruit of Vasta's razor-sharp mind, and Dandi had to admit that the lawyer had arranged things brilliantly. Still, that remarkable order of events struck Dandi as a sign of destiny. At last, a positive signal.

Vanessa was doing her best, and even Nercio was working his fingers to the bone, but regaining control of those pop-brained junkies was a losing proposition. With Trentadenari out and in circulation, it was a whole different thing. Now they could definitely start dealing again. Larinese was soon forgotten. As usual, Dandi had made the right move.

V

RAI TELEVISION WAS doing a live broadcast of Enrico Berlinguer's funeral. The leader of the Italian Communists had popped an artery while he was addressing a rally. A lifetime of dedicated service to democracy, observed the commentators. Man died of stress. Bang, and it's over. Just like the bullet waiting for you at the end of your road back home. However it happens, it's always the same story. The finale is obligatory.

Freddo was watching the broadcast in the common room, wondering what on earth could drive a hundred thousand people to tear their hair out over a piece of dead flesh. Even Giorgio Almirante, the head Fascist, had paid homage to his long-time fierce and uncompromising political foe. Who had that man been? What had he done? Why was his coffin surrounded by such a flood of love? Why such sorrow at his passing?

If Freddo thought about the funeral he'd be likely to have, he pictured his father's austere face, his mama's tears, and he wondered whether Gigio would even show up...How long had it been since he'd heard from his little brother? When had he started to feel so desperately lonely? Had

400

he always felt that way? What makes a man happy and beloved, and what makes a man an untouchable pariah?

The *maresciallo* tapped him discreetly on the shoulder. 'Visiting room. You have a guest.'

'My lawyer?'

'A guest. That's all I know.'

Freddo followed him unwillingly. Then he saw her, and his knees gave way beneath him, and he had to grab the *maresciallo*'s shoulder to hold himself up.

'Are you all right?'

'Fine, just fine, Officer,' he said, regaining his presence of mind. But his confidence concealed a faint hesitation. Desire, perhaps hope, and certainly fear.

Roberta sat pale and chaste on the other side of the partition glass.

'How are you?' she asked. She was dressed in white.

Freddo laid his hands on the glass. Not to be able to touch her. Not to be able to touch those eyes that burned with weariness, regret and disappointment.

'Getting by,' he finally sighed, flopping down onto the stool. 'You?'

'So-so.'

'You with someone else now?'

Roberta stiffened. 'You think there's anyone in the city of Rome willing to date Freddo's woman?'

A veiled contempt, an admonishment. And yet, there'd never been a hint of violence between them. She knew that there never would be.

'But would you want...another man, I mean...'

'No. But I don't want to be Freddo's woman anymore either...'

'That I'd guessed. All this time...'

'I found work.'

'What kind of work?'

'Well, certainly not the kind of work your girlfriends do! A real job. And I'm back in school.'

'Good for you. Good luck.'

With an angry lunge, she hurled herself against the glass.

'Don't you understand that for you...for us...as long as you're in here...there's no...there's no...'

She could barely hold back her tears. Ugly bitter creases were defacing the corners of her mouth, once so fresh and pure. Freddo noticed her acne, barely covered up by a hastily applied layer of rouge.

'Future. There's no future,' he finished her sentence for her. 'But it's my life, Roberta.'

Freddo summoned the *maresciallo* and asked to be taken back to his cell. Better to leave each other like this, without wasting any more words. He couldn't take that heartbreak any longer.

In the corridor of the third cell block, they saw Bufalo looming up before them, blocking their way.

'Just two minutes, *Maresciallo*...'

The guard moved off to one side, discreetly. Freddo tried to head him off.

'This isn't a great time, Bufalo...'

Bufalo shook his big head. 'I know, I know. Roberta came to see you, and now you're a wreck. I just wanted to tell you I understand. And I'm sorry...'

'Thanks.'

Bufalo lit a joint and handed it to him. The *maresciallo* threw his arms wide in exasperation. Bufalo waved for him to keep cool; with what he paid him every month, he ought to understand when it was time to turn a blind eye.

'I have nothing against you, Freddo. I just wanted to let you know that.'

Freddo nodded. Deep down, he felt like he was suffocating.

'You say that Dandi's not doing the wrong thing, eh?'

'No. He's not doing the wrong thing.'

'Well, maybe we should strike an agreement, no?'

'There's already an agreement, Bufalo. We're the agreement.'

'You might be right, Freddo. Still...'

The *maresciallo* came over, at his wits' end.

'Look, any minute now the inspection team will be making the rounds...'

Bufalo stubbed out the joint and sighed in annoyance. Then, without warning, he threw his arms around Freddo and hugged him hard. Freddo overcame his impulse to slam him against the wall and returned the hug without a lot of conviction. The *maresciallo* finally managed to lead Freddo away.

Cunning, patience and poison, Bufalo snickered to himself, pulling another joint out of his pocket. This was only the beginning. You didn't knock down walls by banging your head against them.

That night, Freddo had Ricotta come to his cell.

'Tell Donatella that I need to talk to Vanessa. As soon as possible.'

Ricotta assured him that he'd convey the message on visiting day, Friday.

The Past and the Future
1984–85

I

THE TRAIN BLEW up in a tunnel. It had been almost exactly a year since Sorcio turned state's witness. Fifteen dead and thirty wounded. The evening news broadcast broke into the holiday marathon. Special editions were slapped down on tables set for family banquets.

The train blew up. Uncle Carlo poured himself a glass of Zibibbo white and smiled.

'Merry Christmas and all best wishes. The Father, the Son and the Holy Ghost!' He repeated the last in Sicilian dialect: '*Padre, Figghiu e Spirito santo!*'

The Maestro was frightened. As accustomed as he was to not asking questions, his curiosity got the better of his respect for rules. At first Uncle Carlo ignored him, but when the Maestro returned to the charge, the smile faded from his lips, he looked him hard in the eyes, and he hissed a proverb in heavy Sicilian dialect. If a friend can't hear you the first time, there's no point repeating the question.

The Maestro's fearful thoughts rushed to little Danilo. The child was growing up healthy, strong and intelligent – remarkably intelligent, in fact. An iridescent hot-house flower that, thanks to the light of his remarkable qualities, would surely drown out any memory of his shadowy origins. All that, of course, would be swept away in the face of criminal charges of mass murder. His son might have the brain of Einstein, but he would always and only be the son of a murderer in the eyes of the world.

Uncle Carlo hadn't let slip a hint of what was happening over the past

405

few days. Not even the slightest indication of anxiety. He'd kept him in the dark about that ugly project. The Maestro hadn't known a thing; he wasn't even remotely involved. But try telling that to the judges!

Uncle Carlo stretched luxuriantly and lit a cigar. 'These arseholes were busting our balls! And now we've taken care of it! *'Ddi curnuti ci stavano scassannu 'a minchia! E ora, ci vinniru 'i pinseri!'*

For the first time ever – and they'd been working together for years and years – the Maestro found himself, to his surprise, thinking of Uncle Carlo as a dangerous lunatic.

The Old Man, too, reacted to the news with great anxiety. It was unthinkable that an operation of this kind could have been carried out without his being aware of it. The lack of any claim of responsibility might well mean the extreme right was involved. Unlike the Reds, constantly busy drafting long-winded and fantastically dull documents, the Black terrorists, the right-wingers, preached and practised the mysticism of the act, the wordless idea.

But the Old Man's sources dismissed the hypothesis immediately. Wildcat operators, reckless freelancers, flying shrapnel and, to use a horrible phrase – *schegge volanti* – that had lately become fashionable? It seemed unlikely. The bomb had been constructed with the most advanced technology. That level of expertise belonged to just a few highly refined specialists whose services were available only to a small circle of select clients. In any case, there was a gap in the system of domestic security. Or else the masterminds were foreign, in which case one of his correspondents must be working a double game. But the Old Man's phone was ringing off the hook with assurances and attestations of outrage that the representatives of the leading intelligence agencies were hastening to convey. The Israelis declared their horror at such blind and gratuitous violence. The Arabs swore up and down that the non-belligerence agreements concerning Italy's national territory remained in force, now more than ever. At the agency they were startled, nonplussed, caught flat-footed. It had been a while since anyone had heard talk about bombings in Italy. And the red-flagged legions filling the nation's piazzas and shouting helplessly in their rage at this renewal of the wounds of Bologna? Just one more pain in the arse. The other intelligence agencies didn't count.

Zeta managed to crack the riddle in a few hours. This was the work of a group assembled expressly to carry out that attack. There were Sicilians and Neapolitans involved, the Mafia and a few free agents from the Camorra. The Old Man furrowed his brow. According to Zeta, this was a diversionary strategy of some kind. Since the judges were digging uncomfortably deep, a few clever minds in the world of organized crime had decided to raise their aim and use higher-calibre ammunition. Thus, while everybody was busy chasing after the new terrorist movement, they could go back to their usual work and retake control of the national territory.

'Wrong,' the Old Man corrected him. 'The objective is something else.'

'What?'

'Negotiations. The reason they're aiming higher is to break the will of the state.'

'What would they get out of it?'

'Protection. Agreements. Business. More lenient laws.'

At any rate, an interesting scenario, a variant he hadn't heard before, with something almost Colombian about it. All things considered – intriguing.

Zeta asked whether he should prepare a report for the judges in Bologna. The Old Man recoiled.

'Why on earth would we do that?'

'Then are we supposed to help them?'

'Who?'

'*Them* – the group...'

'Not on your life.'

'Well, then?'

'Well, then,' the Old Man sighed, 'we'll watch and wait. Naturally we'll follow with close attention all the developments of the case!'

Zeta let a malicious little grin play across his lips. He'd held the most succulent piece of news in reserve for his grand finale.

'The timing mechanism...'

'Yes?'

'It's Olandese's work. They paid him a billion lire.'

If he'd hope to see him lose his cool, Zeta was disappointed. The Old Man limited himself to a shrug of the shoulders.

'You know what procedure is required. Good luck!'

DANDI, ON THE other hand, had absolutely no interest in the bomb. This was going to be a great, memorable Christmas. Trentadenari once again had the narcotics business firmly under control. The Sicilian channel, the South American suppliers and the Chinaman had all started to churn along again at full capacity. Shipments came in on a regular basis and the merchandise was first-class. The distribution networks that had been disassembled thanks to Sorcio's revelations were reactivated and newly staffed with Nercio's and Secco's people, working alongside a fair number of the old horses under house arrest or out on bail. Nero had the video poker market under control and he was getting his feet wet again in the poker circuit. The Full 80 was, more than ever, *the* fashionable club. Secco had his heart set on a couple of shops in downtown Rome and some land on the eastern outskirts of the city that, word had it, was soon going to skyrocket in value. Even the simmering feud with Bufalo seemed to be heading towards a promising solution: a rigorous respect for the promises made and great generosity in paying out shares – both seemed to work in his favour. The guys behind bars really had no reason to complain and even the stubbornest ones, in the end, began to see that playing by the rules of the game was in the interests of the entire organization.

But then there were Scialoja and Borgia, of course. The two of them showed no signs of relenting. Every day, some new warrant or other came hailing down, often for some long-forgotten crime, and inevitably without a shred of evidence that rose above the threshold of the merely circumstantial: John Doe was best buddies with Richard Roe, who was notoriously close to John Stiles. John Stiles died, therefore it was John Doe and Richard Roe who killed him. The fact that that was, more or less, what actually happened couldn't be of any importance to a normal judge. There was no solid evidence, amen. The fact was, Scialoja and Borgia weren't normal. There was a screw loose in their heads somewhere. Dandi often wondered whether he'd made a mistake when he spared the cop's life. Then he remembered Uncle Carlo's wise advice, imagined a different future, and resigned himself to the situation. He had to be patient. He had to wait it out. And in the end, he'd be victorious.

Even if the arrest warrants were falling like heavy snow. Even if his court date kept getting postponed.

'There's no chance of it happening until the end of next year,' Miglianico predicted. 'Vasta agrees.'

'You know Vasta?'

'Of course. A fine colleague. But also a naïve innocent. He still hasn't figured out that the way you win trials isn't in the courtroom.'

Dandi hoped to win a full acquittal without ever having been behind bars, but he was ready for any and all eventualities. He moved around unarmed, to limit the risk of a shootout, and he went nowhere without an envelope containing the analyses and diagnosis cooked up with his brother the physician. Dandi really had thought of everything!

But on Christmas Eve he just couldn't resist, and he came knocking at Patrizia's door, buffed to a gleam, clean-shaven cheeks like a baby's bottom, his bull neck close to bursting out of the snug tuxedo collar and bow tie. Patrizia had been expecting this visit. She was waiting for him, alone, in an evening gown. They danced cheek to cheek, they snorted a few lines of coke, they made love, and then they sat down to eat. Just the two of them, with a little charming background music and a long table, candles and an exquisite buffet: lobster, oysters, Cristal and Chablis, apple strudel and chocolate mousse. When the shock troops of the mobile squad came busting through the front door, loaded for bear, Patrizia had just been telling him about her plans for a beauty shop and fitness spa in the Via Veneto neighbourhood.

Dandi, surrounded by policemen, paid his compliments to the team captain. The captain's face darkened and he stepped aside. Behind him, in the doorway, stood the lanky figure of Scialoja. It hadn't been easy but he'd managed to persuade the others. He'd had to foist off a non-existent tip-off as the reason for the raid. He'd sworn that on Christmas Eve Dandi would be paying a call on his woman. He'd made the bet and it had paid off. But there hadn't been any informant. The truth was that he, too, just happened to be tuned in on the right wavelength that night.

'What should we do with the woman?' asked the team captain.

'Nothing,' replied Scialoja, staring at Patrizia.

She looked away. Dandi sketched out a slight bow, sucked down the last of the Marennes-Oléron oysters, and followed the cops out of the apartment with a mocking smile on his broad, round face.

When Miglianico spoke the word 'cancer' to him, Borgia let loose with a hearty laugh. The lawyer put on the mild, pained expression of the petitioner who runs up against blind and unheeding power, but who still knows, deep down, the moral justice of his demands.

'Cancer's an insidious disease, Judge. It lurks in the recesses of our organism and strikes without warning, sometimes without leaving any hope of survival...'

'And in this specific case?'

'In this specific case, we're dealing with an exceedingly rare form of tumour of a pseudo-Hodgkin type. Almost always fatal...'

'Almost always.'

'Of course, this is a difficult moment...The horrible images of the aftermath of that train bombing are still etched into my eyes...I can clearly understand your concerns about the importance of safeguarding the welfare of the collective, but I wouldn't want my client, seriously ill, to wind up paying for the crimes of others...'

Too sick to even attend a deposition, according to the opinion of the illustrious oncologist Professor Gustavo Blinis, Dandi had only a limited amount of time to live and, in fact, was practically on his death bed.

'Perhaps, if he was given adequate treatment, subjected to intense and costly therapy, cared for by a top-notch medical staff twenty-four hours a day, it might be possible to delay – but only delay, I'm not saying we could prevent – the inevitable end...'

Borgia had another truth right before his eyes. The truth of a criminal in all capital letters, six feet tall, two hundred pounds, covered from head to foot with gold the day he was arrested, courteous and cordial with the cops who had busted in on his gilded flight from justice, with an apartment you could only dream about, a religious fanatic of a wife and a prostitute for a mistress – albeit a first-class prostitute – and he was terrifyingly wealthy to boot.

Borgia had, right before his eyes, the image of the spontaneous roar of applause with which the third wing of the prison had greeted Dandi's arrival: a burst of applause that had turned into a standing ovation when he had raised his right arm in a salute, and then, from the ovation, it had

410

moved on to a rhythmic pounding of their lunch pails against their iron cell bars – a concert for Dandi. And for his lawyer, Miglianico: a man with a chequered past involving subversion and extortion, charged, at one point, with having fraudulently obtained both his membership in the bar and his degree in law. He'd been acquitted for lack of evidence, like almost all of his clients. And yet, it was well known how little he knew about articles and sections and clauses. That acquittal, therefore, had come through some other channel. Channels that Dandi had chosen to avail himself of, abandoning good old Counsellor Vasta, a stalwart lawyer from the old school, a bastard, but deep down a clean and legitimate bastard.

Dandi had shifted his alliance, Borgia mused. Dandi had made the great leap forward. But who else had leapt with him? Who else had left Vasta for this cologne-scented fraudster, Miglianico? What was happening in the gang?

'Subordinately, dottore, and out of a stance of extreme defensive tutorism, I herewith request for my client a medical and legal examination and appoint, effective immediately, as a consultant to the defence, Professor Blinis...'

Borgia said his opinion was contrary to the release for health considerations and he further objected to the concession of house arrest. Cancer! But there were the documents – man, these guys were good when it came to juggling documents! And the investigating judge, left with no alternative, ordered the expert examination.

From solitary confinement, Dandi was transferred directly to the infirmary. He came in just as Bufalo was leaving following one of his periodic examinations. They stopped, staring at each other, both feeling equally awkward. Then Bufalo broke the silence.

'I'm sorry they caught you, Dandi.'

Dandi sniffed and then let fly with a faint disdainful hiss.

'Spare me the bullshit...'

Bufalo stood there lost in thought for a moment, then he pretended to haul off and punch him.

'You want to know the truth? I couldn't wait for the day they fucked you too...'

'Now this is the Bufalo I recognize!'

Dandi laughed. Bufalo laughed too. They set a seal on their armed truce with half a handshake. Bufalo handed Dandi a couple of joints and Dandi returned the courtesy with a baggie of coke.

The female nurse was warm and comforting. Security was laughable. Patrizia had arranged to smuggle him a box of Cuban cigars and a case of champagne, which he shared with the doctors and nurses. There was plenty of time for the expert evaluation. Miglianico had guaranteed that the thing would come off without a hitch. The important thing was to make sure that things on the outside moved along smoothly, but as for that, their business interests were in good hands. They could trust Donatella. In fact, once she'd signed her declaration of cohabitation with Ricotta, she came and went as she pleased, like a courier for the Red Brigades. It was just a matter of being patient and waiting it out. Calmly, without pulling any bullshit.

The situation on the inside was improving. Bufalo had stopped busting people's chops. Dandi, Scrocchiazeppi, Fierolocchio and Ricotta had developed a habit of playing nightly games of poker. Ricotta regularly fleeced them. He had a hard time distinguishing between a three-of-a-kind and a straight, but he was devastatingly lucky. Freddo, however, remained an indecipherable phantom. Only once had he stuck his head into the infirmary. Skinny as a skeleton, he'd lingered a moment at the door, staring at the quartet of poker players, indifferent to their invitations. He waved vaguely at Dandi, and then hurried back to his cell.

'What's got into him?' Dandi had asked.

'Heartbreak,' Ricotta replied, sweeping up the ante from the last poker hand. 'Roberta dumped him.'

'It's his bad luck,' Scrocchiazeppi explained. 'He's trying to find a way out of here but he keeps running into brick walls.'

'He wants to play the sick boy too,' Fierolocchio tossed in. 'But not all of us have your luck, Dandi. Think of it – diagnosed with a nice case of terminal cancer!'

They'd all laughed. Dandi had passed around a handful of cigars. Ricotta had drawn a bonus cumulative ante. In short, they were having fun just like in the old days. Too bad about no women, but maybe if the *maresciallo* was willing to look the other way...

Yes, they were having fun. Until one grim day when they threw Secco in with the rest of them, and their story as a gang took another twist.

412

III

WHAT HAD DONE Secco in was the real estate deal involving land to the
east of the city. It all started with Barracuda, a one-time pimp who'd been
rinsed whiter than snow by his marriage to a wealthy widow, now driven
by ambitions in which his grasp clearly exceeded his reach. The land
belonged to an elderly noble, slipping into senility, who wanted a price
approaching the moon and the stars. Then the marquis, or count, or
whatever the hell he was, had gone gaga over one of the girls Barracuda
used to run, a Brazilian chick who was as fiery as she was expensive,
and soon the price had dropped from the orbit of the moon to a much
more reasonable half a billion lire. It was a juicy deal. The main chance
for profitability lay in the land being zoned for construction, a decision
that was thought to be imminent; even the Rome daily *Il Messaggero*
said so.

The pipe dream was an enormous business and industrial park, with
huge office buildings to be rented at sky-high rates to the public sector.
Cooked and served at table. Really, all things considered, an unremark-
able story of bricks and bribes, a classic of the Seven Hills, a totally
ordinary case of real estate speculation. Except that for Barracuda, even
half a billion lire was an unattainable sum. And so he started hunting
around frantically for a partner.

Secco had sized him up at first glance: a spineless pipsqueak, a chicken
to be plucked with the overwrought personality of a *piscimprescia* –
the dictionary definition of a sucker. In the meantime, however, from
between the thighs of Barracuda's one-time protégée and employee had
emerged a preliminary memo of sale, a sort of standard pre-contract,
and having a signed contract in hand rendered Barracuda at once weak,
because he was penniless, yet also powerful, because without him there
could be no deal.

Secco sailed onto the scene in his usual public persona as a dispenser
of credit and friendship, and in less time than it takes to tell, they'd set
up a company to manage and exploit the lands. Barracuda brought the
official documents, Secco supplied the cash, and as for the profits, why,
those would be split fifty-fifty between them, of course. Though Secco
had no intention whatsoever of splitting anything. He could agree on

a fifty-fifty split with Dandi as long as that cut-throat had a position of strength on the market, but to adhere to a promise given to a dickhead like Barracuda would simply have been an unacceptable display of poor taste. Secco was a true artist of the game of bidding up, and cash was his most insidious weapon. He started out with a modest capital increase: unexpected expenses for a greedy city commissioner, he justified the outlay to Barracuda. And his partner, to match the contribution, was forced to put a second mortgage on the widow's home. In no more than three months' time, a new and bigger capital outlay became necessary: this time it was because of the regional oversight commission, which wanted to have its say on the zoning exception. The bankers he approached all judged the potential outcome of that deal to be too risky, and they rejected Barracuda's loan applications. Secco, true friend that he was, told him not to take it personally, and arranged to underwrite the capital increase himself. In exchange, Barracuda handed over half of his half, or 25 per cent of the company's shares.

Finally, the very same day that the city council approved the zoning exception and issued the building permit, Secco lowered the hammer for the last time: an extraordinary one-time bribe, three hundred million lire. In desperation, Barracuda confided to him that he had nowhere left to turn but loan sharks. Secco, who happened to be the acknowledged leader of that tribe, talked him out of such a radical step in his affable way. After a bottle of Orvieto Est-Est-Est and a short bout of tears, the remaining 25 per cent of the company – the other half of Barracuda's half – changed hands. All that was left to Barracuda was the mortgage and the hope that one day he could redeem it by selling the pathetic garage space that Secco had allowed him to keep in the yet-to-be-built shopping centre and office park.

Winning yet another game of real-life Monopoly gave Secco such a thrill that he started bragging around town about how he'd plucked the poor fool clean. The rumour circulated, enriched with a growing array of new details. And since it wasn't as if Secco was wreathed by a cloud of hearts and cupids, as far as general sentiment was concerned, someone who really wanted to put the dagger in him took it upon themselves to get word to Barracuda about the spiciest detail of the story: the fact that the bankers, those heartless wretches who had denied him credit for a deal that was safer than safe could be, were all of them, every last one, on his former partner's payroll.

Barracuda remembered dimly that he'd once been half a stand-up guy, went to see Secco, and shoved his back to the wall. Secco saved himself from a serious beating thanks to his habit of always keeping a pair of enforcers on a short leash. But now he was really pissed off, was old Secco. First he sent a couple of guys to burn Barracuda's car, then paid off the mortgage on his wife's house and demanded Barracuda immediately pay the balance to him. Barracuda bought a third-hand revolver at the flea market of Porta Portese and started stalking Secco, lurking around him and telling anyone who cared to know that he fully intended to see him laid out on a slab. Secco started circulating a rumour of his own: that Barracuda had lost his mind, and that was too bad, because he had a lovely wife and two bouncing boys, and wouldn't it be a terrible thing if one day, in the throes of a fit of insanity, he were to do them some harm.

Barracuda got the message. He threw the handgun into the river and for a little while he was good as gold. Then honour prevailed over his empty stomach. He sent wife and children off to stay with a relative in Australia, and one fine day, in jacket and tie as if he were attending a funeral, he walked through the main entrance of the Via Genova police station and started spilling the beans to a friend who was a cop. In the months during which he was in close and regular contact with Secco, Barracuda had been able to listen, watch, make notes and understand. He had plenty of things to tell the cops. He started with the murder of Angioletto, went on to the narcotics trafficking, the mysterious origins of Secco's wealth, and finished up on a high note, with the con that had pulled him into the real estate deal in the first place. This last charge was, all things considered, the only serious one, the only one that directly involved the accuser. Barracuda himself had never actually seen any white powder change hands; he'd heard about eighteen-carat gangsters but never actually met any. It was all hearsay up to that point. All Secco really had to do was claim that these accusations were the product of a resentful and unsuccessful entrepreneur's anger towards a rival businessman on his way up in the world, and they'd probably release him that same night. But Secco knew nothing about arrests, search warrants, court orders and prison cells. Secco had a clean record. He had a pathological fear of handcuffs.

In his first interrogation session, with a series of partial admissions, references to prominent citizens he knew and could call, threats and tears, Secco screwed up his case with his own hands. The prosecuting magistrate, Morales, a sly old fox who'd at first been inclined to dismiss the matter then and there, started to take a deeper interest in Barracuda's affidavits. A face-to-face confrontation was arranged. Barracuda had his say, clear-eyed and determined; Secco spat out defamatory insults, sweat-drenched and wheezing. The lawyer recommended he keep his mouth shut, and Secco told him to go straight to hell. The judge asked him a question, and Secco replied by blaspheming all of Barracuda's filthy ancestors. Things were not looking good.

When he heard about it, Dandi flew into a rage. Clearly, Secco's nerves were giving out. For the moment, Barracuda had made no allusions to the ties between them. Dandi didn't even know what he looked like, that tremendous son of a bitch. For now. But what if Barracuda suddenly remembered a conversation? A phone call? Some offhand mention of him? It wasn't bad enough that the gang's financial mastermind had wound up in prison: now he was having a nervous breakdown!

Dandi got in touch with his brothers on the outside. But they sent word back, via Miglianico, that their hands were tied. Judge Morales was untouchable. All their appeals were rejected out of hand. Judge Morales sensed that Secco was on the verge of collapse, and he was keeping him in total isolation, twenty-four-hour solitary confinement. From his cell, he wrote and mailed letter after letter to his influential one-time friends. Letters that were unfailingly returned to sender as undeliverable. Judge Morales had guessed that the little real estate fraud could bear much bigger fruit in the form of a wide-ranging investigation. Secco played one last desperate card, offering a bribe to the inmate orderly who swept up the areaways and cells in the solitary confinement wing – the only other prisoner allowed to move freely in that part of the prison. Secco told him he'd give him twenty million lire if he'd punch him a couple of times in the face and kick him in the balls once or twice. The orderly had no interest in earning himself extra jail time just when he was about to be released. But word got around. Bufalo paid a bribe and managed to make his way into Secco's cell.

'What's this I hear that if I beat you up, you're willing to pay me?'

'I have to get out of here. I'm going crazy!'

'And you want to wind up in the hospital?'

'In the infirmary. I want to wind up in the infirmary. See people. Have a chance to think. If I'm stuck in here for another week...'

'What are you going to do? Squeal?'

'I'd rather kill myself!'

Bufalo lit a joint. Secco declined the offer.

'I don't want to get stoned, Bufalo. I want to get out!'

'Then why don't you ask Dandi for help? You're such good buddies...'

Secco began to insult Dandi. Conceited. Incompetent. He'd got himself arrested like a dodo because he was incapable of staying clear of that whore of his. A dictator. If Bufalo only knew the way he talked about them, about the other guys...

'Why? What does he say about us?' asked Bufalo, suddenly interested.

Secco read his mind, understood that there might still be hope, and put on an inspired expression.

'Bufalo, if it hadn't been for me, he'd have let the lot of you rot in here!'

'You? What did you do?'

'Who do you think demanded that an equal share be given to those behind bars? Me! And who do you think accounts for every last lira of your money? Me! He even beat me up, the son of a bitch!'

Bufalo didn't believe him for a second. Dandi was too sly a dog to open his flank to attack like this at such a critical juncture. Everyone knew what had really happened. If there was a snake that was even more venomous than Dandi, that snake was Secco. Still, it was one thing to believe because you were a gullible arse; it was quite another to believe because you wanted to believe. Especially when the wounds kept spilling fresh blood. Especially when, with the snake's help, the future offered you a once-in-a-lifetime opportunity.

'So let me make sure I understand: you want me to beat you up...'

'Sure, Bufalo, sure! But take it easy, eh?'

'As much as I can, given the circumstances, comrade!' Bufalo laughed, rolling up his sleeves. Secco shut his eyes and waited for the first blow.

IT WAS BY a matter of a few hundred yards' distance that the investigation into the Christmas bombing fell under the jurisdiction of the district attorney of the Italian Republic for Florence. A few hundred yards that could very well prove fatal to the Old Man and his cohorts, seeing that their influence over that office had been waning for some time. Two particularly brilliant minds of the anti-terrorism division had managed to lay their hands on Olandese before Zeta could find him. Olandese had cracked open his suitcase of compromising secrets ever so slightly. The name of Uncle Carlo had been mentioned.

One March morning, after fifteen years as a fugitive, they'd picked Uncle Carlo up in a villa on the Via Appia Antica, and with him was his trusted colleague, the Maestro. Two birds with one stone. Out of the extremely neat address book that the Mafioso kept in an old graph-paper notebook, they had found an encrypted telephone number. All efforts to open any discussions of co-operation with Uncle Carlo had fallen on deaf ears – literally, considering that when he was arrested, in order to dispense with the usual formalities, he pretended that he was deaf as a doornail. And so the anti-terrorism squad turned to a famous professor, a major international expert in codes and ciphers. He broke the code in a single afternoon and the phone number, finally unveiled, turned out to belong to a shell real estate company in the Castelli Romani area.

A SWAT team ready for heavy combat broke through the front door. Pigreco was caught manning the otherwise empty office. The secret agent appealed to solidarity among colleagues in law enforcement and was allowed to use the phone. But instead of the welcome sound of the Old Man's voice, however furious he might turn out to be, there was only a dead phone line. While the initial bafflement of the team of policemen slowly grew into a dangerous form of suspicious curiosity, and questions began to pelt him, Pigreco frantically tried to track down Zeta. All efforts were in vain. And so he started hunting for other, less highly placed, colleagues, moving lower and lower down the organizational chart, phone number by phone number, until he was actually calling his own direct reports. All pointless. It was as if he'd been stricken from the list. A man who no longer existed. Even the organization's 'overt' switchboard failed to ring. When at last someone in the SWAT team whispered the words 'mass murder' with an edge of hostility, Pigreco asked to be put in touch with the cop.

'I didn't have anything to do with this bomb, you tell him,' Pigreco implored when, around midnight, Scialoja was finally tracked down.

'Why me of all people?'

'Because they'll believe you. They know we're not friends. I didn't have anything to do with it, I swear it! We've never planted bombs...'

'Should I believe you?'

'Do what you want, but just get me out of here!'

'Why?'

'Because in exchange I can give you something you really, really want.'

'What would that be?'

'Dandi!'

'What else?'

'The Old Man. I'm offering you a link. A connection. You'll be famous. The most famous cop in Italy...'

Scialoja lit a cigarette and handed it to him. The spy greedily sucked down two long drags of smoke.

'How do you think you can pull it off, Pigreco?'

'With the help of Larinese, God rest his soul...'

When Borgia saw him come stumbling into his home at sunrise, rain-soaked and wild-eyed, he assumed that Scialoja was losing his mind. His wife, indignant at this unbelievable violation of their personal privacy, barricaded herself in their bedroom, clutching her weeping children to her breast. With a bitter sigh, Borgia looked forward to the inevitable aftermath: arguments, lasting grudges, gloomy home life, pathetic attempts to make up, the scalding accusation that he was neglecting his family for his job, and so on and so forth. He suddenly realized that he hated that lunatic missionary in a trench coat. He did his best to talk him out of having that conversation right here, right now, and he even tried – but only half-heartedly, without much conviction – to show him the door. But Scialoja shoved him into an unsightly Scandinavian-style armchair from the sixties and refused to let him move a muscle until he was finished.

'Here's how it went: Larinese is a first-class counterfeiter, one of the best in the business today. He's on the Old Man's payroll. They use him for certain dirty little jobs they need done. During the Moro kidnapping, they hired him to organize the disinformation campaign involving Lake Duchessa. Do you remember that famous but apocryphal Red Brigades communiqué that sent half the Italian police force scampering to search for the president's corpse in the icy lake waters? Well, that was Larinese's handiwork. The fact is that Lake Duchessa isn't far from the township of Gradoli. They needed to cover up another tip, and this one was real: Via Gradoli was also the name of the street where, in an apartment completely ignored by the police who were supposedly searching door to door, the Red Brigades leaders were actually hiding. And that's not all. After his masterpiece with the communiqué, Larinese vanished back into the shadows. Until one fine day they asked him to do another little job: organize a robbery. The apparent target was a bundle of cash, but the real purpose was to lay hands on certain documents that the Old Man needed. Larinese puts together a rag-tag gang and pulls off the job. But instead of handing over the documents, he holds on to them and tries to blackmail the Old Man. At this point the Old Man loses his temper. He calls Dandi and orders him to eliminate Larinese and recover the documents. That way, he kills two birds with one stone: he regains possession of what he most needs and he also rids himself of an inconvenient witness...'

'And how did you find out all these things?' Borgia let out his breath, addressing him, without noticing it, with the informal *tu*.

'Pigreco. He's my source.'

Borgia shut his eyes. The story held together. It explained a few of the mysteries of recent years. It provided a code of analysis. It fit perfectly into the mosaic. The story held together goddamned perfectly. What Borgia wanted was a less tumultuous life: a transfer to civil law, the civil service exam to become a notary, a modest university position.

'We'll have to inform the district attorney...' he murmured.

'Let's bear down on them!' Scialoja urged. 'Let's strike while the iron's hot! Today, right now! Pigreco is a hot trail. He has names, dates, locations, numbered bank accounts...Let's not give them the time to reorganize! Let's strike now, immediately.'

'We'll need corroborating evidence…'

'We'll track that down. But first thing we have to do is neutralize the Old Man…'

'If Dandi doesn't confirm this…'

'We'll cut him a deal!'

'Scialoja, we're not in America, you know!'

'Damn it, this isn't the time to start wallowing in scruples!'

Borgia closed his eyes. He sensed that something was about to slip through his fingers. Maybe for good. What he ought to do was go along with the cop. Follow his intuition. Cover his strategy of attack. But he just didn't feel sure of himself, that was all.

'Write up a report for me,' he ordered in a flat voice.

Epidemics
1985–86

I

THE BEATING THAT sent Secco to the infirmary was blamed on the orderly who did the sweeping up. After all, who else but him could possibly have made their way into solitary confinement? The shift commander confirmed that nothing out of the ordinary had taken place. Except for the ten or fifteen minutes when the orderly was cleaning out the cell, no one else had had any contact with Secco. So that must have been when the beating took place. Secco himself babbled out the motive, struggling to emerge from the stunned slumber induced by the sedatives: a few words too many that, in one of his recurring moments of weakness, he'd allowed to escape him when confronted with the orderly's refusal of a requested favour, otherwise left vague.

There was clearly a set-up of some kind; the stink was unmistakable and it left Judge Morales breathless. He tried every trick in the book to get the orderly to confess, but nothing seemed to work. Between an extra six-to-eight months of prison time and an underworld vendetta, the soon-to-be-freed convict had no real alternative. The man confessed he'd inflicted the beating, adducing a long-held dislike for the fat-bellied prisoner, took his extra time without a word, along with the twenty million lire that Secco had already conveyed to his wife on the outside, and the con job went off without a hitch.

Morales did everything within his power to revoke the prisoner's long-term assignment to the infirmary. But the physicians objected, expressing their considered medical view. A couple of good-hearted

423

nuns even squeezed out a tear or two and so, in the end, the judge resigned himself to it.

Dandi wasn't satisfied with that version of the story either. On the one hand, Secco's new assignment within the prison universe kept him safe from further pernicious, hysterical attacks. On the other hand, the details of what had happened worried him considerably. Because, talking to Dandi, Secco denied any collusion. Sure, he was willing to pay someone to beat him, but certainly not Bufalo. That had been his own undertaking and Secco had had nothing to do with it. The reckless act of a dangerous lunatic.

'Mind if I ask what triggered this?'

'What do I know!' Secco whined. 'He started insulting me and insulting you...Bufalo hates you, Dandi! He says that we stole his money, but as God is my witness, there's not a penny missing! Then...I don't know what happened after that. I just remember getting hit. *Mamma mia*, I took a lot of kicks and punches! He's crazy, I tell you, crazy!'

Crazy as far as the judges were concerned, perhaps. But not for Dandi, who knew Bufalo all too well. Bufalo was planning something. He'd wound up resigning himself to his fate, but deep down he was still nurturing the usual age-old ancestral hatred. Dandi decided that he had to get to the bottom of that matter, whatever the cost, before the consequences recoiled against them all.

He cut Botola, Scrocchiazeppi and Fierolocchio loose in search of a contact of any sort with Bufalo. But they were too late. Bufalo had already left for the asylum for the criminally insane. In the end, they'd given him mental infirmity on account of the whole mess with the Gemito brothers.

The fact that the situation had been resolved successfully was entirely to the credit of good teamwork, Vasta's sly and nimble legal work and, as always in this world, pure dumb luck.

What had happened was that Baldissera, the psychiatrist who remained unwilling to come around, the one who was convinced to the bitter end of Bufalo's enormous acting ability, had put in a request for a position as the head physician of a hospital up north. The chairman of the search committee, as chance would have it, was the esteemed Professor Cortina. Baldissera came to see his colleague with his tail between his legs.

'I wouldn't want this courtesy call to be taken for an attempt to put my own name forward...'

'Why, perish the thought!' Cortina had smiled in response. 'In the presence of a professional of your calibre, I take off my hat.'

'That said, I wouldn't want our past disagreements to carry more weight than is proper in your careful evaluation...'

'Don't worry! Intelligent people can always come to an understanding...'

Three days after that conversation, Baldissera resigned his post on the panel of expert witnesses due to 'irreconcilable differences'. With a single blow he'd saved his own face but had demolished the expert witnesses' report. If they wanted to figure out whether Bufalo was crazy or not, they'd have to start over again from scratch. Caught between Borgia, who was urging him to move quicker, and Vasta, who cautioned prudence, the investigating judge had taken as much as he could stomach. He reserved the right to make the decision but put it in abeyance.

At this point, Vasta piped up. Bufalo, aside from the killing of the Gemito brothers, had another dozen or so charges pending against him. One of those – an old armed robbery from before even his connection with Libano, legal proceedings that were lost in the mists of time through a strange, intertwining welter of jurisdictions – had been taken out of Borgia's hands and was now lying fallow between the inboxes of a prosecuting magistrate on the anti-terrorism squad team and an elderly, completely apathetic investigating judge.

Vasta explained that he considered his client to be insane. And if he was insane for the murder, he could hardly be sane for the armed robbery. Therefore, a psychiatric evaluation ought to be ordered as well for that old pending charge. The judge found that proposal to be reasonable and set a hearing for the appointment of the expert witness.

Trentadenari and Nero paid a little visit to the powerful official on whom they'd been lavishing gifts now for two years, without results. In one hand they bore a mink coat and a Rolex, in the other, their firearms. The powerful official promptly took the ultimatum for what it was, and when the hearing rolled around, Dr Polistena was appointed as the expert witness. An up-and-coming young professional fresh out of medical school, where he'd specialized in forms of paranoid schizophrenia with a learned thesis inspired by the classics of the field: foremost among them, Cortina, 1971 edition. Polistena examined Bufalo, a female assistant administered a battery of tests, and in no more time than it takes to say amen, the diagnosis was official: paranoid schizophrenia, obviously, and total mental infirmity.

Vasta went to see the judge on the Gemito case and inverted his reasoning: if Bufalo was insane for the armed robbery, how could he be sane for the murder? The judge summoned Polistena and another hack expert, and *ipso facto* conceded a thirty-day extension for some extra expert witnessing.

In one month's time, Bufalo was declared for the second time to be totally incapable of understanding or intending – the classic Italian wording of all insanity pleas, the equivalent of knowing the difference between good and evil, right and wrong. A lawyerly masterpiece.

The main event was still scheduled to proceed, but the most serious charge had been stricken from the docket.

Borgia was furious. And he furiously drafted a writ of appeal for which he had only the faintest of hopes. He knew from experience that, once a breach of mental infirmity had been opened by the defence, the ensuing chain reaction could prove devastating.

Late at night, Bufalo was hustled out to a paddy wagon, with an attending physician and nurse and an offer of Valium, which he indignantly refused. Crazy, no question, but not a basket case. He'd see the others again in court. In the meantime, he'd bide his time by fine-tuning the ironclad agreement he'd made with Secco. His money was safe and sound. And sooner or later, he'd nail Dandi's hide to the wall.

II

NERO HEARD ABOUT Freddo's problems from Vanessa. Prison tradecraft cautioned against direct contacts in cases like this, but he had to do something for his old friend who was clearly having a breakdown of some sort. Nero remembered Mainardi. They'd been boon companions back in high school, committing minor infractions together. The usual things: stealing everything in the house when the parents were away for the weekend, or crashing clubs, or cracking the skulls of a few Reds. But then in the past few years Mainardi had straightened out and started to fly right. The last time Nero had seen him was on the occasion of a quick abortion for the girlfriend of one of their old comrades from the EUR. Mainardi, then in his second year of medical school, had done the right thing and taken care of business. Now, thanks to the recommendations of his father, a renowned plastic surgeon, he was working in a private clinic outside Rome. At first, when Nero went to see him, Mainardi acted all indignant. Nero was forced to refresh his memory, and the young doctor dropped the high-and-mighty act. He paid a call on Freddo, thanks to a special medical authorization delivered on strings pulled by the powerful official.

'Who sent you?'

'Nero.'

'How is he?'

'He sends his regards. He said I was to place myself at your full disposal. What can I do for you?'

'I need to get out of here.'

Mainardi promised that he'd take the situation under advisement. But even a first-year medical student could see that Freddo was in disgustingly fine fettle. Hospitalization was out of the question, unless he felt like abetting a spectacular piece of fraud that could easily cost him his career. Still, he put together a sufficiently ambiguous report to convince Borgia to order his transfer to the infirmary where he could be 'kept under observation'. That meant Freddo found himself in close contact with chronic patients Dandi and Secco, who hardly seemed excited to see him again.

Scrocchiazeppi and Fierolocchio, who, though not patients themselves, seemed to have the run of the infirmary, openly accused him of having devoted far too much energy to minding his own fucking business. Secco greeted him with unctuous salutations, but the minute Freddo's back was turned, he gossiped viciously about him. Oddly enough, the most expansive of the lot was Dandi. But he had his reasons: he was worried, almost to the point of obsession, about Bufalo. And he was eagerly searching for information, news, perhaps even an alliance. Freddo told him in no uncertain terms that Fierolocchio and Scrocchiazeppi had read him correctly.

'Which is to say?'

'Which is to say that I mind my own business and I'm not looking for trouble. I don't want to have anything to do with your business.'

It had always been Dandi's opinion that real men showed their mettle when things were at their worst. There had been a time when, in terms of brains and guts, no one could measure up to Libano and Freddo. Then Libano got himself that bad case of lead poisoning, and day by day Freddo was fading away into a shadow of his former self. When matters had deteriorated to their worst possible state, his mind had blown. Prison had unhinged him. He was fixated with the dream of an impossible escape. He'd gone soft before his time.

It was a spectacle that Dandi found both sad and exhilarating. Often his memories of times gone by sank him into a grim mood, verging on the maudlin and the nostalgic. But Dandi was a man who lived in the present, not the past. Hence the exhilaration, because with Freddo out of the way, there was no one, aside from Bufalo, who could be a cause for worry. Even Secco was too much of a coward to constitute a danger. As for the others, they were all followers; cannon fodder.

'Forget about Freddo,' Dandi ordered them.

Freddo watched them from his place of internal exile, a bed that he increasingly rarely left, and when he did, only grudgingly. He let time gobble him up, incapable of even the slightest spurt of energy. What was devouring him was an excruciating desire for something that he could only vaguely intuit: Roberta; something warm and lasting; pure air; to be far away from all this filth; real men, friends, not the peckerwoods in their frenzies of reciprocal arse-fucking.

Freddo silently watched and took note. Secco dealt and manoeuvred the cards with the superhuman ability of a prestidigitator. When you were not busy doing, you had the time to understand. Already Scrocchiazeppi and Fierolocchio, poor fools that they were, were looking at Dandi with different eyes. Secco was slowly, inexorably pitting them one against another. Secco was playing at dividing and conquering, and he'd be sure to gobble down the whole cake himself when he was done. And Dandi was too full of himself to be aware of what Secco was doing. When push came to shove – because a reckoning was sure to come – the only one who would stick with him would be Botola. A faithful dog, ceremonious, reliable. But the others? The others were ready to betray him, then maybe betray Secco, and finally betray themselves. Puma's grim prophecy returned to Freddo. He'd robbed, killed and scattered his life to the four winds.

One night, while Dandi was sleeping, Secco lifted his busy little head from the usual mile-long letter of complaint and nodded at him in a friendly manner. Freddo went over to him. He'd decided he wanted to find out what the point was.

'Freddo, I've got a deal in the works...'

'Ah, you do? Interesting.'

'A sure-fire thing...'

'Have you mentioned it to Dandi?'

Secco put on a discontented expression. His voice rose an octave, turning into an almost womanly whine.

'I'm not talking to that guy! He's a turd! You, on the other hand...'

Freddo seized him by the throat and raised his forefinger, warning him to say nothing. Secco let out a gurgling sound, and foam appeared on his lips.

'Listen to me and listen good, you piece of shit: your little tricks don't work with me. Say one more word, just one, and I'll rip that serpent's tongue out of your mouth and I'll kick it down your throat. Do I make myself clear?'

Secco nodded frantically. Freddo released his grip, went back to bed, and fell sound asleep.

III

JUDGES, THE OLD Man thought to himself as Borgia politely extended his hand, shouldn't be too intelligent. That was something his father always used to say. His father was a high-ranking officer in the Italian navy. A war hero. Where he grew up, in the centre of Naples, there lived a judge in the apartment across the landing. An elderly man, tall, white-haired, straight-shouldered and erect, invariably glowering, impeccably dressed. Never a hair out of place, subtle colours, perfectly matching, a rigid demeanour with stiff gestures, more than a hint of arrogance.

The Old Man struggled to place the name. Maggiulli...Massulli...Maioli. That's right, Judge Stefano Maioli. An enthusiastic hunter and a talented bridge player. The Old Man's father would point the judge out to him with a blend of respect and condescension. Maioli: a first-class judge, but in human terms, something of a twit. That's how a judge ought to be: a bit of a twit and not too intelligent. Maioli would never have dreamed of issuing a subpoena for nine in the morning. In Maioli's day, such a thing would have been unthinkable. Moreover, a man of Maioli's class would never have come to the office dressed in a turtleneck jumper and what looked like two days' growth of whiskers.

'Forgive my appearance, dottore, but if I'd stopped off at home to change, I know I would have collapsed on the bed and you'd have had to waste a trip all the way here. The fact is that last night, my son – the older one, the boy, you know, I have two kids, Mirko and Teresa – anyway, Mirko has an ear infection. Poor little guy, you should have heard him scream! Anyway, it was after five in the morning when we finally took him to the emergency room, and what with one thing and another, it was only half an hour ago...'

The Old Man nodded, a sympathetic smile on his thin lips. Maioli would never have dared to proffer such an unseemly excuse. No, now that he thought about it: Judge Maioli would never have dared even to have children at all.

'The reason I've invited you here – in the documents, references seem to surface... We're obliged to ascertain... May I offer a cigarette?'

Tact, good manners, a certain style. And he was vague, very vague, far too vague. The Old Man was starting to feel a certain fondness for Borgia. He was still a kid. Judges like Maioli, on the other hand, were born white-haired and disdainful.

'I'd be grateful if you could skip the preliminaries...'

'An auction of your beloved automatons?' asked a mocking voice from behind him.

The Old Man didn't even bother to turn around. He limited himself to extending his arms in a hieratic gesture.

'Commissario Scialoja...' Borgia began, clearly embarrassed.

'We've been introduced,' the Old Man interrupted, with a disdainful little smile. 'Yes, commissario. That's right. Feurbrunner is selling an exquisite model of the *Frankfurt Chess Player*, AD 1787. I'd really like to be there...'

Scialoja walked around the desk and took a seat next to his judge. Borgia watched him, looking baffled.

'Have you ever heard of an individual called Larinese?'

'I vaguely recall that name.'

Scialoja launched into an assault that was as vehement as it was reckless, and the Old Man soon stopped listening entirely. He preferred to focus on physiognomy. The Old Man had a voluminous dossier on Borgia, as well as on many others. Confidential reports, whispered gossip, analyses of his judicial production, the inevitable wiretaps and bugs. He knew, for instance, that the usual trick of accusing the target of being pro-Communist wouldn't work with Borgia. Borgia had no links whatsoever with those hotheads in Magistratura Democratica. He was a man who favoured law and order. A politically colourless moralist, which constituted both a strength and a shortcoming. As for Scialoja, he watched him work himself up, shambolic in his department store suit that barely contained his muscle mass. Unlit cigar clenched in his teeth. General appearance of a spruced-up street thug. High forehead, dark, penetrating eyes. Quite a customer, but he'd already figured that out. A straight-arrow, and that too came as no surprise, with the added and highly meritorious quality of being no stickler for the fine points of procedure. The first time they met, the Old Man had mentally catalogued him as St George in the act of killing the dragon. A warrior with God on his side. Now that he had a chance to study him more closely, he seemed to detect unnoticed gleams, like shafts of light from some cold, internal flame. Less frenzy, more rationality. With a whiff of cynicism. The young man was growing up, becoming a man, losing his innocence. He was studying to be a bastard, and it looked like he was getting high marks.

Taken together, the judge and his cop henchman formed quite some pair. But they still weren't strong enough to screw the Old Man. At least, not this time. It was that they were both missing a certain something. To use a brutal but effective summary that his partners in the agency would actually have appreciated: Scialoja had the balls but lacked the power, and Borgia had the power but lacked the balls. In the final analysis, they were merely one-dimensional men. Loyal servants of the state. Boh.

'Are you quite done?' the Old Man politely enquired, taking advantage of a pause in Scialoja's diatribe. 'Yes? Very good. Now, if you'll be patient, Dottore Borgia, let me tell you another story. The true story...'

The Old Man, with carefully studied deliberation, clicked open the catches on his attaché case and leafed through a slender sheaf of papers.

'I could talk to you for an hour about an agent under my supervision whom I have been forced to relieve of duty for a series of very grave contraventions and because he was suffering from an officially diagnosed case of psychotic depression. I could talk to you about his resentment, about the slanderous rumours that he's been spreading against me for months now...But instead I'll limit myself to handing over these papers. Please study them, employ the diligence for which you are renowned, and you'll see that the whole episode will become clear to you for what it really is: a colossal soap bubble, signifying nothing!'

Borgia had dug in behind an intimidated little smile that looked very much like an *excusatio non petita*, an unasked-for excuse. There was a little bit of Maioli inside every judge, after all. Scialoja, the proletarian, shouted with every ounce of rage in his body.

'You covered up for Moro's murderers! You ordered Larinese's killing! Pigreco has talked! You won't be able to pass him off as a madman!'

'Now that's enough, Scialoja!' Borgia reacted, and added, mildly, to the Old Man: 'Of course, dottore, this is only an investigative theory...'

'I thank you for that very useful explanation, Judge. I certainly hope that your able assistant – whose many fine qualities I have had opportunities to appreciate in the past – would never let himself be swept away by an impulsive fit of improvisation...'

Scialoja looked daggers at the prosecuting magistrate, who prudently looked quickly away. The Old Man was staring at Scialoja. If Scialoja had been able to read the implicit message hidden in his words, this was how he would have decrypted it: not yet, boy, and not entirely. You do know something, but you don't know enough. You're in a tributary branch of the big river. Settle for being there a while, don't overdo it. But the cop was in the throes of possession, control of his mind seized by one of those really demonic imps that reason struggles to control. The Old Man felt a piercing desire to jump into the game. All of this sweet scent of idealism offended his delicate nostrils. The Old Man made a note to intervene at the earliest opportunity. A little bit of healthy filth would only do the young man good.

The interview was coming to an end. Borgia shuffled his papers, and on his drawn, hollow-cheeked face two opposing expressions were swimming into focus: consciousness and relief. Borgia knew that Scialoja had hit a bull's-eye. But the Old Man was offering a satisfactory explanation. The lack of solid evidence exempted him from the obligation to proceed. Scialoja grasped the situation, turned to stone then and there, and stormed out of the room, slamming the door behind him.

Poor little judge! The Old Man was almost tempted to explain where the trick lay hidden. It had been obvious that Olandese's arrest was bound to trigger a chain reaction. He'd been able to make his moves with time to spare. He'd been forced to sacrifice Pigreco, the weakest link in the chain. A successful gambit. The only unknown factor was timing. Borgia and Scialoja had done a clean, above-board investigation. Too clean, too above-board. They'd given him exactly what he needed most: time. If they'd charged in with a warrant before he'd had a chance to fabricate the dossier on the dismissed agent…

The Old Man rose to his feet, bracing himself on the arms of the chair. To Borgia, in that moment, the Old man looked like an exhausted pachyderm in whose watery eyes a sense of regret for his fading energy was slowly drowning.

'Just who are you, really?'

The Old Man fluttered his long white eyelashes, lowered his head, and said nothing. That was, after all, the only sensible question he'd heard so far.

Twenty-four hours later, the investigation into the murder of Larinese was reassigned by the chief district attorney to a young and ambitious colleague.

Over the next ten days, informants popped up, offering names, dates and numbers. In short order, six two-bit ex-cons were arrested. All of them confessed to having taken part in a major armed robbery masterminded by Larinese. They added, however, that Larinese had held back a part of the loot, in violation of their deal. It was never ascertained which of them actually fired the fatal shots, but still, the case was closed.

Pigreco was acquitted of all charges and declared unable to tell right from wrong.

Once the storm had subsided, the Old Man sent Borgia a signed gift copy of Edward Luttwak's *Coup d'État: A Practical Handbook*. A book that, albeit dated, possessed a certain liveliness. On one page there was an underlined phrase: 'A coup consists of the infiltration of a small but critical segment of the state apparatus, which is then used to displace the government from its control of the remainder.'

Here was the answer to Borgia's question. This was what the Old Man had been doing all his life. Controlling. That's what the Old Man was. A controller. Neither right-wing nor left-wing. Without governments to kick aside and replace with faded photocopies. In it for himself. Always and only opposed to that one infuriating obstacle, mankind, which he refused to understand and accept. A controlling anarchist.

IV

NERO WASN'T GIVING up. There must be some way to save Freddo. Once again, he reached out to Mainardi. But the doctor wasn't having any of it.

'I got legal advice! I spoke to my lawyer! All that crap we did when we were kids, it's all long forgotten. There's a statute of limitations! I'm at no risk and I don't want to hear another word about all this nonsense!'

They were in Mainardi's penthouse, high atop Fleming Hill. Nero threw open the French doors and took the young doctor for a stroll on the terrace. Mainardi went on ranting. Nero lifted him off the ground by sheer force and shoved him, shoulders and chest, over the balustrade.

'How far down do you think it is, from here to the street?'

'Put me down! Have you lost your mind?'

'You ought to know, being a doctor and all. What do you think – would it kill you?'

The doctor kept screaming for help and flailing wildly, but Nero, implacably, kept shoving him further over the edge, inch by inch.

'Maybe you'd get by with a few broken limbs. Think of the luck, though, if you were paralyzed! The rest of your life in a wheelchair...Aw, it might not be all that tragic. Look at it from my point of view, with all the lead that I've got in my skull...'

'Put me down, you animal! I'll do what you want!'

'That's what I like to hear, comrade!'

Two nights later, Freddo injected a syringe full of infected blood directly into his jugular vein. The blood came from an Arab covered with sores who wasn't expected to live more than six months. The examining physicians at San Camillo hospital found his lymph nodes swollen, and certified the reliability of the histology slide. Freddo had diffuse lymphatic adenocarcinoma.

Scialoja went to see him in the hospital ward.

'I don't know how you did it, but I know why. You're sick and tired of jail, of your life, of everything... Those are things even a cop can understand. I just wanted to say to you that there are less destructive ways to clear your conscience. That is, if you ever had one...'

Freddo rolled over and turned his back to him.

At the San Camillo hospital, there was no way they'd keep him, what with sixteen policemen standing guard, the whole ward under lockdown, the other patients lodging protests, the danger of a retaliatory attack, the constant confusion... Only two alternatives remained: either release, pending trial, or else house arrest in some medical care facility.

Mainardi offered use of the clinic where he worked. Everything was ready for Freddo's release when a small obstacle arose. They were willing to take Freddo, only on the condition that in exchange, the clinic be given – as a donation, from one or several benefactors – a certain costly piece of medical equipment.

'Just how costly?'

'Forty-five million lire, to be exact.'

'Just think, if you happened to walk out your front door and a – what are they called? – a hit-and-run driver ran over you without even stopping...'

'It's not up to me,' Mainardi hastened to explain. 'It's the decision of the board of directors. But whatever the case, take it or leave it...'

Nero decided to try to drum up some funds from Trentadenari.

'You want to pay for it out of the general fund?'

'That's what it's there for, right? To help the comrades when they're in trouble. So come on, cough up the money!'

Still, Trentadenari hemmed and hawed. It was a serious sum of money. First they'd have to talk to the others. Lately, they'd already spent plenty of money on Freddo. What with his share, medical expenses, miscellaneous and other various outlays, his end had practically all been gobbled up...

'Are you telling me that Freddo's out of money?'

'It's the truth!'

'From video poker alone seventy million lire a day pour in here, and you have the nerve to deny me chump change for Freddo!'

'Don't get worked up, Nero! Maybe I can come up with ten million or so...'

Nero lost his patience.

'I'd like to take a look at your account books, Trentadenari!'

The Neapolitan reacted as if to an intolerable humiliation, ostentatiously and personally offended. Nero blocked the performance before it could run the customary litany. They all knew that in the time Secco had been behind bars and Trentadenari had been in charge of the treasury, he'd battened shamelessly off it, enriching himself enormously. So he could stop trying to be a wise guy. The very stones and pebbles could hardly have missed it. There was the villa on Capri. And the little apartment in Positano. And the three cars in the garage. And the weeks at a time at Punta Rossa with his little candy striper. And the yacht moored at Fiumicino...

'You're talking crazy talk, Nero! You don't know the troubles I have with the law...'

'What troubles are you talking about, you buffoon! You put on that act at the trial, they gave you just six years, and now you're even out on a provisional sentence! Pay up and be done with it!'

Trentadenari paid. The equipment was purchased. Mainardi phoned Nero.

'It's done. Your friend is at Villa Poggioli.'

'You've saved your own life, sweetheart!'

'Can I ask you a question?'

'Of course, doctor, be my guest!'

'You've behaved like a lunatic to get Freddo out. Do you mind if I ask why?'

Nero sighed. 'You wouldn't get it. It's not the kind of thing you'd understand...'

The night the police took Freddo to the clinic, Secco heaved a sigh of relief. With his unshakable loyalty, that kid really was turning into a serious pain in the neck.

As soon as he was safely in the clinic, Freddo wrote to Roberta: *I'm out. I love you. Come to me.*

V

PUSHING AND PUSHING relentlessly, Secco finally did find someone willing to respond to his desperate pleas for justice. A couple of politicos, ravenously eyeing the real estate opportunity on the city's eastern outskirts, clamoured to have Secco transferred to a medical clinic up in northern Italy. A nice little place: quiet, private, courteous staff, unlimited possibilities of communicating with the outside world. A cushy berth, no doubt about it. The waiting room for house arrest, if not complete release.

Secco took full advantage of the opportunity to launch lukewarm initial contacts with Barracuda. The grand accuser was still pissed off – if anything, worse than before – and would always be that way. But the preliminary investigation was dragging out and Secco, with one letter after another, was working incessantly to blunt its sharp edges, promising the moon, the sun and the stars.

Only Dandi was short-changed in the cancer department. Sure, he's sick, the physicians pronounced sagely, but not in such bad shape that he can't be properly treated within the penitentiary's own medical system. Dandi didn't take it all that hard. The trial was about to begin. And he'd already won: inside the courtroom and outside as well. Miglianico guaranteed it. He'd be walking out the front door. Head held high. Acquitted. Or, worst case scenario, slightly the worse for wear.

Once Secco was gone, Scrocchiazeppi and Fierolocchio stopped frequenting the infirmary from dusk to dawn. So Dandi went wandering the halls in his pyjamas in search of news and ran into Ricotta.

'They're pissed at you,' Ricotta said.

'Again? Now what's the matter?'

'The usual things. They say you don't pay enough, that you're all stiff and formal...'

'Did I ever deny you anything?'

'No, never, but...'

'But what?'

'You know what they're like...'

'They're not good, that's what they're like. Not good at all. I'm sick and tired, and this time I've had it, Rico. Not another lira. And if they want to complain, tell them to talk to Trentadenari, because now he's in charge of the treasury!'

Ricotta looked away. Dandi knew what he wanted. But the others kept hassling him every blessed day, and it was hard for someone who wanted to be everybody's friend.

For a few days, the Maestro transitioned through the infirmary. From the day they arrested him, he'd succeeded in arranging one acquittal after another. The only charge still pending against him was a generic accusation of Mafia conspiracy, but soon that indictment, too, was sure to vanish in a puff of smoke.

The same could not be said of Uncle Carlo, who already had two mandatory life sentences that had been upheld on appeal and a pending indictment for mass murder.

'But that's a different kind of man, right there. He watches *La Piovra* on television and laughs out loud whenever a cop gets blown up.'

Dandi confided his worries. The Maestro recommended he watch out for Secco.

'He doesn't have the balls to come at me!' Dandi replied dismissively.

'Maybe not the balls, but he's got brains and venom aplenty. So mind your back!'

Could it be that the Maestro knew what he was talking about? Could it be that it had all taken place right in front of him without him noticing a thing? Now that he thought back on it, the significance of certain glances, certain sly laughter, certain double entendres tossed off as a joke suddenly became clear to him. They'd plotted in the shadows to isolate him. But what was it they were holding against him? The fact that he'd been smarter than them? That he hadn't squandered all his wealth on orgies and bullshit? Ingrates! Incompetents! Idiots! And the way he'd fought with Secco to make sure they got their fair share, to keep the group united...He should have just left them to their fate. Pieces of shit. Half-arsed jerks. And what a bastard Secco was! But if he thought he could hold together an organization with that herd of goofy womanizers...

If only Freddo, the only one who still had his head on straight, hadn't let himself slip into that state of depression...

At last, the trial got started. Ricotta joined Scrocchiazeppi and Fierolocchio in the courtroom defendants' cage. Bufalo, fatter, smiling and tanned, joined them on the second day and was welcomed with warm hugs. They shunned Dandi and Botola as if the two of them had the plague. Only with Freddo did they exchange a few vague waves of salutation.

Dandi sent Freddo long chains of messages via Botola, but Freddo showed up and left stretched out on a gurney, and throughout the hearings he lay there, under a rough cloth blanket with an administrative serial number stamped on the hem, indifferent to the cancan dances of judges, clerks of the court, turncoats, lawyers, wives, girlfriends...

Sorcio talked for three days running, confirming point by point all of the prosecution's claims. Bufalo never listened to a single word. He was studying Dandi, studying Botola, and studying Freddo. Every so often he'd turn to talk intently with Ricotta.

After the interrogation was over, as they sat waiting in the basement holding cells of Piazzale Clodio to be transported back to prison, Bufalo suggested killing Dandi.

'How you going to do it?' Fierolocchio demanded. 'With your hands?' Bufalo, with an evil leer, pulled a long ice pick, with the tip filed razor-sharp, out of his trousers.

'Gift from a friend,' he laughed, winking one eye. 'Conte Ugolino!'

'The one from Dante Alighieri!' Ricotta cried, jumping up. He was clowning around to suppress the panic that was sweeping over him.

'When?' asked Scrocchiazeppi.

'Tomorrow, even.'

'I'm in.'

'Me too,' Fierolocchio joined in.

'What about Botola?' Ricotta tossed out.

'Well, Rico, if he looks on and leaves well enough alone, fine; otherwise, we'll do him in too!'

Ricotta did his best to make them stop and think. This was madness. They'd all get a blessed life sentence without parole. Or did they think they could pass this off as an accident?

'What do I care? I'm mentally infirm!'

'Fuck me, I'm not!' Ricotta baulked.

Bufalo shrugged his shoulders.

'If you're in, you're in, and if you're not, it's your own fucking problem...'

But the idea of life without parole had proved persuasive. Fierolocchio suggested they think it over first for a bit. Ricotta banged on the bars to get a guard's attention.

'Boss, I have to use the bathroom!'

Waiting on his gurney in the lobby was Freddo. In short order, Ricotta apprised him of Bufalo's plan. Freddo shook his head.

'You're not in, eh? Neither am I! It would just be wrong! What, you kill a guy like Dandi just like that? I'm starting to think that Bufalo's crazy for real!'

'I don't give a damn if he is,' Freddo shut him down. 'That's your fucking problem.'

Freddo returned to the clinic. He found Roberta waiting for him. She was wearing a tight cashmere jumper and a short tartan skirt, white tights and flat shoes. Freddo felt his heart go thump, and he ventured a faint, shy smile. His police guards helped him into a wheelchair. Freddo begged them to leave the two of them alone. The cops left the room.

Roberta was standing at the far end of the room. She was beautiful, my God, she was beautiful. She'd never looked so beautiful and desirable to him before now. Roberta waved her hand at the wheelchair, and a film of tears blurred her eyes. Freddo looked around, then he tossed off the blanket and surged to his feet, athletic and lithe.

'You can walk!'

'Of course I can walk. Even if officially I'm on chemo...'

'I thought that…that you were dying…'

Freddo went over to her, took her hand, and ran it over his face.

'It was the only way to get you to come back to me…'

Roberta threw herself into his arms. They exchanged a long kiss, full of things left unsaid. But when he tried to slip his hand under her skirt, she pushed him away.

'My love…'

'No, no, don't touch me. This can't work…There's no future…'

'I'm going to get out of here!' Freddo roared. 'The trial will be over soon. I'll get out, you'll see. And then…'

'Then you'll start asking around for a gun, you'll start working the street again, you'll start seeing old friends…'

'I'm through with them.'

Roberta burst into tears. Freddo gently caressed her hair, breathing in her sweet, delicate scent, and felt a new wave of strength sweep through him. He could do this. They could do this. The two of them together.

He heard someone cough discreetly outside the door. Freddo got back into his wheelchair and covered his legs with the blanket. A police officer stuck his head around the door.

'Are you all right, signora? Do you need something?'

Roberta shook her head no. The officer withdrew. Roberta and Freddo looked at each other and burst into laughter in unison. He could do this. They could do this. The two of them together.

Ricotta had made his decision, in the meantime. When he got back to prison, he asked to see the doctor, and when he got to the infirmary, he spoke to Dandi.

'Dandi, there's trouble on the way!'

'Bufalo?'

Ricotta nodded. Dandi thanked him, promised a million lire to the male nurse on duty and called Miglianico's law office from the infirmary office phone.

'I'm in trouble. Let Zeta know.'

'I'll take care of it, don't worry.'

Cliffhangers, Escapes
1986

I

A YOUNG WOMAN DRESSED in a black leotard came to open the door. Tall, slender, with large hazel eyes and a swarm of tiny freckles illuminating her décolletage, and a generous pair of breasts. Scialoja, at a loss, was frantically trying to come up with some explanation when Patrizia appeared from behind her. She, too, was wearing a black leotard.

'It's all right, Palma. He's an old friend!'

The girl stood aside with a perplexed look. Patrizia explained to him that Palma was her yoga teacher.

'Just let us finish our class and I'll be right with you, darling. Why don't you get comfortable.'

The two young women moved off, leaving a penetrating scent of woman and sweat wafting in the air behind them, and stirring naughty thoughts in Scialoja. He dropped heavily into an uncomfortable little armchair. The place looked different. Cosy softwoods had taken the place of the solid marble. Signed canvases by noted artists had given way to batiks illustrating the war of the Pandavas from the Mahabharata. Everywhere the air was filled with a hint of incense. Patrizia was probably in the throes of some Eastern mystical period.

For some time after Dandi's arrest, they'd seen each other on a regular basis. As secret lovers experienced in subterfuge, they'd spent afternoons enjoying electrifying sex, rarely if ever exchanging a word. They used hotels, motels and borrowed apartments. Never, by tacit agreement, in that house. But then he forced himself to stop desiring her.

Under Arjuna's furrowed brow, Scialoja mechanically lit a cigarette.

He sucked down half of it in one angry breath. His average varied between two and three packs a day. On weekends he shifted over to cigars. He hadn't been to a gym in months. More and more these days, he heard an unsettling whistling sound deep in his lungs. He looked around in a futile search for an ashtray. There was nothing. Even the knickknacks and accessories seemed to have disappeared, with the exception of a small, potbellied laughing Buddha who appeared to be blessing the room from a vitrine high on the wall. Desolate emptiness. So Scialoja stubbed out his cigarette butt and pocketed it. Guided by the echoing sound of diffuse panting, he ventured deeper into the apartment. On a carpet spread lengthwise across the hardwood floor, the young women were holding the 'downward-facing dog' position: arms extended forward, spine straight, bottom in the air. As if in offering.

He thought he'd glimpsed a sardonic glance from Patrizia, and he hastened to look elsewhere. Palma leapt up, visibly annoyed.

'This isn't right. You're interrupting our focus!'

Scialoja withdrew prudently. The girls came out immediately afterwards. Palma was angry.

'We can continue the lesson tomorrow,' Patrizia said apologetically.

'I'm subpoenaed for a deposition tomorrow.'

Palma collected her things and stole away without bothering to say goodbye. Scialoja watched the scene from his uncomfortable perch on the little armchair.

Patrizia went over to him and kissed him delicately on the forehead, enveloping him in her scent.

'I'll just take a shower and then I'm all yours, handsome.'

He squeezed her arm tight.

'I'm leaving.'

'Are you finally taking a holiday?'

'I'm being transferred to Genoa.'

'To do what?'

'Chief of the DIGOS.'

'Ah, politics! Maybe you can do something to help out Palma. You know, she was in the Red Brigades, and now she's trying – how do you say it? – to rebuild her life, rejoin society…So I'm giving her a hand.'

'Are you two close?'

'Very.'

'She's jealous of you.'

'Prison will play strange tricks on people.'

Patrizia sat in his lap. He plunged his face into her breasts. She caressed his hair. They sat there, sinking one into the arms of the other, for time without end. His superiors had given him forty-eight hours to make up his mind.

To judge from the appointment letter, they seemed to consider him as a sort of saviour of the fatherland. The offer: promotion to assistant chief of police, supervisory position, lots of paper-pushing and public relations. He would oversee the work of underlings. Report directly to the two or three high muckamucks who happened to be in office. Safely steer clear of the mud of battle, evidently on the road towards ambitious summits.

Word had spread rapidly. Colleagues glared daggers at him. Scialoja: another typical example of a brilliant career studded with failures. Workmates theorized a political move on Borgia's part. Grey eminences somewhere moving pawns to abet him. All nonsense. The truth was that there was someone in Genoa who thought highly of him. Nothing more.

'You have a few grey hairs,' Patrizia said suddenly.

'And your hair is dark again.'

'You noticed!' She laughed happily.

Patrizia's hand slipped under his shirt. Scialoja started licking at the drops of moisture all around her neck, until he reached the musky hollows of her armpits. Patrizia moaned.

He thought back to the smile on Dandi's face when he'd questioned him about Larinese's death. A benevolent smile, almost a smile of camaraderie. The camaraderie of two men who were bedding the same woman. It was all wrong. It had been all wrong, from the very first time.

They made love with a strange tenderness. He tasted in her a soft languor that spoke to him of peace, crystal-clear sea water, and limitless freedom. Afterwards, he felt like asking her: will you miss me? But he held back. It was fine the way it was. Patrizia insisted on throwing the I Ching coins for him.

'I don't understand what the hell you're all trying to find in the Far East,' Scialoja snapped. 'Maybe you're just looking for a religion that will allow you to do whatever you want and ignore the voice of your conscience!'

'Nero says that yoga is the mother of all virtues.'

'Nero is a stone-cold killer.'

'You see killers everywhere.'

'And you pretend not to see them!'

'Anyway, ever since I started doing yoga, I've been sleeping really well, and fucking even better.'

'Clearly, you've finally found your place in life.'

Patrizia recoiled, stung by his bitterness. He suddenly felt like asking her to forgive him. To hold her in his arms and rock her until she turned back into a little girl. Or into one of those plush toys that he'd seen so many years before, in the lair of a person so different and yet so similar. To tell her quite simply: it's all right, it's all right, I won't ask you a thing...

She picked up the coins and tossed them, eyes shut.

'Look! *Siau Kuo* – Preponderance of the Small!'

'What the hell does that mean?'

'Read it.'

'Success. Perseverance furthers. Small things may be done; great things should not be done. The flying bird brings the message: it is not well to strive upwards, it is well to remain below. Great, good fortune.'

'It's a sign of retrenchment,' Patrizia explained.

'Does that mean: forget about it?'

'It says: "He who in times of extraordinary salience of small things does not know how to call a halt, but restlessly seeks to press on and on, draws upon himself misfortune at the hands of gods and men, because he deviates from the order of nature..."'

'Bullshit! Why not ask your sacred book whether I ought to leave town or not?'

Patrizia looked him in the eye, suddenly serious.

'It says here that first you should talk it over with Trentadenari.'

II

DAY BY DAY, Freddo was steadily getting poorer and poorer.

What with Vasta's retainer and fees, the bloodsucking charges for the clinic, the gifts to policemen who turned a blind eye, and more often two, he'd already had to sell off two luxury cars, an off-road vehicle, his motorcycle, and even his Rolex. He entrusted the various items to Nasello, a coke-hound hospital orderly, who took care of actually finding buyers. Nasello was an honest soul who limited his take to 15 per cent of the net profit.

Freddo still had a couple of apartments and his parents' villa. But that was property he couldn't touch. Out of the question. If it kept up like this, he might even have to find work!

Trentadenari had clipped 30 per cent off his monthly share. Official justification: the grumbling of the other gang members about the expense of the 'sophisticated medical equipment'. Take it or leave it. Trentadenari was behaving like a jackal. But Freddo didn't care. Money aside, life wasn't bad. The controls were discreet; the medical examinations, under Mainardi's supervision, watered down at best.

Freddo had broken off all contact entirely with his comrades behind bars. From the day that Roberta came back, he'd stopped attending his hearings. He was planning for the future. And if there was a sore point, it was exactly that. Roberta came to see him every day at the clinic, the minute she got off work. They'd make love, watch TV, smoke a joint, order in dinner from a restaurant, or else she'd show up with a hot boxed pizza, and Freddo would sink his teeth into oozing hot Pettinicchio mozzarella cheese and drink warm beer with the enthusiasm of the kid he'd never been. But inevitably the conversation led back around to the same point.

'Let's leave,' she was saying. 'Get your friends to help you, and we'll just go somewhere else.'

'But where?'

'Anywhere you like. You can sell your house and apartments...'

'That's out of the question!'

'I have a little money of my own set aside...'

'That way I'll wind up on the list of people to track down and our lives

447

are over. You don't know these people. They'd hunt me down any place on earth!'

'Why don't you just get plastic surgery?'

'You've been watching too many American films!'

For Roberta, the idea of running away had turned into an obsession. She couldn't figure out for the life of her why Freddo should be so obstinate. But he wanted to get out clean. Vasta had guaranteed he'd get a mild sentence. He'd be able to walk out with his head held high. They'd start a new life together. In their own city, Rome. Freddo couldn't imagine living anywhere else.

One day, Nero came to pay a visit. He and Roberta had never met. Freddo introduced them light-heartedly.

'Roberta, I'd like you to meet my only friend. Nero, I'd like you to meet my only woman!'

Roberta considered, with a certain coldness, that courteous and good-mannered young man who every so often lost his balance because of the lead he carried in his body. To her, anything that belonged to Freddo's past constituted a danger.

'I need to talk to you,' said Nero in a serious voice. Freddo glanced at Roberta. She picked up her handbag and slipped through the door without a word of farewell.

'Good-looking woman,' Nero commented.

'I still haven't thanked you for...'

'I think we've had this conversation a couple of times already, Freddo.'

Freddo offered him something to drink. Nero shook his head no. They remained in silence for a while. Nero had something important to tell him. He was trying to find the best way to begin. Freddo lit a cigarette. Nero decided to cut to the chase.

'Leave.'

'What?'

'Leave. Get out of here. In two days' time, I can have the passports ready for you. If you need to sell something off, I'll take care of it for you.'

'What are you talking about? Vasta guaranteed that—'

'Vasta is full of shit,' hissed Nero, harsh and cutting. 'You want to know how the trial's going to end? Dandi and Botola will get a couple of years each and Bufalo, at the very worst, partial mental infirmity. All you others? They're going to bury you in prison. It's not looking good, Freddo.'

'Yeah, I know about that, Bufalo and Dandi, and all the rest of it… But I'm out of it by now…'

'You're not out as long as you're still in, Freddo. There's going to be a bloodbath. And in the end, the coldest and cruellest of them all is going to take the cake. Trust me. Take your woman and vanish!'

'It's all over, isn't it?'

'That's right.'

Freddo felt a sense of relief. It was strange. The idea that everything could turn rotten would once have filled him with contempt. How far away he was from all that now!'

'Nero, I—'

'Just leave, Freddo. You're not a shopkeeper, you're a warrior. Get out, while you still can.'

'You've already made your decision, haven't you?'

Nero gestured vaguely. They embraced.

'I love you, Nero.'

'Yeah, me too. But you need to leave.'

III

DANDI REJOINED THE trial after two months' absence. He'd spent that time holed up in the infirmary, guarded night and day by Botola and a couple of Moroccans who cost him a million lire a day and were strictly good for window-dressing. Everyone knew perfectly well that if Bufalo had decided to make a determined move on him, they would have taken to their heels and left him defenceless. And his phone calls to his lawyer cost him another million. He was bleeding himself dry, but this was a decisive match. The dispute had to be settled in some way. He needed something he could toss into the pot, to up the ante. Out on the street, things were falling to pieces. To hear Nero tell it, by now Trentadenari was stealing openly and greedily. He'd caught a whiff of the atmosphere behind bars. He was thinking about retirement, the sleaze. But Bufalo was showing no signs of life. In the end, his fellow gangsters had gotten cold feet.

'Let's just say that there's been a reprieve on the death sentence,' Fierolocchio summed up the situation.

Bufalo was foaming at the mouth with rage. What he should have done was gut-stab that bastard Dandi first thing without warning. On his own. Without getting any pant-wetters involved in the job. Not that Dandi hadn't considered striking the first blow himself. But Miglianico kept telling him to keep cool. That Zeta was hard at work on a solution.

Dandi made his first appearance back at the trial on the very day that Borgia began his summation. The night before, Zeta had given him the go-ahead. Dandi asked to be put in the same cage as the rest of them. Mutterings and snickerings greeted his grand entrance. Fierolocchio drew a finger across his throat in a slicing motion. Bufalo grabbed at his balls. Ricotta moved to form a human barrier between Dandi and the others.

'Have you lost your mind?'

'I'm going to the bathroom now. Come in one at a time.'

'Bufalo too?'

'No. Not him.'

Dandi summoned the police escort and had them open the cage. As he was descending the steps to the basement, he saw Ricotta talking intently with the others. Bufalo was vigorously shaking his big head. But in the end, one at a time, they all followed Dandi down. The squad leader left them unattended in the front wash-up area of the bathrooms.

'All right, what the fuck do you want?'

'Yeah, what the fuck do you want, traitor?'

'Pickpocket.'

'Cocksucker.'

'I'll rip you open, arsehole!'

'You bastard.'

Dandi let them get it off their chests, then he announced, in a tranquil tone of voice, that one of them could escape. They all stood open-mouthed with amazement. The first to recover was Ricotta.

'One of us? Why not all of us?'

'Because the people who are helping me can't handle any more than one.'

'And just who would these "people who are helping me" be?'

'Friends. Friends on the outside. Well?'

'So why didn't you ask Bufalo?' Scrocchiazeppi provoked him.

'Because he's going to get himself a declaration of mental semi-infirmity and he'll be out in five. No muss, no fuss.'

'This is a con job,' Scrocchiazeppi snarled. 'He's taking us for suckers!'

'And to think that I was planning to do you the favour, of all people!' Dandi replied sarcastically.

'And why me in particular?'

'Because that would mean that for once and for all you'd stop spouting your bullshit. And because I've always liked you so much...'

Scrocchiazeppi remained speechless. But it was clear that the proposal interested him.

They'd finally stopped insulting him . It was as if the age-old hold Dandi had over them all had begun to glitter again.

Ricotta snorted. 'Dandi, let's just...let's say I went. Then what would happen to me?'

'From the minute you escape, that's your business. In here, whatever you do, it's hard jail time. But we can play on the amnesties and the time off for good behaviour, plus a new law on prisons is coming down the pike. It's your choice...'

'Is that what your lawyer told you?'

Dandi nodded. Ricotta was torn at the prospect of having to choose.

'Say they give me, I don't know, thirty years – how much do you think your lawyer can get taken off the sentence?'

'Calculate fifteen, sixteen years off the top.'

'I'd almost be tempted to stay in...'

Scrocchiazeppi gave him a shove.

'It's a trap, comrades! Don't listen to him! Maybe he can get one of us out of here, but the minute the guy's out, they'll kill him!'

'What good would that do me?' Dandi countered.

'What good does it do you to help me escape? Why don't you take the opportunity, then, if it's such a sure thing?'

'Because they're going to acquit me,' Dandi replied, calm and confident. 'Or at the very most, I'll serve three, maybe four years.'

'What a slick operation! They haven't even handed down the verdict, and he's already out on appeal!'

'You win appeals in hallway sidebars is the way it works, Scrocchia.'

451

'So how come you have hallway sidebars and we have to face the judge in the courtroom?'

'Evidently, I'm smarter than you.' Dandi sighed. 'All right, I'm sick and tired of all this. Make up your mind.'

'I'll go,' said Fierolocchio.

Dandi said it didn't matter to him. He would have preferred Scrocchiazeppi, who was a tougher, more resilient enemy. But that was fine too.

Scrocchiazeppi spewed out some more bullshit. Fierolocchio told him to go to hell. Borgia had just demanded life imprisonment without parole. But now the decision had been made.

'So when is this for?'

'Today. Listen carefully...'

When the hearing was over, instead of shackling and chaining Fierolocchio like the others, they just slipped an ordinary pair of handcuffs on him without locking them tight. All it would take was a twist of the wrist and he could slip out of them without help.

The prisoners trooped off towards the basement. Fierolocchio brought up the rear. In the bathroom wash-up area, where they'd negotiated with Dandi, Fierolocchio hung back. Nobody paid him the slightest attention. He waited for the line of prisoners to move off, then slipped out of his handcuffs and went back into the courtroom.

Judges, lawyers, officers and the public had all cleared the room. There were just two men standing in the litter of crumpled paper, in the miasma of cigarette smoke and foot stench. They were waiting for him. They swung open the gates of the courtroom cage after turning a brand-new key in the lock, flanked him, and nonchalantly hustled him out of the Hall of Justice, scooting right past the bored gazes of the policemen standing guard. A third man was waiting for them in the parking area in Piazzale Clodio, at the wheel of a nondescript Peugeot. They waved for Fierolocchio to climb into the back seat.

'All right then,' the driver asked in a cheery voice as he started up the engine. 'Where are we going this fine day, Scrocchiazeppi?'

'Listen, get one thing straight: I'm Fierolocchio!'

The expression on the man's face changed immediately. He shot a

452

worried glance at the other two men, muttered a curse under his breath, and jerked the car into gear and out into the afternoon traffic jam.

Fierolocchio took fright and curled up on the seat. But nothing happened. They dropped him off half an hour later at Torrimpietra and told him, if he was caught again, not to say anything about them. He should tell them that he'd taken advantage of a guard's momentary distraction and just cut and run. That was it.

Fierolocchio made his way to a public phone box and placed a call to his bereft little widow.

'It's me. I'm out!'

The evening television news headlined the escape. Chief theme: alarm at the unbridled power of organized crime. Ricotta opened a bottle of champagne in Dandi's honour.

'Friend, you're the best! The first guy I·hear say a word against you, I'll cut his dick off!'

Scrocchiazeppi and Bufalo had a furious argument and stopped talking to each other. Scrocchiazeppi, overwhelmed by shame and anger, cut his forearms and spent the night in the hospital.

Borgia put in a phone call to the Old Man, but a courteous secretary regretted to inform him that the dottore was in Istanbul attending a European summit conference on security.

The following day, when the trial resumed, the prosecuting magistrate publicly accused the intelligence agencies of having arranged the escape. Dandi, enthroned between Botola and Ricotta, shot Bufalo a mocking little smile every time their glances crossed.

IV

FREDDO BROKE OUT the night that the rest of the world was riveted by the horrifying story of the nuclear cloud over Chernobyl. For a week now, Borgia had replaced all the police officers with much scarier-looking individuals. Maybe he sensed something coming.

Freddo had spent the last three days in bed. They'd equipped him with a sheath urinal. He was refusing to take food. He was raving. In his delirium, he was invoking Libano and his mama. He'd been chewing tobacco and castor oil seeds procured by the male nurse Nasello in order to make his fever spike.

Mainardi came to see him every three hours. He'd walk out of the room, gravely shaking his head. In the presence of the squad leader, in a fairly audible voice, he informed Roberta that the patient hadn't long to live. Roberta played the role of the sobbing young widow-to-be. The squad leader, overwrought, offered to send for the next of kin. Roberta soaked him with salt tears and, with a touch of class, managed to persuade the leader to send an officer to see her home. It was just too much, poor little thing, to ask her to tolerate so much pain.

The squad leader drew up a detailed service report and got in touch with the prosecuting magistrate, requesting further instructions for the now imminent autopsy. When the time came, Freddo plugged up the toilet with a bundle of rags, stuck a couple of fingers down his throat, and vomited onto the blankets. Then he let loose with an interminable, heart-breaking howl. The police detail hurried to summon Mainardi. Freddo kept on vomiting. The doctor said that there was a suitably equipped bathroom on the ground floor.

Freddo was loaded on the gurney and transported downstairs. Mainardi accompanied him into the bathroom. Freddo stripped off his pyjamas. Underneath he was wearing a pair of jeans and a clean shirt. He didn't want to show up filthy for his big appointment with freedom. He shook hands with Mainardi and then hit him in the jaw, hard enough to leave a nice, visible mark. He climbed out the window. Nero was waiting for him outside in a car with the engine running. The doctor had left a gate open and unguarded.

Then they were gone, rocketing away into a springtime that smelled of exhaust fumes and almond blossoms: the odour of resurrection.

The newspapers progressed from outright alarm to open derision: law and order leakier than a sieve; security below zero; and the judges, of course, guilty for everything that had gone wrong. Soft on crime, with a weakness for the civil rights of criminals. Could they seriously have taken a mob boss at his word when he said he didn't feel well? Oh, right: first they were all rending their garments in pity, humanitarians that they were, because the poor fool had a case of diarrhoea. And now that Freddo had flown the coop, the same judges were swearing up and down that they'd known all along what he had up his sleeve, no doubt about it! If it had only been up to them…

The angriest of all was the district attorney. This big a cock-up could really cost him his office. He summoned Borgia and gave him a proper dressing down. He wasn't about to get set up as the fall guy.

'There should have been better security measures. Two prisoners gone in a single month. Disgraceful. We're a laughing stock!'

'We'll look into it.'

And they did look into it. They detailed a mixed squad of carabinieri and police officers on a round-the-clock basis. They planted microphones. They bugged telephones. They tailed family members and lovers. They even busted the chops of Vasta, but he icily told them to go to hell. Freddo was nothing but another client, and it's not like he ever went to bed with his clients. All pointless, in other words.

Roberta came in to the police station and reported her fiancé's disappearance. She was worried. She was afraid, she told the police, that his old friends might have killed him. The officer on duty phoned Scialoja. Scialoja told him to take an official report of this criminal complaint and then let her go.

When he heard what had happened, Borgia flew into a biblical rage. Outside the office, everyone could hear him shouting that they should have arrested her, indict her for aiding and abetting a known criminal, put the screws on her, for the love of Christ.

He sent for Scialoja. Scialoja sent word back that he was out on a duty call. Borgia peppered him with a hail of notes. No answer came back. Scialoja had no time to waste. Certainly not with Borgia. He hadn't renounced his shot at Genoa just so he could sit around wasting time. They'd been close, tantalizingly close, to the heart of the system. So close that they could sniff at the rotting corruption, distinctly smell the stench. And that was when Borgia had decided to pull back. The judge couldn't bring himself to believe that this horrible stench really existed. He'd refused to acknowledge its existence. And Borgia was one of the best!

Could Scialoja ever bring himself to forgive his boss for it? It didn't really matter. The right question was: what would he do the next time? Scialoja imagined a less direct strategy. It would be the sheer force of things that would take him once again to the Old Man. One more time, straight to the heart of the system. And at that point there would no longer be any room for hesitation. His winning card was named Trentadenari. He'd been to see him. Twice. He'd looked into his eyes and read what he found there: fear and betrayal. But when he'd finally brought himself to offer the man a deal, in violation of every rule in the book, shredding the last fragments of proper legal process he was still draping himself in, the Neapolitan had merely shaken his head.

'That's not going to work, dotto. They're still too strong!'

But he'd been proved wrong. With the rest of the board of directors behind bars, Trentadenari was left standing as the absolute master of the situation. Had he taken advantage? No doubt. His sense of ethics was hardly his finest quality; that is, if he even had one. But that wasn't the important thing; what counted most was the fact that the others were certain that Trentadenari was stealing from them.

Scialoja knew that they were in control of the prison. He'd identified a few prison guards who were the subject of a steady buzz of gossip, and he'd confronted them with the hard facts: collaborate, or jump out the window. That didn't leave the guards with a lot of options.

Now prison radio was openly accusing Trentadenari of theft. Two men, absolutely trusted operatives, shadowed him everywhere. The order: watch, don't intervene, no matter what happens.

They'd shaken the branches of the tree. The fruit was bound to fall, as soon as it was ripe. That's why Scialoja had given up Genoa. For this. And, of course, for her.

V

THEY, TOO, WERE looking for Freddo. Both Dandi and Bufalo were doing their best to establish contact with the fugitive. Freddo on the loose was an invaluable trump card to play in the game they were trying to win. Either an invaluable ally or a dangerous enemy; the important thing was to figure out which of the two.

For Roberta, this marked the beginning of a period of intense visits. Bufalo sent Scrocchiazeppi's sister to see her; Dandi, through Ricotta, sent Donatella.

'I don't know a thing about it,' she replied, predictably. 'I'm sorry.'

Trentadenari, on the other hand, went to see her in person, after a long and circuitous detour to make sure he had shaken the officers who were perennially on his tail. From the minute Freddo made his escape, Trentadenari had been living in terror. The policeman's visit had done nothing other than crank up his fear to breaking point. Recently, he'd made a shambles of the general fund. There were no problems with Fierolocchio. He'd dropped by to collect a handsome dividend and then he'd cut and run. Now he was out of the country, on the Côte d'Azur. Sooner or later he'd run out of money and then he'd show up again.

But with Freddo it was an entirely different matter. Freddo wasn't the kind of guy who'd swallow his bullshit. Trentadenari was seriously considering dumping everything and going on the run. His cousin Baffo di Ghisa had told him about a *fazenda* in Brazil. Bright sunshine, bananas, cocaine and tropical beaches. With the money he had socked away, he could leave tomorrow morning. That is, if he managed to make it all the way to the airport in one piece. That is, unless Freddo broke out with the specific intention of murdering him. Still, there might be a way of striking a deal.

Roberta let him talk and, after listening to him, unlike all the others, she answered neither yes nor no. Trentadenari had shown up with a briefcase full of cash. That could always come in handy. Freddo had given her very specific instructions. She told him to leave the briefcase and promised that, if she had any news for him, she'd get in touch.

Freddo was resting up and regaining his strength in Comrade Cerino's Trastevere penthouse. Cerino was an old friend of Nero's. A man above suspicion. Cerino really was a comrade. What channels had led him to become a friend of Nero's remained a mystery. Cerino had a full-time job, but he'd taken a leave of absence. Cerino knew who Freddo was, but he asked no questions. Cerino was depressed: his wife had just dumped him. He spent his hours watching TV and playing solitaire.

Freddo was waiting for the hurricane to subside. He had passports and a little cash. Nero had arranged for a book of traveller's cheques. Cerino would happen to bump into Roberta along certain agreed-upon stretches of the Rome metro, or else he'd pick up with an air of distracted interest a copy of *Il Messaggero* left lying on a bench in the park of Villa Pamphili, read Roberta's message, destroy it, then report back.

Freddo was sitting, gazing at the television screen, when the verdict was handed down. As Nero had predicted, Dandi's group got off relatively lightly. Bufalo had once again been judged insane. For everyone else: a bloodbath. Thirty years to Ricotta. Twenty-six to Scrocchiazeppi. Between five and eight years apiece for horses and ants. For Freddo and Fierolocchio, declared fugitives from justice, eighteen years each. Puma got fifteen, and so did Carlo Buffoni. It could have been much, much worse; most of the murder charges had folded on the grounds of lack of evidence. Evidently, the judges had made up the difference with the criminal conspiracy charges and the drugs.

The sole consolation: the court had pounded turncoat Sorcio good and proper. Freddo felt no resentment. If, at the right moment, he'd had better luck, Sorcio wouldn't have caused trouble for anyone, and his own life would have followed a different path. But would that have necessarily been a good thing?

In the middle of the summer, Nero showed up at Cerino's.

'We're done tailing people. It's on, for tomorrow.'

'I won't see you again...' Freddo said.

'I hope not, for your sake!'

Roberta picked him up the next morning at nine, driving a rented BMW. Cerino had refused to take so much as a lira for arranging the meet. He was just sad to be going back to his life of loneliness.

They crossed the Swiss border and drove straight to Frankfurt. Freddo had lightened his hair. The guard at the security desk focused on that skinny blond South American. El Señor Neto-Alves, stated the passport. Something about the high-strung gestures of the well-dressed woman travelling with him had aroused his suspicions. Freddo sketched out a smile and pointed at his wristwatch. A chorus of mutterings rose from the line snaking away behind them. The guard shook his head as he handed back their passports.

Roberta only managed to relax once the Boeing lifted off the tarmac. Then she grabbed Freddo's hand and squeezed it tight.

'Are you sorry?'

'No.'

'You've given up everything...'

'I still have you.'

'But we're penniless!'

'We're so rich, my love.'

VI

AFTER THE ACQUITTAL, Bufalo was sent back to the insane asylum. Before leaving Rebibbia, he'd dropped by to say so long to Ricotta, who was plenty depressed about the unexpectedly harsh thirty-year sentence.

'Well, Rico, now that the Gozzini law has passed, you'll see, they'll give you a little discount too!'

'Dandi tells me the same thing...'

'If he says so!'

'What can I tell you? The way I see it, you're making a mistake, Bufalo!'

'Maybe so. In any case, I wanted to tell you thanks!'

'I thought you were pissed off at me!'

'What are you talking about? You saved me!'

Bufalo said that he'd been a thousand times right to oppose his plan. Killing Dandi in prison would have been an enormous fuck-up.

'I have plenty of ideas, there's no shortage there,' he confided, in an impetus of sincerity. 'The problem is, I'm always in too much of a hurry. And when I stop to think, I realize that if I just give it a few minutes' reflection...'

'Sure, it's all water under the bridge,' Ricotta said brightly, filled with hope. 'I say that this is the moment to make peace...'

'If it were up to me,' Bufalo sighed, 'but Scrocchia's furious!'

'I'll talk to him myself!'

'All right, take care, brother!'

'Same to you!'

Sure, time to make peace! Ricotta was so naïve. The thing was, either you did things right, or you might as well not do them. Half measures were what ruined the world. Acting on impulse. Still, what kind of Bufalo would Bufalo be without his headstrong impulses? Sure, it was time to

459

make peace: but peace with oneself. Find a middle ground between the urge to act and the resources available. The first attempt had failed. The second one would have to pay off. There would be no third chance. Cunning, poison and patience. He needed to learn from Secco.

In the insane asylum, Bufalo ran into Conte Ugolino and Turi Funciazza again. The Tuscan was packing his bags. After five years, they'd decided he was no longer a menace to society. Bufalo found himself on the verge of suffocating, wrapped in the man's massively powerful embrace. Conte Ugolino was getting out on Friday, and he'd already planned a nice little Saturday night armed robbery.

'A rich moneybags with a villa in Versilia…You know the way these things are: I'm having cash-flow problems!'

Turi Funciazza, on the other hand, was rather depressed. The judge had refused to give him a miserable five-day leave of absence, on account of outstanding charges. Bufalo, cautiously, let him know that he had a certain amount of cash he was willing to invest in heroin.

'It can be done,' the Sicilian nodded, 'but not from in here…'

'Sure.' Bufalo winked. 'Freedom is a good thing. And not just for this!'

Miglianico was rubbing his hands together, proud to have pulled off a historic coup.

Dandi knew that even if the appeals court upheld his original conviction, it would fall under the statute of limitations in no more than another seven or eight months. And he'd already practically served the sentence. But still, he wasn't a bit satisfied with the outcome.

'Well, I sure expected a little more gratitude!' Miglianico said.

'Why? Bufalo got released as crazy because he was crazy to start with. Ricotta was screwed anyway because they caught him red-handed. Freddo and the others had taken a beating. If this was the brilliant outcome, we might as well have stayed with Vasta!'

Miglianico looked offended. 'What did you expect? What did all of you expect?'

'You said you had all the judges in Rome in the palm of your hands!'

'Not all of them. Some of them. Not these judges, for instance.'

'We haven't won, Counsellor. We'll only have won once they drop the criminal conspiracy charges…'

Because, Dandi thought to himself, now that he'd made a name for himself, now that Bufalo had been sent back to rot in his insane asylum, and now that Freddo, according to Nero, was enjoying life on a sunny beach somewhere in the Caribbean – now the criminal conspiracy charges needed to die. And what was needed was a genuine death, real in every sense of the word. Legally sound. They needed a certification, black and white, that they'd never been a gang. That was the only way to ensure that his plans would have a future.

Miglianico was starting to understand. 'You're asking a little too much of me...'

'With the money I pay you, it strikes me as the very least you can do. You say that you've got the brotherhood? Well, get busy, no?'

It was because of this decision that, when he heard about Secco's acquittal, Dandi sent a message to Nero.

'Give him my regards. For real.'

With all the things that Secco had done to him, he'd decided to spare his life a second time. Because he needed him. There was a clearly defined role for Secco in the new life he had in mind for himself, for Patrizia, and for all those who were close to him. In the meantime, until he could get out from behind bars, everything needed to keep going along just as it was. There would be no more unseemly episodes like what had happened with Bufalo. He needed to maintain an appearance of absolute reliability. Nasty rumours were circulating in prison about Trentadenari. It was time to act. And that was why he entrusted another message to Nero.

'Trentadenari – he needs to be cut down to size. Now he's taking things too far.'

Trentadenari was in a foul mood. The whole thing with Freddo had been a rip-off, good and proper. He'd been afraid that Freddo was out to kill him, and instead the slick bastard had screwed him out of two hundred million lire, and now he was living the good life at his expense. He'd run into that cop two or three times, at a café along the Via Laurentina, while he was trying to track down an out-of-control horse, to straighten the bastard's back for him. All the cop did was smile at him with that mocking monkey face of his, as if to say: *curre, curre, ma 'ddo vaje?* You can run, but you can't hide. Sooner or later, *acca' 'a ferni'*, you'll wind up here, you'll have to deal with me.

461

No, it was time to leave, no question. The moment had arrived. But Vanessa was putting up resistance. She was afraid to stay and she was afraid to go. Afraid of the present and afraid of the future. Afraid of everything, even her own shadow. And it was a paralyzing fear. They couldn't go on like that. Their days were spent in unrelenting tension. He kept trying to talk her into it, and she kept advancing one pretext after another.

One night, as he was returning home after signing in at the police station as required by the terms of his release, someone shot at him from a moving car. If they'd been trying to kill him, they'd never have aimed so high. He thought he'd recognized a familiar silhouette inside the car.

The next morning, he went to see Nero. He found him doing yoga, immersed in the revolting aroma of incense. He tried to sell him the puppet show that he'd dreamed up over the course of a long night of paranoia, snorting and drinking like a lunatic. The essence was this: possibly, in the last few months, his accounts were a little tangled. But he'd been left so alone and for so long! Alone with the responsibility for the treasury, running the dealing operation all by himself, and with all the mess going on behind bars...But there was no question about his loyalty. And if there was anything that Nero had a problem with, why not discuss it openly, the way men of honour have always done?

Nero let him have his say, finished his yoga exercises, then stared at him with his chilly eyes.

'What are you talking about, Trentadenari? I don't follow you...'

'Someone took a shot at me last night.'

'Really? It must have been some drunk. In any case, when a person keeps his promises, why, then he has nothing to fear!'

Trentadenari understood that things were looking black. In fact, blacker than the blackest night. He decided to step up the timing. If Vanessa didn't want to come with him when he asked nicely, then he'd just kidnap her.

There was one last shipment of product to place – thirty ounces of Peshawar that he'd left with a lowlife from Tor Bella Monaca, Cocciamuffa – shit that belonged to the gang, but after all they'd done to him, they didn't deserve a lira from the deal. He had the treasury, he had the shit, he had the documents. What was he waiting for? He put in a phone call to Cocciamuffa and told him to sell it all that same night to the Calabrians from Montagano.

'But those guys only pay half our rate!'

'Who the fuck cares? I want the money here by midnight. Go on, get moving!'

What Trentadenari didn't know was that for the last few weeks, Scialoja had been 'cultivating' Cocciamuffa too. The officer in charge of phone taps picked up the call at 7.30 that morning. At 9.15, a squad car alerted from Giardinetti pulled up outside Cocciamuffa's house and a team of cops knocked at the door. The hoodlum put his hands up, pulled the dope out of the water tank high above the toilet, and spoke a single, devastating phrase:

'I'm just small fry, dotto. The one who pays me is Trentadenari.'

'Well, you don't say!' shot back Scialoja with a sharkish smile.

They picked Trentadenari up that same night. When he saw his apartment being overrun by policemen under Scialoja's command, the Neapolitan was suddenly reminded of the miracle of the liquefaction of the blood of St Gennaro – the blood that looks like a solid brick, but the moment always comes when it dissolves. A message from God Almighty.

'Take me to see the judge,' he implored them.

Borgia came charging into the district headquarters at dawn. He found Scialoja, his face carved in stone, waiting for him. The two men stared at each other, then Borgia extended his right hand. Scialoja shook it warmly, vigorously. No comment needed. Time to start over.

'Dotto.' Trentadenari smiled. 'I'll tell you everything you want to know, but you have to forget about Vanessa!'

Individuals and Society
1987

I

CIVIL AND CRIMINAL TRIBUNAL OF ROME
SPECIAL SECTION FOR REVIEW OF CRIMINAL PROCEEDINGS
IN THE DOMAIN OF PERSONAL LIBERTY OF PERSONS UNDER
INDICTMENT OR INVESTIGATION
CRIMINAL PROCEEDING NO. 5/87 RGPM

THE TRIBUNAL
issuing a verdict on the writ of re-examination submitted by
the counsel for the defence of (redacted) versus the arrest warrant
no. 5/87, executed on (redacted), having heard the arguments of
both parties, notes as follows:

The subject of the current review consists in its entirety in the consideration of the statements of (*redacted*), also known as – significantly – TRENTADENARI, or Thirty Pieces of Silver, with a clear reference to the character from the Gospels responsible for the betrayal of Our Lord Jesus Christ. He is an individual who has been involved with shameless determination in numerous serious crimes but who has now, unexpectedly and inexplicably, found himself suddenly and surprisingly driven to 'collaborate' with law enforcement authorities. In fact, of course, the 'repentance', whether real or alleged – unless it is rooted in a full and genuine awakening of a social and moral sensibility and maturation, impossible to determine from the case before us here – is reduced, unless actual lies are being foisted off

465

upon the judges, to a mere bartering of the individual's freedom for that of others (in the case that the informant is providing true information), and therefore to the attainment of a significant personal benefit, substantially driven by the placement of his own private interest well above that of others, which would make of it yet another demonstration of the same mental attitude that underlay this individual's initial decision to embark on a life of crime.

This fact demands that we show extreme caution in our acceptance of the declarations in question, and tips the balance in favour of a scrupulous scepticism with regard to their veracity. (*Redacted.*)

We must ascertain that the interest in 'benefits' and advantages has not produced false statements concerning matters determined to have been of special interest to the investigators. (*Redacted.*)

We must eliminate the unpleasant, but unavoidable, sensation that the 'collaborator with the law' might not have seized this opportunity to take justice into his hands, inflicting revenge on real or supposed enemies. (*Redacted.*)

What is needed is a painstaking and thorough investigation on each of the points premised in revelations (*redacted*) while taking into account that no valid indicator of credibility can be drawn from the gravity and number of facts deduced by the source and proven to be accurate: how is it possible to know with any certainty how many facts the source really knows and how many he might have remained silent about, and whether he might have suppressed the most important facts that are the most prejudicial to his interests? (*Redacted.*)

Numerous and significant discrepancies emerge between the judicial investigation just completed by the Court of Assizes of this city and a number of statements made by (*redacted*), also known as TRENTADENARI. In fact, there are so many discrepancies that they prompt the more than legitimate suspicion that the very statements in question were intended not to promote the course of justice, but rather to contaminate the trials now underway.

To an even smaller degree can (*redacted*) proof of truthfulness on the part of the prosecution be drawn from the level of detail in the accounts and the inclusion of many elements that are either true or plausible, even where they correspond to the ascertained events of the episodes in question that have been described, because, in any case, there are no elements of direct and immediate verification for the roles attributed to the various individuals by the deponent.

It is not enough to say that John Doe or Richard Roe possessed a certain vehicle that was actually noticed by witnesses in the context of the murder of John Stiles in order to deduce from that fact that John Doe and Richard Roe necessarily took part, as reported, in the murder in question. (*Redacted.*)

Last of all, it should be pointed out that correspondences concerning location, methods and timing of the execution of murders, and the meetings and contacts between the various subjects, can actually be misleading elements, inducing the investigation to circle around the true events without ever penetrating into the facts, to pursue the plausible while losing sight of the actual truth. (*Redacted.*)

THE TRIBUNAL ERGO REVOKES
the arrest warrants issued by the prosecuting magistrate against (*redacted*).

Trentadenari wasn't believable because he was a gangster and had no conscience. Trentadenari wasn't believable, full stop. As if they were supposed to investigate underlying psychic motives! Sure, as if a turn coat witness – a *pentito* – was a shrinking violet. If he was a shrinking violet, what the hell would he have to tell us? Fuck all! He was invaluable precisely because he was foul, corrupt to the bone, rotten, filthy. The more bloodstained his hands, the less he could give a damn about it. Why was it that this logic seemed obvious when you were talking about terrorists, but the minute you started talking about major criminals, everyone seemed to turn into so many daughters of the Virgin Mary, trembling like leaves?

Borgia realized that he'd committed a decisive error. When they'd laid hands on the Neapolitan, he'd redoubled his efforts, consecrating himself to his work, body and soul. Now he believed in it. He once again believed in justice and therefore, finally, in himself. He'd accumulated night after night without sleep, carving a perilous trench between himself and his

467

wife, just a step or two short of waking up one day, puffy-faced and abandoned. He'd caught a whiff of a wind of redemption and, perhaps, even a chance to gather up the threads of that close legal reasoning that had been thrown into disarray by the all-too-convenient truth that he'd allowed the Old Man to slide down his throat like a glib tissue of horseshit…

A tragic, indelible error. Four months of painstaking investigations shot to hell by a skimpy little screed. And one more time, everyone was set free. Except those who had been found guilty and sentenced. Perhaps the appeals court would take care of them, in the end. And, in extreme cases, the Court of Cassation. He'd learned that Uncle Carlo never missed an episode of *La Piovra*. Someone had heard him say that Dottoressa Silvia Conti was a woman with serious attributes. In a moment of dismay, when he received news of his fifth or sixth life sentence without parole, he'd murmured that, if there was such a thing as reincarnation, this time he'd choose to be a prosecuting magistrate.

But actually, the logic needed to be reversed. It was he, Borgia, who'd chosen the wrong profession. He should have become a Mafioso. Beautiful women, plenty of cash, villas, yachts. And, above all, social approbation. Sumptuous dinners with individuals above all suspicion. Maybe even in the notorious restaurant where, it was whispered, the Old Man had installed a sophisticated surveillance system to blackmail his most distinguished guests. And the greatest possible delight of all: gripping a bunch of lawyers tightly by the balls, crushing their heads, worms that they were.

Sick and tired of nodding his way through the endless outburst, Scialoja recommended Borgia take a nice holiday.

'Holiday? Tomorrow I'm resigning. But first I'm going to look those fine experts of the law right in the eye and I'm going to nail them to the wall.'

'Don't talk nonsense. The last thing I want to have to do is arrest you.'

'You or someone else…Maybe, if I'm guilty, I'll get by. If fact, I'll get by because I'm guilty. You know the story about Pinocchio and the judge?'

'Take a week off. Go to Punta Rossa with your wife.'

'That might be a good idea. But first I have to pass the civil service exam…'

'What civil service exam?'

'The civil service exam to become a notary. I start studying tomorrow.'

Scialoja shot him a vague smile. 'You want to become a notary! You!'

'Why, what's so strange about that? Notaries earn good money and, generally speaking, they live to a nice ripe age. No one bothers to organize to get rid of them. No one waits downstairs for them with a shotgun, ready to riddle them with lead. I've reached the age when a man needs to take care of his family. And as far as I'm concerned, the investigation is dead!'

II

THE INVESTIGATION WAS dead, no doubt about it. But the turncoat bastard was still alive and kicking. He needed to be rubbed out. Every day that bastard went on living was another slap in the face to them all. All of them, no one excluded. In the presence of such a filthy pig, there were no rifts that couldn't be overlooked. Fierolocchio had come back especially from the Côte d'Azur. He and Nercio were standing watch outside the bunker-like house on the outskirts of Morlupo, where Trentadenari was enjoying the delights of house arrest. Both men were armed to the teeth. Fierolocchio was thrilled to have the smell of battle in his nostrils. Nercio, fresh out of prison, was in a black fury. But the challenges facing them looked insurmountable. Borgia had deployed four squad cars packed with cops, with a shift change every six hours. Two officers on each shift lived with Trentadenari. They did his grocery shopping for him and kept an eye on anyone who came any closer than a hundred feet from the house. An authentic fortress.

Nercio lit a joint. 'We should do like Cutolo did, that time he planted a bomb under the seat of the turncoat who was trying to dig a grave for him.'

'Were you there?'

'That's where I come from, don't forget it.'

'But you still stank of mother's milk!'

'That just means I got started early!'

They went back to watching. If only they could spot a gap in the security system. The tiniest little distraction could offer them their opportunity. It wouldn't take much time, just a few minutes, even though they'd all much prefer taking their time with this job...

'Those friends of mine up north in Milan, when they catch an informer, first they cut off one hand, then the other. Then they cut off his dick and stuff it in his mouth. At that point, if they're feeling charitable, they give him a mercy bullet in the head...'

'If they're not?'

'If they're not, they all take a nice long piss and then they toss the miserable bag of bones into a vat of muriatic acid. Bullets aren't cheap, after all.'

'Absolutely. That's the way to do it,' Fierolocchio said.

'Every so often they find out later that the poor sap was totally clean after all...'

'And then?'

'And then nothing. There was a whiff of suspicion. And a whiff of suspicion is more than enough, don't you think?'

'Aw, I couldn't say, but with Trentadenari, there's no doubt about it!'

'No, no doubt whatsoever...Hey, take a look at who just showed up!'

It was Vanessa. Trentadenari had treated her with tender loving care as if she were his child. Not a word about her in any of the depositions, and no question that there would have been plenty to say!

Borgia, however, who had a pair of balls on him when it came to being a judge, had arrested her anyway, along with the rest of them. And so the little candy striper had enjoyed the benefits, like all the rest of them, of the benevolence of the Tribunal of Liberty. Now here she was. Nercio clicked off the safety and aimed his rod.

'Hey, take it easy. At this distance, there's a good chance of missing your shot!'

'I've never missed a shot in my life!'

'But how do we know she had anything to do with it?'

'What do I care! She sleeps with him, doesn't she? What more do you want?'

Nercio took careful aim. A police officer walked between him and his target. The street door of the row house swung open a crack. Another police officer stuck his head out, grabbed Vanessa, and pulled her inside. Nercio let his arm drop.

'Now we're going to have to wait for her to come back out.'

But Fierolocchio wasn't convinced. Nercio looked at him pityingly.

'Oh, I get it. You're not up for shooting a woman!'

'What are you talking about? I...well, I never have...'

'Well, as far as that goes, neither have I. But what does that matter? She's not just any old woman. She's the traitor's woman!'

'Maybe we should talk it over with Dandi...'

'If you don't feel up to it, why don't you go get some sleep? I'll take care of it on my own.'

'What, you think I don't have the balls for this?'

The door swung open again two hours later. The officers reprised their pantomime. Vanessa headed off down a long and winding avenue. Nercio and Fierolocchio had already identified her Alfetta, and they were waiting in their Range Rover. Vanessa turned the car around and headed back towards Rome. They followed her with headlights doused.

'Maybe she has police protection too!'

'You'd like that, wouldn't you, Fierolo?'

Vanessa led them back to Trentadenari's old apartment.

'That's just crazy. Either she feels safe or she's incredibly reckless!'

'I don't like this. I'll go in. You keep an eye out. If something happens, you cut and run.'

Nercio snapped open the lock and went upstairs to the third floor. He knocked on the door with the knuckles of one hand.

'Signora, it's the police...'

Vanessa hurried to the door, wrapped in a pink bath towel. She saw Nercio and the muzzle of the semi-automatic, turned pale, and tried to slam the door. Nercio shoved her aside and was in. In the tussle, her towel fell to the floor. Nercio stood rooted to the spot. He'd never dreamed she could be so lovely. A piece of pussy to dream about. The scent of a woman that could make anyone lose their mind.

'I had nothing to do with it! It wasn't my idea! He did it all on his own! I wanted to warn you, but they caught me before I could. Nercio, you tell the others...I'll do anything you tell me to do...I beg you!'

'Come here.'

Vanessa stepped forward uncertainly. Nercio holstered his weapon.

'Come here. Don't be afraid...'

471

Nercio started unbuttoning his shirt. Vanessa gave him a timid smile. Nercio lunged at her and stuffed his face between her large breasts.

Fierolocchio had fallen asleep in the Range Rover. Nercio banged on the glass. Fierolocchio jerked awake, pistol in hand. Nercio let him see it was him. Fierolocchio noticed the girl and his face darkened.

'So we're going to do it somewhere else?'

'It's all cool,' Nercio reassured him. 'She's clean. And now she's with me!'

Fierolocchio burst out laughing. If he'd ever dreamed of this finale, all hugs and kisses, he would have stayed at home on the Côte d'Azur.

III

DANDI AND BOTOLA were ordered to be released from prison on their appeals decision. Their guilty verdicts were upheld, but by now they had done their extra jail time. Sentence served in full, it's been good to know you.

Botola would have been happy to settle for that outcome.

'I'll keep the guilty verdict and time served and to hell with it!'

Dandi had other plans. He wanted to start a new life. The way Freddo had. But not in a rush. Not leaving the country on the run. As a wealthy gentleman, not as a penniless bastard. As a respected citizen, not as a fugitive being hunted by the police forces of half the world. All of the cash piled up over years of shrewd, intelligent administration of his assets would serve one single purpose: the erasure of the scarlet letter G for gangster.

Ever since Borgia's last blitz, Dandi had come to believe implicitly in Miglianico and his cohort of experts. The pitiable fate that had been visited on Trentadenari's depositions was one sure and eloquent sign of the power of his new allies. They'd have to take it all the way to the Court of Cassation to demolish the criminal conspiracy charges. His criminal record would have to become as spotless as the driven snow once again.

Dandi was sick of police intrusions and search warrants, and the cash he had to spend on fronts and shell companies. He was sick of having to carry a stack of false medical certificates and bottles of life-saving capsules to wave under the nose of the mobile squad in case of unexpected arrest. He was determined to never again set foot in prison.

Dandi wanted to be in charge of all his business interests himself. And they would be perfectly legal business interests. Or practically legal. After a reasonable period of time had gone by, that is. At first, there might still be a certain grey area, but then, after that…In the meantime, the important thing was to make a sharp break with the past. Some transitions might be thornier than others. But Dandi had too much respect for his own worth to worry about the complications.

Two days after he got out of Rebibbia, he ordered a meeting at the Full 80. Secco was there, more flaccid and unctuous than ever; so was Nero, all twisted and grimacing at the pain caused him by the change of seasons; Botola, with a Borsalino hat on his head that would make you die laughing; and Nercio and Vanessa, who were now a regular couple.

In just a few words, Dandi explained the situation.

'The corporation is dissolved. The dope dealing is assigned to Nercio.'

'How much do you want?' Nercio asked.

'Nothing.'

'Nothing?'

'Nothing. You take the network and the suppliers and run them as you see fit. Including Secco's contacts and every other conduit into the market. But from now on the people you have working for you are your problem. You decide whether to give them a share, and if so, how much. Do what you think's best. We're out of it. Starting from today, the dope is no longer any of our concern.'

Before Nercio accepted, he asked to have a few details cleared up. Dandi told him that they were still friends, and if needed, they could help each other out. But no more general fund. No more partnership. No more reciprocal obligations. They hugged. Dandi kissed Vanessa on the cheek.

Nero asked about the video poker circuit.

'Just the same as it always was,' Dandi reassured him.

Nero nodded.

Dandi remained behind, alone, with Secco. Dandi lit a cigarette and blew the smoke into Secco's face. He knew how much Secco detested the odour of tobacco. Secco coughed.

'We're walking away from a lot of money, Dandi.'

'Are you talking about the drug dealing? We don't need it anymore. Gambling brings in more and we're not facing twenty years in prison for it. Let me take a look at the accounts...'

The fat man laid open an imposing ledger book and started blathering on about investments, loans, guarantees, surety bonds, payments due and collectable, stocks to trade in. Dandi asked him exactly how much the capital amounted to.

'I don't get the question...'

'If I decided to sell everything today, how much would I get?'

Secco named a figure. Dandi furrowed his brow.

'Is that all?'

'Look, if they were to draw up a ranking of the richest Italians, we'd be near the top...'

'We?'

Secco mopped away a drop of sweat.

'I was just talking about our money, obviously...'

'And I was just talking about my own money, obviously...How much is mine, and how much is yours?'

'Well, just like that, here and now, how could I say...?'

'Listen good, now: exactly half of everything – and I mean everything – transfer it now to an overseas account in Gina's name. When it's all ready, I'll bring her here and she'll sign. The rest of it, keep it moving like always. But half of every lira that comes in, from every new and old deal, I want it to go to that account. Got it?'

'Eh, no, that's highway robbery!' Secco blurted out.

'Oh! Look at Secco now! Try to touch his wallet and all of a sudden he grows a pair of testicles! What wouldn't you do for money, eh, Secco? Traitor!'

Secco closed his eyes and clutched the armrests of his office chair tight. But Dandi had no intention of laying hands on that filthy tub of lard. He laughed and lit another cigarette. Secco made an effort to come up with the right words. His tone of voice became courteous, even humble.

'So you're still pissed off about what happened behind bars?'

'Me?'

'But you know I had no alternatives! You know what Bufalo's like! I pretended to be on his side to avoid even worse trouble. Dandi, I just don't know how to live in prison!'

'You poor little thing!'

'But now that you're out...it's all okay, right? We'll do exactly what you tell us to, and...'

Dandi stopped laughing. His eyes turned icy.

'Just remember that you're alive only because you're useful to me, you piece of shit. And only as long as you stay useful!'

But with the Maestro, there was nothing Dandi could do. They were in a cinema featuring old films, almost the only spectators enjoying *Once Upon a Time in America*. Dandi had chosen it at the lawyer's suggestion. Miglianico was right: it wasn't a brand-new film, and it was full of exasperating slow patches, but it was about them. About an hour or so into the picture, it was clear what was going to happen. James Woods was obviously going to fuck Robert De Niro. Woods had finally had enough of De Niro's bitter loyalty. He stank of defeat. It was as if the director had taken his inspiration from Freddo. Dandi saw himself as the winner in the film. But the finale was all wrong. All that wallowing in remorse! If he'd ever managed to kick the shit off his shoes the way James Woods had, the last thing on his mind would have been remorse!

Patrizia had brought a girlfriend. But the Maestro didn't deign to look at her. A strange man. A rock-solid fidelity to his wife, a drab little woman who almost never appeared in public. If Dandi thought that sex was going to brighten the Maestro's mood, he'd miscounted his cards.

After they left the cinema, they put the girls into a cab. Dandi and the Maestro went to Piazza Navona to drain a large whiskey nightcap together. Dandi said that he'd been giving a lot of thought to the film business. He hadn't been kidding around, all those years ago, with that famous director.

'You want to become a producer?'

'Why not? It could come in handy for you, too. A clean, classy way to move money.'

'The film business is in trouble. It's just losing money, everywhere you look.'

Dandi reeled off one project after another and the Maestro shot them down mercilessly. Dandi was starting to think it might be tougher than he'd expected. The Maestro stared at him with a baffled expression.

'So in other words, you're trying to get clear!'

'What are you talking about? I...'

The Maestro lit a cigarette and heaved a sigh.

'I understand you. Really, I do. I've had the same thought. Lots of times. Why do you think I'm so in love with my baby boy? But getting clear...it's just not possible. No way!'

The Maestro explained to him that he didn't care in the least about his relations with his old partners.

'But things are different with us,' he contined. 'This is something that involves me personally. I vouched for you...'

'Look, the real estate deal goes on as before. There's no question about the money. Nothing changes. It's just that—'

'It's just that,' the Maestro interrupted firmly, 'you don't want to get your hands dirty anymore...'

Dandi nodded. The Maestro laid his cigarette down in the ashtray and took a sip of his whiskey.

'If you're ordered to move a kilo of shit tomorrow morning, then you have to do it. And if it's necessary to do someone a favour – any type of favour, for anyone – you have to do it.'

'I know the rules, Maestro, but—'

'And if you fail to do it, if you fail to behave properly, then someone else has to do it in your place. Usually, whoever vouched for you has to do it. And even in that case, there's no guarantee that afterwards – for both people; both the voucher and the vouchee – things don't end badly!'

'You seem to be forgetting that I'm not a made man!'

'That's exactly why you can't say no.'

'What about if someone else took my place?'

'Who?'

'Nercio. I gave him the dope-dealing circuit...'

'Nercio's no good. He's too impulsive. The bosses don't like him. There were things that happened down south…It can't be done. I'm sorry, Dandi…'

Dandi understood that no matter how far he pushed, he'd never be able to break the meshes of that net. And a wave of helpless fury washed over him. The Maestro tossed him a lifeline.

'I'll make mention of your situation. They might even let you go. It's happened before. Just don't do anything stupid!'

'I'd never dream of it!'

'And one more thing…'

'Yes, I'm listening.'

'You're one lucky fellow, brother. If Uncle Carlo were still out on the street, tomorrow morning you'd wake up in Prima Porta cemetery!'

IV

CORRIERE ROMANO

The Mafia? The Government Finds it Comes in Handy!

Commissario Nicola Scialoja of the judicial police shares his views with our correspondent, Sandra Reynal

Rome

27 December 1987

Commissario Nicola Scialoja, a highly placed official in the judicial police, stops a waiter and orders his third martini of the evening. A crowd of fetching starlets takes the Club Hemingway by storm, the place on Via delle Coppelle that has lately become the favourite hangout of the Eternal City's film and political elite. The noise is deafening. Scialoja cocks an appraising glance at a blonde fashion model wrapped around a famous film producer. The waiter comes to the table. Scialoja throws back his cocktail in a single gulp and immediately orders another. Our compliments on the way you hold your alcohol, commissario! I turn on the tape recorder.

Q: Commissario Scialoja, for years you've been stubbornly stitching together trials against the so-called 'Roman Mafia'. A few months ago, the courts dropped all charges against forty people you ordered arrested at one fell swoop, declaring that the accusations were fanciful. Who is right? You or the judges?

A: If the Tribunal of Liberty had applied the same standards to the Red Brigades terrorists, Moretti would be out on the street today. Those judges quite simply didn't know how to read the documents. Or even worse, they did read them and decided to turn a blind eye.

Q: That's a serious accusation.

A: What happened was a serious thing. Still, I can appreciate your question. You're accustomed to thinking of judicial error as something resulting in the arrest of an innocent person or, worse, their conviction and imprisonment. Instead, every day the exact opposite is taking place: we're setting free genuine criminals.

Q: I understand your point of view. After all, you are a policeman. But I choose to go on thinking that it's preferable to let a hundred guilty men free than to see a single innocent man in jail!

A: I respect all opinions.

Q: Well, that's nice to know! All the same, voices come from all sides objecting to the general decline of judicial respect for civil rights. People don't want to live in a police state. That's why so many people are hailing the imminent passage of the new criminal code...

A: Many? Who? Are you referring to the Mafiosi who are dancing in the streets? The corrupt politicians who can finally heave a sigh of relief? The lawyers who'll make their millions sliding through the cracks in criminal procedure? You can have them, all these fans of the new trial system!

Q: And yet, thanks to the new trial procedures, Italy will finally catch up with the most advanced European standards...

A: You want to know when we'll really be European? Once we're free of the perverse connections between politics, organized crime,

478

corrupt entrepreneurs and out-of-control intelligence agencies. Once this cancer has been uprooted – if it ever can be...

Q: Are we really such a basket case, commissario? I'm sure you know that just a few months ago, Italy rose to the ranking of the fifth-biggest industrial power in the western world!
A: If you say so...

Q: It wouldn't happen to be that you're just resentful of your country because if everything is moving along in an orderly fashion, an ambitious policeman has less of an opportunity to advance his career?
A: Listen to me, and listen carefully. We were just one step away from the rotten heart of the whole affair. Just one single step. We'd happened onto the trail by pure chance, in an investigation into the murder of a two-bit organized crime soldier. We discovered unbelievable things. A thread that ran from what I call the 'Roman Mafia', linking the assassination of Aldo Moro, the bombing of the Bologna train station, a ten-year-long chain of murders, leading finally to the bunker headquarters of a special branch reporting directly to the intelligence apparatus of the Italian state. A department that officially doesn't exist, with a phantom director who is at the crossroads of all the biggest mysteries of our country's recent history. And we were about to rewrite that history. Then...someone decided to pull back. The names are of no importance. They made it clear to us that it would not be possible for us to push past a certain threshold. That someone got the message and complied obediently. And now we're back where we started. This country may very well be wealthy, as you point out. But deep down, it's rotten, believe me!

Q: Rewriting history! What an ambitious goal! But don't you think that the idea of rewriting history falls outside the bounds of the duties of a magistrate or a policeman?
A: Since nobody else seems to be doing it...

Q: So we're in the heart of the realm of conspiracy theory then, aren't we? You sound just like a representative of the opposition. And yet you know that for years, a certain political party has stubbornly insisted on pursuing the theory of 'state massacres'. Unsuccessfully, so far...

A: Listen, I'm a servant of the state. I can't really imagine the government planting bombs and knocking passenger planes out of the sky. But one thing is certain: whenever a spectacular crime takes place, the intelligence services we're talking about seem to be capable of reconstructing the background and assigning guilt in a remarkably short time. That is, assuming they didn't know all about it in advance. Whatever the case, exactly what would the responsible – and the legal – requirements be for a government body that had information about serious criminal acts of violence? Prevent the violence, if possible; punish, if it proved impossible to prevent. The first thing to do, in any case, would be to put all available information into the hands of the judiciary...

Q: And that isn't what happens?

A: Never. If they know in advance, they never intervene. If they find out afterwards, they work to cover it up. If they really have no other options, they overwhelm us with hot air: meaningless, contradictory papers, ambiguous documents, disinformation campaigns...

Q: Couldn't it be nothing more than a matter of shoddy performance, amateurism, a loose adherence to duty? You know that there's a vast and amusing body of literature concerning our security agencies...

A: It's a goddamn trick. They pass themselves off as fools to keep from paying the price. In reality, they're genuine scoundrels.

Q: Why on earth would they do such a thing?

A: Broadly speaking, they're political considerations. They want to maintain order. Keep the general situation under control. Make sure nothing really changes. Bombers could turn out to be useful. So they do nothing to stop them. They use them. They pet them and caress them. It's all a function of anti-Communism. The initial driving force was fear of the Reds. Personally, I haven't voted in years. But I'm horrified at the idea that, just to keep people like Amendola and

Berlinguer from gaining power, our government finds itself becoming bedfellows with murderers and assassins. Protecting drug traffickers. Giving money to neo-Fascist terrorists. Giving the Mafia a free hand.

Q: Is that what the government is doing?
A: Yes. Anyone who has the slightest impact on the marketplace is immediately co-opted. Once they no longer know what to do with them, they unceremoniously dump them. As I was saying, that's in broad outlines. Then there are others who play these questionable games for love of risk or danger.

Q: You don't say!
A: Listen, at certain levels, the exercise of power becomes an art for its own sake. People go on out of inertia, or because it's too late to turn back, or because it's just too much fun to move the men on the chessboard. The ultimate ends – if there ever were any – fade, vanish, are lost from sight. What survives is only a vast, tragic game…If I think back to certain police officials I've had an opportunity to meet, people who live in the shadows and dress in grey, the only comparison I can think of is Dr Strangelove. You remember the film by Kubrick, no? Bombs for bombs' sake, for the sheer love of the bomb, or something like that…

Q: Perhaps so. But let's get a little more concrete. What do you think of the increasingly common opinion, according to which the Mafia – or the Mafias, if you like – are endemic presences and we have no choice but to coexist with them?
A: You don't take cancer out to dinner. You do everything you can to uproot it.

Q: Do you think that that's something that can be done?
A: The right question is another one: do you think that anyone wants to do so?

Q: That's a little provocative, don't you think?
A: The Mafia's very useful. Lots of people make money off it.

481

Q: Listen, someone like you, with such a black outlook on current affairs – have you ever given any serious thought to the idea of looking for another line of work?

A: Nothing could be further from my mind! I'm keeping my job and moving forward!

Q: And what lies ahead for you, if you don't mind my asking?

A: I want to screw as many bastards as I can.

Nicola Scialoja, chief commissario of the judicial police, is a man who never experiences doubt. Italy, in his view, is a democracy with limited sovereignty, dominated by an oligarchy of corrupt men, mass murderers and Mafiosi, bound together by the cement of anti-Communism. His determination is impressive. His faith in his own professional ability appears as unshakable as it would seem to be ill-founded, at least to judge from results achieved. The history of Italy – the history of a country that approaches the last decade of the century solid, intact, rich and flourishing – slides past him and he, indifferent, twists it to fit his own highly personal vision of things. Scialoja is a man obsessed with evil. We can understand him – he must have seen plenty, in his professional life! – but that certainly doesn't mean we can justify him.

As a citizen, I am frightened at the mere thought that such a man has the power to determine my fate.

Sandra Reynal

V

TWO HOURS AFTER the Sunday supplement of the *Corriere Romano* hit the newsstands, Scialoja was suspended from duty. His statements had set off an institutional bomb. Parliamentary inquiries were being rapidly organized. The highest officials of the security agencies had issued fiery statements. The chairman of the Commission on Massacres was agitating for an immediate hearing. Colleagues from Palermo and

Milan, concealed behind the cover of anonymity, had let it be known that, however critical they might be of the way Scialoja had done it, they fully subscribed to the content of what he had said.

The lawyer hired in haste and hurry by the policemen's guild recommended Scialoja issue a flat denial, followed by a lawsuit against the journalist and her paper. Scialoja explained to him that that wouldn't be possible: the article was accurate down to the last detail. He'd met with the journalist, he'd had too much to drink, and he'd said everything she quoted him as saying. He'd said those things because that was what he believed.

'If that's the case, we haven't the slightest chance of saving your career. We can drag it out, but sooner or later you're going to have to pay.'

Scialoja unplugged his telephone. Now his bed was impregnated with the scent of Patrizia. It was cold out, but she'd refused to let him turn on the radiators. It was dark, but she preferred to keep the lights off.

Patrizia had rushed over to his apartment after seeing the afternoon television news report. She was wearing a red jumper that emphasized the carefree lines of her breasts and a soft tartan skirt. Her hair was pulled back to the nape of her neck, and there wasn't a speck of make-up on her face. She looked like the classic girl next door. A sweet, upstanding, kind-hearted girl next door, eager to console the suffering hero.

With his head plunged into her lap, Scialoja told her as little as possible. Once upon a time there was a girl named Sandra Belli. She'd travelled to Paris and made her fortune there. She came home with a new last name and a prestigious job – a correspondent for a major daily newspaper. She'd thanked him for a certain favour he'd done for her once, long ago. He'd modestly said it was nothing, really. They'd spent an enjoyable evening together, with maybe a little too much to drink. Then she'd made a fool of him. And now he was screwed.

'But why'd she do it to you? You helped her out…'

'Maybe someone asked her to do it. Maybe one of your friends.'

'Not likely. I'd have heard about it.'

'Or else maybe she just couldn't stand the idea that she had a debt of gratitude towards me…'

'You ought to smash her face in.'

'What good would that do? The damage is done!'

Patrizia couldn't wrap her head around his resigned attitude. It was almost as if he were happy, as if a burden had been lifted from his shoulders.

'What are you going to do now?'

'I don't know.'

'We could take a holiday together. Let's go somewhere. Like that time we went to Positano…'

Scialoja stroked her cheek.

'Patrizia,' he said in a whisper, 'when I saw Sandra again, after all these years, the first thought that came into my head was to take her to bed and sleep with her. I would have given up ten years of my life to have sex with her…'

He felt Patrizia's body stiffen in the darkness. He sensed her urge to run away from him. He grabbed her by the wrists. He held on to her, hard.

'I thought about the two of us, me and her, in bed. In this bed, or in a hotel, or in a doorway somewhere, or on the back seat of a car… What does it matter where? All night long, I couldn't think about anything else. Her coming back and me fucking her. And Sandra's not the only one. It happens to me all the time, you know? More and more often. With all the women I meet. I'd like to take them all to bed…'

Patrizia shoved him away, firmly.

'I don't want to stay here, listening to this…'

'But you have to,' he resumed, still in the same tone of voice, 'because in all these other women, I only see one woman. You.'

'I want a cigarette,' she said softly. 'I want something to drink.'

'You're the only woman I want.'

'You can have me whenever you want.'

'But I'll never be able to be the most important thing in your life.'

She slid, shivering, out of bed. She grabbed her fur coat and handbag, then lit herself a cigarette.

'You know where to find me,' she said in a flat voice.

He let her leave.

Two thugs from Campo de' Fiori brought her back to Dandi in the middle of the night. Her left eye, half-shut, was swollen and bruised blue.

'She was putting on a show with a sailor on shore leave and it was a good thing the barman recognized her, otherwise she'd have been arrested sooner or later. We had to get a little rough with her because she didn't want to let go of the guy...'

Dandi surveyed, with a sense of some distaste, her torn jumper, the stockings with stepladder runs, and the penetrating rancid and sickly sweet odour that came wafting off her, and then gave the thugs his blessing.

'One more thing, Dandi...'

'What now?'

'The Jaguar... You should see what a wreck it is!'

'The upholstery's torn to shreds.'

'The car radio's been ripped out.'

'Someone even pissed in it.'

Dandi cocked an eyebrow.

'Fine, okay, I get it, now get the fuck out of here!'

Drunk beyond all decency, completely out of her gourd, a crazed, malicious smile altered Patrizia's features. And that phrase that she kept repeating, between the repetitive laughter and the persistent belching:

'The most important thing in my life! The most important thing in my life!'

Dandi knew that there were times when the best thing to do was nothing. So he let her vent. Anyway, how long was it likely to go on, the shape she was in?

After ten minutes of that goddamned litany, Patrizia fell flat on her face on the wall-to-wall carpeting. Dandi undressed her and put her to bed. To see her like that, naked, filthy, lips chapped, hair dry and wispy, breathing laboured – especially with how important appearance was to her, the way she still insisted he shower every blessed time – it made Dandi unbelievably horny. He started to take his clothes off. After all, she belonged to him, didn't she?

Then Patrizia moaned softly, like a little girl crying, and his desire vanished, only to be replaced by a blend of pity and regret. He went off to hibernate on the six-foot-long sofa that he'd just picked up from the furniture shop in Via del Pellegrino. Still, she'd be paying for the upholstery in the Jaguar. With her own money.

The Certainty of the Law
1988

I

NERCIO LET THE guys behind bars know that, as far as he was concerned, they could still consider the agreement to be in force. But they could forget about the good times they'd gotten used to. Trentadenari's betrayal had not been entirely without consequences. Junkies were notoriously less than lion-hearted when it came to that sort of thing. Some of them had been lost along the way. Others had taken that long one-way junkie trip via overdose. The drug-dealing network would have to be reorganized and reinforced with some of the boys from Primavalle. Their share of the turnover was going to plummet sharply.

Scrocchiazeppi indignantly rejected the offer of charity and started looking around for people to do some dirty work. Scrocchia still enjoyed a modicum of prestige, but there wasn't a soul willing to listen to his plans. There was no going against Dandi. Even the worst Moroccan desperadoes said no; even the gypsies who weren't afraid of anything or anybody, not even Christ; even the most worn-down junkies, including the certified psychopaths. He'd whipped them all into line. He was the top. He was number one. The one and only.

During a transfer for a court hearing, Scrocchiazeppi found himself in the same prison van as Bufalo.

'When I get out, I'm going to kill Dandi,' Scrocchiazeppi said.

'If you get out...How much did they give you?'

'Who cares? Wait to see what the Court of Cassation has to say.'

'Damn, Scrocchiaze, you've got some fangs on you! Too bad that last time, when there was some biting to do, all you did was bark!'

'And you're so good at talking, what are you doing? Giving up?'

'Maybe I've turned pacifist!'

Scrocchiazeppi had always been too much of a talker. But threats were just hot air, if you didn't know how to put them into effect. All that threats were good for was to keep your enemy nimble.

But Bufalo had his own plans. Secco was keeping him informed of the situation. Dandi was quickly getting a swelled head, losing touch with reality. Excellent, excellent. Secco was paying. Generously and without any questions. As far as that went, the money was actually his. Let him just try and pull a move! No, no, everything would take care of itself in good time.

In the meantime, the security provisions were giddily running out, past their expiration dates. The Court of Cassation didn't really scare Bufalo all that much. At the very most, they'd confirm his ten-year sentence. He'd already served nearly five. He was the uncontested boss of the insane asylum. The only ones who could claim to be his peers were Conte Ugolino, who came and went, and Turi Funciazza, who was just hoping for the ultimate hair-splitting objection to spare him the unavoidable life sentence without parole. The three musketeers, they were. Champagne, unlimited phone calls and, a couple of times a month, whores procured by the Tuscan. It was a good way to stay in practice. Otherwise, Bufalo scrupulously followed the prescriptions of the medical commission and hadn't incurred a punishment since 1986. At the end of every session, the doctors complimented him for the progress he was making. He could already feel it in his gut: the scent of freedom. And that nasty thorn in his back that had tormented him ever since he was a boy – day by day it hurt less and less.

Fierolocchio got himself arrested, like a fool, at the widow's house, because fate seemed determined to let a nice pair of tits trip him up. Forget about the Côte d'Azur! He asked to be allowed to go to the bathroom, snorted down the last line of coke left over from the night before, and followed the team of cops, loaded for bear, out of the front door with a mocking sneer on his lips.

'Hey, Commissa, this is a rerun of last time, but I'm getting out quicker, guaranteed.'

'There's never two without three, Fierolocchio!' the cop shot back, citing an old Italian proverb.

He'd drawn the only cop in the Eternal City with a sense of humour!

They put him in the same cell as Ricotta, who couldn't resign himself to what had happened.

'I don't believe that Dandi would ever do such a thing to me! This is all Nercio's idea, that Sicilian piece of shit!'

'You've been in here for a lifetime and you still don't get it? Dandi is the piece of shit!'

'But he got you out!'

'And they caught me again. So what? One–all, and the ball's back in the middle of the field!'

'Well, whatever you say, but I can't believe it!'

So Ricotta sent Donatella to convey his complaints. They met at Patrizia's.

That day, Dandi was in fine fettle. He fired off one wisecrack after another and was frantically hunting for the right shirt to wear with an oversized and improbable regimental striped necktie.

'He's come up with the idea of going into politics,' Patrizia sighed mockingly as she filed her nails.

'So? What's so funny about that? Cicciolina did and she got elected, so I can do it too...'

Donatella repressed a giggle and cautiously introduced the subject of a cut. Dandi was brotherly and reassuring. First of all, she should give Ricotta his best wishes. A true friend, a friend that he'd never forget. He'd talk to Nercio, everything would be taken care of. In the meantime, as a sign of his good will, he hoped he'd accept this thirty million lire. Nothing to do with his share; almost a reimbursement for the misunderstanding.

Ricotta rubbed his hands and gave Fierolocchio the arm, slapping the interior of his bent right elbow with his left hand.

'Take that! And you were saying he's a piece of shit!'

'So? He gave you a gracious concession...'

'Forget about it, go on!'

'Rico, you're such a sucker! He's just working it like the Horatii and the Curiatii: me today, you tomorrow, but in the end, he'll arse-fuck us all!'

489

THE SUPREME COURT OF CASSATION
APPEALS COURT OF ASSIZES OF ROME
(*redacted*)

The Grand Inquisitor Tomas De Torquemada, in 1460, began writing a series of disquisitions on confessions and accusations of complicity, identifying them as variously: *legitima, vitiosa, libera, coacta, simplex* or *qualificata*. These definitions were meant to resolve definitively any given trial, whether or not the confession or accusation actually corresponded to the facts. And what was even more serious was he legitimized – and indeed called for – the use of torture.

Which brings us to the triumph of torture: legalized and subjected to a complex, refined and highly detailed ceremonial, designed to extract both confessions and accusations against accomplices. (*Redacted.*)

The experience of the Column of Infamy, the stations of the cross suffered by the commissioner of public health Guglielmo Piazza, who, after withstanding torture, identified as an 'anointer', or spreader of the plague, the barber Mora, who was of course innocent, driven by the promise of absolution or at least a reduction of his sentence, (*redacted*) proves only that during the inquisitorial trial of medieval tradition, confession and accusation of complicity came to acquire a distinct and determinant physiognomy (*redacted*) while with the current flourishing to new life of the deep respect for the human person, we have come to affirm, finally, how little interest there is for the ascertainment of the truth, which is the ultimate and effective purpose of all and any trials, in the word of informants.

Then what is the figure of the 'repentant' turncoat, or '*pentito*', in the present trial? Who is this (*redacted*), also known as 'Sorcio', upon whose words we are being asked to stake the liberty of a significant number of defendants? (*Redacted.*)

This man, a criminal by nature, a drug addict, a confessed user of cocaine, heroin, and every and all other possible and imaginable psychotropic substance, by his own admission and by the behaviour displayed within the houses of detention, as well as the set of behaviours manifested in his interactions with the investigators, certainly expresses an abnormal and doubtless unbalanced mental characterization. The difficulties in social adaptation manifested from the earliest age, the failure of his educational career, his inability to obtain a dignified job and to keep it (when he did manage to obtain one), his malaise in terms of an adult emotional life, his inadaptability to function as a responsible citizen, to accept and comply with social norms, his inclination to engage in illegal activities, his numerous arrests, his disturbances in the emotional sphere, with frequent depressive and maniacal episodes, culminating in his attempted suicides in prison, his irresponsible tendency towards drug abuse – these are all elements of a weak mind with antisocial character traits that fully confirm a grave degree of psychic abnormality, rendered even more acute by deleterious environmental influences buttressed by a cognitive deficit that can be identified as that of a 'mental defective'.

It hardly denotes a favourable diagnosis for a normal development of this individual's cerebration that, as he himself has informed us, he was accustomed to use unfortunate drug addicts as guinea pigs in order to 'test' the authenticity of the narcotics that he intended to market. That activity was not entirely foreign to the party in question himself. (*Redacted.*)

The numerous abnormalities that can be detected in the deposition of (*redacted*), also known as 'Sorcio', while it is not possible to exclude a marked propensity on the part of the subject to untruth and unbridled invention, do lead us to suspect, given the uncommon volume of the accounts proffered, given the sheer number of accusatory declarations, given the contradictory nature of the discourse, given the confusion of ideas demonstrated even in the daily activities in the context of restricted incarceration, that we have identified a paroxysmal logorrhea with a clear fugue state in terms of ideation and a general condition of mental obtundation in this individual.

It is a well-known fact that in cases of accusatory logorrhea, the mythomaniacal subject conceives a sequence of ideas at such a rapid pace that he is entirely unable to dominate them, thus releasing a gushing flow of disorganized thinking, in which representations vary continuously without any opportunity for superior powers of concentration and determining tendencies to guide them and order them in the manner that they require, in accordance with the norms of logical thought.

Thus, however true it may be that confused ideation should be kept quite distinct as a concept from fugue state ideation, it remains undebatable that in both the former and the latter condition – and (*redacted*), also known as 'Sorcio', does present both these deviant mental aspects – the dysfunction is a clear indicator of a less than lucid consciousness, of obsessive ideation, various states of delirium, mental confusion and dissociation, and in any and all cases entails a complete lack of reliability for the fabulator and his imprecise and distorted accounts of events. (*Redacted.*)

III

MIGLIANICO AND VASTA were standing side by side for the delivery of the verdict when the judges established that there had never been any criminal conspiracy. Vasta hastened to provide the press with an official statement.

'This is a great day for me, but especially for Italian justice. Yet again, we have seen proof that the theoretical houses of cards built on the statements of this or that state's witness fail to stand up to the analysis of the better sort of legal probing. I hope that this lesson will serve as a warning to those who obstinately insist on methods that are obsolete and condemned by history. And I hope that the impending implementation of the new code of criminal procedure, based on the accusatory principle, will once and for all put an end to the ignoble abuse of the institution of the accusation of confederates...'

The reporters dutifully took down every last word. Miglianico locked arms with Vasta, a wicked smile on his face.

'Esteemed colleague, please accept my compliments for yet another triumph of the rule of law...'

'No, allow me to extend my compliments, esteemed colleague, considering that you've been involved in this trial for four years now and you've never bothered to read a single document...'

'Esteemed colleague, with all your years of experience, I'd expect you to know that documents count for little or nothing in this world we live in...'

'If I were you, I'd be very careful not to attribute merits to me that I don't deserve, especially outside of our milieu, esteemed colleague...'

'But what are you talking about? If you only knew how much this trial has cost me!'

'Horseshit, your excellency. You never paid a lira. The verdict is clean.'

'You wouldn't be accusing me of taking false credit, *carissimo*?'

'What else would I be saying, *carissimo*?'

'You really ought to be more sporting, *carissimo*, considering that the only guilty verdict confirmed on appeal was for your own client!'

'To tell the truth, *carissimo*, you've taken quite a beating yourself...'

'All part of the cost of doing business, esteemed colleague; all factored into the equation!'

'My best regards, colleague.'

'See you soon, colleague.'

But credit for the fact that the criminal conspiracy charges had been overturned really belonged neither to Vasta nor Miglianico, nor to the rule of law nor to the brotherhood, or whatever the hell name one chose to give it. Credit was due only and exclusively to good old Libano, God rest his soul. Dandi was absolutely convinced of it. It was Libano who had gotten rid once and for all of the vast array of bullshit that Calabrians and Mafiosi could never seem to get enough of. Pinpricks to fingertips, knife cuts and ritual tattoos, burned holy cards, molten wax, oaths sworn on the heads of each and every saint in heaven...Strictly medieval shit. Libano was a practical man with an eye on the future.

And the judges had fallen right into step. In the legal opinion, laying out the grounds for the decision, it was written, clear as day: what kind of criminal conspiracy can we be talking about if the members never swore an oath? If they gleefully kill one another at will? If they don't even have a headquarters, and when they need to plan out a murder, they meet at the bar downstairs?

493

A good old Roman criminal conspiracy, Libano would have replied, with that smile of his that invariably left its mark. What do you think – that we're the kind of folks that wear Sicilian shepherd's caps and tote sawn-off shotguns? Not us, we're Romans!

Even so, the judges had gone well past anyone's rosiest hopes. The arms deposit? Sure, there might have been a few people making use of it, but from the outside, this showed only that a number of criminals had chanced upon a handy hiding place for their gats. And Sorcio and Trentadenari: they were treated high-handedly, like a couple of rotten turncoats, nothing more.

Certainly, not even Dandi could have predicted such a definitive knuckle-rapping! In the great calm sea of the law's certainty, even the Barbetta incident had vanished, sinking like a stone. Sorcio had told them: go. The cops had gone, and they had found Barbetta and the dope. But if Sorcio was crazy, then who had given Barbetta the dope in the first place? The Holy Ghost? No. The fact was that turncoat informants were just as roundly reviled by certain judges as they were by everybody else. The good-hearted judges. The judges who thought things through like real men. Sometimes it seemed that there wasn't really all that much distance after all between the two worlds: the world of the street and the world of the office building. Which was just one more reason that Dandi was so anxious to take that great leap forward. Deep down, everyone could be the same. All that it took was an understanding of the basics.

Dandi poured himself a glass of Cristal and drank a toast to his ideal judge – a guy you could spend the evening with, drinking happily, maybe even dive into a little pussy together. He was enjoying the most wonderful birthday of his life. Secco's villa, requisitioned for the occasion, glowed like a Hollywood set. Dandi enjoyed humiliating his business partner at any opportunity that presented itself. He had taken immense enjoyment from the horrified expression on Secco's face when, as homeowner, he informed him that his presence as a guest would not be welcome.

The orchestra was playing its heart out on the podium, and the hardest rock alternated with piano ballads. There had been a stormy dispute with Patrizia over logistics. She'd had her heart set on Antonello Venditti. She said that his romantic songs put a certain something in her body that she couldn't express in words. He wanted to have Amedeo Minghi perform instead. Then, he'd grumbled, I don't like that Venditti: he's a dyed-in-the-wool Red. Patrizia had let him listen to '*Grazie roma*', and Dandi, moved to tears, decided to reconsider the situation. But when he made the offer to the middleman for a guy who claimed to be a personal friend of the rock star, he was told that Antonello never played private parties. Dandi considered how much fun it would be to buy the record company and kick the star down the front steps.

He went back to Patrizia with the suggestion that they hire the Caliph. She resisted: Venditti or nobody. In the end, they decided to forget about big-name performers and went for something less demanding. Not to save money, but to avoid complications. For that matter, those guys were all first-rate professionals, recruited by his old friend Surtano.

Dandi hadn't given up the idea of going into films. He was financing Surtano, who had a certain amount of experience in the business and was willing to try to bring his project to fruition. It would be a story of sex and violence. It would be about life on the streets. A way to make money by telling the story of a band of men with real balls. Men willing to do what it took. When the smoke cleared, only one would still be standing. The best of them all. Him. For the starring role, he'd considered Al Pacino. But how much money would he cost him! In the meantime, Surtano had managed to assemble a caravan of starlets for the party. Okay, maybe one or two of them were also part-time whores, but as far as that went, his guests had a right to enjoy themselves. Dandi was footing the bill. He could afford it.

The Maestro was strolling all alone in the garden. Dandi offered him a glass of bubbly. He'd barely seen him since that night the year before. No one from the Sicilian side had ever contacted him. The Maestro protected him in silence.

The Maestro was in a grim mood. He took the glass of champagne and gave him a melancholy smile.

'Is it true that Freddo and Ricotta got screwed?'

'Freddo took to his heels without paying his last legal bill, and Vasta, old-school gentleman that he is, let his appeal lapse. As for Ricotta... Well, there was no saving him, what with the story of the Gemito brothers. Now that the sentence has been upheld on every appeal, we'll see what we can do with the Gozzini law and the accumulated mitigating factors...'

'What about the others? Bufalo, Scrocchiazeppi...'

'Scrocchia is serving an old concurrent sentence. Fierolocchio still has to serve out the extra time for his escape attempt. Anyway, who cares about the others?'

'So, in other words, it couldn't have gone any better?'

'So it would seem!'

'I wish I could say the same thing for myself...'

The Maestro was worried. In fact, he was losing it. By protecting Dandi, he was protecting himself. But down south, there were people who were completely out of control.

'Well then, Maestro, could you tell me what you're so worried about? Is it that longhair they shot down in Trapani? The one from Lotta Continua who had those programmes on the radio?'

'No. That wasn't our doing, no...'

'Really?'

'Yeah. No, it wasn't. The real problem is the judge they killed the other week...'

'Hardly the first. And after all, it sounded like he deserved what he got, right?'

'Sure, that's how I see it. The jury was practically on salary with our friends from down there. He figured it out and you know what he did? He locked the jury room doors and kept them holed up in there until they finally came up with the verdict he was looking for.'

'Oh, well then...'

'Eh, but the handicapped son, what did he have to do with anything?'

'They killed him, too?'

The Maestro nodded, lost in thought. He told him that when they told Uncle Carlo the news, he'd exclaimed: 'Praised be the Lord! How was that poor child going to survive alone?' According to the Maestro, in other words, Uncle Carlo was going too far.

Dandi said he agreed. But he was too revved up to let the Maestro's gloom drag him down. He politely offered him more champagne, a girl, a line of coke...Whatever he wanted, in other words, as long as he'd cut it out with his tale of woe.

But the Maestro, just as politely, said that he'd rather go home.

'It's been a hard day. And tomorrow Danilo has his piano recital.'

Dandi saw him leave, hunched over, weighed down with concerns and thoughts. No question, the older his son got, the more the Maestro turned into an idiot about him. Dandi definitely never wanted to have that kind of worry. If he did, he sure wouldn't have picked someone like Patrizia.

IV

THE FULL 80 DJ mixed '*La isla bonita*' with hectic disco music. Rossana seemed to emerge from her trance.

'I feel like dancing.'

'At your orders, princess!'

Doctor Mainardi followed her out onto the dance floor. The way she swung her hips was a spectacle to behold.

They'd met at a party. She'd looked down on him scornfully. He'd noticed her tendency to overdo it with drink. By midnight Rossana could hardly stand upright. Mainardi managed to catch her alone at the edge of the swimming pool.

'You're an unrivalled cocktail of purebred racehorse and man-eating panther, whiskers dripping with blood from your last kill...'

That was his come-on line. Rossana had tilted her head to one side, tittering cheerfully like a dumb bimbo. Mainardi assumed that she was drunk out of her mind. Too impaired to resist his advances. He'd seized her by the waist and was trying to force open her bee-stung lips when she gave him a single good hard shove and knocked him into the water.

'Rinse off your brain, you idiot! Racehorse, panther...I don't like animals!'

Mainardi wasn't about to give up. After all, what was at stake was the kind of thing that could change your life. Rossana was the daughter of Ugo Lepore. Professor Lepore. Sole owner and chief executive officer of the Case Associate: eleven super-deluxe clinics distributed throughout Rome, Florence and Bologna, along with a series of affiliated clinics in Spain and Greece. An authentic empire of bandages and silver spoons that would one day – to a considerable extent, at least a 30 per cent share – belong to that spectacular blonde who was twisting and jerking in the circle of psychotic strobe lights under the ravenous gazes of the dance-hall hunks.

The recovery had been slow and laborious, but in the end he'd managed to tame her. The wedding was planned for November. Mainardi was aiming at a grand slam in all areas of his life.

Lepore felt a certain fondness for him. And Nero – when all was said and done, better to have him as a friend than an enemy – had made it clear to him that certain business partners of his might be interested in investing in the clinics. If the situation looked right. If they could find the right intermediary.

Mainardi could already see himself on the bridge of the great ship. He had in mind a bundle that would take care of him for the rest of his days. In the meantime, joint property. Then, after a reasonable lapse of time, a nice, clean divorce between civilized people. He'd never planned for an instant to spend the rest of his life with Rossana. He didn't love her. He didn't even particularly like her. In fact, to tell the truth, he deeply detested her. All right, fair enough, in bed she was a force of nature. But, that aside, she was a genuine concentrate of all the worst aspects of the female soul: lazy, always bored, hungry for powerful sensations, fickle, eager to flirt with every drug imaginable... The classic spoiled daughter of a self-made man – an entrepreneur more likely to wield a club than a scalpel.

That night, in particular, Rossana was even more intolerable than usual. Problems with her split ends and the hem of her skirt, problems with her rouge and with her Chanel perfume, problems with a girlfriend and with an art auction, problems with her father and with her studies, continually off-track and off schedule. Problems with the universe at large, which never seemed willing to bend in instant obedience to her latest whim. Eh, but he'd put the noose around her neck! Then the shoe would be on the other foot! With a woman like her, the only way to make it out alive was with a commando operation, zap! – take the money and run. In the meantime, dancing seemed to have drained her of some of her evil spirits.

Mainardi smiled at her. Personally, he hated dancing, but this was just part of the difficult climb to the summit. The nicely dressed young man, who for the past few minutes had been leaping and spinning around them, chose that exact moment to land on his foot.

'Excuse me!'

'Watch where you put your feet!'

The young man, with a sad smile, was practically bowing in his apology.

Mainardi seized Rossana by the arm and dragged her a few yards away. Even though the music was frantic, Rossana was standing there in something close to a trance, a smile wandering across her face. Mainardi knew that smile all too well. It was a danger signal. Rossana had noticed something or someone, and this something or someone had managed to make a breach in her eternal, exasperating armour of apathy...

He turned to follow the direction of her gaze and nearly ran headlong into the face of the nicely dressed young man. What with his moves and dance steps, there he was again, hard up against them, and now he was actually trying to worm his way between the two of them...

'I'm sick of this!' Mainardi shouted, in a vain effort to make himself heard over the obsessive pounding of the beat.

'I can't hear you!' Rossana replied.

'Shall we go?'

'Why? I'm having fun!'

In the end, Rossana brought the nicely dressed young man to their table.

'I wouldn't want to intrude...'

'What on earth are you talking about! We can have a drink together, what's wrong with that?'

'But maybe the two of you would prefer to be alone...'

'Not at all. Come right over, have a seat!'

Mainardi had no choice but to make the best of a bad situation. Rossana loved to tease him just as much as he hated to have his will thwarted. He would have happily wiped that oily smile off the baby-bottom-smooth face of that overgrown toddler in an Armani suit with a quick one-two punch. But he couldn't afford to cause a scene. She would never forgive him. It was like kicking in an own-goal at the ninetieth minute.

The youngster was small, not a hair out of place, with natural charm. He said his name was Pietro. A law student, falling behind in his studies. Rossana laughed and ordered champagne.

'If I may, allow me to take care of this,' the kid hastened to offer. 'But first, if you'll excuse me, I have to make a phone call.'

Mainardi watched him go. As he expected, the young man headed straight for the toilets.

'I'll be right back.'

'What is this?' Rossana snickered. 'The prostate hour?'

Ha, ha, ha. Laugh to your heart's content, my beauty. I'm going to go fix your little student good.

The young man was washing his hands. In the mirror he saw Mainardi coming in and turned around with an awkward expression. Mainardi walked towards him with a broad smile on his face, and once he was within reach, he shoved him hard against the sink. A glint of genuine malicious evil appeared in the young man's eyes. But Mainardi was too wrapped up in his mission to notice it.

'Listen up and listen good, arsehole. You're starting to be a pain in the arse. Understood?'

The young man checked to make sure that his jacket hadn't gotten dirty or torn, ran a hand through his smooth black hair, and threw his arms open in mute appeal.

'You could have put it a little more politely...'

'You need to get the fuck out of my hair. Do it now. Get it?'

'Maybe the signorina feels differently about it...'

'Why am I still looking at you? Do you want to understand what I'm telling you? Scram! Beat it! *Raus!*'

The young man didn't seem to be upset in the slightest. In fact, he looked as if he were actually enjoying himself. This was a development that Mainardi hadn't taken into account. For that matter, it was one thing to shove someone, another matter entirely to get into a full-blown brawl. Physical combat wasn't his forte. For all he knew, the young man might be a black belt in karate. Plus there was the added consideration that fisticuffs would be quite unseemly; he couldn't afford a scene, much less a fist fight! But he couldn't pull back now. One more false step and that little midget would laugh right in his face. And how would Rossana take that? He decided it was time to change technique.

'Listen,' he said in a fluted voice, 'put yourself in my shoes. I'm spending the evening in delightful company when suddenly a little arsehole pops out of nowhere and starts flirting with my fiancée...'

'But you were the one who invited me over!' the young man sighed sweetly.

At that, Mainardi lost it.

'Now you've busted my balls for the last time! I'm going to call Nero and have you tossed out of here with a good swift kick in the arse!'

'Nero?'

'That's right. He owns the place. And he's not the kind of guy to take things lightly, my young dickhead law-student friend!'

The young man thought it over for a while, then shrugged his shoulders and held out his hand.

'All right. My mistake. Forgive me. No hard feelings?'

No hard feelings. Mainardi was feeling cocky when he got back to the table. Rossana hadn't even touched her champagne.

'Where's the young man?'

'Ah, well, he...said to say goodbye, that he had to leave...'

'This is your doing!'

'Me? What are you talking about! I ran into him and he asked me to tell you...Where are you going?'

Rossana had grabbed her bag and jumped to her feet. Mainardi tossed three hundred-thousand lire notes onto the tablecloth and ran after her. Out on the street he stopped and listened, then turned in the direction of the furious tapping of her high heels on the *sampietrini*, the Roman cobblestones.

'Rossana, my love!'

The blow came from behind and caught him right at the base of his neck. He fell to his knees, stunned as if someone had fired a round of New Year's fireworks right into his ear. A split second later he felt something metallic slide into his mouth. It was a hard object, with a revolting taste of rancid oil – the barrel of a pistol. Mainardi desperately tried to lift his head, but a second blow whipped down, and then a third, and the weapon was crushing his throat, and a retching surge of vomit almost suffocated him.

'Make sure you don't get any of that filth on me, you animal!'

The young man withdrew the pistol, and now he was checking to make sure no stains of vomit had spattered his clothes. But everything was immaculate. The young man cocked the gun and placed it against his temple. Mainardi vomited again.

'Now listen to me and listen good. The only reason I don't shoot you right here and now is that I don't want to ruin a perfectly good suit. You know, you can get blood out, but spattered brain material, that just stains like a bitch!'

Mainardi started crying. The young man heaved a sigh and snapped on the safety.

'Come on, come on, buck up! This one time, you got off easy. But if I ever see you again, you'll be one dead doctor. Now go get washed up, you're a disgusting mess!'

The young man put both hands under his arms and lifted him to his feet.

'One more thing. If you see Nero, tell him that Pischello sends his best regards!'

Mainardi looked around for Rossana. She was leaning against her Volvo, a cigarette clenched between her teeth. She didn't seem even slightly shocked at the spectacle she'd just witnessed. The young man holstered his pistol and went over to her.

'Frightened?'

'Not in the least!'

'Shall I take you home?'

'So early?'

'Then offer a suggestion...'

'I want to go to the beach!'

'I like the beach...'

'We can go in my car...'

'You deserve something better.'

Pischello stole an Arab's yellow Ferrari Testarossa for her and took her to Fregene. They walked on the beach, hand in hand. Pischello told her his story. She told him that when she was fourteen, she ran away from home with a girlfriend. They'd lived together for three months. Her girlfriend was shooting up. To buy drugs for her, they'd both turned tricks and made a porno film.

'I'm rich,' she said.

'So am I. I like money...'

'What else besides money?'

502

'Lots of other things. Cars. Clothes. Dancing. Cats. Dope. The smell of salt water. Excitement. Beautiful girls. But let me warn you: I'm fickle, and I'm a little bit crazy.'

'It strikes me we'll get along famously, the two of us!'

They made love in the pine grove. At dawn he took her home, then he parked the Ferrari Testarossa exactly where he'd found it.

Mainardi went to see Nero with a bandaged head. He couldn't find Rossana anywhere. Her father had told him that she'd left home.

Nero listened to the litany of complaints with some irritation and when it was over, coldly informed Mainardi that he couldn't care less about his misfortunes.

'I'm not a pimp, Doctor...'

'But she's my woman!'

'She was. Now she's with Pischello.'

'What should I do?'

'Are you asking me? Take her back, if you think you can do it. But if you want my advice, forget about her. Pischello's heart beats on the right side of his chest!'

V

THE TWO INDIVIDUALS who had picked him up an hour earlier – short, taciturn, venomous, probably gypsies – dropped him off in front of a small door with a plaque stating 'Private', and made it clear to him that as of this exact instant, they were washing their hands of him. Scialoja rummaged through his pockets, as if he were looking for some change to tip them with. Something in the razor-sharp glance of the shorter of the two gypsies told him that he'd be smarter not to try to be too damned funny. He walked in without knocking.

'Take a seat,' Dandi ordered.

Scialoja lit a cigarette. Just a few dozen feet below them, in the luxurious restaurant of the Full 80, murderers and powerful men were working on their meals, plying forks and knives shoulder to shoulder, soon to move on to the adjoining bar. Before they led him upstairs for his audience with the boss, Scialoja had noticed a princess of the blood royal share bread and salt with Botola. Nero, rubbing shoulders with a well-known television personality, had ironically raised his glass in salutation, and then immediately went back to toying with the remnants of a goblet of caviar. There was more: two models, or whatever they were, were pretending to have the times of their lives laughing at the incomprehensible wisecracks of a fat Arab with mirrored sunglasses. A cabinet minister in the current government, visibly tipsy, pressing the flesh of a couple of ladies with bountiful bosoms. A legion of bodyguards camping out in the cramped corners of the restaurant room, making no effort to go unnoticed. A young man with a freshly scrubbed face had looked him right in the eye as he whispered something funny into the ear of a bored-looking blonde. She'd burst out laughing: a raucous, full-throated laugh. A spectacular laugh.

'Sit down!' Dandi said again, as if he were using up the last little bit of an already scanty reservoir of patience.

Scialoja was doing his best to remember where he'd seen the smooth-faced youngster before. Such a good-mannered young man: too nice to be true. But Scialoja had been drinking heavily all afternoon and he could barely focus. Even if he could place the face, what good would it have done him? He stood there, savouring one drag of smoke after another. Dandi snorted in annoyance.

'Stay on your feet if you prefer. So here's what this is about—'

'Let me guess: you've decided to turn state's witness and you called me in to spill the beans...'

'You think I'd tell you if I did?' Dandi laughed. 'Have you taken a look at yourself lately? You look like a bum!'

Scialoja looked down and considered his sagging jumper, the jeans that urgently needed laundering, his two-days' growth of whiskers. Dandi had a point. Lately, he'd been letting himself go. He kept telling himself that it was only a passing phase. Still, he was starting to have his doubts. He looked around and chose a red-leather chair next to the antique writing desk.

'Oh, at last! Now, listen carefully, I don't have any time to waste. If there are men who are busting your balls, there are two solutions. Either you buy them off or you eliminate them...'

Dandi was quoting Machiavelli!

'And just where does that come from?' Scialoja prodded him provocatively.

'From personal experience. And from this brain!' roared Dandi, tapping temple with forefinger. 'But what the hell am I wasting time on you for? With all the things I've got going…All right then: eliminating a guy like you, these days, brings little glory, if any. You're practically done for already. Finished. Fucked. You've got two verdicts against you on appeal and a fucking host of old charges. They've even repossessed your mattress. You're worthless – as a cop and as a human being. Not worth a plugged lire. And it serves you right, because you made too many of us weep and wail! If I were in your shoes, I'd fire a bullet into my brain and say goodnight nurse! So, even if I was to buy you, I wouldn't be getting much for my money. Still, all the same, the one thing you have is you're lucky. Because, like that old line from a film, "somebody up there likes me". You know what I'm talking about, don't you, cop?' Dandi slammed a hand down on the desk. 'All right, then. I'll buy you. I've made up my mind. You're going to come work for me!'

Scialoja burst out laughing. Dandi relaxed against the back rest.

'Go ahead and laugh; laugh all you like. Your mama's made you gnocchi for dinner! Oh, but nothing serious, eh, let's not get a swelled head or anything! After all, you're still just a weasel and a rat! If you knew how much work it was to bring the others around! But here's the thing: when Dandi sets his mind to something…Just a few little jobs, now and then, so you can afford the pussy you seem to love so much…'

Scialoja closed his eyes and tried to evaluate the situation objectively. He felt like punching a hole in that fat bastard's belly. A piercing urge, almost physically painful. There had to be a pistol around somewhere. Lunge at him. Immobilize him. Find the weapon, or get someone to tell him where it was. Use it. Kill him, right here, in his lair. Right where he felt safest. Then to hell with it. He could claim self-defence.

Dandi's voice faded into an evil whisper.

'I know exactly what you're thinking. You just give it a try and you'll be a dead man. This time it's not the way it was at Patrizia's. Accept the offer, and I'll have spared your life twice. Try it and *bang, bang* – you're dead!' Dandi mimed the sign of the pistol.

505

Scialoja clenched his fists. No one would ever fall for the idea of legitimate self-defence. He'd get a life sentence without parole. One of this guy's friends would cut his throat in the shower. He needed to live, to survive. A still picture of Patrizia – the way she hooked her bra back up, after making love – suddenly made a smile flash faintly across his face.

'Well?'

'I'll think it over.'

She was the short-lived triumph, and she was also the long-ensuing drift. Somewhere at home he must have a bottle.

Dandi was concentrating on a ledger of some kind. He looked up distractedly.

'Well, when you've made up your mind, send me a postcard!'

At the bar they told him his drinks were all on the house. Scialoja insisted on paying for his double whiskey. The gypsies materialized behind him. He followed them obediently. In the middle of the dance floor, glowing with psychedelic lights, he found himself with the baby-faced young man and the sophisticated blonde.

'I know you,' he shouted, doing his best to make himself heard over the roar of the music.

'Excuse me?'

'You're the guy they call Pischello.'

'I can't understand you!'

Scialoja grabbed the blonde.

'Your boyfriend is a murderer, did you know that?'

She shook her head with an embarrassed smile.

The gypsies lifted him by his shoulders. There must be a bottle somewhere back home.

Liberty
1989

I

THAT'S LIFE. AND this is Rome. Instead of the little corner bar where you used to be king, there's a beer hall full of kids so young they're still wetting the bed; kids who don't know you or remember you. At the social club there are new faces that when you go to nod hello, they steer clear of you worse than if you'd just tested seropositive. Sidelong glances, muffled laughter. Everyone minding their own business, in line, arses covered, squirming under the almighty heel of Dandi, that complete bastard. That's life. And this is Rome.

You're behind bars and you think to yourself: the minute I get out, I'll fix you guys good. So you get out, and now you're nobody. Respect dies after X number of years in prison. With nothing but small change in your pocket and a rage deep in your belly so poisonous that if a rattlesnake bites you, it'd kill him.

Scrocchiazeppi felt like the Russian at the Porta Portese market who'd sold him his piece: a survivor. That guy was escaping from Communism; what Scrocchiazeppi was running from was his own luck. And the past. That's right, a veteran. Out on his arse, with patches on the seat of his pants. His apartment under judicial sequester. Forced to sleep in one of those *pensiones* over behind the train station. A Makarov pistol and a bag of tarnished-looking bullets that had practically cost him the last penny he had to his name. The only way he could have got anything better would have been by trading his Rolex. But better dead with the Rolex on his wrist than alive without it.

The first one he went to look up was Secco. Secco reminded him that the organization had been dissolved. If he was looking for a share, the guy he needed to see was Nercio.

'And how would you like it if I shoot you here and now?'

'What good would that do you? I don't keep cash on hand. It'd be less trouble to organize a nice armed robbery!'

'I'm going to kill that bastard. Give me a hand, Secco!'

'I'll think it over. In the meantime, try and stay out of trouble.'

As soon as Scrocchiazeppi left, Secco informed Dandi. What the hell benefit was it to him to sponsor a zero like Scrocchia? Just one look at the state he'd been reduced to was enough to tell you that he had two, three days tops, left to live. Dandi would be grateful to him for the tip. This manifestation of loyalty would make a favourable impression on him. Slowly, ever so slowly, his mistrust had been lessening. The final blow – because there was no doubt that sooner or later there would be a final blow – would have to arrive like the angel in the fable, who passes by, says amen, and the bad little boy stands rooted to the spot, mouth wide open, and he can no longer shut it...

Dandi sent Botola to talk with Scrocchiazeppi, who had become nightmarishly skinny, with an unkempt beard and frantic eyes. Botola handed him ten million lire or so. Scrocchiazeppi spat on the money and set fire to a hundred-thousand lire note.

'You trying to buy me with this pittance, Botola? My God, look what's become of you! You and the penguin remind me of Don Quixote and Sancho Panza!'

'What is it exactly that you're looking for?'

'I want thirty per cent, a passport, and a plane ticket for South America.'

'Planning to get lost? Just like Freddo, eh?'

'Better to take off and get lost than to lick your master's arse!'

'Thirty per cent's too much, Scrocchia...'

'Freedom isn't cheap!'

'Thirty per cent is outrageous...'

'A lead bullet is worse, Botola!'

Botola faithfully reported the message. To see an old comrade in such pitiful shape had aroused his tenderest feelings. He put in a good word for Scrocchia.

'As far as I'm concerned, he's just done too much dope. Let's give him a couple hundred million lire, put him on the first plane to Rio, and it's live and let live!'

Secco fell back on his perfidious diplomacy.

'Sure, after all, he's just an isolated individual, nobody's scared of him. He won't find a stray dog to listen to him. He must be out of his mind! All these threats...Well, one things certain, Dandi: he must really hate you! All things considered, is it wise to let a nutcase like him run around loose?'

Dandi stared at Nero.

'I don't care either way,' Nero said. 'All I say is that if we're going to do it, we should do it fast. And right.'

'He's an old comrade...' Botola insisted.

Dandi understood that the decision was up to him, and him alone. For that matter, he was the boss. What would Libano and Freddo have done in his place? An idle question. Libano and Freddo would never have dissolved the gang. Botola had said it right: Scrocchia was an old comrade. But how many old comrades had fallen by the wayside, struck down by other, equally old comrades? Was there still anyone to mourn them? Who even remembered Satana? And Trentadenari, the traitor? Wasn't he every bit as much of an old comrade? And he hadn't thought twice about betraying them! Old comrade was a meaningless phrase. Straight-up comrade at least made sense. But who was right and who was wrong?

Freddo hadn't thought twice about having one of the Buffoni twins killed. Sure. But the Buffoni brother was stealing. The Buffoni brother was breaking the rules. Scrocchia, poor thing, felt victimized. But victimized by what? Easy to say: Dandi had made his fortune and Scrocchia had remained penniless. In that case, he could just take it up with God Almighty, who'd decided to scrimp on his brains! Hadn't Dandi told him a million ways come Sunday that if he wanted to prosper, he had to think, invest, move money...Fucking gangster had put more coke up his nose than an elephant and now he wanted to complain? If he'd only come to him, humble and obedient to ask for some help, then maybe...But instead, that arrogance, that truculent challenge...Did that mean that somehow Scrocchiazeppi had got it into his head that now that Dandi was on his way to becoming a respectable citizen, he'd forgotten what the street was all about? Did he think for one second that Dandi had gone soft because he hadn't fired a gun in years? What the fuck? Shooting was like driving a car: learn it once and you never forgot. Enough talk, already! He was the boss. He'd made his decision.

'It's him or us,' Dandi concluded. 'But we'll have to plan it out carefully. We'd be the first logical suspects. We'll do it two days from now. The Maestro's renting the Full for his son's birthday...'

The carabinieri pulled up at Alberone with sirens wailing and tyres screeching not fifteen minutes after the shooting. Scrocchiazeppi's corpse was still warm and there was even an eyewitness: a little old man who was just coming out of the local shop with a bottle of milk, and he wouldn't stop whining in fright. He said that a high-performance motorcycle had roared up. The two men aboard the bike were wearing black motorcycle suits and full-face helmets. The guy on the back had fired two shots from behind and the tall skinny gentleman had fallen to the ground and hadn't moved again.

The investigation wound up on the desk of the ADA on duty that day, an older guy who hadn't even bothered to lift his arse off his chair for a pro-forma investigation. With Scialoja in disgrace and Borgia hot on the trail of shopkeepers accused of skimming off their taxes, there was nobody out there who could give less of a damn about that kind of a murder.

Trentadenari, who'd read the news in a short item in *Il Messaggero*, wrote a letter to the prosecuting magistrate: Dandi did this. Scrocchiazeppi had gotten out of prison without a penny to his name and wanted revenge, but the other guys were faster on the draw. More corpses would be forthcoming. But Trentadenari, notoriously, was an unreliable witness, discredited, psychopathic, you name it. A couple of shoe-leather operatives were sent out to check on it anyway.

Dandi, questioned during a soirée at the Full 80, was exquisitely courteous, offering them drinks and throwing in their teeth a videocassette of the birthday party: while Scrocchiazeppi was breathing his last, the full leadership contingent of the Empire of Evil was toasting the little boy's health. The case was rapidly archived 'because of the impossibility of identifying the guilty parties.'

Fierolocchio's sentence was up on the day of the funeral. Before picking up his duffel bag and cheque, he swung by to say so long to Ricotta. Ricotta was weeping over his dead friend. Fierolocchio gave him a good hard slap on the back.

'But I thought the two of you weren't even talking anymore!'

'What's that got to do with anything! He was still a friend!'

'I heard that Dandi sent a couple of outside torpedoes...Neapolitans, apparently. He gave them fifty million lire and they pulled the job.'

'I don't believe it. Dandi would never have done such a thing!'

'Ri-i-i-ight...Next thing you know, Scrocchia committed suicide!'

'Not Dandi. He's a stand-up guy. It's the guys around him, the bastards!'

Fierolocchio enjoyed a hearty laugh.

'Listen, Rico, you know that you reminded me of Libano just now? One time we were talking about Mussolini...'

Ricotta sniffed loudly. 'Eh, Libano! No doubt about it, he was fixated on Mussolini!'

'Eh! Fair to say: Libano used to talk and talk: Il Duce this, and Il Duce that, and he built railroads, and reclaimed swampland, and fought the wheat war, and built houses, and developments..."Hey, Libano," I told him, "if this Mussolini guy was so damned good, how come they hung him up by his heels like a slaughtered veal calf?" And you know what he told me?'

'What did he tell you?'

'And he said to me: "It was the guys he had around him! They betrayed him! There were things he didn't even know...He didn't have time! He was thinking about the fate of the nation..." And you know what I said to him? I said: "Look, Libano, maybe that's the way things went, but if a leader doesn't know how to choose his men, then that's his fucking problem!"'

'I don't know, Fierolo...I say that if Libano was still around, something like this couldn't have happened. And it couldn't have happened if Freddo was still around. It strikes me that the ones who come along later are always worse...'

'Hey, Rico, it strikes me that this Pasolini ruined you!'

They hugged roughly.

'What are you going to do now?' Ricotta asked.

'I'm leaving. Then we'll see!'

When he heard about Scrocchiazeppi, Bufalo spread both arms.

'He talked too much!'

'Amen!' laughed Conte Ugolino. And he sank his teeth into the massive leg of wild boar that he'd just pulled out of the oven.

II

IT ALL STARTED with a stabbing pain in his right arm. It was followed by dizziness, pinwheels in his eyes and, last of all, the hardest thing to take: the loss of that sense of invulnerability, that expectation of eternity that had never abandoned him throughout the course of his life, long though it had been. The Old Man was lucky: his secretary had just stuck her head in the door to say goodnight. She saw him, blue in the face and gurgling, one hand on the chess-playing automaton and the other on a Piranesi etching of Piazza del Popolo, and half an hour later the chief physician of the resuscitation unit had declared him out of danger. All told, a minor incident. They hadn't even had to defibrillate.

'Now rest, I insist. Absolute rest. Cancel all your appointments and don't let any funny ideas get into your head. This time you survived, but the next time you might not!'

Damn it. With all the things that he still needed to do. With all the things that he'd never done, things he kept putting off. With all the missed opportunities, the regrets concealed in a little corner of his heart...at the word *heart* a wave of rage swept over him. The warning was like a low blow from an hourglass, a sudden acceleration as he barrelled straight for the brink, a substantial tear in the fabric...was there a meaning to all this? Was it the voice of God appealing to his conscience or was it simply an old and worn-out piece of clockwork finally running down and dying?

Zeta came to see him on the third day. However hard he worked to put on a show of concern, it was obvious that he was disappointed at his rapid recovery. Zeta aspired to succeed him. As long as it would undermine him, Zeta was even willing to throw himself into the arms of the left. But the Old Man was proudly recovering his strength. He had come to the conclusion that, all things considered, perhaps there was a message behind that sign from above. Don't waste time, that voice was saying. Get as much done while you still have time. But only do you what you really want to.

Years before, if fate had posed that question, he would have answered, without hesitation: I want it all and I want it now. The whole world. Absolute power. Eternity.

With the passing of the years, though, the range of ambitions had narrowed dangerously. But the intensity of his desire had grown disproportionately. There were times when he felt an acute, intense physical pain. This was where the extremes came together and the heart attack became a desperate appeal. No time to waste. Now what he wanted was fresh young flesh. He wanted a collection of vintage canvases that he could admire in the muffled silence of his study. He wanted a life-sized Coppélia with a music box cylinder playing the original music by Léo Delibes. He wanted to go skinny-dipping in Marrakesh. He wanted to go out with a huge orgy of pleasure, with one last, snarling burst of laughter.

Everything he wanted had a price. The highest price imaginable. But most of all, what he wanted was to play, damn it, to play. The Old Man called for a telephone.

The first gambling parlour to be shut down was the one in the Via Merulana. The video poker machines were placed under judicial sequester and seal, and the operator, an old thief who had spent thirty years in prison, was released on his own recognizance after being charged with operating games of chance and violation of the terms of his parole. Over the following week, various other parlours fell: Via Ostiense, Via di Pietralata, Via Livorno, Via Prati Fiscali and the Via degli Orti di Trastevere.

Dandi, furious, threw a tantrum with Miglianico. The lawyer met with Zeta at the gardens of the Orto Botanico. The agent was smoking a long Cuban cigar and was in a foul mood himself.

'I'm done with this whole thing. Orders from the Old Man. You'll have to talk with Peloso.'

'How's the Old Man doing?'

'He's losing his mind. It's a good thing retirement isn't far off now.'

Peloso was the Old Man's latest masterpiece. Half a gangster: cleaned up just enough to keep from causing a scandal in certain settings, but still with a foundation of innate brutality that rendered him invaluable when it came to negotiations that might prove to be – how to put it? – complex.

When Dandi heard from him in person that, in order to provide protection to the social clubs, Peloso expected 20 per cent of the net profit on the gambling machines, he lunged at him and knocked him back against the wall. Peloso wriggled out of his grip with a judo move that sent Dandi sprawling onto the floor. They were in Miglianico's law office. Dandi got to his feet brandishing a heavy onyx ashtray. The lawyer stepped between them. They should try to be reasonable. Try to find an agreement. Open warfare wasn't helpful to anyone. Not to Dandi, who might be about to see his main source of income seriously crippled, nor to Peloso and his investors, because if the social clubs decided to go out of business, it would only hurt them both.

'If the cow stops giving milk, what will the farmer drink?' Miglianico summed up the problem, never far in his mind from his long-ago origins in the countryside of the Ciociaria, outside Rome.

But Dandi stubbornly refused to budge. Peloso waved farewell with a raised middle finger and promised that this wasn't the last they'd hear of him.

Dandi reached out frantically for a direct contact with Zeta, but he failed to show up for two meetings of the brotherhood.

A week later they arrested Nero and hauled him up on fabricated charges of money laundering. It was brought home in no uncertain terms to Dandi that the other man was pure wolf, and so he went to see Peloso with his best lamb-face on.

'All right. But in the meantime, since you decided to act out and throw a tantrum, the twenty per cent I mentioned before has now gone up to thirty per cent.'

Dandi paid up. He was frothing with rage, but he knew that Peloso was no Scrocchiazeppi. Peloso was untouchable. Peloso, from a certain point of view, was a partner. But how it rankled! The businessman's life was truly beginning to fill up with unwelcome surprises. There were times when Dandi thought how much better it had been to be a stone criminal. Still, it didn't take him long to get back on his feet from the thumping he'd taken from Peloso. Property values in Sardinia were finally skyrocketing. All of the sales had gone through without a hitch. The Maestro offered to let him reinvest his share of the profits.

'But it's fine if you pull out, too. Word came from Palermo that there are no problems.'

'In that case, if you have no objections, I'd like to pull out.'

Who wouldn't jump at an opportunity like that? One step closer to freedom! True liberty!

III

WHAT WAS FREEDOM? Having no restrictions.

Bufalo was released from the insane asylum the day that German kids were demolishing the Berlin Wall. A five-day leave of absence, obtained through the intercession of a kind-hearted nun and an affidavit from Professor Cortina, who swore up and down that Bufalo presented no active danger to society.

The farewell hug that Conte Ugolino gave him practically crushed his spine. Turi Funciazza limited himself to a half-hearted handshake. The Sicilian was down in the dumps. The Court of Cassation was going to be ruling soon. It looked like a life sentence without parole. Bufalo gave him his last bottle of coke. They snorted a line together, then Bufalo said that he needed his advice on a fine point of the rules.

'Let's hear it,' the Sicilian conceded in a bored voice.

'Turi, what happens if someone from outside the family kills someone from the family?'

'Who would be fool enough?'

'I'm just asking… What would you do to him?'

'Why would you need to ask? The family is the family, and anyone from outside the family is just shit. Fuck, Roman, talk straight!'

'Dandi,' Bufalo said clearly, looking him in the eye.

Turi emitted a baffled grunt. 'Dandi's not in the family…'

'Well then, there's no problem…'

'But he's a friend of the family…'

515

'Understood. So a person would have to ask permission?'

'Sometimes they would, sometimes they wouldn't. You'd have to ask…'

'Okay, I'm asking you!'

'What can I tell you? Dandi's a friend of Uncle Carlo, but Uncle Carlo is behind bars, and not everyone in Palermo agrees with him…Now out on the streets things are in the hands of the Maestro, so you'd have to talk to him. Sometimes they'll tell you not to ask again, or else, if the family does you this favour, then you owe a favour to the family…I'll let you know.'

Waiting outside the prison gates was a brand-new Mercedes Benz. A gift from Secco. Bufalo tossed his backpack to the scar-faced gypsy who had welcomed him with a respectful nod of the head and set out on foot for the Bar della Luna.

Two and a half years in prison. Six years in the insane asylum. Trials. Verdicts. Anger. Resignation. Again, a new and more determined anger.

The sign outside the little bar attracted him like a magnet. For six long years he'd watched the place from the window of the common room. He'd watched the elderly owner age and grow stooped. His wife, a diminutive woman dressed in black, vanished one day. For a week, the bar was closed. A black-bordered poster appeared on the metal shutter. Then the man reopened for business, older and more stooped than ever. The guards went in in groups and left scratching their crotches. At night, just before last call, a sad prostitute stopped to count her change for one more grappa. Springs, summers, autumns, winters…Sun and snow…Seasons spent watching. Dreaming. He could already taste the wine. Freedom was like a colossal bender.

He hesitated outside the entrance. He shifted the strands of the fly-barrier curtain aside, as if to peek inside, then let it fall back into place. He had no desire to drink. He wanted to stretch out indefinitely the short time that they'd given him. He wanted to take back the time that they'd stolen from him. He wanted all the time in the world. Temporary leave wasn't freedom. As for the past, let it all remain just as he'd imagined it. In his memory. Including the bender.

Bufalo went back to the Mercedes Benz. A bottomless weariness made his movements slow down exhaustingly.

'Take me to see Secco,' he ordered the gypsy.

He adjusted the backrest and shut his eyes. Neither man spoke a word for the entire length of the trip. The gypsy had put on a cassette of gypsy music. Lulled by the sound of violins and guitars, seduced by the voices of fiery women, Bufalo soon dropped off into a heavy, dreamless slumber.

Secco gave him a hug, then pretended to give him a jocular punch.

'Accounting report.'

Secco named a figure. Bufalo lit a cigarette.

'Is that all?'

Secco started up with the usual litany. With everything that was going on, it was just a miracle that they weren't reduced to starvation. Dandi had turned into a wild animal. There was no talking to him, no reasoning with him. He checked everything down to the last lira, had something to say about everything, only cared about his own business, and left nothing but crumbs for the others. It was worse than it had been with Sardo. Worse than in the darkest times. And anyone who failed to knuckle under wound up like poor old Scrocchiazeppi. A dictator: that's who was boss now. At this rate, everything that they'd built over the years would be nothing but a field of rubble.

Bufalo interrupted with a curt gesture.

'I want fifty in cash and two clean sets of IDs.'

'You're not coming back?'

'No.'

'They're going to be looking for you...'

'How long will it take for you to put it all together?'

'Two, maybe three days...'

'That's fine. In three days. At Il Fungo. Send the gypsy. I've decided I like him.'

Secco mopped a drop of sweat.

'What about...Dandi?'

'Give him my best. Tell him I decided to take some time off. I'm not looking for trouble.'

'So much the better.'

Secco was playing the role of the contented peacemaker, but disappointment was unmistakable on his mouth shaped like a hen's arsehole, in the twitches of his fat rubicund cheeks.

'One more thing: send me a couple of whores.'

The girls showed up in the afternoon. They had to knock and knock before Bufalo woke up and opened the door. He looked the two blondes up and down: pneumatic tits, miniskirts, fishnet stockings. They told him he had them on an unlimited basis: all the time he wanted, anything he wanted to do. Bufalo pulled a couple of C-notes out of his wallet and sent them packing, apologizing for having asked them over in the first place.

'But we've already been paid!'

'That's fine, take it.'

At home, all alone, he felt safer. He still had a place to live, after all. A woman that Secco paid kept the place clean. There was fresh food in the fridge.

That night, he went by the carabinieri station to sign the register, then he walked into the first cinema he passed. They were showing a sexy light comedy. He practically slept through the whole show. He was still sleeping when the usher shook him roughly.

He slept the full five days of his leave of absence. He only left his apartment to sign the register and to take delivery of the package that the gypsy, punctual and laconic, handed him out front of Il Fungo. He slept until time was up for him to return from his leave.

It was only when the evening television news reported that he'd escaped from prison that he finally felt free.

IV

LEANING ON AN elegant walking stick with the head of a greyhound for a handle, backlit by the flames in the fireplace with a Vermeer over the mantelpiece – either a genuine Vermeer or a first-class counterfeiter's masterpiece – the Old Man informed him that only a few very privileged individuals had ever been allowed to set foot in this private pied-à-terre of his.

'Should I consider myself honoured?' Scialoja murmured in a chilly voice.

'You should evaluate the situation objectively. A month ago, you were a piece of bobbing human flotsam, an alcoholic dragging himself from tavern to park bench. Today you're a man who's ready.'

He should have retorted: ready for what? Instead, he limited himself to hoisting his tea cup in the air with an ironic smile.

'Well then, to my rebirth!'

The Old Man laboriously picked up a long fireplace poker and bent over to rake the embers. Exhausted by the effort, out of breath, he collapsed onto an overstuffed chair upholstered in a fetching pink fabric. He'd lost weight. His cheeks were hollow and red with age. He was wheezing. A man close to the jumping-off point, thought Scialoja.

'I don't expect gratitude. Like I told you once before, gratitude is a sentiment I abhor. But I do expect…in fact, I demand that you listen to me. Then, when I'm done, it's your decision!'

Scialoja put down his cup on the small round table, between the lamp with a base consisting of a licentious young cherub and a framed photograph of the Old Man as a young man, in a paratrooper's uniform and beret. Did he really have a choice? A month ago, some guy they called Peloso had grabbed him and jerked him away from the table where he'd sat guzzling his last litre of sweet Olevano wine. Since then, he'd been a guest at that farmhouse, somewhere between the rustic and the pretentious that looked out over the rolling Umbrian countryside. Two men and a woman, servants of some kind, had taken turns guarding him. They'd kept him from drinking alcohol or smoking cigarettes. He'd been forced to walk ten or even fifteen miles in the open countryside, followed by his guards in an off-road vehicle. Armed guards. He hadn't doubted for an instant that, if he'd only given them the excuse, they'd have been delighted to test the efficacy of their pistols.

The first few days had slipped by in a sort of alcoholic haze. He'd put up a minimum level of passive resistance. Just enough to make it clear that he was, in fact, a prisoner. Once the urge for alcohol became less pressing, he started looking around for a way to escape. He'd tried to play on his guard's sensibilities with cunning, cultivating their human sympathy. He found they had none.

Starting on his fifteenth day of captivity, his body had begun to roar again, just like in the old days. He'd started to wake up spontaneously, at dawn, a few minutes before his jailers came to yank him out of bed with a rude jerk. He'd started shaving again. He'd been surprised to find himself yearning for those long excursions over slopes and through clearings, the smell of winter soil, the sudden downpours of rain, the distant flash of lightning. On one of the last days, at sundown, he'd entered into some kind of harmony with the bells of the livestock coming home from pasture. Their mooing had given him a strange sensation, midway between regret for something that would soon be gone forever and the racing pulse that, as a boy, he'd always felt at the thought of the marvellous, unparalleled adventures that tomorrow had stored up for him. He'd stumblingly tried to convey this sensation to the least moronic of his guards. The man had smiled at him, for the first and only time.

Now the Old Man, sprawled in his armchair, was telling him that he had no idea what to do with his gratitude.

'I'm all ears.'

The Old Man nodded.

'In terms of heart attacks, I've got two under my belt, Dottor Scialoja. Ditto, in terms of indictments. But that's not my main problem...'

The Old Man was annoyed by the reactions to the collapse of the Berlin Wall. What irritated him was the cheap burlesque atmosphere in which the most exhilarating years of his life were about to be engulfed. The austere, tragic and anarchistic game to whose construction he had dedicated every last gram of his highly superior energy was about to be transformed into a giddy little costume operetta. Obtuse magistrates devoted to an insipid faith in piddling legalities and yet who yearned, in their heart of hearts, to go down in history as the cunning latter-day Sherlock Holmeses who had finally solved the mystery of the Great Italian Enigma. Communists who shrilled about the handcuffing of democracy. Hawkish Christian Democrats who re-vindicated their militant anti-Communism under the umbrella of NATO. Dovish Christian Democrats who questioned the distortions of the Atlantic Alliance in the confessional. Socialists who struck blows both left and right only to continue on their way, down a path paved in gold ingots. And all them marching in procession to his front door: why, oh why don't you resign? Why don't you take advantage of the extremely advantageous conditions we're offering you? A more than dignified pension...A proud isolation...

And everyone panicking and wondering to themselves: what if he talks? Did he leave a written memorial somewhere? What if he decides to spill the beans? All of them worms. Disgusting, filthy worms. Hack actors in a *commedia all'italiana*!

They denied grief and mourning to the victims and stripped the murders of all honour. The way they so often did, with a smile on their lips. Italian-style.

And the minuet of noble spirits that thrilled the government's pet scriveners...Opinion pieces and illustrious bylines: the Berlin Wall, my role in its downfall. A modest proposal to build another one, new and improved, stronger and longer-lasting. And of course, deeply humanitarian! What do they know about it? What do they ever know?

The Old Man would never speak. And the fact made him feel a certain sadness and a slight giddy thrill of contentment. He was planning to take it with him to the grave, this cruel joy of being the one to know, the only one to know...The Old Man and his secrets...Red terror and Black terror...Feh! The *Untermenschen* must be eating their hearts out over his silence. But something had to perpetuate itself, whatever else happened. A bequest, an inheritance. No, perhaps the right word was heritage...

Then, without warning, in a lunge that was an odd mixture of violence and tenderness, the Old Man seized Scialoja's hand in a paternal clasp.

'I need you to do something for me.'

V

FIEROLOCCHIO HAD COME back because he didn't have a lira to his name, and Bufalo had been his salvation. Pischello was there because he was fed up with Rossana: too clingy. After all, what he liked was adventure. And nothing else.

They were getting the dope from Turi's brother in Palermo and from Turco. Pippo Funciazza charged them prices with a special discount for friends. Turco – whose name meant 'the Turk' – was a contact of Conte Ugolino's. In his youth, he'd been an idealist of the neo-fascist Grey Wolves. He boasted a personal friendship with Ali Agca himself. He'd been sentenced to a total of three hundred years on various charges.

He'd been officially declared dead in a firefight. The police had displayed a disfigured corpse. But Turco had established an agreement with the intelligence agencies. They had provided him with a new identity, weapons and cash. In exchange, he'd promised to bring them the hide of the leader of the Kurdish separatists. Which was a spectacular, bald-faced lie. Once he had the money, Turco eliminated the middleman and went into hiding in the Balkans. He supplied weapons to all the count-less movements – more or less nationalistic and more or less bent on liberation – that were plotting the wholesale destruction of Yugoslavia.

Ever since the collapse of Communism, the routes through the Balkans had turned into a superhighway open to anything and everything. The wealthy Western nations stocked up on all manner of merchandise at the supermarket of dirty business. Whores and underpaid labour for the fathers. Heroin of all grades and qualities for the sons. Turco was a deceitful bastard and did everything he could think of to rip them off.

Bufalo said that sooner or later he'd find a way to pay him back. But in the meantime, he helped them stay afloat. All told, Bufalo and his men moved two or three kilos of dope a month. They only sold in Tuscany, working with certain friends of Conte Ugolino. Bufalo steered clear of Rome. On account of Dandi, he said. Pischello had nothing personal against Dandi. They'd met each other in passing, without ever becoming friends. But if Bufalo had decided to rub him out, that was fine with him. What Pischello loved above all else was action. And he failed to see the reason for such an excessive display of caution.

'Dandi's causing trouble? Then what are you waiting for? Let's go eliminate him from the picture!'

Still, Bufalo was determined to wait. What he was waiting for, nobody knew but him.

In the meantime, after Pippo Funciazza and Turco both got their cuts, there was plenty left over to enjoy the *bonne bonne vie*. That's what Pischello was doing: a different woman every night, binge drinking, snorting lines of coke till his nostrils were ready to explode, driving in the wrong direction down the superhighway. There wasn't a kinky weirdness that he was unwilling to try. Pischello was just basically weird himself. When he went loony, there was no way to hold him back. Like a younger, cleaner, nastier Bufalo.

One night they caught him with a transvestite. Fierolocchio ridiculed him mercilessly: wasn't he afraid of catching AIDS? Pischello pulled out his gun. Bufalo looked him hard in the eye. Pischello was ashamed, but he wasn't going to back down. The transvestite was slithering away, whimpering in terror. Pischello shot him in the leg. The transvestite screamed and shat himself. Bufalo walked over to Pischello and let fly with a kick to the crotch. Pischello remained standing, teeth clenched. Bufalo ragged him.

'If you were a real man, you would have shot me just now.'

Pischello had lowered his pistol. They filled the transvestite's pockets with cash and then dumped him outside the hospital. They'd had to burn the blood-spattered car. None of it had been fun.

Bufalo talked Fierolocchio into becoming his business partner. They regularly handed over money to Secco. The courier was Pischello. He could come and go as he pleased. He'd paid his debt to society. A perfect example of successful rehabilitation: always impeccable, always unfailingly courteous. But that didn't mean he'd become a man. Every time he saw Rossana, she turned his stomach. But he still slept with her. He still hadn't found anyone who was better in bed than she was.

Then, one day, the refinery was raided and Pippo Funciazza went into hiding. From his hideout in Cinisi, he sent a foot soldier to bring them an urgent message. He needed two kilos of shit. The courier was already standing by. If Bufalo could help to solve this situation, the family would be very grateful to him indeed. Bufalo contacted Turco. They agreed on a meeting two kilometres away from the airport of Ronchi dei Legionari. The foot soldier was nervous as a cat. Evidently Pippo was in bad shape, if he was forced to rely on such worthless personnel. Turco showed up exactly on time. He must have suspected something was up, because he said the dope was available, but the price had doubled. The foot soldier said that that was extortion, plain and simple, and invited Turco to reconsider. It wasn't in his interest to make enemies of them.

Turco spat out a gob of tobacco-brown phlegm.

'I'm not afraid of you. Fucking Italians. Take it or leave it.'

Pischello made a move. Bufalo laid a hand on his shoulder and squeezed hard. He knew that the kid had a gun in his trench coat pocket with a bullet in the chamber.

'Fine. It's a deal,' Bufalo said. 'Where's the dope?'

'Where's the money?'

Bufalo nodded to the foot soldier. The foot soldier clicked open the lock on the attaché case. Turco nodded, a smile of triumph spreading across his face, and invited them to come with him. The dope was in the car, a hundred yards away. As they were heading off, the foot soldier took Bufalo aside.

'What are you doing? Why'd you take the deal? It's too much money! Pippo's going to be furious...'

'Just let me work, you little piece of shit.'

Turco opened the car trunk and pulled out two sacks of brown sugar. 'The money?'

Bufalo pulled his revolver and fired a bullet into Turco's forehead.

'Holy shit!' the foot soldier gasped. And then he started vomiting. Fierolocchio gathered the sacks of brown sugar. Bufalo waited for the foot soldier to calm down, handed him the sacks and the attaché case, and told him to give his regards to Pippo.

Later, on their way back to Tuscany, Pischello apologized to Bufalo.

'That thing with the faggot...'

'Water under the bridge.'

Two days later, Pippo Funciazza informed him that, as far as Dandi was concerned, the family was indifferent. Bufalo invited them all out to dinner in a fancy restaurant. For the first time since he'd gotten out of the insane asylum, they saw him laugh. He drank practically half a bottle of Veuve Cliquot on his own and solemnly announced that the *dies irae* – the Day of Wrath – was close and coming closer. All they were waiting on now was for Conte Ugolino to be released: a matter of weeks, possibly only days.

VI

As soon as he set foot in his new office, Scialoja felt an urgent desire for something to drink. He looked around for a bottle. To calm the urge, he forced himself to do forty push-ups. Asceticism. Purity. He had to be up to the task.

He had his own personal bathroom. The mirror over the sink reflected back the image of a toughened forty-year-old, crew cut, clear, somewhat indifferent eyes. Colleagues and underlings lined up to pay homage to him. He dismissed them with the proper blend of courtesy and kindness.

That afternoon, a note from Borgia was hand delivered. Welcome back, Deputy Police Chief. He felt a secret thrill of pleasure that he took care to reveal to no one, least of all the judge. For dinner, he had yogurt and prosciutto.

The lawsuits had been withdrawn. The civil actions had expired. The prosecution for libel had been archived. The suspension from duty had been transformed into a promotion on the field. Deputy Police Chief Dr Nicola Scialoja. Be up to the challenge.

It was the Old Man who'd sent him Sandra Belli. It was the Old Man who'd plunged him into the filth. It was the Old Man who'd grabbed him by the hair and lifted him back onto the high road. He'd taught him a lesson. Shown him the plot. How to play the game. That's what the Old Man wanted him to do: take the game in hand. Take the game to its extreme, logical consequences. Make them dance, make them jump, make them burn, make them collapse.

'You're ready now. You'll have men, resources, all the help you need. Doors wide open everywhere you turn, no bumps along your road.'

The Old Man had been impressed by the interview. The comparison with Dr Strangelove had flattered him.

'Soon, there are going to be some changes made. Take advantage of them. You are going to be one uncontrollable variable. You owe no one any justifications. Ignore everything and everyone. There will be changes made, then everything will go back just exactly as it was. Worse than before. Swinish humanity never changes. In the meantime, you remember? In the meantime, *cependant* – manoeuvre for position. Climb the ladder. Shake off any and all forms of supervision...'

'Including yours?'

'Oh, I'll continue to help you out, long after I've left this vale of tears...'

The Old Man had said goodbye with an awkward caress of sorts.

'Screw as many of the bastards as you can,' were his last words.

He owed everything to the Old Man. If he'd had time to do it, he would have repaid him by crucifying him. But death would be inexorably faster.

Scialoja ordered the latest-generation computer and assigned a couple of trusted secretaries to feed the complete archive of the investigations into it, from the kidnapping of the baron to Bufalo's escape from prison. When they delivered the device to him, he did something he'd been secretly dreaming of trying for years: he navigated to the central memory and typed in the word 'Rolex'. The device set to work with a whirling hum and produced a list of three hundred and fifteen documents. There wasn't a single subject arrested or searched who hadn't displayed a Rolex. To say nothing of the dead bodies. Mister Rolex. The authentic trademark by definition, the ritual tattoo that so obsessed the judges of the Court of Cassation. If it wasn't for them, Bandiera & Bedetti, the Italian retailers of Rolex, might just as well go out of business.

Patrizia's name appeared in two or three reports. He was amazed to realize that the sight of it sparked no emotion whatsoever in him.

Now there was serious business to take care of. He spent hours furiously cross-referencing data. In the last few months, the financial police had been doing excellent work. A new judge was tracing the flows of cash from the gambling industry. Scialoja made a mental note to pay a call on him.

Many ostensibly unrelated threads ran from Dandi only to converge on Secco. Dandi stepped out; Secco stepped in. Dandi was doing his best to get out of the spotlight. He was building an image for himself of an entrepreneur indifferent to factions and alliances. Secco was the man of the future. A Bufalo, but free and on the loose: an uncontrollable variable.

Scialoja smiled: he'd just used the same jargon as the Old Man. He started drawing up a report on Secco's assets. He'd request a judicial confiscation in accordance with the old anti-Mafia law. Strike directly at the heart: that is, the wallet.

At the dawn of a new day, after a night spent happily without sleep, Scialoja found himself concentrating once again on those three names. Secco-Dandi-Bufalo. Secco-Dandi-Bufalo. Secco steps in, Dandi steps out...

An impulse that he couldn't restrain – not yet, at least – guided him towards the telephone. Dandi answered on the tenth ring.

'Who is it?'

'Scialoja.'

'Ah, there you are! If it's about that job we discussed, you're too late. I already hired another failure instead of you...'

'If I were Secco, I'd ask Bufalo a favour.'

'Really? What favour?'

'Your head on a silver platter.'

'Those guys can take turns sucking my cock.'

'Good luck, Dandi.'

'Fuck yourself, cop.'

Scialoja imagined Dandi as he slammed down the receiver, tousled his hair, took a look at his Rolex, and then maybe screwed Patrizia.

The chill of indifference that Scialoja felt deep in his heart scared him.

VII

TURI FUNCIAZZA HAD talked to the Maestro. The Maestro had forwarded the message to Palermo. From Palermo, no answer. The Maestro knew that silence could mean only one thing: the Sicilians had taken offence at Dandi's efforts to slip loose of the partnership. Technically, the matter had stopped concerning the Maestro in any way once the real estate deal had been concluded and the partnership had been dissolved. Still, he was a sentimental old man. He couldn't help feeling a deep fondness for Dandi. Sure, he was foppish and vain, he had a swollen head, he paraded around like a magnificent gentleman, at times he verged on the ridiculous, with that obsessive, almost grotesque aspiration of his to attain an unachievable respectability. Whatever the case, the person who replaced him would certainly be no better.

Theoretically, it was incumbent upon the Maestro to maintain a neutral stance. The neutral and indifferent stance that the family had chosen to assume. But he wasn't breaking any rules if he made an effort to warn Dandi in advance.

The Maestro was trying to get in touch with Dandi when they arrested him for an old case of extortion. A financier in Milan – a miserable nobody that they'd fed, housed and saved once or twice from bankruptcy – had suddenly discovered that he had a conscience and now he'd dragged half the family into the mud with him. Relegated to solitary confinement, the Maestro had only one chance: the brotherhood. He mentioned it during a conference with his lawyer.

'Dandi's in danger. You need to talk to the Old Man.'

But the Old Man sent word to get in touch with Dottore Scialoja, and refused to see the Maestro. The Old Man had lost touch. It wasn't clear why they couldn't get rid of him. He just got crazier and more uncontrollable with every day that passed. The bond that tied him to that cop was incomprehensible. And dangerous. The Old Man was losing his mind, and the hot potato was now in his hands.

Given the context, Counsellor Miglianico decided that the best policy to follow would be to imitate the ostrich. All things considered, the Maestro's interest was strictly on a personal basis. All things considered, the Old Man was done for. All things considered, Dandi was an arrogant ruffian, and his fate was a matter of no particular importance.

Once Conte Ugolino was officially declared of sound mind and had been released from the criminal insane asylum, Bufalo went to see Secco and told him that he'd like to have a face-to-face meeting with good old Dandi. Secco stalled for time. At least ten days. He'd have to churn the accounts for a while, see how much he could claw back. He'd have to put into operation a complicated mechanism involving companies and invoicing. A part of the estate would, in any case, wind up in the hands of Dandi's heirs, but he believed that the lion's share could still be saved. Moreover, ever since Dandi had decided to live a life of gilded leisure, it had become impossible to track him down. It would take him some time just to trace his whereabouts, as he never even came around to Secco's office anymore.

'The only thing I know for sure is that he spends a lot of time at the Pagnottone...'

The Pagnottone was a seafood restaurant in Parioli. Pischello went to lunch there with Rossana, and reported back that there would be no problems.

'We can even go there tonight.'

'But the place is full of people, at all hours!' Fierolocchio objected.

'So what? All you need is four Kalashnikovs, and then you'll see the place empty out!'

'But families with little kids go there to eat! What're we doing now, shooting little kids?'

'Well, how's that saying go? It would have been better to die when you were little...'

Bufalo was opposed to the plan. No moral misgivings, just the awareness that if you shot a kid, they'd be sure to make you pay for it. Kids were sacred. Just like cops, judges and priests.

Pischello listened to the sermon but he wasn't conviced, it was plain to see. Bufalo told him that sometimes it was best to listen to experience. There were things you could do and there were things you couldn't. There were people who could do whatever they wanted and there were others who had to stop in time. Sometimes respecting boundaries could save your life.

'Holy crap, Bufalo! You got all educated when you were in the insane asylum...I guess you had plenty of time on your hands, didn't you?'

'You wanna hear something funny? You know who taught me this? Dandi, none other!'

It took Secco ten days to clean up his account ledger. One Saturday morning, he called Bufalo, who was holed up in an industrial shed along the Via Laurentina.

'Today he's coming by to sign the last powers of attorney. And tonight at seven he's going to pick up a couple of pieces of stained glass at Savona, the antiques place on Via dei Coronari.'

Dandi's Blues
1990

I

ON THE MORNING of his last day, lolling in his jacuzzi, Dandi felt himself swell with a boundless surge of energy. The time had come to rid himself of all the old detritus of the past. He was starting a new life. He'd worked hard, but at last the mechanism was capable of operating on its own. The clean money coming in was considerably more than the revenue from loan sharking and video poker machines. He could cut his ties without losing a lira. The income from his landholdings had been invested in broad daylight. A couple of jeans shops, a chain of dry cleaners, a hotel in Abano Terme, a real estate development on the Gargano, an idyllic tourist resort that certain OPEC sheiks were eyeing with interest – the list of properties that he controlled either directly or by proxy was growing longer day by day. He could afford the whim – and it was, in fact, nothing more than a whim – of buying a restaurant that was on the verge of bankruptcy in the historic centre of Rome. And just because he liked the owners, an elderly couple with one foot in the grave who exchanged love letters and called each other by names of endearment. He could afford anything he wanted. He was the top; number one.

Dandi thought about a future of travelling and joyful serenity. He still had ambitions to make films. He'd unceremoniously fired that incompetent Surtano, who was good for nothing but sucking cash out of his bank account and converting it to cocaine to blow up his insatiable nostrils. He'd paid a call on a genuine film producer with a bag of cash and a sensational proposal. Negotiations were underway. Films! No more pistol. No more prison. Retirement? Why not? He'd given so much to so many, it was only fair that he enjoy the fruits of his labours. No more video poker. No more loan sharking and fixed football games. He would be as generous in the leaving of the business as he had been in his triumph. The one and only, the invincible, the chosen one. Dandi was dreaming of a freedom without restrictions.

The Filipino houseboy, Ramon, announced that Nero had come to call. Dandi welcomed him in a dressing gown, stretched out on his new peccary-hide chaise longue.

'Nice, eh? It used to belong to Rock Hudson. He liked to fuck his little boyfriends on it...'

'That didn't go too well for him.'

'I'm not superstitious.' Dandi laughed. 'And, after all, we have different tastes! Can I offer you something to drink?'

'A cup of tea. Without sugar.'

At a gesture from Dandi, the Filipino moved off silently. Nero handed him the briefcase with the week's take and got comfortable at the far end of the B&B Italia sofa.

'We have a problem in the Nomentano quarter. A cop's getting out of line. Botola tried to cut a deal, thought it was a matter of gifts, and the cop arrested him. Miglianico got him out immediately, of course, but in the meantime, the social club's been shut down...'

Dandi made a vague gesture.

'I think you ought to have a chat with Peloso,' Nero concluded.

Ramon served the tea. Nero took a long swallow of the boiling hot liquid. Dandi told him that he was pulling out of the social clubs deal.

'Are you serious?'

'I'm going by Secco's today to sign the powers of attorney. But that won't change anything as far as you're concerned. In fact, if anything, you'll have one less mouth to feed!'

'You seem to be pretty confident...'

'Absolutely confident! And wipe that look off your face. Come on, let me show you something...'

Dandi locked arms with Nero and took him downstairs.

'You want to know why I bought this palazzo? For the simple reason that my mama – may God elevate her in glory – broke her back polishing the marble staircase of some fucked-up *Marchese*. Let's call it a form of redemption…The renovations alone cost me half a billion lire. Look here, this is the ballroom…'

Nero couldn't keep from gazing in open admiration. The pieces were all authentic, and all arrayed with excellent taste. He'd come a long way, the old bandit! Dandi got the message and smiled.

'As you can see, in the end I came back to Tor di Nona. And I came back as the boss!'

On the ground floor, right next to the seventeenth-century front door, Dandi had renovated the old servants' quarters. And now he possessed a glittering new *salle de jeu* – as he liked to call it – with a fully equipped gym, a billiard parlour, an emergency fuck-room, just in case any of his friends felt like they needed a quickie, with circular mirrors and black satin sheets, a ballroom with a perch for the DJ and a dance floor, and a private screening room, complete with giant screen.

'So you can enjoy a film in blessed peace. Oh, whenever you want, my house is your house, Nero! Now to finish in glory: a whole collection of rare antique books…There's even a copy of that book that the professor gave me. Do you remember the professor?'

'*The Protocols of the Elders of Zion…*'

'Right. It's worth a pile of money. I even read a little bit of it. Now, Nero, tell me: do you really believe that stuff?'

Nero said nothing. Dandi had had enough of his black mood.

'All right, then, Nero, unless there's something else…I've got lots of things to do today…'

'Bufalo's back.'

'Too bad for him. He's going to get himself arrested.'

'That appointment with Savona…'

'What about it?'

'I wouldn't go. It's not safe.'

'Who? Savona? I pulled him back from the brink of bankruptcy! No, Savona's totally clean…'

'Bufalo's pissed off, Dandi.'

'Bufalo, Bufalo, Bufalo…You remind me of that cop, Scialoja. Bufalo should just bless the Virgin Mary he's not a yard deep underground right now…'

'Maybe so, but he's here. And he's got Fierolocchio and Pischello with him.'

'I've settled matters with Fierolocchio. As for Pischello...Who the hell is this Pischello?'

'He's a guy who's capable of anything.'

Hell, Nero really had made his mind up to ruin his day! If it weren't for the fact that he was an old comrade...

'Do you want to get it through your head once and for all that I don't give a damn about those four renegades? They're powerless against me! They reek of dead carcasses! I'm Dandi, you understand? I gave a huddled mass of street thugs a path and a sense of confidence. I own Rome! And you know why I own it? Because I created Rome. That's right! Before me, there wasn't anything here, just a bunch of outsiders grazing on the open fields. Sicilians, Calabrians, Frenchmen from Marseilles, smart-arses, the scattered masses of you slaves, licking the bones the rich masters tossed under the table for you. Before me, there were a bunch of two-bit loan sharks and cut-throats ready to shit their pants when they ran into the first few *caramba* with a pair of balls on them. Same for you, Nero! With all that crap you used to go on about – the Idea, and the Act and the Revolution...You wound up on my payroll like the rest of them – like the cabinet ministers, and the lawyers, and the judges, and the military commanders with their fine uniforms...So if you think that a crowd of raggedy-arsed losers can scare me...'

Dandi was shouting. He wasn't used to being told no. He was shouting louder and louder, and he could be heard all over Trastevere. But Nero didn't seem to care in the slightest.

'We'll see you tonight, at seven, at Savona's. I'll bring Botola with me. Better to be alert.'

'If I see you, I'll shoot you, Nero. I'm not kidding.'

'When was the last time you packed a gun, Dandi?'

'Hey, Nero, don't get carried away with yourself!'

'You're the boss. But I'm still out there. I'll call you later.'

Finally alone, Dandi put on his Armani jeans and the monogrammed Battistoni shirt, the mirrored sunglasses and the jacket with the crest of the Circolo di Voga rowing club, the Rolex and the fine gold chain with the holy image of the Virgin Mary set in a golden oval, with the phrase engraved: *Watch over my loved ones*. He picked up the briefcase and the keys to his scooter.

Outside there was a bright March sky. Don Dante was in the forecourt of the basilica.

'I kiss your hands, Padre.'

'Bless you, my son! I've told you a thousand times never to use those words...'

'Then I kiss your robe, Monsignor!'

Don Dante shooed away two tattered little boys who were playing ball in the waiting room and led Dandi into the sacristy. Dandi extracted the already filled-out cheque from his breast pocket and handed it over, eyes lowered and hands trembling in humility. Gina refused to discuss the idea of divorce. Miglianico had put Dandi on guard against the vendetta of a wounded wife, especially one who was given to religious frenzies. The only way forward was the Sacra Rota, the ecclesiastical court. And the road to the Rota ran through that greedy and hypocritical man of the cloth.

'But I can't accept this, my son!'

'It's for the poor...'

'Ah, the poor! If you only knew how hard life is for a humble priest, struggling day in and day out to wrest those unfortunate creatures from the clutches of Satan!'

The priest snatched at the cheque. He read the numbers and turned pale.

'I have many sins of which I hope to be absolved, Padre...'

'Your request has been granted,' murmured Don Dante, hastening to conceal the cheque beneath a Moroccan leather paper-holder. 'The hearing of the ecclesiastical tribunal is set for next month...'

Patrizia was still in bed when Dandi arrived.

'What a miserable night,' Patrizia moaned. 'Three South Americans stuffed to the gills with cocaine. Friends of Nercio, so they said. Real losers, hicks that give you this feeling, you're not sure what they're looking for, but it's not likely to be anything good... They all came two minutes into it, spraying jizm all over the furniture, and then they just wouldn't pack up and leave.'

When Botola told Dandi that Patrizia had taken up her old profession again, he'd given her a good smacking around. She hadn't even bothered to deny the accusation.

'I was bored. You've gotten fat.'

He'd never completely tame this woman. Every time he got distracted by business concerns and lowered his guard, she'd slip out of his grasp. A whore by vocation. The only person in the whole city of Rome who could confidently tell him to go to hell. His woman. It was some struggle, though. And in the end, he knew he'd win. The way he always did.

'What are you doing? I'm sleepy…'

Dandi was excited by the scent of bed and sleepiness, Patrizia's watchful sleepiness. He took her violently.

'We're getting married in June. And you're going to stop working.'

Patrizia stiffened and shoved him away.

'Not on your life. You know how I feel…'

'You're going to be Dandi's wife. And Dandi's wife is no whore.'

Patrizia ran her hand through her long hair. An amused sigh made her small breasts heave.

'If I'm a whore, then pay me what I deserve!'

Dandi picked up the briefcase and poured a waterfall of crumpled cash out over her. Disgusting filthy banknotes that had passed through the grubby hands of miserable white-collar employees and imperious professionals. Patrizia grabbed handfuls of the notes and stuffed them into her mouth, under her perfectly plucked underarms, between her legs.

'Tell me that you've never seen so much money in your life,' he murmured in a hoarse voice as he turned her over on her tummy.

He took her again, from behind, and this time Patrizia seemed to participate more passionately.

'Tell me you won't take anyone else to bed but me!' he groaned as he was coming.

Patrizia pushed him off her with a mischievous smile.

'That will just mean that I'll have to do it with the others in the basement, or in the bathroom!'

She showed him to the door. 'I'm expecting the ambassador,' she said. 'The one who likes to be whipped.'

'So what happens if I shoot him between the legs?'

'You can't even remember what a pistol looks like!'

It was the second time someone had said the same thing to him in just the past few hours. Were they trying to tell him something? But Dandi was too thrilled with his freedom to think about it.

He returned home. On his answering machine he found two messages from Miglianico and one from Nero. The lawyer was summoning him for a meeting of the brotherhood. His comrade urged him to call him back an hour before the appointment at Savona. He'd leave him a message with Patrizia.

Nero was paranoid. Maybe Dandi could give Bufalo a little cash to get him out of his hair. A fleeting thought. Dandi wasn't doing any more negotiating. Dandi wasn't afraid of anything or anyone now.

For the meeting with Miglianico, he chose a Versace leather suit, custom-made shoes from London, a light overcoat without a lining and, on his right pinkie finger, impossible to miss, the ring of the masonic lodge.

The lawyer seemed worried when Dandi arrived. Dandi noticed that a rivulet of sweat now dotted his impeccable sunlamp tan. He extracted a black hood, a mason's apron and a fencing sword from his wall safe and invited Dandi to follow him into the musty parlour that he used only for his clients without much money.

'Come on. We were only waiting for you.'

There were four of them. Dandi exchanged an icy nod of greeting with Peloso. He'd never seen the other three before. Physiques that were clearly the product of time at a health club, faces of well-to-do snobs, wrinkles visible under a hasty application of foundation. Brothers from Milan, said the lawyer, and added that, considering the circumstances, they might as well skip the ritual.

'Sure, let's just get busy.'

One of the three strangers, the one that seemed to be in charge, unfurled the classic rug-merchant smile, opened a glossy folder and started his pitch.

'In view of the upcoming football World Cup, which as you know will be held in just a few months, the consortium that we represent, a pool of companies specializing in the construction of highly specialized infrastructure—'

Dandi made a sign for him to cut to the chase. The Milanese froze. Miglianico took the situation in hand.

'The project in hand involves the renovation of a metro station and the construction and equipment of four utility buildings. The brother won the contract.'

'Congratulations. So how do I fit in?'

The Milanese cleared his throat.

'The contract's already been signed. Unfortunately, the consortium that we represent finds itself going through a temporary crisis of liquidity—'

'Ah, now I get it!' Dandi snickered. 'You all don't have a lira to get started!'

'Perhaps stated somewhat brutally,' the Milanese sighed, 'but substantially accurate!'

In other words, they were offering him a partnership at a loss. The northern polenta-eaters would put in the signed contracts and he'd provide the cash.

Dandi lit a cigarette. He blew smoke into the lawyer's face.

'What's the state of progress on construction?'

'We're supposed to get started this week...'

'Tell me something, counsellor: these guys are still bowing and scraping and they think they're going to be finished in time for the World Cup? There's no way!'

Miglianico dry-washed his hands.

'Who said anything about being finished? The important thing is just to get started...'

'And you think no one will mind getting short-changed?'

'Italy's going to win the World Cup and certain minor details will easily be overlooked.'

'I don't give a damn about Italy. The only team that matters to me is Roma.'

There was a burst of laughter. The lawyer took a folder full of papers from the desk and invited Dandi to sign. Zero risk. Three hundred and sixty degrees of coverage on all imaginable fronts: political, banking, legal. When he pulled out the stops, Miglianico knew how to be convincing. Dandi started to see the good side of the project.

538

'I'll think it over and let you know.'

The smile faded from the Lombard's face and appeared on the lawyer's face.

'Good friend, brother of mine – lentils can't grow without being watered, and if the rain comes late, the lentil wilts and dies...'

Dandi signed. In the past, he'd trusted Miglianico and he'd had no regrets. He left without saying goodbye. Peloso came after him. Dandi pretended he hadn't seen him and quickened his step.

'Just a word, Dandi...'

'If it's about the social clubs, talk to Secco. I'm out of that circuit.'

'This has nothing to do with the social clubs. There's a problem.'

'Another one?'

'You remember what happened with Pidocchio?'

'Everyone in Rome knows that I had nothing to do with Pidocchio...'

'Well, I've heard that there's a judge who doesn't seem to think that's the case...'

It sounded serious, said Peloso. The judge was one of the new generation. A Communist. Absolutely uncontrollable. Word was that he'd gone into partnership with Scialoja. New and more thorough investigations had been ordered.

'Still, the whole thing could be made to die on the vine at the level of a report from the judicial police. But they'd have to move fast...'

'How fast?'

'Thirty times faster...'

Dandi opened his chequebook. Peloso recoiled in horror.

'A cheque? Have you lost your mind?'

'Hey, Peloso, what a pain in the arse! Drop by and see Botola tomorrow.'

'Tomorrow could be too late...'

Peloso let him use the radio-phone installed in his Alfetta.

'Aren't you afraid of someone listening in?'

'Who could? Me and who else?'

Dandi called Botola and told him to get thirty lobsters ready for Peloso.

'Half an hour,' he told Peloso.

'Half an hour's the right amount of time.'

'Let me make another call.'

'Be my guest,' said Peloso, and moved away.

Dandi called Nero. No answer. Then he tried Patrizia's number. She picked up on the tenth ring. Her voice was languid, drawling, deeply irritated.

'It's me.'

'As if you have to tell me. What's up? I'm working.'

'I want you.'

'I'm sorry, I don't have a single hole in my schedule.'

'Not even one little hole?'

'Not today, I'm dead tired.'

'Did anyone call for me?'

'I'm not your secretary.'

'If Nero calls—'

'If Nero calls, I'll invite him over for a drink.'

Patrizia hung up with a deep, throaty laugh. Dandi experienced a stab of irritation. Now Patrizia was overdoing it. It was an enjoyable struggle, sure, as long as he was the winner. Let me just take you to the altar, *bella mia*...

Dandi was of a mind to give Patrizia a nice little lesson. Yes, she'd overdone it this time. One last little lesson, before spreading all Rome at her feet like a spectacular offering.

At Secco's too he found himself signing a seemingly endless stack of papers. After the umpteenth rip-off, Secco poured champagne and raised a glass to friendship. Dandi took the merest sip, barely wetting his lips. Secco had had two new gold teeth put in. He was wearing a pink shirt and a carnation in his buttonhole. Dandi asked him if he knew anything about what was up with Bufalo.

'He was here,' Secco said, looking him straight in the eye.

'I'm so scared!'

Secco laughed.

'You know how Bufalo is – says he has a business deal in Greece, I loaned him some money...If you ask me, he and his friends have already left town.'

'Your own money, I hope!'

'Of course, Dandi, I'd never dare to—'

'That's right, good boy. Keep it up and you'll live to be a hundred.'

At a quarter to seven – he'd returned home for another session in the jacuzzi – Dandi found Nero waiting for him outside.

'Hey, Nero, I hear that Bufalo's on the run.'

'Yeah, I heard the same thing.'

'Peloso says there's trouble about that thing with Pidocchio.'

'I'll talk to him.'

'Okay, see you tomorrow, Nero.'

'Ciao, Dandi.'

Handshake. Back aboard the scooter. Ten minutes to the appointment.

Savona took his money and hurried over to the shipper. The delivery of the stained glass was expected about eleven. Ramon would take care of it.

The stained glass panels were magnificent. Something out of a dream. The touch of class that had been sorely missed. He'd been waiting for them for six months now. They used to be in the home of a famous actress, Sarah Bernhardt, one of the great Gabriele d'Annunzio's lovers. A poet and a legionnaire, a man who was equally adept with the pen and with the sword. Maybe one day Dandi would make a film about him. He needed to remember to tell the director to include them in a shot or two. When he finally made his film. Someday soon. Any day now.

At a minute to seven, Dandi turned into Via dei Coronari, riding against traffic. Fierolocchio honked the horn of his Fiat Tipo twice. From the opposite side of the road, a Honda 750 pulled out, headlights doused. Pischello was driving. Conte Ugolino, seated behind him, took careful aim. Dandi passed through the glow of light from a shop sign. When he heard the shot, Bufalo smiled faintly and lit a cigarette.

II

BASILICA OF SAINTS AMETHYST AND TODARIAN

Most Reverend Eminence,

At the express request of our parishioner, Gina ****, I venture to request of this Vicariate of Rome the *nihil obstat* to allow the deceased husband of the above-mentioned parishioner to be entombed in one of the mortuary chambers located in the subterranean crypts of the basilica in question.

The work on the sepulchre itself will be undertaken and completed by craftstmen and labourers specializing in this sector, who have previously taken part in the entombment of the most recent supreme pontiffs in the Vatican.

The deceased was generous in his assistance to the poor who worship in this basilica, the priests and the seminarians, and in his suffrage, our parishioner Gina **** promises to continue to perform charitable deeds, especially with contributions to the construction and implementation of a diocesan project.

The deceased, ****, a popular figure throughout the city, under his nickname of 'Dandi', died in Rome several days ago.

I herewith pay my deepest respects to Your Reverence, and I ask your holy blessing upon myself, the priests who assist in the pastoral service provided by this basilica, and the poor whom we assist.

Don Dante Decenza, Rector

VICARIATE OF ROME
Prot. no. 4456/90 rse

It is hereby declared on the part of the Vicariate, *nihil obstat*, as far as it is within its jurisdiction, to the entombment of the mortal remains of **** ****, also known as 'Dandi', recently deceased in Rome, in one of the mortuary chambers located in the subterranean crypts of the Basilica of Saints Amethyst and Todarian.

Signed,

(x)

The Cardinal Vicar

III

Bufalo, Fierolocchio and Pischello celebrated with a trip to Amsterdam. A few days before that, Pischello had picked up a blonde in a disco, a Dutch girl, Gherda. They'd hit it off. Rossana threw a tantrum. Pischello told her to go to hell.

Gherda raised no objections when he asked her if she could put a couple of his friends up for a few days. The whole drive to Amsterdam they were beside themselves with excitement, reliving every detail of the killing. The two cars, with Fierolocchio and Bufalo at the wheel, barring the street, ready to intervene in case the marksman failed to hit dead centre. Dandi's scooter roaring arrogantly the wrong way up the one-way street. The single shot fired by Conte Ugolino, shooting from the hip, on the fly, had hit the target square in the heart. Dandi had continued another fifty feet or so down the street before hitting a parked car. It was a scooter driven by a corpse: a touch of class that would have made even the dearly departed gangster smile.

The cute little Dutch blonde had brought a couple of girlfriends to meet them. Black girls, but magnificent. They let the men feel them up and were laughing in the private back room of the Amsterdam coffee-shop full of stoners of all races and ages. Neither Bufalo nor Fierolocchio could understand a word anyone was saying, unlike Pischello, who spoke pretty good English. It was a thrilling situation. They were smoking joints and getting brewed on Mary Jane tea. Everyone in Holland was doing it. Basically in front of the cops. All you had to do was keep yourself somewhat under control.

Fierolocchio declared that Holland was his new favourite country.

'This is where I want to live and this is where I want to die!'

Bufalo smacked him lightly in the back of his neck.

'Because you're an idiot. The day they start selling dope at the local tobacco shop is the day we go out of business!'

Pischello said that he'd like to send a postcard to Judge Borgia.

'Sure, good thinking,' Bufalo mumbled, 'and tomorrow Interpol pulls up out front.'

'I'd like to give Borgia a joint,' laughed Fierolocchio, 'then maybe he'd start to understand the right way to live!'

'And throw in a couple of puffs for Scialoja,' Bufalo conceded.

The thought of the judge high on pot drove them crazy. They started laughing and couldn't stop. The girls caught the giggles too.

They went on like that for a whole week. But it couldn't last forever. Somebody had to think about business.

IV

'OH MY GOD, oh my God! They killed my friend! It was that bastard Freddo!' shouted Secco at the funeral, tearing out his hair in the solemn surroundings.

And the fat man's version of what happened was approved by acclamation, while Don Dante pronounced the homily, and Gina, wrapped in a mournful mink stole, looked around her, accepting with cold eyes the homage of the Roman underworld and the Roman overworld that mattered. Among those attending were: Er Bavoso, Er Bavosetto, Caccola, Puzzafiato and Pesciolino. There was Cachezio with Monnezza, Mollichetta with Er Pilletto, and Striozzo with La Vecchia. Then there was: Er Zebra, Fragoletta, Er Sicco and Zimbo; Er Kilovattaro, Capretta and Bardocchietto; Canappa, Er Tadù, Camera-a-Canna, Melle, Balena and Staccaletto. Then there was: Trippa, Er Cornuto, Micio, Nuerga, Er Pippetto; Toro, Filotto and Burino; Er Sisone, 'A Biancona and Er Bighimeo; Gufo, Caciotta, Marisa 'a Zinnona, Fiasco, Coccetta, Darè, Adolfo (also known as the 'Fürhere coi Baffi'), Paperone, Tizzo and Mammoletta. 'A Zagheria, Er Zamondo and Barone. And there was: Galletto and Mirella l'Albina, Pietro Puzza-Barone, Er Lupetto; and Suino, Pallesecche, Gianni 'a Vacca, and lots and lots of others – an honour guard of gypsies and certain others that no one had ever seen before.

It was a chilly morning, with a fine drizzle and a biting wind that carved into your temples. From a third-floor apartment overlooking the venerable old piazza, with a pair of precision binoculars, Scialoja took in the human comedy of grief while his men watched, took notes and filmed. He'd given orders to stay well clear of the stage. The long manhunt was now over. Dandi had been a capo, a chieftain. He was a man with a plan, after his fashion. He deserved some degree of respect.

Scialoja was going to nail his murderers in the end. His would be the ironic, belated hand of the vendetta. The Old Man would have savoured the twist. Yes, they really were all here. The sharks, the minnows, and even the plankton. The only one missing was Patrizia. Scialoja felt sure that there'd been no need to even negotiate with the widow. Patrizia could figure it out for herself: her attendance wouldn't be welcome.

Botola couldn't hold back the flood of tears. Nercio was surrounded by a squadron of black-clad thugs and heavy-hitters. Donatella was holding a wreath with Ricotta's signature. Ricotta had wept as he watched the news report. Because on the one hand it was obvious that, after what Dandi had done to Scrocchiazeppi, no one could really say a good word on his behalf. But at the same time, with Dandi's death, the film had a sad ending, and Ricotta really couldn't take a film with a sad ending. Of course, Nero was there too, refusing to look anyone in the eye, and the one person he did look full in the face, and hard, was Secco. And Secco trembled: he understood that the other man knew, and that all it would take was a word from Nero to destroy the façade of his innocence. Nero was on the brink of saying that word, but he changed his mind, and at the last minute turned his head away and sank back into silence. He'd have had to explain, first of all, why he'd pretended to swallow the horseshit about Bufalo escaping to Greece. Why he hadn't warned Botola. Why he hadn't protected his boss right up to the very end. Why he hadn't stopped him in that last meeting. Why he'd rushed over to Patrizia's and the two of them had stretched out comfortably with the soft background music and a nice glass of Chinotto, while he talked to her about history and life, and the man of destiny. And then he'd told her that there was no such thing as the man of destiny – that everything was written in the sacred river of life, the river that runs and runs, inexorably carrying off both good and evil forever... They hadn't even fucked. Patrizia was exhausted, practically falling asleep right then and there. When it became clear to him that she was no longer listening, Nero tiptoed out of the room.

After all, he and Secco were cut from the same cloth. Neither of them believed in anything. They both detested dreams. That one dream that had undone first Libano, then Freddo, and finally Dandi – the dream of building something that was destined to last. But you can't build on the void. You don't win the game with young, handsome heroes. You win the game by remaining on the field long after the others have cried, 'Hold, enough!' And more often than not, the last ones standing were the hunchbacks, the bladders of fat, the accountants, the miserable grinds you wouldn't lend five lire. It was all written in life.

Everyone was looking for Freddo, but no one knew where he was. They staked out likely locations. They tailed the parents. They turned Rome inside out like a sock. Nothing.

Pischello came back and it didn't take long to figure out that there were no problems. No one even dreamed that they were the ones who eliminated Dandi. And everyone was looking for Freddo. Pischello was about to take the good news to his comrades when Rossana insisted on one last date.

They met at the Zodiaco. Rossana was swollen with sedatives and alcohol. Puffy face, her hair a mess, she wasn't clean, with a stink on her that was a mix of days spent in bed, like a she-goat. Pischello recoiled in disgust. The more she rubbed up against him, the more he asked himself how he could ever have felt anything remotely resembling desire for this walking corpse. Pischello was ashamed even to be seen in public with someone like her. He dragged her away from the club, and by now she could barely stand upright.

They were walking along the Via Panoramica when, without warning, she clawed his cheek. Pischello struggled to control himself and managed to do no more than push her away. But Rossana renewed her attack. Pischello picked her up by sheer force and hurled her away from him, in no particular direction. Rossana crashed through the wooden safety fence and tumbled into the street below. A truck just happened to be passing. Too late to brake.

Pischello saw her body disintegrate under the impact of that over-whelming onrushing mass and understood that things had just gotten very heavy. The two of them had been seen together. Her family knew all about their relationship. Pischello was sincerely sorry for what had happened. He wished there'd been a different ending, but it was too late to do anything about that now.

That same night, from the airport, he called Rossana's father and tried to explain that it had only been an unfortunate accident. A week later, he boarded a ship in Amsterdam and set sail for Kenya.

Everyone was still looking for Freddo when Carlo Buffoni found Gigio.

V

FREDDO DROPPED THE receiver and ran a hand over his forehead. He felt an overwhelming urge to break down in tears. But he couldn't do that. Not there, not in front of the wealthy South Americans and the European tourists who were crowding into the Paloma Blanca, gulping down plates of lasagna and washing it down with robust Chilean wine. Not in front of Roberta, who smiled as she took orders and fed them back to the kitchen, delivering food to the tables and exchanging greetings and chitchat with regular customers.

Cerino looked up from his accounting and asked a wordless question.

'I'm going home,' Freddo explained. 'See you tomorrow.'

His mother had screamed and sobbed over the phone until she couldn't breathe. They'd found Gigio's half-charred corpse in the burned hulk of an Alfetta, under Ponte Mammolo. Nero said that Gigio had been seen with Carlo Buffoni. But he wouldn't repeat that under oath. His mother had cursed him on the phone.

Freddo walked through the mild evening, skirting the bands of drunks who were singing rude songs as they rattled their bottles against the flaking old walls of Managua. Freddo could picture the scene in his mind: Gigio begging for mercy and Carlo lifting the knife, plunging it down into his brother's tender, lamb-like youth. Because Freddo had taken no pity on Aldo, and that was the coin in which they'd repaid him. Brother, brother, and I never even said farewell to you!

Unsteady on his feet, he stumbled to the bed swathed in mosquito netting and let himself drop onto the fresh, lavender-scented sheets. The household staff must have sensed lowering storm clouds, because he didn't hear them coming and going as usual, and their inevitably queru-lous voices had fallen silent.

The shivering began. Then the clammy sweat. The doctor said that there was nothing to worry about. At least, not for the moment. Still, better to keep a watchful eye on things. But Freddo could feel the nodules growing day by day. They were growing, swelling, and one day they'd burst. The infected blood that he'd injected into himself in order to get out of prison had entered his circulatory system. For the past year, he and Roberta had been using condoms. There hadn't been any other women. Nor would there be, ever.

Why had Gigio gone back, Freddo kept asking himself?

The telephone rang. Dolores stuck her head in the door. Someone for El Señor Alvarez. Freddo dismissed her with a brisk wave of the hand. *El Señor Alvarez.* That was what they called him now. He'd been Alves, and Neto, and Tabarron. He'd learned Spanish and Portuguese. He'd spent months with Baffo di Ghisa at La Frontera overseeing coke shipments. It didn't take long for him to figure out that this was no longer his line of business, though. And he'd let it drop. He'd run into a small group of Nero's old comrades – professional torturers who were working the dictator circuit, with their thick black moustaches, their mirrored sunglasses, and a caravan of diseased *putas*. They hadn't hit it off. They reminded Roberta of the skulls painted on pirate flags.

Now they had the restaurant, and regulation identity papers that Cerino had managed to procure in the name of his age-old solidarity with the Sandinistas. Later, Cerino really had tried to kill himself. They'd saved him in time, but he'd lost the power of speech. Now he was helping Freddo and Roberta to run the restaurant.

There had never been any problems with Roberta. Only a single argument between them, many years earlier. A Chilean in exile had happened to dine at the Paloma. He was a diminutive, chubby guy. He told them he was an author.

'What book are you working on now?' Roberta had asked him.

'It's the story of a friendship between a cat and a seagull. The cat raises the baby seagull, which grows up thinking it's a cat. But the cat explains to him that a seagull isn't a cat. And the cat teaches the seagull to fly.'

Roberta's face had turned all dreamy and she'd refused to take any money from the Chilean or his girlfriend for their meal. Later, Freddo had told her that the story of the cat and the seagull made no sense to him.

'You don't understand a thing. You're an animal.'

'Come on! It's just a fairy tale for kids…'

At the word 'kids', Roberta had burst into tears. Freddo understood that however much they loved each other, that boulder would always exist between them. So he'd become even sweeter to her. And after a while it was over. But those were old stories. Water long past under the bridge. Now all that stayed with him was the lamb's disfigured face and his own immense pain and grief. There were things you could never run away from. Sooner or later, you wound up paying for everything.

Freddo went to the phone and requested a long-distance call to Italy.

When he was told about the phone calls, Scialoja remained relatively unruffled. He knew Freddo. He knew them all. He could predict every move they'd make with his eyes closed. Freddo had nothing to do with that whole thing. Freddo had turned his back on the bunch of them years ago. He was nothing but a scapegoat. And Gigio's death was further proof of that.

No, this was something else: Dandi leaves the picture, Bufalo opens the door, and in scoots Secco. The trail led to Nicaragua. Troublesome country, entirely possible that Freddo could pass himself off as a victim of political persecution.

Scialoja sent dispatches via Interpol. The Managua police went to knock at the door of a well-respected local citizen, Señor Alvarez. An ordinary, routine administrative matter, said the officer, almost apologetic about having bothered him.

'Forget about it. It's me,' said Freddo.

Scialoja flew to Managua under complete secrecy.

'I don't have anything to say to you,' Freddo said. 'I want to see Borgia.'

The commissario flew back to Rome. Borgia had been mercilessly dismissed from the running in two civil service exams for positions as notary public, and he'd resigned himself to living off the crumbs of financial wrongdoing.

When he saw the cop walk into his office, Borgia threatened to throw him bodily out the window. Scialoja softly shut the office door and removed his jacket.

'With all due respect, dottore, now you've really busted my balls for the last time!'

The plane for South America was scheduled to take off at six that afternoon. Borgia went by the French day school to pick up his son. The boy was talking with a friend.

'Papa, this is Danilo. He wins all the prizes!'

The little boy extended his hand with an exaggeratedly polite gesture.

'Danilo, what's your surname?' laughed Borgia, his curiosity piqued by the sight of that tall child, with perfectly combed hair and a relaxed expression.

When he heard the last name, Borgia turned pale. He looked up and found himself face to face with the Maestro, impeccable in his haute couture overcoat.

Epilogue
Rome, 1992

ONE SATURDAY EVENING in September, around sunset, Scialoja and Patrizia met at Tre Scalini in Piazza Navona.

'I'm happy to see you again,' she smiled, kissing him on the cheek.

'So am I.'

'You're really in great shape!'

'So are you.'

Pigeons fluttered on the piazza. Tourists brushed past them, indifferent. The dying disk of the sun cast its reddish light over the fountains.

He was in a dark double-breasted suit. She was wearing a mud-grey Armani skirt suit and a few – eminently tasteful – pieces of jewellery. A tranquil pair of busy professionals at the end of their long workdays. She was unhurriedly enjoying a chocolate truffle. He was idly sipping a glass of fresh orange juice.

She told him that she'd been going to school. She was reading books. She no longer worked. Now she owned a health club in the centre of Rome. An exclusive place, with a very select clientele.

'Glad to hear it,' he said approvingly.

She manifested the unmistakable signs of a permanent suntan under her sleek pageboy hairstyle. She'd turned blonde again. Her skin, unnaturally smooth, suggested the handiwork of a skilled plastic surgeon. But maybe, Scialoja thought, no scalpel had even been necessary. Everything had slid over her without leaving a trace. A fleeting thought.

Patrizia talked and talked. She'd gone back to using her real name. The past was dead and buried. Her giddy, excited tone of voice revealed an authentic happiness over their meeting. He didn't have a lot to say. She let him walk her part of the way back. When they passed the Jaguar parked in Via dell'Anima, he recognized the model and the number plate. It was one of the jewels of Secco's fleet of cars. In just a couple of months, a verdict was expected from the tribunal on a judge's request to confiscate the car.

'So you're with Secco!'

She rolled her eyes with the expression of a clever little girl.

'He doesn't expect much and he solves a lot of problems. After all, life goes on, right?'

'Sure,' he commented in a flat voice.

'For you, the door's always open, cop!'

She leaned forward, her lips seeking his mouth. He kissed her unenthusiastically. She handed him a set of keys. Just like that time at Ranocchia's funeral.

'But call ahead; give me at least half an hour's warning,' she added, pragmatic as ever.

As he watched her walk away, he realized that he no longer recognized her scent. It was blurred, at this point, mingled irretrievably with the scents of the dozens of women he loved to collect. He devoted the same maniacal dedication to that pursuit as the Old Man had devoted to his automatons. But the Old Man was faithful to his beloved creatures, whereas Scialoja always made sure to get rid of his after a single night. Only one night: that was his rule. He got rid of the keys by dropping them into a bin on the street.

Later, as he was changing for dinner with the Minister of the Interior, he thought back to the old days, and he wondered how he could ever have wanted to give it all up for Patrizia. Water under the bridge, anyway.

Ten months ago, the third massive coronary had finished off the Old Man. Some time later, Scialoja had received an anonymous package. It contained the Old Man's diaries. The note that came with it said: *Enjoy the game!*

Enjoy the game! Yes, the Old Man was right. The game was infinitely more thrilling than any other kind of adventure. All he'd had to do was scatter the occasional allusion, make a distracted reference, a well-placed wink and a nod, and everyone who needed to know had been duly informed. He possessed the Old Man's diaries! He was the holder of the secret history of the Italian Republic! He could destroy cabinet ministers, grill unsuspectable businessmen, trigger unthinkable waves of scandal. He could do practically anything he wanted. He had the power. He was the power.

Panic had spread like wildfire. Scialoja insinuated reassuring words. This new broom would sweep clean, certainly – *pero con juicio*, he added, using the Spanish phrase advisedly. There were cases that could never be solved. Other cases that would only bear the partial light of truth. The continuity of underlying intent had never been open to debate, nor had Scialoja's basic loyalty to the institutions. They'd believed him, or they'd pretended to believe him. They had no alternatives. He had the power. He was the power.

As he was knotting his tie, he wondered whether he should accept the offer from the cabinet minister – director of the intelligence agencies, or national chief of police, take your pick – or hold out until the next round of elections, which the opposition hoped to sweep, hands down. The judges in Milan were kicking up their heels. He pretended to take no interest in it. There should be quite a shake-up at the top. But, as the Old Man had once told him, there would be changes, then everything would go back exactly as it was.

He'd follow the Old Man's approach. Lurk in the shadows. Stay in an outlying office, protected by an anodyne acronym, with a band of cut-throats ready to lunge at the slightest blink of an eye. Ah, the game, the game! To clutch them all in one's grip, to be the anonymous, indifferent arbiter of their destinies!

But as he was stepping into the lift, after checking the knot in his tie one last time, he felt a small, painful stab of pain to his heart. Just a pinprick, nothing more. Odd. In his moment of triumph, from what shadowy recesses of his past could this incomparable sense of defeat be blooming?

Closing Credits

Freddo was extradited to Italy, where he collaborated with the law. In the months that followed, **Fierolocchio**, **Ricotta** and **Donatella** all chose to become state's witnesses.

Bufalo was arrested a few months later. A police car pulled him over at the wheel of a car filled with weapons. No one ever knew what that shipment of weapons was for.

On the basis of sworn declarations by the state's witnesses, **Bufalo**, **Botola**, **Nero**, **Secco**, **Carlo Buffoni** and many others were sentenced to lengthy jail terms.

All **Secco**'s property was confiscated. **Secco** made every lira back in a relatively short time.

The **Maestro**, **Zeta** and **Peloso** were acquitted on all charges.

Conte Ugolino died of AIDS.

Lawyer Miglianico continues to practise his profession successfully. **Lawyer Vasta** is retired.

Sorcio lives under a fake name in another city.

Trentadenari was killed as he was leaving a bar.

Pischello was never arrested.

Patrizia continues to run her health club and hosts a fitness television show on a network of local channels.

Pidocchio's murder was never solved.

Judge Borgia was transferred to a civil part of the court of appeals.

Dottore **Nicola Scialoja** is in charge of the Logistics and Crime Reporting Office in the Ministry of the Interior. He lives in a luxurious penthouse apartment in the Via Chiana. He never married.